P9-DOH-906

"Don't move, you idiot! I can manage."

Jack stiffened as if she'd slapped him.

She shot him a mutinous glare, then shuffled back, tugging the injured man out from the carriage's shadow.

His hearing was acute; he heard her muttering beneath her breath, "I'm hardly a weak, fainting female, you dolt."

Entirely unexpectedly, his lips kicked up at the ends.

"You can let it down now."

She'd pulled the man onto the grass. Jack slowly let the carriage down, then followed.

He set about methodically checking the man for any injury, straightening limbs, noting the breaks.

Still frowning, she watched his hands. "Do you know what you're doing?"

"Yes." He glanced at the lady. "I don't suppose you'd consider sacrificing the flounce from your petticoat?"

"Of course I will."

An instant later, he heard cloth rip.

He bent to the task. She helped, working under his direction, in silence.

But in Jack's experience, females were rarely silent.

The Bastion Club Novels*

#1 THE LADY CHOSEN
#2 A GENTLEMAN'S HONOR
#3 A LADY OF HIS OWN
CAPTAIN JACK'S WOMAN (*prequel*)

The Cynster Novels

THE TRUTH ABOUT LOVE • THE IDEAL BRIDE
THE PERFECT LOVER • THE PROMISE IN A KISS
ON A WICKED DAWN • ON A WILD NIGHT
ALL ABOUT PASSION • ALL ABOUT LOVE
A SECRET LOVE • A ROGUE'S PROPOSAL
SCANDAL'S BRIDE • A RAKE'S VOW
DEVIL'S BRIDE

Also Available the Anthologies

HERO, COME BACK • SECRETS OF A PERFECT NIGHT
SCOTTISH BRIDES

Coming Soon in Hardcover

WHAT PRICE LOVE?

*See members list on pages vi–vii

STEPHANIE LAURENS

A Fine Passion

A BASTION CLUB NOVEL

AVON BOOKS
An Imprint of HarperCollinsPublishers

This is a work of fiction. Names, characters, places, and incidents are products of the author's imagination or are used fictitiously and are not to be construed as real. Any resemblance to actual events, locales, organizations, or persons, living or dead, is entirely coincidental.

AVON BOOKS
An Imprint of HarperCollins*Publishers*
10 East 53rd Street
New York, New York 10022-5299

Copyright © 2005 by Savdek Management Proprietory Ltd.
Excerpt from *The Truth About Love* copyright © 2005 by Savdek Management Proprietory Ltd.
ISBN-13: 978-0-06-059331-5
ISBN-10: 0-06-059331-8
www.avonromance.com

First Avon Books paperback printing: September 2005

Avon Trademark Reg. U.S. Pat. Off. and in Other Countries, Marca Registrada, Hecho en U.S.A.
HarperCollins® is a registered trademark of HarperCollins Publishers Inc.

Printed in the U.S.A.

10 9 8 7 6 5 4 3 2 1

A Fine Passion

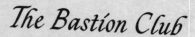

The Bastion Club

"a last bastion against the matchmakers of the ton"

MEMBERS

Christian Allardyce,
Marquess of Dearne

#2 ~~Anthony Blake,~~
~~Viscount Torrington~~

Alicia
"Carrington"
Pevensey

Jocelyn Deverell,
Viscount Paignton

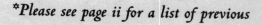

*Please see page ii for a list of previous

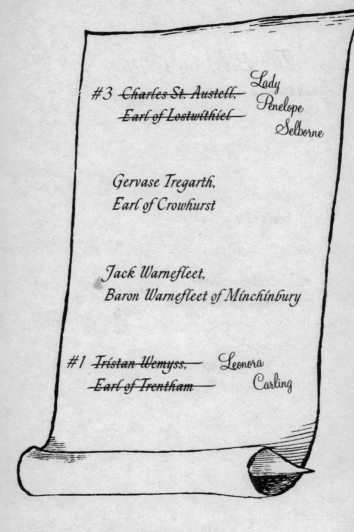

#3 ~~Charles St. Austell,~~ Lady Penelope Selborne
~~Earl of Lostwithiel~~

Gervase Tregarth,
Earl of Crowhurst

Jack Warnefleet,
Baron Warnefleet of Minchinbury

#1 ~~Tristan Wemyss,~~ Leonora Carling
~~Earl of Trentham~~

titles in the Bastion Club series.

Chapter 1

Early May
Avening village, Gloucestershire

Apple blossoms in springtime.

Julius—Jack—Warnefleet, Baron Warnefleet of Minchinbury, reined in on the rise above Avening valley and looked down on the pink-and-white clouds surrounding Avening Manor. His first sight of his home in seven years could, he felt, have been more apt.

Apple blossom always reminded him of brides.

Regarding the blossoms with a jaundiced eye, he twitched the reins and set his gray gelding, Challenger, ambling down the long hill. Everything, it seemed, was conspiring to remind him of his failure, of the fact he hadn't found a bride.

Avening Manor had been without a lady for most of his life. His mother had died when he was six years old; his father had never remarried.

Jack had spent the last thirteen years fighting for king and country, almost entirely behind enemy lines in France. His father's death seven years before had brought him briefly home, but only for two days, just long enough for the funeral and to formally place the running of Avening into the hands of old Griggs, his father's steward, before he'd had to slip back over the Channel, back to the varied roles he'd played in disrupting French shipping and commercial links, draining the lifeblood from the French state, weakening it.

Not the sort of battles most people imagined a major in the Guards engaged in.

Along with an elite group of fellow officers, he'd been seconded to work under a secretive individual known as Dalziel, who'd been responsible for all covert English operations on foreign soil. Neither Jack nor any of the six colleagues he'd met knew how many operatives Dalziel had commanded, or how wide the arena of their activities had been. They did know those activities had directly contributed, indeed been crucial, to the final ultimate defeat of Napoleon.

But the wars were now over. Along with his colleagues, Jack had retired from the fray and turned his mind to picking up the reins of civilian life. The previous October, he and his six colleagues, all gentlemen blessed with title, wealth, and the consequent responsibilities, and therefore all sorely in need of wives, had banded together to form the Bastion Club—their bulwark against the matchmakers of the ton, their castle from which each would sally forth, do battle with society's dragons, and secure the fair maid he required.

That, at least, had been their plan. Matters, however, hadn't fallen out quite as they'd supposed.

Tristan Wemyss had stumbled across his bride while overseeing the refurbishment of the house that was now the Bastion Club. Shortly after, Tony Blake had even more literally stumbled across his bride along with a dead body. Charles St. Austell, fleeing the capital and his too-helpful female relatives, had found his bride haunting his ancestral home. And now Jack was fleeing the capital, too, but not because of female relatives.

The rattle of carriage wheels reached him. Through the screening drifts, he glimpsed a black carriage bowling along the road from Cherington. The carriage crossed the junction with the Tetbury lane down which Jack was descending, and continued west toward Nailsworth.

Jack wondered who the carriage belonged to, but he'd been away so long he had no idea who might be visiting whom these days.

On returning permanently to England, he'd had to decide which of his responsibilities to attend to first. He was an only child; his father's death had set Avening in his lap with no one else to watch over it, but he knew the estate from the ground up—he'd been born and raised there, in this green valley on the northwest slope of the Cotswolds. Avening had been in sound hands; he trusted Griggs as his father had. Much more pressing had been the need to come to grips with the varied investments and far-flung properties he'd entirely unexpectedly inherited from his great-aunt Sophia.

His mother had been the daughter of an earl and his father the grandson of a duke; an eccentric spinster, Great-aunt Sophia had been a twig somewhere on his paternal family tree. Her hobby had been amassing wealth; although Jack could only recall meeting her briefly twice, on her death two years ago, Great-aunt Sophia had willed a sizable portion of her amassed wealth to him.

By the time he'd returned to England, various decisions associated with that inheritance had grown urgent; learning about his new holdings and investments had been imperative. He'd duly suppressed a deep-seated longing to return to Avening—to reassure himself it was all as he remembered, that after all his years away, after all he'd had to do, witness, and endure, his home was still there, as he remembered it—and instead had devoted the last six months to coming to grips with his inheritance, welding the whole into one workable estate.

Although he now owned numerous elegant country houses, to him, Avening was still the centerpiece, the place that was home, the place that held his heart.

That was why he was there, slowly ambling down the lane, letting his jaded senses absorb the achingly familiar sights and sounds, letting them soothe his abraded temper, his less-than-contented mood, and the dull but persistent ache in his head.

Temper and mood were due to his failure to find a suitable bride. He'd accepted he should and had bitten the bullet; while in London organizing his inheritance, he'd applied himself to looking over the field. Once the Season had commenced, he'd assumed suitable ladies would be thick on the ground; wasn't that what the marriage mart was all about? Instead, he'd discovered that while sweet and not so sweet young ladies littered the pavements, parks, and ballrooms, the sort of lady he could imagine marrying had been nowhere to be found.

He would have said he was too old, and too finicky, yet he was only thirty-four, prime matrimonial age for a gentleman, and he had no physical preference in women. Short, tall, blond, or brunette were all the same to him; it was being female that counted—soft, perfumed skin, feminine curves and, once they were beneath him, those breathy little gasps falling from luscious, parted lips. He should have been easy to please.

Instead, he'd discovered he couldn't bear the company of young ladies for longer than five minutes; beyond that, he grew so bored he had difficulty remembering their names. For reasons he didn't comprehend, they possessed no power whatever to focus, let alone fix his attention. Inevitably within minutes of being introduced, he'd be looking for an avenue to escape.

He was good at escaping. Or so he'd thought, until he'd met Miss Lydia Cowley and her gorgon of an aunt.

Miss Cowley was the daughter of a wealthy industrialist, her aunt distantly connected to some Midlands peer. Jack had found little in Miss Cowley to interest him. He, however, had been of great interest to Miss Cowley and her aunt.

They'd tried to entrap him. His mind elsewhere, he hadn't seen the danger until it had been upon him. But the instant he had, his well-honed instincts had sprung to life, the same instincts that had kept him alive and undetected through thirteen years of living with the enemy. They'd thought they'd cornered him alone with Miss Cowley in a first-floor parlor, yet when her aunt had swept in, with Lady Carmichael in the role of unwitting witness by her side, the parlor had been empty, devoid of life.

Put out, confused, the aunt had retreated, leaving to look elsewhere for her errant niece.

She hadn't looked out on the narrow ledge outside the parlor window, hadn't seen Jack holding Miss Cowley locked against him, her eyes starting above the hand he'd clapped over her lips.

He'd held her there, silent and deadly, precariously balanced two floors above the basement area, until the parlor door had closed, and the retreating footsteps died, then he'd eased the window open, swung her inside, and released her.

One wide-eyed look into his face, and she hadn't been able to get out of the parlor fast enough. He hadn't tried to hide his understanding of what had happened, or his reaction to that, and her. She'd stumbled through a garbled excuse and fled.

He'd canceled all further social engagements and retreated to the club to brood over his situation. But then Dalziel had sent word that Charles needed assistance in Cornwall. The information had seemed godsent; he'd finished dealing with his inheritance, and, he'd decided, he was also finished with searching for a wife. In company with Gervase Tregarth, another club member, he'd ridden away from London, back to a world he understood.

While the action in Cornwall had ultimately ended in success, he'd suffered a crack on the head that had been worse than any he'd received before. Once the villain had been dispatched and Charles back in his own fort, he'd returned to London, head still aching, for Pringle to check him over. An experienced battlefield surgeon the members of the club routinely consulted, Pringle had informed him that had his skull not been so thick, he wouldn't have survived the blow. That said, there was nothing seriously amiss, no damage a few weeks of quiet rest wouldn't repair.

He'd stayed at the club for a few more days, finalizing business, then headed down to Cornwall for Charles's wedding.

That had been two days ago. Leaving the wedding breakfast, he'd ridden across Dartmoor to Exeter, then the next day had taken the road to Bristol, where he'd rested last night. Early in the morning, he'd set out along the country lanes on the last leg of his journey home.

It had been seven long years since he'd set eyes on the limestone facade of the manor and watched the westering sun paint it a honey gold. He knew just where to look to glimpse the manor's gables through the trees lining the lane and the intervening orchards. The scent of apple blossom wreathed about him; for all it meant bride, it also meant home. His heart lifted; his lips lifted, too, as he reached the junction of the Tetbury lane and the Nailsworth–Cherington road.

To his left lay the village proper. He turned Challenger to the right; head rising, he touched his heels to the big horse's flanks and cantered down the road.

He rounded the bend, heart lifting with anticipation.

A little way ahead, a phaeton lay overturned by the side of the road.

The horse trapped in the traces, panicked and ungovernable, attempted to rear, paying no attention to the lady clinging to its bridle, trying to calm it.

Jack took in the scene in one glance. Face hardening, he dug his heels in, urging Challenger into a gallop.

Any second the trapped horse would lash out—at the lady.

She heard the thunder of approaching hooves and glanced fleetingly over her shoulder.

Eyes glued to the trapped horse, Jack came out of his saddle at a run. With hip and shoulder, he shoved the lady aside and lunged for the reins—just as the horse lashed out.

"Oh!" The lady flew sideways, landing in the lush grass beyond the ditch.

Jack ducked, but the iron-shod hoof grazed his head—in exactly the spot he'd been coshed.

He swore, then bit his lip, hard. Blinking against the pain, weaving to avoid being butted, he grabbed the horse's bridle above the bit, exerted enough strength to let the animal know he was in the hands of someone who knew, and started talking. Crooning, assuring the horse that all danger had passed.

The young bay stamped its hooves, shook its head; Jack hung on and kept talking. Gradually, the horse quieted.

Jack shot a glance at the lady. Riding up, all he'd seen was her back—that she had a wealth of dark mahogany hair worn in an elegantly plaited and coiled chignon, was wearing a plum-colored walking dress, and was uncommonly tall.

Sprawled on her back on the bank beyond the ditch, she struggled onto her elbows. Across the ditch, their gazes locked.

Her face was classically beautiful.

Her dark gaze was a fulminating glare.

Jack blinked. She looked like she wanted to rend him limb from limb, metaphorically at least, and had every intention of doing so—soon. He would have looked again, more closely, but the horse shied, still skittish; he refocused his attention and crooned some more.

From the corner of his eye, he caught a flash of petticoats and slim ankles as the lady got to her feet. He glanced at her again, but she didn't look his way; instead, she nimbly leapt the ditch and went quickly to the side of the over-turned carriage.

Jack realized the driver was nowhere to be seen. "Is he conscious?"

After an instant, the lady replied, "No." The carriage rocked as she tried unsuccessfully to lift the side. "He's trapped. His leg's broken and possibly one arm. Once the horse is calm enough, you'll have to help me get him out."

To Jack's relief, her voice showed no hint of agitation, much less hysteria. Her words were brisk, her tone commanding, as if she was used to being obeyed.

He looked at the horse. "I can't let the horse go—he's too nervous—but he's calm enough for you to hold. Come and take the reins, and I'll get the driver out."

The lady straightened; hands on hips, she rounded the wrecked phaeton and stopped five feet away, regarding him through dark, narrowed eyes, her ruby lips a thin line, her sculpted jaw set.

He'd been right; she was tall. Only a few inches shorter than he.

"Don't be asinine." Her glance was measuring—measuring and dismissive. "You can't lift the carriage and get him out at the same time."

Jack narrowed his eyes back; pain stabbed through his skull. His tone verging on lordly arrogance, he retorted, "Just take the reins and leave getting him out to me."

He offered the reins he'd gathered to her.

She made no move to take them. Instead, she caught his eye. "Unharness the horse." Her words were a clipped order. "If he panics again, I won't be able to hold him, and if he drags the carriage, he'll harm the driver more." She turned back to the side of the phaeton. "Or worse, you'll drop the carriage after you've lifted it."

Jack bit his tongue and manfully swallowed his less-than-civilized response. It was, he told himself, only because his head was throbbing that he hadn't thought of unharnessing the horse himself.

Talking nonsense to the horse, he played out enough rein to reach the harness buckles along one side. The lady returned and, without so much as a glance his way, went to work on the buckles opposite. Tugging the leather straps free, he studied her face, alabaster ivory, exquisitely molded features set in aloof dispassion. Arched brows and lush dark lashes framed large dark eyes; he hadn't yet got close enough to be sure of their true color.

Then they had the harness loose. The horse edged forward; the poles threatened to fall to the ground.

Jack grabbed one. "Here—take the reins and walk him forward. I'll hold the poles steady." If they fell, the driver's trapped limbs might be crushed even more.

Grasping the reins, the lady went to the horse's head, caught its attention, then, talking soothingly, slowly urged the bay forward step by step. Jack took the weight of the poles as the harness loops slid off.

With the horse free, the lady looked around. Jack glanced over his shoulder. Challenger had returned and stood cropping grass on the other side of the road. "Tie him to the hedge near my horse."

She did, although she cast him another of her irritated looks on the way.

By the time she returned, he'd found the height at which the poles were balanced; he held them resting on his palms. "Stand here, and support these until I tip the carriage. Once I do, you can let go and come and help drag the driver free."

Her gaze raked his face, then she looked at the poles, quite clearly evaluating his plan. Then she nodded, stepped up beside him, and grasped the poles.

Jack bit his tongue. Again. She was the most aggravating female, and she didn't even need to speak.

He rounded the side of the carriage and saw the driver. A young gentleman, he'd obviously done everything he could to save horse and carriage, and had stayed on the box too long. The carriage had rolled onto its side, then farther, pinning and crushing one leg. Luckily, the slope of the ditch wasn't that steep; the carriage hadn't continued rolling onto its hood, but had rocked back to settle on its side.

Hunkering down, Jack checked the man's pulse. Strong enough, steady enough. At least one leg was broken; a quick survey revealed that one shoulder was dislocated, a collarbone broken, and an arm as well. On top of what must have been a hellish knock on the head. Jack winced, then rose and studied the wreck. The fine wood of the ornamented sides was splintered, but the carriage was well made; the skeleton remained intact.

It took a minute to identify the best points on the frame to grasp to lift. Positioning himself with his back to the carriage, half-crouched, the edge of the lower side resting on his hands, Jack glanced at the lady. She was watching him in surprising silence and with grudging approval.

"When I lift, let the poles rise as they will. When we're sure the carriage is going to hold together and not break apart, come around and help haul him out."

She nodded.

He straightened, lifting the side up to waist height, then he braced, bent, heaved the carriage higher, and ducked his shoulders beneath the bones of the side. Bits of panel fell away; wood creaked, groaned, but the frame held.

Without waiting for any word, the lady rushed up. Bending, she grasped the man's shoulders.

"No! One's dislocated. Hook your hands under his armpits and drag him out."

She stiffened at his tone but did as he said.

Although he couldn't see her face, Jack could imagine her expression. Shifting, he tried to ease the weight of the carriage onto one shoulder so he could reach down and help—

"Don't move, you idiot! I can manage."

Jack stiffened as if she'd slapped him.

She shot him a mutinous, distinctly black glare, then shuffled back, tugging the man out from the carriage's shadow.

His hearing was acute; he heard her muttering beneath her breath, "I'm hardly a weak, fainting female, you dolt."

Entirely unexpectedly, his lips kicked up at the ends.

"You can let it down now."

She'd pulled the man onto the grass. Jack slowly let the carriage down, then followed.

Frowning at the man's face, she dropped to her knees beside him.

"Do you know him?" Jack knelt on the man's other side.

She shook her head. "He's not from around here."

Which meant she was, and that surprised him. She certainly hadn't been living in the vicinity seven years ago. Funeral or not, he would have noticed her, and remembered.

He set about methodically checking the man for injury, straightening limbs, noting the breaks.

Still frowning, she watched his hands. "Do you know what you're doing?"

"Yes."

Her lips tightened, but she accepted the assurance.

His assessment of the man's injuries had been largely correct. With one quick, expert jerk, he reset the shoulder, then, using sections of beading broken off the carriage, he used his and the man's cravats to splint the broken arm and bind it and the shoulder. That done, he turned to the leg, broken in two places. He had plenty of wood for splints.

He glanced at the lady. "I don't suppose you'd consider sacrificing the flounce from your petticoat?"

She looked up, met his gaze; faint color bloomed in her pale cheeks. "Of course I will."

Her tone belied her blush; no missish sentiment permitted or acknowledged. She swung around so her back was to him, and sat. An instant later, he heard cloth rip.

Rising, he went to the carriage to hunt for longer splints. By the time he returned, a long strip of fine lawn lay waiting by the unconscious man.

He bent to the task. She helped, working under his direction, in silence.

In Jack's experience, females were rarely silent.

Her hands, gripping where he directed, holding the splints in place, were as fine as her features, long-fingered and elegant, palms slender, skin fine-grained and white.

Distinctly aristocratic hands.

He glanced briefly at her face, closer now they were both leaning over the man. Distinctly aristocratic face, too. As for the rest . . .

Looking down, he forced his mind back to the man and his broken limb. Not easy; the distractions were manifold.

She had the sort of figure commonly described as an armful.

Words like "voluptuous" sprang to his mind. Phrases like well endowed.

Then he remembered her earlier scorching gaze and found the perfect adjective. Boadicean.

Very English. Very female. Very fierce.

He finished tying off their improvised bandage. The injured man was as comfortable as they could make him.

Boadicea sat back with a small sigh.

Jack rocked back on his heels and rose. He dusted off his hands, then held one out to her.

She was staring past him, down the road. Without looking at him—apparently without thought—she laid her hand in his and allowed him to pull her to her feet.

Retrieving her hand, she looked down, surveying their patient. "The manor's the nearest house. How are we going to get him there?"

She'd surprised him again. Not only had she volunteered his house, her question was rhetorical.

Although tempted to see how she would solve the problem, he took pity on the unconscious unfortunate. "There's probably some part of the carriage we can use to lay him on."

He went to look. One side door was smashed beyond use; the other was intact, but by itself too small. The board beneath the seat was splintered.

"Will this do?"

Jack turned to see Boadicea pointing at the rear of the phaeton. Joining her, he examined the long, slightly curved backing board jarred loose at one end but otherwise intact. "Stand back."

Of course, she didn't move; arms crossed, she watched while he got a firm grip, yanked the board loose, then pried it free.

He resisted the urge to see if her toe was tapping.

He carried the board to the unconscious man; she followed at his heels. Together, with no need for instructions, they lifted the man onto the board. Boadicea set down the man's legs, turned, and disappeared behind the phaeton. A second later she reappeared lugging a traveling bag.

She dropped it beside the man and bent to open it. "He's sure to have more cravats. We can tie him to the board with them."

Without bothering to nod—she wasn't looking at him— Jack left her and went to fetch the bay. When he returned, she was securing their patient to the improvised stretcher with a pair of cravats. "That should hold him."

Jack checked her knots; they were perfectly serviceable. Bending, he looped the long reins around and over their patient, and under the cravats.

She watched his every move; when he tied off the last rein, she nodded in regal approval. "Good." She dusted off her skirts, placed the man's bag on the board at his feet, then waved down the road. "The manor's less than a quarter of a mile."

About a quarter of a mile, most of it the long drive. Fetching Challenger, Jack hoped Griggs and his butler Howlett had kept the drive in good repair.

Leading Challenger, he fell in beside Boadicea, who was coaxing the bay forward in an even, steady walk. The reins pulled taut; their stretcher eased into the lane, riding the dry, reasonably even surface smoothly enough.

Satisfied they'd done all they could for the injured man, Jack turned his attention to his companion. No hat, no gloves. She had to live close. "Do you live hereabouts?"

She waved to the left. "At the rectory."

Jack frowned. "James Altwood used to be rector there."

"He still is."

Jack remembered her hands. No ring, no hint she'd ever worn one. He waited for her to elaborate. She didn't.

After a few moments, he asked, "How did you come to be in the road?"

She glanced at him; her eyes were very dark brown, even darker than her hair. "I was in the field mushrooming."

Again she waved to the left. "There's an old oak on a knoll—there are always mushrooms there."

Jack knew of it.

"I heard the accident, dropped my basket, and came racing down." She reached a hand to her hair, grimaced. "My hat fell off somewhere."

She didn't seem overly perturbed.

A second later, she slanted him a glance. "Where are you headed?"

"The manor."

He looked ahead and said nothing more. He felt her gaze, felt it sharpen, but, hiding a grim grin, refused to meet it. Two could play at withholding information.

They walked on through the glorious morning in silence. A strange silence—contained, controlled, assured. She, it seemed, was no more susceptible than he to the intimidation many felt when subjected to silence.

He should, of course, introduce himself, but she'd volunteered his house; telling her who he was might embarrass her, although somehow he doubted it would. He wasn't playing by the social rules because . . . she was different.

And he wanted to knock her off her regal perch.

The wrought-iron gates of the manor appeared on their right, flanked by oaks that had been ancient when Jack was born. As usual, the gates were propped wide. Together, he and Boadicea guided the bay in a wide arc, towing the stretcher smoothly through the turn and onto the long, rising drive.

Jack looked around as they walked on. Most of the fields within a mile were his, but these acres, the stretch between the drive and the rushing stream, a tributary of the Frome, and the gardens around the house, played host to most of his childhood memories.

They crested a rise and the house came into view. Lifting his head, he scanned the facade; everything was in excellent repair, yet it was the simple solidity of the house and its welcoming ambiance that reached out and closed about his heart.

He was aware Boadicea was watching him; he could feel her gaze, uninhibitedly curious.

"Are you expected?" she asked.

"Not precisely."

From the corner of his eye, he caught her narrow-eyed glance, then she looked ahead and lengthened her stride, leaving him to lead both horses.

He let her go ahead; striding up to the portico, she tugged the bell. Halting the horses in the forecourt, he waited.

Howlett opened the door. He immediately bowed. "Lady Clarice."

Lady Clarice?

Then Howlett saw him. The smile that broke across his butler's face was a welcome all on its own. "My lord! Welcome home!"

Boadicea stepped back, slowly turning to face him.

Howlett rushed out, then realized and turned back to call to the footman, Adam, who'd poked his head around the door. "Go and tell Griggs and Mrs. Connimore! His lordship's back!"

Jack smiled at Adam, who grinned and bobbed his head before racing back into the house. Howlett bowed, beaming, before him; Jack thumped him on the shoulder and asked if all was well. Howlett assured him all was. Then gravel crunching beneath a lumbering gait heralded the arrival of Crabthorpe, the head stableman, known to all as Crawler. Rounding the house, he saw Jack, and his face split.

"Thought as it must be you—too much carry-on to be anyone else." Then Crawler saw Howlett examining the makeshift stretcher. "What have we here?"

"His phaeton overturned in the ditch."

Crawler ambled across and bent over the injured man. "Another young larrikin with more hair than wit, no doubt." After a cursory examination, he straightened. "I'll send one of my lads for Dr. Willis."

"Do."

Stepping back from the stretcher, Howlett remembered

Boadicea. "Lady Clarice!" Howlett rushed back to her. "I do apologize, my lady. But, well, his lordship's come home at last, as you can see."

A smile softened Bodicea's face as she met Howlett's eyes. "Yes, indeed." She looked at Jack; her gaze sharped to flint. "I do see."

His slow, easy smile had charmed women from one end of England to the other and through at least half of France. It had no discernible effect on Boadicea.

"My lord! You're back!" Mrs. Connimore rushed out, followed more slowly by his steward, Griggs, leaning heavily on his cane.

In the ensuing melee, Jack lost sight of his recent companion; he surrendered to Mrs. Connimore's wild hug and nonstop exclamations. He was instantly aware of, and seriously alarmed by, Griggs's frailty. When had he grown so old?

Perturbed, distracted, he deflected their solicitiousness onto the unknown, still unconscious man. Mrs. Connimore and Howlett rose to the occasion and quickly organized to spirit the poor soul indoors and into a bed.

Crawler took charge of both horses and assured Jack he'd send his lads to clear the wreckage from the road.

Jack directed Adam to the traveling bag. As the crowd cleared, he was almost surprised to see Boadicea still standing by the front portico, still watching—he suspected still waiting to exact retribution. "I'll be in shortly, Griggs." Jack smiled and took Griggs's arm to help him back to the house. "Everything seems in excellent order—I know I have you to thank."

"Oh, no—well, everyone here quite understood . . . I daresay your new responsibilities are quite onerous . . . but we're so glad you've come home."

"I couldn't stay away." Jack smiled as he said it, not his polished smile but one of real feeling.

He stopped before the portico and urged Griggs to go in. "I must speak with Lady Clarice."

"Oh, yes." Reminded of her presence, Griggs halted and bowed low. "Please do excuse us, my lady."

She smiled, warm and reassuring. "Of course, Griggs. Don't concern yourself."

Her eyes lifted to meet Jack's. The look in them stated very clearly that she had no intention of forgiving him so easily.

He waited until Griggs had gone in and the footman had shut the door before strolling the last few feet to her.

She met his gaze directly, her dark eyes accusatory. "You're Warnefleet."

Not a question. Jack acknowledged the comment with an inclination of his head, but was at a loss to account for the condemnatory nuances clear in both her inflection and stance. "And you're Lady Clarice . . . ?"

She held his gaze for a definite moment, then said, "Altwood."

Jack frowned.

Before he could ask, she added, "James is a cousin. I've been living at the rectory for nearly seven years."

Unmarried. Living buried in the country. Lady Clarice Altwood. Who . . . ?

She seemed to have no difficulty following his train of thought. Her lips thinned. "My father was the Marquess of Melton."

The information only intrigued him all the more, but he could hardly ask why she wasn't married and managing some ducal estate. Then he refocused on her eyes, and knew the answer; this lady was no sweet young thing and never had been. "Thank you for your assistance with the gentleman—my people will handle things from here. I'll send word to the rectory when we know more."

She held his gaze, brows lightly arching. She considered him for a totally unruffled moment, then said, "I vaguely recall hearing . . . if you're Warnefleet, then you're also the local magistrate. Is that correct?"

He frowned. "Yes."

"In that case . . ." She drew a deep breath, and for the first time Jack glimpsed a hint of vulnerability—perhaps a touch of fright—in the dark depths of her eyes. "You need to understand that what happened to the young man was no accident. He didn't overturn his phaeton. He was deliberately run off the road by another carriage."

The image of a black carriage rattling off to Nailsworth flashed through Jack's mind. "Are you sure?"

"Yes." Clarice Adele Altwood folded her arms and sternly suppressed a shiver. Displaying weakness had never been her style, and she'd be damned if she let Warnefleet, the too-charming prodigal, see how unsettled she was. "I didn't see the overturning itself—the noise of it was what brought me running—but when I reached the road, the other carriage had stopped, and the man driving had got down. He was approaching the phaeton, was about to go around it to the driver, but then he heard my footsteps and stopped. He looked up and saw me. He stared at me for a moment, then he swung around, walked back to his carriage, climbed in, whipped up his horses, and drove away."

She could still see the scene, frozen in her mind. Could still feel the menace exuding from that large, heavy male figure, feel the weight of his consideration while he'd debated. . . . She blinked and refocused on the man before her, on his green-and-gold eyes. "I'd take an oath the man in the carriage meant to murder—to finish off—the gentleman in the phaeton."

Chapter 2

"I came into the road there, through that gap in the hedge." Clarice pointed, then looked at the wreckage a hundred yards farther on. "I stopped, surprised to see the other carriage there, then I remembered I'd heard shouting just before the crash—the young man swearing, I think."

She glanced at the man beside her; she kept expecting him to play the autocratic male, pat her on the head, assure her all was right, and dismiss all she'd seen and more importantly sensed. Instead, he was listening, quite as grimly as she would have wished.

Instead of dismissing her assertion of foul play, he'd studied her, then asked her to accompany him back to the scene. He hadn't tried to take her arm, but had walked beside her back down the drive. He'd ordered Crabthorpe's lads to wait at the gates until he'd finished examining the phaeton, then asked her to show him where she'd entered the lane.

Eyes narrowed, he stood beside her, looking toward the wreck. "Describe the man."

Any other day, any other man, and she would have taken umbrage at the bald order; today, from him, she was simply glad he was paying appropriate attention. "Tallish—taller than me. About your height. Heavily built, thick arms and legs. Close-cropped hair, light-colored, could be salt-and-pepper, but I can't be certain."

Folding her arms, she stared down the lane, reinvoking the moment in her mind. "He was wearing a drab topcoat, well cut enough but not of the first stare. His boots were brown, good-quality but not Hoby, not Hessians. He was wearing tan driving gloves. His skin was pale, his face rather round." She glanced at Warnefleet. "That's all I recall."

He nodded. "He was going around the phaeton when he heard you, halted, and looked at you." He caught her eye. "You said he stared."

She held his gaze for an instant, then looked back down the road. "Yes. Just stared . . . thinking. Considering." She resisted the urge to rub her hands up and down her arms to dispel the remembered chill.

"And then he turned and left?"

"Yes."

"No acknowledgment, no sign at all?"

She shook her head. "He just turned, got back in his carriage, and drove away."

He waved her down the road, but along the verge on the opposite side. He paced beside her. "What sort of carriage?"

"Small, black—from the back that was all I could see. It might have been one of those small carriages inns have for hire."

"You didn't see the horses?"

"No."

"Why do you think the black carriage ran the phaeton off the road?"

She was positive that's what had happened, but how did she know? She drew breath. "Three things—one, the swearing I heard just before the crash. A young man's voice, and he was swearing at someone else—not his horse or a bird or the sun. *Someone*. And he was frightened. Scared. I heard that, too. I wasn't surprised to hear the crash, nor to find the wreck."

Glancing briefly at her interrogator's hard-edged face,

features angular and austere, as aristocratic as her own, she saw he was concentrating, taking in her every word. "I hadn't truly been listening, not until I heard him swearing, so I hadn't heard the wheels of two carriages—truth be told, I hadn't even registered one." She looked ahead. "But the second reason I'm so sure the carriage driver intended the accident was the position of his carriage. It had stopped in the middle of the road, but skewed away from the phaeton, because it *had been* on the same side of the road as the phaeton."

They were almost level with the wreck; she slowed. "And lastly . . ." She halted. Warnefleet stopped and faced her. After a moment, she met his eyes; she owed it to the injured man to report all she'd seen. "The way the carriage driver walked toward the phaeton. He was intent. Determined. He wasn't in a dither or upset. He was intending to do harm." She looked across the road at the wreck. "He'd already done that much—he intended to finish what he'd started."

She waited for Warnefleet to make some disparaging remark, to tell her her imagination had run away with her. She steeled herself to defend her view—

"Where did the carriage stop?"

She blinked, then pointed to a spot some yards farther along the road. "About there."

Jack nodded. "Wait here."

He had few illusions about being obeyed, but at least she let him go ahead, trailing some yards behind him as he stepped onto the lane proper and walked along, studying the surface in the area she'd indicated.

A yard farther on he found what he was looking for. Crouching, he examined the shallow ruts left by the carriage's wheels when the driver had braked. Swiveling, he glanced back at the wreck, gauging the distance and the angle of the carriage.

Rising, he circled the area where the carriage had stood, aware Boadicea was following in his footsteps, more or less literally. Eyes on the ground, he scanned as he slowly worked his way toward the phaeton. He'd ridden over this ground; she'd led the bay from the phaeton over it. He didn't hold much hope . . . but then fate smiled. He crouched again, studying the single bootprint, all that was left of the unknown driver's trail.

Boadicea's observations had been accurate. The print was from an ordinary, leather-soled gentleman's boot. Its size, almost as large as his own, was consistent with the description she'd given. The even imprint, with neither toe nor heel unusually deep, suggested the wearer hadn't been in any panic. Deliberate, she'd said; deliberate it looked.

Head tilted, she'd been watching him; when he rose, she raised her brows. "What can you tell from that?"

He glanced at her, met her dark eyes. "That you're an observant and reliable witness."

Watching her swallow her surprise made uttering the compliment all the more worthwhile.

She recovered quickly. "So you agree that the carriage driver intended to harm—probably to murder—the young man?"

He felt his face harden. "He wasn't intending to offer succor—if he had, he wouldn't have left as he did." He glanced from the wrecked phaeton to where the carriage had pulled up. "And you're right on the other score, too—the carriage driver deliberately ran the phaeton off the road."

That was what she'd been wanting to hear, yet he was instantly aware of the shiver that slithered through her, even though she turned away to hide it. Before he'd thought, he'd taken a step toward her. Self-preservation reared its head and halted him; he knew better than to touch, to reach for her and draw her into his arms . . . but he wanted to.

The realization made him inwardly frown. He'd never met a female more prickly and independent than Boadicea, more likely to spurn any comfort he might offer, because to offer meant he'd seen her weakness . . . wryly, he realized he understood her perfectly, he just hadn't previously met a female who thought that way.

"Come." He had to stop himself from taking her elbow, converting the instinctive movement into a wave down the road. "I'll walk you back to the rectory."

She hesitated, then started walking. After a moment, her head rose. "You don't need to. I'm hardly likely to get lost."

"Nevertheless." He signaled to the waiting stable lads; they saw and headed for the phaeton. "Aside from all else, I should call on James and let him know I'm back."

"I'll be certain to tell him."

"It wouldn't be the same."

He waited, but she made no further protest. A dark flash of her eyes when they reached the gap in the hedge and she led him through told him she knew he would trump any argument she made.

Such a small victory, yet it still tasted sweet.

Beyond the gap, the field rolled down to a dip, then the land gently rose to the knoll on which the old oak tree stood. Once past the hedge, Clarice looked around. Eventually she spied her hat hanging from the branches of a tree along the hedge line; without comment, she detoured to fetch it.

Warnefleet followed, also without comment.

Clarice tramped through the long grass, supremely conscious that her senses remained focused a few feet behind her, on the large, lean, athletic body, broad-shouldered and sleekly muscled, trailing her. In her mind's eye, she could readily conjure not just his face, all hard angles and planes with that edge of ruthlessness peculiar to certain males of her own class, not just his body, long limbs strong, every movement both graceful and controlled, but even more telling—more evocative, more exciting—the aura that clung like a cloak about him, redolent of danger, exotic, illicit, and unnervingly tempting. Even more unsettling, and more puzzling, was a feeling that he saw her—the real her—clearly, yet found nothing in the sight to send him running.

None of that, however, explained her physical response, the sudden tension that gripped her, that tightened her nerves, the anticipation that stretched them—and left them taut when he didn't touch her.

For her, susceptibility of that sort was unprecedented; she'd heard of such affliction, seen other ladies fall victim, but not her. Never her.

Such a reaction was definitely not her style.

Then again, he wasn't the usual run of arrogant male. Not that she was fool enough to think him *un*arrogant, simply that she'd not met his like before.

Reaching the tree, she stopped and stared up at her hat. It dangled above her head, swinging gently in the breeze. She stretched up, but it was out of her reach. She jumped, but missed; she stretched as far as she could . . . and was still an inch short.

From over her head, a hand appeared and plucked the hat from the branch.

Her breath caught; she hadn't known he was so *close*.

She whirled. Her boots tangled in the long grass, and she fell.

Directly into him.

He caught her, steadied her breast to chest against him.

Her lungs seized; she looked up on a strangled gasp.

Mortification should have slain her, except there was no room for it in her mind. Sensation welled and swamped her, trapped her wits in a web of new experience, of novel feelings.

She'd been held in men's arms before, but it had never been like this. Never had the chest against which her breasts were pressed been so hard, never had the arm around her been so steely. Never had large hands held her so gently, or so securely. Never had her senses sighed, as if she'd found heaven.

Never had her pulse sped up, never had her skin shot with heat.

She stared into his eyes, green and gold melded into a true hazel, framed by long lashes and heavy lids, and sensed . . . strength. A strength as powerful as her own, not simply a strength of muscle and bone, but of mind and determination.

A strength not only on the physical plane, but manifest in other ways, in other arenas. . . .

The direction of her thoughts shocked her.

She blinked, mentally shook free of their hold, and refocused on his eyes, his face.

Realized he was watching her intently.

Realized he hadn't moved, that he'd made no attempt to set her on her feet.

The look in his eyes was blatantly predatory and frankly interested; he made not the slightest effort to screen it, to disguise it, to hide it from her. The image that popped into her mind was of a large, powerful, prowling beast contemplating his next meal.

But he made no move to seize her. He was waiting to see what she would do.

She knew better than to turn and flee.

Clearing her throat, she discovered her hands were pressed to his shoulders; she pushed back, and he let her go easily—smoothly—but still he watched her.

Chin rising, she met his gaze and reached for her hat, with her eyes dared him to make anything whatever of that accidental moment. "Thank you."

Before she could grasp her hat and twitch it from his fingers, he lifted it and dropped it on her head.

And smiled. Slowly, intently. "It was entirely my pleasure."

If she'd been a weak female, easily distracted by a handsome face, a warrior's body, and a smile that promised experience beyond her wildest dreams, after the incident with her hat she would doubtless have preserved a safe silence all the way to the rectory.

Instead, in order to ensure Warnefleet understood she wasn't susceptible, she felt compelled to make conversation—the sort of conversation to put him in his place and make clear her opinion of him, an opinion unaffected by their recent interactions.

"So, my lord, do you plan on remaining at Avening for

long?" The old oak lay ahead, her discarded basket sitting in its shade.

He didn't immediately reply, but eventually said, "Avening's my home. I grew up here."

"Yes, I know. But you've been absent for years—I understand your interests keep you in the capital." She put subtle emphasis on "interests," enough to let him know she had an excellent grasp of what interests kept gentlemen like him in London.

She ducked under the ends of the oak's lower branches, walking into the cool shadows.

He followed. "Some interests are best dealt with in town, true enough." His drawl was easy, but as he continued, she sensed steel beneath. "But no sensible man would let business tie him to London, and most other interests are portable, not tied to any location."

He, too, put a similar subtle emphasis on "interests"; it was patently clear he was calling her bluff.

"Indeed?" She bent and picked up the basket, then straightened, turned and met his eyes. "However, I daresay you would find it difficult to transfer sufficient of your other interests here, to the manor or village. Consequently, after dealing with whatever estate matters brought you here, I imagine you'll be off once more, hence my question. How long do you plan to stay?"

Jack held her gaze. After a moment, he quietly said, "You don't look like a female given to disordered imaginings."

Her dark eyes flared; her chin set. "I'm not!"

He nodded amenably. Reaching for the basket, he took it from her; she surrendered it with barely a thought, too distracted. Too incipiently incensed. "So I'd thought," he agreed with unimpaired calm. "That's why I listened to all you had to say about the accident that wasn't any accident. You were right about that."

"Naturally." She frowned at him. "I don't imagine things."

"Is that so?" He caught her dark gaze, held it for a pregnant instant, then quietly asked, "So why, Lady Clarice, have you taken against me? What have you imagined about me?"

She saw the trap, recognized she'd stepped into it; faint color tinged her cheeks—anger and irritation, not embarrassment. Purest alabaster, her complexion reminded him of rich cream, smooth, luscious; his fingers itched to touch, to stroke. To feel.

To make her flush with something other than anger.

She must have seen some hint of his thoughts in his eyes; her chin rose, but there was defensiveness in the gesture. "In your case, my lord, no imagination was necessary. Your actions over the years speak clearly enough."

He'd been right; for some mystical reason she held him in contempt, even though they'd never met, never set eyes on each other, let alone communicated in any way. "Which actions are those?"

His tone would have warned most men they were treading on extremely thin ice. He was quite sure she heard the warning, read it correctly, felt equally sure as her eyes flashed that she'd dismissed it out of hand.

"I can understand that while your father lived, there was no pressing need for you to live here, no reason for you to curtail your military service."

"Especially given the country was at war."

Her lips thinned, but she inclined her head, acknowledging the point, conceding that much. "However"—she turned and walked out of the tree's shade toward the rectory, a low, rambling house partially screened by the high hedge bordering the other side of the field—"once your father died, you should have returned. An estate like the manor, a village like Avening, needs someone to manage the reins. But no, you preferred to be an absentee landlord and leave Griggs to shoulder the responsibilities that should have been yours. He's done well, but he's not young—the years have taken their toll on him."

Pacing beside her, Jack frowned. "I was . . . with my regiment." He'd been in France, alone, but he saw no reason to tell her that. "I couldn't simply sell out—"

"Of course you could have. Many others did." The glance she cast him was scornful. "In our circle, elder sons—those who will inherit—don't usually serve, and while I understand your father died unexpectedly, once he had, your place was here, not"—she gestured dismissively—"playing the dashing officer in Tunbridge Wells or wherever you were stationed."

In France. Alone. Jack bit his tongue. What had he done to deserve this lecture? Why had he invited it—and even more pertinently, why was he putting up with it?

Why wasn't he simply annihilating her with a setdown, putting her firmly in her place, reminding her it was no place of hers to pass judgment on him?

He glanced at her. Head up, nose elevated to a superior, distinctly haughty angle, she paced fluidly, gracefully, beside him. She had a long-legged, swinging, confident stride; he didn't have to adjust his by much to match it.

Annihilating Boadicea wouldn't be easy, and for some unfathomable reason, he didn't want to meet her on any battlefield.

He did want to meet her, but on another field entirely, one with silken sheets, and a soft mattress into which she would sink. . . . He blinked and looked ahead.

"Then came Toulouse, but you didn't bother to return even then. No doubt you were too busy enjoying the Victory Celebrations to remember those who'd spent the years working here for you, supporting you."

He'd spent the months of false victory in France. Alone. Mistrusting the too-easy peace as had Dalziel and certain others, it had been he who had kept a distant eye on Elba, he who'd sent the first word that Napoleon had returned and raised the eagles again. He kept his tongue clamped between his teeth; his jaw had set.

"Even worse," she declaimed, condemnation in every syllable, the same emotion lighting her dark eyes as she glanced, fleetingly, at him, "when everything ended at Waterloo, you compounded your slights of the past and remained in London, no doubt catching up on all you'd missed in your months abroad."

Years. Alone. Every last week, every last month for thirteen years, all alone except for that brief, supremely dangerous, reckless three days that for him had been Waterloo. And after that, once he'd sold out, there'd been a line of pressing, very real and weighty responsibilities waiting to claim him.

Her final words had been scathing, her meaning crystal clear. He couldn't recall the last time he'd indulged in the manner to which she was alluding; no doubt that accounted for his current state—the intense, urgent, remarkably powerful urge to slake his long-suppressed carnal appetites.

With Boadicea.

Not with any other woman. Now he'd met her, no other would do.

It had to be her.

Clearly he had his work cut out for him, but he loved challenges, especially of that sort.

An image of Boadicea—*Lady Clarice*—lying naked beneath him, heated, desperate, and wantonly begging, those long, long legs tensing about his hips as he thrust into her, helped immeasurably in focusing his mind. In clarifying his direction.

They'd reached the hedge surrounding the rectory. She lashed him with another of her cutting glances; he caught it, held her gaze as, by unvoiced consent, they paused in the archway leading into the rectory gardens.

He read her face, examined the dismissive contempt written in her fine features, that glowed, alive, in her lovely dark eyes. Slowly, he arched a brow. "So . . . you think I should remain at Avening and devote myself to my responsibilities?"

She smiled, not sweetly—condescendingly. "No—I believe we'll all do better if you return to London and continue with your hedonistic existence there."

He frowned. She continued, without hesitation answering

his unvoiced question, "We've grown accustomed to managing without you. Those here no longer need a lord of the manor—they've elected someone else in your place."

She held his eyes for a defiant instant, her gaze direct and ungiving, then she turned and swept on, heading for the rectory's side door.

Frown deepening, Jack watched her—let his eyes drink in the quintessentially feminine sway of her hips, the evocative line from her nape to her waist, the promise of her curves . . .

She couldn't mean what he thought she'd meant, surely?

There was one certain way to find out. About that, and all else he now wanted to know about Boadicea. Stirring, he followed her into the rectory.

He found the Rector of Avening, the Honorable James Altwood, in exactly the same place he'd left him seven years ago—in the chair behind the desk in his study, poring over some tome. Jack knew the subject of said tome without asking; James was a renowned military historian, a Fellow of Balliol among other things. He held the livings of numerous parishes, but other than overseeing the work of his curates, he spent all his days researching and analyzing military campaigns, both ancient and contemporary.

Boadicea, predictably, preceded him into the study. "James, Lord Warnefleet has returned—he's come to speak with you."

"Heh?" James looked up, peering over his spectacles. Then his gaze found Jack, and he dropped the book on the desk. "Jack, m'boy! At last!"

Jack managed not to wince as James surged to his feet. Very aware of Boadicea's critical gaze, he went forward to grasp James's outstretched hand and let himself be pulled into a fierce hug.

James gripped tight, thumped his back, then released him. Retaining Jack's hand, he drew back to examine him.

Now in his fifties, James was starting to show his age; the brown hair Jack remembered as thick and wavy had thinned, and the paunch around his middle had grown. But the energy and enthusiasm in James's brown eyes was still the same; if anyone had been responsible for encouraging Jack into the army, it was James.

James blew out a long breath, and released Jack's hand. "Damn it, Jack, it's a relief to see you hale and whole."

Along with Jack's father, James had been one of the very few who knew that Jack hadn't spent the last thirteen years in any regimental barracks.

Jack smiled, no screening charm; with James, he was never other than himself. "It's a huge relief to be back." He couldn't resist adding, "*At last*, as you so sapiently note."

"Indeed, indeed. *Such* a shambles with your great-aunt and her holdings. But here—sit, sit!"

Waving Jack to a chair, James went to resume his, then remembered Boadicea. "Ah, thank you, Clarice." James looked from her to Jack, at whom she was now staring, her expression, to James, impossible to interpret. Jack had no such difficulty. Boadicea was quick. She'd heard James's reference to his great-aunt . . . and now wondered.

When James looked at her, he flashed her a tauntingly superior smile.

"Ah . . . I take it you two have met?" James looked from one to the other, sensing undercurrents but unable to read them.

"Yes." When Jack raised his brows at her, Clarice transferred her gaze to James. "I was mushrooming, and there was a carriage accident along the road, just past the manor gates."

"Good gracious!" James waved Clarice to a chair, waiting for her to sit before sinking into his. "What happened?"

"I didn't actually see the accident, but I was the first to the wreck"—Clarice glanced Jack's way as he sat in the other armchair—"then his lordship rode up."

"Was anyone hurt?" James asked.

"The driver," Jack replied, "a young gentleman. He's unconscious. We've moved him to the manor and sent for Dr. Willis. Mrs. Connimore's taking care of him."

James nodded. "Good, good." He looked at Clarice. "Was he anyone from round about?"

"No." She frowned.

Jack recalled she'd done the same, out on the road.

"But . . . ?" James prompted before Jack could.

Her lips twisted; she glanced at Jack, then looked at James. "I know I've never met him—I don't recognize him at all—but he looks familiar."

"Ah!" James nodded sagely.

Jack wished he knew why.

Clarice went on, "He seems too young to be anyone I knew in the past, but I wondered . . . he could be someone's younger brother, or son, and I'm picking up the resemblance."

Jack wondered which circles she'd inhabited in her "past."

As if reading his mind, she shrugged. "All that means is that he's most likely some scion of some tonnish family, which doesn't get us far."

"Hmm—I must drop by. If he doesn't regain his wits soon, I will, although if you can't place him, it's unlikely I will." James shifted his gaze to Jack. "And even less likely you'd draw a bead on him. I don't suppose you've been haunting the clubs and hells lately, heh?"

Aware of Clarice's saber-edged gaze, Jack humphed. "I barely had time to visit my tailor."

A tap on the door heralded Macimber, James's butler. He beamed at Jack and bowed. "Welcome home, my lord."

"Thank you, Macimber."

Macimber looked at James. "Mrs. Cleever wishes to know if his lordship will be remaining for luncheon, sir."

"Yes, of course!" James looked at Jack. "You'll stay, won't you? I daresay Mrs. Connimore would love to have you back at your own table, but I've a greater need to hear your voice and learn what you've been about."

Jack kept his gaze on James while gauging the quality of

that other, sharp, dark-eyed gaze trained on his face. "I'd be delighted to stay for luncheon"—turning, he met Boadicea's eyes—"if it's no trouble?"

If she didn't object. She understood his question perfectly. James, puzzled, glanced back and forth; they ignored him.

Holding her dark gaze, Jack saw her decision, knew the moment the scales tipped in his favor, when her curiosity got the better of her scorn.

"I'm sure it will be no trouble. . . ." She paused, then went on, her voice regaining its customary decisive note, "And indeed, with the young man to look after I'm sure Mrs. Connimore has enough on her plate, especially as she wasn't aware you'd be arriving today."

That last was delivered with a predictable bite; Jack bit back a retort to the effect that he'd grown out of short-coats many years ago.

While James instructed a delighted Macimber to set the table for three, Jack turned his mind to planning how best to exploit the advantage Boadicea and her unjustified disapproval had handed him.

When dealing with warrior queens, no advantage should be squandered.

One point that nagged at him was her age, the first point he should address in learning what she, a marquess's daughter, was doing living buried in the country with James. A scandal was the only situation he could conjure that might account for it, yet Lady Clarice didn't seem the sort to throw her bonnet over any windmill. A less flighty, less flibberti-gibbety female was hard to imagine.

"So!" James sat back and regarded Jack with fond anticipation. "Start at the beginning of recent events. How did you find London after what? Thirteen years?"

Jack grimaced. "Not much different, truth to tell. The names were unchanged, the faces older, but the game was still the same."

"And still left you largely unmoved, heh?" James grinned.

"I always told your father he'd never have to worry over you being seduced by the delights of the capital."

"Just so," Jack rejoined, his tone dry. He was careful not to glance at Clarice, to see what she was making of James's more accurate view of him; he was itching to know, but if he looked, she'd realize. . . .

"Griggs told me that Ellicot—it is Ellicot, isn't it—your great-aunt's solicitor?"

Jack nodded. "Solicitor, agent, and executor combined, and he'd inherited the position just a month before Great-aunt Sophia departed this mortal coil, so he was as green as I was in terms of her estate."

"Difficult." James nodded understandingly. "As I was saying, Griggs told me Ellicot was close to panicking, so I wasn't surprised when you remained in town."

"It took months." Jack sat back and let the frustrations of the past months show; the easiest way to convince Boadicea she'd read him entirely wrongly was simply to be himself. "Ellicot had held the fort as well as he could, but in truth, some decisions should have been made, steps taken, even without my knowledge and consent. However, I do understand he was walking a fine line, especially as he hadn't even met me."

"Indeed. Not an easy charge to fulfill, managing estates in the name of an unknown client."

Jack agreed, describing some of the multitude of difficulties that had faced him on returning to England courtesy of his inherited holdings. Most concerned matters of estate management; although female, Boadicea clearly understood the ramifications, even those less obvious to the untrained. From the corner of his eye, he saw a frown gradually etch a line between her finely arched brows.

After half an hour, he'd largely finished with recent events, excepting those concerned with his ill-fated attempts to find a suitable wife; those he kept to himself. Boadicea listened as he and James discussed some of the measures he'd set in place to better facilitate his grip on the day-to-day running of the numerous properties he now owned; Jack inwardly smiled at the grudging respect he glimpsed in her eyes.

Macimber looked in to tell them that luncheon was served. They all rose; Clarice led the way into the dining room. James took his seat at the head of the table; Clarice sat on his left, Jack on his right, in a companionable group.

"Well, then." James reached for the platter of cold meats. "You seem to have overcome all hurdles—your great-aunt would, I'm sure, approve. So now you can go back seven years. You filled me in on your duties when last you were home—did your assignment vary much between then and Toulouse?"

Jack shook his head. "Not materially. There was still a great deal of sleight of hand involved—misdirection, and, of course, the main purpose was to scupper all the deals I could, especially with the New World. There were times when I spent weeks in dockside taverns teasing out and piecing together information on the deals planned. As the war dragged on, less and less was done through official channels, which made it that much harder to discover what was really happening—what was being brought in, what sent out, when, how, and by whom."

"And you were still under the command of that certain gentleman in Whitehall?"

"Indeed. He's still there, still active."

James nodded, chewing. He swallowed, then said, "So what happened after Toulouse? Things must have changed then?"

Clarice fought to hide her interest. She kept her gaze trained on her plate, kept her lips firmly shut, did all she could to make herself the proverbial fly on the wall. She'd encouraged Warnefleet to join them for luncheon because she'd known James would interrogate him, and she'd wanted to be there to watch him squirm and be made to appreciate his shortcomings.

Instead, she was the one squirming. Or at least, she would be, if she wasn't so engrossed. She'd obviously misread things, misinterpreted comments made about Warnefleet, not just by James but by all around, including the manor staff, but before she could decide just how badly she'd been off target—just how much of an apology she would have to make—she had to piece together the truth by reading between the lines of James and Warnefleet's conversation.

Their annoyingly imprecise conversation, but she could hardly insist they speak plainly.

"Yes for most, but not for me." Warnefleet paused as if selecting his words, then he glanced at James. "There were many in our particular line of defence who were skeptical of the abdication. We all had roots in French society. None of us thought the battle was truly won."

"Yet most came home."

Warnefleet nodded. "But I and a few others remained. In my case, I had a good and reliable line to Elba. Others stayed in the ports most likely to see first action. How long we'd have stayed, keeping watch as it were, I don't know, but as it transpired, we didn't see out a year before it was war again."

"And then what?" James leaned forward, the eagerness in his face transparent.

Clarice found herself holding her breath; she risked a quick glance at Warnefleet's face.

He was looking at her, but not seeing her.

She got the impression he was looking into the past.

Then his lips twisted, and he glanced at James. "Waterloo came on quickly."

"You were there, weren't you?"

"I and a group of others were technically involved in the engagement, but we didn't get within ten miles of the battlefield."

James's eyes narrowed. "Supply lines?"

Warnefleet nodded. "We went first for the munitions, then the mounts, and lastly the reinforcements."

James frowned. "I can see how you'd manage the first two, but the last?"

"Confusion and preferably chaos." Again Warnefleet's lips lifted in a wry grin. "We had to be inventive."

To Clarice's dismay, Macimber came in and started to clear the dishes. The meal had ended, but she hadn't yet heard all she wished. How had he been inventive? How inventive had he been? What . . . ?

James drained his wine, then set the goblet down and grinned engagingly at Warnefleet. "Well, m'boy, let's go for a constitutional and you can tell me the details."

Before she could think of some way to delay them, James rose and smiled at her. "Excellent meal, m'dear."

She hid her disappointment behind a cool facade. "I'll be sure to pass your commendation to Mrs. Cleever."

"And mine, too, if you'd be so kind."

She looked up and met Warnefleet's eyes. He'd risen with James and now stood looking down at her. His gaze held a certain weight; she had no difficulty interpreting his message.

He was too clever to gloat, but he knew just how wrong she'd been, how awkward and untenable her attitude to him now was, and he wasn't above letting her know it. He expected an apology, and she would have to give him one.

Her customary expression of serene calm anchored in place, she nodded graciously. "My lord. No doubt we'll meet again."

One brow quirked. His eyes cut to James, then he inclined his head. "Lady Clarice." His hazel eyes recaptured hers; his lips lifted in a charming, wholly untrustworthy smile. "It was a pleasure to make your acquaintance."

He bowed gracefully. She bit her lip on an acid retort and nodded in regal dismissal. She didn't look his way as he left the room in James's wake.

She might have to eat crow, but she wasn't about to do it in public, not even in front of James. Instinct warned that whatever concessions she was forced to make to appease Warnefleet would definitely be better kept between themselves.

Chapter 3

Jack followed James out onto the rectory's front lawn, a
green and peaceful place surrounded by large trees.

"I still enjoy my after-lunch constitutional." James waved
to a worn track circling the lawn; Jack fell in beside him.
"Now, tell me *all*."

Jack obliged, supplying the details he'd omitted earlier,
those aspects of his activities during the Waterloo campaign
of most interest to James. "And that, thank God, was the end.
Once Napoleon was on his way to St. Helena, there was no
need for any of us to remain in France."

"So you returned to the fray here. I take it you're satisfied
your inheritance is under control?"

Jack nodded. "It took longer than I'd thought, but I'm
happy with the new system we've instituted—it should allow
me to manage the reins from here." He looked around at the
well-remembered vistas, noted how much the trees and
shrubs had grown. He glanced at James. "Now *you* can brief
me on all that's happened here."

James smiled, and did, rattling through a potted history of
the births, deaths, and marriages in the area, of those who'd
moved away, and those who'd arrived to take their place.
"As Griggs no doubt has told you, all your tenants are still in
place. Avening village is much as it was, but . . ."

Jack listened intently, committing much to memory; all that James let fall was information he needed to know.

Eventually, however, James wound down, without revealing what Jack *most* wanted to know. He inwardly sighed, and remarked, "You've forgotten one major event—Lady Clarice. When did she arrive?"

James grinned; they strolled on. "Two months after your father left us. Quite opportune, as it happened."

"Opportune?"

"Well." James grimaced. "Your father had always been the bulwark of village life. His word was law, not just in the legal sense but everyone about relied on his advice and even more his judgment—adjudication, if you will—in disputes large and small. People round about had grown to depend on him, and then suddenly he wasn't there, and neither were you."

Jack glanced at him. "But you were here."

James sighed. "I fear, dear boy, that gaining a research fellowship from Balliol falls far short of giving one the expertise to step into your father's shoes. By the time Clarice arrived, matters were well-nigh chaotic."

Jack hid a frown. "And she fixed things?"

"Yes. Unlike me"—James smiled self-deprecatingly—"she's been trained to the role."

Jack's inward frown deepened. "She mentioned she was Melton's daughter." So what was she doing there?

"Indeed. Melton, her father, was a cousin. My father was his father's younger brother."

When James said nothing more, Jack kept his lips firmly shut, and simply waited. . . .

Eventually, James chuckled. "All right, although it all seems ancient history now. Clarice was Melton's fourth child by his first wife, the only daughter of that union. Her mother, Edith, definitely ranked as a *grande dame*, a very forceful woman."

Presumably the source of Boadicea's steel.

"Edith died of a fever when Clarice was young. Four or five years old, I can't recall. Melton married again and sired a quiver of daughters and a fourth son by his second wife—I don't know much of them. Nevertheless, Clarice's life would no doubt have followed the predictable pattern—there's never been any shortage of families keen to ally themselves with the marquisate—except that at sixteen, she formed an attachment for a local neighbor's son, a guardsman. Not quite what Melton had in mind for her, but the lad was heir to a nice enough estate, so Melton allowed Clarice to persuade him. All well and good, but then the Peninsula campaign came along and the young man went to Spain, and died in an engagement there. Clarice was devastated. Instead of being presented and doing the Season, she spent the next years quietly at Rosewood, Melton's principal estate."

"So what brought her here?"

"Ah, we're barely halfway through the tale." James paused, ordering his thoughts, then went on, "As I said, there's never been any lack of gentlemen with an eye to Melton's coffers, and Clarice is six years older than her next sister. A cad named Jonathon Warwick got wind of Clarice. He went to Rosewood and pursued her, but was cunning enough to hide his true colors."

"I remember Warwick." Jack heard the hardness that had infused his voice. "We met during that long-ago year I spent in town, before I enlisted. Even then, 'cad' would have been a generous description."

"Indeed. By the time he took up with Clarice, Warwick's estates were mortgaged to the hilt, he was being dunned left and right, but he still looked and played the part of an impeccably turned-out, thoroughly eligible gentleman. And he was well experienced in knowing just how best to trade on his pretty face."

Jack made a mental note that should he ever meet Warwick again, he'd find a way to rearrange said pretty face.

"As I heard it, Warwick led Clarice on to the point where, when Warwick approached Melton for permission to marry her and he, of course, tossed him out on his ear, Warwick was able to convince Clarice to elope. Not, of course, that Warwick planned on following through with such a plan—he wasn't about to jeopardize his entrée into polite circles. Instead, he sent a message to Melton, along with a demand. From Melton's point of view, it was easiest to simply buy him off. What neither Warwick nor Melton expected was that Clarice would unexpectedly turn up and overhear the transaction. According to Melton, she stormed in, pinned Warwick with a glare, then slapped him hard enough to knock him out of his chair. After giving him her opinion of his antecedents, she walked out. Melton was quite proud of her."

Jack frowned. "So to escape the consequent whispers, she came here?"

"No. Stop getting ahead of me, boy." James snorted. "Anyway, can you imagine Clarice being bothered by whispers? Indeed, I'm not sure there's many would dare whisper about her. Regardless, her reaction to the incident with Warwick was that it was clearly past time she returned to the capital and found herself a husband. She was twenty, and it was time to leave her father's roof. An estimable conclusion, one with which both Melton and his second wife wholeheartedly concurred, so with her customary single-mindedness, Clarice sallied forth to do battle the following Season."

Jack had no trouble envisaging that.

"However—and here I'm extrapolating from what my correspondents told me—Clarice proved difficult to please. Not one of the horde who prostrated themselves at her feet found favor. Worse, after two Seasons she'd gained the reputation of being an aristocratic iceberg, unlikely to melt for any man."

Jack blinked. Icy was not an adjective he would have applied to Boadicea.

"Which brings us to her third and final Season. To the very start of it, when her stepmother, Moira, and Clarice returned to the capital. There had been some correspondence between Melton and a Viscount Emsworth, of which Clarice was initially unaware. The long and short of it was that

Emsworth had title, estates, but insufficient wealth, and he was also ambitious, so he was looking for a well-dowered and also well-connected bride."

"Clarice fitted his bill, I take it." Jack heard his grim tone, and wondered why he felt as he did, as if he'd willingly plant Emsworth a facer.

"To a tee. Emsworth had written to Melton asking for Clarice's hand. He presented his offer as a suitable-to-all-parties marriage of convenience. Moira was by then desperate to get Clarice married and off her hands—her own eldest daughter would be presented the following year. Of all his daughters, Clarice was Melton's favorite, was the best dowered as she'd also inherited considerable funds through her mother, and she has a much more . . . *commanding* presence than her half sisters. Indeed, with her in the room, they fade into the wallpaper, so one can at least understand Moira's attitude."

James paused as they turned to retrace their steps; Jack held his tongue and waited for him to continue.

"Moira pressed Melton to accept Emsworth's suit. Melton wished to consult Clarice, but Moira convinced him letting Emsworth woo Clarice in romantic fashion during the Season was more likely to sway Clarice—eventually, Melton gave way. However, he agreed to the match on the condition that Clarice agreed.

"It transpired," James said, his tone hardening, "that Moira and Emsworth had an agreement, too. Moira knew Clarice would never accept Emsworth—the man's a priggish tyrant, I've heard—but Moira wasn't going to allow Clarice's capriciousness to stand in her and her daughter's way, so . . . once Moira and Clarice were in town, and, despite Emsworth's marked attentions, Clarice showed no signs of being swept off her feet, Moira and Emsworth took matters into their own hands."

"How so?" Jack's words were clipped; foreboding rang in them.

"Much as you've guessed. They arranged for Clarice and

Emsworth to be discovered in a compromising situation by two of the more prominent hostesses. Scandal threatened, but Emsworth promptly stepped forward to do the honorable thing and offer the protection of his name."

"How neat."

To Jack's surprise, James grinned at his cuttingly sarcastic remark. "Actually, no. Moira and Emsworth thought they had the whole sewn up tight, but they'd reckoned without Clarice."

Jack blinked. His experience of the ton wasn't vast, but it was enough to appreciate the situation and the forces ranged against Clarice. "She refused?"

James's grin grew. "Categorically. She saw through the whole scheme in a blink and simply, unwaveringly, refused to, as she put it, be socially blackmailed into such a union."

Jack frowned. "But there was a scandal." That had to be the reason why Clarice now lived there.

"Oh, indeed!" James sighed. "The scandal to top all scandals, most of which can be laid at Moira's door. She was determined to force Clarice into the marriage and stopped at nothing to increase the pressure. By the time Melton heard of it and arrived in town, the damage to Clarice's reputation was done—or rather, her reputation was hanging above the abyss by a single thread. If she agreed to marry Emsworth, all would be forgiven—you know how these affairs are managed."

Jack said nothing, but he did, indeed, understand.

"And that, unfortunately, was where Melton's less-than-admirable side came to the fore. He was a stickler for keeping the family escutcheon pristine and unblemished. Despite understanding the whole, including how he himself had been manipulated, he nevertheless insisted that now things had come to such a pass, Clarice had to wed Emsworth to protect the family name."

Jack made a disgusted sound.

James nodded. "Precisely. You can imagine the arguments, the rants and raving. Yet despite all the forces arrayed against her, Clarice refused to budge. She adamantly refused to marry Emsworth." James paused, then continued, "If she'd been a less *formidable* female, I daresay some rather less savory methods of persuasion would have been applied, but when Clarice declared a position, no one, not even then, doubted she would hold to it to her grave. So . . ."

"Stalemate," Jack said. His nickname for the lady seemed remarkably apt.

"In a fashion, but it wasn't a situation that could remain unresolved. Melton forced the issue by threatening to banish Clarice from his houses and estates."

Jack's jaw clenched tight. The notion of a lady of Clarice's standing being tossed into the streets brought out every protective instinct he possessed. What had he fought the last thirteen years for? So well-heeled aristocrats could treat their daughters like that?

His disillusionment with tonnish society plumbed new depths.

"So you stepped in and brought her here." He looked up at the rectory as they drew near once more.

"Not directly. Her three older brothers were appalled by Melton's decree. They interceded and persuaded him to allow Clarice to retire from society and live here, with me." James's lips twisted wryly. "Within the family, I'm considered a black sheep, having gone into the Church and not even in the pursuit of power. Researching military strategies was never considered a suitable occupation for an Altwood. On the other hand, there are times the family is quite grateful to have a member of the Church as one of their own. And in this case, living so quietly here as I do, so cut off from society, my house seemed the perfect solution—much like those convents to which recalcitrant young ladies used to be sent to consider the follies of their ways."

James's slow smile returned. "Much to everyone's surprise, Clarice agreed."

Jack shot James a glance. "Did you know her? Did she know you?"

"Yes, but we'd only met a handful of times at family gatherings. Nevertheless, while I would hardly describe us as kindred souls, we'd both recognized the other as an amenable companion. We rub along quite nicely."

Jack couldn't imagine it, not for himself. "You don't find having such a . . . lady"—termagent, battle-hardened warriorqueen—"constantly about distracting?"

"Not at all. While Clarice is hardly quiet or restful, there's much to be said for having one's house run by a highly competent female. And as I mentioned, she's dealt with all those problems and questions that in your father's absence, and yours, devolved to me—her presence has been a boon."

Jack knew enough to read between the lines; James was frequently absentminded, and could go for long periods completely immersed in his researches, oblivious to all about him and crotchety if interrupted.

They drew level with the steps leading up to the front porch. Jack halted. "So . . . having had her fill of offers of marriage—three attempts, all devastating failures for one reason or another—Clarice retreated here, more or less turning her back on the usual young lady's romantic dreams."

James paused beside him; a considering frown on his face, he looked up at the house, somewhere in which the object of their discussion was no doubt busily managing something. "Do you think so?"

Jack glanced at him.

James stared unseeing at the door. "You know, I always saw it as the other way around. That far from turning away from love, Clarice dismissed as well lost a world without it."

Jack blinked. He considered for a moment, then glanced at the front door. "Perhaps." Another moment passed, then he stirred. "I'd best get back to the manor."

James clapped him on the shoulder and they parted. Pensive still, Jack walked off down the drive.

For Clarice, the afternoon flew too swiftly, filled with myriad tasks and duties that had found their way onto her shoulders. Mrs. Swithins, the curate's mother, called, wanting to discuss—again—the roster for providing flowers to the church. Later, Jed Butler from the inn dropped by to ask her advice on the changes he was thinking of making in the taproom.

It was close to four o'clock, the shadows starting to paint the hollows a misty lilac before, throwing a light shawl over her shoulders, she set out to walk to the manor to check on the young gentleman.

And if Warnefleet was about, to admit her error in thinking him a wastrel, absentee landlord, although how she might have guessed he was . . . whatever it was he had been, she didn't know.

She still didn't know precisely what role he'd played in the late wars, but she knew enough of James's interest in military matters to make an educated guess.

Warnefleet had been a spy of sorts, not simply the type who observes and reports, but an active . . . operative—was that the word?

From what she'd seen in him, she rather thought it was.

The irony of the situation wasn't lost on her; the one excuse she would without question accept for any degree of neglect was that of a man serving his country in a dangerous and potentially self-sacrificing way. To her mind, only one duty transcended the one she and her class owed to the people on their estates—the overarching duty to the country itself.

She'd been raised to rule large estates, raised to honor, observe, indeed live by a certain code, one based on the concept of *noblesse oblige,* but driven from the heart, from a true appreciation of how the many layers of people in the common community of an estate interacted, how they relied on each other, and how important it was for all to be valued, encouraged, ultimately cared for.

Fate might have decreed that she wouldn't gain the role she'd been bred to hold, that of lady of a castle, through marriage, but circumstances had placed her in much the same role here, in Avening, caring for James and his household on the one hand, on the other overseeing the welfare of the broader community of the village and the surrounding houses and farms.

It was a role she enjoyed, one that gave her what she needed—something to do, a role she filled well, that required her particular skills.

She heard the cry of birds on the wing; halting, she looked up and spotted two swallows swooping and looping high overhead. She watched them for a moment, streaks of blue-black against the soft blue, then resettled her shawl and continued across the field. Despite the situation that had brought her there, she was content enough, as content as she imagined she might be.

Warnefleet. Passing through the rectory gates, she frowned. Was he going to disrupt her peace? Get in her way?

Continuing down the road toward the manor, she considered the likelihood; there was no *per se* reason he should. He might not be the wastrel care-for-nought she'd thought him, yet he was still just a man, moreover a man without a wife. As things stood, he would no doubt be glad to leave the guidance of the local populace to her.

Mentally nodding, endorsing that conclusion, she turned in at the manor gates and walked briskly up the drive.

She was halfway to the house when the rattle of carriage wheels had her scanning ahead. Dr. Willis appeared in his gig, the horse trotting evenly down the drive. Smiling, she stepped to the verge.

Willis drew his nag to a halt alongside her and lifted his hat. "Lady Clarice. I've just left your young man."

She grinned. "Hardly mine, but he is indeed young."

"And male." Willis's gray eyes twinkled. "But as for his condition . . ." The animation drained from the doctor's face, leaving a frown in its wake. "He's still unconscious. We tried the usual methods to revive him, but none did the trick, so he's as comfortable as I can make him, and Connimore will keep a close watch on him. I've left orders to be sent for the instant there's any change."

"What's the damage?"

Clarice listened as Willis rattled off a list of broken bones and bruises. He and she had met over sickbeds and deathbeds constantly over the past seven years; they'd formed a working partnership.

When he ended his catalog, she nodded. "I'll make sure you're kept informed of his condition."

"Thank you, my dear." Willis tipped his hat, then gathered his horse's reins. "It's a relief to know you're close by. Warnefleet's experienced with injuries, too, indeed, he must have a certain sympathy with our patient, but I don't know him well, and I trust your judgment."

With a nod and an easy smile, Clarice watched him go, then turned and walked on.

The fact that Warnefleet was experienced with injuries circled in her brain. Presumably he'd sustained injuries during his years of . . . spying. Common sense suggested that such an occupation could be rather more dangerous than simple soldiering, and that was quite dangerous enough.

But what had Willis meant by saying Warnefleet would be in *sympathy* with the injured man? Warnefleet presently had no broken bones, of that she was quite sure. He—his strength—hadn't appeared in any way impaired when he'd lifted the wrecked phaeton, or when he'd caught her.

Frowning, she reached the manor's front porch. The front door was propped open, as it often was in fine weather; she didn't bother knocking but went in. She found a footman at the back of the hall; he told her which room the young man had been put in.

She started up the stairs. The manor was a substantial house, solid and comfortable; she always enjoyed the brightly colored tapestries that hung on the walls beside the stairs. The same jewel tones featured in the arched, three-paneled leadlight window on the landing; the sun shone through in bright-hued beams to dapple the lovingly polished woodwork.

The banister was smooth under her palm as she gained the top step. Turning to her right, she headed down the corridor.

"If you ask me that London surgeon of yours needs a talking-to." Mrs. Connimore's voice floated into the corridor through the open door halfway along. "Fancy telling you it'll all just pass with time!"

"But it will," Warnefleet soothingly replied.

Clarice slowed.

"I assure you Pringle is an expert in such injuries." Warnefleet sounded certain, yet patiently resigned to Connimore's disbelief. "A few months' rest, meaning no undue exercise, and I'll be as right as rain. Besides, what other remedy could apply? There's no potion to magically cure it, and considering the location, surgical intervention is hardly something I'd invite."

Connimore's reply was a disapproving humph. "Well, we'll just have to ensure you don't go *exercising* it *unduly* for the next few months."

Clarice blinked at Connimore's emphasis. Just what part of Warnefleet's anatomy was injured?

"We can only hope," Warnefleet rejoined, amusement running beneath his words.

Clarice had three older brothers, and one younger; there was something in Warnefleet's tone that made her think . . . with a humph, she shook off the distracting thought, lifted her chin, and walked on.

She paused in the open doorway. Courtesy of the hall runner, neither Warnefleet nor Mrs. Connimore had heard her. Both were concentrating on the body in the bed. Warnefleet had been helping his housekeeper bathe the young man; they were engaged in pulling a clean nightshirt down over his lean frame.

"There!" Connimore straightened. She reached for the covers as Warnefleet tugged the neck of the nightshirt into place, then stood back. Connimore drew the covers up and patted them down around the young man. "Snug as a bug. Now if only he'd wake. . . ."

The instant he shifted his concentration from the young man, Jack sensed another's presence. No—he sensed *her* presence; he was not at all surprised to see Boadicea, tall and regal, commanding the doorway.

She met his eye and nodded. Mrs. Connimore noticed her and bobbed a curtsy. Boadicea smiled and inclined her head. "I met Dr. Willis. He told me the gentleman hadn't yet regained his wits."

Jack wondered why he hadn't rated a smile.

"Aye, that's right." Connimore glanced at the bed and grimaced. "Tried everything—burnt feathers, spirits of ammonia—but he's still deep."

Boadicea's gaze flicked to Jack; her next question was addressed to him and Connimore both. "Was there anything in his things to tell us who he is?"

Connimore looked to Jack; Boadicea followed suit.

"Coat by Shultz, and his boots *were* by Hoby."

Boadicea frowned. "One of the ton, then."

"It seems likely. The phaeton was from one of the better makers in Long Acre." After a moment, Jack asked, "Still no revelation over who he might be?"

She met his eyes, then shook her head. "None." She looked again at the young man laid out under the covers. "He's definitely familiar. I just can't place the resemblance."

"Stop worrying about it." Jack rounded the bed to stand beside her; he, too, studied the young man. Brown hair, brown brows, clean lines of forehead, cheeks, nose, and jaw; the patrician cast bore mute witness to its owner's aristocratic antecedents. "If you stop trying to force it, the connection will come to you."

She glanced at him briefly, then turned to Mrs. Connimore. Jack remained, unmoving, beside her. And waited.

Boadicea proceeded as if he didn't exist. She asked for details of Willis's visit, and Connimore reported, as if Boadicea were a centurion and his housekeeper a trooper . . .

except the relationship was more cordial than that. Boadicea was understanding, supportive, and encouraging as Connimore aired not just all they'd done, but her concerns over the young man's state.

Unwillingly, unexpectedly, Jack was impressed. Having heard of the role Boadicea had assumed in the community, he'd expected her to appear, to attempt to take the reins even though he was there now. However, despite being at some level aware of Connimore's concerns, he hadn't drawn them from her, hadn't soothed them.

Boadicea accomplished both with calm serenity, rocklike, unshakable, reliable. By implication hers was a shoulder Connimore could be certain would be there to lean on. By the time she and Connimore ended their discussion, Connimore was heartened, and Boadicea was in possession of every last snippet of information they'd gleaned about the young man and his injuries.

In light of the former, Jack couldn't begrudge her the latter. Yet still he waited, and she knew it.

He was due an apology, and had every intention of extracting maximum enjoyment from receiving it. He doubted Boadicea apologized all that often.

At last, with no alternative offering, she turned to him; he stood between her and the door. Her dark eyes bored into his—in warning?

"If I could have a word with you, my lord?" Her voice was even, her tones clear.

He smiled, stepped back, and waved her to the door. "Of course, Lady Clarice." She swept past him; as he followed he murmured, voice low so only she could hear, "I've been looking forward to hearing your thoughts."

She shot him a glance sharp enough to slice ice, then sailed down the corridor. He followed; with most women, he'd have to amble slowly, but to keep up with Boadicea he had to stride along, if not briskly, then at least without dawdling.

Reaching the top of the stairs, she paused. Joining her, he

was about to suggest they repair to his study. Chin firm, she glanced at him. "The rose garden." Looking forward, she started down the stairs. "I should take a look at it while I'm here."

His mother's rose garden? Jack remembered it as a wilderness. It had been his mother's especial place; after her death, his father had turned from it, ordering it be left undisturbed. Jack had never understoood that decision, but everyone had obeyed; the rose garden had bloomed fabulously for a few more years, a vivid and scented reminder of his mother, but neglect had taken its toll, the paths and the arches in the enclosing stone walls had become overgrown, and it had become an area into which nobody any longer ventured.

Distracted by memories, not sure what awaited him, he trailed close behind as Clarice led the way through his morning room, onto the terrace, down the steps, and across the lawn . . . to the now neat, stone archway leading into the rose garden.

Slowing, he followed her through, pausing under the archway. For one instant, he thought he'd stepped back in time.

The garden was exactly as his seven-year-old eyes had seen it, a shifting sea of colors and textures, of rampantly arching canes and bright green leaves, of sharp thorns and the unfurling bronze of new growth.

Clarice had sailed on, down the central path heading for the alcove at the far end of the garden, with its stone bench overlooking a small pond and fountain. He stepped down to the path; transported by memories, he slowly followed.

His mind conjured visions from his childhood, of him, blond hair flopping over his eyes as he raced down the paths. All the paths led to the alcove where his mother would be waiting, laughing and smiling as he pelted toward her to tell her of the best bloom in the garden, of the dark, blood-red rose he'd liked best, of the rich, almost overpowering perfume that wafted in waves from the deep pink rose that had been her favorite.

Without conscious thought, he looked for it, and found it there, covered with fat buds.

Eventually, he reached the end of the path. Eshewing the stone bench, Boadicea had paused by the pond; she was idly examining buds on a cascading bush, patiently waiting for him to join her.

Drawing in a deep breath, savoring the almost forgotten scents that came with it, he relutantly drew his mind from the past and focused on her. "Did you do this?"

She blinked. "Not personally. I did suggest Warren, the gardener Griggs found after Hedgemore left, tidy the place and get it back in order."

Jack translated easily; tidy and back in order meant restored to the most exacting standards—Lady Clarice Altwood's standards. He glanced around; obviously Warren had understood her, too.

"Did they—Griggs and the others—tell you why the garden had been left to go to seed?" He brought his gaze back to her face.

Far from coloring, as many might have done, she merely raised a brow. "They told me your father had ordered it be shut up, but he was gone by then, and, frankly, I've never seen the point in celebrating a death rather than celebrating the life."

He held her dark gaze; it didn't waver in the least. She was, at least over the garden and its present state, as calm and assured as she outwardly appeared. For all she knew, she might have trampled his toes and be in for a nasty altercation . . . he glanced around again, unable to help himself. She couldn't know she'd given him back something he hadn't realized he'd mourned, and had just put into simple adult words exactly what he, as a boy, had always felt but been unable to express.

"It's as I remember it." That was all he could find to say, that he could easily say.

He looked back at her. To his surprise, faint color had now risen to her alabaster cheeks. Aware of it, and of his gaze, she shifted, then admitted, "I found a notebook of your mother's, with a detailed plan of the garden. I didn't think you'd mind me consulting it to bring the garden back to what it was."

He studied her face, then glanced around. "I don't mind."

He sensed a certain relief ripple through her; her stance—her stiffness—eased a fraction. But then she drew breath, and drew herself up, and faced him. "Now—I believe I owe you an apology, my lord."

The words were brisk, even. They effectively drew him back from the past, into the present.

He smiled at her. Intently. "You perceive me all ears, my lady."

She didn't frown, but her gaze sharpened. For a moment, she studied him, as if debating whether to inform him gloating was uncouth, then she raised her chin and fixed him with a challengingly direct gaze. "When we first met I misjudged you, my lord. Pray accept my apologies."

Clarice waited, willing him to simply nod.

Instead, he raised his brows. "Misjudged? How so, if I might make so bold as to ask?"

His hazel eyes held hers. She felt her temper stir. Make so bold, indeed. "As you're perfectly well aware, I thought—had deduced from what I'd heard from others here—that you cared nothing for your acres, and were wholly absorbed with the typical, frivolous, and inconsequential entertainments of gentlemen of our class. That view, it appears, was incorrect."

His brows rose higher. "I thought it was my prolonged absences that invoked your ire?"

She pressed her lips tight, then nodded. "Indeed. But I now understand those absences were . . . excusable. Understandable."

"Perhaps even laudable?"

She drew in a breath, held it, then nodded again. "Even that."

He smiled, all gratified male.

She exhaled, pleased to have the deed over and done—

"You didn't hear anything specific from those round about, and you didn't ask what they thought of me, either. You leapt to unwarranted conclusions."

She snapped her eyes up to his and caught her breath. Felt her own eyes widen as he stepped closer, and she was afforded a glimpse of the man behind the charming mask—one whose honor she'd impugned, at least as he saw it. Looking into his face, at his squared jaw, the etched line of his lips—and most especially the changeable, now clear and agatey-hard hazel of his eyes—she understood that clearly.

He was one of the few men she'd ever met who made her feel . . . slight. And some part of her knew he wasn't even trying, not deliberately trying to physically intimidate her.

Eating crow suddenly seemed easy. Even advisable. Holding his hard gaze, she nodded. "Yes."

He blinked. His brows rose again; this time, when his eyes met hers, she detected surprise, swiftly superseded by an untrustworthy amusement that warmed the hazel depths, softening them. His lips eased, but he managed not to smile. "Just yes? No equivocation?"

She narrowed her eyes to slits; folding her arms, she fixed him with a gaze just short of a glare. "You're determined to be difficult over this, aren't you?"

"Difficult? Me? Everyone round about will assure you I'm the most easygoing gentleman you're ever likely to meet."

She sniffed. "More fool them."

"It would be unwise to leap to any further conclusions about me, don't you think?"

She held his gaze, then succinctly replied, "Overlooking the obvious would be more unwise."

Amusement again flirted about his mobile lips. With any other, she'd be incensed; with him, she was intrigued. . . .

The oddity of that brought her back to earth with a thump.

She lowered her arms. "You've forgiven me—I know you have." She started to turn away. "There's no point dragging this out—"

"I haven't forgiven you." Jack moved across and into her, with one step trapped her against the edge of the pond. The basin of the fountain within it stood shoulder high, preventing her from leaning back. He studied her eyes from close quarters; such dark, dark brown was hard to read, but he sensed from their wideness, from her quickened breathing, that he'd succeeded in claiming her entire attention.

Tauntingly, he let his lips quirk, let his eyes light with understanding. "Perhaps an olive branch? That might sway me." Beyond his control, his gaze dropped to her lips. "Might appease me."

And my demons.

He had to fight not to move closer still, to crowd her even more . . . to feel her body against his, teasing, tempting . . .

She licked her lips. He watched the tip of her tongue slide over the lush, lower curve; something inside him clenched. Tight.

"What olive branch?"

She'd managed to find enough breath to speak evenly, to infuse the words with a veneer of her customary haughtiness—enough to spark his less-civilized instincts.

"A kiss."

He hadn't even needed to think. That was what he wanted from her, now, here in her resurrection of his mother's garden.

She blinked, but he sensed she wasn't shocked. Nor was she unwilling . . . he had to drag in a breath and fight to hold his instincts back, to give her time enough to agree before he took, seized.

Her eyes returned to his; she eyed him, not warily so much as assessingly. Measuringly.

He wasn't entirely surprised by her unmissish reaction. From James's revelations, he'd calculated that she was twenty-nine. She'd been betrothed twice, had farewelled a guardsman going to war once, had been about to elope once. She'd been pursued by many. He knew the males of his class, knew the females, too. She wouldn't be—couldn't be—totally innocent.

And she'd been living here for seven years, buried in the country with no one—no gentleman of the style and class with whom she might dally. His style, his class, and now he was home. To stay.

He could almost see the procession of facts cross her mind.

He wasn't the least surprised when she said, "In return for a kiss—one kiss and nothing more—you'll agree never to mention or allude to my leaping to unwarranted conclusions again?"

Holding her gaze, he nodded. "Yes."

Her head rose; her dark eyes flashed. "Very well—one kiss."

He smiled, and reached for her.

Chapter 4

One kiss. Clarice hadn't been able to resist. She had to know, had to reassure herself he was just like all the others—of no real consequence. That the response he evoked in her was an aberration that meant nothing, that she could ignore it. And one kiss—just one—could pose no great danger. She'd been kissed before; in her opinion, the activity was overrated.

The instant his hand touched the back of her waist, the instant her breasts touched his chest, she realized her mistake.

Her breath tangled in her throat.

One large hand clasped her nape; his thumb beneath her jaw tipped her head back as he lowered his. For a heartbeat his lips hovered above hers; she glimpsed his hazel eyes gleaming from beneath long lashes—in that instant realized he fully intended this kiss would be anything but easily dismissed.

Then he swooped and captured her lips.

Claimed them and her senses, her entire mind . . . not with force, not with strength, but with temptation. His lips moved on hers, confident yet beguiling, searching, learning, then, as if satisfied he'd reconnoitered the terrain, his lips firmed.

She kept hers shut, tried to remain passive—and failed. Stunned, she found herself responding; she hadn't intended to at all. Certainly hadn't intended to part her lips for him, but then his tongue slid between and found hers, and pleasure bloomed.

Lured. Beckoned.

Was there a male version of a siren?

If there was, he and his lips qualified. She knew what he wanted, knew what he intended, yet still she went forward, following his artful, highly skillful lead. Into an exchange that was fascinating, intriguing, exciting—all the things kisses for her had never been.

Just a kiss, she mentally swore, but her limbs didn't answer her call as he smoothly gathered her into his arms, surrounded her with his strength, a strength that, at such close quarters, warmed and reassured.

Tempted and enticed.

She hadn't expected that. She usually couldn't abide being held, confined, restricted. Controlled. Yet when he drew her against him, against his hard frame, all resistance fled; she had to fight a far-too-revealing urge to abandon all sense and sink against him.

And still the kiss went on, a shifting blend of subtle yet blatant exploration inexorably superseded by flagrant demand. He wasn't in any way less than direct; even less was he hesitant. He asked for no permission as he angled his head and deepened the kiss—sweeping her into deeper waters.

Waters in which she'd never before swum. The distant part of her mind that still functioned was shocked to discover herself outflanked, outmaneuvered, totally out of her depth. Plunged, not gently but forcefully into a world of sensation and hunger, where passion swirled, indistinct as yet, more mist and promise than solid reality, yet hot, demanding, and exciting nonetheless. Each press of his lips, each too-knowingly languid thrust of his tongue sent a lick of desire sliding through her.

Sent heat through her flesh, weakening her limbs, melting her steel.

Jack felt her hands slide up his chest, hesitate on his

shoulders, then rise to frame his face. To grasp and hold tight as their lips fused, as he tasted her, as he learned just how much to his liking she was. Even locked deep in the kiss, in the immersion of his senses, he felt the touch of her cool fingers on his cheeks, on his jaw, felt reaction streak through him.

Nearly cheered.

He tightened his arms about her instead, greedily drawing her more fully against him. Flush, so he could feel her softness cradling him, sense the promise in the long, taut thighs pressed to his. Glory in the firmness of her breasts, in the ruched nipples poking his chest.

Then she kissed him back—not just responded but clamped his head between her hands and pressed a voracious, hungry, defiantly passionate caress of lips and tongue upon him. She sent his senses careening as she leaned into him, into his embrace, and blatantly incited not just him, but herself.

He knew that last instinctively, knew she was exploring as much as he had earlier, but not, in her case, the physical, as he had; she was wholly engrossed in the sensual. She wanted it, grasped the moment and all he offered, and stroked, caressed, learned, and left him aching.

Beneath the clamor of his senses, something primal stirred, some part of him that hadn't prowled in years but that now scented the right prey, lifted its head, and stretched. He savored her, luxuriated in her promise, in the heady invitation inherent in her bold and challenging response.

And started to plot, to plan.

Some small part of his mind was congratulating himself on the superiority of his instincts—he'd been wanting to kiss her for hours—and his good sense in acting so promptly in that regard, when footsteps sounded on the paved path.

He lifted his head, instantly alert.

He was smugly aware that a finite moment passed before, blinking, she refocused.

And tensed. Before she could struggle he released her,

setting her back on her feet. "The side path," he said, voice low. "They haven't seen us."

She glanced around, still a trifle dazed. She shot him a glance to see if he'd noticed; he pretended to be oblivious, looking past her to where Crawler had come into view, walking along a secondary path leading to the alcove.

Crawler saw them; his grizzled face cleared. "Howlett said as he thought you'd headed this way."

Nearing, Crawler nodded to Jack, then his gaze switched to Clarice. "Begging your pardon, m'lady, but if you've a minute when you're finished with his lordship . . . ?"

Clarice flicked a glance Jack's way. "I'm quite finished with his lordship. What can I help you with?"

She moved, stepping closer to Crawler; Jack quashed a powerful urge to reach out and haul her back, and whisper in her ear that she was very far from being finished with him, or he with her.

Not after that kiss.

"I was wondering," Crawler said, "if you've any ideas about that new mare Mr. Trelliwell's been riding. Seems he feels she's not up to his weight and wants rid of her. He's asking a fair price, but I wondered if you'd heard any whispers—whether there was any other reason he wanted shot of her?"

Boadicea smiled. Knowingly. Crawler's eyes lit.

"I heard," she said, "that Mr. Trelliwell suffered a rather embarrassing accident when out with the Quorn a few weeks ago. I heard he was riding a bay mare, and that mare is a bay, isn't she?"

Crawler snorted. "Tipped him over a fence, did she? Well, that suits me—I want her for breeding. She has right nice lines"—this Crawler directed at Jack—"and I'm always in favor of spirit in a mare."

"Indeed." Jack smiled, jovially man-to-man. "Spirited fillies make quite the best riding all around."

Darting a glance at Boadicea, Crawler manfully swallowed his guffaw.

But Clarice had looked down, absorbed with flicking out her skirts. When she looked up, her expression was as usual, serenely calm with a touch of hauteur. "If you'll excuse me, gentlemen, I must get back to the rectory."

Crawler immediately bowed. "Thank you for the advice, m'lady. I'll be off to see Mr. Trelliwell tomorrow morning."

She directed a gracious smile at Crawler, but when she turned to Jack, there was nothing but dark warning in her eyes. "Lord Warnefleet." She inclined her head regally, then added, more softly, "Welcome home."

With that, she turned, and sailed away up the central path.

Jack watched her go, the frown in his mind due to more than the simple fact that he hadn't wanted her to leave, yet she had. He found it difficult to tear his gaze from the elegant line of her back, the perfect inverted heart shape of her hips and bottom as she walked away . . . and left him standing.

Mentally gritting his teeth, he forced his gaze to Crawler. He felt he should have known about Trelliwell's mare, that it should have been he who Crawler had come to. He knew that was irrational, yet . . . outwardly relaxed, he met Crawler's gaze. "So tell me about this mare. And what else have you been dabbling in breedingwise, you old reprobate?"

Crawler chuckled and told him as together they walked to the stables.

But the main part of Jack's mind remained in the rose garden, with the opportunity he'd sensed, and was determined to pursue, despite—or perhaps because of—the complex mix of reactions a certain warrior-queen evoked in him. And those he evoked in her.

He was quite certain she'd guessed he wouldn't be content with one kiss, not now; that was what that warning in her eyes had been about, why she'd so slickly seized the opportunity Crawler had presented to escape.

Did she truly think he wouldn't pursue it, and her—that she could with just a censorious look warn him off?

Probably.

Unfortunately, she'd misjudged him—again. He had every

intention of pursuing her, and would, but he was too wise to simply ride forth to engage with a warrior-queen secure in her domain. He'd pursue her, but on his terms.

In his own time, in his own way, in a place of his choosing.

After that kiss, definitely in a place of his choosing.

One that eliminated all chance of interruptions.

Jack spent a quiet evening letting his staff fuss over him. The dinner Mrs. Connimore set before him would have done justice to a king; it was a pity, he later reflected, nursing a glass of brandy in the library, that a certain warrior-queen hadn't been there to share it.

He sat and sipped, letting the peace and tranquility of home sink in, the quiet tock of the longcase clock, the comforting crackle of the log in the grate, feeling the glow from the brandy spread through him, reminiscent of the fire Boadicea evoked . . .

After a long moment, he shifted in his chair, then resolutely redirected his mind to his alternate plan to ensure his succession. It was the only alternative, but if matters fell out as he hoped, it would do.

Gradually, the day caught up with him; his head still ached, but no longer throbbed. Draining his glass, he went upstairs, along the way noticing this and that, little items, glimpses of the past . . .

He was home.

He slept well, better than he had in thirteen years. He awoke with a clear head, rose, washed, and dressed for the day, a sense of anticipation buoying him.

Walking through the gallery, he saw Mrs. Connimore come out of the bedchamber in which the young man lay. Pausing at the top of the stairs, he waited for her to join him.

"Good morning, my lord." Mrs. Connimore beamed at him. "And it's a pleasure to be able to say that, you may be sure."

He smiled. "Thank you, and good morning to you. How's the patient?"

Mrs. Connimore's face fell. "Still not with us."

Jack nodded and started down the stairs, knowing she'd insist he go first.

Connimore followed. "I'll send word to Dr. Willis, and to Lady Clarice."

Jack paused, then shook aside an urge to ask why Lady Clarice Altwood needed to be informed; it would only fluster Connimore, and Boadicea had, after all, been instrumental in rescuing the gentleman. He continued down the stairs and headed for the breakfast parlor. He was disinclined to allow anything to dim his ebullient mood.

After demolishing a plate of ham, eggs, and pikelets, washed down with a mug of strong coffee while perusing the latest news-sheet, he headed for the study, and Griggs. He expected his faithful agent to be eager to go through all that had been done in his absence and reacquaint him with the current state of the manor. In that, he wasn't disappointed; Griggs, old cheeks flushed with pleasure, laid out ledgers and accounts with not a little pride.

Justifiable pride; the estate was doing better than Jack had imagined it could.

Something else he hadn't expected was the number of times Clarice's name figured in Griggs's explanations for the manor's improved state.

"Now." Pince-nez perched on his nose, Griggs set another open ledger before Jack. "We've managed to increase the yields from the south fields."

Jack couldn't stop himself. "Lady Clarice . . . ?"

"She suggested—oh, a few years ago now—that Hidgson might rotate his clover with his grains. Seemed no harm trying it, so he did." Griggs pointed to a row of neat figures. "Improved the yield by ten percent the first year, then another five percent the year after. We're now running the same system in the east fields, and they're coming along well, too. If you look here . . ."

Jack looked, and absorbed, and asked himself why he minded.

He hadn't been here. She had.

A trip to the stables before lunch should have restored his mood; instead, while listening to Crawler bring him up to date on his horses and his herds, he learned that Clarice knew a remarkable amount about horses, cattle, and sheep, and their husbandry. Enough, at least, to have gained the respect of Crawler, a confirmed misogynist, or so Jack had always thought.

Lunchtime arrived; when, later, he visited Connimore and Cook in the kitchens, he discovered the recipe for the asparagus soup he'd so enjoyed had been introduced to his household by . . . Lady Clarice.

He forced a charming smile and asked after the young gentleman.

"No change." Connimore shook her head. "Lady Clarice sent word she'd drop by this afternoon."

His smile grew tight. "I'm afraid I'll miss her—I'm going to ride around the estate."

With a nod, he left the kitchens, strode out to the stables, called for Challenger to be saddled, then swung himself up and thundered off across the fields. *His* fields. *His* land.

He prayed his tenants wouldn't fill his ears with tales of Lady Clarice and her suggestions.

They did, of course.

By the time he turned Challenger's head for home, he had a very clear idea of how Boadicea had filled her time, buried down there in the country. And while some part of his brain told him his instinctive response to her actions was irrational—she *wasn't* trying to interfere, nor had she deliberately usurped his position—yet still he smarted, justifiably or not.

He still felt . . . slighted in some indefinable way.

Illogical, irrational, and given Boadicea, probably idiotic, yet he couldn't shake the feeling, couldn't free himself of the emotion.

When he turned into the village street and, looking ahead, saw her talking to the innkeeper, Jed Butler, then saw them go into the tap, he couldn't stop his reaction.

Leaving Challenger with Jed's son in the yard behind the inn, he entered the tap quietly through the side door. Neither Clarice nor Jed heard him; they were standing facing the long, scarred bar, studying it and the wall behind it. Halting in the shadows behind them, Jack listened.

"I thought as how, if we knock out that wall there, we'll be able to open up that back parlor. Hardly ever used, it is, and Betsy says as we could serve food for the lads in there. They won't go into the dining room, o'course, and with their boots an' all, we'd not want them to, and summer they do like the tables outdoors, but in winter, we could make this place right snug, and they'd have some place by the bar to eat as well as drink."

Boadicea had been nodding slowly throughout. "I think that's an excellent idea, but—"

"Lady Clarice." Jack heard the hard command in his voice; he softened it as Clarice and Jed swung to face him, and nodded genially to the innkeeper. "Jed."

Jed blinked, then bobbed his head. "M'lord."

Clarice scanned his face. She opened her mouth.

Before she could speak, Jack seized her hand. "If you'll excuse us, Jed, I want a few words with Lady Clarice." He met her gaze briefly as he turned to the door. "Outside."

He would have hauled her out with him—towed her—but after that fleeting exchange of glances she went with him readily if not willingly, giving him, his temper, not even that much satisfaction. Her hand in his, he led her out of the side door, across the grassed lane that led to the rear yard, making for the inn's orchard beyond. He strode for the gap in the orchard wall, registering that Boadicea's long legs kept pace without hurrying in the least.

The distracting observation only sharpened his flinty mood.

Three stone steps led into the orchard; he went down them and continued beneath the trees. Without warning, Boadicea halted, dug in her heels, and pulled back. "Lord Warnefleet!"

"Jack." Curt, abrupt, he flung the name over his shoulder and jerked her on. With a gasp—stifled—she was forced to follow; he wanted to be far enough from the lane so no one passing would be able to hear them. "If you're going to be me, you might at least use my name!"

"Wh—what?"

"Don't play the innocent—it doesn't become you."

An instant passed, then she said, "I beg your pardon?"

Her voice had turned to ice, dripping with chilly warning. He ignored it. "As well you might."

"Have you taken leave of your senses?"

They were in the middle of the orchard with nothing but trees and apple blossom for company. Jack halted and swung to face her. "Not yet."

He still held her hand; they were close, only a foot between them.

She read his eyes; he thought hers widened.

"It may interest you to know that while reacquainting myself with my estate, with all the numerous aspects of it, one refrain has sounded again and again—'Lady Clarice suggested.' Lady Clarice suggested this, Lady Clarice suggested that—there seems very little of my business, madam, in which you haven't had a hand!"

Clarice drew breath, straightened, stiffened. A deadening feeling swelled in the pit of her stomach; she was fairly sure she knew what was coming. She fought to keep her expression impassive, to hide any reaction to his biting words.

She continued to meet his aggravated hazel gaze. Irritation—very male, highly charged—poured from him.

"And now, after an entire day of hearing just how busy you've been over the years I've been away, I discover you consulting over structural alterations to the inn."

He paused, his gaze pinning her. "It may interest you to know that I own the inn." His tone was cutting. "No changes should be made without my express approval—"

"Indeed." She kept her tone even; if they both lost their tempers, there would be hell to pay. "And if you had let me finish what I was saying to Jed, you would have heard me tell him that as the manor owned the inn, before he made any alterations to the fabric he should seek the estate's permission, and as you were now home, he should approach you directly."

He shut his lips. But there was no taking back what he'd already said. Already revealed. They both knew it.

She wondered what he would do. Their gazes remained locked, but she couldn't read what passed behind the hard agate of his eyes.

Eventually, he drew in a huge breath; his chest swelled, his long fingers uncurled, releasing her hand, but the dangerous tension riding him abated not one jot.

"Lady Clarice." His accents were still clipped, his tone still cutting. "I would greatly appreciate it if henceforth, should any of my people approach you for assistance on any subject that falls within Avening Manor's purlieu, you would refer them directly to me."

Before he could add anything further, she nodded, as abrupt and curt as he. "As you wish, Lord Warnefleet."

He blinked. Lifting her head, she grasped the moment to add, "I'm sorry that my advising your people has discomposed you. In my defence, their need was real, you weren't here, but I was. For seven years, that was the case—asking me has become their habit. It will, necessarily, take some time for them to realize that you are now here for them to approach. I fear I cannot pretend to any regret that I helped them, however, I can assure you that I will from now on refer all their requests to you."

With her most regal nod, she turned away. "I bid you good day, Lord Warnefleet."

She took two steps, then stopped. Head rising, she asked without turning, "Incidentally, did you discover any instance in which my advice to your people caused any detriment of any kind to them or to the estate?"

After a moment, he replied, "No."

She nodded, lips twisting. "Just so."

Without glancing back, she walked calmly to the lane, and then around the inn.

Jack stood in the orchard, under the blasted apple blossom, and watched her go. Watched her walk away, her spine stiff, her movements gracefully controlled, yet somehow screaming of injury.

But he'd done the right thing. He was home now, there for his people to consult. Their dependency on her had to stop, and there was realistically only one way to achieve that. . . .

He exhaled; hands rising to his hips, he looked up at the clouds of pink and white blossoms, and inwardly swore. Perhaps he should have been more tactful. Perhaps he shouldn't have lost . . . he wasn't even sure it was his temper that had driven him, rather than something more primitive, some form of territorial imperative.

Regardless, he'd been within his rights, yet . . . he was sorry to see the back of her like that, walking away from him.

Sorry to have her faintly contemptuous, definitely cold "Lord Warnefleet" ringing in his ears.

He'd definitely done the right thing. Jack repeated that refrain as, after breakfast the next day, he settled in his study to go over the projected accounts. He was adding figures when Howlett tapped on the door.

Jack looked up as Howlett entered, carefully closing the door behind him.

"My lord." Howlett looked confused. "Mrs. Swithins is here—she wishes to discuss the roster for supplying the church flowers."

Jack looked blank.

Howlett hurried on, "Lady Clarice usually—"

"No, no." Jack laid down his pen. "Show Mrs. Swithins in."

Howlett looked uncertain, but did. Mrs. Swithins proved to be a large, regrettably hatchet-faced lady dressed in a style both more severe and more formal than generally favored by country ladies of her station. Her woollen coat had a fur collar; her poke bonnet was anchored by a wide ribbon tied in a large bow beneath her second chin.

Rising, Jack smiled his charming smile, rapidly revising

his guess of who Mrs. Swithins was. He'd heard James's new curate, whom he'd yet to meet, was a Mr. Swithins; Jack had assumed Mrs. Swithins to be the curate's wife. This woman, however, had to be Swithins's mother.

"Mrs. Swithins." He waved her to a chair.

"Lord Warnefleet." She bobbed a curtsy and swept forward to perch, spine rigid, on the edge of the chair. "I'm exceedingly glad to see you returned, sir, hale and whole and prepared to take up the duties that are rightfully yours."

She smiled up at him, but the gesture failed to soften her stony eyes. Jack wondered why hearing her declare his state perfectly accurately made him want to deny it, or at least equivocate.

"I understand you have some questions about some roster for the church." Resuming his seat, Jack assumed a wryly apologetic expression guaranteed to gain the sympathy of the most hard-hearted. "I'm afraid you have the advantage of me. Having just returned, I'm unaware of just what roster you're referring to."

"Well!" Mrs. Swithins's bosom swelled impressively. "I can assist you there. It's the supply of the flowers for the Sunday and Wednesday services."

Jack sat back and listened as Mrs. Swithins described the roster that Clarice had set in train, which had Mrs. Swithins supplying the flowers for every second Sunday, and the alternate Wednesdays.

"It would simplify matters considerably, my lord, if the roster was reorganized so that I supplied the floral arrangements for each Sunday, and the others between them took care of every Wednesday." Mrs. Swithins paused, eyeing him, then added, "So much easier for all of us not to have to try and remember which week is which."

Jack raised his brows. "That seems reasonable enough." A tiny voice whispered that Clarice wouldn't have instituted a complicated roster if a simple one would have sufficed; he ignored it and leaned forward. "I see no reason not to revamp the roster as you suggest. Now." He drew a sheet of paper to him. "Who are the other ladies involved?"

Mrs. Swithins beamed. "Oh, you don't need to bother informing them, my lord." She all but preened as she stood. "I'll be happy to spread the word."

Instinct flared, combining with that tiny voice to niggle; rising to see Mrs. Swithins out, Jack quashed both. It was only the church flowers, for heaven's sake, hardly a matter of life and death.

With Mrs. Swithins gone, clearly delighted with her first encounter with the new Lord Warnefleet, he settled into his chair once more and returned to his projections.

He was still wrestling with his crop returns—there was some element contributing to the past years' progressively increasing totals that he couldn't identify—when Howlett looked in to announce luncheon.

Jack rose and stretched, inwardly savoring the sense of sinking back into the deeply familiar but long-denied regimen of country life. Following Howlett from the study, he reached the front hall just as the doorbell pealed.

And pealed.

Howlett hurried to open the front door. Curious, Jack followed.

"I want to see his lordship!" an agitated female voice demanded. "It's important, Howlett!"

Jack hung back, screened by the door. There was an incipient catch in the young woman's voice that sent a shudder through him. Tearful scenes had never been his forte.

"What's it about, Betsy?" Howlett sounded concerned, kindly and soothing.

"The church flowers!" Betsy wailed. "That old bat Swithins said as how his lordship had '*quite agreed with her*' that she should do all the Sundays! It's not fair—how could he give them all to her?"

Jack blinked. Howlett slid him a sidelong, questioning—clearly lost—glance.

Jack reminded himself he was a battle-hardened warrior. Mentally girding his loins, he stepped around Howlett, into the doorway.

Betsy saw him. She bobbed a quick curtsy. "My lord, I—"

"Come inside, Betsy." Jack smiled his practiced smile and hoped charming the innkeeper's wife would work. "I understand there's some problem about the church flowers. I don't quite follow—why don't you come in and explain it to me?"

Betsy eyed him rather warily, but nodded and followed him in. Jack showed her into the study, where she sat perched, rather more nervously, in the same chair Mrs. Swithins had earlier occupied.

Jack had just resumed his seat behind the desk when Howlett tapped and looked in again. "Mrs. Candlewick and Martha Skegs are coming up the drive, my lord."

Mrs. Candlewick was the cooper's wife, and Martha helped in the inn.

Some of Betsy's confidence returned. "They'll be here 'bout the flowers, same as me. Swithins must have been real quick to find them to gloat."

Jack inwardly sighed; he looked at Howlett. "Show the good ladies in."

Howlett did, but rather than aiding in clarifying the situation, listening to three females simultaneously bewail the forwardness—the most complimentary term they used for what they saw as Mrs. Swithins's encroaching on their rights and privileges—of the curate's mother left Jack ready to pull out his hair.

His head was throbbing when he held up a hand, silencing the diatribe. "Ladies, I fear my decision on the roster earlier today was based on insufficient information." His jaw set as he recalled how Mrs. Swithins had presented her case without any mention of the wishes of others. "I'll revisit that decision, but first I want to consult with others to make sure that what I decide is fair to all." To make sure he didn't commit some other unwitting faux pas.

All three women appeared mollified by his pronouncement. They nodded in acceptance, their color still high but their agitation subsiding.

Rapidly canvassing his options, he asked, "Under the previous roster, who would do the flowers this coming Sunday?"

The three exchanged glances. "Her," Betsy said. "Swithins."

Jack nodded. "So there's no real change, regardless of which roster we're following, until next week. I'll revise the roster and have it to you all, and Mrs. Swithins, before Monday. Will that suit?"

"Yes, thank you, my lord," they chorused.

"Just so long as Swithins doesn't get more than the Sundays she's due." The light of battle still glowed in Mrs. Candlewick's eyes.

Jack rose as they did. "I'll ensure the final roster is a fair and equitable one."

They all accepted that assurance; Betsy even smiled as she shyly shook his hand and with the two older women took her leave.

Jack watched them retreat down the drive, then finally headed for his waiting lunch.

He suspected they thought he'd consult with Clarice, even if he hadn't mentioned her name. However, there had to be others who could advise him as well.

Connimore blinked at him when he sought her out after lunch. "I'm sure I couldn't say, my lord." Then she grimaced. "Well, truth is, I wouldn't like to say. That Mrs. Swithins is a right old stick, but she is the poor curate's mother, after all, and what else does she have to do? But then Betsy and June Candlewick and Martha do get their noses out of joint—well, I'm glad I'm not in your shoes having to weigh up the rights and wrongs of it."

Jack wasn't sure he wanted to be in his shoes either, not over this, but . . . there were three days yet to Sunday. He'd work something out by then.

The young gentleman had yet to regain his wits. Connimore told him Willis would call later in the day. "And no doubt Lady Clarice will drop by."

Jack sincerely doubted it. He wondered whether he should disabuse Connimore of her expectation. Instead, he left her counting pillowcases and headed back to his study.

To the profits from his crops that, it seemed, ought somehow to be higher than he could reasonably predict. That was the only way the figures from previous years would align with his projections for the current year. There had to be some positive something he was missing.

He considered asking Griggs, but he couldn't put his finger on what question to ask, short of going through the profits from the whole estate, segment by segment. Head in his hands, vainly trying to suppress the thudding between his temples, he was, once again, totting up figures when Howlett looked in.

Jack looked up, grateful for the interruption.

"It's Wallace, my lord. He'd like a word."

One of his tenant farmers, Wallace was a slow, steady country type Jack had known all his life. He sat back with a smile. "Show him in."

Wallace lumbered in. Jack rose, still smiling, and shook hands.

"Does my heart good to see you again, my lord, and looking so hearty." Wallace nodded at Jack as he sat. "And just as it should be, to see you behind your father's desk and all."

Jack relaxed. Wallace sat in the chair before the desk, his bulk filling it, his slow country humor pure balm after Jack's difficult morning.

Once they'd indulged in the customary exchanges, bringing him up to date with Wallace's family and his acres, Jack asked, "You seem to have everything running as smoothly as ever—what can I help you with?"

"Aye, well." Wallace rubbed his stubbled chin. "Some things one can order, others . . ." He drew breath and went on, "It's my daughter, Mary. She's been walking out with John Hawkins's boy, Roger. They're thinking of tying the knot, and I was wondering what would be right to make over as Mary's portion. I don't want to be miserly, and John's an old friend, so we're all pleased with the match, but I do have two other girls and, of course, there's my lad, Joe, who'll get most."

Wallace met Jack's gaze. "I wondered if you had any advice as to how much Mary's portion should be?"

Jack blinked. He had absolutely no idea what amount would be a suitable marriage portion for Mary Wallace. Not an inkling, not a clue. But Wallace was looking at him as if he should know. "Ah . . . leave it with me." There had to be someone he could ask, someone other than a certain lady who, he was perfectly sure, would know the answer. "I'll ask around quietly. You'll be at church on Sunday—I'll let you know what I come up with then."

Wallace beamed. "Any help would be greatly appreciated, my lord."

Transparently relieved, Wallace departed.

Jack sank back in his chair, wondering how the devil to live up to Wallace's expectations.

He'd barely refocused on the sheet of figures still taunting him with his inability to make sense of them when the doorbell pealed once more. Jack sat back and waited. Howlett eventually appeared, closing the door behind him—a telling sign.

"A Mr. Jones, my lord. He's an apple merchant from Bristol—he supplies the cider makers."

Jack's brows rose. The apple crop from the valley traditionally went to the Gloucester merchants. "Show Mr. Jones in—let's hear what he has to say."

The gentleman Howlett ushered in was, at first glance, short, rotund, and jovial, very like an apple himself. But as Jack lazily rose and extended his hand, he noted the hardness in Jones's eyes and the tight, rather mean line of his mouth. "Mr. Jones. I understand you're interested in our apples?"

Jones shook his hand. "Indeed, my lord. Just so."

"Please be seated." Jack waved to the chair before the desk and resumed his own. "Now, how can I help you?"

"Ah, well, my lord, I rather fancy the shoe's on the other foot. If you've a moment, I'd like to explain how I believe I can help you."

Jack inclined his head, with a gesture indicated Jones should proceed, and withheld judgment. Jones's glib patter prodded his instincts—certainly not, judging by his too-genial smile, what Jones intended.

Jones settled in the chair. "I have to say, my lord, that I'm delighted you're back in the saddle here."

Jack suppressed a blink. "You've dealt with the estate before?"

Jones grimaced. "Tried to. I've called for the past five years. The first two years I met with some old gentleman—a Mr. Grigg, I think it was. Then the last three years, there was this . . . lady."

Jack was certain Jones had been about to say "female," but had changed his mind.

Jones looked inquiringly at him. "Your sister, would that be?"

Jack met his eyes. "As you say, the reins are now in my hands. I take it you have a proposition to make?"

Jones looked slightly taken aback at the abrupt focus on business, but quickly rallied. "It's quite simple, my lord. I can take your entire crop for a shilling more per bushel than you'll get from anyone else."

"I see." Jack was certain he didn't—not all, not yet. "We usually supply the merchants in Gloucester."

Jones opened his eyes wide. "But this is business, my lord. You have a crop to sell, and I'm offering the best terms. No reason you should feel obliged to settle for a lower price because of the past. The Gloucester merchants will manage, no doubt. There are plenty of other orchards, but my clients are most fussy about the quality of the apples that go into their vats."

A glimmer of a suspicion crossed Jack's mind; the figures he'd been wrestling with all day . . . if a premium was built into the apple crop, that would balance his projections with the previous returns.

He refocused on Jones, waiting, expectant. "Your offer is tempting, Mr. Jones, but I'll need to consider carefully." Aside from all else, the manor negotiated for the entire valley; his decision would commit not just the manor crop but those from his tenant farmers and from the few freeholders in the area. "Have you been up Nailsworth way yet?"

"No, no—just starting in this neck of the woods. Avening ranks high on our list for quality crops, so I always start filling my quota here."

"I see." Jack registered the subtle pressure in the mention of a quota; his inclination was to dismiss the offer, but he didn't yet know the full story. "In that case, I imagine, as Avening does indeed have the highest-quality crop, you would be happy to call back in two days to learn of my decision. I must consult with the other growers and determine where we stand as to expected yields."

"Yes, of course." Jones smiled, stood, and held out his hand. "We're prepared to take all you have at one shilling above the best offer you've had from anywhere else. However much the valley can supply, we're willing to take every last bushel."

Jack inclined his head and showed Jones out. Closing the study door, Jack slowly returned to his desk. Jones's poorly concealed delight on hearing he would consult with the other growers revolved in his mind; the man clearly thought avarice over that extra shilling per bushel would swing the deal his way, but there had to be a catch. A worm in Jones's bright and shining apple.

Or, perhaps, poison?

Jack knew what his instincts were telling him, but he couldn't yet see what Jones truly intended. Dropping into his chair, he pulled his sheet of figures to him. Ten minutes of factoring a premium into the price for the apple crop and he had numbers that at long last tallied.

But that only raised another question. If, as he'd intimated, Jones hadn't succeeded in buying Avening's apple crops for the last five years, where had the consistently paid premium come from?

Jack pushed back his chair, rose, and went to find Griggs. At least he now knew what questions to ask.

Chapter 5

Late that evening, Jack sat in the armchair in his library, nursing a glass of brandy along with his aching head. He'd started the day feeling reasonably well, reasonably certain. Confident he'd done the right thing and that everything would quickly sort itself out.

He was ending the day not just in uncertainty but facing the very real prospect of having to approach Clarice for advice on precisely the subjects he'd informed her he no longer wanted her meddling with.

Closing his eyes, he tried to will away the insistent thudding in his brain. He really didn't want to contemplate just how difficult she was likely to be to charm and bring around, but no one else, it seemed, could help him with any of the problems that had come his way.

Not Howlett, not Connimore, not Griggs. He knew better than to bother consulting James.

He'd found Griggs, and asked first about the appropriate portion for Mary Wallace, but Griggs, a bachelor who'd worked all his life for the estate, had never had to deal with such an issue and had no better idea than he.

Setting that matter aside, he'd moved on to the more definite question of Jones and his offer. Griggs had confirmed that Jones had visited for the previous five years; Griggs had found the man overbearing and difficult to deal with. He'd appealed to Clarice, who'd assisted Griggs in sending Jones on his way, but in recent years, Clarice had dealt with Jones by herself, on Griggs's behalf. Griggs confirmed that to date, none of the Avening apple crop had gone to Jones. The premiums paid for the crop had come from the Gloucester merchants, with whom Clarice, through Griggs, had corresponded, bargaining on behalf of the Avening growers.

Griggs, however, wasn't clear on the details of Clarice's understanding with the Gloucester merchants.

The situation resembled a battlefield where one step the wrong way could be fatal.

He couldn't adequately respond to any of the situations facing him without the insights Clarice possessed. Reliving their exchange in the orchard, recalling not just his words but his tone, he closed his eyes and groaned.

He was going to have to crawl.

He woke the next morning, and immediately turned his mind to how to accomplish that act while minimizing the damage to his ego. With any other female, he wouldn't have been concerned, would have relied on the ready charm that to date had never failed him, but with Boadicea . . . he hadn't given her that nickname without cause.

He was sipping his coffee and pondering when to do the deed when a footman came in to clear the chafing dishes. Jack watched the familiar scene, all but unseeing—until the footman slipped a silver serving spoon into his coat pocket.

Jack sat up; lowering his cup he stared at the footman's back. The man turned to leave, dishes piled in his arms. "One moment." The man was new to the household, at least in Jack's terms; Jack didn't know his name.

The man obligingly faced Jack, his expression the usual footman's blank mask. "My lord?"

Jack pointed to the end of the table. "Put those down."

The footman did.

"What's your name?"

"Edward, my lord."

"Turn out your pockets, Edward."

Edward blinked, and slowly complied. Consternation filled his face as his fingers drew forth the silver spoon. He stared at it as if it were a snake.

Jack sat back. "Ring for Howlett." He kept his voice devoid of emotion. He watched as, now anxious, Edward crossed to the bellpull and tugged it.

A minute later, Howlett appeared. "Yes, my lord?"

He'd barely glanced at Edward, but, seeing Jack's face, looked again.

Edward hung his head.

Jack inwardly sighed. "I just discovered Edward about to leave with a silver spoon in his pocket. I suggest you accompany him to his rooms while he packs, then escort him from the house." Rising, Jack walked past Edward to the door; he paused beside Howlett. "Draw what wages he's owed from Griggs and send him on his way."

Howlett's eyes were wide. "Ah . . . yes, my lord." He looked shaken, even stricken.

Jack nodded and walked into the hall, inwardly frowning. Did Howlett think he'd blame him for taking on an untrustworthy footman? Surely not? Edward's accent marked him as a Londoner; easy enough to hide a nefarious past when far from one's home turf.

Still unsure how best to approach Clarice, or even if there was a best way, he headed out onto the terrace to get some fresh air. Beyond the neatly clipped lawn, the rose garden beckoned; giving in to temptation, knowing it would make him feel even more guilty for being less than appreciative of her "help," he went to stretch his legs there.

He returned half an hour later, and found Howlett and Connimore waiting to waylay him. Howlett spoke as he entered the hall. "If we could have a moment, my lord?"

Jack waved to the study; they followed him in. Howlett shut the door, then came to join Connimore before the desk.

Jack didn't sit, but stood behind the desk, studying them. "What is it?"

"It's about Edward, my lord." Connimore exchanged a glance with Howlett, then drew in a breath and met Jack's eyes. "He's staying in his room for the moment, but . . . before we send him on his way, like you ordered, could you . . ." Connimore started to wring her hands, then blurted, "Would you *please* speak with Lady Clarice about him?"

Howlett cleared his throat, equally uncomfortable. "There's something you rightly should know about Edward, my lord, but it isn't our place to say."

Jack looked from one to the other. Both had known him from birth. Both were urging him to consult Clarice before he committed some blunder. . . .

Exasperation flared, but died swiftly. Neither Howlett nor Connimore was given to nonsensical acts, and neither they nor anyone else knew of the situation between him and Clarice. A situation that, after half an hour of peace in the rose garden, he felt forced to admit was largely of his own making. It had been his overreaction that had sparked it, and he was honest enough to acknowledge to himself if no one else that if she'd been a less-formidable female, he wouldn't have reacted as strongly as he had.

Lips setting in a grim line, he nodded. "Very well. I'll speak with Lady Clarice, and then we'll review Edward's position."

Connimore sighed with relief. "Thank you, my lord. You won't regret it, I promise you."

"Indeed, my lord." Howlett smiled, relieved.

They both bustled out, leaving Jack wondering what on earth was going on—why his normally reliable, entirely sane, and determinedly correct butler and housekeeper thought having a thief on the staff was a good thing.

There was only one way to find out the answer, to that and all else that had plagued him for the past twenty-four hours. And there was no sense dallying. He hadn't yet thought of any wonderful way to approach Boadicea to ensure her hackles stayed down; perhaps this latest issue might be his salvation? Explaining why he had a thief on his staff might just leave her at a disadvantage, however slight.

With her, he'd accept help from any quarter.

He set out to walk to the rectory. On impulse, rather than stick to the road, he crossed it and pushed through the gap in the hedge, idly wondering if Clarice had guessed who had made it in the first place. As a boy, he'd been military-mad, and James had been, if not his idol, then certainly his inspiration. With his father's blessing, he'd spent countless afternoons at James's feet, learning of this battle, that campaign. Strategy was something he'd learned from James; much of the understanding and patience that had enabled him to survive the last thirteen years had in one way or another derived from that.

Passing the oak, he strode across the field, his mind engrossed with the questions facing him. He came to the archway through the rectory's hedge and looked up.

A quick movement to his left had him glancing that way. The house lay to his right, the rear gardens running down to end in an extensive vegetable plot to the far left. Between that and the shaded rear lawns lay a strip of grass open to the sun along which washing lines were strung; the movement he'd glimpsed had been a sheet being flicked as it was taken down and folded.

By Boadicea.

The notion of a marquess's daughter taking in the washing intrigued him; he was heading her way before he'd thought. Then he did, and kept walking. The washing lines were far enough from the house to afford them privacy; at that hour, there was unlikely to be anyone in the kitchen gardens beyond.

She heard his bootsteps on the path and looked up. Their gazes touched. Her face smoothed to marble, cool and unyielding, her expression unreadable, uninformative—shielded. Reaching for the next peg, she unhooked it and shook out a pillowcase.

He inwardly sighed and walked around the lines to where a low stone wall separated the grassed area from the vegetables. "Good morning, Lady Clarice."

"Good morning, Lord Warnefleet. James is in his study as usual."

Suppressing his reaction to her cold and pointed greeting-cum-dismissal, he sat on the wall five paces from her, behind and to her side. "It's you I've come to see."

She made no response. At all.

He watched her fold the pillowcase and lay it in a basket by her feet. The line was a movable circuit; when she tugged it around and reached for the next peg, he asked, "Would you mind telling me why I have Edward the footman from London, who is also a thief, in my household?"

She shot him a glance, dark and unfathomable, then looked back at the line. "He's Griggs's nephew."

Jack blinked. That was, quite definitely, the last thing he'd expected to hear. "*Griggs's* nephew?" Griggs was as honest as the day was long.

"His only living relative." After wrestling a sheet into submission, Clarice went on, "Griggs received word about two years ago that his only sister had died. He was worried about her boy, her only child. The father hadn't remained long enough to claim paternity." Folding the sheet, she met Jack's gaze. "Griggs is old. He fretted and grew so anxious we were worried about his health. Through James and the church, we traced the boy—Edward—and managed to get him here. Along the way, we realized he's a thief, but . . ." She paused, lips compressing, then continued, "He's a compulsive thief. He can't seem to stop, and indeed, we're not even sure he realizes he's taken things."

Jack recalled the look of consternation on Edward's face when he'd drawn the spoon from his pocket. "But . . ." He frowned. "He's still a thief."

"Yes, *but* he's all the family Griggs has. We all—literally everyone in Avening *bar* Griggs—know Edward takes things. Every week, Connimore and Howlett go through his room and return everything they find to wherever it belongs. Edward's been at the manor for over eighteen months, and nothing has gone missing permanently in that time."

Jack sat and absorbed that. Turned the matter over in his mind, weighed it, looked for options . . . reluctantly concluded he would have to allow Edward to continue as his footman. Griggs was too frail, and meant too much to the entire household, Jack especially, to have his peace threatened.

"What are you going to do about him—Edward?"

Jack glanced at Clarice, industriously folding napkins. He humphed. "Nothing—what else?"

He thought she might have smiled—just a little, very fleetingly. "Is there some problem with James's maids?"

She threw him a look. "Why do you ask? Because I'm doing this?"

He nodded. "Unfamiliar though I am with the ways of tonnish ladies"—he ignored her soft, incredulous snort—"I'm certain folding washing isn't a gazetted occupation for daughters of the nobility."

"This daughter of the nobility finds the occupation relaxing. While my hands are busy, I can think."

He longed to ask her what she was thinking about; instead, he watched her deftly unpegging, shaking out, and folding, and decided she was right. There was something inherently soothing in the simple domestic task.

"There are a number of issues on which I need to consult you." The words came without effort, without real thought. He paused, considered, then decided they would do; they were the simple truth.

She glanced briefly at him, but he could read nothing in her eyes or face. "Such as?"

"The church flowers for one." Exasperation colored his tone. A slight smile curved her lips; the sight sent a shaft of unexpected desire through him. He remembered all too well how they felt, how she tasted. Frustration on a number of counts lent an edge to his voice. "Can you explain what the devil's behind this roster?"

Clarice sighed, and shook out a sheet, her gaze traveling up the garden to the house. "It's all about status, I'm afraid."

Succinctly, she explained what lay behind Mrs. Swithins's desire for preeminence. "Poor Swithins—his mother expected much better from him, but although he's just a curate, she's determined to make the best of it, indeed, to push the standing his position affords her as far as it will go. Doing the flower arrangements for the Sunday services, as distinct from the minor Wednesday offices, is but one feather she's determined to seize for her cap."

"Thus putting Betsy's and Mrs. Candlewick's and Martha's noses out of joint."

She glanced at Jack. "Not just theirs. You'll discover Mrs. Swithins is at odds, in one way or another, with most of the females in the parish."

He groaned. "Just as long as I don't have to adjudicate between them."

She didn't say anything to that. She was acutely aware of him two yards away, large, lean, and incredibly vital, sitting on the wall, his gaze on her.

"What about you?" he asked. She looked at him, and found him eyeing her with spurious innocence. "Does Mrs. Swithins think to lord it over you?"

She met his eyes, then flicked out a napkin; it cracked like a whip. "Not even Swithins is that foolish." Creasing the napkin, she bent and set it in her basket. "No—to me she's ingratiating, which I find equally obnoxious." She glanced at him, realized with a jolt that his gaze had lowered—to her breasts, partly exposed by her scooped neckline. She straightened. "Wasn't she the same with you?"

He wrinkled his nose; his gaze slowly made its way back up to her face. "Yes, now you mention it. She could toady with the best of them."

Turning to the line, she tugged it and the next napkin to her; she'd wager her pearls he hadn't even registered he'd been ogling her breasts.

"So what should I do about the roster?"

She unpegged the napkin, folded it, kept her gaze on it. "Tell them all that, after due consideration, you've decided to revert the roster to what it was. Swithins does every second Sunday and the alternate Wednesdays, and between them, the other three do the other Sundays and Wednesdays. Mrs. Cleever and the maids from here freshen the vases in between, and for all the major celebrations, Mrs. Connimore and the maids—and indeed all the others except Swithins—use the flowers from the manor to decorate the church."

Without looking his way, she dropped the napkin in the basket and reached for the tablecloth.

"All right. Next, how much should Mary Wallace's marriage portion be?"

She looked at him, and saw no sign of irritation that he'd been forced to retreat and support her decision over the roster. She raised her brows, outwardly in inquiry, inwardly in surprise.

He explained, "Wallace tells me his Mary and Roger Hawkins are close to tying the knot. I assume he told you?"

"Everyone knows, but I didn't ask what advice he wanted."

"He's trying to decide on the right size for Mary's marriage portion given the match, his other daughters, and his son's inheritance, but I've no idea what sum would be appropriate."

She looked past him as she folded the tablecloth, mentally calculating. "Thirty guineas. A goodly sum Wallace can afford, not just for Mary but later for her sisters. A nice start for the new couple, and one Hawkins can match, either in cash or kind." She met Jack's gaze. "It's important neither family is seen to be overwhelming the young couple."

His brows rose. "I hadn't thought of that."

The light in his eyes as they met hers made her feel ridiculously pleased, as if he appreciated her insight, even valued it.

"Now, what about Jones, the apple buyer for the cider makers?"

"Jones?" She paused. "Yes, I suppose he would come calling about now."

"So what's the story there? Griggs told me you've negotiated with the man on Grigg's behalf for the last three years."

Clarice laid the tablecloth in the basket, slowly smoothed it while her mind raced. He might have accepted her advice on the church roster and Mary's marriage portion, but this—essentially her direct assumption of his authority—was distinctly more touchy. More likely to grate on his male pride.

Why should she care? Men, especially gentlemen of his ilk—of her own class—had never cared about her pride.

She drew breath, and straightened. She met his eyes; this time they'd remained on her face. "The first thing you need to know about Jones is that he's an outright bully, to those he thinks he can intimidate, at any rate."

His eyes narrowed. "Not you, obviously. Griggs?"

She nodded, and turned back to the line. "The first year Jones appeared—five years ago—Griggs came to me in an absolute lather. He was close to panicking and consigning the entire crop into Jones's hands, believing he had no real option." Her lips thinned as she remembered. "I stepped in and made Jones explain the whole to both Griggs and me again. Needless to say, the situation, and Jones's offer, wasn't quite as he'd painted it to Griggs."

"What exactly was the offer then? This time, it's a shilling a bushel above the general market price."

She nodded. "Eight pence above, that year. It's a swindle of sorts, of course. Not that Jones and those behind him won't happily pay what they promise, but the intent is to break the long-standing connection between the Avening growers and the Gloucester merchants. Avening supplies more than twenty percent of the Gloucester market. If the crop was sold to Jones instead, the Gloucester merchants would be forced to turn to other suppliers—they couldn't simply ride out the shortfall. But once they'd established new deals with other growers, then the next season, Avening would have to sell to Jones, because the Gloucester merchants wouldn't need the Avening crop."

"So then Jones and his masters could offer whatever price

they pleased, and Avening would have to sell for what might then be a shilling *less* than the market price."

"Precisely." She shook out another pillowcase. "The Gloucester merchants have always dealt in good faith. They're a large conglomerate, and there's little benefit to them in haggling unreasonably, especially as Avening is one of their more reliable suppliers, both for quality and quantity."

He was silent for a moment, then he rose. She glanced at him as he stepped closer. Hands in his pockets, he was frowning, but vaguely at the ground, not at her.

"There's been a premium paid to the Avening growers for the last four years. Griggs said it came from the Gloucester merchants. How did that come about?"

Trickier and trickier. She drew breath, and evenly said, "When Jones turned up the second year, I realized he wasn't going to go away. So I wrote to the Gloucester merchants, and without exactly stating sums, explained how torn the Avening growers were, that of course we'd prefer to continue to sell to Gloucester, but we needed to make improvements to our orchards, and so on."

"And so they stumped up the extra."

"Yes, and no." She met his eyes. "We worked out a sliding scale. They've paid a decreasing premium for the last four years, but over those years, the overall Avening crop has increased. More trees have been planted. We divided up the premium on the basis of the harvest, and then advised all the growers to invest in increasing their acreage under trees. All of them did."

Jack thought of the figures he'd spent all day yesterday analyzing. "So now . . . ?"

"So now, this year, we'll be able to sell our usual crop to the Gloucester merchants for the current market price, and at the same time sell a crop of nearly the same size to Jones, at his inflated price."

It didn't take much arithmetic to realize just what a windfall that would mean to the local growers.

"And next year?"

"If Jones tries to lower his figure, we don't need to sell to him—the Gloucester merchants will take the lot, at market price."

"That's brilliant." Jack made the statement spontaneously, but it was indeed the truth. He glanced at her, hesitated, then more quietly said, "I suspect Avening would do better if I reverted more than the responsibility for the church roster." He drew breath, surprised to find his lungs tight, and forced himself to go on, "Perhaps we'd do best to go back to how things were before I returned. You've made such a good fist of things, I can plainly leave all in your hands."

Those hands, fine-skinned, slender-fingered, until then working steadily folding napkins, faltered, paused. He was standing nearly shoulder to shoulder with her, but she didn't look up; he could read nothing, no reaction to his words in her profile, all he could see of her face.

He'd managed to keep his tone level, easy, managed to make his statements sound like a straightforward matter, not something that bothered him, affected him, deeply.

Clarice let the silence lengthen; she was very aware of him so close beside her, very aware that, if she was thinking of just herself, his offer had much to recommend it. Her being clearly in charge again would make life much simpler, more comfortable, as it had been before . . . but what about him?

She glanced at him, knew her gaze was sharp. "You're leaving?"

He met her eyes steadily. "No."

She nodded, turned back to the napkin in her hand . . . then forced herself to look back at him and meet his eyes. Steadily. "I don't want your position. I have no ambition, absolutely none, to be lord of the manor."

He blinked, thick lashes fluttering over those changeable, intriguingly complex hazel eyes. But then his lids rose, and he met her gaze, equally direct, equally sincere. "I don't want your position either." His lips—lips she was trying hard not to focus on—quirked. "Indeed, after my short adventure tangling with the ladies of the parish, I suspect taking your place would drive me demented within a week."

She couldn't stop her lips from twitching, curving. She looked down and dropped the last napkin on the pile.

"Perhaps . . ." He sounded not precisely hesitant but diffident, unsure—unsure how she would react. "In the interests of Avening as a whole, we—you and I—could come to some arrangement."

It was her turn to blink. She looked at him; his eyes told her he was in earnest, but, like her, wasn't at all sure how such an arrangement—between him and her, people like them—might work. Yet he'd spoken her thoughts aloud; perhaps, if they both wished it, they could rub along together . . . somehow.

"What did you have in mind?" She was under no illusions that he wasn't an arrogant, accustomed-to-command gentleman of her class; however, she'd already discovered he wasn't as bad as others of that ilk, and he had suggested it. She wasn't the sort to cut off her nose to spite her face.

He studied her; there was something in the line of his lips, the cool steadiness of his gaze that assured her her earlier suspicion that he saw her clearly wasn't wrong. He knew—appreciated—just how strong she was, just how steely her will would be.

He'd made his offer and was going forward with his eyes fully open.

For quite the first time in her life, she felt a touch giddy.

His brows rose consideringly. "All I can suggest is that we play it by ear. You're hardly the sort to suffer in silence." His untrustworthy smile flashed. "And neither am I. Why not simply proceed, and deal with matters as they arise?"

The only sensible solution. She nodded, brisk and businesslike, and held out her hand. "Agreed."

His gaze dropped to her hand, then rose to her face. His hand engulfed hers, then he smoothly wrapped it, her arm and his behind her and drew her to him.

Before she could blink, she was in his arms, breast to chest, eyes widening as he bent his head.

"Agreed," he confirmed. His lips curved in a wholly male smile, then swooped and captured hers.

Captured *her*. She didn't understand how it happened, how he did it, but the instant his arms closed around her, the instant his lips touched hers, the field on which they stood changed, shifted.

She'd started her day distantly hurt, reminding herself his attitude to her was no more than she'd expected. Gentlemen of her class didn't like ladies who managed, no matter how well they accomplished the task. She'd half expected him to take umbrage at the role she'd assumed in his absence; she hadn't been surprised by him claiming it back. But she had been, somewhere inside where she hid what she termed her foolish self, been disappointed.

His lips firmed and she met them, and felt that foolish self slip her leash. And dance a little jig.

This—this sensual exchange—had nothing to do with the bargain they'd struck, yet that bargain was both intriguing and, to her, fascinatingly tempting.

Something unexpected.

As was he.

As was this.

His arms locked about her, and tightened, slowly, easing her against him—and she went. Without any missish hesitation, but with foreknowledge and intent. She pushed her arms up, draped them over his broad shoulders, clasped his nape between her hands, and boldly kissed him back. Then she parted her lips and let him take, let him lead her where he would.

Into an engagement that spoke of hunger and need, that promised mutual pleasure.

Pleasure of a sort she'd thought had passed her by, that had long ago drifted beyond her grasp. Pleasure of a sort that despite never experiencing it she understood very well.

He concealed nothing, pretended nothing; he let her see

his need, feel his hunger. Let his desire rise unfettered and caress her with fingers of flame.

Evoking hers. Inciting hers in a way that had never happened before. Physical desire wasn't something she'd felt before; the realization had her mentally blinking, then the challenge—the pressure of his lips on hers, the subtle taunt of his maurading tongue—firmed, and she, not just her foolish self but with conscious decision, responded.

Why shouldn't she know, experience? Why shouldn't she take?

She moved into him, deliberately meeting him breast to chest, hips to hips, thighs to thighs. Through the now flagrant mating of their mouths, she sensed his reaction, a brief hiatus while he caught his breath, and his control. Not because she, with her wanton response, had weakened it, but because his response to her action had.

Fascinating. Her newfound interest in physical desire escalated. She twined her arms about his neck and settled to returning the heated caresses he pressed on her.

Jack met her, matched her, dueled with her for supremacy, a tug-of-war that neither could truly win. The exchange—she—held his attention utterly, so completely it scared him; he couldn't think. With her in his arms, with her lips under his, her mouth freely offered in a scorching, viscerally tempting exchange—a viscerally arousing engagement of lips, tongues, and heated breaths—lust fogged his brain. Only one thought penetrated it, the thought of penetrating her.

Of having her beneath him, arching as she took him deep into her firm, curvaceous body, into her scalding feminine heat.

He wanted her naked and abandoned. Wanted her with a need, an elemental hunger that shook him. That snared him so deeply he didn't want to look too closely, to examine why it should be, why of all the ladies with whom he'd dallied, or who he now could have, she—a haughty termagent he was going to have to deal carefully with on a daily basis—was the one who struck sparks to his tinder.

All he knew was that with her, for her, he burned.

And not by one inch did she retreat. She encouraged him, not with the eager urging of a younger woman but with the mature, self-assured, almost blatant invitation of a lady who knew what she wanted, who knew she wanted him.

As he wanted her. Hers was the perfect counterpart to his need, the perfect match for his hunger.

The urge to let his hands roam, to take the next step they both clearly wished for, burgeoned and grew . . . but they were in the open, with the folded laundry beside them. Anyone who walked down the garden past the trees edging the lawn would see them. Some maid might come to see if Clarice needed help . . .

Stopping, calling a halt, drawing back from the depths of her luscious mouth was one of the hardest things he'd ever done.

He managed to lift his head an inch, immediately felt the loss of the connection keenly. His wits were still locked, still focused on her. Her lashes fluttered, then rose. Her dark, dark eyes met his.

"I didn't thank you for restoring my mother's garden."

Excuse enough to dive back into her mouth, to take one last, long, lingering taste of her, of the passion within her, simmering, very feminine, precisely the right mix of haughty will and heady promise to sate him.

But . . . he drew back from the flames, from her scorching temptation. Eased her back, eased back himself until there was air between them. He had to force his fingers to release her, to let her go.

She drew breath, stepped back, opened her eyes, blinked once, then studied him; she seemed as puzzled as he, and beneath that, as curious.

Looking into her dark eyes, to his soul aware of the rising of her breasts as she drew in a huge breath, he felt . . . not as assured as he usually was in such situations.

Presumably because she was who she was—Boadicea. A point he'd do well to bear in mind.

His gaze fell on the washing basket piled high with folded linen. He stooped and hefted it up. "I'll carry this up to the house for you."

She met his eyes, but other than a pretension-depressing, amused quirk of her lips, made no response. She fell in beside him, her long-legged stride keeping pace easily as they passed beneath the trees and headed across the lawn.

By the time they reached the back porch, their usual roles had reclaimed them; their customary polite distance had returned. He set the basket on the wooden table by the back door, then faced her. "Jones. I told him to come back tomorrow afternoon. I think it would be best if you were present when I meet with him. Perhaps if you would join me for luncheon tomorrow, we could discuss how best to deal with him?"

She held his gaze, her own steady and direct, then nodded. "Very well." She hesitated, then said, "As usual, the other growers have given approval for the manor to strike the price for the valley. Griggs should already have estimates from the other orchards—he'll have a tally of the expected crop."

He nodded equably. "I'll get the details from him."

Again, she hesitated, then asked, "The young man from the phaeton?"

He grimaced. "Still unconscious." He didn't add that the longer the man remained so, the more worrying his condition became. "I don't suppose you've had any revelation over why he seems familiar?"

She shook her head. Frowned. "I'll . . . look in on him tomorrow."

Jack suspected she'd intended looking in on their patient that afternoon, but that would mean stopping in at the manor, thus chancing another meeting with him . . . and that, he accepted, was too soon.

Too soon for her; too soon for him, too.

With a graceful bow, he took his leave of her. He strode away, conscious of her gaze on his back. Passing through the archway in the hedge, he consoled his suddenly uncertain

self that, over the matter of whatever was burgeoning between them, at least Boadicea was as uncertain as he.

The next day, Clarice spent what she would normally consider an inordinate amount of time dressing for lunch at the
manor. She told herself her filmy apple green muslin with its
heart-shaped neckline would distract Jones, and wondered at
such self-deception.

She knew precisely whom she wanted to distract, and
why. She was amazed at her interest in the hunger she stirred
in Jack and in the answering response he drew from her.

"Pure curiosity," she told her mirror as she checked her
plaited chignon. It lay heavy on her nape; she thought of his
strong fingers sliding beneath the heavy mass, across her
sensitive skin . . . and shivered.

"A temporary madness—no doubt it'll pass." With that
firmly stated verdict, she rose and headed for her bedchamber door.

With a wide-brimmed hat shading her white skin, a light
shawl draped over her elbows, she walked down the rectory
drive and turned into the road.

A form of madness. Her assessment of their state was unde-
niable; they were walking a tightrope on two planes, and both
knew it. That last only seemed to heighten the exhilaration.

The danger.

Neither she nor, she was perfectly sure, he, knew where
they were headed, not with the physical attraction that
flared between them, not with their "arrangement." Whether
the latter would work was anyone's guess; neither of them
was used to that type of working partnership, and neither
was patient, or undemanding. They both had their share of
arrogance, of being accustomed to leading, to being in
charge.

As for the former . . . that was a total unknown.

It had been a very long time since anything had claimed
her attention as it did, as he did when she was in his arms.

She didn't know what she thought, had yet to form any

view on the activity, on what she was doing, what she wanted. The unvarnished truth was that when in his arms, she didn't—couldn't seem to—think at all.

Such a situation should have disturbed her; she certainly thought it should, yet it didn't. As she swung up the manor drive, no hint of trepidation bloomed, no vestige of even caution dimmed her anticipation. She was eager to see him again, keen to see where next they would stray, to observe how she affected him, to experience again how he affected her.

Shocking.

She was twenty-nine; she didn't give a damn.

Life had long ago passed her by. As long as neither he nor she were hurt by their exchanges, where was the harm?

Confident, assured, she reached the manor's door and rang the bell.

Howlett opened the door and beamed.

Clarice smiled back, and spotted Warnefleet—Jack—in the hall, hovering behind his butler.

Almost as if he'd been waiting for the bell to peal.

Howlett stepped back and she entered. Her expression perfectly gauged—calm, serene, with just a hint of warmth—she advanced and gave Jack her hand, very aware that as he bowed over it his gaze slid down . . . then slowly rose as he straightened.

He smiled, devilish appreciation in his hazel eyes. "You look ravishing. I believe Mrs. Connimore is assembling a small feast . . ."

He broke off, his gaze going to the door. She turned, too, as the sound of carriage wheels rattling up the drive reached them.

"I wonder who that is . . . ?" Jack inwardly frowned. Retaining Clarice's hand, drawing her with him, he stepped to the side of the hall, to where he could see past Howlett, once again opening the door.

The sight that met his eyes momentarily flummoxed him; a plain black carriage, clearly from some posting house, drew up in the forecourt.

Boadicea, also peering past Howlett, put his thoughts into words. "Perhaps they're lost?"

The carriage door opened, and a young gentleman stepped down. Of average height and average build, with a pleasant face and pale brown hair, he held his hat in his hands and looked about curiously, then he saw Howlett and made for the door.

"Can I help you, sir?" Howlett intoned.

"I hope so," the gentleman replied. "I'm looking for Lord Warnefleet."

Jack stepped forward; her hand locked in his, Boadicea moved with him. "I'm Warnefleet."

"Oh!" The gentleman looked up, a certain wariness in his open face. "I . . . ah, I'm Percy Warnefleet. You sent for me."

Jack suddenly realized who the gentleman was.

Smiling a trifle nervously, Percy confirmed it. "I believe I'm your heir."

Chapter 6

"What the devil are you about?"

Jack sat behind his desk and watched Boadicea march back and forth. Her arms were folded beneath her sumptuous breasts; her expression, however, was a warning. So much for softening her up with sweetmeats and wine.

They hadn't even progressed to luncheon yet; after the introductions—inevitably stilted—he'd had Howlett show Percy upstairs to unpack and refresh himself before joining them in the dining room.

Boadicea wasn't impressed. "You can tell just by looking at him. He's a milksop, wet behind the ears and gullible to boot. You can't seriously be intending to leave Avening and, if I understood what you were discussing with James, all the rest, to him." She halted and glared at him. "Besides, he can't be more than what, ten years your junior?"

"Eight. But that's beside the point. Percy can marry and have sons who'll inherit after him." Her glare turned to a slack-jawed stare, stunned speculation dawning. He hurried on before she could ask the question blooming in her mind. "I have no wish to marry, so I thought it prudent to get Percy here and take charge of his estate education. By the time Griggs and I are finished with him, he'll be a shining example of lordly acumen."

Boadicea snorted. She swung away, but he heard her mutter, "He might just finish Griggs."

It was a thought . . . but then he did have someone else who could, and assuredly would, share the burden of knocking Percy into shape.

He watched her, mentally sifting through the possible avenues to solicit her help. "Actually"—he met her gaze as she glanced at him—"I rather thought you'd approve, if not of Percy himself, then at least of my getting him here. As matters stand, it's highly likely he will at some point inherit my estate, and given the size it's now grown to, he'll need to know how to run it when the reins fall into his hands."

She considered him for a long moment; he couldn't read the expression in her dark eyes. Then she humphed and looked away, out of the window.

On leaving her the previous day, he'd returned to the manor and discussed the vexed question of Edward the footman with Howlett and Mrs. Connimore. He'd agreed to let Edward stay under the parameters already established. That settled, this morning, he'd called on Swithins, James's curate. The man was as Boadicea had intimated, a mild, unprepossessing sort; after due consideration, he'd left his decision on the church flower roster with Swithins, to be included with the parish announcements at the end of service that Sunday. It wouldn't hurt Swithins to be seen as allied with Jack in curbing Swithins's mother's ambitions.

A note dispatched to Wallace, and a half hour spent in the taproom with Jed Butler had taken care of all outstanding business. Jack had returned in good time to watch for Boadicea, conscious of a mild-yet-pleasant sense of triumph, a satisfaction he owed in large part to Clarice; her advice had smoothed his way back into the local community, into the position in which he belonged.

He studied her as she stood before the window, head up, spine straight.

A knock fell on the door, then it opened; Howlett looked in.

"Mr. Warnefleet has come downstairs, my lord—I've shown him to the dining room. Griggs is there, too."

"Excellent." Jack rose. Rounding his desk, he offered his arm to Boadicea. "Shall we?"

She met his gaze; a frown in her eyes, she briefly studied his, then, her face smoothing to its usual serene mask, she placed her hand on his sleeve. He escorted her from the room; head high, she glided beside him.

Once they were out of Howlett's hearing, she murmured, "You were a spy in enemy territory for seven years *after* your father's death, without any great concern over your succession. Yet you return to England, and within a few months decide to groom your heir. Why?" She glanced sharply at him. "You're far less likely to die now—I'm sure you're not anticipating an imminent demise. So what happened in a few months to convince you you'd never have a son of your own?"

He couldn't stop his jaw from firming. Impertinent though her question was, he answered succinctly, "The Season happened."

Her gaze remained fixed on his profile. "You can't possibly mean to tell me that in just a few months you took against the entire female nation?"

"Not the entire female nation, just the marriageable part." The dining room door drew near. "You've inhabited the ton, seen the young ladies on the marriage mart. Tell me, if you were in my shoes, would you marry one of them?"

She frowned, then looked ahead. And said no more.

Jack suppressed a feral smile and steered her into the dining room. He noted how Griggs's expression softened when he saw Boadicea, noted her gracious nod to Percy as she allowed Jack to seat her in the chair beside his.

That done, he moved to the head of the table. Even as he sat, and Griggs and Percy followed suit, it was transparent that Clarice's presence made a difference. She might not think highly of Percy, but she let no sign of her opinion show; she immediately engaged him in an exchange of the usual sort of background information, a conversation that quickly put him at ease. As for Griggs, it was plain he thought she was wonderful.

They passed around the dishes. Relieved of the necessity of making conversation himself, Jack sat back and listened, increasingly appreciatively as he realized just how wide-ranging Clarice's inquisition was. She cloaked it brilliantly in the usual social chatter; although it seemed she imparted information on the local scene in return, it was Percy who revealed most, and that with surprising readiness, soothed by Clarice's gracious interest and the calm serenity in her dark eyes.

"I own to some surprise," she eventually said, "that you presented yourself in Avening so promptly. It is April, after all, and the Season's in full swing . . ." Her dark brows rose in quizzical interrogation. "Or was it a case of a sojourn in the country being the lesser of several evils?"

That question had occurred to Jack, too. He'd issued his invitation-cum-summons to Percy via his solicitor on the day he'd quit the capital; he hadn't expected to see Percy inside of a few months.

Leaning back in his chair, he watched as, far from displaying any signs of unease—shifting, a blush—Percy's expression remained open and earnest. After nothing more than the slightest of hesitations, plainly to consider his words, he replied, "I have to admit Lord Warnefleet's summons came at an opportune time. Not that I'm under the weather, but cutting a dash in town on limited funds is a trifle difficult—unless one excels at cards, but I don't."

"Are the hells along Pall Mall still the pinnacle of their type?" Clarice asked the question as if a lady would, of course, know, and there was no solecism attendant on admitting to frequenting such establishments in the presence of a marquess's daughter.

Jack managed not to blink at her bald-faced gambit; Griggs, of course, knew nothing of the hells of Pall Mall.

Percy squirmed, just a little; Clarice pretended not to notice, overtly busying herself selecting a date. Eventually, Percy said, "I visited there once or twice, but . . . I've decided gaming is really not for me."

Clarice glanced at Percy with, Jack felt, a touch more approval. "The gamesters never do win, not in the long term. So, are you looking forward to learning about the estate?"

Percy looked at Jack, clearly unsure.

"Perhaps," Jack said, "you'd like to ride out and take a look around this afternoon, then . . ." He paused, confused by the dismayed expression that bloomed on Percy's round face.

"Ah . . ." Percy paused, then blurted, "I'm afraid I don't ride."

Clarice blinked, slowly. "You don't ride?"

It was obvious Percy had just lost what little ground he'd made with her; Jack felt a smidgen of sympathy. Mildly, he said, "You can learn. Crawler, my head stableman, will be happy to teach you."

Griggs cleared his throat. "Meanwhile, I could show you maps of the estate. You could become acquainted with the holdings that way."

"An excellent idea." Jack leaned back in his chair and smiled encouragingly. "Why don't you take Percy to the office and introduce him to the estate, fill him in on the nearer fields and farms? Lady Clarice and I have some business to attend to. We'll be meeting with Jones later this afternoon."

"Yes, indeed." Griggs nodded and rose.

Percy pushed back his chair and rose, too. "Ah . . ." His gaze went to Clarice, then returned to Jack.

Jack smiled. "Go with Griggs. I'll speak with you at dinner."

Percy studied him for a moment, then bowed. "Thank you." Turning, he bowed very correctly to Clarice. "Lady Clarice."

She softened enough to bestow a gracious nod.

Percy escaped.

The instant the door closed behind him and Griggs, Clarice met Jack's eyes. "He'll never do."

Jack merely smiled. "Jones. How should we tackle him?"

Clarice studied him for a moment, wondering if she dared prod him, if she should push her point that he really should marry rather than pass the estate to Percy—a nice enough fellow, honest at least, but one without the requisite steel in his spine. Deciding to leave that subject for the present— there was no urgency, after all—she turned her mind to his question.

"Jones doesn't like me, doesn't like having to deal with me." She considered Jack, letting her eyes drink in the simple elegance with which he habitually dressed, a white linen shirt screening a muscled chest, pristine cravat in a classic knot, well-cut coat hugging broad shoulders, buckskin breeches clinging to long, strong legs, shining top boots upon his large feet. He looked precisely what he was, a wealthy country gentleman. Her lips quirked. "He was probably delighted to find you at home."

"He was."

"Well, then, if our purpose is to extract the highest price from him . . . ?" She raised her brows inquiringly.

Jack nodded. "It is."

She smiled. "Then I suggest . . ."

They spent the next twenty minutes devising and honing their tactics, then, aware of an anticipatory tightening of her nerves that had nothing to do with Jones's visit, she decided caution would, in the circumstances, be wise, at least until after they'd triumphed over Jones. Excusing herself to Jack, she headed upstairs to look in on the still-unconscious young man.

"Mr. Jones." From the chair behind his desk, Jack rose and offered his hand.

Jones came forward to take it, the expectation of victory shining in his eyes. "My lord. I trust the other growers found my offer to their liking?"

"Indeed." Jack waved Jones to the chair he'd placed directly in front of his desk. "There's no question that your offer is an attractive one."

"A very generous one, but then the quality of the Avening crop is second to none."

Jack smiled, his amiable, gentlemanly mask in place. "Just so. It's not your offer that has raised concerns."

"Concerns?" Jones straightened in his chair. "What concerns would those be?"

Jack looked down. He toyed with a pen, eyes fixed on the nib as he flicked it back and forth. He frowned. "The growers in the valley are used to selling to the Gloucester merchants. Most feel disinclined to change their ways."

"What? Not even for a shilling above the market rate?"

"Of course, if you would settle for taking half our crop, that might appease them."

"Hmm." Jones frowned as if considering; Jack was perfectly certain the expression was false. "I really don't think, not when I'm offering a shilling *extra* per bushel that just half the crop is fair . . . no." Jones straightened, jaw bravely squaring. "I'm afraid, my lord, that it's the whole crop or nothing."

"I see." Jack tapped the dry nib on his blotter, then looked up at Jones. "For myself, I'm willing to agree—this is, as you said, business, after all. Our difficulty lies in bringing the others around. I wonder . . ." He broke off as if struck, looked at the door, then back at Jones. "There's one person whose opinion will sway the other growers. If we can convince them, then you can be sure of the full eight hundred bushels, and, as it happens, they dropped by this afternoon. If I ask them to join us, are you willing to work with me to bring them around?"

Jones's smile was all ferretlike anticipation. "Just bring them in, and we'll have the deal done, I promise you."

Jack smiled, rose and tugged the bellpull. "Would you care for some refreshment?" He waved at the tantalus.

Jones's eyes gleamed. "Thank you, m'lord. Most kind."

Jack poured him a glass of brandy and took a small measure for himself. He handed the glass to Jones, then, hearing Howlett's footsteps approaching, met his butler at the door.

Instructions received, Howlett retreated; Jack turned back to see Jones savoring the brandy entirely unaware, increasingly relaxed.

Hiding an expectant grin, Jack returned to his chair.

A minute later, the door opened. Jack looked up. Clarice walked in. Because of the placement of Jones's chair, Jones couldn't see her.

Jack smiled, innocently genial. "There you are, my dear." He didn't rise, but waved to Jones. "Mr. Jones." He met Jones's eyes. "I believe you've met Lady Clarice previously."

Jones jettisoned his manners and swiveled as Clarice walked regally forward. Jones's gaze had some way to rise to reach her face; he stared, then tried to haul in a breath and choked on his brandy.

Clarice paused beside his chair and looked down dispassionately on his convulsing form. When he'd stopped wheezing, she spoke. "Good afternoon, Jones."

If Jack had harbored any doubts over the nature of Jones's previous encounters with Boadicea, and who had been the victor, Jones's reaction to her dispelled them. Horror was the mildest emotion that flitted across his face.

Understandable. With a nod that would have depressed the pretensions of a prince, Clarice glided, as they'd arranged, forward and around the desk. She paused beside his chair, one slender hand resting on the curved back as she viewed the hapless Jones.

Jack could no longer see her face; he could, however, feel her presence. Feel the icy chill enough to be grateful it wasn't directed at him. He'd not previously seen her in this mood, in this persona, in full war paint. He was acquainted with some of the most powerful *grandes dames* of the ton; none could hold a candle to Boadicea.

It was an old power she wielded; a distinctly female power, it seemed to well up and flow through her. It wasn't a power any sane man would willingly challenge.

"I assume, Mr. Jones"—Clarice rounded his chair, her

tone cold and unencouraging—"that you've come with your usual proposal?"

Jones swallowed heroically, and managed, "A shilling above market price, this year."

Clarice's brows rose. "A shilling?" She sank gracefully into the chair beside the desk, on Jack's left, angled to face Jones.

Every aspect of her entry had been carefully staged to give Jones the impression she and Jack were close.

"My dear." Jack leaned forward, all effortless charm. Clarice switched her dark gaze from Jones to him. He smiled easily, almost intimately. "Mr. Jones's proposition is really a very good one. I do think I, and all the other growers, too, would be well advised to give it serious consideration."

Clarice let her gaze rest on his face, then turned her head to study Jones. "Consideration, perhaps, but it's tradition that the Avening crop goes to Gloucester."

"Perhaps, my dear," Jack replied, "but this is a new age, and traditions can't last forever."

"Indeed, my lady." Jones sat forward, his gaze fixing on her. "It's as his lordship says—we must move on. New ventures, new business deals. That's the way of the future."

For the next ten minutes, Clarice sat and let them work to sway her. Jones grew increasingly desperate, which was precisely what they wished. As for Jack, his role of easygoing amiability was perfectly gauged, and never faltered; if she hadn't known better, she would have believed, as Jones clearly did, that he was, if not precisely weak, then easily led.

As their arguments rolled on, she allowed a frown to come into being. "It just feels as if, in turning from the Gloucester merchants, we'd be committing some sin, a betrayal as it were . . ."

Her tone suggested she was weakening, that she might be amenable to persuasion, if they could assuage her doubts. Jones leaned so far forward he nearly fell out of his chair. "Now, now, my lady—this is business, you see. Shouldn't ever allow your heart to rule your head, not in business."

She frowned more definitely—at him.

"Perhaps"—Jack cast Jones a look of appeal—"if there were some degree of compensation, to help the growers overcome their reticence . . ." He looked a tad uncomfortable. "I suppose, to speak plainly, to act as incentive for them to turn away from the Gloucester merchants and sign with you instead."

"Incentive? But . . ." Eyes widening, Jones sat back. "What about the shilling per bushel more?"

Clarice regarded him steadily. "But that's the price you're offering. There's no *extra* incentive there. Nothing to recognize the difficulty of what you're asking the growers to do. Nothing to address their moral dilemma."

Jones's expression stated that he'd never before encountered a moral dilemma, at least not in business. "Ah . . ." He opened and closed his mouth, then looked at Jack. "I'm not sure I follow."

"Oh, come now, Jones." Jack looked faintly peeved, a weak man faced with a vacillating conspirator. "You said you were keen to seal the deal—here's your chance. A token of esteem, as it were, in appreciation of the Avening growers selling you their crop, and eight hundred bushels of the best quality apples will be yours."

Jack widened his eyes at Jones, urging him to seize the moment, and their bait.

But Jones suddenly blinked. "Eight hundred?" He glanced at Clarice. "I thought it was over one thousand bushels last time."

"The crop varies considerably year to year." Unperturbed, Clarice glanced at Jack. "I understand that this year, eight hundred bushels is what we could contract to sell you."

Her tone was cold, distant—discouraging. Jones clearly considered questioning them further, but after studying her haughty, unyielding expression, he sank back into his chair.

A moment ticked by. Jones frowned into the remnants of brandy in his glass.

Clarice pointedly shifted to look at the mantelpiece clock,

then she turned to Jones. "Mr. Jones, if you've nothing further to add, I have matters awaiting my attention—"

"No, no! Please . . ." He looked at Clarice, then Jack. "I was just considering what I could do. . . ." He swallowed. "By way of incentive."

It was clearly a difficult notion for him to digest. Clarice remained in her chair, lightly tapping her nails on the wooden arm.

Jones looked at her fingers, then at Jack. "How many growers are there?"

Jack pulled a face. "I'm not sure."

"Seventeen." Clarice leveled her gaze on Jones. "Why?"

"I was thinking, shall we say two pounds apiece to each grower in er . . . recognition of them selling to me?"

"Three pounds," Clarice said.

Jones stared at her. They watched as he calculated swiftly in his head.

"Three pounds to each grower, plus a shilling per bushel above the market price, and you'll have eight hundred bushels of Avening apples." Clarice held Jones's gaze, then raised a coldly arrogant brow. "Do we have a deal, Mr. Jones?"

Jones swallowed, then nodded. Quickly. "Yes. A deal."

"Excellent." Jack leaned back in his chair, his genial smile wreathing his face. "Here—I had my man draw up a contract for the sale. You just need to fill in the figures, and sign there . . ."

Clarice preserved her haughty distance as Jack had Jones put his signature to the deal. They'd had no idea if they could wring more from Jones; the satisfaction in having succeeded was sweet.

The contract duly signed and witnessed, Jones rose. He stared at the document as if he couldn't quite understand how it had come into being.

"Well, Jones, come harvesttime we'll deliver eight hundred bushels to your store in Bristol." Jack clapped him on the shoulder and turned him, unresisting, to the door. "Once you send me the draft for the incentive, the deal will be locked up tight. Congratulations!"

Jack offered his hand. Jones seemed to come out of his daze; he reached for Jack's hand, his face clearing. "Thank you, my lord." Jones actually smiled as he shook hands. "A pleasure doing business with you."

Jones turned back to the room and bowed low. "Lady Clarice."

Even from across the room, Clarice could read the smugness in Jones's eyes; he thought he'd at long last bested her. Regally, she inclined her head. "Until next time, Jones."

His smile faltered for a moment, but then broadened again; he turned to the door Jack held open. With an almost cheery nod, he left.

Jack saw Jones to the front hall and left Howlett to show him out. Returning to the study, he found Clarice still regally ensconced in the chair by the desk. He closed the door, then crossed the room. Halting before her, he held out both hands.

She looked up at him, then placed her hands in his and allowed him to draw her to her feet. Leaving them a mere inch part. Their eyes met; their gazes locked.

"Victory is ours." The smile that curved his lips had nothing to do with charm and everything to do with intent.

Her lips curved in response, one of her elusive, subtly taunting half smiles.

He released her fingers; sliding his hands lightly up her arms, he reached for her—

They both heard the hurrying footsteps outside the door a second before someone tapped.

Swallowing a curse, Jack moved to the end of the desk as Clarice shifted to lean against the chair. "Come."

One of the upstairs maids poked her head around the door. "Mrs. Connimore sent me, m'lord. She said as to tell you and Lady Clarice that the young man's stirring. She thought as you might want to come, in case he regains his wits."

"Yes, of course." Clarice straightened from the chair and headed for the door.

Smothering a sigh of frustration and disappointment combined, Jack muttered an oath, and followed her.

Griggs looked out of the estate office to ask him a question; Jack caught up with Clarice as she entered the sickroom and approached the foot of the bed. Upon it, the young man lay lifeless and still, as he had for the past two days. His eyes were closed; there was no animation in his face.

Mrs. Connimore heaved a gusty sigh. "He was restless, shifting—I thought for a moment he could hear me, then . . . off he went again."

Jack glanced at Clarice. She was studying the young man's pale face, a definite frown on her own. He looked back at Mrs. Connimore. "At least it shows he's not beyond the reach of consciousness yet. With some injuries, the body decides sleep is what it needs and refuses to allow anything else. His stupor may be for the best—his bones will be setting, if nothing else."

Mrs. Connimore accepted his words with a nod. Clarice seemed barely to hear them.

Jack bent his head to better see her face; she looked up and met his eyes. "What is it? Have you recognized him?"

She shook her head. They looked back at the young man. Clarice gestured at him. "The more weight he loses, the more gaunt his face, the more I'm *sure* I should know which family he hails from. But I just can't place the resemblance."

They both stared at the young man for a minute more, then Jack jogged her elbow. "Standing here trying to force your memory to cooperate isn't going to work. Come on— I'll walk you back to the rectory."

She sighed and turned away. He escorted her down the stairs, waited while she picked up her hat from the hall table and with no fuss set it on her head, then he opened the front door for her and followed her through.

Together, they stepped down onto the graveled forecourt. Instead of heading down the drive, Jack touched her arm and pointed to the lush lawns rolling down to the stream. "Let's go that way." He glanced up at the sky, a pure cerulean blue unmarred by any clouds; at least the weather was cooperating. "It's a nicer walk, especially on a day like this."

Clarice acquiesced with a nod. She seemed absentminded, presumably still thinking of the unconscious young man.

His hands in his pockets, ambling beside her as they descended the lawn to the path beside the stream, Jack set himself to redirect her thoughts. "The last time I spent any length of time here was over thirteen years ago." He glanced at her. "Is it still quiet socially, or did the arrival of a marquess's daughter in this sleepy backwater spark a frenzy of balls and dinners?"

She lifted her gaze, looking ahead to where the stream rushed and gurgled between its green banks; the curve of her lips was wry. "Initially. But"—she glanced briefly at him—"the truth was I arrived here entirely out of charity with tonnish society. The last thing I wished was to plunge into a round of balls and parties, being introduced to every eligible male within twenty miles. Of course"—her tone turned cynically resigned—"there was no help for it, but once the first rush of novelty faded, and I showed no signs of wanting to be the lynchpin of an active social circle, that, indeed, my interests were entirely otherwise, the pace slowed to what I suspect is its normal rhythm, and I was largely left in peace to do as I prefer."

"Organizing and managing, specifically my estate. I know, I know"—he caught her gaze as she glanced at him and smiled to take any sting from his words—"you were here and I wasn't." They walked on in silence for a moment, then he added, his tone less flippant, "I'm actually very grateful."

The fleeting glance she threw him, one dark brow arched, told him she was perfectly aware he had good cause to be so. "Reluctantly, but sincerely?"

Wryly, he inclined his head. "Just so."

They reached the narrow path that followed the meandering stream and turned along it; it would lead them through the manor's fields, under the bridge over which the road crossed, then on into the fields attached to the rectory.

He studied her profile as they strolled along, neither hurried nor dawdling. How was he to learn what he wanted to know? "And so after that first rush you've lived quietly here?"

"I doubt much has changed in the years you've been gone. Local society remains peaceful and undemanding."

"Perhaps, but I'm finding it difficult to accept that the local gentlemen are all such slow-tops. Surely they come calling?"

Her eyes narrowed. "Unfortunately, they do. Too frequently. You'd think after seven years they would have realized . . ."

Her words faded. When she failed to go on, he evenly supplied, "That you've no intention of marrying any of them?"

"Precisely." Her eyes flashed; her tone was clipped.

He smiled easily, his expression one she could read as mild amusement if she wished; beneath, he was congratulating himself on having teased from her the answer to his most important question. "You'll have to excuse them—they're only men."

Her soft snort was eloquent. His smile deepened.

So she had no current suitor, nor any wish to have one, and if he was any judge, she wasn't enamored of gentlemen in general, at least not those who vied for her hand. Given her history, he wasn't surprised. No lady of her ilk, well connected, wealthy, and attractive to boot, reached the age of twenty-nine unwed, not just on the shelf but dusty, without having made some definite decisions regarding matrimony. But he'd wanted to be sure, and now he was.

However, while she might have turned her back on matrimony, that didn't mean she didn't have some lover in the area, some gentleman who saw her as he did, and came riding over every few days to meet with her.

He slanted her a glance, recalled how she'd kissed him.

Hungrily, if not ravenously. Even if she'd had a local lover, given her response to him, did he need to know?

"As we're speaking of society and its marital preoccupation, what happened to drive you from town?"

The question, uttered in her usual even tones, jerked Jack from his preoccupation. He blinked at her and found himself staring into a pair of dark eyes that held a great deal of shrewdness and an ability to see through social masks that was, quite possibly, the equal of his.

"You've clearly had some run-in with the matrons and their charges." Clarice raised her brows, challenge and faint amusement in her eyes. "I admit I find it difficult to imagine they routed you so comprehensively."

Despite his outward ease, the mind behind his hazel eyes remained sharply focused as he waved her assertion away. "I was ready to decamp." He looked ahead, then continued, "What was being offered was not to my taste. As for *how* it was being offered"—his jaw set—"that was the last straw."

"I see." She said that conversationally, but she could indeed see it. After three Seasons let alone the social world she'd been immersed in from birth, she knew just how the ton behaved, knew what he would have encountered, could see that perhaps, with him, the matrons might have misjudged and so mismanaged their approach. He'd clearly taken against, as he'd phrased it, the marriageable portion of the female nation; he appeared to view that stance as ineradicable. Not only was he in the country while the Season was in full swing, but he'd sent for Percy and was grooming him as his heir.

She found his decision not just interesting and enlightening, but something of a relief. She had no wish to become involved with a gentleman of his type, his status, who was searching for a bride. Not again. *Never* again.

However, all thoughts of matrimony aside—and how encouraging that they'd both had done with that complication—there was the intriguing question of her reaction to him. She wasn't sure what such a reaction presaged, and whether pursuing it was wisdom or folly, yet said reaction was sufficiently compelling to have her wondering where it might lead, what might be possible.

Between them. Between her and the lord of Avening Manor.

She slanted him a glance. He walked with easy grace beside her, his gaze following the stream. She seized the moment to let her gaze roam, swiftly confirming her earlier view. His was a strength that was so pervasive it needed no action, no specific movement, to draw attention to it; it simply was.

Just being this close to him, only a foot or so apart, she was acutely conscious of his physical presence, a distinctly male presence ruffling her female senses like a hand lightly rippling the very ends of a cat's fur. Not quite a touch, more the suggestion of a caress.

Under its influence, her senses purred and wanted more.

Much more.

And that was the point where she stepped into uncharted territory. She had more than her fair share of experience of what gentlemen regarded as "more." What she didn't know was what *she* truly wished, for she'd never wanted more before. Not from any man, gentleman or otherwise; never before had her senses been so tweaked, even less had her desire, in any form, been so irresistibly piqued.

He had succeeded where all others had failed. Until now, she hadn't even known that was still possible; along with most of the ton, she'd wondered if, after three less-than-satisfying "engagements," she'd become one of those females who would never again be interested in a physical liaison.

But she was interested now, thanks to him. And in the back of her mind was the unsettling notion that the attraction she felt wasn't solely due to appreciation of his physical form.

She'd enjoyed today, enjoyed joining with him to best Jones and deliver the most for the local growers who relied on them, who trusted them to guide them. A job well-done, unquestionably, but it wasn't just the victory that had buoyed her; she'd enjoyed both the planning and the execution far more than she would have if she'd dealt with Jones alone. She'd never worked with anyone in such a way before, let alone known the joy of sharing an endeavor with someone who thought as she did, who understood her ideas and followed her reasoning so effortlessly.

Their mutual triumph was one she savored on more than one plane.

A pity Connimore had sent for them when she had.

The thought brought to mind Jack's injury, the injury he seemed inclined to dismiss or at least play down. She slanted another glance his way. If she hadn't overheard him admit to being injured, she'd have sworn he was hale, whole, and in the best of health. Even now, the notion that he was suffering from some mortal affliction that would kill him before he could marry and sire an heir—hence Percy—occurred only to be dismissed.

Which left her wondering if his injury was anatomically restricted—he'd implied as much to Connimore—and if the existence of said injury wasn't linked to his determination to groom Percy as his heir . . . and, possibly, to his dismissal of matrimony.

He halted. Jerked from her thoughts, she stopped walking and looked at him. He'd turned to view the stream; she followed his gaze and realized they were standing beside the deep pool within the wood that divided the last of the manor's fields from the road and the bridge. The trees had just come into leaf, screening the area in spring green, dappling the sunlight that shone through to illuminate the darker green of lush grass, the rich brown of the path.

The birdsong was louder, more concentrated; the flutter of wings drifted through the trees. The burbling of the stream changed into a sigh as it slid into the deep pool, then quietly flowed on.

"This was my favorite spot when I was a boy. I used to come here to fish whenever I could."

"By yourself?"

"Usually." Jack looked at the opposite bank, where the trees and shrubs crowded down to the water. "The village is a fair distance away, and there's no other farm close. To get here any of the local lads had to cross a lot of manor land, and they were scared of Cruikshanks, our gamekeeper."

Beside him, Boadicea stared at the smooth surface of the pool. "There's rarely anyone here." She glanced up and caught his eye. "I often walk this way. It's a lovely spot and almost always deserted."

Precisely why he'd steered her there. He raised his brows at her. "You fish?"

Her brows rose even higher, infinitely more haughty. "Not here, but I do fish, as it happens."

He blinked. "Another activity not on the list of recommended occupations for a marquess's daughter."

She laughed and turned along the path. "I have three older brothers. When we were children, they disappeared with their rods whenever they could."

"And little sister followed?"

She inclined her head. "Whenever I could. Which was more frequently than my stepmother would have wished, but then she was one of the principal reasons I used to slip away."

"You didn't get along with her?"

"No, but my going fishing wasn't only because of that. Much to her disgust, I was never particularly concerned with being a 'proper little lady.'" She glanced back and caught his eye. "I was never little, for a start, and, of course, I was always being lectured that fishing was for boys, which only made me more determined to enjoy it."

Jack smiled. He found no difficulty imagining a much younger Boadicea determinedly forging her own path through life. Elements of her background as James had described it floated across his mind; clearly willfull self-determination was a deeply ingrained trait.

She was drifting along the path, not strolling as they had

been, but nevertheless moving on. He shifted, soundlessly followed. A beam of sunlight struck through the canopy and caught in her hair; it glowed richly, facets of blood-red garnet flaming in the dark mass of her chignon.

His fingers itched to slide into the silky weight. Burned to stroke the fine satin of her nape, the evocative curve exposed and vulnerable as she looked down at the path.

He closed the distance between them, caught her arm, drew her to face him, halted, and smoothly drew her into his arms.

She blinked, eyes widening as she realized. He smothered a gloating, too-hungry smile. "We haven't yet celebrated our victory over Jones."

She didn't pull back, didn't even tense; there was no recoil, no resistance in her. Her eyes searched his, then her brows rose lightly. "No—we haven't."

Her voice was a touch breathless, but there was no trepidation—no equivocation—in her lovely eyes. Her direct gaze sent desire lancing through him; she was waiting, calmly agreable, to see what he would do. . . .

"I think we should." He bent his head.

She lifted her lips. "So do I."

Chapter 7

❧

The kiss started innocently, a light brush of lips; that lasted for all of one second. Hunger erupted, unexpected, unprecedented, and roared through them both. Their lips fused, melded; she pressed closer as he gathered her to him.

Her lips parted beneath his, inviting, inciting; he plunged in, seized, plundered, and sensed her delight.

He molded her to him, urged on by the flagrant fire in her kiss, in the wordless but eloquent invitation she blatantly laid before him. She wanted as he did, with the same single-minded purpose, with the same urgency, the same need.

A need he for one didn't fully understand, one that overwhelmed with just a kiss, that too easily—effortlessly—swept them into a conflagration that threatened and demanded but one end. An end they both transparently desired; she sank against him, her arms locked about his neck, her fingers spearing through his hair to hold him, to snare him, to willingly surrender to him.

Her wish was implicit in every shifting, seductive slide of her long, sumptuous body against his. In every shared gasp as they kissed, in every tantalizing stroke of her tongue against his. Desire answered, roaring through his veins, thudding in his fingertips.

Here. Now.

He heard the clamor clearly, sensed it not just in the throbbing hardness of his body but in the heated softness of hers.

But . . . the same instincts that had kept him alive through thirteen long years still functioned. It was unlikely anyone would venture by, yet they were in the open. Taking her here, now . . . no.

Such a coupling, however passionate and satisfying, would necessarily be restricted by their clothes, and when he first sank into Boadicea, he wanted her naked beneath him. Wanted to be naked, too, to feel her skin against his, feel the satin smoothness of her thighs grip his flanks as he rode her. . . .

Not here, not now.

At least, not that.

Strategy, tactics, had long been second nature; he didn't need to think but simply knew, as he toppled her hat from her head and eased her down to the thick grass, what would suffice for now, and pave the way for later.

Clarice sank to the grass, smelled the crisp tang as it crushed beneath them, felt the coolness of the earth only momentarily before it heated beneath her. And him. He was all hot, hard muscle, fluid strength and potent masculinity; at close quarters, he was devastating. She couldn't think beyond the need to spread her hands across his naked chest.

But that wasn't to be, not yet.

He lay beside her, propped on one elbow, one hard hand framing her face as, leaning over her, he plundered her mouth and besieged her senses. His body was close, yet not close enough. She ached to have him against her; she tried to draw him down, but he didn't budge.

Instead he moved his hand from her jaw to her breast.

Pleasure, pure and sharp, arced through her, stole her breath, made her arch, pushing her breast more firmly into his hand, a flagrant invitation he accepted as his due. His long fingers firmed, stroked, caressed, through the fine muslin found her nipple and tempted, teased, then squeezed.

She forgot about breathing; it no longer seemed necessary. The sensations he pressed on her claimed her mind, claimed her senses. Set her wits whirling giddily, artfully pleasured as they'd never been.

So this was sensual delight.

At last.

Her body responded, unfurling, or so it seemed, like a rosebud beneath the sun. He was heat and she was yearning; he gave and she took. Or so it seemed.

She felt gentle tugs at her side, felt her bodice loosen.

Felt his fingers press aside the muslin and the fine lawn of her chemise to slide beneath and cup her breast. Skin to skin, the sensitive satin of her breast against his hard palm. She shuddered with sudden understanding, with anticipation and wonder.

Deep within, some emotion, some primal, until-now-buried compulsion stirred. Distantly aware of it, she let it rise, unconcerned, curious.

Then his lips left hers. Before she could summon enough decision to open her eyes, she felt the soft brush of his hair on her bare skin, immediately followed by the hot brand of his mouth.

His lips skated over the upper curve of her breast, and her lungs seized. Then he dipped his head; that scalding heat closed over her nipple, and she gasped, arched, felt more than heard a growl of male satisfaction and inwardly glowed, with a satisfaction of her own, one she'd never expected to feel.

Lips curving, she let her fingers firm on his skull, encouraged him to feast, caught her breath on a gasp when he did, rode out the blissful spike of pleasure, then let the desire that raced in its wake drive her, guide her.

She shifted, lifted beneath him; inexperienced, untutored, she might be, yet she knew enough, could guess enough. With her body she tempted him, lured him. There was no thought in her mind beyond seeing how much further the pleasure might stretch, how much more he might share with her.

He responded, not with any calculation but in instinctive reaction, with a shuddering gasp he couldn't suppress, with a sudden tensing of muscles already tight, with a flaring of wholly male need.

His erection rode against her thigh, rigid, impressive, not threatening so much as tempting. She longed to reach down and caress him, to take that hardness into her palm and learn of it as he was learning her, but she couldn't press her arm between them, not without pressing him back.

She cracked open her lids and glanced down, felt desire grip her as she watched him minister to her swollen flesh. From beneath his lids, his eyes flashed, and caught hers; he held her gaze as he slowly laved, then drew one nipple into the hot wetness of his mouth and suckled.

Her lids fell; a moan escaped her, a sound she'd never before made in her life. A sound of feminine need, of female entreaty.

He heard, but didn't respond; all he did was shift his attention to her other breast and make her moan again.

She wanted, throbbed with a need she'd never felt before, yet recognized. She knew what she wanted, was certain she could have it, if she dared. If she made her wishes plain.

Twisting beneath him, she slid one thigh against him, let her hip and thigh caress him, and was instantly rewarded. He sucked in a tight breath, held it, then he lifted his head, framed her jaw, held her face steady as his lips covered hers, as his tongue plunged between and ravaged her mouth.

Through her giddily whirling senses she felt the touch of spring air on her legs as he lifted her skirts and slid his hand beneath. Long fingers traced upward, over her stockinged knee, skated over her garter to lightly grip bare skin. For an instant, he savored, his palm running over the delicate skin of her upper thigh, then he reached higher, boldly touched her curls, stroked down, through, and parted her.

Slid one long finger into her.

She managed not to gasp, not to tremble at the unexpected invasion. For one moment, her struggle to suppress any reaction that would scream of just how unused to such easy intimacy she was distracted her. Then he shifted his hand, pressing deeper, then stroked.

Her mind fragmented, senses spinning, then abruptly refocusing as he repeated the act.

Again, and again.

Suddenly nothing else mattered. Nothing beyond the heat racing through her, the flames consuming her. The conflagration built, and built. Although his lips remained on hers, his body shielding hers while he pandered to her needs, while he gave her one element of what she wished, some part of his mind watched, cataloged, and gave her the ability to do the same.

To override the distraction of her panting breaths, her fiery skin, her ever-tightening nerves, and view the exchange critically, and see what they each drew from it.

Pleasure. For her physical and sensual, for him the same but in a different way.

He knew what he was doing; never once did she doubt it. He didn't rush, but drove her steadily up some peak of sensation, held her there so they could both savor the moment, then coolly, calmly, tipped her over the edge.

Into sensual abandon, a state where her senses disintegrated in rapture, leaving her floating on waves of delight and golden pleasure.

Jack let her slide into the glory of aftermath. He drew back from their kiss, lifted his head to watch. He studied her face—blissfully radiant, more than relaxed—and felt vindicated. They'd both wanted; they'd both got.

Enough, for now.

Momentarily disengaged, his mind wandered. He hadn't foreseen this when he'd initiated their "celebration." He'd been pursuing his well-thought-out agenda; he'd forgotten Boadicea would have an agenda of her own. Fortunately, their agendas had been highly compatible. When he'd steered her down to the stream, he hadn't envisaged anything so explicit, hadn't imagined that, together, mutually intent, they could by mutual consent dispense with the preliminaries and conjure . . . heat enough to cinder all sense, to make it near impossible to think.

That heat had risen and engulfed them, igniting desire, sending it searing down their veins, driving them on, demanding more, whipping their senses with a lash of expectation and the promise of estatic delight.

For them both, expectation and promise still beckoned, still waited, not patiently, in the wings.

Her lashes fluttered, rose to reveal eyes dark and lustrous with passion. Her hands, lax on his shoulders, firmed, gripped. She urged him back down to her, lifted her lips as he obliged, and kissed him.

With a wholly feminine confidence. Never had any invitation to intimacy been so explicit; he felt it to his bones, felt its potency slide through him. He fought to resist. *Not here, not now.*

She didn't have the same reservations. She drew back just enough to whisper against his lips, "Come to me . . . now."

The last word glided over his lips, distilled temptation. He felt himself literally harden, muscles growing rigid with the effort to hold back. He savored her lips, but kept his mental distance, then drew back and murmured, "Not here. Not now."

She opened her eyes and looked into his, searched them. Then asked, "When then? And where?"

The simple, straightforward, oh-so-direct questions sent lust spiraling through him; no equivocation, no obfuscation, no falsity. She wanted him, and knew he wanted her. He shifted in a vain attempt to ease the ache in his loins. "Soon." The tension in the word had a smile teasing her lips. He held her gaze for an instant, then suggested, "Tonight?"

She didn't nod, but her eyes, her expression signaled her wholehearted agreement. "Where?"

That was harder. Concentrating was difficult. The warmth they'd generated wafted the perfume from her skin, from her gorgeous breasts, bared and still swollen, elementally tempting; it combined with the headier scent of the slickness he'd drawn forth, an even more evocative invitation to sink his body into hers. Hardly surprising he could barely focus.

"Hmm . . ." Reluctantly he withdrew his fingers from the heated haven between her thighs.

"Not the rectory, and not the manor either." Helpfully she stated the obvious.

He couldn't bring himself to lift back from her, from the promise she embodied. "The folly on the hill—is it still habitable?"

Her lips curved. "Yes. And yes, that will do very nicely."

He studied her smile, tempted to ask why "very nicely," but he'd learn the answer soon enough. "Tonight, at the folly, after dark."

Her smile deepened. She held his gaze, her own mysterious and yet open and direct. After a moment, her gaze lowered to his lips. "Are you going to let me up?"

Her tone suggested she was in two minds about what answer she wanted.

So he gave her the answer they would both prefer. "Eventually."

Then he bent his head and again set his lips to hers.

Twilight was fading from the sky, leaving it a deep indigo flecked with brilliant stars, when Clarice slipped out of the rectory. She paused on the porch to draw in a deep breath, to savor the sweet smell of night-blooming flowers, then calmly flicked her shawl about her shoulders and set off down the drive.

The spring night closed around her, familiar yet, tonight, faintly exotic, spiced with the subtle thrill of impending adventure. She often walked in the evening; no one would miss her until morning, and she would be back long before then.

Her expectations of the coming hours wound her nerves tight, sent excitement sliding down her veins. Normally she walked simply to ease the energy pent up inside her; tonight, she turned out of the gate accepting that when she returned, she might well be exhausted.

She didn't truly know what to expect, not specifically. She didn't even know whether she would enjoy the exercise, but she wanted to find out.

With Jack Warnefleet, she could. With him she would finally learn about those aspects of herself, the sensual, elementally female aspects that she'd thought would remain forever untried, unbroached.

She'd parted from him when they'd reached the rectory; he'd gone to talk with James while she'd turned her attention to the numerous household matters awaiting her decree. Countless times over the ensuing hours, she'd asked herself whether she was mad, or if it was a case of her reckless, hedonistic streak, the one her stepmother so deplored, overcoming her good sense.

Viewing the question dispassionately, she rather thought the latter was indeed true. But what she couldn't quite fathom was why, after all these years of quiet, even docile existence, it had taken Jack Warnefleet less than twenty-four hours to bring that long-buried part of her not just back to her surface, but back in full strength.

Back in mature strength; she felt the impulse to act, to seize and wrest from life what she wanted, far more powerfully than she had before, seven and more long years ago.

She crossed the stream at the stone bridge, then left the road. Climbing over a stile, she unerringly followed the path through the lower meadow and up the gentle hill that commanded the upper reaches of the valley; built high on stilts, the folly sat within a small wood just below the crown. From the valley, the folly was all but invisible, but from the single room high in the canopies, the views were extensive, an arcadian panorama of quiet valley and distantly burbling stream, of woods and orchards and green pastures.

The folly belonged to the manor; it was on manor lands, but no one from there or anywhere else visited any longer. She'd discovered it within a month of coming to Avening, on one of her first nighttime walks. It had fallen into disrepair, so she'd claimed it as her place, something no one from either the manor or the rectory had thought odd, or had questioned. She'd spent her own money to have the shingles repaired and the leaks in the roof patched, the windows reset and the floor restored. Howlett had volunteered furniture from the manor's attics. Connimore had taken to sending up two maids every few weeks to dust and sweep, while she had brought what comforts she wished—a rug, books, cushions, and more—from the rectory.

Passing into the cooler, denser shadows of the trees surrounding the folly, she looked ahead, senses sharpening, anticipation digging in its spurs.

He would have come via the other path, the one that led directly from the manor. Both paths cut through the trees to converge before the folly; as she stepped out from the shadows into the small clearing, she noted the door at the top of the wooden stairs was open, propped wide.

No candle glowed, no shadow stirred behind the wide windows of the room high above, but she was the only one who ever came this way; he was already there, waiting.

She climbed the stairs; they still creaked, an oddly comforting sound. The door at the top opened directly into the single room that was the folly; she went in, and, through the gloom, saw him. Waiting, as she'd supposed.

He was sitting in one of the cane armchairs, shoulders wide against the chair's broad back, one booted ankle balanced on his knee, elbow on the chair arm, jaw resting on his fist, his eyes fixed on the doorway, on her.

The fine day had mellowed to a mild evening; he'd doffed his coat and opened his waistcoat. The white of his shirt drew what little light remained, drew her eye, held it.

Stationary, seated in such an elementally masculine pose, he exuded an even more powerful aura of harnessed strength, as if without the distraction of his fluid, graceful movements, the truth shone more clearly.

For a moment, she considered the picture he made, took note, then, reaching behind her, closed the door.

He watched her, unmoving, yet she sensed the tightening

of the rein under which he held himself, sensed, too, his careful gauging of her. For this moment, the initiative was hers; wisdom urged her to grasp it.

Thanks to the wide windows that filled the folly's front wall, framing the views, there was light enough to see by. Crossing to the dresser that stood along one wall, she let her shawl slide from her shoulders, caught it, folded it, and laid it down.

She walked past the wide daybed, set before the windows, its thick mattress draped with colorful throws, the cushions strewn upon it bright and inviting. One of the bank of windows was open; pushing it wide, she looked out, breathed in. The scents of the wood laced with apple blossom from the orchards slid through her.

"About this." Her voice was even, steady. Turning, through the gloom she met his gaze. "Before we go further, I want to make one point clear."

Seeing him sitting there, waiting for her, confident, arrogant even though he hid it well, she'd realized just how much of a danger he was—could be—to her, and what form that danger might take. He was the personification of a gentleman of her class; no matter she didn't imagine he intended it, she wasn't going to fall victim to one such. Not again. *Never* again.

"I want you to know—and to agree—that no matter what passes between us, what happens here or elsewhere, that this will be nothing more than a limited liaison." Leaving the windows, she drifted, her gaze on him as she circled the room toward him. "Whatever else might come to be, this, between us, is only a temporary relationship, one that will last as long as we both wish, but that ultimately will fade and be no more."

She halted beside the chair, looked down through the shadows into his eyes. "I want it understood that in even beginning this, we both recognize it will end, and with no repercussions. No obligation, no implied understanding, no expectations of anything."

His eyes held hers. "The moment, and nothing more?"

"Precisely." She held his gaze for two heartbeats longer. "That's my price. Are you willing to meet it?"

He rose, in one fluid movement came to his feet a hand-breadth away.

She suddenly found herself looking up, feeling slight.

Jack looked down into her face, acutely aware of the tug of desire, the compulsion she so easily evoked just by being in the same room, by being within arm's reach. Her price was a rake's dream; no repercussions guaranteed. A clean start, and a clean end; if asked to state his own preferred rules of engagement, he would have said the same.

Why, then, did her saying it—demanding that that was how their relationship would be, setting down the very rules he normally preferred to play by—evoke such a contrary reaction in him?

Why was he suddenly absolutely certain—more, fixed upon—getting more, taking more, from her?

It had to be some form of momentary madness. He shook it aside, and reached for her. "Yes."

He drew her to him, bent his head, paused just long enough to watch her lids fall, see her lips part, then he kissed her.

Sank into her mouth, not just sure of his welcome but assured of it, a fact implicit in the way she came into his arms, not passively but actively seeking to be closer, to impress her flagrantly female body on his harder male form, to entice, then incite.

Their mouths melded, tongues mated. She spread her hands on his chest, fingertips sinking into muscle in wordless demand. He splayed his hands over her back, pressed her to him, then swept his palms down, over her waist, over her hips to boldly cup her bottom and draw her fully to him.

She was tall enough that his erection pressed against her mons; he molded her to him, suggestively shifted against her, and felt the urgent shudder that racked her spine.

They were both adults, both mature, both experienced

enough so that while there was no hurry, there likewise was no need for any slow introduction, especially not this first time. The need that rose through them was powerful, full-fledged, a hunger that had depth and breadth and claws. They surrendered without a fight—more, they welcomed it, let it ride them, flow through them. Take them. He sensed her commitment, that moment when she let go of all restraint and gave herself up to their passion; he followed without thought.

Raising his head, breaking from the kiss that had already set their pulses racing, he backed her to the daybed. She shuffled back at his direction, let him steer her, her hands, her whole focus, on the buttons closing his shirt. Her legs bumped the side of the daybed as the last button slid free; she spread the halves of the shirt wide, paused for a heart-beat while her eyes devoured, then set her hands to his skin.

His reaction shocked him, for one instant rocked him; no other woman's touch had ever made him feel weak. But then her nails lightly scored, and desire came rushing back, more demanding, more commanding.

He reached for her laces.

They stood beside the daybed exchanging occasional, explicitly intimate kisses as they helped each other from their clothes. Hands reached, touched, grasped; fingers stroked, then gripped and stripped away.

Shadows fell over them, welcoming, enveloping. She'd sent one fiancé to war, had been ready to elope with another, had been wooed and pursued by how many males of his ilk he didn't know.

He did know what type of male she would attract: men like him. Men who wouldn't settle for just a kiss, however explicit, but who would want, and press for, more. So he wasn't surprised by her calmness, her boldness in reaching for what she wanted, what she transparently desired; he wasn't surprised that she showed no sign of modesty, of hesitation when he drew her chemise off over her head. He would have been more surprised if she had.

Instead, she stood within the loose circle of his arms and marveled—at him. That he hadn't expected. The chemise fell from his fingers, disregarded, to the floor, while he drank in the sight of her drinking in the sight of him.

He was naked; she'd helped him dispense with boots and breeches, insistent while he'd been distracted by the fine buttons on her chemise, so he'd complied. So now they stood close, naked in the soft dark, but with their eyes well adjusted to the night they could both see well enough.

She reached for him, reached out with fingers spread to touch, to trace, in wonder. That was all he could read in her face, in the pale features that in the weak light were stripped of all pretense; she was a female, but one who ruled. Her expression was not impassive but contained, not aloof so much as in control. He ached to shatter that, to break through her barricades to the sensuous female he knew her to be, to stroke, caress, to rip away that control and bring her to writhing ecstasy.

To conquer. Ultimately to make her his.

Such a possessive urge was unfamiliar, not something that had struck him before. Yet in the dark, standing naked before her, he accepted it, accepted that they were both pagan warriors at heart.

She confirmed that when she lifted her gaze to his eyes. She searched for but an instant, then boldly stepped into him, into his arms as they closed around her and locked, into his kiss as he bent his head and covered her lips.

There was no question over what they wanted.

He pressed her back to the daybed, lowered her to the silky covers, followed her down. Covered her. Spread her thighs with his and settled between, locked her hands in his and anchored them to the cushions on either side of her head. He plunged into her mouth and laid claim, dropped all restraint and took from her what he wished, what the real man behind his charming mask, the far-from-civilized warrior wanted.

Perhaps needed.

The thought drifted into his brain, then out, unable to find purchase with his senses locked on the heated silken feminine form trapped beneath him. His predatory instincts were fully awake, tracking her responses, noting with growing satisfaction how abandoned, how wanton, those became.

Then she seemed to gather her strength; her fingers curled around his, and she kissed him back.

Met him, matched him, challenged him.

The kiss turned incendiary; flames roared through his head, through his body, licked around his soul. Her hips lifted beneath his, tilting, driving him, directing . . .

On a gasp, he drew back, raised up on his elbows to look down at her breasts, then he bent his head and feasted.

Ravenously.

Clarice cried out. Beyond thought, beyond concern, beyond everything but sensation. Sensation that poured through her, that with every sharp pull of his mouth on her flesh thrust deeper into her, that with every shift of his hard, muscled, hair-dusted body against hers seared and burned.

She drank it in, embraced it, opened her heart and soul to it. Felt it to her bones, and gloried.

Gloried in being female, in being herself, fully, wholly, completely.

Then he shifted again; releasing one of her hands, he reached down between them, and found her. Touched, stroked, pressed in where she was hot and slick and wet. She gathered herself, her wits, steeling herself to withstand the shattering sensation of his finger boldly entering her.

Instead, his fingers left her. He released her breast; shifting higher up her body, he found her lips again, took them as he gripped her thigh just above her knee and moved it wider, opening her more fully, then he shifted his hips, pressed nearer, and she felt the broad head of his erection press against her.

Slide into her.

Her senses unraveled. She tried to breathe, tried to relax and let it happen, let him in. He pressed deeper. The physical impact was devastating; the onslaught of sensations, all new, all sharp, hot, and searingly exciting, overwhelmed her. Held her completely in thrall, her entire being focused on the slow, heavy, inexorable penetration of his body into hers.

The slow, steady, and inexorable possession.

That realization slid through her, shivered down her spine, made her fingers clench, her nails sinking into his upper arms as her body arched beneath his. Not fought but tried to hold on, to hold back . . .

His hand slid up her thigh, pressed beneath her and cupped her bottom, gripped and tilted her hips, holding her steady, anchored beneath him for that slow, steady impalement.

And then, with one last thrust, he was there, deep inside her, and she couldn't catch her breath. A sharp sting was all she'd felt; she hadn't expected more, but her lungs had seized. What little air she took came through him, through the kiss that suddenly seemed her only anchor in a world transformed. A world where sensation ruled, where pleasure was king, where emotions swirled and eddied, built and surged, and dragged her down.

A world that had closed in to just her and him, joined intimately on the daybed in the moonlight.

He was hard and heavy, potent and so male, so foreign within her. Eyes closed, she clung as he slowly withdrew, then powerfully surged in, sinking deep, then thrusting deeper yet. A sound escaped her, a whimper of pleasure. He repeated the action, even more forcefully, and the sound came again, more definite, more revealing.

She felt his satisfaction, felt his determination to drive her further as if it were tangible, something she could touch.

Then he lowered his body to hers, let her feel his weight, his chest hard, crinkly hair against her swollen breasts, abrading her excruciatingly sensitive nipples as he withdrew and thrust in, setting the pace for a long, steady ride.

The arms her fingers had wrapped around were warm steel, flexing with the rocking of his body into hers, but otherwise solid and unmoving. She held on tight, lungs locked as sensation swelled, welled, then the dam broke and she let passion take her. Let it sweep through her, consume her, drive her body against his in a primitive dance, rising again and again to the escalating rhythm.

Reality fractured. There was no life beyond their shared breaths, beyond the dance of thrust and retreat, of acceptance and release, of need and fire, and the flames of passion that flared and coalesced and drove them.

On. Unrelentingly demanding. Not just him but her, too; her own demands swelled and filled her. She let her body free, let it take him as it would, as he gave himself and took her.

They were matched. Despite the unforgiving, brutally hard body pinning her down, plunging deep, powerfully driving her on, despite the fact that in the presence of his strength she felt so much weaker, despite all the physical advantages he held, she held advantages, too.

Her power showed in his touch, not reverent so much as covetous, in the hunger that drove him, that seemed to well from his soul as he drove himself into her. As if he needed to be there, deep inside, and that need was not physical alone.

That knowledge was hers, instinctive and sure, but understanding was beyond her. The flames grew, roared; sensation built, nerves steadily coiling, tight, then tighter. Hot, then hotter. Then the kaleidoscope of passion and desire swirled about them, swooped and caught them, whipped them high to some pinnacle of earthly bliss, held them there for one bright, indescribably intense instant, then flung them down.

Released them.

Shattered them. Fragmented their senses with that release. Emptied them.

Of thought, of will, of feeling.

The little death, they called it; she now knew why. But unlike death, in the aftermath came . . . not feeling, not sensation, but a warm sea of emotion, flooding in, filling her, buoying her.

Blindly, she shifted one hand, found his head on her shoulder, lightly riffled his soft hair. He'd collapsed and lay heavily upon her, pressing her into the bed, totally immobilizing her.

It didn't matter; she couldn't move, and his weight felt curiously right.

Just as the whole, first to last, had felt . . . meant to be.

So easy.

So . . . amazing.

She felt her lips curve. Eyes still closed, she gave herself up to the golden glory sliding through her veins, and let the peace and the sense of fulfillment soothe her, let them both seep to her soul.

Jack stirred. Eventually. Not because he wanted to; he could happily lie on her, feeling her soft and sated beneath him, feeling her sheath hot and wet occasionally contracting about his sated flesh, for any number of hours.

But although she was relaxed beneath him, he was worried he was crushing her, and as he had every intention of persuading her to repeat the exercise later, not just tonight but frequently in the future, it seemed wise to exercise some degree of restraint and not push his luck.

Besides . . .

He rolled onto his back, lifting her half over him, draping her long limbs about him, securing her, still boneless, within the circle of his arm.

Where she belonged.

That wasn't a thought he'd intended thinking, but he couldn't deny what he felt. That, however, was only one of the disturbing mysteries their actions of the past half hour had uncovered.

Head back on the cushions, he looked up at the ceiling, at the dappled shadows that shifted as the breeze played in the treetops outside. He stared unseeing at the changing patterns while he cataloged what he knew, and what he didn't yet understand.

Minutes passed, then she stirred. He felt the infusion of tension into her muscles, the change in her breathing as she came fully awake. He didn't move. For a long moment, she lay cradled in his arm, then, hand splaying on his chest, she pushed back and sat up. He let his arm slide down, permitted her to move away. Smoothly, without looking at him, she swung to sit on the edge of the daybed, then rose.

He had to fight to squelch the urge to reach out and haul her back. He watched as she walked, not to where her clothes had fallen, but to the window. She stood and looked out. The moon had risen; half-full, it shed a gentle light, one that bathed her white skin in an unearthly radiance, making it glow softly, pearl-bright. Her hair . . . he'd avoided disarranging it earlier; now it hung in a heavy knot low over her nape, still coiled and partly anchored in her usual chignon, but with dark tendrils their lovemaking had teased loose curling over her shoulders and down her long, exquisitely lovely back.

Her spine remained regally straight; her stance gave no hint that she was uncomfortable in her nakedness. She'd moved through the room with her usual grace.

He shifted onto one side, coming up on one elbow, settling, raising one knee. "You were a virgin."

Clarice turned her head and looked at him. Studied the body that had so recently joined with hers. " 'Was' being the operative word." She'd foreseen the comment, one reason for her clear rules of engagement. "I was, now I'm not. That's all there is to it."

She couldn't see the frown in his eyes, but she knew it was there.

"You should have told me—I could have hurt you."

She raised her brows, faintly skeptical. "I'm twenty-nine. I've ridden all my life. It was unlikely there'd be much pain." Just the faintest of stings, as it had happened; she'd hoped he hadn't noticed. She kept her gaze on his face. "My virginity wasn't something I valued. It was something I'd been left with long past the date it should have been gone. Pray accept my thanks for eradicating it."

A ripple of something passed through him, but she could

read nothing in his shadowed face. He lay there, flagrantly male, blatantly strong, his chest—that glorious expanse that fascinated her—wide and heavily muscled, tapering past a rock-hard abdomen to much narrower waist and hips, and long, strong, legs. All naked, blatantly displayed for her delectation.

Except . . . was it her imagination, or had some dangerous quality, one she couldn't name, crept in, infused his body, his stance, something that was not quite a threat, but a hint of displeasure?

"Your thanks . . ." His voice was low; she hadn't noticed before how gravelly it had grown. Now she felt it slide through her and fought to quell a shiver.

His gaze hadn't left her; she could feel it like a flame. Slowly, he let it slide down her body, a caress, intimate, frankly possessive.

Oh, yes, she'd been right to state her terms, and make them clear.

Slowly, his gaze rose, returned to her face. "Perhaps you should tender your thanks in more than just words?"

She couldn't help hear the challenge in his voice, couldn't help read it in his frankly masculine pose. Couldn't help meet it. Coolly, she raised her brows.

With slow deliberation, he held out one hand. "Come here."

For one long moment, she studied him. Then she pushed away from the window, crossed the room unhurriedly, and placed her hand in his.

Walking home through his fields in the dark hours before dawn, Jack detoured via the rose garden. He sat on the cold stone bench in the alcove and stared at the still pond, giving his mind, his thoughts—hell, his body—time to rediscover their equilibrium.

She'd thrown him. Not just off-balance but into some disordered reality where he wasn't entirely sure which way was normal, which was safe.

He'd started the evening sure he was in control, that he had the reins of their affair—that's how he'd thought of it—firmly in his grasp. Even after she'd surprised him with her unexpectedly straightforward view of the matter, he'd believed all was, if not quite as he'd anticipated, then only slightly off-track. His urge to oppose her, to disagree and change her rules, even if he hadn't previously been one to react to feminine suggestions with mindless, instinctive opposition, he'd assumed that was all his reaction was.

He was no longer so sure that was true.

Not after she'd blindsided him with her statement about her virginity, serenely absolving him of any and all responsibility for taking her maidenhead.

Not after what had followed.

He didn't, even now, understand his reaction. All he did know was that it was real, that it was a fundamental part of him, no fleeting response but something grounded in who he truly was, in the man he was, not superficial, not something he could discard. His taking her virginity might not have meant anything to her, but it had meant, and still did mean, a great deal to him.

Her dismissal of her virginity as valueless, her casting of her allowing him to take it as a matter of no account, had triggered that response. When she'd so calmly put her hand in his, he hadn't been able to suppress it, whatever it was. Not temper; that didn't even come close. Something akin to an unquenchable need to conquer.

The passion she'd unleashed in him had been frightening. It had pushed him to sweep her into sexual arenas of which she couldn't possibly have had any experience, into realms of sensuality that should have shocked her, that should have had her retreating if not outright fleeing.

Instead, she'd met him, matched him, risen to every challenge, every blatantly sexual demand he'd made of her.

One point was clear; the gentlemen who'd labeled her an iceberg had had no notion of what she truly was. It was true she wasn't a woman who melted into a man's arms. Boadicea didn't melt—in the throes of passion, she was like flaming steel, hot, searing, malleable, giving in her way, but not weakly. Never weakly.

He'd wanted to conquer her, and in the end she'd surrendered at least enough to appease him, but along the way he greatly feared that she had returned the favor.

His head was still spinning, an unsurprising response to discovering the one lady who could affect him to that extent, while simultaneously realizing that she hadn't intended to.

Didn't intend to; she had no interest in any long-term relationship. It wasn't hard to understand why. Even while he'd been inwardly rebelling at her insistence that their liaison was strictly temporary, he'd recognized why she'd taken such a stance, and declared it so clearly.

But that had been before he'd thrust inside her and felt the telltale give, so slight that if he hadn't been concentrating so intently on her body's responses, he would have missed that fractional instant of pain. Most other men would have; he hadn't. He'd known.

And the knowledge had made him feel . . . like a conqueror who had found his rightful queen.

Putting his head in his hands, he clutched his hair and groaned.

He'd turned his back on marriage, deliberately, unequivocally, so fate had sent him a lover, one who possessed the ability to satisfy him, all of him, as no other ever had, one who wanted marriage no more than he. . . .

It *should* have been perfect. He should have been deliriously happy.

Instead, there he was, sated to his teeth, sitting on a cold hard bench trying not to think of how his entire life had, in one night, turned on its head, so that his future—any degree of future contentment—now depended on him succeeding in a task that was as close to impossible as made no odds.

He had to get Boadicea to change her mind.

Chapter 8

He'd charmed women by the hundreds, ladies by the score. All he had to do was charm Boadicea.

Jack stood at the manor's drawing-room window and watched Clarice walking briskly up his drive. So briskly, she appeared set on storming his castle; from the look on her face, pale and serious, he doubted charm—any amount of charm—would get him far today, but what concerned him most was the figure struggling to keep pace by her side. James.

Clarice was only an inch shorter than James; she had the longer legs. Jack watched as she halted, rather grimly waited for James to catch up, then stormed on.

James didn't look upset; he looked concerned but, Jack would swear, not about Clarice. He didn't waste time wondering what might have happened; he headed for the front door.

The doorbell pealed. Howlett appeared, tugging his coat straight as he made for the door. Jack fell in behind him. He waited until Howlett swung the door wide, then stepped forward to greet Clarice as, head up, spine rigid, she marched in.

He reached for her hand, squeezed it, met her dark eyes. "What's happened?" This close, with her hand in his, he could sense her agitation.

She drew breath, then said, "Over the breakfast table this

morning, I realized who that unfortunate young man reminds me of." Turning, she waved at James, who, almost puffing, had followed her in. He exchanged a nod with Jack as Clarice continued, "The young man reminds me of James."

Jack blinked; the young man looked nothing like James.

Clarice made a dismissive sound. "Not as James is now, but there's a portrait in the family collection of James when he was sixteen." She viewed James critically. "*Now* James looks more like the Altwoods, but *then* he looked more like his mother's family, the Sissingbournes."

James met Jack's eyes. "If Clarice is right, I greatly fear the young man might be one of my relatives." James's face clouded. "I should have come earlier, done the right thing and put my books aside—"

"Never mind that." Clarice took his arm and drew him on. "You're here now, so let's go upstairs and see—" She broke off.

Clattering footsteps drew their eyes to the stairs. A maid came hurrying down. Seeing them, she blushed, slowed; stepping off the stairs, she bobbed a curtsy. "Begging y'r pardon, m'lord, m'lady, Reverend Altwood, but Mrs. Connimore says as the young man's stirring again. She thinks he might wake this time."

Clarice nodded. "We were just on our way up." Determinedly, she steered James to the stairs.

Jack came up on James's other side in time to hear James murmur, "I wonder if it's Teddy."

Clarice glanced sharply at James. "Were you expecting him?"

James shook his head. "But he's the most likely of that lot to come calling." To Jack, he added, "Teddy's a canon with the Bishop of London."

Jack grimaced. "Not many canons drive high-perch phaetons."

James's face cleared. "True." Then his frown returned. "So . . ."

Clarice stepped off the stairs into the gallery. "Come along, and you can see who it is, and then we can puzzle over why he's here."

Her bracing, faintly exasperated tone got James moving down the corridor. They came to the open sickroom door. Clarice led the way in, then stepped to the side. James followed, his gaze going directly to the young man lying in the bed.

"Not Teddy." James studied the young man, now restless and twisting fretfully beneath the sheets, frowning as if in the grip of some nightmare. James frowned, too, then his face cleared. "Anthony—it's Anthony." James glanced at Jack. "Teddy's younger brother."

At the sound of his name, the young man stilled, then, with obvious effort, he lifted his lids. James was standing at the end of the bed, directly in his line of sight.

"James?" The young man blinked, struggling to focus. "Is that you?"

"Yes, indeed, my boy." James went around the bed so Anthony could more easily see his face. "But what brings you here? And what happened?"

Anthony licked dry lips. Instantly, Clarice was at his other side, holding a glass of water. Jack pushed past James and supported Anthony's shoulders. He gratefully sipped the water, then weakly motioned that he'd had enough. Jack laid him back on the pillows Mrs. Connimore plumped behind him, relieved to see a little color returning to his face.

"I came to warn you. Teddy sent me." Anthony looked at James. "He found out there's some report within the church that names you a military spy through the last decade. You're under investigation."

"What?" James looked stunned.

"That's nonsense." Clarice stared down at Anthony.

Anthony waved weakly. "We all know that, but, well . . . something's going on." His lids fluttered; he seemed to gather his strength, then he gestured to the bed. "Well, it's obvious. How else did I get here?"

Jack's face set. Dragging an armchair from the side of the room, he set it beside the bed, then bundled James, still shocked and stiff, into it. Mrs. Connimore, on the other side of the bed, had pulled up a chair for Clarice; Jack fetched a straight-backed chair for himself.

Clarice turned to Mrs. Connimore. "Perhaps a little chicken broth?"

Mrs. Connimore, eyes on Anthony, nodded. "Just what I was thinking myself. I'll get it heating."

She left the room, closing the door behind her.

"Now," Jack said, "tell us first about the accident on the road."

Anthony's lips twisted. "No accident. I'm not such a ham-fisted clod that I would run my cattle into a ditch, and I swear I was stone-cold sober."

"There was another carriage," Clarice prompted, and was immediately treated to a hazel-eyed glare. She was taken aback for a second, then met it belligerently. "We know there was."

Anthony, eyes half-closed, nodded. "He drove me off the road."

"Can you describe him?" Jack kept his eyes on Clarice; she mutely sniffed, but kept her lips closed.

Anthony frowned. "Largish, pale face—rather round. A gentleman . . . of sorts."

Clarice's description had been more detailed, yet they were clearly describing the same man. "Had you met him or seen him before?" Jack asked.

Anthony started to shake his head, then winced and stopped. "No. But . . . just before it happened, before the phaeton tipped, I knew—knew he meant to run me off the road. He stared at me, looked into my face." Anthony's gaze found Jack. "He did it deliberately."

Grim-faced, Jack nodded. "So it seems."

Anthony grimaced. "When I knew there was no help for it, I jumped, but the phaeton rolled on top of me." He glanced down at his legs.

"One's broken, but mending well, as is your arm. Other than that, it's all bruises and wrenched muscles." Jack caught Anthony's gaze. "You'll be hale and whole in a few months."

Relief filled Anthony's face, making him look much younger.

"Now," Clarice said, "what's this about James being under investigation?"

"Before you get to the message your brother sent," Jack smoothly cut in, "fill in the gap between leaving your brother and reaching here."

Anthony smiled, faintly apologetic, at Clarice, then turned to Jack. "Teddy sent for me. I met him in the shrine in the grounds at Lambeth. I was surprised he'd told me to go there, but as it turned out, he didn't want anyone to see him speak with me."

Clarice, lips tight, raised her gaze and, across Anthony, met Jack's eyes. Clearly, despite Teddy's caution, someone had seen the brothers talking.

"Teddy told me about the allegations against James and asked me to come straight down and warn you." Anthony looked at James, rather sheepishly. "I had a dinner to attend that evening, but I left first thing the next morning."

"You stopped somewhere along the way." Jack leaned forward. "Swindon?"

Anthony nodded. "I left Swindon after breakfast but I wasn't entirely sure of the way, so I went to Stroud first. Longer, but at least I didn't get lost."

His voice was less strong; he was clearly tiring. Clarice kept her lips shut, but caught Jack's gaze and widened her eyes at him.

He looked at Anthony. "All right, now tell us about these allegations. Better yet, try to tell us exactly what Teddy told you."

Anthony sighed; he closed his eyes, a frown creasing his brow. "Teddy overheard a conversation between the bishop and the dean. He was passing the bishop's study, and the door was slightly ajar—Teddy heard James's name, so stopped and . . . he heard that there'd been allegations made that James had been hand in glove with the French, not just recently but over the past decade.

"The accusations were that James was passing on strategic analyses of Wellington's campaigns, as well as information he'd gleaned about troop strengths and movements from the soldiers he interviewed. When one of the deacons at the palace first warned the bishop about it, the bishop dismissed the whole as scurrilous rumors, but then the deacon returned with more details and . . . the conversation Teddy overheard was the bishop telling the dean that they would have to treat the matter seriously—that it did indeed appear truly serious—and so they would have to investigate James."

Anthony paused, then opened his eyes. "That's all Teddy heard because Deacon Humphries—he's the one who'd brought the allegations to the bishop's notice—came into the corridor and Teddy had to move on. Teddy saw Humphries go into the study, presumably to give the bishop all the information he had."

James had stiffened at the mention of Humphries' name. Studying James's face, Clarice found it unusually unreadable. "Who's Humphries?"

James blinked, then grimaced. "He's another scholar . . . well, would-be scholar. He also specializes in military strategy, although in his case purely battlefield tactics."

"So he's a competitor of sorts," Clarice said.

James grimaced again. He glanced at Jack. "Years ago, Humphries and I were the principal candidates for the fellowship I still hold."

"So," Jack replied, "not just a competitor but a rival."

James sighed. "Unfortunately, Humphries does see it that way."

"Still?" Clarice asked. "You were made a fellow more than twenty years ago."

James nodded, his expression one more of sorrow than anger. "When I go up to town to do research, I stay at the palace. The bishop has always been interested in my work, which of course means Humphries hears of it, too. He's never been slow to show that my success, then and now, rankles. You see, without the fellowship, and without the livings I hold, he has to support himself via his duties, and so has little time for his research."

"So he resents you," Clarice said.

"I fear so." James looked troubled.

Jack straightened. "Regardless, if there's to be an investigation, then we need to learn the substance of Humphries' allegations."

"Teddy might have learned more by now. I'm sure he would have tried . . ." Anthony's lids had fallen; his voice was increasingly weak.

Clarice exchanged a firm glance with Jack and James, then patted Anthony's hand where it lay on the covers. "I daresay, but you don't need to worry about that now. You've delivered your message, and may leave the rest to us. You should rest. Mrs. Connimore will bring some broth for you in an hour or so."

She pushed back her chair and rose, forcing Jack and James reluctantly to follow suit.

Anthony lifted his lids enough to look up at her, and smile, rather sweetly. "You're Clarice. Teddy said you'd be here. You probably don't remember me. I was still at school when you . . . left, but Teddy said to remember him to you."

Clarice was surprised—if James was the black sheep of the family, then she was obsidian—but she smiled and inclined her head regally. "Thank you. Now you should sleep."

She turned and led the way from the room, with one glance ensuring that James and Jack followed, then headed for the stairs.

With a nod to Anthony, Jack left in James's wake, closing the door behind him. He paused, then ambled after James, wondering if he'd read that last exchange between Clarice and Anthony correctly.

Teddy and Anthony both viewed Clarice warmly, something she hadn't expected. Jack couldn't help but wonder how deep the break with her family had been, how acrimonious. Apparently enough for her not to expect to be fondly thought of by other family members.

He started down the stairs some steps behind James. Clarice was already sweeping across the front hall toward the drawing room, presumably expecting a serious confabulation over Anthony's revelations, when the front doorbell was rung with considerable force.

Clarice stopped at the drawing room door. James stepped off the stairs and halted, too. Jack continued his descent, outwardly unperturbed, inwardly aware of his instincts stirring even though he couldn't yet see why.

Howlett appeared and swept majesterially to the door. He opened it; over Howlett's shoulder Jack saw Dickens, James's groom.

Dickens nodded to Howlett. "I've a message for the master and Lady Clarice. Urgent, it is."

Howlett stepped back as Clarice, James, and Jack converged on the door. Clarice got there first. "Dickens." She nodded at the man. "What's the message?"

Dickens bobbed to her, and to James and Jack behind her. "M'lady, m'lord, sir, Macimber sent me." Dickens's gaze settled on James. "The dean's come from Gloucester and he's waiting to see you, sir. He's not staying, but he has an urgent communication from the bishop and must see you right away."

Standing beside James, Jack felt reluctance sweep over his friend, closely followed by resignation. James sighed. "Thank you, Dickens. I'll come straightaway."

James went to move past Clarice, but she briskly descended the steps, tightening her shawl about her shoulders as she swung to glance at James. "I'll come, too, of course."

Jack hid a faint smile and followed at James's heels. "We'll all go." He met Clarice's dark gaze. "Of course."

She hesitated for a heartbeat, then nodded, and turned to follow Dickens down the drive.

* * *

"I'm afraid, James, that I must insist that you abide by the bishop's stated wishes." Dean Halliwell, the rural dean representing the Bishop of London, tried his best not to meet Clarice's eyes. "You must remain within your parish of Avening until the investigation into these allegations is complete."

"These allegations are nonsense," Clarice stated, haughty censure coloring her tone, "but if the bishop is so misguided as to give them any credence, then clearly the best person to refute them is James himself."

Seated in one of the armchairs in James's study, his fingers steepled defensively before him, Dean Halliwell carefully inclined his head her way. "Be that as it may—"

"To suggest anything else would, I feel sure, be tantamount to a miscarriage of justice." Seated regally in the other armchair, Clarice speared the hapless dean with her gaze. "It could hardly be construed as fair were my cousin not to know of the charges brought against him, nor be given the opportunity to defend himself against them."

Dean Halliwell drew in a tight breath. "The Church has its own procedures in such matters, Lady Clarice."

Clarice's expression grew even more stony. She raised her brows. Before she could utter the blistering setdown forming on her lips, Jack shifted in his chair, set beside hers, drawing the dean's attention.

"Perhaps," Jack said, his tone even and unthreatening, "you might explain those procedures."

As he'd hoped, Dean Halliwell was eager to offer whatever he could in the hope of appeasing the irate personage on Jack's right.

"I believe the matter will be heard by the bishop himself in the first instance, purely within the palace, you understand." Halliwell hurried to add, "Regardless, the procedures are the same as a full ecclesiastical court. There will be a prosecutor and a defender appointed."

"And who will those individuals be?" Clarice asked.

Her accents were arctic; Dean Halliwell tried not to

shiver. "I understand the prosecutor will be the deacon who first brought the allegations to the bishop's notice."

Clarice opened her lips, doubtless on a withering denunciation of Deacon Humphries; Jack evenly cut in, "And the defender?"

He ignored Clarice's fulminating glare.

"Another deacon named Olsen." Dean Halliwell appeared grateful for Jack's intervention; he looked at James. "I understand Dean Samuels himself wished to defend you, but the bishop ruled that such overt partisanship on his principal advisor's part was unwise."

From the corner of his eye, Jack saw Clarice's narrow. She'd no doubt interpreted that last comment as he had; unwise for the Church, not unwise for James. He was relieved that, although her lips thinned, she kept them shut.

After his initial disbelief at the bishop's edict effectively confining him at Avening, James had grown increasingly subdued, leaving all subsequent questions to Clarice and Jack. Jack continued to probe, to glean all they could from Dean Halliwell, ably assisted by Clarice, although her contributions were primarily nonverbal.

Eventually, Dean Halliwell made his excuses and fled, Clarice's saber-edged gaze fixed between his shoulder blades. Once his carriage had rattled away down the drive, the three of them returned to the study.

James sank into the chair behind his desk slowly, as if he still couldn't quite believe the turn events had taken. His gaze was distant, fixed on the opposite wall, his mind far away.

While Jack could certainly sympathize—two hours ago James had had no idea there were any clouds on his horizon, let alone a storm of this magnitude—Jack's reaction was more in tune with Clarice's.

She paced back and forth, arms folded beneath her breasts. Her skirts swished as she turned. A definite frown drew down her fine brows; she was clearly wrestling with the problem of what next, of how best to react. How to proceed to clear James's name.

"Well!" James blew out a breath. His gaze remained distant.

Jack caught Clarice's eye and raised a brow; she frowned at him for a moment, then waved dismissively. "Oh, sit, for heaven's sake. This is hardly the time for standing on ceremony."

Of course, she'd held to every iota of ceremony while poor Dean Halliwell had been there; suppressing a smile, Jack sank into one of the armchairs. He studied James.

This was James's battle; while Jack had every intention of doing all he could to assist, he needed to know James's mind.

"I'll have to go to London and rally the family."

Clarice's statement, delivered in a tone that brooked no dissension, let alone argument, brought James's head up.

"Oh, no, my dear. There's really no need . . . The bishop will see sense, I'm sure." James looked at Jack. "Don't you think, m'boy?"

Jack didn't, but was saved from explaining by Clarice.

"If the bishop is ready to waste his time, and that of numerous others, in convening a private court to hear this matter, then there's no grounds to suppose he won't be swayed by whatever trumped-up arguments were laid before him in the first place."

Precisely. "I think," Jack said, once again grateful to be able to take the even, reassuring tack, taking the sting from the acerbic truth Clarice so unflinchingly dispensed, "that we do need to respond to this, James."

James frowned at him, then at Clarice. She ceased her pacing and met James's stare steadily. After a long moment, James seemed to shake aside his thoughts. "No." He leaned back to look at them both. "This is a storm in a teacup, no doubt whipped up by Humphries' regrettable envy. The most appropriate response is to ignore it. The less said, the soonest mended."

Above her arms, Clarice's breasts swelled.

"No, James. Not with this." Jack's voice was no longer reassuring, an edge of steel creeping in. "If you don't challenge and defeat these 'allegations,' and the bishop determines you have a case to answer, then the charge that will go before any secular court will be one of treason."

James smiled. "But that's just it, dear boy. No one in his right mind would accuse an Altwood of treason."

Clarice's snort was eloquent. "For goodness sake, James! The only reason the bishop has convened a private court is because of the family, but *he's still convened that court.* He's still investigating the allegations."

"But the allegations are false."

Clarice looked at the ceiling so James wouldn't see the exasperation in her eyes. "The bishop doesn't know that. Indeed, it's clear he doesn't know what to believe, and without you or anyone else acting in your best interests, he might never see the evidence that will show the allegations to be false, only evidence that leaves a large question mark over your integrity."

"Over your honor, James." Jack caught James's gaze as it swung his way. "Clarice is right. You need someone more devoted to your interests than just an appointed cleric looking into this on your behalf. Do you know this man Olsen?"

A glimmer of uncertainty passed through James's eyes. He looked down; reaching out, he lifted a paperweight. "I have met him."

They waited, Clarice by Jack's chair, staring down at James, then she prompted in a tone that held clear demand, "And?"

James grimaced, sighed. "He's young. He was only appointed last year. He was a chaplain with the army, one of the regiments. The bishop took him on when he returned after Waterloo."

Jack felt the flare of Clarice's temper even though she wasn't directing it his way.

"So your defense rests in the hands of some wet-behind-the-ears whelp—"

"Actually," Jack said, "Olsen might be useful." He glanced at Clarice. "A man with experience of a battlefield—better, in this case, than one with none."

She met his eyes, then shut her lips and nodded. "True." Swinging around, she started pacing again. "Regardless, as you yourself can no longer attend, James, you need supporters who will ensure this Olsen has all the right arguments and whatever proofs he needs to reveal these allegations for the fabrications they are."

After a moment, she added, "I'll leave for London in the morning."

"My dear!" James looked distressed. "Truly, there's no need."

"Yes, there is." She didn't stop her pacing. "Regardless of how *private* the bishop's court is, the story will out, of that you may be sure. The family will be horrified." She glanced at James. "I'm perfectly aware of what sort of reception I can expect from the family were I to approach them on my behalf. On *your* behalf, by way of quashing a potential scandal—in such a case I'm sure they'll not only listen, but act in whatever way is necessary."

"No." James started to look mulish. "I won't have you subjecting yourself—"

"She's right, James." Jack was treated to a surprised but approving look from Clarice. He didn't know why James thought she'd be subjected to anything untoward, but he knew she was right, and the way his plans were unfurling in his head, she wouldn't be subjected to anything untoward, either.

"Precisely." Clarice nodded decisively. "I'll leave at first light—"

"However"—without raising his voice, Jack spoke over her—"before I leave for London, I'll want all the relevant facts. Dates, James, and a list of all the papers you've published in the last decade—indeed, a summary of all you've researched over that time, whom you've corresponded with, and when, what dates you traveled and to where, and whom you spoke with while there, all the soldiers you've interviewed . . . once I have all that, I'll go up to London."

He wasn't surprised to hear Clarice state, "I'll wait and go with you."

Looking up, he met her dark eyes. "As James said, there's really no need, and I do have the right contacts to do what needs to be done."

Clarice read the calm certainty in his eyes, took a moment to consult her instincts, all too reckless as she'd been told often enough. But she'd never be able to sit and wait, wondering what was happening. "No doubt. Regardless, I'll accompany you to London."

She glanced warningly at James, her decision clear in her face. She would listen to no argument. She was her own person; neither James nor any other had any authority over her. "The family will need to know." She looked at Jack. "They don't know you, but, for my sins, they definitely know me."

Jack had merely inclined his head—whether in true acceptance of her decision, or with some vain hope that she might later change her mind he didn't know—but he'd let the matter slide.

James hadn't, but had only succeeded in wasting his breath, and pricking her temper to boot.

She knew what she was doing.

Both in that, and in this.

Calmly, Clarice walked through the night's shadows, crossed the bridge and climbed the stile, then headed through the meadow toward the hill and the folly.

And Jack. His arms, his body, and the excitement she'd found with him.

She wasn't sure it would be the same, as absorbing the second time—more accurately the second night—but she was keen to find out.

He'd excused himself soon after her declaration that she'd go to London with him. She'd escorted him to the front door; following close behind her, he'd whispered in her ear.

She'd had to fight a reactive shiver, but had calmly agreed to meet him again tonight.

The folly rose before her, the door once again left enticingly open. Anticipation leapt in her veins; smiling to herself, at herself, she quickened her pace and strode eagerly on.

From behind the wide windows of the folly, Jack looked down, watching as Clarice left the shadows of the trees and, with an easy, confident stride, crossed to the stairs. And started up them, to him.

Expectation rose through him, definite and unusually powerful, strangely compelling. Not simply the expectation of sensual delight, but of a chance to engage more fully with her, of another opportunity he would grasp to woo her, another step in his campaign to win her.

He knew what he wanted; what he didn't truly understand was why. What he felt was beyond question; what he wanted and needed—what he had to have—was crystal clear. But he saw her clearly, and knew himself well; he couldn't comprehend what had given rise to the connection that already existed, that was already so strong, at least for him.

Strong enough to bind him, to compel him.

He turned as she came through the door. She saw him, smiled with her customary assurance, then closed the door and crossed the room to him.

He waited for her to come to him through the dappled shadows, her gown, a pale, fine evening gown, flirting about the long line of her legs. She let her shawl slide from her arms to trail across the head of the daybed. Her head tilting slightly, studying his face in the poor light, she came steadily on, slowing to a halt only when she was breast to chest with him.

He closed his hands about her waist as she lifted her arms and draped them over his shoulders.

She examined his face from closer quarters. "Did you want to talk about James?"

"No." He held her dark gaze, marveled at the feel of her between his hands, supple, warm, strong in a quintessentially female way, marveled at what she made him feel. "I don't want to talk, not even about James . . . at least, not yet."

His voice was low, rough, gravelly with the promise of passion.

Her lips curved as he bent his head. "Good."

Then she kissed him. And he kissed her.

For one long moment, they wrestled for sensual supremacy, then, with a soft sigh he felt to his bones, she gave way, willingly ceded him the right to script their play.

As she had last night.

It was that, that willing, not surrender but trust, that struck him, that provoked such a primitive response in him, that spurred him to take all she offered, consume, want, and demand more.

Having her could easily become an addiction.

As he closed his hand about one sumptuous breast and kneaded possessively, and felt her flaring response—a response she was helpless not to make, but one she brazenly made no attempt to deny—he felt the talons of his need sink deeper and knew he was already lost.

No sense in trying to fight it, not her or the powerful surge of feeling she evoked in him.

He surrendered, too, simply gave himself up to the passion that rose so readily between them. They stood by the window and swiftly yet unhurriedly shed their clothes. Naked, they stood locked in each other's arms, lips tempting, tongues enticing, mouths melding only to part on a sigh, skins heating, brushing, hands touching, exploring, explicitly caressing.

She possessed none of the hesitancy, the modesty of a woman new to this game; it was her confidence, her assurance in going forward, in facing the challenge of intimacy and embracing it with such unshakable will that had cloaked her inexperience. Even now, he sensed her as a true physical partner, one who would consent to be led, but who, if he relinquished control to her, was strong enough to lead, too . . .

The notion taunted, teased. Last night, driven by primal

impulses he didn't wish to examine too closely, he'd held her beneath him, captured in the cushions, and filled her, ridden her to ecstasy three times. She'd sobbed, moaned, in the end screamed her surrender, yet she hadn't been vanquished; it had felt more as if he had, as if in drinking her screams, in taking her so possessively, he'd acknowledged her as his queen—she who could command him.

Now she met him, matched him, and urged him on. Used her body to flagrantly, blatantly incite him.

He couldn't think, just reacted. Did what felt right, what would appease him, and her.

Grasping her waist, he turned her around so she was facing away from him; he drew her back, hard, against him, felt her stretch, then mold her back to his front, arms gracefully reaching down and back, long slender fingers splaying over the tight muscles of his thighs and gripping, then sliding to caress. Boldly she used the swell of her hips to press against, then brush his loins, used her lush bottom to caress his erection.

She was tall enough; locking one arm about her waist, closing his other hand about her hip, he hosited her hips up against his, heard her breath catch as the broad head of his erection slipped between her thighs. Almost instantly he found her entrance, already damp, welcoming. He pressed in, easing her down, back, inch by inch filling her. The scalding heat of her slick sheath closed powerfully around him; head bowing beside hers, he couldn't hold back a growl of pleasure.

An answering ripple of delight coursed up her spine; she arched against him, lightly panting. He drew her down the last inch, embedding himself in her body. Her toes touched the ground.

She immediately tried to wriggle against him, to experiment; he caught his breath and locked his arm about her, hand splaying over her stomach to angle her hips to him, his other hand clamped tight, anchoring her, holding her immobile as he withdrew a little way, then more powerfully forged in.

Clarice lost her breath on a shuddering sigh. Head tipping back, eyes closed, she savored the heated strength of him surrounding her, as he held her body just so, and filled her, slowly, repetitively, until she thought she would scream with frustration. But she'd learned enough last night to know he knew what he was doing, that his way would ultimately bring her pleasure beyond anything she, in her innocence, could imagine. So she acquiesced and let herself follow rather than vie for the lead; she rode the sensual wave he created, let it sweep her up, rise through her, and build.

Constantly higher, further. Deeper, only gradually faster.

Until heat raced through them, flamed beneath their skins, until a furnace burned within them, and still the coiling wave rose. With every sure thrust, every shift of his thighs against the backs of hers, with each penetration, every rocking invasion of his body into hers.

His hand left her hip, rose, and closed over one breast. Hard. Kneading possessively, the action of his hard palm and strong fingers diverting her attention, then his fingers found her nipple, and rolled it. Drew on it, tauntingly stroked, then he closed his fingers and squeezed.

Just as he thrust even deeper into her.

Sensation bright as lightning lanced through her. She gasped, the sound sharp, echoing through the quiet room. She suddenly became aware of their breathing, hers ragged and thready, his harsh by her ear. He dipped his head; his lips traced the sensitive side of her throat.

Then his fingers closed again, tight, tighter; he squeezed in time with the flexing of his hips, with the rhythm of his more intimate possession. The hand splayed over her stomach tightened, lifting her half an inch, angling her hips a fraction more. He thrust deeper, harder, deeper still.

Her senses fractured.

Like spun glass, they shattered; sharp sensations rushed

down her nerves, leaving each one raw, abraded, aching, and open. Her skin burned, sensitive beyond measure; her whole body came alive to every touch, every brush, every deep thrust. Each sensation became a spur, sharp, crystalline in clarity, disjointed pieces of a kaleidoscopic whole that whirled higher, faster, coiling ever tighter, until she flew apart.

Until completion claimed her, fragmented her reality and let ecstasy pour in. Her body convulsed, clenching tight for one long moment, then release swept her just as he joined her, as he stiffened behind her, and filled her one last time.

She felt his warmth flood her, felt the heat of his rasping breath on her throat. His hands held her locked to him, his body a hard cage about her. His head moved; he placed a kiss, heated yet delicate, on her shoulder.

Lips lightly curving, she sank against him, into the haven of his arms.

She wasn't at all sure how they made it to the daybed, but when she opened her eyes, he and she were horizontal. Her cheek rested on the heavy muscle of his chest. His skin was warm, as was the rest of him; she could still feel a great deal of his skin against hers.

He was lying on his back, with her lying atop him, loosely cradled in his arms. Her hips lay between his spread thighs, his long legs outside hers.

Lifting her head required more effort than she could summon; shifting, she squinted up at his face.

One arm lay across his eyes, but he felt her gaze and raised it. From beneath heavy lids, his eyes met hers. He studied them for a moment, then he lowered his arm. "I got us this far—don't think about moving anytime soon."

She smiled, and returned her head to its previous, comfortable resting place. Savored this, too, the quiet moments afterward when, wrapped in glowing warmth, peaceful and still, they both seemed so free, so much just themselves without having to be what the world had designated them—

lord, lady. In these moments, they were just them. Him, her, no social structures . . . in some ways, no shields.

The concept intrigued her, focused her mind on how close, how open, she felt with him. How unrestrained. It wasn't simply the physical intimacy that made her feel so; indeed, that was a symptom, an outcome, not the cause. The cause, the reason she felt so differently about him and treated him—treated with him—in ways so far removed from her norm was more complex.

Or perhaps more simple.

He understood her, or seemed to, and she, in large measure, understood him.

Because of that, he was the only man of her class she'd ever considered, ever even thought of, asking for advice. The only one whose advice she considered might have value.

Her skin was cooling; a light breeze drifted through the open window and trailed chill fingers along her body. She quelled a shiver; she didn't want his arms to close around her again, not just yet.

She shifted and sat up. Ignoring the look he cast her from under his arm, she reached up behind him and tugged her shawl free. Shaking it out, she swung it about her shoulders, then, uncurling her legs, she clambered from the daybed.

Without looking back, she walked to the windows; as the heat beneath her skin faded, the night air seemed less chill. Halting before the casements, she looked out. The night was a medley of shadows and faint moonlight, of distant, muted rustlings, and the soughing of the breeze.

If she invited his advice, would he expect her to heed it?

Did she value his views enough to cross swords with him?

Did she want to know what he thought?

Turning, she looked at him, through the gloom met his eyes. "I'm worried about James."

Chapter 9

Jack looked across the room at her; she stood still and straight, the shawl in no way hiding the mesmerizing lines of her body. Those long lines decorously clad and lit by the sun distracted him; clad only in the pearly sheen of moonlight they exuded a magical power that ensnared his mind. It took effort to lift his gaze to her face, to fix it there. "Worried in what way?"

She frowned. "He doesn't seem to be reacting to the threat of these allegations as he ought."

He thought about that, thought of what he'd sensed of James's reaction, and how that differed from his, and hers.

"He doesn't seem to understand"—she made a sweeping gesture—"that it's not enough just to bear the family name. That that alone won't shield him."

It puzzled him that she saw it so clearly, then again, his nickname for her had proved surprisingly apt. "James doesn't understand about power." He eased up, then relaxed against the daybed's raised back. "He never really has. He was born to a powerful family—he assumes that that power will be his, or at least will serve him, purely by virtue of him carrying the name."

She made a sound suspiciously like a snort. Folding her arms, folding the shawl about her body, she leaned back against the window frame and studied him. "You and I know he's wrong. Power isn't a passive thing—something that sits waiting to do its job, like a door or a fence. Power doesn't even exist unless you wield it."

She spoke as one who knew. He inclined his head. "James won't change. He doesn't see the need, and in truth, I doubt he has it in him—the ability to wield the power the Altwood name would give him if he chose to exercise it. . . ."

Even before she nodded decisively, he saw where she'd led him. "Precisely." She walked back to the daybed. "That's why *I* need to go to London, to wield the family's power in his stead."

She paused beside the daybed, by his side, and looked down at him, into his eyes. "*You* understand."

Statement, not a hint of a question.

Jack felt his face harden. He reached for her hand. "I understand why you feel as you do."

He drew her down to the bed, down into his arms, drew her to him and kissed her. Knew from the way she so readily put aside their discussion and responded, ardent and eager to experience more, that she imagined that discussion was finished with, over. Won.

It wasn't, but he wasn't yet ready to pursue the point of her journeying to London in James's defense. She was right; he did understand about power, about how to wield it. That being so, there was no real reason for her to return to the capital, especially if that would involve some difficulty on her part. But . . . there were other issues to consider, such as whether, no matter how persuasive he was, she would consent to remaining at Avening.

That, however, was an argument for another day. Tonight . . . he followed her lead, set the matter aside, and devoted himself to one much nearer, much dearer to him, to the warrior-lord he truly was.

Drawing her to him, dispensing with her shawl, he devoted himself to conquering her.

That, at least, was his intention, but this time, when he

tensed to roll her beneath him, she pulled back from their kiss. Pushed back; planting her hands on his chest, bracing her arms, she rose above him in the deepening dark.

He'd already parted her long legs and drawn her knees high, had already caressed the swollen flesh between her thighs to slick readiness, so when she pushed back she was straddling his abdomen, and the musky scent of her wreathed through his brain . . . he was already aching, tense with the expectation of sinking his throbbing erection into her welcoming heat.

He had to catch his breath, clench his jaw, and hold that breath, hold himself back long enough to discover what her new tack was. To decide whether he would permit it, or instead change their direction.

Upright, she sank down, her well-toned thighs, ivory white against his darker skin, gripping his sides, her calves tucking along his flanks as she settled astride him. Her gaze was locked on his chest. She pressed her hands, fingers spread, across, sweeping from the center outward, tracing the wide muscle bands, then sweeping farther, over his shoulders and along and down his arms; she followed them to his wrists and locked her fingers about them.

Lifting both wrists, she raised them, then leaned forward, and pressed them back until he felt the carved wood of the upper edge of the daybed against his hands.

"Keep your hands there." An order. She didn't even look to see if he obeyed. Releasing his hands, she returned her attention to his chest.

The look on her face, intent, focused yet still considering, still planning, had him curling his palms over the carved wood.

"Don't move them unless I give you leave."

He suppressed a smirk at her commanding tone; he'd keep his hands off her for exactly as long as he wished, and no longer. But he waited to see what she would do, what new aspect of herself his warrior-queen might reveal.

Knowledge was the surest route to victory, with her as with anything else.

She lifted her gaze to his eyes; decision clearly made, her plan defined, she leaned forward, her hands on his chest once more, fingertips sinking in as she pressed close, and kissed him. Covered his lips, then, when he parted them, swept her tongue into his mouth. Exploring, learning . . . he relaxed beneath her, remained as passive as he could, and let her lead where she would.

Let her take from him what she would, let her give what she would in return.

Remaining unresponsive beneath the heated sweetness of her kiss, the increasingly definite demands of her lips and her tongue, was beyond him; he responded, but tried to hold to minimal involvement so he could continue to think, to watch her.

She wasn't appeased; the kiss turned sultry, not just siren-like but bewitching, calling forth the beast in him. She deliberately taunted until that less-than-civilized male shook free of the shackles he'd set, and roared forth to do sensual battle with her . . .

That was what she wanted.

In the instant he thrust rapaciously into her mouth, he sensed her satisfaction. A satisfaction that bloomed, that patently thrilled her as she shifted and closed both hands around his face, rising above him, holding him steady while she met him in a glorious exchange—of heat, of fire, of promise.

The battle continued until they both burned, until flames seemed to crackle, the very air about them spark.

Abruptly, she pulled away. Looked down on him with dark eyes glowing with passion and something he recognized as feminine will. They were both heated, both wanting, their breaths already coming hard and fast.

Slowly, she looked down at his chest. Then she drew breath—her breasts swelled—and she edged back, still straddling him. Pressing his jaw up, she bent her head and set her lips to his throat. Kissed, licked, laved. Set her teeth to the steely tendons and grazed.

Sensation and need swamped him. He closed his eyes, locked his hands about the carved wood above his head and endured . . . her touch, her ministrations, all the while burningly conscious of her body, all flushed silk and wet heat, supple and strong, a unique match for his moving above him, not touching except where her thighs and calves gripped his flanks, instead hovering, the ultimate temptation, mere inches above his rigid flesh.

It was all he could do to lock his jaw and survive.

She was thorough, yet she didn't dally; she worked her way steadily down his throat, paying attention to the indentation between his collarbones, pausing briefly to lave, then close her mouth over the pulse raging at the base of his throat and suck, before shifting lower.

To his chest. Her fingers swept through the crinkly hair adorning it, then curled, lightly tugged. He cracked open his lids, but found she didn't want his attention; she was busy examining, then setting her mouth to one flat nipple. Her tongue flicked, then her teeth gently closed, tightened . . . he sucked in a breath and closed his eyes. His jaw felt as if it would break.

But she was far, far from finished.

Eyes closed, he tracked her direction, tried to predict her intention, tried to mute the storm her innocent yet bold experimenting was wreaking on his senses, and only partially succeeded.

Only partially held back the inevitable rise of passion, of a hunger that, once it hit in full force, would not be denied. He could feel it rise in her, too, feel the escalating flames in her touch, in the grasping of her fingers on his skin, in the increasingly voracious plundering of her mouth and tongue.

When, having explored his navel to her satisfaction, her lips slid lower, tracing the line of hair that led to his groin, he exhaled. Soon, she'd sit up. Sometime during her exploring, she'd scooted down his thighs; she had his legs trapped between hers, under her.

He filled his lungs and exhaled again; he'd survived her torture. He started thinking of an appropriate response, of those tortures he could use on her; he was about to open his eyes, release his grip on the top of the daybed and lower his arms, when she took him into her mouth.

Sensual shock streaked through him. Every muscle froze, tensed so hard they hurt, further engorging the flesh she'd taken deep between her lips, sending all thought winging from his head.

She curled her tongue and licked, then sucked.

His lungs had seized. He hauled in a breath, then let it out in a shuddering groan as she bent to her task. His entire body tightened beneath her; his fingers straightened from the wooden edge.

"Don't move your hands."

The words were sultry, low, heavy with feminine power. She'd spoken over him; her breath added another level of sensory heat playing over his aching erection.

She closed her mouth about him again, sucked powerfully, and he was sure he saw stars on the insides of his lids. She was innocent, yet she had a very good idea of what she was doing.

He focused on that, clung to the contradiction. How had she known?

A flash of memory answered him, a picture of her writhing beneath him, then other visual memories of how far he'd pushed her the previous night crowded in. He'd driven her far farther than he would normally have taken even a mildly experienced lady, but despite her practical inexperience, she'd been neither shocked nor afraid . . .

Her theoretical knowledge was greater than the norm. As his body rose beneath her ministrations, as another, deeper, more heartfelt groan shuddered through his chest, he grasped the point, understood more completely who this was, who he had engaged with.

A warrior-queen denied for far too long. One who had wanted, and hadn't been able to have, but who had known what she was missing.

She was determined now to seize opportunity, to revel in it, to enjoy it, and him, to the full.

He had to fight to breathe, had to battle to regain and retain some degree of control, to form some idea of where the engagement was headed, and how he could seize the initiative back. If he didn't soon . . .

Her questing fingers found his balls. Rolled them, gently squeezed. Her other hand left his stomach, slid down to close, firm and sure, about the base of his rigid length, to hold him while she ministered with her mouth, her lips, her tongue.

"Enough!" He barely got the word out.

Releasing the top of the daybed, opening his eyes, he looked down, saw her release him and look up, one brow faintly arched, a look in her dark, blatantly provocative eyes that patently said, "If you're sure."

Lowering his arms, he reached for her, but she came up on her knees, met his hands with hers, laced her fingers with his and used his hold for balance as she shuffled upward, moving over him, still straddling him.

"I'm not quite sure how this works . . ."

Speech was beyond him. Through his hands, he directed her, pressed back on her hands when he wanted her to ease her hips down . . . he watched, saw the empurpled head of his erection touch, slide against her swollen flesh . . . he couldn't stand any more torture.

With a flick of his hands, he had them free; he clamped them about her hips, nudged upward and into her, then he pressed her back, down . . . closed his eyes and groaned as her scalding sheath took him in, as her fire engulfed his, then closed around him. Tight.

On a shuddering, strangled sigh, he opened his eyes and met hers, dark and burning.

"I told you not to move your hands."

She wasn't so much complaining as asking.

"You need them now." He used his grip on her hips to raise her, then guide her back. In seconds, she'd caught the rhythm, then rode him of her own accord. He was half-sitting, his shoulders raised, courtesy of the daybed. She was straddling him, her hands on his chest; he had a perfect view, one he drank in.

When she started experimenting, sinking more deeply, then stroking shallowly, then grinding her hips against his, he sucked in a breath, lifted his gaze, and tried to think of something else.

Her breasts, sumptuous, swollen, all flushed satin skin and pert, furled nipples, rose and fell before his face. His lips curved in his otherwise passion-locked face; dispensing with his now-redundant hold on her hips, he raised his hands to her breasts. Closed them around the lush mounds, kneaded, and heard her gasp.

He set himself to pander to her heavily aroused senses, to drive her, to render her as mindless as he. She rose and fell on him unceasingly, taking him deep, caressing him with abandon. The long muscles in her thighs, well toned by years of riding, stood her in good stead; he was increasingly certain she would last longer than he.

Not something he would allow. Rising, lifting his shoulders, he set his mouth to her breasts and heard her muted shriek. Remembered the screams he'd drawn from her the previous night, set himself to hear the same again.

He ministered to her breasts while she rode him steadily, unswervingly to ecstasy. When the peak and the inevitable precipice loomed, when he felt his body gather inexorably beneath her, he freed one hand and sent it skating, pressing hard and possessively down the front of her body, sliding over her hip to close briefly about her bottom and squeeze, then to trace the line between thigh and hip forward and down to the damp curls between her thighs.

The tight knot of flesh he sought stood erect and begging beneath its hood. He caressed it, felt the immediate rush of her response. Bending his head, he drew the peak of one breast deep, suckled strongly as he stroked and pressed, as she rose and fell harder, faster . . .

She broke apart and took him with her. Head thrown back, her cry rose to the ceiling while he feasted on her breast, while her body closed in tight contractions around his, while he groaned and shuddered beneath her, and surrendered.

To the power she'd evoked, to the power with which he'd replied.

The moment of ecstasy, of infinite pleasure, held them locked in its bliss for an incalculable time . . . then left them, released them. Let them fall from the heavens into sweet oblivion.

They collapsed, sated, in a jumble of limbs. She shifted, eased. He sank back, closed his arms about her; she rested her head on his chest. They lay still, aware, watchful, wondering, as the power slowly faded.

Jack laid his cheek on her dark hair, felt it like silk against his stubbled jaw.

Power was something they both understood. It was not a passive thing; it didn't exist unless you wielded it.

Now they had . . . they would again. That was simply their natures, a fascination they shared. Warrior-lord and warrior-queen. Well matched.

The shadows slowly lengthened as the moon traversed the sky. He felt no urge to move; neither, it seemed, did she. Neither slept; the aftermath coursing their veins was not, this time, of physical exhaustion. What held them awake, quiet and watchful, was their predator's sense of that power in the air.

A power neither was yet sure they understood.

He let his senses stretch, acutely aware of her, of the svelte body, the long, feminine limbs tangled with his. Of the heat cooling between them, of desire for the moment appeased. Given all he could feel, all he sensed, all he now knew, it was difficult to comprehend why she'd been as she was, unclaimed. Supremely conscious of her warm weight, of the satin skin dewed with passion pressed tightly, intimately, about him, it remained a mystery that his peers had been so blind.

To him, she was sensual challenge personified, give and take demanded . . .

He inwardly paused, then silently acknowledged that perhaps that was why, with her, no other had succeeded; they hadn't been willing, hadn't been strong enough to let her have her way. To let her come to them, to let her be as she truly was, all she truly was.

A plausible, very likely accurate thesis, yet he couldn't see in it any hint of how to make her pledge herself to him. Not just for a night, or a week, or a year, but forever.

The peace of the night enveloped them; peace of a different sort cradled them. Eventually, she stirred. He helped her lift from him, shifted so she could slump by his side, still lying half over him, her head pillowed on his chest.

Folding one arm behind his head, the other locking her against his side, he squinted down at her dark head. "Where did you learn all that?"

She didn't pretend to misunderstand. She glanced fleetingly up at him, her lips lightly curving, then looked away. Gently, absentmindedly, she traced patterns on his chest. "The library at Rosewood, the family seat. The collection's been there, being added to by succeeding generations, for centuries. Some of the volumes were highly informative, highly detailed."

"I take it you were an avid student." He had to fight to remain still under her trailing fingers.

"I was interested . . . intrigued. And I have an excellent memory, at least for pictures." She shifted against him, sliding around so she could lift her head and look into his face, as her hand drifted lower. "If you must know, I've been waiting for years to put into practice all I learned."

Her voice was beyond sultry; it purred, low and soft in his ears, slunk around him like an artful cat, rubbing her power over him.

He held her dark, blatantly challenging gaze while his mind raced. "In that case"—he swallowed and repitched his voice to a more normal level—"perhaps you'd like to try . . ." Leaning close, he whispered in her ear.

Then he lay back and looked at her, giving her back raised brows, and a challenge of his own.

For a long moment, she held his gaze, then she smiled, slowly. "Why not?"

He grinned, and reached for her as she rose and came eagerly into his arms.

The next morning, Jack awoke with a familiar urgency riding him. It was the same sense of time ticking by, defined and limited, that he always felt when going into a mission; there were things he had to do first, arrangements to set in train, or the need to act would come and find him unprepared.

In this case, he had to get all he needed from James before Clarice decided to embark on her rescue precipitously, alone.

He headed down to breakfast, plans revolving in his head. Clarice was right; James did need to be rescued, they did need to act. Exactly how, however . . . that he'd yet to define.

In the breakfast parlor, Percy was tucking into ham and eggs. Jack waved and went straight to the sideboard. Thanks to Clarice, his appetite had definitely improved; his plate piled high with samples of everything Cook had sent to tempt him, he took his seat at the head of the table.

After dinner last night, he'd warned Percy that he would have to go to London for a few weeks; they'd agreed that, in the few days before he left, he would introduce Percy to the locals and show him around the estate, enough to be able to hand Percy and his induction into the vagaries of estate management into Griggs's able hands. Griggs might be old, but he knew all there was to know about estate management.

"So." Percy pushed away his empty plate and eyed Jack hopefully. "Where do we start?"

Jack chewed and considered. Reaching for his coffee cup,

he took a long swallow. "There are some nonestate matters I need to get organized first, but you can help with those."

Percy's eagerness didn't dim. Jack had realized his young relative was the sort who preferred any activity to none; Clarice should approve.

"What do you want me to do?"

"Young Anthony upstairs." He'd introduced the two yesterday evening. They were of an age; Percy had commiserated with Anthony over being confined to bed and had offered to play chess through the evening. Looking in on his way to the folly, Jack had found them both engrossed. "I want a list of his relatives likely to be in London, or within half a day's reach, how each is connected to James, and those most likely to lend James their aid. In addition, names and directions of any others Anthony thinks might be of use."

Percy nodded; he'd heard the gist of the problem facing James. "Anything else?"

It struck Jack that it was a pleasant change to have someone simply accept and not argue. "No, that's it." He pushed back his chair. "I have a letter to write, then I'm going to the rectory to get James started on another list. I'll be back before luncheon." He joined Percy; side by side they walked out into the hall. "If you have time before I get back, try to memorize the layout of the fields and cottages to the east. I'll take you out that way this afternoon, introduce you to the tenants, let you get a feel for the lie of the land that way."

"Umm . . ." Percy looked at him with wide eyes.

Jack grinned. "You can take the gig. There are lanes we can follow."

Percy didn't try to hide his relief. "Good." He glanced up the stairs. "I'll go and beard Anthony."

Jack parted from him with a nod. He went to the library, sat at his desk, and dashed off a letter to the one man he'd expected never to need to write to again. Sealing the letter, he went looking for Howlett; leaving the missive with him for urgent dispatch to London, he looked in on Griggs, checked there was no urgent business awaiting his attention, talked over Griggs's opinion of Percy—surprisingly positive; it seemed Percy had a head for figures—then he headed down the drive and cut through the hedge, taking the shortest route to the rectory.

There was no warrior-queen at the washing line today. With a grin at the thought, Jack climbed the steps to the rectory porch, circled around to the side door, and so through the hall to James's study. He knocked, heard James call, as always distractedly, "Come."

Opening the door, Jack went in, to find a harassed-looking James seated behind his desk with Clarice standing over him.

Her arms were folded—rarely, he was coming to learn, a good sign. He resisted the urge to check if her toe was tapping.

He smiled, charmingly. "Good morning." He made the greeting general. Clarice accorded him a regal nod and looked back at James.

James had looked up, incipient relief on his face; it faded as he looked at Jack. "Ah . . . good morning, my boy." James looked down at the sheet of paper on his blotter. "I suppose you're here to demand information, too."

Clarice's lips thinned. "I explained, James. We need to know all you can tell us before we go to London."

James looked at Jack.

Who shrugged. "She's right."

"But"—James's tone turned querulous—"I really don't see the need—"

"This is serious, James."

Jack looked at Clarice; she looked at him. They'd spoken in unison, with very similar inflections, hers a touch more impatient.

Looking back at James, Jack continued, "We can't not act, James. You can't expect it of us."

That made James think; after a moment, he grimaced, then waved his pen at the sheet before him. "Clarice said you'd need as much detail as I can recall . . ."

Clarice reached around James and twitched a fresh sheet

of paper free. "I think it would be best if Jack listed all the information he needs." She laid the sheet on the desk opposite James, along with a pen she filched from a rack by James's hand. "Then you can do your best to assemble the goods."

Under her forceful gaze, Jack drew up a chair and sat before the blank sheet. He picked up the pen, tested the nib. "This might take a while."

Over the tip of the nib, he met Clarice's eyes. She was never a restful female; at present, the energy pouring from her—as if she was impatient to attack an as-yet-unsighted enemy—while in one sense reassuring, was otherwise distracting. He sympathized with James; he'd never be able to focus his thoughts if she remained in the room in her present state.

If she remained in the room at all.

She met his eyes, clearly heard his suggestion. Considered it, then asked, "How's Anthony?"

"Better and steadily improving." Jack dipped his nib in the inkwell, then looked again at her. "He's getting restless over being confined to his bed."

"Hmm." Lowering her arms, she walked around the desk. "I'll call on him this afternoon."

"That might be wise." Jack bent over the paper. "I'll be out this afternoon, and I'll have Percy with me. Anthony would probably appreciate the company."

James looked up. "I'll go, too. Must do all I can, given it was me he came to speak with—"

"The best way you can repay his bravery and all he's suffered in bringing Teddy's message to you is to compile all the information Jack is about to request from you."

Clarice hadn't raised her voice, yet there was a note in it that brooked no argument. Jack shut his lips against the urge to soften her words; in this case, she was absolutely right, and he knew James more than well enough to know he would seize any opportunity to drag his heels over the business.

There was stubborn—James's rather weak brand—and

stubborn, Clarice's battle hardness. The latter might not be comfortable; it was, in this instance, necessary.

James sighed; a touch of grimness about his mouth, he nodded. "Very well." He glanced across the desk. "What do you need?"

Jack told him; once James had started making a list of all his journeys over the past decade, Jack settled to write down the other questions regarding James's work he wanted answered.

Clarice paced, slowly, behind him, watching them both; occasionally she drew near and read his list over his shoulder. Jack simply bided his time.

So did James. When Macimber put his head around the door and summoned Clarice to deal with some household matter, James waited only until the door had shut, cutting off Clarice's final narrow-eyed glance, to lay down his pen and appeal to Jack. "My boy, you have to help me. I really do not wish Clarice to go to London on my behalf."

Why? was the first word that popped into Jack's mind, but he hesitated . . . instead felt compelled to make James see something he was clearly missing. "It's not that simple, James. For a start, Clarice is under no man's thumb. If she decides to go to London, neither I nor you can prevent her doing so—indeed, I doubt if hell or high water would suffice."

James grimaced. "I suppose persuading her is the only real option."

Jack met his gaze. "My powers of persuasion are considerable, but they're not that good."

James frowned.

Jack paused, and chose his words with care. "I'm not sure, in this, that she's wrong. With you confined here, someone from your family does need to alert the other members, more definitively than by letter, to explain to them what the situation is, and regardless of her past, Clarice is the late marquess's daughter, the current marquess's sister. The family will listen to her."

"Perhaps." James looked unconvinced, strangely uncertain.

Puzzled, Jack raised his brows.

James sighed unhappily. "Very well, I concede they'll most likely listen to her, because she'll make them. She'll engineer an audience, and get her point across, but at what cost to her?"

Jack blinked. "I don't understand."

"I know." James closed his eyes, then opened them. "Clarice isn't spoken of within the family. She was cast off by her father, disowned, or as near to it as his sons would allow."

Jack frowned. "So you intimated, but I didn't imagine—"

"No, why would you?" James shook his head, concern in his eyes. "I didn't explain as clearly, as completely, as I might have. Melton, her father, wasn't the only one in the family who was furious with Clarice and, as they saw it, her intransigence. Her aunts, Melton's sisters, and even Edith's family were horrified. In holding to her refusal to marry Emsworth, in the eyes of the family, Clarice stepped far beyond the pale."

Jack held James's gaze, read his eyes. "Are you saying that she might not even be *acknowledged* by the family, that they might still, seven years later, treat her as an outcast?"

"Yes." James nodded very definitely. "The Altwoods aren't renowned for their forgiving natures. I greatly fear that, regardless of what she allows to show, their . . . rejection hurt Clarice deeply. Returning to the fold to plead my case will unquestionably exacerbate long-buried wounds. Worse, certain members of the family might take advantage of having her at their mercy, in the sense of having her in a position of begging for their help for me, to . . ."

In imagining what vindictiveness his and her family might visit on Clarice, James was out of his depth; that showed in his confused, distressed expression as he searched for words. "Well," he eventually admitted, "I don't know *what* they might take it into their hard heads to do, but whatever." James fixed Jack with a for him belligerent and decisive look. "I don't want Clarice placed in such a situation on my account."

A minute ticked past, then Jack exhaled. "I see."

"Indeed." James leaned across the desk. "So will you help me, dear boy, in dissuading her from going to London?"

Jack held James's gaze, read his sincerity. Knew the matter wasn't as simple as James had painted it. But . . . he grimaced. "The best I can promise is to think about it, along with every other option."

James smiled. "Good, good."

His immediate relaxing made Jack inwardly smile, fondly, if cynically. Having explained his problem and handed it to Jack to resolve, with his customary single-mindedness James turned back to the task on his desk. He dipped his pen in the inkwell, then frowned at the sheet on his blotter. "I'd better get on with these lists, then, heh? Don't want to delay you, and they'll take a few days as it is."

Jack finished his list and left it with James to fulfill. He departed the rectory without encountering Clarice; he considered, but didn't seek her out. Opting to take the longer route home, he sank his hands in his breeches' pockets and ambled down the drive, and did what he'd promised James he would.

He thought about dissuading Clarice from going to London.

Unlike James, he could see some distinct pros as well as the obvious, now he'd heard the full story of Clarice's past, cons.

There was no denying that once in London, she would command the family's immediate attention. More, they would accept that she would not let them stand aside and not support James; if they wanted her to leave them in peace, they would have to act in James's defence. Not having to convince people of one's steely and unbending nature was an advantage he appreciated.

On a darker note, he hadn't forgotten the not-quite-a-gentleman with the round face. If he persuaded Clarice to remain here and leave the London mission to him, in stirring matters up in London, might he precipitate some action directed against James here—here where Clarice would undoubtedly insist on standing in front of James?

Not a comforting scenario. In such a situation, he would be second-guessing himself constantly, hamstrung in prosecuting James's defence in London.

In similar vein, given he seriously doubted his ability to convince her to remain at Avening, if he refused to take her with him, she would travel to London on her own. Not only would that leave her facing the con James sought to avoid, it would also leave her a free agent, one beyond his immediate reach.

In London.

If, alerted by her activity on James's behalf, the round-faced man took it into his head to silence her . . . London was a far more dangerous stage if she became a target, and he wasn't prepared to allow her to become a target here, in the sleepy country where she was surrounded by people who knew and valued her. As Anthony's carriage accident had proved, the sleepy countryside wasn't all that safe, not if one was stalked by one skilled in the art.

Jack knew all about such things; he didn't need to dwell on them. Turning out of the rectory gates, he headed down the road and turned his mind to London, to the nature of the welcome James was sure awaited Clarice there.

Was James right? He might have been right seven years ago, but was that how matters still stood within the Altwood clan? Certainly Anthony and his clergyman brother didn't view Clarice as *persona non grata*, as a female ostracized by their family. Swinging through the manor's gates, Jack looked up at his house and made a mental note to charm Anthony that evening and see what he could learn.

However . . .

He looked down, staring unseeing at the graveled drive as he climbed the long slope to his front door. Even if James was right, and Clarice faced a hostile reception in London, regardless of whatever pain that might cause her, did he, or James, have the right to interfere, to make that judgment—the judgment that she shouldn't face that pain—for her?

He mentally replayed that moment when she'd first decreed that she would go to London on James's behalf. She hadn't made the decision lightly, in haste, without considering the pros and cons. She knew better than James what she would face in town; she'd known what she was doing in deciding to go.

James hadn't asked; she'd insisted on making a sacrifice on James's behalf. Was it right for him to dismiss that as meaningless? Offering themselves as sacrifices was what warriors did . . . and she was a warrior-queen.

Jack grimaced and kicked a larger stone out of the driveway, then paused to look down the rolling meadows to the stream. He wished he didn't understand her quite so well; in some respects, it made life more difficult.

Protectiveness, especially with respect to females, especially females of his class, was second nature, something bred into him; as with James, it was an instinctive reaction. If the lady in question had been anyone but Clarice . . . but it wasn't. With her, unlike James, *because* he understood, he had to think before he acted, because for her—for a warrior-queen—protecting her might not mean the obvious.

Protecting Clarice, acting in her best interests, might actually mean taking her to London with him. Allowing her to brave the wrath of her family and beard the dragons of her past and their rejection, potentially to conquer it, to overcome it, all while he was there, by her side, for support. That she had the right to face whatever battles she chose was, in dealing with her, a very real consideration. To his mind, he had a corresponding right to stand by her side, but not to stand in her way.

He stood for a time, assessing his logic while the burbling of the stream soothed his senses. He couldn't fault his analysis, his reading of her. Eventually, he turned and continued up the drive.

There were other, to him highly desirable outcomes that would be served by taking Clarice with him. He didn't underestimate the logistical difficulties, yet the chance of placing him and her together in a situation tailor-made to help him persuade her to look at him more deeply, to consider him as her consort, was hard to resist. In London, especially given their misson, she would see sides of him few ever had, and all against the backrop of his and her rightful circle, the ton.

At some point, he would have to jar her into seeing him as more than a brief liaison, as a lover for all seasons rather than just one. Spending time together alone, not necessarily private but without being constantly surrounded by people who relied on them and demanded their attention would be essential; the chance of spending time together in London seemed god-sent.

At the back of his mind lay the notion that in order to succeed in his pursuit of her, to change her mind and convince her to consider matrimony again, he would need to exorcise the ghosts he presumed must exist given her past history with men and marriage. Dispatching such ghosts would be much easier if he could see them, and London was their haunt.

His front door rose before him. He halted before the steps, stared at the door, and let the final thread of his argument run through his head.

The final consideration. Him.

Taking Clarice with him to London meant he would know she was safe. Regardless of all else, in order to function efficiently, to concentrate and accomplish all James needed done, he would need that assurance. Fussing over her, hemming her in, here or there, would put her back up, and perhaps reveal too much of his intentions too soon, but if she was with him, he would know without needing to ask.

Drawing in a breath, taking his hands from his pockets, he climbed the steps to his front door. James would have to live with his fears; he did not intend to put a foot wrong in his pursuit of his warrior-queen.

Chapter 10

🪷

ack joined Griggs and Percy in the estate office. Percy produced the list he'd extracted from Anthony; Jack read through the workmanlike effort, then commended Percy, who glowed.

Howlett appeared to announce luncheon. In the dining room, they found Anthony propped in a Bath chair, looking pale but grimly determined.

"If I can be forced to remember the entire family," he said in response to Jack's raised brow, "in all its glory, root and branch, I can sit up."

Jack smiled and took his seat. "You'd better be sure not to damage anything, or Connimore will be unbearable."

Anthony arched a brow. "Spoken from experience?"

"Just so," Jack affirmed.

The meal passed comfortably. Jack, Griggs, and Percy discussed the farms Percy would see that afternoon. Anthony teased, but mostly simply listened. Despite his bravado, his broken bones were still painful.

At the end of the meal, they strolled into the front hall, Percy wheeling Anthony in the chair. Jack caught Anthony's eyes. "If I were you, I'd get what rest you can. Clarice said she'd come by this afternoon to bear you company."

Anthony's face lit with delighted, almost childlike enthusiasm. "Excellent!"

Percy was less sure. "Perhaps she plays chess?"

Anthony raised his brows. Both he and Percy looked inquiringly at Jack.

What did they think? "I wouldn't be surprised, but don't feel too badly if she trounces you."

Anthony chortled. Two footmen carried his chair upstairs; Anthony waved cheerily as they carted him along the gallery back to his room.

Jack repaired to the estate office with Griggs and Percy. After a final round of conferring, with Percy armed with a detailed map of the estate, Jack and Percy set out to do the rounds, Percy in the gig behind a calm and stately mare, Jack on Challenger.

Jack hadn't had the gray gelding out for two days; Percy eyed Challenger's consequent snorting and cavorting with overt distrust.

Jack grinned; tightening the reins, he brought Challenger to pace, aloof and unrepentant, beside the gig as Percy steered the mare down the drive. "How are your riding lessons going?"

Percy cast Challenger a look, then pointed at the mare. "Crawler had me out on Matilda here yesterday."

"And?"

Percy shrugged. "It went well enough, but we didn't get past a trot." He glanced again at Challenger. "I'll never be able to manage a horse like him."

Jack smiled and looked ahead as they turned out of the drive. "You don't have to. Being able to ride Matilda will get you around the estate well enough. You don't need to ride like the wind."

They rattled and clopped across the stone bridge. Scenting the open fields beyond, Challenger tugged at the bit, restless and not understanding why Jack didn't want to gallop. "Speaking of which"—Jack ruthlessly held the gelding on a tight rein—"one of the consequences of riding horses like this is that they need to run." He nodded ahead to the fields north of the road. "You know where we're headed—the Delancey farm. If I leave you here, can you find your way there? I'll let Challenger stretch his legs and meet you in the lane outside the farm gate."

Percy nodded. "I won't get lost. I've got the map, and Griggs said it was accurate."

Jack saluted and wheeled away.

Two minutes later, he was streaking across a field not yet planted with its summer crop. Challenger crushed the stubble of winter wheat beneath his pounding hooves; the scent of the dried stalks and the smell of bare earth warming in the sunshine rose and flowed over them.

Jack gave himself up to the moment, to the race that was not a competition but simply a private joy, that sent a rush of exhilaration down his veins unclouded by any risk, any consequence. He and Challenger flew across his lands purely because they could, and wanted to.

Perhaps needed to.

The sun shone down; the breeze was a mere wisp of sensation. For one finite moment he understood what it meant to feel his heart was singing.

In the same moment, he realized what it truly meant to be home.

It was odd how, sometimes, different things connected, or more accurately made a connection in the mind. While riding free on Challenger's back, thundering across his lands, his fields, Jack had felt a sense of rightness, of home and all that meant to him—not before, but now—click like a jigsaw about him. As if him being there was the final necessary piece to make his life whole . . . bar one.

With Percy beside him, he visited his tenants and refreshed his memories of his eastern holdings. When the afternoon waned, he returned to the manor with Percy, well pleased on all counts. Sending Percy in to report to Griggs, he took Challenger to the stables; he spent a companionable half hour chatting to Crawler, who also approved of Percy, untutored town whelp though he was. All was progressing well on that front.

Returning to the house via the garden door, Jack walked into the front hall, his bootheels ringing on the flags. Pausing at the foot of the stairs, senses suddenly prickling, he looked up—and saw Clarice poised on the landing. She'd been on her way down, had heard his footsteps, and paused; their gazes met, locked, then calmly, regally, she continued down.

Jack watched her descend. Watched the subtle shift of her hips under the fine muslin of her gown, a creation in rich burgundy that highlighted the full curves of her breasts, the long lines of her thighs fleetingly outlined with each downward step. He drank in her queenly self-assurance, her fine features serene, her dark hair coiled, a lustrous coronet about her head.

In his bones, he sensed her strength, that deep well of feminine unruffleability, of elemental power that called to him, captured him, anchored him. It was blindingly obvious what the ultimate piece of his jigsaw was. All he had to do was secure it, seize her and bind her into his life, fit her into his picture, to make that picture whole.

Complete.

He reached for her hand as she neared. She surrendered it, no doubt expecting him to bow over it. Instead, he closed his hand about hers, engulfing it. "Come with me."

He turned and made for the library, his stride unhurried, but definite. Her hand locked in his, he towed her behind him. Surprised, she thought about resisting; even facing the other way, he sensed when she decided to humor him, to see what he wanted of her.

As it transpired, that was precisely what he wished to make plain.

He set the library door swinging, towed her through, caught the edge of the door with one hand, and shoved it closed. Twirled her so her back was to the door, then walked into her. Backed her until she was pressed against the panels, then moved closer yet, until the lush curves of breasts, stomach, hips, and thighs were trapped against him.

The sensation sent a surge of possessive lust through him; he dammed it, but didn't hide it as he looked into her eyes, dark and darkening, widening not so much with surprise as interest, a simple uncomplicated wish to know what he thought he was about. Not the slightest tinge of fear clouded those glorious eyes.

He caught his breath, bent his head, found her lips, and let her feel what he wanted.

Her.

Not in any civilized way, but in every way imaginable.

He wasn't the least surprised when she met his invasion with a challenge of her own; she didn't know that her acceptance of his unrestrained ardor as if it were simply her due was a potent challenge in itself. She might have learned the techniques of sexual interaction from a library of learned texts; she hadn't learned the nuances that could apply, that might be brought to bear.

In that respect, with her, even he was learning.

Her arms had been trapped between them, her hands gripping his sides; as desire flared and the kiss ignited, she released her hold, pushed her arms up over his chest, over his shoulders, then reached higher and speared her fingers into his hair, holding him to her.

He wasn't going anywhere, and neither was she.

The kiss raged, sensual battle joined . . .

Footsteps in the hall, a footman passing, jerked them from the spell, had them both hesitating, considering, assessing.

Clarice pulled back from the kiss, broke it. Her breathing quick and shallow, from under lids suddenly heavy, she met his eyes, green and gold etched with desire.

A desire that sent her own need spiraling. He wanted her, here, now, and she wanted him.

"How?" She licked her dry lips, held his gaze, let him see she was serious.

He studied her eyes, then reached to the side. She heard a dull click; he'd locked the door.

His hand returned to her side, then slid down to her thigh. His eyes hadn't left hers. "Like this."

His fingers curled, and her skirts rose. Up, then higher. He drew them to her hips, then slid his hand beneath; reaching down between their bodies, he found her curls. His questing fingers blatantly stroked, then pressed past, parting her damp flesh, stroking lightly, then probing more deeply.

He didn't kiss her again, but watched her, leaving her wholly aware, totally undistracted from the physical sensations. Aware to her fingernails of the intimacy as he shifted his hand between her thighs and slid one hard finger into her.

Her lungs seized, her gasp strangled in her throat. She gripped his shoulders, fingers sinking in as he pressed deeper and stroked. Her lids lowered, but she couldn't not watch his eyes, not watch him watching her . . .

He eased his body back a fraction; she felt his other hand working between them, realized he was dealing with the buttons at his waist. Then the rigid length of his erection sprang free. His fingers left her; he drew his hand from between her thighs. She felt his hard palms glide down and around her thighs, then he closed his hands and lifted her.

Hoisted her up against the door. Spread her thighs as he did and stepped between.

She gasped and grabbed his shoulders. He closed with her, pressing between her thighs; she felt the broad head of his erection seek her entrance, find it, and sink in. Just a little.

Then he thrust home.

He filled her. Then he thrust that last inch until she felt him high, near her heart. Then, slow and controlled, he withdrew and slowly filled her, inch by inch, once more.

Then he repeated the sensual torture, one that had her gasping, too soon softly moaning. Tightening about him, locking her legs about his hips, she tried to urge him on, but he kept to his slow, deliberate rhythm, one that unraveled her senses, that sent waves of dark, illicit delight coursing through her, that steadily, inexorably, yet unhurriedly built the familiar blaze within them, but held the conflagration back.

He didn't kiss her; they were both more or less fully clothed. Yet they stood pressed against his library door, intimately joined, and there was nothing to distract her from the sheer, unadulterated physicality of the moment, not just the powerful need that drove them both but the reality of him inside her, of the heavy weight of his erection sliding into her sheath, of her body so eagerly welcoming him in.

Of his taking her, filling her, possessing her.

She came apart on a breathless cry, glory imploding, pleasure enveloping her, swamping her, coursing down her veins, releasing her.

Jack covered her lips in the instant she crested the peak; he drank her cry, rode out the waves of her pleasure, then his body, held too long in check, slipped its leash. He surged powerfully into her, one, twice, three times, then with a groan muffled between their lips, joined her. Felt his seed release deep within her, felt in the deepest depths of his soul that he was home.

"I'll meet you at the folly tonight."

They'd rested for half an hour, even managed decorously to consume a pot of tea and a plate of cakes; Jack hadn't been keen to see her walk out of his door, not so soon after they'd both been reduced to staggering.

But, as usual, she'd recovered well. He'd accompanied her to the front door; they now stood side by side on his front step.

At his words, she cast him one of her direct, faintly reproving glances. "You're getting greedy."

He held her gaze, without a blink replied, "And you aren't?"

She humphed and looked ahead. After a moment, she conceded, "Very well." She stepped down to the gravel and started off down the drive. "But I might be late."

She didn't look back but waved a hand in farewell.

Jack grinned, and savored the view, along with the knowledge that she'd be at the folly not a minute later than usual. After that interlude in the library, he'd wager his life on it.

The dip in the drive hid her from his sight; turning, he went into the house, grin fading as he realized just how true his previous thought was. With her, it was his life he was gambling with.

He paused in the hall, instinctively searching for ways to tip the odds in his favor; this wasn't a game in which he had any intention of throwing in his hand. That being so, knowledge, as always, would be his best weapon.

Looking up the stairs, he considered, then headed for Anthony's room.

His reluctant guest was growing increasingly restless, but Connimore had decreed that if he wished to take his place at the dinner table, then he had to rest until the first gong. Consequently, Anthony was glad of any distraction, even one that involved discussing his family.

"I wasn't much about when it happened—away at school, and even when I was at home, the subject was never really discussed. Just the occasional comment one of the elders would make, you know the sort of thing."

Jack nodded. "How would you describe your parents' view of Clarice?"

Anthony screwed up his face. "I'd say that while they were shocked speechless at the time, it was a dashed long time ago, and it wasn't as if she committed a crime, for heaven's sake. Plenty of scandals much worse than Clarice refusing to marry that stick Emsworth. I know Melton—her father—raised a dust to end all dusts over it, but at least in my branch of the family, I've never detected any opprobrium that would make it difficult for Clarice to return to town."

"What about the other branches? The connections?"

Anthony frowned. "I've heard that at the time it was all rather dreadful. The elders were in the main shocked to their toes. Melton's sisters—the Countess of Camleigh and Lady

Bentwood—were livid. Clarice's maternal aunts and uncles were also furious. You can imagine the refrains—that she was blackening the family name, that she was insulting her mother's memory, and so on." Anthony looked somber. "All pretty awful stuff."

Jack waited a moment, then prompted, "But . . . ?"

"But while I can't speak for the immediate family, as far as I've ever known, within the wider family the whole matter blew over long ago." Anthony met Jack's eyes. "I really don't think even the elders of the wider family would cut Clarice, would care to cut her if she returned to town now." He smiled. "I know the younger generation wouldn't."

Jack grinned. "I gathered Teddy, and you, too, don't view her in any unfavorable light."

"Good God, no!" Anthony met his eyes. "If you'd ever met Melton, her father, you'd understand. Anyone who stood up to him and walked away the victor—well, that's the sort of deed that guarantees instant hero status, and Clarice is a female, what's more."

Jack studied Anthony's open face. "So within the wider family, Clarice's returning to town won't pose any difficulties."

Anthony nodded. "The only group I'm unsure of is the principal line. They hold themselves aloof these days, mostly thanks to Moira, Clarice's stepmother. Clarice's father may have died, but Moira's still a force within the marquisate. The present Melton, Clarice's brother, allows Moira's wishes to hold sway. Well, he hasn't married yet, so Moira's his hostess, and the senior lady of the house."

Jack considered. After a moment, he asked, "So you can't tell me how Clarice's immediate family—Melton, her other brothers, her half sisters and half brother—will react if she reappears in town."

Anthony grimaced, and shook his head. "Perhaps Teddy . . . but no. He sees them less than I do." He frowned. A moment passed, then he said, "I can't think of anyone who could tell you how her immediate family view Clarice now.

Her father died two years ago, and while he was alive no one dared mention her name in his house or his hearing. That I do know."

"But what the real feelings are now, you can't say?"

"Other than for Moira." Anthony met Jack's eyes. "Moira was always jealous of Clarice. You might say she hates Clarice—she certainly acts like it—but it's hate driven by jealousy."

"Jealousy of the weak for the strong?"

"Precisely. I've never heard that Clarice did anything to account for Moira's hatred."

"Other than being Clarice?"

Anthony grinned. "Other than that." After a moment, he ruefully admitted, "She didn't trounce me at chess. She wiped me off the board, and I'm not even sure she was paying all that much attention."

Jack smiled and rose. "I did warn you." With a salute, he turned to the door. "My thanks for the information. I'll see you at dinner."

He headed downstairs and returned to the library. Sitting in the chair behind his desk, leaning back, eyes fixed unseeing on the far wall, he went over all Anthony had told him, creating a framework of expectations of what they would meet when he and Clarice went to London.

By the time the gong for dinner sounded and he rose and headed for the door, he had a better notion of what she—they—would face.

Gaps, blanks, still covered crucial areas, but he could see enough to realize and appreciate Clarice's courage in, without hesitation, insisting on going to London on James's behalf.

Even though she'd known it would mean bearding the dragons of her past. Even though going back would almost certainly mean dealing with a woman who hated her, and who very possibly still possessed the means to hurt her deeply.

* * *

Much later that night, Clarice stood at the folly windows, looking out over the sleeping countryside. Sprawled on the daybed, sated to his toes, Jack watched her. She wasn't brooding—she rarely brooded; she was thinking, planning.

Turning, she looked through the heavy shadows at him. After a moment, she asked, "When do you think we should leave for London?"

He considered her phrasing, then evenly replied, "The day after tomorrow."

Enough moonlight spilled in for him to see her blink. She stared at him, unmoving, for a long moment, then pushed away from the window. On bare feet, she padded closer; stopping by the daybed's side, she looked into his face. There was a frown in her eyes. "I said 'we'—you heard me."

Not a question, so he made no response, merely lay there, looking up at her, at her long, curvaceous, luscious body, totally bare, his to savor.

Her frown materialized. "Aren't you going to argue?"

Lifting his gaze to her face, he settled his head more comfortably on the daybed's back. "Is there any point?"

She studied him; gradually, a smile replaced her frown. "You're a strange man, Jack Warnefleet."

Her voice had lowered to that intimate tone that never failed to arouse him, that hinted of the sultry, more deep-throated purr that acted on his libido like a sharpened spur.

His lips curved in blatant anticipation rather than humor. He made no reply, just reached for her hand and drew her down to him.

Drew her into his arms, and turned his mind to her conquest, even though he knew the truth. He wasn't strange, he was addicted. To the taste of her, the smell of her, the warmth of her. He wasn't strange, he was committed.

To having all that for the rest of his days.

Two evenings later, Clarice looked about her as Jack handed her down from James's traveling carriage. "I told you I usually stay at the Crown and Anchor in Reading."

"And I usually stay at the Pelican, also in Reading." Unperturbed, Jack looked around.

Clarice looked up at the sign swinging above the inn's side door. "The Maiden & Sword" was neatly lettered on it.

Reading was half an hour behind them. They'd made good time from Avening, and Jack had suggested they should travel on, only to stop a little farther along in the much smaller town of Twyford.

Taking her arm, he turned her toward the inn's door. "I rather think this place will be more comfortable for us." He caught her eye, faintly raised a brow.

She realized. "Oh." She looked ahead and allowed him to guide her up the steps.

"Indeed." His voice was low, pitched just for her. "The fewer who see us, the less chance of being recognized."

She'd forgotten that by tonnish standards, an unmarried female of her station traveling alone with a gentleman such as he would be fodder for scandal. Having turned her back on tonnish life she truly didn't care, but given her intention of appealing to her family, avoiding further scandal at that point would unquestionably be wise.

Absence from society had made her rusty; she made a mental note to exercise greater care.

Ostlers were unharnessing the horses; two boys had hurried out to fetch their bags. The innkeeper, beaming, swung his door wide and bowed them through. She swept in, then turned to speak with the innkeeper—only to hear Jack, charm to the fore, smoothly engage the man.

"I'm Warnefleet. My wife and I require your best room."

She managed to keep her jaw from falling. Jack didn't even glance her way, but kept his persuasive gaze fixed on the innkeeper.

"Of course, my lord." Short, rotund, and irrepressibly genial, the innkeeper bowed to them both. "My lady. Our best chamber is always kept ready and aired, and my wife will be pleased to serve you dinner. We have a private parlor if you wish?"

Clarice thought of the lack of any ring on her left hand, then remembered she was wearing gloves. She nodded regally, and found her voice. "That will suit admirably. I wish to wash away the dust of the day. We'll be ready to dine in an hour."

"Excellent!" The innkeeper gestured to a set of well-polished stairs. "If you'll come this way?"

Clarice followed him up the stairs, supremely conscious of Jack climbing steadily after her. The inn was on a side street off the London road; although the large room the innkeeper led them to was set above the front of the inn with wide windows looking out on the cobbled street, with only trees and fields beyond, it was quiet.

It was also comfortably furnished with a dressing table, dresser, washstand, wardrobe, and a large four-poster bed.

Clarice swept across the room and set her traveling reticule down on the dressing table. The ewer and basin on the washstand were spotless, as were the towels neatly folded on the dresser. Tugging the ribbons of her bonnet loose, she turned to the innkeeper. "This will do nicely. If you could have some hot water sent up?"

"Of course, my lady." The innkeeper bowed low. "At once!" He turned to Jack.

Jack nodded easily. "Dinner in the private parlor in an hour."

"Indeed, sir. I'll have your boxes brought up immediately." Beaming, the innkeeper backed out of the door, closing it behind him.

Clarice caught Jack's eye. "Wife?" She kept her voice low.

He shrugged, all graceful elegance as he crossed the room. "Do you have a better idea?"

She didn't, not one that would pass muster. Setting her bonnet on the dressing table, she sat before the mirror to tuck the wayward strands of hair that had escaped through the long day back into her chignon.

A knock on the door heralded the boys with her traveling trunk and Jack's large bag. He let them in, then shut the door behind them. Shrugging out of his greatcoat, he dropped it on a straight-backed chair by the wall, then crossed to the armchair angled before the windows and dropped into it with a sigh, stretching out his long, booted legs.

Going to her trunk, Clarice unbuckled the straps, then opened the lid.

"We're not dressing for dinner."

She cast him a repressive glance. "Of course not. One doesn't dress for dinner at an inn. But I do want my brushes, and one or two other things."

She'd wrapped her brushes and comb in her nightgown; she pulled out the bundle and set it on the dressing table.

"No point dressing for bed either."

She glanced at him again, then looked at her nightgown. "That's as may be."

He snorted softly; she ignored him.

A tap on the door announced a maid with a pitcher of steaming water. Clarice relieved her of it, and assured her she didn't require any assistance, then or later.

Shutting the door with her hip, she carried the pitcher to the washstand. Ignoring the lounging figure in the armchair, she poured water into the basin, washed her face and hands, then blotted them dry. And felt considerably better.

Lowering the towel, she looked at Jack. His eyes were closed. He appeared to have fallen asleep. His chest rose and fell in a slow, regular rhythm; his hands lay lax, long fingers relaxed on the chair's broad arms.

She glanced at the bed. It had a dimity-covered comforter spread over crisp white sheets. The pillows were plump and plentiful. The bed-curtains gathered at each post with wide ribbons matched the comforter; once released, they'd cocoon the bed in spring clouds of tiny blossoms.

Just like the apple blossom in the orchards at Avening.

The idea of rolling in that cushioning expanse, naked, with Jack, filled her mind; the mental vision she conjured stole her breath.

"Just think of it as an extrawide daybed."

Jack watched her gaze flash to him. He lifted his lids fully and met it.

She hesitated for a heartbeat, then, chin lifting, she walked to the bed, with a swish of her skirts, turned, and sat on the end. "What are we going to do once we reach London? What should we do first?"

He noted the change of subject, noted, too, her defiant stance. He'd foreseen the need for them to share a room, to pretend to be man and wife. That didn't mean they had to share a bed, yet it wasn't in his nature to pass up such an opportunity to steer her in the direction he wished.

"First, you should explain the situation to your family and see what support they're prepared to give, what connections and contacts they have to exploit. I, meanwhile, will alert my own contacts and see what I can learn, what's known from outside the Church." He hesitated, then added, "I sent a letter a few days ago to someone who should know what's going on."

She studied him. "To the man you used to work for—that 'certain gentleman in Whitehall'?"

He recalled she'd been present when James had used that phrase, their private code for Dalziel. "Yes. He was in command of His Majesty's covert operations on foreign soil for years. He's still in the position, but now in the sense of tying up loose ends."

"Loose ends like traitors as yet uncovered?"

He heard the rising concern in her voice. "I told him about James because there's one fact that more than any other proves James is no traitor, one my ex-commander in particular won't miss."

She looked her question.

He smiled. "Me. The very fact I'm here, alive, proves beyond doubt that James is not a traitor."

"He knew what you were doing?"

"Not only what I was doing, but where I was. And I'd lay odds my ex-commander knew that James had that information. Very little escapes him."

She frowned. "But surely that means James is in no real danger?"

"Not of being *convicted* of treason, no. But neither you, your family, nor I, nor my ex-commander, and even less the government, would want this business to go to a public trial. The current charges against James are private, entirely within the Church. If they can be dealt with and dismissed within that forum, all will be well. But unfortunately, with the case being within the Church, the secular authorities can't simply intervene and quash it. All we can do is provide information and evidence to James's defender. However . . ."

He stopped, visited by an urge to keep the more dangerous aspects from her.

Too late. Lightly frowning, she studied him, then said, "We know James isn't guilty, which means someone is going to considerable lengths to fabricate these charges. Why? There has to be a reason."

He grimaced. "That's the point I imagine my ex-commander will find most interesting."

A knock on the door brought a summons to dinner.

"Ah, yes." Clarice dismissed the maid with a wave. "We'll be down in a moment."

Puzzled, Jack closed the door. He watched as Clarice crossed to her open trunk; bending over it, she rummaged beneath the layers, then rose, a jewelry box in her hands. Placing it on the dressing table, she opened it. He drew near, blinking at the blaze of jewels revealed. He frowned as she sorted swiftly through the pieces. "This is an inn."

"Indeed." She nodded. "An inn where we're supposed to be man and wife. Ah—there it is."

She picked out a simple gold ring supporting three small emeralds. Holding up her hand, she slid the ring onto the ring finger of her left hand. Turning the emeralds to her palm, she flexed her fingers. She examined the ring, now masquerading as a wedding band. "That should do."

Shutting the jewelry box, she replaced it in the trunk. Straightening, she fixed him with a superior look. "If one is going to carry off a charade convincingly, one has to think of such little things."

He raised a brow, then offered his arm. She took it. He led her to the door, opened it, and murmured as she passed him, "I'll remember that the next time we play at man and wife."

Dinner was a relaxed affair, the food excellent, the wine more than passable. Comfortable and secure in the small private parlor, Clarice directed the conversation, determined to give Jack no further opening to discompose her. The next time they played at man and wife, indeed!

They filled the time discussing the various points they'd uncovered while combing through the sheets of information James had supplied. They'd spent the better part of the journey comparing one list to another, connecting time, place, and people James had spoken with. It was tempting to speculate on exactly what facts the allegations against James hinged upon.

"There's really no way to tell, not until we see the details presented to the bishop."

She wrinkled her nose but had to admit Jack was right. Still, it was hard simply to wait and not plan.

"You'll just have to possess your soul in patience."

She glanced across the table, met his amused but understanding gaze, and humphed.

The maid entered to clear the dishes, followed by the innkeeper with a bottle of port. Clarice seized the moment to beat a strategic retreat; pushing back her chair, she nodded to the innkeeper. "Please convey my compliments to your wife. The meal was excellent." Rising, she looked at Jack, who tensed to stand, then recalled they were supposedly married. She smiled lightly. "I'll leave you to your port."

To her surprise, he changed his mind, uncoiled his long legs, and rose. He waved her to the door. "I'll take a glass in the tap."

The innkeeper beamed and bustled away. She headed for the door; Jack followed.

He paused just outside, briefly scanning the hall and the stairs. "I'll be up shortly." His eyes returned to hers. "Don't lock the door."

One of the little things one had to remember. She read the message in his eyes. Elevating her nose, she turned to the stairs, and for one of the few times in her life, swept away with no pithy parting shot.

Discretion was sometimes the wiser course.

Especially given he stood in the hall and watched her until the upper gallery hid her from his view. Although she could no longer see him, she would have wagered her pearls that he stood listening until she shut the door to their room. Then and only then would he have stirred and headed for the tap.

She suspected he intended to learn who else was passing the evening at the inn, whether there was anyone whose notice they needed to avoid when they left in the morning.

It was what she, in his place, would have done; as she stood before the dressing table and unpinned her long hair, the notion that she trusted him in the same vein she would herself floated through her mind.

Definitely strange. Definitely not something that had happened with anyone else.

Oddly, that only made her more determined to be undressed and in bed before he came up. Nonsensical to feel shy given all that had passed between them in the folly, yet there was something quite different about undressing before him in a fully lighted room.

Illogical, of course. She considered that while she quickly brushed out her hair. She was rarely illogical; why now, over this?

The answer popped into her mind as she laid her gown neatly over her trunk, then reached for the hem of her chemise. It was the implied domesticity that struck her as unwise, as belonging to those scenarios they'd agreed didn't apply to them.

Pondering that, she drew off the chemise, dropped it on her gown, reached for her nightgown—and heard his voice in her head. No point.

And, perhaps, one domestic touch she didn't need to make. Turning, she crossed naked to the bed.

Chapter 11

*J*ack climbed the stairs congratulating himself on having chosen the Maiden & Sword. Not only was the inn comfortable, but situated as it was just on the London side of the major posting town of Reading, it was generally overlooked by tonnish society. There were no members of the aristocracy or the upper echelons of the ton staying that night. A few well-to-do merchants, businessmen, and their wives, a clientele that no doubt accounted for the inn's quality, but no one who would place either Clarice or him.

He opened their door to a room steeped in darkness. He glanced around; Clarice had doused all the candles and left the curtains over the windows drawn. All he could see of her was a mound under the covers on the window side of the bed. She'd loosened the bed-curtains but hadn't drawn them tight. Closing the door, cutting off what little light had come from the corridor, he crossed soft-footed to the window and drew the curtains wide.

Pale moonlight spilled in, enough so he could see. He sat in the armchair and eased off his boots, then unhurriedly undressed, hanging his coat in the wardrobe, draping shirt and waistcoat over the straight-backed chair.

Eventually naked, he went to the bed, lifted the covers,

and slid under them. The instant his weight settled into the mattress, Clarice rolled into him.

He'd expected that; she hadn't.

She valiantly smothered a shriek; he wisely smothered a chuckle as he caught her, then expertly juggled her until they were face-to-face, nose to nose.

She looked into his eyes. In the same instant, he registered that she was as naked as he. She was all warm silken limbs and lush curves.

Her gaze lowered to his lips. He looked at hers.

She reached for him as he closed his arms about her. Who kissed whom first was moot.

What followed was their usual tussle for sensual supremacy. In the kiss, she ultimately gave way, let him plunder her mouth as he wished, as he wanted. But even while she accommodated him there, with her hands on his shoulders, she pressed him back.

Distracted, he obliged, rolling onto his back.

Lying back, he watched her rise over him in the moon-drenched dark, watched her straighten, watched her arch as she slowly, smoothly, with total control impaled herself on him, as she sheathed him in her body's lush heat.

Then she rode him, slowly, deliberately driving both him and herself inexorably on, harder, faster, until the peak of fulfillment beckoned.

He caught her hips and rolled, tipping her, then trapping her beneath him. Settling between her thighs, he spread them wider, urging her long legs over his. Pinning her deep in the cushioning mattress, he thrust deep. Home.

Bending his head, he found her lips and filled her mouth as his body joined with hers, plundering to the same primitively erotic beat.

Clarice couldn't think, could only respond and embrace the moment. Drink in the sensations, the familiar, comforting, freeing dimness, the heat pouring through them, a delicious flame, the powerful flexing of his body as he covered her, possessed her, as they danced within the cocoon of the apple blossom covers, enclosed in a world of passion and desire.

Hot passion, wild desire.

At his urging, she wrapped her legs about his hips, felt his hand spread beneath her bottom, tipping her hips to his. Gasped as he drove deeper into her willing body, into her heat, into the furnace that built and built as he stoked, stroked, until nothing else mattered but the raging flames, the drive for release, the need for completion.

The shattering desperation that it should claim them both.

It came in a rush, and did.

For one long moment, they clung to the peak, trapped in and consumed by the glory, then they tumbled and fell, into blessed oblivion.

He collapsed upon her. Limbs like jelly, she held him, slowly stroked the long muscles of his back. Listened to his heart thunder, then slow. Felt his heartbeat within her, felt her own in her skin, in her fingertips, easing.

Eventually, he stirred enough to lift from her. Slumping onto the bed, he slid an arm beneath her and drew her to him, settled her against him.

Boneless, she let him; laying her head on his chest, she murmured, "That was *not* how it was supposed to be."

She'd intended to stay in control, to use her body to overwhelm him, to watch as she sated him. She was still curious over, fascinated by, the fact that she could.

He relaxed, sinking deeper into the bed. "You won't always get what you want."

Her lids were too heavy to lift, to stare, to react to his tone, one that suggested he'd understood her intent but hadn't been of a mind to indulge her.

If she'd had the strength, she would have taken issue with such arrogance, but pleasure lay too heavy in her veins. Some other time.

Right now, the principal issue claiming her mind was how to prolong their liaison in London. That's what she'd been thinking about while she'd waited in the dark for him to join her. Somewhat contrary to her expectations, she was in no hurry to terminate their affair, not yet. There was a lot she'd yet to learn, and a great deal he could teach her. Arrogant lord though he might be, he definitely had his uses.

Stirring, she leaned back against his arm, lifting her head so she could look up at his face. A heavy lock of his hair, a medley of light browns shot with blond, had fallen across his forehead. Reaching up, she brushed it aside just as he turned his head to look at her. The side of her hand connected awkwardly with his temple.

Even in the poor light, she saw him wince. Felt the spike of pain that raked him.

"What is it?" She heard alarm in her voice, realized it was because she saw him as invincible, yet knew he wasn't. He was only flesh and blood, and flesh and blood could so easily die.

She half expected him to say "Nothing," but after a moment's hesitation, he relaxed back on the pillows. "A recent injury."

"Recent?" She struggled to sit the better to examine him; his arm tightened and held her down. She frowned at him. "How recent?"

"A few weeks."

She blinked. "So *that's* the injury . . ."

When she didn't go on, he raised his brows. And waited.

"When I first came to the manor to see Anthony, you and Connimore were talking of some lingering injury."

He was silent for a minute; from the look on his face, he was replaying his words to Connimore. "I see." He refocused on her face, studied it. "What sort of injury did you think I had?"

His tone was curious, wondering, and suspicious. She was tempted to declare she hadn't thought about the matter at all; the expression in his eyes warned he wouldn't be fooled, more, that he was starting to suspect just what she had thought. She lifted one shoulder. "I have three older brothers. And then you summoned Percy . . ."

She broke off as his face split in a grin. His chest, beneath her, started to shake. She narrowed her eyes at him. "And *then* you declared you wouldn't have children. What the devil do you imagine I thought?"

He threw back his head and laughed, trying vainly not to make too much noise.

She waited with quite terrible patience.

He noticed; hilarity reducing to a chuckle, he grinned at her. "Wouldn't, not couldn't." Beneath the covers he nudged her hip. "I would have thought that distinction would by now have occurred to you."

"I daresay it would have *if* I'd given the matter any recent thought." Despite her haughty tone, that was indeed the truth; he was so transparently virile and vigorous, she'd forgotten he was supposedly carrying an injury.

Yet he was. If a frown could change in tone, hers did. "How is it? What exactly is it? Does it hurt much?"

He grimaced. She read in his eyes the usual male reaction to female fussing. "It hurts sometimes, but lately not as much. It was just a bad knock on the head."

A knock on the head that still hurt weeks later? "What on earth were you doing to get such a clout?"

He studied her eyes, then resettled her against him, and somewhat to her surprise, told her. She listened, alternately intrigued, shocked, and amazed. She made no comment when he described how he'd been taken in and then coshed by the spy he been left to guard against. Although he clearly considered that a failure, one that still rankled, he'd acknowledged it and set it behind him; he neither dwelled on the mistake nor tried to excuse it. She had experience enough of life's vicissitudes to appreciate the maturity in that.

When he ended his tale, she frowned. "So you're retired from the services, yet still at the beck and call of the government?"

He shook his head. "It's more that we'll oblige in pursuit of a good cause. Those of us who've served in our particular capacity are better equipped, better trained to respond to certain situations. And in this latest instance, we were assisting a friend, an ex-comrade-in-arms so to speak."

"So am I right in assuming that those contacts you intend to speak with in London will be your ex-comrades, along with your ex-commander?"

"Indeed." Stifling a yawn, he sank lower in the bed. "I'll speak with those of the crew still in town." His voice had grown sleepy. "And yes, they will help us."

His tiredness was catching; her lids felt increasingly heavy. She snuggled down on his chest. His hand rose to stroke her head, his fingers gently tangling in, then smoothing out strands of her hair.

Peace enveloped them, warm, still, undemanding. They hadn't shared a bed before, yet the closeness felt right; she felt unexpectedly secure.

His certainty that his friends would help, would rally to James's cause, reassured some part of her that was still in shock at the very thought of James being accused of traitorous dealings. But more intriguing had been the view of him his tale had revealed—how his friends viewed him, that he was a member of such a group of gentlemen, loyal defenders even in peace upon whom those charged with the defence of the realm did not hesitate to call.

Her original vision of him as a dissolute wastrel floated into her brain. Her lips curved; how very wrong she'd been.

The more she learned of him the more she approved, the more she appreciated. Heaven knew she was halfway to thinking him admirable. There were few other men she'd admitted to such status; indeed, as sleep slowly fogged her brain, she couldn't think of one.

She felt the last of his wakeful tension fade, sensed him slide into sleep. Listened to his slow, steady breathing. His heart beat beneath her cheek, a muffled, solid thud, regular and reliable; his arms held her, not tightly but securely. Not restraining but comforting, a protection, not a restriction.

Sleep beckoned, and she let herself go, let herself relax in his arms.

Warm, comfortable, sated, and secure. Playing man and wife with him wasn't bad at all.

The errant thought jerked her from that comfortable slide into slumber, made her inwardly blink, but then she smiled, let the thought drift away, and fell asleep.

For the first time in his life, Jack woke at dawn with a woman in his arms.

He'd slept with countless women, but he'd never before shared a bed with one through the night.

But this one, his warrior-queen, was different in such a multitude of ways. Waking to the feel of her warm, soft, quintessentially female limbs draped over him, her curves pressed provocatively against his side, seemed the ultimate warrior's reward.

He wasn't even thinking when he lifted his hand and ran it lightly over her arm, over the swell of her breast. Down over the swell of her hip to the long sweep of her thigh.

It required no thought to appreciate, to worship. To gently arouse her, to bring her body awake, responsive and instinctively ardent. She unfurled like a flower to his touch, her mind still drifting in the realms of sleep, soft sighs falling from her lips as he stirred her to an awakening of a different sort.

To power of a different sort.

Sensual, covetous, yet reverent, it seemed to flow from his fingers, from his hands as he caressed her.

When he lifted over her and settled between her thighs, her lids fluttered, then rose a little way.

Rose fully as he filled her; she looked up into his eyes, hers widening, then he thrust home. Her lips formed a soft O, then relaxed, curving. Her lids fell again, veiling dark eyes now glowing with passion.

Passion he'd evoked.

He bent his head, covered her lips with his, and gently rode her as dawn painted the sky and sent soft golden light reaching across the chamber to where they rocked in the bed, surrounded by clouds of dimity apple blossom.

No rush. A slow traverse across a landscape they now knew well, pausing, breaths tight, strangled, as they savored here, then there. As they let their senses expand and together absorbed the passionate beauty of each stage, each step in the progression to fulfillment.

A fulfillment neither doubted would come, that was implicit in the shift of their bodies, in the repetitive movement that held them both engaged, absorbed, aware of little beyond the heated dampness of their skins, their ragged breathing, their desires and needs.

A true communion of bodies, of minds. Ultimately, as they crested the peak and together surrendered and fell, a communion of souls.

Later, they lay twined in each other's arms. Neither spoke. Each recognized the power growing between them, knew the other would sense it, too, but it was too new for either to name, to describe.

Shifting his head, he dropped a soft kiss on her shoulder. Felt, an instant later, her hand stroke his head, gently riffling his hair.

And was content. For now.

Yet his ultimate goal, the goal he wanted, needed, and would fight for, was now not just clear but defined. He wanted to wake up in this way, just like this, every morning for the rest of his life.

They rocked into London in the early afternoon. As Clarice would keep the carriage with her, Jack gave the coachman directions to Montrose Place.

Focused on their campaign to exonerate James, Clarice had paid scant attention to the sights they'd passed. But when the carriage pulled up outside Number 12, Montrose Place, she ceased her recitation of the facts they already knew to peer out at the house. "This is your club?"

"The Bastion Club." Jack opened the door and stepped down to the pavement. He'd explained that the club was a private one set up by him and his six ex-comrades as a personal stronghold against the matchmaking mamas and their legions. "Wait here. I'll just leave my bag with Gasthorpe—he's our majordomo—and be back."

A footman had already materialized from the club and was retrieving his traveling bag from the boot. Clarice nodded, her gaze fixed on the club's facade as if searching out its weaknesses. Jack quashed the thought and followed the footman up the path.

Gasthorpe met him at the door. Consigning his bag into Gasthorpe's keeping, Jack informed him he would be staying for an as-yet-undetermined time.

"We're delighted to have you back, my lord. All will, of course, be in readiness here. If you require any further assistance, please inform me."

Jack smiled his charming smile; he was about to turn away when he thought to ask, "Who else is here at present? Crowhurst?"

"I regret the earl returned to Cornwall yesterday, my lord. But Viscount Paignton returned to us last week. I believe he intends to remain for some weeks. And the marquess is in town. He frequently drops by of an evening."

Jack saluted and turned away. So Deverell was about, and Christian Allardyce, Marquess of Dearne, was also on hand. Excellent support, should he require it, and he'd certainly pick their brains and use their contacts, too.

He was still smiling when he reached the carriage. Clarice sat back, studying his face as he climbed in and sat opposite her.

"You look . . . expectant."

His smile deepened. "Just the scent of prey on the wind."

She snorted and looked out of the window as the carriage lurched once again into motion. Jack noted she was watching the facades now, no longer absorbed in James's predicament. A slight frown creased her brow.

"So where are we headed?" he asked.

"I gave the coachman directions." After a moment, she realized she hadn't answered him and glanced at him. "To Benedict's Hotel in Brook Street."

Jack blinked. He'd assumed when she'd mentioned putting up at a hotel that she'd meant Grillons, that bastion of all things proper; he couldn't have risked visiting her there. Benedict's was another matter entirely. From what he'd heard, it was an extremely exclusive establishment catering only to the highest echelons of the aristocracy. It didn't have rooms; it had suites.

When the carriage pulled up before the elegant facade in Brook Street, and he escorted Clarice inside, it was immediately apparent by the subtle-yet-obsequious welcome that she was a known and honored guest.

"We've held your usual rooms for you, my lady." The dapper concierge relegated his desk to an underling and came to conduct Clarice upward himself. "Naturally, anything—anything at all—that I or my staff can do to assist you during your stay, we'll be only too delighted to do."

Leading the way up the main stairs, as wide as in any ducal residence, the concierge went to a door just along the sumptuous gallery, inserted a key, then threw the door wide. He bowed Clarice in.

Strolling at her heels, Jack paused to glance around, taking note of the side stairs visible at the end of one corridor. His gaze returned to the concierge's face and found it encouragingly blank; the staff at Benedict's clearly knew who paid their piper. With a slight smile, Jack inclined his head and moved past the concierge into the room.

It was a luxurious suite, the first room a large, well-appointed sitting room, the bedroom leading off it via an ornate arch. A gilt-framed mirror filled the wall above the marble mantelpiece; gilt sconces in the form of cupids hung on the walls. Despite their fine fabrics, both chaise and chairs looked well stuffed and inviting, and all the woodwork glowed. Two long windows looked out onto Brook Street; Jack moved across to glance out as Clarice swept into the bedroom, directing the footmen who had arrived with her trunk.

Like a well-trained butler, the concierge harried the footmen out, then bowed and departed. Jack turned as Clarice came to join him. She met his eyes, then looked out at the street. "Now we're here, what next?"

He followed her gaze; it was midafternoon, and Brook Street was awash with carriages ferrying matrons from one afternoon tea to another. "There's not much we can accomplish in what's left of today. Unless you want to approach your family?"

"Late afternoon is hardly a good time to call unexpectedly, not during the Season. Everyone will be rushing to get ready for their evening's engagements."

He nodded. "I'm hoping for some word from my ex-commander. I told him I'd be at the club from tonight. I should be there in case he contacts me." He would also meet Deverell there and alert him to their likely need for his services.

Clarice faced him. "Perhaps an early night would be best, then we can commence our campaign refreshed in the morning."

He studied her dark eyes, wondered if she, like he, was considering ways and means . . . but he'd yet to reconnoiter, to confirm that he could come and go from her room without risking scandal, that the hotel was as accommodating as it appeared. "That probably will be best."

"Very well." She hesitated, then placed a hand on his chest and stretched up. She'd intended to kiss his cheek but he turned his head and his lips met hers.

His arms slid around her; he drew her to him, against him, and let the kiss slide into that realm of heated sensuality they both craved. When he raised his head, they were both breathing more rapidly; her eyes were darker, softly glowing with stirred passion as she pushed back and eased out of his arms.

"I'll . . ." To his delight, she had to blink to refocus her wits. "I'll call on my brother in the morning. Best to catch him before he goes out."

"I'll call here at noon. We can discuss our outcomes to that point and plan our next foray over luncheon."

She nodded graciously, softly smiling. "Until tomorrow, then."

He stepped back, bowed elegantly, and left her while he could.

Circling the gallery, he took the secondary stairs down, and confirmed that they led to a small foyer with a door giving onto a narrow side street. He checked the lock; it posed no barrier to one such as he. Hands in his greatcoat pockets, he strolled through the ground floor, committing the layout to memory, then exited the building by the front door, inclining his head to the concierge as he passed that worthy's desk.

Benedict's was, indeed, an excellent hotel.

On the pavement, Jack halted and took stock. He had no doubt Dalziel would interpret the events thus far as he had. His ex-commander would be in touch as soon as was practicable; he didn't need to chase him. However, bearding the Bishop of London would necessarily need to wait until after Dalziel and Jack had discussed matters. There was little he could do until then.

Frowning, he let himself consider the pounding gradually building in his skull. He'd been steadfastly ignoring it for the past hour. Experience suggested it wouldn't go away, not for the rest of the day, and, indeed, would likely become worse. What bothered him most was that the pounding hadn't been this bad for weeks.

Pringle's surgery was in Wigmore Street, only two blocks away. Jack turned his feet in that direction. At this hour, the surgeon would be in; he could use a little reassurance.

"You've made excellent progress!" Pringle turned away from Jack, propped on the edge of Pringle's desk and still blinking owlishly in the aftermath of the magnesium flare Pringle had used to check his pupils.

"I'm really most impressed." Pringle started putting away the numerous devices he'd used to test Jack's responses.

"Whatever you've been doing has been just the ticket. I would never have imagined you'd be this much improved in, what? Just over two weeks?"

Jack nodded, and massaged his temple. "But it's back. Why?"

"You've just arrived in town. Did you ride?"

Jack shook his head. "Carriage. Two days on the road."

"Well, there you are." Pringle started polishing other implements; he'd seen Jack immediately his last patient had left. "A jolting carriage over that distance would give anyone a sore head—in your case, a pounding one. Just don't do it again until you're fully recovered. To ease the ache, I'd suggest doing whatever it is you've been doing recently. It's clear that works for you."

Jack frowned more direfully. "I haven't been doing anything—anything medicinal—at least not that I'm aware of."

"Ah, yes." Pringle squinted at a scalpel, then polished harder. "Take it from me, you've definitely been doing something medicinal, but I agree you might not have realized how effective some activities can be. For instance, Turkish baths, or certain herbal ointments, or even perfumes, although you probably haven't been using those." With a grin, Pringle continued to recite common habits that were known to alleviate head pain.

Jack listened, eliminating all; most seemed as likely as the perfumes.

Until Pringle airily concluded, "And then there's the old standby, sexual release."

Jack blinked. "That works?"

"An ancient remedy, doesn't work for all head pain, and works best when indulged in before the pain actually sets in. I've always imagined it works by way of some pressure-release mechanism."

Jack was rapidly thinking back, aligning his interludes with Boadicea and the recent absence of his headaches. "How fascinating." He realized Pringle was watching him, an amused light in his eye. Jack grinned; he straightened from the desk, then winced as his head throbbed. "Thank you." He extended his hand to Pringle. "For your excellent advice."

Pringle grinned back and shook Jack's hand. "A few more weeks of rest interspersed with your patent remedy, and I predict your headaches will be consigned to your past."

Jack left the surgery and turned his feet toward Montrose Place. As he had no recourse to his patent remedy that evening, he'd have to make do with fresh air. He wondered what Clarice would say to their interludes qualifying as medicinal acts.

The thought of her reaction brought a smile to his face, and made him forget his throbbing head for the short while it took him to reach the club.

The headache hit with a vengeance in the early evening. Surrendering to the savage pain, to the nauseating sensations every time he tried to move, to the excruciating agony when he tried to think, Jack retired to his room and his bed before Deverell returned.

It was more important that he be alert and functioning in the morning; consulting Deverell could wait. As Jack crawled under the cool sheets and laid his head on the pillow, he prayed Dalziel wouldn't send for him that evening.

Dalziel didn't. He did, however, appear downstairs before Jack had had breakfast the next morning. Despite the comfortable bed and his best intentions, he hadn't slept well, but at least his headache had subsided to a level at which he could listen and talk. Muttering beneath his breath over the early hour—it wasn't even nine o'clock—Jack followed Gasthorpe down to the first floor; Gasthorpe had conducted his unnerving guest to the library. Jack paused, eyeing the door. "Bring coffee. As soon as you can."

Gasthorpe bowed. "Immediately, my lord."

Jack opened the door and went in. Closing it, he took a moment to study the tall figure standing before the long windows overlooking the back garden. Dalziel—they had yet to ferret out his real name—shared many characteristics with the men he'd commanded. He was much the same height as Jack, with a similar, fractionally leaner, build. Finer build, finer bone structure, finer, more austere features—that was really all that separated him physically from his men. In menace, however, Dalziel had them all trumped. In his presence, anyone with the slightest ability to sense danger was inevitably on full alert.

Releasing the doorknob, Jack let the latch click and watched Dalziel turn from the window to face him. As if he hadn't, until then, been aware Jack was there.

Jack inwardly scoffed. Put simply, Dalziel was the most dangerous man he'd ever met. His ex-commander was the ultimate epitome of the predatory warrior lords the Normans had left scattered throughout England.

"Good morning. I won't ask what's brought you here." Jack waved Dalziel to an armchair and subsided into its mate, fighting to keep any hint of his headache from his face.

"Indeed." Dalziel's tone stated he wasn't the least happy about the matter in question. His dark eyes examined Jack's face. "I greatly fear that your friend, James Altwood, has become embroiled, entirely innocently, in a scheme to discredit me."

"You?" Jack frowned. This was Dalziel; it would be a waste of time to question his statement; if he said that was so, it was. "What scheme? And how did James come to be drawn into it?"

Dalziel steepled his fingers; his gaze fixed beyond Jack. "At this point, I can only speculate, but I imagine the scheme has come about because, as I'm sure you and the other members here are aware, I've been searching for one last traitor, who for various reasons, none unfortunately within the realm of hard fact, I believe remains undetected, unrepentant, and unpunished, buried within the higher echelons of power."

A knock preceded Gasthorpe carrying a tray.

Dalziel waited until the coffee had been dispensed and Gasthorpe had left, then met Jack's gaze. "Just what connections this man might have, and what type of power he wields, whether simply that of money, or alternatively status or governmental position, I don't know. However, I've tripped over too many inconsistencies over the past years not to suspect he exists. Unfortunately, to date, that's all I have—my suspicions."

Jack narrowed his eyes, sipped. "So you believe this scheme has come about because he, whoever he is, doesn't appreciate your entertaining such suspicions?"

Dalziel nodded. "An apt enough way to put it."

"But at present, this scheme—its existence, just like that of your last traitor's—is pure conjecture on your part?"

Dalziel's lips twisted in a very wry grimace. "Precisely. What I believe has occurred is that, knowing I'm still searching for him, the real traitor set out—initially at least—to give me a scapegoat, someone I might confuse for him, remove, and so deem my job done."

"And retire?"

Dalziel inclined his head. "For all of us, the war is past, and it's time we returned to the civilian world and our responsibilities therein. This traitor thinks to appease me by feeding me some other prey in his stead."

"So he looked around for a suitable scapegoat . . . and found James." Jack instantly saw why James had been chosen.

"Indeed. James Altwood was an inspired choice. He had access to, gathered, and studied information potentially damaging to the military cause, information Napoleon and his generals would indeed have paid a high price for. I haven't seen the substance of the allegations, however, as we both know"—Dalziel smiled at Jack, a smile that didn't reach his eyes—"James Altwood is no traitor."

Dalziel paused, then went on, "I never asked whether you, against my orders, had divulged your status and mission to Altwood, but when your father died and Altwood came straight to me to get a message to you, it was fairly clear he knew more than enough to, were he a spy, ensure your disappearance." Dalziel shrugged. "As you're here hale and whole, Altwood is no traitor, especially given your watch on Elba. Of all my agents, you would have been the most vital to nullify when Napoleon was planning his return. You're still alive because they never knew you existed, because James Altwood isn't a traitor. No traitor, no matter how fond of you, would have omitted, in the circumstances, to mention you. Fortunes have been made for less."

Setting aside his cup, Dalziel continued, "That, however, was a series of telling facts the real traitor didn't know. If it is he behind this, then he discovered Altwood, and then realized the potential, how very sensational a charge of treason against Altwood would be, and how even more sensational the *failure* of such a trial would be, and how such an outcome would reflect on whoever was so unwise as to instigate the prosecution of Altwood."

"You." Eyes still narrowed, Jack followed the argument. "The real traitor thought you'd leap on James, get him by the throat, and drag him before the courts—and then . . ."

"Once the case failed, and the real traitor would ensure it would, and in the most spectacular fashion, that would render any future charge I might make against anyone not just ineffective but laughable."

"He'd essentially nullify you, at least with respect to bringing traitors to justice."

"Indeed." Dalziel frowned. "However, before we get too ahead of ourselves, none of what I've just told you is provable fact. As far as James Altwood passing secrets to the French, I can report that there is no evidence whatever, not an iota, to support such a contention, nothing beyond the purely circumstantial fact that Altwood had access to sensitive information and the ability to comprehend that intelligence."

Dalziel met Jack's eyes. "That, of course, would be known to many. On the face of it, there's nothing to say that this charge against Altwood hasn't arisen from some petty jealousy or need to make trouble. It may not even be directed at

Altwood, but at his superiors, or at clerical scholars in general. There's no reason *per se* that the situation has to be a scheme by any traitor, yet one reason my instincts are pressing me in that direction is that it's just too pat that it's Altwood involved. Not only is he a renowned scholar, a long time Fellow of Balliol, but a *clerical* scholar very well regarded by his bishop and by the Church heirarchy. Bad enough, were I to get involved, but on top of that, he *is* an Altwood, albeit it, as I heard it, something of a black sheep. That's by the by. To all the ton, all the government, he's still an Altwood. If the family comes to his support, as I fully expect they will, then anyone seeking to prosecute him is going to have a very messy battle on his hands."

Jack could only agree. The cold-blooded calculation behind such a scheme, if indeed it was a ploy of the last traitor to discredit Dalziel, was breathtaking. Tony Blake and Charles St. Austell had advised the other Bastion Club members of Dalziel's continuing search for a deeply buried traitor. Some might consider such perseverance an unhealthy obsession; Jack wasn't of that number, nor were the other club members. They all knew Dalziel; his instincts, his ability to read intelligence, and the orders that had flowed from that, sometimes apparently counter to safety, had kept them all alive for many long years behind enemy lines. If Dalziel believed a traitor was still free, they'd back his judgment.

"So the charges against James could be a traitor's scheme to discredit you, or alternately something more innocent— for instance, a jealous rival's plot."

Dalziel nodded, his gaze on Jack's face. "Is there a rival involved?"

Jack grimaced. "Seems to be. He's the one who brought the allegations before the bishop, and has a history of losing out to James in the fellowship stakes."

After a moment, Dalziel murmured, "That would make him an excellent pawn for the real traitor to exploit."

Jack nodded. "He's at the top of my list to question." He looked at Dalziel and raised a brow in mute query.

Dalziel sighed. "Yes, I do realize your presence here is a godsend—without your connection to Altwood, I couldn't directly investigate at all. So by all means poke around, ask questions, investigate, and do whatever necessary to get the charges against Altwood dismissed. Just keep me informed of all you learn."

"And in return?" Jack needed Dalziel to open doors, but exactly which doors his ex-commander had keys to he had no clue.

"In return, I'll inform you of anything pertinent that crosses my desk, and I'll write to the Bishop of London and inform him of two things. One, that having heard of the allegations about to be tested in his court, I've looked into the matter and can find no evidence of James Altwood selling secrets to the enemy. Of course, his lordship will have to make up his own mind based on the facts laid before him." Dalziel held Jack's gaze. "I can't make any declaration that reads as if I'm preempting the church's judgment."

Jack nodded.

"The second thing I'll tell the bishop is that you're a government servant experienced in such matters, and that regardless of your connection to Altwood, you are to be trusted as if you were me."

Jack allowed his surprise to show. He hadn't expected Dalziel to open the Lambeth Palace doors; that had seemed too much to hope for. The fact he could go even further only confirmed, as they'd long suspected, that he was a member of one of the very old families, those with members and connections throughout the various strata of the ruling elite.

Refocusing, Jack saw amusement lurking in Dalziel's dark eyes. Eyes very like another pair he now knew well. . . .

Dalziel rose. "I take it that will suffice?"

"Indeed. For the moment." Jack stood and held out his hand.

Dalziel gripped it, then releasing him, turned to the door. "If you can discover who, exactly, is behind the allegations against James Altwood, I, and the country, too, will owe you yet another boon." He paused before the door, and met Jack's eyes. "And the Altwoods will, too, of course."

The limpid intelligence in Dalziel's eyes assured Jack that, in the event of the Altwoods being in his debt, Dalziel knew precisely what he might request of them. Dalziel already knew of his involvement with Clarice; the only question remaining in Jack's mind was how much he knew. How he knew would, as always, remain a mystery.

Resigned, Jack merely smiled and reached for the doorknob. The door opened before he could grasp it.

Revealing Gasthorpe. Seeing them, Gasthorpe stepped back. He met Jack's eyes. "A . . . person has called to see you, my lord. They're waiting in the parlor."

Jack instantly knew who had called. Dalziel, of course, didn't; he didn't know that the parlor was the small room beside the front door reserved for entertaining females.

Smiling easily, Jack nodded. "I'll see Mr. Dalziel out, then see my visitor."

With a wave, he indicated Dalziel should precede him down the stairs. Following unhurriedly in his ex-commander's wake, Jack saw—too late—that the door to the parlor was set wide. Gasthorpe wouldn't have left it so, but given who was waiting in the room, it wasn't difficult to imagine how the door came to be open.

Ahead of him, unaware of any danger, Dalziel crossed the hall to the front door, walking into view of anyone in the parlor.

This, Jack thought, was going to be interesting.

Chapter 12

Not just interesting, but revealing.

Dalziel reached the front door and paused before he sensed another's presence. He turned toward the parlor; from where he was standing, he would have a clear view across the room.

Strolling up behind him, because he was watching, Jack detected the infinitesimal stiffening of Dalziel's shoulders beneath his well-cut coat, but then he bowed, correct and distant, toward the parlor, and turned away.

Jack kept his expression easy, unconcerned, apparently unaware of that minor incident and its implications; he opened the door and saw Dalziel out. As soon as his ex-commander's boots hit the gravel, Jack closed the door. Intrigued, he walked into the parlor.

Clarice stood before the window, peeking through the curtains at Dalziel's departing back. Jack closed the parlor door; she turned to face him, a familiar frown etched between her brows.

"Who is he?"

Clarice looked up at him, and blinked. "Don't you know?"

"I told you we only know him as Dalziel."

"*He's* your ex-commander?"

"Yes." Jack halted before her, studying her face. "You recognized him, didn't you? He certainly recognized you."

"Damn!" She frowned harder. "I hate that."

"What?"

"That he knows who I am, but I can't think of his name."

"But you do know him?"

"Not exactly. I have met him, but it was years and years ago, at Miranda Ffolliot's birthday party. I was . . ." She paused to work it out. "Nine. It was one of those parties one had to attend. He—whoever he is—was older, fifteen at least. He was at Eton with Miranda's eldest brother, I think, although that wasn't why he was there. All the guests, children though we were, had been invited with the usual in mind."

"Matchmaking from the cradle?"

"It was considered wise to encourage us get to know each other from an early age." She smiled wryly. "That was the circle from which we were ultimately supposed to chose our spouses."

Jack smiled into her eyes. "What are you doing here?"

"I came to plan what we should do."

"I thought you were going to alert your brother."

"I decided it was pointless broaching the subject with the family before we know what the allegations actually are. I don't want to appear hysterical, as if I'm reacting to some imagined situation they'll think can't possibly be true."

Somewhat to her relief, he nodded. "Dalziel didn't know the details of the allegations either, although he has confirmed that assertions that James passed information to the enemy are being heard in the bishop's court."

Clarice saw he had a great deal more to relate. Crossing to one of the armchairs, she sat and waved to the other, facing her. "What else did your ex-commander say?"

He considered how much to tell her as he sank into the chair. Then he relaxed, shoulders back against the cushions, and proceeded to talk without reservation. She couldn't say why she was so certain of that last, but she was. Listening intently, she questioned, and he answered as he gave her chapter and verse of his ex-commander's crusade to uncover one last traitor and why that might be the prime cause behind James's plight.

"How . . ."—she searched for the right word—"diabolical! That James, his reputation, even the family's reputation should be so cavalierly jeopardized. Whoever this person is, he has absolutely no scruples."

"I think we can take that as read."

Jack's dry tone registered. She met his eyes. "Is it always like this in spying? That you assume the other side has no real morals?"

He considered, then said, "It's safer to work on that basis."

She inwardly frowned, wondering what working constantly within such a framework, where you didn't dare trust in anyone or anything, would be like. "Lonely" was the word that leapt to her mind.

But such thoughts were a distraction. Glancing at Jack, she was about to ask what next they should do when she saw pain fleetingly fill his eyes; it was gone in an instant as he focused on her. "Is your head hurting?"

He hesitated, then his lips thinned. "Yes." Dispensing with all pretense, he raised his hands and massaged his temples. "The carriage journey . . ."

Alarm of an unfamiliar sort lanced through her. "You need to see your doctor." She stood and headed for the bellpull. "What's his name?"

"No, no." He waved her back to her seat, away from the bellpull. "I've already seen him. Yesterday, after I left you."

She sank back, reluctantly, into the armchair. "You were in pain then?"

He grimaced. "It was building."

Now he'd been forced to admit it, he seemed less reluctant to discuss his state. She pressed. "What did your doctor say?"

Jack continued to massage his temples. "Actually, he was highly impressed by my progress."

She humphed dismissively. "You're in more pain now than you have been since you returned to Avening."

"Pringle said it was because of the long hours in the carriage, compounded by not having—"

The look that crossed his face as he broke off was as close to self-conscious as she imagined he ever got, like a guilty little boy having let out some secret. She narrowed her eyes at him. "Not having *what?*"

He glanced at her, but didn't meet her eyes. "Exercise of a certain sort. Apparently, it reduces the incidence and possibly the severity of head pain."

"Well, then!" She straightened. "You clearly need to attend to this exercise before we do anything else."

His lips weren't straight, but she wasn't sure if he was grimacing, or, strangely, struggling not to laugh. She frowned. "What is this exercise?"

"Don't worry about it—it's not a ride in the park or a stroll around the garden." Lowering his hands, he met her eyes. "If you must know, I plan on taking care of it tonight. I'll just have to suffer until then."

"Don't be nonsensical!" She studied his eyes. "You're in pain—you look like your head's splitting. You can't possibly think clearly, and we—James, me, the Altwoods, and the government—need you functioning at the top of your bent. So what is this exercise? Can it be performed at any time, and if so, why not now?"

When he simply looked at her—that stubborn look she now knew meant he wasn't going to fall in with her demands—and kept his lips firmly shut, she sighed. "Very well." Rising, she reached for her reticule. "I'll just have to visit this doctor—Pringle, I think you said?—and ask him what sort of exercise you need."

The look on his face was priceless, horror and disbelief mingling. "You can't do that."

His tone was flat, a statement of reality as he saw it.

Looking down at him, she raised her brows. "Of course I can." And would. The fact she could actually see the pain clouding his lovely hazel eyes worried her more than she cared to admit, shook her in some way she didn't fully understand. She told herself it was because the long carriage drive had been undertaken on James's behalf, and so ensuring he recovered swiftly from any ill it might have caused was the correct and honorable thing to do.

Head back against the chair, he stared up at her. His expression had turned impassive; it no longer told her anything. Yet despite the dulling pain, she could see the thoughts passing through his mind, him weighing up telling her against her asking Pringle. Then his chest swelled as he drew in a breath. "Lovemaking."

She blinked at him. For one instant she was totally unsure what her own expression was: stunned amazement, most likely. "*That's* the exercise that eases your head?" She dropped her reticule back on the table.

"Apparently." Jaw tight, he waved her to her chair. "So I'll just have to bear with my headache until this evening, then we can attend to it. I'm sure I'll be well again by tomorrow morning."

She stood her ground, frowning down at him. "There are times when your mental processes defy my comprehension. There's no reason we need to wait to ease your head." With a swish of her skirts, she turned and sat on his lap.

He jerked upright, stiffened, but his arms instinctively rose to hold her. "Clarice—" He seemed shocked.

Framing his face, she succinctly replied, "Shut up, and let me fix this."

Then she kissed him.

Hard.

Demandingly, commandingly, a summons he didn't have it in him to refuse. His lips parted under her onslaught, and she boldly tasted him; a minute passed while he tried to hold aloof, then he gave up, clamped one hand at her nape, surged into her mouth, and took control.

Through the kiss she smiled, smugly satisfied. The idea that with this she could heal him, that through dallying with him she could banish the dullness from his hazel eyes, succor him, and ease his pain, seemed nothing short of miraculous. She had to put it to the test. She certainly wasn't going to wait until that night.

Heat bloomed, then raced down their veins, pulsed beneath their skins, pooled low. Jack broke from the kiss, his breathing ragged, his control sliding away far too fast. "Damn it, woman!" He growled the words against her swollen lips, luscious, so tempting. "There's no lock on the door."

She calmly leaned back and reached for his waistband. "Your exceedingly stiff majordomo is far too well trained to interrupt. Now"—laying the flap of his breeches wide, she slid her hand inside—"how do we go about this? Show me."

He gave up, and did; he simply didn't have the strength to fight against that order, not with her, all long rounded limbs and lush curves, squirming in his lap, not with her clever lips and even cleverer fingers urging him on. Not with his head in its present state.

Yet when he lifted her hips, then lowered her, easing his aching erection into the slick haven of her scalding sheath, even as he struggled to bite back a groan of sheer sensual pleasure, he realized that the throbbing in his temples had ceased.

Something else was throbbing now.

Apparently his body couldn't throb in two places simultaneously.

Making a mental note to tell Pringle he'd been right, he slumped back in the chair; hands locked about her hips, skin to skin beneath her rucked up skirts and petticoats, he guided her and let her have her wicked way with him. He was simply glad she was facing the other way, and couldn't see the blissful expression he was sure had claimed his face.

He didn't even want to look too closely himself, to analyze the breadth and depth of the joy that filled him as she rode him, driving him and herself to a shattering completion.

Driving away his pain, replacing it with marrow-deep pleasure.

When she finally lay slumped back against him, boneless as a rag doll as they waited for their hearts to slow, for their breathing to even out, for the blissful golden aftermath to fade, he bent his head and pressed a lingering kiss to her temple. "Thank you."

She reached up and gently riffled his hair, letting the strands fall through her fingers. "I think it's my turn to say it was entirely my pleasure." He could hear the smile in her voice. "Is your head better?"

"Amazingly, yes." The saber-edged pain had reduced to a vague shadow. He suspected his head might ache dully later, but the difference was striking; he could think without pain.

Yet as she lay in his arms, languidly sated and replete, his first thought remained one of simple disbelief that she had acted as she had. He couldn't imagine any other lady of her standing doing the same. This, apparently, was what came of treating with warrior-queens who would, without a blink, sacrifice social strictures to succor their consort's injuries.

The thought made him smile.

Then she shifted, and he sucked in a breath. His body reacted predictably to the warm boneless weight of her, to the hot clasp of her wet sheath.

Tempting fate was never wise.

He stirred her, then lifted her to her feet. She came back to life, shook out her skirts, readjusted her bodice while he righted his clothes. Then she sat once more in the chair facing his; as coolly collected as any dowager, she looked inquiringly at him. "Right then. What should we do first? I rather think we need to visit the Bishop of London."

Mildly amused by her sudden focusing—and the effort he knew it cost her to achieve it—he agreed. They spent the next fifteen minutes reviewing their plans, whom they needed to speak with, and the best order in which to do so, then a tap on the door heralded Gasthorpe with a tray.

"I took the liberty, my lord, of bringing your usual breakfast fare."

Looking over the selection of dishes Gasthorpe set out on the low table, Jack recalled he hadn't yet broken his fast. "Thank you, Gasthorpe."

Gasthorpe had also brought a pot of tea for Clarice and a plate of delicate cakes. As he set those out, he glanced at Jack. "Indeed, my lord—we must remember you need to keep up your strength."

Excruciatingly correct, Gasthorpe bowed to Clarice, who nodded regally, then he bowed to Jack and departed.

Clarice met Jack's gaze, raised her brows.

Jack shrugged and reached for the coffeepot. "Make of that what you will."

While they ate, they concentrated on how best to approach the Bishop of London. Not only was his approval critical to allowing them to meet with and assist James's defender, but without the bishop's specific consent, they were unlikely to learn the details of the allegations.

"And without those details, we won't get far." Clarice sipped her tea.

Jack watched her; he wondered if she'd noticed how very domesticated their present behavior was. Chatting over the breakfast cups, discussing family matters. Her dark hair, once again neat in its chignon—he wondered which of the club members had thought to hang a mirror in the parlor—sheened as a sunbeam slanted through the curtains, striking garnet glints from within the dark mass. She leaned forward to place her empty cup on the table, the regal set of her head and the vulnerable line of her nape apparent as she straightened.

Regardless of all else, through the last hours one aspect of their London adventure had become much clearer in his mind. Together, he and Clarice would be a formidable force in countering the threat to James, if Dalziel's instincts told true in exposing the last traitor's distracting scheme—and potentially exposing the last traitor, too.

They would become a threat to the last traitor.

And that would be dangerous.

His instincts had already been stirring, awakening; now, they quietly switched to full alert. Regardless of all else, he was going to be keeping his eyes wide open and trained most especially on her.

Clarice glanced up, met his eyes, studied their expression, but couldn't read it. She raised her brows, faintly haughty. "Well, shall we go?"

Nearly two hours had passed since Dalziel had departed. Jack knew how fast his ex-commander acted; the bishop should have received Dalziel's missive by now. He rose and held out his hand; she placed her fingers in his, and he drew her to her feet. "Indeed, let's make a start."

The Archbishop of Canterbury's London residence, Lambeth Palace, sited in its own extensive gardens, lay just over Lambeth Bridge. The Bishop of London was currently residing there, together with his administration and household. They took a hackney to the impressive front gates, then walked up the graveled drive. At the porticoed entrance, a footman took their names and conducted them to a small waiting room.

They didn't have long to wait. Dean Samuels, whom James had mentioned as the Bishop's right-hand man, appeared in less than five minutes.

White-haired with a round, rather careworn face, he smiled, introduced himself, then ushered them out of the room and toward the towering stairs. "I'm extremely glad you've come." Climbing the stairs beside them, he glanced sidelong at Jack. "The bishop has received a communication from Whitehall. I have to say, from my own perspective, it's reassuring to have someone with a professional background involved."

Jack inclined his head. Before he could ask, the dean went on, his gaze flicking up the stairs ahead of them, "I should perhaps warn you that the bishop is nevertheless in two minds over allowing the details of the allegations against James to pass beyond Church walls at this stage." The dean heaved a small sigh. "I hope, once he meets you, he'll change his mind."

Thus alerted, they were shown into a long room, the far end of which was filled with a dais on which the bishop's throne sat, supporting the prelate, all red robes and gilt-embroidered ivory linen.

Clarice swept in, head high, her silk skirts swishing. Ten feet from the dais, she halted and sank into a deep curtsy. Halting beside her, Jack bowed as Dean Samuels announced them.

Straightening, at the bishop's signal they approached the dais. The four of them were the only people in the audience chamber.

The bishop was not as old as Dean Samuels, more James's age. Sharp, pale blue eyes studied them, first Clarice, then Jack, then the bishop's lips pursed querulously. "This is all most irregular, and indeed most distressing. I'm really very exercised about these allegations. I had hoped to keep them entirely within the Church—I really can't believe James Altwood guilty of any misdemeanor, yet of course I'm honor-bound to test the case brought against him. However, it appears news of the matter has reached Whitehall."

Jack heard the irritated note in the bishop's voice. He'd met such men before; they held their position by virtue of their connections, and the smooth running of their enterprises was almost entirely due to the efforts of their underlings. Like Dean Samuels.

In the bishop's defence, Jack could readily appreciate that a scandal of the scope the allegations against James promised would not be to the liking of any man in high office, secular or clerical.

Lifting a sheet from his lap, the bishop scanned the lines thereon, then looked, somewhat peevishly, at Jack. "Whitehall has sung your praises, and suggested that, in light of the gravity of these allegations and their sensitive nature, that justice would best be served by allowing your input at this stage, in my court, rather than allowing views that a professional such as yourself would see as unwarranted or misjudged to adversely color our conclusions and potentially precipiate a more serious, public situation."

The bishop paused, his gaze fixed on Jack, then more quietly said, "I'm not as yet convinced that that is our best course."

Jack held that dyspeptic blue stare, but before he could draw breath and, logically and with charm, turn the bishop to his bidding, Clarice spoke.

"My lord Bishop, if I may speak to this point?" The bishop's gaze deflected to her; she caught and held it. "Specifically to admitting myself and Lord Warnefleet to the confidence of your court, as you have intimated, the charges against my cousin, the Honorable James Altwood, are indeed serious, but more, they deal with fields of endeavor not well understood by the layperson, nor yet by clerical officers. To adequately test these charges, knowledge of the field with which they deal will be vital, and I would submit it will be in no one's interest to have these charges upheld because of misunderstanding, and thus unnecessarily passed on to a high civilian court, only to be subsequently shown as groundless.

"Lord Warnefleet is eminently qualified to assist your officers with determining the truthfulness of these allegations"— she nodded to the sheet still held between the bishop's fingers—"as confirmed by his superiors in Whitehall. The fact he is acquainted with James is unlikely to cloud his judgment given his long service to the crown. Indeed, he would have been one of those placed most at risk if the allegations were true."

She paused; the bishop was frowning, following her free-flowing words, clearly caught. She lifted her chin, consciously regal. "As for myself, I will, of course, be representing the family in this matter. I will be reporting to my brother, Melton, on what transpires. I hope, on leaving here today, to be able to explain to him precisely what the allegations made against our cousin are. The family will be pleased to know that this attack against one of our name is being dealt with as expeditiously, and as appropriately, as may be."

The bishop's frown turned faintly harried. "I see." It was transparently clear he'd heard and correctly interpreted Boadicea's battle cry.

He glanced again at the missive in his hand, then at Jack, and finally at Dean Samuels. "I suppose," the bishop said, "that all things considered, it is, perhaps, appropriate"—he inclined his head toward Clarice—"as you point out, my dear, for you both to have access to our court, Lord Warnefleet in giving professional advice on these unusual charges and Lady Clarice as the family's representative."

He didn't quite make the statement a question, but Dean Samuels was quick to bow. "Indeed, my lord. That seems most wise."

Jack smiled charmingly. Boadicea smiled, too.

After tendering their appreciation for the bishop's dispensation and exchanging the usual social remarks, they bowed, preparing to retreat.

"I'll introduce Lady Clarice and Lord Warnefleet to Olsen, my lord," Dean Samuels said.

"Indeed, indeed." The bishop smiled at Clarice. "Do remember me to your aunt, my dear."

With a noncommittal inclination of her head, Clarice returned his smile. Dean Samuels led them away, out of the audience chamber and into the heart of the palace.

"Olsen is the deacon appointed to argue James's defence." Dean Samuels led them on. "He's young, but I believe will do an excellent job. He'll be in his workroom."

The farther they went, the more labyrinthine the palace became; eventually Dean Samuels led them down a corridor lined with doors. He stopped before one, tapped, then opened the door.

"Olsen? Allow me to introduce two people who, I believe,

will be of great help in quashing these ridiculous charges against James Altwood."

A clearer statement of sympathy couldn't be imagined; Jack caught Clarice's eye as she passed into the room. He followed. The room was a small square delineated by stone walls, just big enough to hold a desk and chair, three other straight-backed chairs, and three piles of leather-bound tomes, along with Deacon Olsen, a cleric in his late twenties, who rose as they entered, his eyes widening in surprise.

Dean Samuels introduced them, describing Jack as an expert sent by Whitehall to assist the bishop's deliberations. Olsen stammered engagingly over Clarice's hand and hurried to set a chair for her. She consented to sit. Seeing Jack and Dean Samuels helping themselves to the other chairs, Olsen scurried once more behind his desk.

"I have to say I'm exceedingly glad to see you." Sinking into his chair, he waved a hand at the papers scattered over the desk. "I may know something of war, but this is beyond me. And although I've heard much of James Altwood and his researches, I've only met him once."

Jack smiled and grabbed the reins before Boadicea could. "What regiment were you with?"

The question proved the start of a useful friendship; Olsen was sensible, straightforward, and in this case, knew he was in over his head. He was very ready, even eager, to share with them the details of the allegations.

Once assured they were comfortable together, Dean Samuels left.

Clarice looked at Jack as the door closed behind the dean. "What odds he goes straight to the bishop to report that all is well on the way to being taken care of?"

Jack grinned. "No wager."

Bright-eyed, Olsen looked from one to the other. "The bishop has to appear impartial." He grimaced. "Indeed, more than that—he has to appear to be prosecuting these charges with all due vigor. Humphries ensured that. He's made quite a stir with his claims."

Jack leaned back in his chair. "Tell me about Humphries."

Olsen grimaced again. "You'll meet him once the court convenes, or more likely sooner—as soon as he hears you've been permitted to assist me." Olsen considered, then went on, "Humphries has been on the bishop's staff for decades. He's a loner, dour, pious in a rather pompous way, not one given to smiles and jollification of any stripe. He seems entirely sincere in his conviction that James Altwood was involved in, at the very least, selling his more sensitive researches into English military strategy to the French."

Sorting through the papers on his desk, Olsen pulled out three sheets. "While some part of the allegations are general—more inferences drawn than fact, and there's some jealousy on Humphries' part that would account for that— the most damaging and potentially damning of the allegations are these." Handing the papers to Jack, Olsen leaned forward to point to various entries. "Three dates, times, and places where Altwood supposedly met with his courier, and a list of some of the information passed over the years."

Holding the sheets so Clarice could read them, too, Jack examined the crux of Humphries' allegations. If they'd been true, they would indeed constitute a damning indictment of James. Reaching the end of the list, Jack looked at Olsen. "How did Humphries get such information?"

"From the courier." Olsen sat back with a sigh. "And before you ask, he refuses at this point to reveal the man's name."

Jack looked again at the listed details. "Without the courier to testify to the accuracy of these assertions, then proof will rest on witnesses."

Olsen nodded. "Indeed, and that's just what Humphries has. For every incident, he has at least two witnesses who can place Altwood at that place, at that time, with another man."

Jack stared, unseeing, at Olsen for a moment, then refocused. "Can we have copies of this—the three dates, times, and places—and do you have access to the list of witnesses?"

"Yes, and yes." Olsen pulled out a fresh sheet of paper.

"I'll make you a copy, but I warn you, I've already spoken to all the witnesses, and they confirm all that Humphries has claimed is true."

Jack smiled; Olsen glimpsed the gesture, looked more closely, then blinked. Jack let his smile deepen into a more genuine expression. "There's a significant difference between you asking witnesses for confirmation and me asking them to relate exactly what they saw. Aside from all else, I don't wear the collar."

Olsen's lips formed an O. His hand had frozen, the pen poised above the paper.

Clarice stirred. "The list, Deacon Olsen." From her tone, she was unimpressed by Jack's abilities, or rather, considered them a given. "The sooner we have that, the sooner Lord Warnefleet can begin disproving the allegations and the sooner I can reassure my family of the situation here."

Olsen flushed and quickly redipped his nib. "Of course, Lady Clarice. At once."

Fifteen minutes later, Olsen conducted them back to the main stairs. He parted from Jack as a comrade in arms, but Clarice he treated with patent caution and extravagant respect.

The list of details in his coat pocket, Jack descended the stairs beside Clarice. The patter of Olsen's footsteps died away behind them. Jack grinned. "Olsen's instincts appear sound."

Clarice shot him a glance, haughtily censorious. She knew to what he referred—Olsen's reaction to her. "Nonsense." She looked ahead. "All that shows is that he can recognize well enough what's good for him."

Jack laughed.

They crossed the huge front foyer, nodded to the doorman, and went out through the massive front doors. Sunshine and brightness greeted them; Jack squinted. Clarice glanced at him. "Are you all right?"

He paused to take stock, then smiled. "The effects of your ministrations appear to last for some time."

She humphed and started down the steps. "Good."

They strolled down the drive, neither fast nor slow, both, Jack would wager, considering that perennial question: what next? The drive curved toward the gates; a high hedge hid the last yards of one side of the drive from the palace. At that spot, in the lee of the hedge, a figure in clerical garb stood waiting.

As they drew near, his eager expression and a marked resemblance to Anthony suggested who the man was. Clarice confirmed it. "Teddy."

"Clarice." Teddy grinned engagingly as they joined him in the shade; he warmly clasped the hand Clarice gave him, drawing her close to kiss her cheek. "I can't tell you how delighted and relieved I am to see you."

"This is Lord Warnefleet." Stepping back, Clarice waited while they shook hands, then asked, "You have heard about Anthony?"

Teddy sobered. "Indeed. Thank you for your letter. Anthony wrote as well. I had started to wonder, but then thought, perhaps, scamp that he is, he'd delivered my message and then gone on to some house party somewhere."

"No party," Jack murmured. "He was lucky to come out of the accident so well."

"Oh?" Teddy looked at Clarice.

She nodded. "But when we left him, he was well on the road to recovery. He'll be back in London soon enough."

Teddy accepted her reassurance but still looked concerned. "About James." He looked from Clarice to Jack.

"We've spoken with the bishop and been granted the confidence of the court. We've just been with Olsen—he's given us details of the allegations, or rather, of the allegations that aren't conjecture." Jack studied Teddy; he looked about thirty years old, sensible and steady. "What can you tell us about Deacon Humphries? We know about the fellowship he lost to James."

Teddy grimaced. "Humphries is now the most senior deacon under the bishop, which is why he's been able to push these charges to the extent he has. Apparently he always was jealous of James, even before that old fellowship was awarded, and ever since, he's . . . well, one-eyed in his dislike would be an understatement. Whenever James comes to London, the bishop and Dean Samuels do all they can to keep Humphries and James apart. Last time, they sent Humphries to visit the rural dean in Southampton on some trumped-up mission. In the five years I've been with the bishop, I've never heard Humphries say one good word about James."

Jack frowned. "Leaving aside the present incident, has Humphries gone out of his way in the past to attack James?"

Teddy considered, then, frowning, shook his head. "No. Indeed normally Humphries goes out of his way to avoid any mention of James, any raising of James as a subject at all."

"So"—Jack slid his hands into his pockets—"this is an unusual turn for Humphries, a change in his normal behavior toward James."

"Yes." Teddy looked at him, puzzled.

Jack grimaced. "My next questions would be, what happened to change Humphries' behavior, why did whatever it was happen, and why now?"

Teddy stared, then blinked, his eyes slowly widening as he followed Jack's deductions.

Clarice already had; she snorted softly. "The courier-cum-informer. It had to be he. He turned up with information, information that, even discounting Humphries' animosity toward James, Humphries would have felt honorbound to bring before the bishop."

Jack nodded. "However, having done so, Humphries' animosity toward James *would* have ensured he'd keep pressing the point, demanding the allegations be investigated."

He and Clarice exchanged a glance, then they both looked at Teddy. "Do you have any idea who Humphries' informer is?" Jack asked.

Wide-eyed, Teddy shook his head. "Until you mentioned him, I didn't know he existed."

Succinctly Clarice outlined what they'd learned from Olsen.

"While we can attack the details of the informer's information, and we will, ultimately we'll need to speak with the man himself, but as yet Humphries has refused to divulge his name."

Watching Teddy, Jack saw the resemblance to Anthony manifest more clearly; a determined light filled Teddy's eyes.

"I'll watch Humphries and see what I can learn. Of course, he knows my relationship to James, so I'll have to be discreet." Teddy met Clarice's eyes and grinned. "He ordered me not to speak to James of the allegations, but I'd already sent Anthony off by then."

"Did you tell Humphries that?" Jack asked.

"No, but . . ." Teddy grimaced. "The porters report to Humphries, and they knew I'd sent for Anthony and that he'd come and we'd spoken."

Jack studied Teddy for a long moment, then said, his tone making the words an order, "*Don't* follow Humphries out of these grounds. Not in any circumstances. What you *can* do is try every avenue possible to learn the identity of Humphries' informer. Cultivate the porters, see what they know. Ask whoever cleans Humphries' rooms if they've seen a note with a name or address. Does he ever ride out, or only walk? Anything that might give us some idea of this informer and where he can be found."

Teddy nodded. "I'll do that." He looked at Clarice. "How's James taking this?"

Clarice assured him that, in typical James fashion, James was somewhat less exercised than they were.

Teddy grinned. "He always excelled at ignoring what he didn't want to concern himself with."

Parting from Teddy, they went out of the gates, then turned toward Lambeth Bridge to find a hackney.

Eyes down, frowning, Clarice paced beside Jack. "Why did you warn Teddy not to follow Humphries outside the grounds?"

"Because we've already had one Altwood with a close to broken head." Jack glanced around. The area surrounding the palace and its gardens was well-to-do, genteel, and stultifyingly neat, but just blocks away in multiple directions lay stews and squalid tenements where not even clerics would be safe. "I don't want another one, and I don't even want to think about what might occur if Teddy meets your almost-a-gentleman with a round face, and you and I aren't there to scare him off."

"Ah." Clarice lifted her head; her lips set in a determined line. "In that case, I suggest you and I repair to the Benedict and over luncheon sort out what we need to do to disprove these allegations."

A hackney came clattering over the bridge; Jack waved it down, then with a flourishing bow, waved Clarice into it. "Your charger awaits. Lead on."

The look she threw him as she entered the carriage was elementally superior. "Are you sure there's not some deeper problem with your head?"

Jack laughed and followed her.

Chapter 13

❦

$\mathcal{T}$he following morning, Clarice sat at the little table before the window in her suite, sipped her tea, crunched
her toast, and considered calling on her brother.

She really should call on her modiste. If she was to go out
among the ton at the height of the Season, she would need at
least one or two new gowns.

Glancing at the mantelpiece clock, she confirmed it was
close to ten o'clock. She'd risen late, long after Jack had left
her in a sated tangle of limbs and sheets at sometime close
to dawn.

Yesterday, they'd returned from their audience with the
bishop and had immediately set to work, nibbling on luncheon dishes while they correlated the details of the three
meetings cited in the allegations with James's lists of journeys and interviews. Their first setback had occurred when
they'd discovered that the dates of the three incidents did indeed align with three visits James had made to the capital,
three visits during which he'd interviewed various soldiers
and commanders.

Her heart had temporarily sunk, but Jack, reading her expression, had remarked that it would have been more surprising if disproving the allegations had indeed been that easy.

She'd acerbically replied that she would have been quite happy to be so surprised.

With the meetings established as possible, they'd turned their attention to the people involved, both the witnesses and those James had interviewed. There seemed little correlation between those interviewed and the information James had allegedly passed on.

"We'll have to check," Jack had said, "but even if the substance of the interviews doesn't match the information supposedly passed, that won't really help. James could have amassed the information by some other route, or through earlier interviews."

"But there does have to be reasonable cause to suppose James actually knew the information he passed, surely?"

Jack had nodded. "True. So we'll investigate both aspects—the witnesses and the information passed. We'll need to learn the specific facts supposedly passed at those three meetings. So far, Humphries hasn't revealed that, but that will be the most crucial point for James's defence to attack."

It had taken them until dinnertime to decide precisely how they were going to refute the allegations, to list all the points they could challenge and then define every avenue that might lead to the contrary evidence they sought. All in all, the possibilities were extensive, but Jack cautioned that they would need more than one contrary fact, possibly more than two, for each of the three incidents to be sure of laying the allegations to rest.

At eight o'clock, they'd called a halt and went down to dine in the hotel's dining room, in an atmosphere more commonly found in the most august of the gentlemen's clubs. Quiet conversation and total blindness as to the other occupants was the unwritten rule; even Jack, who'd initially balked on the grounds of calling unnecessary attention to their association, had had to admit there was no danger there.

Returning to her suite, they'd reviewed their work and

agreed that Jack would initially devote himself to finding and speaking with the witnesses. Clarice, meanwhile, would inform her family, rally them to James's cause, and establish what connections they had that might prove useful in influencing the bishop, investigating the courier, and also in verifying James's movements. And one way or another, they would extract from Humphries the details they required.

That decided, Jack had risen and given every indication of departing. She'd quickly made plain, in the most effective manner she could devise, that she expected him to remain and share her bed. Aside from all else, as she'd astringently remarked, there was his injury to consider. In furthering James's cause, it clearly behooved her to do all she could to ensure Jack's brain was functioning as incisively as possible. She hadn't wanted him spending another day with a throbbing head.

He'd laughed, then whispered in her ear that while he fully intended to leave her and her room, and waltz out of the hotel by the front door, past the concierge who had noted his arrival hours earlier, he also fully intended to return by the side door, and the side stairs, to her room, and her.

She'd let him go and waited, not patiently.

He'd returned as promised, not fifteen minutes later, and she'd taken his hand and led him to her bed.

She was quite sure, given all that had passed between then and this morning, that if any part of him was aching, it wouldn't be his head.

Lips quirking, she set down her teacup, and took a moment to savor the odd feeling of accomplishment, of having been able to successfully ease his injury, of being able to tend him in such a fashion . . . and the benefits that had ensued in the form of his thanks.

His expert and all-too-knowing attentions.

A tap on the door drew her back from her reverie and forced her to banish the silly smile from her face. Calling to the maid to enter, she returned to the bedchamber while her breakfast tray was cleared away.

Sitting before the dressing table mirror, she tidied her hair.

Her brother Melton, or her modiste?

The clocks in the suite chimed, ten light pings.

Fashionable gentlemen rarely left their beds before noon during the Season; clearly there was no point in calling on Melton too early in the day.

Dilemma solved, she reached for her bonnet.

Celestine had been her modiste for the last nine years. Initially a newcomer to Bruton Street, over the years *Celestine* had grown to be a name connoting the very *haute* of *haute couture*; Clarice now shared her services with the cream of the ton.

And only the cream of the ton; no one else could now possibly afford the most minor of the modiste's creations.

There had been a time in her more scandalous days when Clarice had slipped into the salon at the unfashionable hour of nine o'clock to avoid the eyes of the censorious. Standing behind a screen in one corner of the salon allowing one of the modiste's assistants to help her into a rather daring gown in her favorite plum silk, she reminded herself those days were long behind her.

It was nearly eleven o'clock, and the tonnish matrons with their daughters in tow would be pulling on their gloves preparatory to making their first foray of the morning, to a morning tea or a fashionable at-home, or to Bruton Street. Despite her years away, she still sensed the ebb and flow of the hours, without thought knew what activities should fill each if she were still a fashionable lady.

But she wasn't, so she could do as she pleased.

Lifting her head, hands smoothing the silk down over her hips, she stood straight and tall as the assistant tightened the laces. That done, she half turned, then paraded before the long mirror, examining the fall of the skirts, the way the silk clung to her figure.

Imagined what Jack would see, imagined how he would react.

Lips curving, she was about to send the assistant to summon Celestine when the main door to the salon opened to admit what sounded like a gossipy horde. Clarice heard Celestine coolly greet the newcomers, Lady Grimwade and Mrs. Raleigh the elder, two eminently well connected old battle-axes who perennially vied for the title of most avid gossipmonger in the ton.

"I tell you, Henrietta, it's *true*!" Lady Grimwade paused to draw in a wheezy breath. "Just fancy!" Behind the screen, Clarice could easily envision the gleam in her ladyship's beady black eyes. "*What* a comedown for that horrible woman to have a traitor in the family."

A sudden chill spread over Clarice's shoulders.

"I really find it difficult to credit, Amabelle." Mrs. Raleigh's quieter tones were mildly censorious. "This is the Altwoods, after all. One would want to be quite sure before one were heard whispering such tales."

"Indeed, Henrietta, but you may be sure I have it right. Apparently the Bishop of London has already referred the matter to the authorities."

Clarice didn't wait to hear more. She was an expert on the advisability of nipping scandal in the bud; it was what she'd failed to do seven years ago. She whisked gracefully around the screen. "Celestine? If you would . . ."

Across the expanse of the salon, she came face-to-face with Amabelle Grimwade and Henrietta Raleigh. Not one element in Clarice's manner or demeanor suggested she'd heard their prattle. She stood relaxed, arms gracefully extended as if waiting for Celestine, frozen between the parties, to admire the fall of the gown. Both Lady Grimwade and Mrs Raleigh stared, initially Clarice suspected at the daringly glamorous gown with its deep decollete; it took a long-drawn silent moment before they recognized her.

She knew when they did; their eyes grew round, then rounder; their sagging jaws sagged even farther. Satisfied, she looked at Celestine. "I rather think this gown will do." She swirled so the even more daring back was presented to her goggle-eyed audience; she thought she heard a small gasp. "Don't you think?"

Celestine rose to the challenge. "It becomes you *parfaitement*. Now if you would, while you are here, I would like you to try the forest green satin." Coming forward, she gestured to the area behind the screen.

Clarice moved as if to retreat, but then halted, and looked back at the two harpies. "Incidentally, you might like to know that regarding the matter you were so recently discussing, I was speaking with the Bishop of London only yesterday. His understanding of his own mind seems curiously at odds with yours." She paused, holding their startled gazes, then added, her tone dripping with icy hauteur, "You might recall that, expert though you might be, when it comes to scandal, few know the ropes more thoroughly than me."

With that parting shot, she swept behind the screen.

Celestine followed on her heels. "*Cherie,* I am so sorry."

"Don't be. It's useful that I heard of the rumors so soon." With a wave, Clarice urged the assistant to hurry and unlace the gown. "I'll take this incidentally. Send it to Benedict's. I'll return tomorrow morning to see what else you have."

Celestine sighed. "It was not you hearing those two *beldames* that I was apologizing for."

In the mirror, Clarice met Celestine's eyes. "What, then?"

"Why, that I mentioned the green satin." Celestine shifted to glance out at the salon. "Those two have departed, but there are six others here who heard and saw. If you wish to quash this rumor, then you must try on the green satin, no?"

It was Clarice's turn to sigh. "Yes, you're right." She dipped her shoulders, wriggled them, then straightened; the plum silk gown slithered down to puddle at her feet. Interesting; at least she felt sure Jack would think so. "Bring on the forest green satin, then I really must go."

As usually occurred with any gown Celestine specifically recommended, the forest green satin became her admirably, so the time spent in trying it on could not be counted a real loss.

But she'd spoken truly; she did know all there was to know about gossip within the ton. She might have temporarily gagged two of the foremost practitioners, but that wouldn't be the end of it. If Grimwade and Raleigh had heard the news, others would have, too. No one seeded a rumor in just one ear. The situation called for immediate and decisive action.

Further, Grimwade's gloating over "that horrible woman's" downfall, strongly suggested that her stepmother, Moira, had not grown more lovable or well respected with the years.

The defense of the family might well fall to Clarice. She was clearly going to have to do her part and go out into the ton, which meant her new gowns would be as essential as armor on a battlefield. Nevertheless, as soon as she decently could, she left the salon and descended the stairs to the street.

No more excuses, no more procrastination. Even if Melton was still abed, she'd simply order him dragged from it and make him listen.

She sincerely hoped he wasn't suffering the aftereffects of a night on the town.

One of the assistants had hurried down to hold the door for her; smiling absentmindedly, Clarice stepped out onto the pavement. She paused for an instant, her eyes adjusting to the glare of the bright sunshine.

"There you are, luv. We've been waiting for you."

She blinked, and nearly stepped back, but the door was directly behind her. Before her, on either side, not quite but almost hemming her in, stood two large men. Their clothes declared them workmen, not gentlemen. What on earth were they doing in Bruton Street?

Why on earth did they think they were waiting for her?

"I'm afraid you've made some mistake."

One of the men smiled and opened his mouth—

"Clarice?"

Turning her head, she saw Jack striding up from the corner. He was focused on the two men and didn't look pleased.

She smiled reassuringly and waved; she turned back in time to see the two men exchange a look. Then the one who'd been about to speak touched the brim of his cap. "You're right, miss. Looks like a mistake. If you'll excuse us."

The other touched his cap, too, and hurried around her. The pair strode off in the opposite direction to Jack. They reached a corner, and turned, disappearing from view.

She raised her brows, then turned to greet Jack as he came up.

He was scowling after the two men. "Who the devil were they?"

"I have no clue. They were waiting for someone and mistook me for her . . ." Hearing her own words, she realized the unlikelihood, or rather the impossibility. She glanced up at Jack.

The look he bent on her was disbelieving. A touch patronizing, too.

"Regardless, we don't have time for that." Grasping his arm, she steered him around. "I take it you got my note." She'd left a note of her whereabouts with the concierge just in case Jack needed to speak with her. "Unfortunately, matters have deteriorated. News of the allegations is out. Rumors are already spreading." She drew breath and determinedly lifted her chin. "I have to go and beard my brother."

Jack glanced at her, at the angle of her chin, and swallowed the acid words burning his tongue; now was not the time to lecture her on the dangers that lurked on even the most fashionable streets. He could quiz her about the two men later and check with Deverell over whether seizing women off the streets had become more prevalent in recent years. Now, however . . . "I'll come with you."

She shot him a sidelong glance, then looked ahead and walked on.

He could almost hear the arguments passing through her head. If she tried to refuse, he would insist, but he'd much rather she accepted his support, preferably in the vein in which it was offered—as her husband-to-be—although he was fairly certain she hadn't yet realized his intent. They walked briskly along, heading into the heart of Mayfair. The farther they walked without her declining his escort, the more likely she was to agree.

"Where does your brother live?"

"Melton House. It's in Grosvenor Street."

They'd circled the end of Berkeley Square and turned into Mount Street. Without speaking, Clarice turned up Carlos Place.

"So what rumors have you heard? Where, and from whom?"

She told him. Lightly frowning, she also related her suspicions regarding her stepmother. "Moira was seen as something of a social upstart when she married Papa, yet thinking back, I can't recall any adverse behavior toward her, not when I used to go about with her."

"When you used to go about with her, you were there." He glanced at her profile. "Those who might offer your stepmother a cold shoulder might not have done so in your presence."

Her frown grew more definite. "You're right, of course. I wonder what's been going on, how Moira has been managing in that respect since I've been gone."

"Not well by the sound of it."

They reached Grosvenor Street, and she pointed to a large mansion across the road, one door back from the square. "That's it." She paused, then drew breath. "Come on."

He took her elbow; together they crossed the street and climbed the steps to the narrow front porch. Releasing her, he reached out and jerked the doorbell. From deep within the house, they heard a loud jangle.

Clarice stood facing the door, her father's door, although

he was now gone and her eldest brother Alton ruled in his stead. Behind her right shoulder, Jack stood, not exactly relaxed yet elegantly at ease, taller than she, stronger, able, and willing to, even likely to, step in should she need his aid.

That knowledge was a very real comfort, and that surprised her. Even unnerved her, just a little. She'd never been one to lean on others, and had learned long ago that it was better not to have witnesses if things went wrong. She'd never liked others seeing her weaknesses, seeing her vulnerabilities. Yet with Jack . . . somehow, he was different.

Aside from all else, he was very like her. She trusted him to react as she would, to know how to react as she needed and wanted.

It seemed surpassingly strange to be standing on her father's stoop with a gentleman like Jack beside her.

Ponderous footsteps approached on the other side of the door, then the sound of a heavy latch lifting reached them.

The door swung slowly wide. "Yes?"

Head high, Clarice looked into her father's butler's face, and watched his expression change from a hauteur to rival her own to beaming welcome.

"Lady Clarice! My lady—come in!" Edwards contorted his ancient frame into a sweeping bow; he beamed as she stepped over the threshold onto the black-and-white tiles. "It does my old eyes good to see you again, my lady."

"Thank you, Edwards. This is Lord Warnefleet." She paused while Edwards bowed to Jack. "Is Alton in?"

"Indeed, my lady, and thrilled he'll be to see you after all these years. He's in the library."

Clarice hid a frown as she turned to the corridor to the left of the grand staircase. Alton in the library at this hour? At any hour? Clearly things weren't as they used to be.

She hadn't set foot in this house for seven years, not since she'd left it on her way to family-decreed banishment at Avening. Over the years, she'd fallen into the habit of not approaching her family, not even her brothers; although she probably could have done so once her father and his decree against all mention of her had died, after five years of no contact, she'd grown accustomed to the lack.

Presumably so had they, for they'd never written or traveled down to see her, even after her father's demise. During her visits to town, she'd therefore made no effort to reestablish contact, and as she'd eschewed the drawing rooms and ballrooms, she hadn't met them at social events.

She halted before the library door, and was surprised to find within her nothing more exercising than a slightly puzzled curiosity over what, for her and James, lay beyond the dark panels. Alton, perennially good-natured, had always been somewhat frivolous, lighthearted, with an insouciant smile that accurately protrayed his outlook on the world. And he was arguably the most serious of her brothers. Her father's three sons by his first marriage had been feted and indulged from birth; although blessed with good health and even tempers, the outcome, nevertheless, had been predictable.

Edwards had preceded them down the corridor. She allowed him to set the door wide and announce them; Edwards would have been hurt if she'd waved him away. The instant he intoned, "Lady Clarice, my lord, and Lord Warnefleet," she swept into the room.

And saw Alton sitting behind the huge desk, more haggard than she'd ever seen him, lifting his head from his hands where he'd been clutching it—apparently in something close to despair—his expression turning dazed as he focused on her. His gaze deflected to Jack, but almost instantly returned to her.

Clarice blinked, and seven years vanished. "Good God, Alton! Surely you're not foxed at this hour?"

She hadn't thought it possible, but his too-pale face grew paler.

"No! Of course not! Haven't touched a drop, not since yesterday. I swear . . ." His words faded; for one instant, he stared at her, then he surged to his feet and rounded the desk. "Clary! Dear Heaven, it's so *good* to see you!"

Hauled into a crushing embrace, squeezed tight as if she were some lifeline, Clarice felt thoroughly disoriented. She returned the hug, albeit rather more weakly, and patted Alton's shoulder. "I'm . . . ah, back for the moment."

Alton released her and stepped back, but caught her hands and, smiling delightedly, studied her. His dark eyes, not quite as dark as her own, all but burned with unabashed happiness and, equally clearly, with massive relief.

Before she could speak, Alton, still grinning fit to split his face, turned to Edwards. "A celebration, Edwards! Bring something—not champagne"—his gaze swung to Clarice—"it's too early, isn't it? How about some ratafia or orgeat, or is it sherry the ladies like now? I never know that sort of thing."

He was like a child, eager and wanting to welcome, to impress.

"Perhaps tea and cakes, my lord?" Edwards suggested.

Like a hopeful puppy, Alton looked inquiringly at Clarice.

"Thank you, Edwards. Tea and cakes will do admirably." She had a sudden premonition she was going to need the sustenance. What was going on here?

"Oh, and Edwards?" Alton met the aged butler's eye. "No need to tell her ladyship that Lady Clarice is here."

"No, indeed, my lord." Some silent communication passed between master and servant, then Edwards bowed majesterially to Clarice. "My lady, permit me to convey the welcome of all the staff, and to say how very pleased we are to see you once more beneath this roof."

Clarice inclined her head regally. "Thank you, Edwards. Please remember me to those I knew from before."

They waited while Edwards retreated; as he closed the door, Clarice introduced Jack.

"Lord Warnefleet was kind enough to accompany me to town. He's a close friend of James's."

Transparently happy to greet anyone who'd shown his sister a kindness, Alton grasped Jack's hand readily, but almost instantly his attention diverted to Clarice. "We'll have your old room prepared, just like old times. No one's been in there since you left. Roger heard Hilda and Mildred planning to steal things from it, so he locked the door, and we hid the key, so I expect there'll be a bit of dust, but Mrs. Hendry will be thrilled to have you home again, so—"

"Alton." Clarice waited until he met her eyes. "I'm staying at Benedict's, as I always do."

He blinked, then looked faintly hurt. "Always do?" He studied her face. "Do you often come up to town, then?"

His tone made her inwardly frown. "I come up at least twice a year. I may live in the country, but I still need gowns. But I wrote and told you. You never replied, and none of you ever came to see me—"

"I've never received any letter from you, not since you left." The hollow note in Alton's voice left no doubt he was speaking the truth. "I never knew that you came to town, and Roger and Nigel didn't, either."

Clarice let her frown materialize, let a hint of disgust into her voice. "Papa, I suppose. I had wondered . . . but I wrote again after he died." Alton shook his head. "You didn't get that either?"

"We had no idea you were ever in town. We thought you'd buried yourself in the country, made a new life and forgotten us. You were so disgusted with us all when you left."

She patted his arm, then moved past him to a chair. "Not you three. I knew what Papa was like, remember. I never blamed you."

Sinking into the armchair, she sat back and looked up at Alton, who had turned to face her; Jack watched her eyes trace her brother's face. "But you never came to Avening to see me, either."

Alton waved. "When you didn't reply to our letters . . ." He broke off, then looked at Clarice, who shook her head. "You never got them?"

"I assume you left them on the salver in the hall for Papa to frank?"

Alton swore beneath his breath, swung back around the

desk, and flung himself heavily into his chair. "I didn't think the old goat would go so far. He refused to allow anyone to mention your name, but he never said anything about us writing to you."

"He didn't bother saying, he just acted."

Leaning on his elbows, Alton frowned across the room. Calmly seating himself in the other armchair facing the desk, Jack saw what he hadn't until that moment, a fleeting touch of Clarice's steel in her brother's brooding eyes. After a moment, Alton looked at Clarice. "I wrote again after he died."

Brother and sister shared a long look, then Clarice raised her brows. "I see."

Jack presumed that meant someone else—his money was on their stepmother—had ensured that the conduit between brothers and sister remained broken. The question that instantly arose was: why?

The same question filled Clarice's dark eyes. He was getting much better at reading their expression, at sensing her feelings, her thoughts. From the moment she'd walked into the library, she'd been . . . groping, knocked off-balance by a welcome that had been very different from what she'd anticipated. He was beginning to understand she'd expected coolness at the very least, even from her brothers, beginning to understand why, beginning to appreciate the depth of the wound she'd carried for so long.

But, like him, she was starting to sense just how far from the expected matters really were.

"Alton"—she trapped her brother's dark gaze with her own—"I came here to ask for your help for James, on a matter that concerns the whole family. But before we discuss that, I think you'd better tell me exactly what's going on here."

Alton held her gaze for a moment, then heaved a huge sigh, scrubbed both hands over his face, then drew his fingers back through his hair, as he'd been doing when they'd entered. Then he lowered his hands, slumped back in the chair, and looked at Clarice. "That's why I was so glad to see you. What's happening here is very simple. Moira's in charge. She pulls the strings, and we—all of us—dance to her tune."

Clarice frowned. Before she could ask her next question, a tap on the door heralded Edwards with a tray, followed by the housekeeper carrying the teapot. They had to wait while Clarice greeted Mrs. Hendry, smiled, accepted the house-keeper's welcome, and gently but firmly dashed all hopes that she would be staying at Melton House. When the door eventually closed behind butler and housekeeper, Alton had recalled Jack's presence.

Alton cleared his throat. "Perhaps we should leave this discussion until after Lord Warnefleet has left us."

Jack caught the glance Clarice sent him—a warning—before she smoothly said, "Lord Warnefleet won't be leav-ing, not without me at any rate." Ignoring Alton's frown, she calmly went on, simultaneously pouring tea into their cups, "I told you he's a close friend of James's. He's also a close friend of mine. Jack knows all about the family. His assis-tance will be critical in helping James, which will equate to helping all the Altwoods. If he doesn't hear what you're about to tell me directly, then I'll need to relate it to him any-way. So stop quibbling, and explain this to me." She handed Alton his cup; Jack reached across and lifted his own.

Sitting back with hers, Clarice fixed Alton with her most inquisitorial gaze. "*You're* Melton—*you* now run the mar-quisate, this house, and all the others, too. What has Moira to say to anything?"

Alton glanced at Jack, then looked at Clarice. "Figura-tively speaking, she has us by the short and curlies."

The look Clarice flashed him rebuked him for his crude-ness and simultaneously urged him to go on.

"I'm thirty-four, Roger's thirty-three, and Nigel's thirty-one." Alton held up a staying hand when Clarice opened her mouth to remind him she knew that. "Even before Papa died, we'd each of us found the lady we wanted to marry. All perfectly aboveboard and all that. But . . . Moira knew, of course. She told us there was no rush, that there was plenty of time, given who we were, to declare our choice, and that we should take the time to make sure we'd chosen correctly . . ." A slight flush rose to Alton's pale cheeks. "Looking back, I can see she played to our own uncertainties, but . . . one thing and another, we all held off mentioning the matter to Papa, and then he died before anything had been said or any formal announcement made."

"But then you were the head of the family. You don't need anyone else's approval."

Alton's lips curled in cynical disgust. "That, unfortunately, is the rub. After Papa died, Moira took over. It's *her* approval I now need, and she's not about to give it, not easily. Not, I suspect, anytime soon."

Clarice studied his face, then calmly asked, "What is she holding over your head?"

"Our own pasts, of course." Alton glanced briefly at Clarice, then fell to examining the liquid in his cup. "You know what we're like . . . what Papa was like. We were all but encouraged to dally with whoever took our fancy, especially at Rosewood."

Her voice even and entirely nonjudgmental, Clarice asked, "You're talking of maids, laundresses, milkmaids?"

Alton nodded without looking up. "It was always so easy, and even when the inevitable happened, as, of course, it did with all three of us, Papa never turned a hair, but just arranged to have the girl taken care of, the babe raised within one of our worker's families . . . you know how it's done." Lips thin, he grimaced. "What none of us knew—not even Papa, I suspect—was that Moira not only knew of each incident, she kept track. More, when we—me, Roger, and Nigel—came up to town, she somehow kept track here as well." Alton looked up and met Clarice's eyes. "For each of us she has a list of every encounter, every affair."

He drew breath, with one hand made a helpless gesture. "For each of us, there's at least one association, one liaison, that if it became known could . . . scupper our plans to marry, or at least marry the ladies we've chosen."

Holding his gaze, Clarice murmured, "We do tend to move in a very small circle . . ."

Alton's lips twisted; he nodded. "Precisely. You can see how it might be."

Jack frowned. When neither Clarice nor Alton said more, he asked, "So Moira uses the information to do what? Drain money from the marquisate?"

A large diamond winked in Alton's cravat; a smaller stone was embedded in the heavy gold signet ring on his right hand. His coat was by Schultz, his linen impeccable. Despite his haggardness, he was perfectly—and expensively— turned out.

Alton's expression lightened; he laughed, but it wasn't a happy sound. "Oh, no. That's not her bent at all. Indeed, she'd be the first to encourage us to spend more, to make an even bigger splash. She would never want us to appear as anything less than as wealthy as we are. She delights in her role as the Marchioness of Melton. She continues to entertain lavishly as my hostess. We always have to be seen to be top of the tree." Alton paused, the bitterness in his tone reflected in his face. "No, for her it's not money. It's control— of us." He glanced at Jack. "The power to make us dance to her tune."

After a moment, Alton looked at Clarice. "Moira tried to control you, and that backfired, but she got rid of you nevertheless. With the three of us, she was much more careful. By the time we realized, after Papa had died, she already had us in thrall. Worse, we'd handed her the ropes ourselves by telling her of our intentions to wed. She gets an unholy joy from knowing she can jerk our strings, make us obey her at any time, and that our futures—for each of us our future happiness—will only be granted at her whim."

Clarice said nothing, yet her disgust with Moira was a palpable thing. "What have you done about it?" When Alton blinked, she rephrased, "Have any of you challenged her, tested her will, or have you simply accepted her threat as real?"

Alton's haggard expression, temporarily eased, returned. "Roger tried. He said he'd tell Alice—Alice Combertville, Carlisle's daughter—tell her all and throw himself on her mercy, and he did. At first, it seemed he'd triumphed. Alice was incensed at Moira's game and swore she wasn't concerned . . . but then two days later, Roger got a note breaking off their understanding. He tried to see Alice, to find out why she changed her mind, to persuade her . . ." Alton looked faintly ill. "That was last November. He still hasn't been able to speak with her."

"He's still trying?"

"Yes! What else can he do? It's driving him out of his mind. She's been dancing with Throgmorton, and Dawlish. He's terrified she'll accept one of them, and then it'll be all over . . ."

Clarice regarded Alton steadily, then calmly said, "Tell Roger he needs to speak with Alice, even if he has to abduct her to do it. He has to ask her what Moira told her."

Alton frowned. "It wasn't Moira, but Roger himself who told her."

Clarice made a dismissive sound and set down her tea cup. "Tell Roger I'll make him a wager—that after he'd spoken with Alice, she, incensed, approached Moira and took her to task. But Moira retaliated with something—some fabrication, something truly horrendous—that Alice couldn't overlook. That's why she changed her mind and broke things off with Roger." The look she cast Alton was one of fond exasperation. "You really are too easily manipulated."

She sat back. "Now what about Nigel?"

"He and Emily—Emily Hollingworth—well, I suppose you could say that in typical Nigel fashion, he's toeing the line in the hope that everything will somehow resolve itself, meaning that either Roger or I will discover some way around Moira." Alton grimaced. "Emily's just twenty. They have time."

Clarice raised her brows. "But you don't?"

Alton lifted his eyes and met her gaze. "No." He gestured helplessly. "That's what I was wrestling with when you came in." He drew in a shuddering breath. "I have no idea what to do."

"Who?" Clarice asked.

"Sarah Haverling, old Conniston's eldest daughter."

Clarice pursed her lips, then nodded slowly. "An excellent choice." She focused on Alton. "You have an understanding, but you've made no formal offer yet?"

"I haven't even hinted at such a thing, not to her father."

"I take it something's made the matter pressing?"

"Yes! Sarah's twenty-three, nearly twenty-four. This will be her last Season. We've been talking of marrying for the last year, but with Moira holding what she is over my head . . ." Hopelessness deepened the lines in Alton's face. "Her father and stepmother are encouraging her to marry, hardly surprisingly. They've lined up Farleigh and Bicknell, both seem increasingly smitten. If either makes an offer . . . if I can't make a counteroffer, Sarah will be pressured to accept them."

Watching Clarice, Jack saw her stiffen; Sarah Haverling's immediate future was exceedingly reminiscent of Clarice's past.

"The worst part," Alton went on, his voice lower, his gaze fixed on his tightly clenched hands, "is that Sarah doesn't understand why I won't speak. She's not enamored of either of the others, and they're older, too. She keeps looking to me, and I have to keep making excuses . . ." His voice wavered; he drew in another huge breath. "I haven't slept for days. I don't know what to do."

A moment ticked by, then Clarice softly asked, "What is it that Moira holds over you?" When Alton looked up, she met his gaze. "If you don't tell me, I can't advise you."

Alton stared at her for a moment, then his eyes cut to Jack. "Don't worry about Jack." Clarice's tone was dry. "His discretion is assured, and indeed, you're liable to get more sympathy from him than me."

Alton didn't smile. He looked at Clarice. "I had an affair with Sarah's stepmother, Claire."

Clarice raised her brows. "How very unwise. But I take it this was before you took up with Sarah?"

Alton looked irritated. "*Years* before. She was still in the schoolroom."

"Indeed. In that case, I'd advise you to confess. Unless Claire has changed greatly in the last seven years, I seriously doubt she'll make any waves."

Alton looked directly at Clarice; Jack could suddenly see a stronger resemblance. "I can't confess. After Roger tried, Moira told me that if I did, she'd speak, not to Sarah, but to Conniston himself. We may all know that Claire has been taking lovers for years, but Moira will assure Conniston that if he allows me to marry Sarah, then she'll ensure that the tale of Conniston meekly handing over his daughter to a man who'd cuckolded him will be spread the length and breadth of the ton."

Clarice held Alton's dark gaze, then grimaced. "Oh."

That, Jack thought, summed it up perfectly. He was starting to develop a very real interest in meeting Clarice's old nemesis—now, it appeared, her brothers' nemesis, too. He was curious to see just what sort of female could, and would, so brazenly run such nasty, sticky coils around people of the caliber of Clarice and Alton. Despite Alton's state, Jack was catching enough glimmers of steel and hard arrogance to guess that on a good day, Alton was no weakling. His inner steel might not yet be tempered to quite the same saber-edged hardness as Clarice's, but it seemed Moira was working on that.

To his mind, that might prove a very dangerous game. Especially for Moira. The woman must be blind not to know with what manner of people she was dealing.

He'd barely finished the thought when the library door burst open.

They all looked. A blond harpy stood on the threshold, blue eyes flaming, heavy breasts heaving with uncontrolled fury.

"Alton!" The voice was shrill, barely controlled. "How *dare* you entertain this . . ." The harpy's eyes cut to Clarice and spat flames. "This *female* in your father's house?"

Chapter 14

❧

$\mathcal{I}$t was like watching a chrysalis crack and a new life-
form emerge.

Alton didn't stand; he didn't actually move, yet he seemed
to grow. His face hardened, stripped of all humor; his dark
eyes burned. When he spoke, anger growled, barely restrained beneath his words. "Leave us, Moira."

Shock showed briefly on the harpy's face, almost as if
he'd slapped her. Then she hauled in a breath and marched
over the threshold. "I most certainly will not! How dare you
permit *that woman*." Advancing, she jabbed a finger at
Clarice. Jack glanced at Clarice, and had to fight to keep his
lips straight.

After that first glance, she'd apparently decided she didn't
need to accord her furious stepmother any further attention;
Clarice had calmly served herself another cake and now sat
in her chair, the very picture of ladylike decorum eating the
cake off a delicate china plate, to all appearances deaf and
blind to the fraught scene being enacted before her.

Enraged, Moira drew in another breath. "That *scandalous
female* into this house! Your father *forbade* it."

Jack suspected he should follow Clarice's lead, but the
temptation was too great. He sat back, watching both Moira
and Alton.

Moira flung to a raging halt by the desk. She was over forty years old, her too-white face starting to show the first lines. Her figure was full but she was rather short, her hair a brassy shade, her eyes a stormy blue sparking with vindictiveness. She all but vibrated with fury as she glared at Clarice.

Jack's eyes narrowed as his senses informed him there was a great deal of fear behind Moira's furious facade.

He glanced at Clarice as with awful control, Alton stated, "My father is dead. This is now my house. Within it, I will see whomever I please."

Moira turned to stare at him. For an instant, she seemed struck speechless. Then she stiffened. "I believe, Alton, that you've forgotten—"

"I haven't forgotten anything, but I have remembered one or two things. *I* am master here. I suggest you leave this room."

Moira's jaw fell, then it snapped shut. "If you think—"

"*Edwards!*"

"Yes, my lord?" The butler answered so quickly it was clear he'd been hovering just outside the door.

"Please escort her ladyship to her room. I believe she needs to lie down until dinnertime." Alton's eyes, hard and beyond furious, locked on Moira's. "If you encounter any difficulties, summon a footman or two to help."

"Indeed, sir."

Quivering with outrage, Moira stiffened. "If you think I'll let you get away with this," she hissed, "you'd better think again."

Edwards touched her arm and she uttered a furious shriek. Jerking away, she glared at the butler, then flung around and stormed from the room. The butler turned to follow. "In her bedchamber, my lord?"

Alton nodded.

"Edwards." Without looking up, Clarice said, "If there's any nastiness over this, do let Alton know."

Edwards bowed to her. "Indeed, my lady."

When the door shut, Alton exhaled heavily; the tension in his shoulders and arms visibly eased.

"There." Clarice set down her empty cake plate. "You see how easy reclaiming your life can be?"

Alton snorted, but his expression turned thoughtful. "I never thought of shouting before."

Clarice humphed, the sound suggesting he should have thought of it long ago.

"Well, Papa always shouted and ranted enough for everyone."

"Precisely. So if you want Moira to understand that you now wear his shoes . . ."

Alton frowned. "I never thought of it like that." After a moment, he glanced at her. "You were the only one of us—not just the four of us but any of us—to stand up to him. Until he died, he rode roughshod over us all whenever he had a mind to." He uttered a short laugh. "As for Roger, Nigel, and me, he never let us forget what he called his leniency in listening to us over sending you to James."

An awkward flush rose to Alton's cheeks; he caught Clarice's eyes. "That wasn't said to make you feel you owe us anything. You don't. We should have protected you better . . . somehow."

"I'm not sure you could have, or that I'd have let you," Clarice calmly replied. "But regardless, that's the past. It's the present we have to deal with, and the future to protect. Which is why Jack and I are here."

Briskly she informed Alton of the allegations against James, succinctly outlining the ramifications to the family name. She appealed to Jack; he confirmed the seriousness of the allegations. Alton was a quick study; they didn't have to spell out the likely effect an Altwood being tried for treason would have on his and his brothers' matrimonial hopes.

Alton looked from Jack to Clarice. "What do you want me to do?"

"Is there any way you can influence the Bishop of London?" Clarice asked.

Alton thought, then nodded. "I know his older brother. He's a member of White's and was a crony of Papa's. I could approach him."

"Good," Jack said. "What we need is permission for me as the family's agent to question Deacon Humphries, not as prosecutor of the case but as the bringer of the original allegations. We already have access to the information thus far made available to the bishop's court, but it's by no means all Humphries knows. We need to ask him about details he's omitted before he presents them at the hearing, so we'll know what evidence we need to refute the allegations *in toto*, not just to chip away at the edges and cast doubt, but to quash them whole."

"It's urgent," Clarice added.

Alton nodded, busily jotting notes. "I'll see what I can manage." He paused, then added, his tone grim, "Heaven knows, there's precious little else I'm likely to accomplish."

Clarice watched him for a moment, then rose and rounded the desk. Pausing by Alton's chair, she laid a hand on his shoulder, bent, and kissed his cheek.

Jack saw Alton's expression as he glanced up, surprise blended with achingly sweet memory. He looked up to see Clarice smile at her brother. She patted his shoulder. "I'll put my mind to your problem with Moira. There has to be a way. Say hello to Roger and Nigel for me, and don't forget to give Roger my message." Leaving Alton, she headed for the door; with a nod to Alton, Jack rose, and followed her.

"Incidentally"—Clarice paused just before the door to look back at Alton—"you might try telling Sarah you love her to distraction and fully intend moving heaven and earth to wed her. Then tell her of Moira's threat. Being trusted with the truth might make her more inclined to do all she can to *avoid* receiving an offer from anyone else."

With that, she turned to the door. Jack opened it for her, then followed her from the room; the last sight he had of Alton Altwood, Marquess of Melton, was of him sitting at his desk, faintly stunned, but with the light of hope dawning in his eyes.

They returned to Benedict's, and had lunch in Clarice's suite. The meal passed in unusual silence. Clarice was transparently digesting all she'd learned at Melton House, and not approving of any of it. Jack watched her face, appreciating the frown she didn't bother to hide. That she no longer sought to conceal her worries and emotions from him was, he felt, an encouraging sign.

After they'd finished and the dishes had been cleared away, Clarice sat back in her armchair, met Jack's eyes as he sat in its mate, and grimaced. "I fear I'm going to have to go back into the ton in a much more *emphatic* manner than I'd planned."

He studied her. "I'd thought you were set on riding to James's social rescue."

"I was. I am. And I will. But it seems I'm going to have to intercede, and act, too, on my brothers' behalfs." She gestured. "You saw Moira. She's thoroughly devious, and she knows them—all four of us—well."

"You don't think Alton can manage on his own, with your support? He seemed to come alive this morning, simply because you were there."

Clarice frowned more deeply. Eventually, she conceded, "You're right in a way. Alton has it in him to rule as he should. I know he has. Unfortunately, previously he was always in Papa's shadow, and with Moira's manipulation, Alton hasn't fully realized Papa's shoes are now his, that he can step into them and take control." A moment passed, then she murmured, "It wasn't so much my being there as Moira attacking me that spurred Alton to action."

Jack held up a staying hand. "If you imagine setting yourself up as a target for that frightful woman to spur your brothers into acting as they ought, then I strongly advise *you* to think again."

Clarice met his eyes, read the warning therein; a subtle glow warmed her, but she humphed dismissively. "I wasn't about to suggest any such thing. Self-sacrifice isn't my style. However, I will, clearly will, need to go about in society more widely than if I'd had just James's defence on my plate. *That* I can accomplish by making contact with a few key people. Nullifying Moira's manipulation will require much more. For a start, I'm going to have to meet with my brothers' chosen ladies, and, I hope, ease the strain there. Meeting Conniston himself, and perhaps Claire—I know her of old—might help. . . ."

Steepling her fingers, she rested her chin on the tips. Staring across the room, she continued to frown. "The major difficulty is how. How can I, quickly and acceptably, step back into the fray I turned my back on so decisively seven years ago?"

After a moment, Jack asked, "Just how decisively did you dismiss the ton?"

She shifted her gaze to meet his. "Totally. I was disgusted with them all, and made no bones about it."

He grimaced, then added, "However, you're an Altwood."

"Indeed. If after seven years I wish to swan back"—she shrugged—"I doubt many would attempt to cut me."

She noted Jack's swift grin, could imagine the vision flitting through his mind, of her depressing the pretensions of any who might try. As indeed she would. She'd suffered the adverse aspects of being a marchioness's daughter; she wasn't about to deny herself the benefits. "I can, and will, return to the ton, but I need advice of a sort that's not easy to gain."

A minute went by, then Jack shifted, drawing her attention. He met her eyes. "I have two aunts. They'll help if I ask."

Clarice raised her brows; it was the first mention she'd heard of any family beyond his father. "And they are?"

"Lady Cowper and Lady Davenport."

She stared at him. "Just like that, you can command the support of *two* of the most formidable hostesses in the ton?"

He grinned. " 'Command' might be stating the matter a trifle strongly, but they know I fled town recently, at the height of the Season. They'll be only too pleased to assist you once they learn it was you who brought me back."

She considered him, searched his hazel eyes, but couldn't tell whether there was anything more than the obvious, anything ambiguous, in his smooth words. Slowly, she nodded. "Lady Cowper and Lady Davenport would indeed be useful allies in combating Moira. As for James . . ."

Jack pulled a face. "My aunts have a close friend, a lady I tend to avoid. She's terrifying. However, when it comes to wielding influence in the upper echelons of power, I doubt there are many her equal. Chances are, if I send word to my aunts, when we visit, she'll be there, too."

She could read his uncertainty over this other lady. "She who?"

"Lady Osbaldestone."

She sat up. "Therese Osbaldestone?"

He nodded.

She blinked, recalled. "She was a close friend of Mama's—Papa's sisters told me that—but I didn't meet Lady Osbaldestone until the day I was presented. She was there, and spoke kindly to me, but then Moira came up, and Lady Osbaldestone looked down her nose and left us."

Jack raised his brows. "Sounds as if she might be inclined to assist in lifting Moira's paw from your brothers' throats."

Clarice grinned. "What an image."

A knock on the door had them both turning. "Come!" Clarice called.

The door opened to admit a footman carrying a silver salver. He crossed and offered the salver to Clarice.

She picked up the three cards lying on it, read them, then smiled a touch ruefully. Over the ivory rectangles, she met Jack's eyes. "My brothers. All three of them."

Dropping the cards on the tray, she looked at the footman. "Show the gentlemen up."

When the door closed behind the footman, she looked at Jack. "I wonder . . . ?"

She didn't have to wonder for long. Barely a minute passed before her brothers, led by Alton, came striding into the room. Roger and Nigel, beaming in patent delight, dragged her from her chair and hugged her exuberantly, blithely ignoring her warnings not to crush her gown.

For one instant, she could almost believe nothing had changed, that the years had vanished, and they were again the slightly older-in-years brothers she'd forever had to keep in line, to guide and in some ways protect. But then she saw them glancing at Jack, sensed their reaction, and his, and knew things would never again be as they'd been.

"Lord Warnefleet escorted me to London. He's a close friend of James." She made the introductions, deftly steering the conversation away from herself and Jack, sitting so patently at ease in her suite, and doing not one damned thing to look any less predatory than he was. Her brothers' overt suspicions seemed to evoke a blatantly possessive stance in him, even more possessive than he normally was.

She longed to kick them all. Hard. "Alton, have you done anything yet about influencing the bishop in our favor?"

"Yes." He grinned at her, suddenly very much the Alton of her memories. "I remembered that old Fotheringham often settles to snooze in White's library after lunch—a good place to corner him, I thought, and so it proved. He's always grumbling about his brother the bishop, about the Church getting above itself, and so on. He was very ready to pen a letter to his brother pointing out the, as he put it, advisability of acceding to the Altwoods' perfectly reasonable request to have a private agent examine the evidence to be presented to the bishop's court prior to the official hearing."

Alton glanced at Jack. "I saw the letter off with one of White's footmen myself. I'd be surprised if the bishop didn't comply. He's considered very astute in judging which way the wind's blowing, and has predictable ambitions. I suspect he'll grasp the opportunity to . . ."

"Ingratiate himself?" Jack supplied.

Alton smiled cynically. "Precisely."

Turning to Clarice, he continued, "But now I've done my best for James over that, we"—his gesture included himself, Roger and Nigel—"have come to throw ourselves on your mercy. We're in over our heads with Moira and her schemes. We're determined to break free, but we need your help."

"Before you say yea or nay"—Roger hauled up a straight-backed chair and sat beside Clarice—"we've an offer to make in exchange. You want to exonerate James, and for that you'll need help, help of the sort we can give." Roger glanced at Jack measuringly, but not antagonistically. "You'll need foot soldiers, and we're good at following orders. Whatever you want us to do to help James, we'll do it and gladly. In return—"

"In return, dear sister"—Nigel curled up at Clarice's feet and grinned up at her adoringly—"we want you to help us to the altar."

"Not one altar, mind," Roger clarified. "Three altars, one for each of us. Different dates, different ladies."

Clarice sent him a withering look.

Alton moved to stand before the fireplace, drawing her gaze. He met it, held it, simply said, "Please."

Watching Clarice, Jack sensed something of her inner struggle. She'd fully intended to do what she could to help her brothers, but to commit herself to doing so, to them . . . that was something else, something she, once the commitment was given, would consider binding.

When her gaze dropped from Alton's face to his, he sat unmoving, giving her an unreadable face and inscrutable eyes. In truth, he couldn't advise her in this; she knew her brothers, knew their caliber, whether they could indeed help effectively in clearing James's name, far better than he. Whatever she decided, he would support her stance.

The frown that had formed in her eyes slowly dissipated; she looked up again at Alton. "If I actively help you in winning free of Moira—"

"And winning the hands of our chosen ladies," Nigel interjected.

Clarice glanced down at him. "And *clear the way* for you to win your ladies—I refuse to be held responsible for the outcome of any ham-fisted attempts at wooing—*if* I do that for you, then you'll devote yourselves to helping us exonerate James in whatever ways Jack and I require."

In unison, the brothers shot a swift glance at Jack, which he met with impassivity, then the three exchanged glances, weighing Clarice's words, wordlessly communicating. Jack noticed the phenomenon with a pang, realized Clarice was following the exchange, too. He'd never had siblings, not even close friends. Never shared that type of communication with anyone.

Then Clarice looked across and met his eyes. He read her assurance that her brothers' help would be worth her effort, and she'd help them, regardless, so her deal was more in the nature of making hay while the sun shone.

She glanced away, and he blinked.

"If it's any help in making your decisions"—Clarice looked at Roger, then Nigel and finally up at Alton—"do consider what having a suspected traitor in the family will do to your matrimonial aspirations."

Alton's lips thinned. Roger's jaw set; his eyes turned bleak. Nigel swore beneath his breath and received a swift kick from his sister.

"Well," he complained, "it's true. Anyway"—he grinned up at her—"you know we'll help you regardless, and you won't be able to resist helping us, so all this haggling is purely by the by. So!" He looked from Clarice to Alton, then back again. "Where do you want us to start?"

Clarice studied Nigel's eager face, then glanced at Alton, before meeting Jack's gaze. "Jack and his friends are checking the facts surrounding three meetings James allegedly had with a French courier. They're better qualified than we are to do that. We"—she looked up at Alton—"need to deal with the other side of this threat—the rumor mill and the scandalmongers. The first thing to do is find out how widespread the rumors are. Once we know that, we can decide on the best way to counter them."

Alton frowned. "I haven't heard any rumor."

"*You* won't." Jack caught Alton's eye. "No one will say anything before members of the family. You'll be the last to know."

"I only heard," Clarice said, "because I was behind a screen at my modiste's and those old witches Lady Grimwade and Mrs. Raleigh didn't know I was there. However, it sounded like the rumor had only just started."

"Grimwade and Raleigh?" Roger frowned. "If you wanted to spread malicious rumors, those two biddies would be an obvious place to start."

"Indeed. Someone had clearly whispered in Grimwade's ear. Raleigh hadn't heard until then. However, I don't believe either will say another word, not until they hear more." Clarice glanced at her brothers. "It's the middle of the afternoon. Many gentlemen will be stopping by their clubs. If you do the rounds, you should get some idea of how widespread the whispers are."

"You'll have to ask friends to help," Jack said. "You won't hear anything directly."

"And whatever you do hear, don't—*do not*—react. Not yet." Clarice met each of her brothers' eyes sternly. "We need some notion of what scale of problem we're dealing with, then we can devise the most effective way to counter it. If anyone does the unthinkable and corners you over the matter, plead complete ignorance. Pretend you've no idea what they're talking about." She paused, then went on, "If we meet again this evening—"

"Oh, we're definitely meeting this evening." Alton glanced at his brothers, then back at Clarice. "We want you to meet our fiancées-in-all-but-name. We've arranged for invitations to be sent here for the balls we'll be attending tonight. We'll meet you at the Fortescues'. We've agreed that Roger's case is most urgent, then mine. Nigel"—Alton nudged his youngest brother with the toe of his boot—"can wait his turn."

Clarice looked up at Alton, her expression an unresolved mixture of haughty umbrage and cool calculation.

Jack managed to hide the smile he knew she wouldn't appreciate. She'd wanted Alton to take charge of his life and the marquisate, but Jack doubted she'd envisaged him taking charge of her, too.

But calculation won out; she inclined her head. "Very well. We'll meet you at the Fortescues at ten o'clock."

Jack felt Clarice's glance, but didn't meet it; she knew he'd escort her to whatever balls and parties she chose to attend. Instead, he watched her brothers and their reaction to her "*We'll* meet you." They weren't at all sure how to take that, weren't at all sure they approved.

Alton shifted his stance, fixed his dark gaze on Clarice; Jack got the impression he was girding for battle. "There's one other thing, Clary—we want you to come home. To come and live with us again at Melton House."

She looked up, distracted, surprise clear in her face, then came that moment of hesitation, of looking inward, that Jack knew signified that she was considering, thinking before she acted . . .

His heart stuttered. She hadn't expected any of this, hadn't known her brothers had missed her so sorely, that they would welcome her back so warmly. That far from ostracizing her, her family would embrace her, falling on her neck, perhaps, but being needed and appreciated was balm to ladies such as she.

Jack drew in a breath, held it, and waited. There was nothing he could do to sway her decision, not with her brothers looking on, ready to leap to her defence if she gave the slightest sign; they would come between her and him in a heartbeat if they thought she would allow it.

He glanced briefly at them, confirmed they were watching not her but him. Regardless of their current state, none of them were slow-tops, nor truly weak. It was as Clarice had said; they hadn't yet realized their potential, their ability to get things done. And they loved her; that was transparent. All three had seen enough, sensed enough to realize there was some connection, a relationship of some ilk between her and him. They would watch him like a hawk from now on; he didn't care. They wouldn't see anything to raise their hackles, because his intentions were all they might wish . . .

The notion of enlisting their aid in his campaign to win her swam into his mind; he blinked, then metaphorically shook it from his head. No matter how tempting the thought, no matter how supportive they might be, she'd learn of any conspiracy and be furious. Not a wise way to woo Boadicea.

From the brothers' dark glances, it was clear they knew and understood her as he did; all four of them knew she'd make her own decision about him, about any relationship between them, and woe betide any who sought to interfere.

Her pause lasted for no more than two breaths, then, without glancing Jack's way, she looked at Roger and Nigel, then met Alton's gaze.

Jack's heart solidified in his chest. Regardless of the past, her family was important to her; returning to their bosom might be something she truly yearned to do—

"Thank you, but no. I prefer to stay here." Clarice suppressed the urge to look at Jack, to reassure and to see his reaction. Alton frowned and opened his mouth to argue; she held up a hand. "No. The last time I was at Melton House . . . the memories are too painful. I put them behind me when I left, a clean break. There's no reason to go back, no reason in the present circumstances that I need to reside under your roof. I'm perfectly comfortable here"—she glanced briefly at Jack; despite her best efforts to appear aloof a faint smile lit her eyes, teased her lips—"and so here I'll remain."

Alton, Roger, and Nigel made grumping sounds denoting their unhappiness, but none of them attempted to argue further.

"Besides"—she sat straighter—"while you might think

having me about to shield you from Moira is a good idea, in reality, having me and Moira under the same roof, especially *that* roof, is an untenable proposition." She glanced at them, her gaze sharp. "The disruption would be significant, not just for you, but for the staff as well. Such an arrangement simply would not work."

They grimaced, but accepted her decree. They all rose. She waited while they shook hands with Jack, then, before they could be difficult, steered them to the door, leaving Jack by the fireplace. Alton, the last to go out, threw a frowning glance back at Jack, but, after reiterating that the necessary invitations would arrive shortly, reluctantly left.

Jack watched her walk back to him. As she neared, he raised a brow. "They feel responsible for you, unsurprisingly. You're not making matters easy for them."

"My life is no longer any concern of theirs, as they well know." With a swish of her skirts, she sank back into her armchair and watched while Jack subsided in a relaxed sprawl in its mate. "Now, how should we proceed?"

They agreed that the obvious division of labor was likely to be the most efficient. Jack, through his contacts, would investigate the three alleged meetings, searching for sufficient facts to disprove each one. Meanwhile Clarice, with her brothers' assistance, would do whatever necessary to quash any rumors circulating through the ton, and via the family's influence open any doors they might discover initially closed. In between, she would do what she could to counter Moira's influence and smooth her brothers' matrimonial paths.

"However, I absolutely refuse to propose for them. That they must do for themselves."

Jack hid a grin at her sternness. He felt like grinning in general, no excuse needed, lighthearted—his heart lightened—by her choosing to remain at Benedict's. Despite what she'd told her brothers, some part of her reasoning had to do with him. That brief smile she'd sent his way had assured him that was so. "I didn't want to say anything while they were here, but your decision not to stand as a physical shield between your brothers and your stepmother was eminently wise. They're at the point, Alton especially, of dealing with her themselves, but if you were there . . ."

"Precisely." She nodded. "They'd regress."

The promised invitations arrived. They read them, mutually grimaced, and agreed to meet at Benedict's at half past nine to commence the journey to Fortescue House.

Jack stole a quick kiss, one that lasted five minutes, then left, still grinning. He walked back to Montrose Place, a light breeze in his face, grateful for the chance to stretch his legs.

His head remained clear, without a hint of pain.

Deverell and Christian arrived at the club shortly after Jack, and brought Tristan Wemyss, Earl of Trentham, another club member, with them. The three joined Jack in the library; stretching out in the large comfortable armchairs, gratefully accepting the mugs of ale Gasthorpe served them, they traded quips, sapiently remarking on their farsightedness in establishing this, their London bolt-hole.

"I swear to you," Tristan said, "society being what it is these days, we'll always need a place to vanish to. After the wedding, I thought I'd be safe, but no. Now it's the married but dissatisfied matrons who set their caps at me."

"I should think Leonora would have something to say to that." Christian's eyes twinkled. Leonora, now Tristan's wife, originally the lady living in the house beside the club, was no meek and mild miss.

"Oh, indeed." Tristan nodded. "But there's only so much hiding behind her skirts I can stomach. Dashed demoralizing after facing and surviving Boney's worst."

They laughed, and caught up with news of their other comrades—Charles St. Austell, the most recently married, settling into domestic bliss in Cornwall, Tony Blake, also now married, learning to cope with a ready-made family at his seat in Devon, and Gervase Tregarth, Earl of Crowhurst, presently out of town dealing with family business.

"As for Christian and me"—Deverell stretched out his long legs—"we've been skulking around the fringes of the ton, reconnoitering as it were."

"Trying our damnedest not to get noticed." Christian grimaced. "Not the easiest assignment. I'm actually exceedingly glad to have something else to occupy my time for the nonce. I haven't seen any prospect worthwhile pursuing in the ballrooms. I'd much rather pursue some villain." He cocked a brow at Deverell. "What about you?"

"Same story." Deverell sighed. "You know, I had such a lovely conceit when we started this club that finding the right lady would be . . . well, a dashed sight easier than infiltrating French business affairs and pretending to be one of them for over ten years."

Christian nodded. "So, leaving the demoralizing subject of our matrimonial endeavors, what have we to report?"

"First," Tristan said, "tell me what the game is. I want to play a hand in this. Far more to my taste than doing the pretty in the ton."

Jack briefly outlined the threat to James Altwood, why they knew he was innocent and Dalziel's suspicions, and their current plans to quash the allegations. "Before they transmogrify to outright charges of treason. Courtesy of the Altwoods, it's likely I'll be able to interview the man behind the allegations—Deacon Humphries—tomorrow. We've already got the dates, times, and places of three recent meetings the courier supposedly had with James—Deverell and Christian were looking into those. We've verified that James was in London on all three occasions, so theoretically the meetings could have taken place."

"Just so." Deverell nodded. "All three places are taverns in Southwark, within walking distance of Lambeth Palace, which is where James Altwood stays when in London. And the taverns are exactly what one might expect of such places in the stews. The only way we'll learn anything is to watch, quiet and unthreatening, until we get a feel for each place. No point cornering the witnesses until we know how the ground lies and so have a chance of catching them out. They'll have been paid to tell their tale, but if we can shake it, they'll most likely retreat, but we'll need a better understanding of each tavern to do that. No other way than the long way, I'm afraid."

"I agree." Christian looked at Jack. "We'll set up the necessary surveillance. The information you drag from the good deacon might help us narrow our scope."

"I have a suggestion." Tristan set down his ale mug. He glanced at Christian and Deverell. "All three of us are at present fixed in London. All three of us have useful contacts here. But our contacts prefer to work only with people they know." He looked at Jack. "You have three principal incidents you need disproved. I suggest each of us take one tavern and throw our people on that one incident alone. Concentrating, focusing, will get us further faster."

Christian was nodding. "An excellent notion. Each of us will be able to press harder. The chain of command will be clearer and more direct."

"I agree." Deverell set down his mug and fished in his coat pocket, drawing out the sheet on which Jack had previously written the addresses of the three meeting places. "So let's see . . ."

Later, before he dressed for their evening among the ton, Jack sat at the desk in the club's library and composed a note to his aunt, Lady Davenport, requesting she share its contents with Lady Cowper.

He expended considerable effort on the wording; with such ladies, a hint was more intriguing than a statement. Nevertheless, when he read the completed letter through, the nature of his request shone clearly; he wanted them to assist Lady Clarice Altwood to return to the ton at the level to which her birth entitled her.

He alluded to the reasons behind her need to return, a serious but unfounded threat to a near relative and to assist her brothers. No need to be more specific; the bare phrases would be enough to ensure his aunts, powerful *grandes dames* that they were, would be agog to learn of Clarice's needs.

Of his reasons for helping her, he said not a word.

Their imaginations would run amok. If they granted him and Clarice an interview the next morning, as he requested, he fully expected both ladies to be bright-eyed and nearly bouncing with curiosity.

Smiling, he signed his name, then recalled, and added a postscript, mentioning that if they knew of any lady they would trust to help influence matters in the political sphere, he'd be grateful for an introduction.

Sanding the letter, then sealing it, he grinned. He'd wager any amount that when he and Clarice met with his aunts, Lady Osbaldestone would be there, too.

Chapter 15

By Jack's side, Clarice entered the Fortescues' front hall and joined the line of guests slowly inching up the main staircase. Had it been left to her, she would have chosen a different venue for her reappearance in the ton. The Fortescues had two daughters to establish; their ball would therefore be the usual crush beloved of tonnish society during the Season.

Glancing around at the other guests thronging the stairs, she murmured, "Not much chance of accomplishing much in James's defence here." For that, she would have chosen one of the more select gatherings of the powerful elite.

Jack shrugged, his hand lightly stroking hers where it rested on his sleeve. "We'll be able to learn from your brothers if there are any rumors circulating yet. Until we know that, there's not much you can do."

She grimaced, acknowledging that truth, wishing it were otherwise. Her nature was to forge ahead, to get things done, but in defending James, they did indeed have to tread carefully. "I sent notes to my aunts, my father's two sisters and my mother's sister, and to my maternal uncle, informing them that I was in London and would be going about among the ton at Alton's request, primarily to ensure that the unfortunate allegations against James are not made unnecessarily sensational."

Jack's lips curved in an appreciative smile. "I take it your aunts and uncle are not fans of the 'unnecessarily sensational'?"

"Not when it's *their* families involved." Clarice noted the many swift glances thrown their way. Leaning closer to Jack, she lowered her voice. "At least we're attracting a satisfactory degree of notice."

"Hardly surprising given that gown."

The crisp note in his voice had her blinking up at him, meeting his eyes. "It's the latest style."

The line of his lips grew more grim than appreciative. "For a lady of your age, status, wealth, and figure, no doubt. Unfortunately, such a gown merely serves to emphasize how few ladies of your age, status, wealth, and figure there are among the ton."

She stared at him; he sounded so disgruntled she didn't know whether to laugh or frown. "Don't you like it?" She'd opted for the forest green satin; the very dark green was a dramatic hue few ladies could carry off well. With its beaded heart-shaped neckline and the elegant fall of its sheening skirts, the gown was perfect for drawing the eye and fixing attention. Time enough, once the ton had realized she was indeed back, to shock them with the plum silk.

Jack held her eyes, then let his gaze lower; briefly, he scanned, then again met her gaze. "I like the gown, as you're well aware. What I'm not enamored of is who else might find it . . . overly alluring."

She nearly laughed; certainly she smiled, rather thrilled if truth be known. That he approved of the gown had been evident the instant he'd set eyes on her in her suite that evening, but she'd never before had any gentleman intimate that he was jealous of the attention—other male attention—she drew. It was a rather heady feeling. Lightly squeezing the steely muscles beneath her fingers, she glanced away.

One more step upward and Jack swept her forward to greet their host and hostess.

Lady Fortescue's eyes widened with delight and avid curiosity. "Lady Clarice." She touched fingers. "How lovely to see you back among the ton. I was quite bowled over when your brother told me the news."

Clarice merely smiled and made no reply.

Extending her hand, Lady Fortescue beamed at Jack. "And Lord Warnefleet! This is a *double* pleasure. I'd heard you'd retired to the country, my lord."

Jack smiled charmingly. "I've returned to escort Lady Clarice about town."

Clarice suppressed the urge to raise her brows haughtily at him. When, intrigued, Lady Fortescue turned to her, she gestured lightly. "We're neighbors in the country."

"Ah . . ." Her ladyship wasn't sure what to make of that.

With no intention of helping her out, Clarice turned to greet Lord Fortescue, as did Jack, then they moved briskly on into the ballroom.

"My brothers should be here somewhere." They were both tall; both scanned the room.

Without luck, but as she turned back to Jack, Clarice saw any number of interested faces; surveying Jack, still searching the room, it wasn't hard to see why. She might be supremely elegant, but he was her equal; where she was regal and gracious, he was charming. Physically, they were well matched, both imposing, long-legged and graceful; they made a strikingly handsome couple.

It was clear many viewing them thought so; there was a much-struck quality in the glances thrown their way. Few had recognized her; she hadn't appeared in these circles for seven years. But the whispered questions had already started. By tomorrow, all London would know that Lady Clarice Altwood was back.

"Come. Let's stroll." Jack settled her hand on his sleeve and turned down the long room.

Clarice kept pace beside him, her innate hauteur cloaking her, making her appear as minor royalty. Which, Jack reflected, was not far from the mark. Some of the older ladies they passed recognized her and opened their eyes wide at them, but when Clarice, calm and serene, inclined her head to them, they returned the gesture readily enough.

Jack sensed a slight easing in the fine tension thrumming through her.

Then she tightened her grip on his sleeve and nodded toward a set of windows. "There they are—Alton and Roger."

They joined them; both brothers perked up as they did.

"What did you learn at the clubs?" Clarice asked.

"Not a great deal," Roger replied.

"It seems," Alton said, "as if quite a few have heard whispers, but they're puzzled by them, and are playing cautious until they learn more."

"Good." Clarice's lips firmed in cynical satisfaction. "Our sainted name is buying us a little time, at least." She glanced at Jack.

He nodded. "Time enough for us to devise suitable countermeasures." He met Alton's gaze. "I seriously doubt that whoever is behind this will allow the whispers to fade and die. Their plan calls for as much sensation as they can generate, but exonerating James will nullify that."

Roger glanced at Clarice. "Now you're here, if you can think of any way to help me with Alice, I'll be your slave for life." His tone sounded hopeless.

Clarice raised her brows. "Very well. Jack can be my witness. Now!" Turning, she surveyed the crowd. "Where is she?"

Roger pointed to a young lady standing beside a chaise on which a bejeweled matron sat conversing with two others. The young lady was steadfastly looking the other way. Although two gentlemen hovered, neither seemed to be holding Alice Combertville's attention.

Clarice grinned, eyes narrowing, the gesture intent. "This should be easy." It was obvious to Clarice that Alice's attention—her senses, her focus—were firmly fixed on their group, on Roger. "Wait here."

She left them and smoothly circled the chaise. With Alice so busy looking the other way, it was easy to approach her, to come up beside her with a smile. "Miss Combertville?"

Alice started, and turned to her. She frowned, puzzled; she had no idea who Clarice was.

Likewise intrigued, the two gentlemen drew closer; Clarice turned to them and smiled graciously. She was sure neither recognized her, equally sure from the looks in their eyes that she could, if she wished, enslave them.

"Harry Throgmorton, fair lady." Harry took the hand she extended and bowed with extravagant flair.

"Miles Dawlish, ma'am." Mr. Dawlish, not to be outdone, was studiously correct.

Clarice hid a smile; they were far too young for her. Too inexperienced, too lightweight to be thinking what they were. "Gentlemen, if you don't mind, I would like a private word with Miss Combertville."

She'd given them no name; she gave them no explanation. Put on the spot, effectively dismissed, although clearly disappointed, they both summoned smiles, murmured "Of course," and reluctantly moved away.

Turning to Alice, Clarice smiled. "I'm Lady Clarice Altwood, Roger's sister."

Alice blinked; her frown deepened. "His half sister . . . ?" She scanned Clarice's features. "No."

Clarice let her smile turn grim. "No, indeed. Moira isn't my mother. However, there's no reason you should recognize me. I haven't been out in the ton for many years. I'm presently in town on business, and in light of Roger's interest in you, I thought to make your acquaintance."

With lustrous brown hair, and brown eyes that should have been bright but instead looked dull and weary, Alice stared up into Clarice's face. She looked as lost in hopelessness as Roger. "I . . . Roger . . ."

Clarice held up a hand. "Just listen, if you would, and let's see if I have this straight. Roger told you of the youthful misdemeanors Moira thought to hold over his head to prevent him from offering for your hand. Is that correct?"

Alice's lips firmed. She nodded.

"Roger thought you understood, that you were as determined to go forward as he to formalize your engagement. Then, however—do correct me if I'm wrong—you spoke to Moira, to upbraid her over her attempt to blackmail Roger into dancing to her tune."

Alice's face fell. She looked faintly ill, but she didn't contradict Clarice; she simply stood there, her large eyes fixed on Clarice's face.

Clarice felt her features harden, fought not to sound too harsh when she said, "My dear Alice, I think you'd better tell me what Moira said to you—what else she told you about Roger—because I'm prefectly certain whatever it was, she lied to you."

Hope welled in Alice; it showed in her eyes, but she didn't know whether to trust in it or not. She searched Clarice's face with painful intensity, then she glanced at her mother, reached for Clarice's hand, and tugged her back a few steps from the chaise.

Alice retained Clarice's hand, pressing her fingers. "You said you haven't been in London for years. If so, how can you truly know Roger, know him well?"

Clarice smiled reassuringly. "Part of the reason I no longer grace the ton is because I grew up closer to my brothers than was probably wise. Until the age of sixteen, I spent every hour I could with them. I do know all three of them very well indeed."

She let her memories and her fondness for her brothers show in her eyes.

Alice saw, read the truth. She hesitated, once more searching Clarice's eyes, then she drew a huge breath, and let it out in a strangled whisper. "Moira said he preferred boys."

"What?" Clarice only just managed to mute her exclama-

tion. She turned her back on the room and pressed Alice's hand. "Sorry. I . . ." Stunned, she shook her head, then set her jaw, and met Alice's wide, almost pleading eyes. "Moira made that up from whole cloth. There is absolutely no truth in it. Well—" Dragging in a breath, she turned and with a gesture directed Alice to look at Roger, standing across the room with Alton and Jack.

"Roger has been in purgatory thinking he'd lost you, struggling to win you back, not for weeks, but *months*. That, Alice, is not the behavior of a man who in reality prefers boys."

Even saying the words, she felt ill. How *dare* Moira invent such a thing?

Alice looked up at her, her expression clearing, transforming as belief strengthened and happiness beckoned. Clarice herself felt torn. Should she tell her brothers what poison Moira had spread, or would it be better to keep silent?

Alice shook her hand to regain her attention. "I . . . feel so happy"—she swallowed—"almost. I love Roger so, and I've been so miserable, but . . . how can I face him now without telling him what I believed?"

Releasing Alice, Clarice lifted her chin. "I'll tell him. I'll explain how you felt, and make sure he understands . . . it's not something a lady can ask a gentleman about, after all."

She met Alice's eyes, saw incipient joy flaring like a beacon in the brown. "I'll speak with him now, then send him to you. After that . . . his heart truly is in your hands. *Don't* disappoint me."

Alice started to smile, blinking back tears. "Oh, I won't, Lady Clarice. I promise I'll always love him."

"Just Clarice if we're to be sisters-in-law." Looking at Roger, Clarice patted Alice's hand, then she looked one last time at Alice, smiled and turned to go. "Oh!" She turned back, met Alice's eyes. "One last thing. Be especially careful around Moira. She won't take this well. You'd be well-advised, once Roger has formally offered for you and been accepted, and that better be done as soon as possible, to take your parents into your confidence over the tricks Moira's played. Moira is not to be trusted, not in any way."

Alice's eyes narrowed, her lips firmed. "Once Roger marries me, I'll keep Moira away."

There was steel beneath Alice's soft brown, distinctly feminine exterior. Entirely satisfied with Roger's choice, Clarice swept back across the ballroom to inform him the reins of his future were once again in his hands.

Telling Alton and Roger about Moira's lie wasn't the easiest thing she'd ever done, but she did it without a blink, then, as she'd expected, spent the next ten minutes damping down her brothers' understandable wrath.

"We do *not* want Moira to know you're retaking control of your lives, not until *after* the reins are firmly in your grasps." She eyed Alton and Roger sternly. "There's no benefit to us in ranting at her over this, unconscionable though it is. Now!" She faced Roger. "I've done my part. What comes next is up to you. If you have any nous at all, you'll reassure poor Alice that you quite understand how it was, and then together you can decry all Moira's works and, as soon as possible, grab your chance and offer for Alice's hand. Once you've been accepted, explain about Moira. *Don't* try to protect her. If you do, she'll just use the opportunity to scupper your happiness again. Just hold off any formal announcement until we have Nigel and Alton settled, too."

Slightly dazed, Roger nodded. His gaze drifted across the room to where Alice stood watching, nervously waiting.

Clarice made an exasperated humming sound, grabbed Roger by the shoulders, turned him to face Alice, and gave him a shove. "Go."

With hope in his eyes, Roger went.

Clarice blew out a breath, then turned to Alton. "Now, where next? The Hendersons'?"

They separated, Alton going ahead to the last ball on their list, at Lady Hartford's, there to speak with his Sarah.

Clarice and Jack would meet him there after they'd waltzed through the Hendersons' ballroom and met Nigel and his Emily.

Nigel was heartened to hear of Clarice's success in clearing Roger's path. Greatly encouraged, he introduced them to Emily, who proved to be a sweet-tempered young lady but no meek miss. She searched Clarice's face in rather studious fashion, then shook hands, and murmured, "I always thought the snide remarks your half sisters made couldn't possibly be true."

The smile that went with that statement drew an answering response from Clarice. Despite the difference in age and experience, they found common ground in discussing Nigel and his manifold shortcomings.

"Here!" he protested. "I thought you were supposed to help me win Em's hand, not tell her all my weaknesses."

Clarice rolled her eyes. "I'm quite sure Emily knows of them already. We're merely passing the time."

Jack smothered a laugh at the look on Nigel's face.

But Alton's assessment proved true; Nigel's case was the least urgent. After bestowing her clear approval, Clarice and he took their leave. He steered her up the long ballroom, noting, as she did, the interest they provoked, the quick looks, the questions whispered after they'd passed.

Music rose from the dais at the end of the room, the lilting strains of a waltz. Halting, he caught Clarice's eyes. "We're here supposedly to enjoy the ball. Shouldn't we dance?"

He raised a brow and watched her slowly raise one in return as she considered just what he was suggesting, that their appearance at three balls in a row with absolutely no attempt to enjoy the entertainment offered would assuredly raise speculation as to their purpose and potentially focus interest on whom they had met, whom they'd been speaking with.

Clarice smiled. "Yes. Let's." As he stepped onto the dance floor and swept her into his arms, she murmured, "I warn you it's been years since I last waltzed."

"Just relax." He stroked his fingers along her spine as his

hand came to rest on her back. "I believe you'll find it's not something you forget."

He drew her to him, and revolved, immediately reminded how well matched they were, how delightful it was that she was so tall, that her legs were so very long. With her in his arms, the waltz took on another dimension, one of deeper, more specific pleasure.

Clarice felt it, knew it, let her mind drink in the sensations of being held so masterfully, captive to a strength far greater than her own, surrounded by it, by him, yet not threatened.

She looked into his face as they whirled, the rest of the dancers dissolving about them, studied his clean-cut, almost austere features, and wondered why. Why, with him, it was so different.

Never before had she liked being held, not in the sense of being controlled, of being confined, of a strength that could accomplish that. His strength, the warm steel she could sense enveloping her, could, if he wished, immobilize her, trap her, restrict her, yet nowhere in her was there even the slightest fear that he, it, ever would.

They were lovers, and if she didn't feel threatened when he held her beneath him, or before him, then no fear was likely to surface here. Instead, this, the dance, the exhilarating precession of the waltz, became another element of their loving, another landscape in which they could explore their physical and sensual connection.

A connection carried through the heat of his hand as it rested, heavy, on her back. In the strength in the fingers that held hers, that powered their sweeping turns, in the effortless control that guided them unerringly through the swirling throng. Their thighs brushed, forest green satin softly swooshing as her skirts caressed, then fell back. She felt alive in his arms as she never had before, more conscious of her body, of her breasts lightly brushing his coat, of the heady promise in the muscled body so close to hers, of the beckoning heat in his eyes.

A heat that welled and rose through them both.

The music faded, then died. Together with the other dancers, they swirled to a halt. She didn't need to speak, simply smiled into his eyes, let her eyes acknowledge their passion.

She saw his response etched in gold and green, then his lashes lowered as he raised her hand to his lips and kissed.

Then his lids rose; their eyes met. The moment held, stretched.

To them both, for that instant, they were the only people in the room.

Then reality returned on a wash of sound. She let her smile deepen as he changed his hold on her fingers and set her hand on his sleeve. "I think that's the first waltz I've ever truly *waltzed.*"

He didn't say anything, merely smiled, satisfied.

They resumed their progress to the door—and saw Moira, mouth open in stunned amazement, standing with two younger ladies by the side of the room, all staring, dumb-founded, at them.

Distantly, supremely haughtily, Clarice inclined her head without breaking her stride. Jack briefly studied the three ladies, then followed her lead. Once they'd merged with the still-considerable crowd, he murmured, "Who were the other two?"

"My half sisters. The darker-haired one is Hilda, the other Mildred."

"Clearly they hadn't expected to see you in such surrounds."

"No." They gained the stairs and started down. "Given she intercepted my letters to Alton, Moira must know I've been coming up to London every year, but I've never before ventured back into the ballrooms."

"Do you think she'll guess why you've broken with habit tonight?"

"Possibly, but possibly not. She and her daughters are avidly devoted to all the gadding about, the balls, dinners, and parties, especially during the Season. It may not immediately occur to them that my return to the ballrooms isn't simply due to social starvation."

"She obviously hadn't seen you until just now, so she didn't see you with Nigel and Emily."

"Or earlier at the Fortescues'." Clarice nodded. "Good. Let's get on to Lady Hartford's."

They did. Like Lady Fortescue, Lady Hartford was thrilled to greet Clarice. Not having any daughter to establish, she hadn't previously met Jack, but smiled and welcomed him effusively. "Your aunt Cowper was here earlier, but I believe she's gone on. She mentioned she was exceedingly pleased that you'd returned to town."

Jack used his charming, completely noncommittal smile to escape. Leading Clarice into the crowded ballroom, he murmured, "I sent a note to my aunt Davenport—she'll have passed the message on to Aunt Emily. I requested a meeting tomorrow morning, if possible. No doubt there'll be a note waiting at the club when I get back."

Clarice caught his eye with a speaking glance. "Just as well Amelia Hartford thought to mention Lady Cowper."

Unrepentant, Jack shrugged. "I would probably have remembered to tell you, but you'd have coped, regardless."

Clarice humphed and gave her attention to the massed throng. Lady Hartford's ballroom was smaller than the norm, yet if anything, there were more guests than the usual crammed within its walls. "We're unlikely to achieve much here." She leaned close as Jack steered her protectively through the crush. "Private conversation will be impossible."

Reaching the center of the ballroom, they paused to search for Alton.

Jack bent his head, and murmured, "By the windows. They just came in."

Clarice turned and looked. Alton was just shutting a door leading out onto the terrace. Beside him, eyes only for him, stood a young lady, blond, well coiffed and gowned, graceful and slender.

Because she was watching, Clarice saw their expressions in the instant before they turned to the crowd, in that moment before they set aside the topic they'd been discussing.

The sight made her catch her breath in empathy. Was love always so painful?

"Come on." Gripping Jack's sleeve, she tugged him in Alton's direction.

Jack caught her hand, linked her arm with his, and by dint of his broad shoulders and grim determination, forged a path through the milling guests.

Sarah was at first trepidatious over meeting Alton's powerful sister, but she lost all reticence when Clarice mentioned Moira. Color returned to Sarah's cheeks and sparks lit her fine blue eyes. Unfortunately, with too many eager ears far too close, they had to converse using subtle references; openly discussing the matter presently exercising them was simply not possible.

Clarice took Sarah's hand and squeezed it meaningfully. "We'll meet again soon, in more congenial surrounds. Meanwhile, if I can—" Clarice stopped, studying a lady she'd glimpsed between two gentlemen's shoulders. "That's Claire, isn't it? Over there?"

Sarah couldn't see, but Alton looked over the heads and nodded. "Yes."

Clarice glanced at Jack. "Stay here—all of you. I want to speak with Claire alone." She grimaced as she surveyed the crowd. "If I can manage it."

She tacked through the crowd, conscious that both Jack and Alton watched her. It was only fifteen feet to where Claire stood chatting to some gentleman; it took a full ten minutes to cover the distance. Emerging through the crowd opposite Claire, Clarice caught her eye and held it. Claire blinked, recognizing her, paused, then, realizing why Clarice was standing back, she smiled at the gentleman and quickly brought their exchange to an end.

The gentleman moved on. Claire came to Clarice.

"Clarice." They exchanged nods. Claire cast a glance at

the shoulders all around them. "This is not a suitable venue in which to discuss the topic I surmise you wish to talk about."

Clarice met her eyes. "Indeed. What about the withdrawing room?"

Claire hestitated, then said, "There's a small parlor I know of. We could try there."

Clarice waved. "Lead on."

They slipped from the ballroom. Somewhat to both their surprise, the parlor was empty. "Lucky." Claire sank into one armchair. She waited while Clarice sat in the other, then said, "I take it you wish to speak of Alton's wish to marry Sarah. It seems an eminently suitable match to me. I'll certainly tell Conniston so when he asks."

Clarice held Claire's gaze and swiftly considered how much to reveal. Claire was a few years older than she, more Alton's age, yet years ago they'd been contemporaries of sorts. Not friends, perhaps even, in the hothouse of tonnish matchmaking they'd been rivals, yet they'd had much in common; Claire had been a viscountess's well-dowered daughter, beautiful enough to attract the attention of many, sensual and clearheaded enough to know her own mind. To make her own decisions.

Sitting back in the armchair, Clarice nodded. "While I'm happy to know you'll support the match—and yes, while I've barely had time to make Sarah's acquaintance, I agree it's an excellent match on all sides—I'm actually here to discuss Moira." When Claire's brows flew up, Clarice smiled grimly. "Moira and her blackmailing schemes."

Briefly, she outlined Moira's threat.

Claire's features hardened. "The bitch."

Clarice nodded. "Indeed. The reason I thought to speak with you is that you're in the best position to assess how this situation might play out." She studied Claire's face. "How will Conniston react? Are you under threat, too?"

Frowning, Claire shook her head. "I'm really very fond of Sarah—not as a daughter, of course, more like a younger sister." She met Clarice's eyes. "Conniston and I have an agreement, have had from the first. I always tell him who my lovers are. He doesn't care, but it does make for less awkwardness all around. He knows that Alton and I . . . but that was nearly ten years ago!"

"So Conniston won't mind?"

"Not about Alton *per se*, but he won't stand for what Moira's proposing. Well, what gentleman would?"

Clarice grimaced. "So we have to shut Moira up."

"Can you?"

Clarice wrinkled her nose. "Yes. But it's reminiscent of descending to her level, not something I'm keen to do."

Claire studied her. Clarice would have said that of all the ladies in the ton, Claire understood her the best.

Eventually, Claire nodded. "A word of advice then, if you'll take it, from one who has remained within the ton while you escaped it." She met Clarice's eyes. "Ladies like us, we're not the sort to let the river of life toss us where it will. We make our decisions and steer our own courses. You and I, we chose different tacks, but choose them we did. We made our own beds, and, once done, we have to lie in them. In this case, that means that whatever you need to do to stop Moira, you will indeed do, because that's the sort of lady you are. However, while dealing with Moira and managing the outcome, don't forget that you haven't yet finished your bed."

Clarice didn't follow. She frowned, openly inviting elucidation.

Claire smiled lightly and rose to her feet. "Years ago, I chose to turn my back on love and accept Conniston's marriage of convenience. For me, that was the right choice, and I don't regret it in the least. You, on the other hand, chose to turn your back on society and leave the door open for what might come . . . you haven't yet chosen finally, haven't yet completed your bed."

Frowning more deeply, Clarice rose, too. "You're saying I still have . . . but no. In that respect, I made all my decisions long ago."

Mildly shaking her head, Claire turned to the door. "No, you didn't. You made the first part of a *two*-part decision. Now you're back in the ton, trust me, you won't be allowed to let that second decision remain unresolved, as you patently have for all these years."

Hand on the doorknob, Claire looked at Clarice, and grinned. "You know, I'm quite looking forward to seeing what your bed looks like when you finally tuck in the last sheet."

Clarice made a disbelieving, dismissive sound, and followed Claire out of the room.

Clarice found Jack and the other two waiting where she'd left them; after confirming that Claire was on their side, she warned them that they had to tread warily. Until they decided how to spike Moira's guns, then needed to lie low. In pursuit of that aim, Clarice and Jack left.

"Well!" She blew out a breath and settled back against the carriage seat. "I must say, I'm amazed that Alton, Roger, and Nigel have all chosen so wisely. Sarah, Alice, and Emily all seem lovely but capable, with the requisite backbone to manage in our circles."

Through the shadows intermittently lit by the streetlights outside, Jack studied her face, read her satisfaction. "The males of your family seem to have a penchant for choosing strong women. Your father married your mother, after all."

Clarice looked struck, then grimanced. "Even Moira. One can hardly describe her as weak."

Jack nodded, his face hardening. "Unprincipled, but not weak."

They said little else as they clattered through the streets. When the carriage, Alton's town carriage borrowed for the evening, halted, Jack descended, handed Clarice down, and let the carriage go on without him. He escorted Clarice into Benedict's foyer, kissed her hand, caught her eye, then bowed and left her.

Fifteen minutes later, after dismissing the maid who'd

been waiting for her, Clarice opened the door of her suite to him. He wasn't surprised when, without a word, she led him to the bedroom. But when she turned to him, and paused, studying his face, he reached for her, drew her to him, and kissed her.

Ravenously. Making no secret of his need for her.

She responded, ardent and willful, demanding and commanding in her own right. Yet tonight he wasn't in any mood to let her distract and deflect him; she was still wearing her green satin gown.

In the instant he'd seen it on her, he'd been visited by a fiery fantasy to strip it from her, inch by slow inch. To reveal each creamy curve, each ivory limb, ultimately to let it fall away, leaving her clad only in the shimmering gauze of her chemise.

When, at length, the green gown did indeed swoosh to the floor, to his infinite satisfaction, she was heated and urgent. Wrapping her arms about his neck, she pressed herself to him in flagrant entreaty, meeting his lips, his tongue with a bold challenge of her own, taunting and daring, wanting him to take her.

Lips locked with hers, he shrugged out of his coat and waistcoat, let them fall unheeded to the floor, then he lifted her. To his surprise, she raised her long legs and wound them about his hips.

Temptation didn't whisper, it roared.

Far too loudly to ignore. His arms circling her hips, holding her to him, he walked the few paces to the bed; without breaking from the kiss, without releasing her, he clambered onto the silk coverlet on his knees. Juggling her, he reached beneath her and opened the placket of his trousers, releasing his already aching erection; guiding the head immediately to the slick, swollen flesh of her entrance, he pressed in.

Then he shifted his hold to her hips, and drew her down. Sank slowly down to sit on his ankles as he did, pulling her down over him, impaling her fully upon him, feeling her squirm, adjust, then gasp as he thrust the last inch and filled her completely.

Eyes closed, she drew back from the kiss, panting, breasts rising and falling dramatically before his face. He grinned, focused and intent; with one hand, he trapped the fine fabric of her chemise and drew it up, over her head. She had to let go of his shoulders to untangle her arms, to draw them free and let the chemise fall. While she did, he bent his head to her breast, with his mouth traced a path to one tightly furled nipple, then drew it deep.

Her gasp filled the room.

She straddled him, naked but for her silk stockings and garters, while he remained fully clothed; catching her breath in something close to desperation, she started to ride him. To rise up, then sink down, easing her scalding sheath about his rigid length, tightening, then releasing, then rolling her hips down and across his, experimenting, searching, it seemed, for the fastest way to drive him beyond all control.

At first, he indulged her, indulged his curiosity over what she might do, indulged his taste for her luscious breasts. Part of his mind kept track of their escalating hunger, their burgeoning need; when the time was right, he rose to his knees and tipped her back, caught and straightened her long legs, stripped off her stockings and garters, then wound her bare legs about his waist.

Instinctively, she locked her ankles in the small of his back, then realized. He caught a glimpse of dark fire beneath her lashes as the vulnerability—the helplessness—of her position struck home. Before she could react and shift, he caught her hips fully to his again, lifting her and working her over him, about him.

She tried to move with him, against him, to direct, to press, only to discover that without the leverage of her legs, she could do nothing but accept every stroke he pressed on her, every sliding penetration of his body deep into hers. Lids falling on a strangled gasp, she surrendered, letting her shoulders fall back on the bed, breasts heaving as she struggled to catch her breath, struggled to retain some degree of control, but he'd already stripped the reins away.

He moved her on him, and she writhed; he watched and drove her on. Ultimately, he lowered her hips to the bed, bracing over her to thrust deep into the scalding heat of her body, totally open to him, his to take.

To fill, to complete.

Clarice felt the wave of completion start from her toes, swelling as it rose through her, sweeping all she was, her mind, her wits, her senses up, ever upward into a shattering climax. He joined her bare seconds later; together they clung, burned as the glory raged and took them, then at the last, faded, leaving them slumped, exhausted, wrung out and boneless, tossed like rag dolls on the wide expanse of her bed.

Sometime later, she recovered enough to smile, to feel her lips curve at the now-familiar glow of aftermath washing through her. Delicious. So desirable.

Fingers riffling through his hair, she lay beneath him, mentally chuckling for no real reason as her naked body cooled beneath the hard warmth of his. He was still clothed, which seemed rather ridiculous.

Apparently he agreed. With a grunt, he lifted from her, then sat up, and stripped off his clothes, apparently no more able to walk than she. Eventually naked, he rose, staggered the few steps to her dressing table, and doused the lamp. Returning to kneel beside her, he lifted her to the pillows, wrestled the covers from beneath them both, then drew them up, settling her against him in the billows of her bed.

He relaxed; she felt all tension leave his muscles, then his breathing deepened, and he slept.

Still boneless in the grip of sated languor, she smiled, feeling her lips curve against the skin of his upper chest.

She loved this, loved him, loved the way they shared, the way he allowed her to lead, then took the reins himself, passing them back and forth . . .

She heard her words in her head. She blinked, stopped.

Tried to tell herself she hadn't actually meant that word in quite that way . . . knew in her heart, to her soul, that she was lying.

Carefully, without disturbing him, she eased back in the arm that even now held her close, and rolled onto her back. Staring up at the shadowed ceiling, she frowned. Tried to focus her mind, to work it out, to see where the path she'd so blithely followed until now truly led.

It seemed to have taken an unexpected turn . . . or was it simply that she'd gone a trifle further in her journey into this until-him-forbidden landscape than she'd anticipated? She'd certainly ventured into unforeseen terrain.

Unbidden, Claire's words floated through her mind, Claire's conviction that, contrary to her expectations, she hadn't finalized the details of her life.

She'd thought she had, that accepting banishment to the country had defined her entire future, that there would be no more new possibilities, no different roads opening up before her feet.

But . . .

She glanced at the man lying sleeping beside her, felt his body hard against the length of hers.

Felt a tug deep in her heart, followed by a painful wrench at the thought that this—this unexpected comfort and peace—might not continue to be hers.

She might not yet be able to define where her life was headed, but one point was crystal clear.

Things *had* changed.

She had changed.

Chapter 16

Having again returned to the Bastion Club before dawn, Jack set out after breakfast, feeling in excellent health. Hailing a hackney, he hied himself to Brook Street, Benedict's, and Boadicea.

He found her in her suite, entertaining her brothers over the breakfast cups. He smiled genially at them all. Alton eyed his transparent content with suspicion. Clarice poured him a cup of coffee and handed it to him with a warning glance.

"We were about to discuss how best to counteract any rumor, to ensure it's dismissed out of hand, or at least denied any chance to spread and grow." Clarice paused to sip as Jack drew up a chair beside her. "I think"—she glanced at Jack—"that raising the matter *ourselves*, before any whispers can gain hold, and stating, flatly, that such an outrageous notion is, quite obviously, untrue, might be our best approach. What do you think?"

He considered, then nodded. Across the breakfast table, he met Alton's eyes. "In most instances, I'd consider such a tack unwise, but in your case, you have the name, the status. It seems pointless not to use it."

"Precisely." Clarice nodded decisively. "Especially as we know James *is* perfectly innocent. There's no risk whatever in the family's supporting him."

"And the fact that we are openly rallying behind him will give even the most inveterate gossipmongers pause," Alton said.

"That certainly worked with Lady Grimwade and Mrs. Raleigh." Clarice set down her cup. "I saw them last night, and if their expressions were anything to judge by, they were still being extremely cautious."

"Actually"—Nigel pushed aside his empty plate—"I rather think old James will be safe enough, at least for the next week or so." He glanced at Alton. "From what I saw and heard last night, the ton have found another Altwood to speculate about."

"Alton?" Clarice frowned.

"No." Nigel looked at her. "You."

"*Me?*" Clarice sat up. "Why on earth . . ." Her words trailed away, but her puzzled frown remained. She studied Nigel. "What are they saying?"

"Not saying—speculating. Everyone's wondering why you're back, and regardless, who will, as many see it, pick up the gauntlet."

"*What* gauntlet?" Clarice asked, her tone tending dire.

"The one you threw down last night," Nigel replied. "When you waltzed with Warnefleet here down Mrs. Henderson's ballroom."

When Clarice looked stunned, Nigel snorted. "Good God, you haven't been out of town *that* long. You know what subject's closest to the old biddies' hearts. French spies and traitors will do in a pinch, but give them the prospect of a highborn spinster still handsome and weddable, still eminently well heeled and eligible, and they're not going to bother with treason."

When Clarice continued to stare, apparently struck dumb, Nigel grinned. "At least you've solved the problem of them gossiping about James."

Clarice groaned, shut her eyes, and slumped back in her chair. "I don't believe it!"

But she did. As Nigel had said, her returning to the ton for the first time in seven years, and then waltzing in the arms of a handsome lord, himself a matrimonial target, was behavior guaranteed to capture the ton's fickle interest.

"Never mind." Abruptly she sat up, opening her eyes. She wasn't going to dwell on it. "What's done is done, and as you say, it will help shield James."

"As long," Alton said, "as you continue to feed the gossips."

Clarice looked at him, caught him exchanging a glance she couldn't interpret with Jack beside her. "What do you mean?"

Alton shrugged. "Just that, for James's sake, it would be helpful if you continued to swan around in the evenings, being seen about generally, the usual sort of thing. While they're focusing on you, they won't be wondering about James."

Clarice expressed her deep antipathy to the notion with a disgusted and dismissive humph.

Jack set down his coffee cup, drawing her attention; he caught her eye. "Think of it as achieving the objective you were aiming for, just by a different route. Just because you hadn't planned it doesn't mean it won't work, and as Melton said, keeping the ton focused on you won't require much effort."

Jack wasn't surprised when her gaze turned considering. He kept his lips shut, slanted a sharp glance at Alton to ensure he did the same. Somewhat taken aback by the unvoiced directive, Alton did, and was rewarded when Clarice wagged her head from side to side, weighing the matter, then reluctantly conceded, "All right. But only if there's nothing definite to do in furthering James's defence.

"Incidentally"—she looked at Alton—"before I forget, while I don't imagine Moira will do anything truly drastic, like poison anyone, thinking back over her campaign to control you, I kept wondering why. She's wealthy enough—as you said it's not the money. So what else?"

Roger looked at his brothers, then replied, "We don't know. She's a female. Does there have to be a 'what else'?"

Clarice narrowed her eyes at him. "Yes. There does. And I think I know what, or rather who, it is. Carlton."

Her brothers blinked at her. Jack had no idea who Carlton was.

Alton frowned. "The succession?"

Jack recalled hearing that Moira had borne the youngest of the previous marquess's four sons.

"Not precisely." Clarice sat straighter "It would be amazing by any standard were he to inherit, with the three of you, all hale and whole, before him. *However*, while none of you are married, and there are no children in your nurseries, then . . . well, Carlton does have some claim. He's third in line and is ten years younger than Nigel, after all. If the three of you go to your graves bachelors, then Carlton will inherit, no matter he might be old by that time. So as long as the knowledge that all three of you are about to marry remains secret, the *perception* that Carlton has some chance to eventually succeed to the marquisate continues unchallenged as the commonly held notion."

"So it is money. Moneylenders . . ." Alton broke off, frowning. "No, that won't wash. If he's deep in debt, I would have heard."

Clarice snorted. "I told you it wasn't money—that's not the point. *Weddings* are the point, on all fronts, Carlton's included. While the three of you remain bachelors, Carlton can look reasonably high for a bride, but the instant even one of you marry, Carlton's matrimonial stocks fall. If all three of you wed, Carlton's standing falls to that of a mere younger son with no real prospects. Moira wants her daughter-in-law's family to be as wealthy and influential as possible, so the last thing she wants is for you three to marry—or more specifically for the ton to realize all three of you are about to marry—before she can get Carlton wed."

Her brothers looked shocked. "He's only twenty-one!" Roger protested.

Clarice met his eyes. "Do you think that'll stop Moira?

Especially now she knows you're all on the verge of making offers that, of course, will be accepted?"

"Good God! I never thought I'd be sorry for the little twerp." Nigel looked horrified. "Fancy being leg-shackled at the age of twenty-one."

Clarice, predictably, wasn't impressed. "Never mind Carlton. Unless he's changed mightily, I'd wager he has no intention of offering for any well-bred miss that Moira selects. He just won't tell her until that point is reached. He never was one for unnecessary effort."

"True." Roger frowned at Clarice. "So Moira doesn't really care about *whom* we wed, just that we shouldn't make our intentions public yet?"

"That seems likely, so that gives you time to arrange your affairs. If you make offers all at once, or rather if the announcements all appear in the *Gazette* on the same day, and Moira hears nothing from any other source until then, then all should be well."

Alton caught Roger's eye. "We'll have to be careful what we say, do, or even write inside Melton House. That maid of Moira's is the very devil—she sneaks around all over the place, poking here and there."

"But it should be doable," Nigel said. "We just have to get our affairs in order, make our offers formally and be accepted, then we can trump Moira all at once, and have done with this business."

Clarice nodded. "Indeed. That's exactly what you should do, and meanwhile I'll do my best to distract the ton from James. Regardless of all that, however, we still need to accomplish what I came to London to do—exonerate James of these nonsensical charges."

There was a note in her voice that made her brothers sit up. "Yes, of course," Alton said. "What do you want us to do?"

Clarice looked at Jack; her brothers followed her lead.

He'd come prepared. "There are three specific meetings at which we want to prove James was not present." Drawing a sheet of paper from his pocket, he handed it to Alton. "If you can check around the family and all James's friends, his clubs, anywhere he might have been, and see if anyone remembers seeing him on those dates, at those times, we'll have the first nails to drive into the coffin to bury these allegations."

Alton read the list, then nodded. "Right. We'll get on with this."

"While you do, I'll see what I can devise to free you and Sarah from Moira's web. Just don't do anything more until I tell you." Clarice looked at Roger and Nigel. "Meanwhile, you two reprobates are free to make best use of your persuasive talents and get formal acceptance of your offers for Alice and Emily's hands."

Both Roger and Nigel looked delighted.

"But only after you help Alton with gathering information for James's defence."

With a rumble of reassurances, the brothers rose, kissed Clarice's cheek, glanced askance at Jack when she wasn't looking, but left without challenging his presence.

He felt for them, but . . .

When Clarice closed the door behind them and turned back to him, he had a slim notelet in his hand. He waved it. "Lady Davenport and Lady Cowper request our presence at Davenport House."

She halted, wide-eyed. "When?" She glanced at the clock on the mantelpiece.

"Half an hour."

"*Arrghh*!" She glared at him. "Why is it that gentlemen never understand how long it takes to get dressed?"

Given she swung on her heel and strode into the bedroom, he surmised the question was rhetorical. He followed more slowly; leaning one shoulder against the doorjamb, he watched her strip off the morning gown she'd been wearing, then hunt through a wardrobe that appeared remarkably well stocked. Pulling out a bronze-and-ivory-striped silk confection, she donned it, then imperiously presented her back to him and demanded he do up her laces.

Lips twitching, he complied, then watched as she redid her hair.

He'd never before found observing such female primping all that interesting, but watching Clarice . . . every graceful movement, every feminine gesture, fascinated. Almost mesmerized. He watched her brush out her long hair, remembered what it felt like swirling about him in the night . . . meanwhile another, more grounded part of his mind trod a more serious path.

He was increasingly certain he didn't want her going about alone, even during the day in the heart of Mayfair. He hadn't forgotten the incident with the two strange men in Bruton Street, nor the inherent threat of the round-faced man. And now, it seemed, her stepmother had good reason to wish Clarice elsewhere, removed from interfering in her schemes.

Unlike Clarice, he wasn't so ready to excuse Moira from any felonious intent; the harpy he'd seen would have scratched Clarice's eyes out given half a chance. And losing her grip, a grip she'd probably thought secure, over Alton, his brothers, and the marquisate in general, would be galling. Especially if hand in hand with such a loss went a lessening of social standing. That last would definitely occur if Clarice returned permanently to the ton.

She wasn't planning to do so, but Moira didn't know that, and probably wouldn't believe it even if told by Clarice herself. From Moira's perspective, the pleasures of Avening couldn't hope to compete with those of London.

Clarice tied a modish bonnet over her dark hair. Jack straightened. She would scoff at any warning of personal danger, at any request to take greater care. To take a footman or two as escort.

He smiled charmingly as she swept toward him, and offered his arm. No point arguing; he'd escort her himself.

"Lady Clarice, it's a pleasure to welcome you." Tall and imposing, handsome in a severe, well-bred way, Lady Davenport nodded approvingly and touched fingers with Clarice, then her gaze deflected to Jack, standing by Clarice's elbow. "And you, too, Warnefleet. As it's due to Lady Clarice that you're here, I can only be grateful for her influence."

Jack summoned his most charming smile and bestowed it on his aunt.

She humphed and turned to introduce Clarice to the small, round lady by her side. "I believe you'll recall my sister?"

"Indeed." Serenely assured, Clarice smiled and bobbed a curtsy of nicely judged degree. Despite Emily, Lady Cowper's, preeminence among the ton's hostesses, Clarice was her better in terms of birth.

Emily was more overtly expressive than her sister, more openly keen to embrace Clarice and all she promised; Jack read her enthusiasm with ease.

"My dear Lady Clarice, I'm delighted to meet you again." Smiling radiantly, Emily pressed Clarice's hand, then waved to the third *grande dame* gracing the elegant drawing room. "And no doubt you'll remember Lady Osbaldestone, too."

"Ma'am." Clarice nodded, a touch reserved, rather careful, to the impressive and distinctly intimidating older lady who studied her, then Jack, with a sharply assessing black gaze.

Then Lady Osbaldestone's brows rose; her expression eased. She beckoned imperiously. "Come sit by me, gel, so I can see you better." Sinking back onto the chaise, Lady Osbaldestone waited until Lady Davenport and Lady Cowper had resumed their seats, and Clarice had obeyed and sat beside her, before, shooting a saber-sharp glance at Jack, standing with one arm braced on the mantelpiece, she thumped her cane lightly on the polished floor, for all the world as if bringing some meeting to order. "Now, then," she said. "What's this I hear about your cousin James and treason?"

Clarice drew in a breath, glanced briefly at Jack, then proceeded to outline in severely abbreviated form James's, and by extension her family's, difficulties. She avoided any mention of specifics, including how they knew James was innocent, only saying that they were working to prove it and were certain to succeed.

During her recitation, Lady Osbaldestone and Jack's aunts shared a number of meaningful looks, ones that pricked Jack's instincts and left him alert. He and Clarice had agreed that if the three ladies had heard of the as yet insufficiently suppressed rumors, then they would have to appease their curiosities if they wanted their help in dealing with Moira.

Smoothly, Clarice switched from the unjustified threat to the family name to the problems her brothers were facing in their pursuit of matrimony. Again, she didn't explain fully, leaving it to the ladies' imaginations to fill in the details she omitted, such as the substance of Moira's threats. With three such ladies, there was no risk they wouldn't leap to the correct conclusions.

Unsurprisingly, all three ladies were even more interested in that subject; as Clarice told her tale, their eyes glowed with awakened zeal.

"So," Clarice concluded, glancing around at the three older faces, "I'm hoping that I can prevail on you to lend me your aid in assisting my brothers to achieve their ends. I've been absent from the ton for so long, and, given the events surrounding my leaving it, I'm well aware that I'll require such aid to successfully clear my brothers' paths."

Again she glanced around; this time, she met each pair of eyes. "Will you help me?"

The three ladies exchanged glances, an unspoken communication that held an element of excitement. Jack wasn't surprised when, decision wordlessly reached, it was Lady Osbaldestone who delivered it.

"My dear, we're very pleased that you've returned to the ton, regardless of the reason. Of course you will have our help in whatever way seems best, but there's two points we would like clarified. First, we take it that in terms of the charges of treason, that it's not only the Altwoods, but ultimately Whitehall and the government who, should the matter proceed to a trial, would be . . . shall we say 'inconvenienced'?"

When Clarice blinked, and didn't reply, Lady Osbaldestone looked at Jack. "Dalziel, I take it? A holy terror, but he does have his uses."

Jack felt his expression blank. From the other two ladies' calmly inquiring looks, Lady Osbaldestone's words came as no surprise to them. How the devil did they know about Dalziel? And if they knew about him, what else did they know?

Lady Osbaldestone's smile took on a distinctly evil edge. "You didn't seriously imagine we were unaware of such things, did you?"

Jack shifted, rapidly canvassing his options; remaining silent seemed the wisest course.

Lady Osbaldestone's expression grew cynical. "You might be relieved to know that, unlike some of our menfolk who fall prey to convoluted dilemmas over concepts of honor whenever the word 'spy' is uttered, most ladies of our station are only too relieved to know that others—those entrusted with the realm's defence—are not so squeamish."

Her last word carried a distinctly censorious edge.

Jack wasn't sure her reference was as general as it had sounded, that she didn't have some specific dilemma-afflicted male in mind. Regardless, he acknowledged, "Whitehall would, indeed, prefer to see the allegations against James Altwood rebutted in the bishop's court rather than in a public one where details submitted in evidence would be widely desseminated."

Lady Osbaldestone nodded. "Just so." She looked again at Clarice. "Our other question is, with the matter of your brothers, do you intend to fully nullify your stepmother's influence for all time, or do you think simply to help your brothers to the altar, leaving them to manage otherwise on their own?"

Clarice looked into Lady Osbaldestone's black eyes, and

couldn't tell which answer the old ladies wanted, yet it seemed clear her response would determine the degree of help they would give. She needed their help. Without it, returning to the ton and countering Moira's schemes would be exceedingly difficult. But they were matriarchs all, absolute rulers within their homes and families; would they disapprove if she told them the truth?

Lifting her chin, she grasped the nettle. "I can't see any prospect of freeing my brothers without in the main eliminating Moira's influence. Not just over their marriages, but in general, and more permanent, terms." She refocused on Lady Osbaldestone's eyes. "It would be neither realistic nor fair to expect my prospective sisters-in-law to deal with Moira. I have more insight, and a great deal more standing and experience behind me, at least in terms of countering her."

Only when her last word had faded did Lady Osbaldestone smile—with relish. "Excellent! When it comes to that upstart, it must be *you* who puts her in her place—or rather, displaces her from the position she's been abusing for so long."

Glancing at Lady Davenport and Lady Cowper, Clarice found a similarly approving and determined light in their eyes.

Lady Cowper's chin was unusually firm as she nodded. "Indeed, my dear. Therese is quite right. We—not just us but the rest, too, all the hostesses and those of us who guide the ton—have had quite enough of Moira, but it isn't in our power to oust her, not without affecting the entire family. Our dilemma has been quite excoriating for some years—indeed, since shortly after you left. Achieving something in that regard will be a *considerable* relief."

The glint in Lady Cowper's eye, the hard note in her usually soft voice, confirmed that Moira's unrestrained use of power had spread far wider than within the family.

"Indeed." Lady Davenport's expression suggested she could hear the call to battle and was very willing to answer. "We're so glad, my dear Clarice, that you see it as we do, that you understand and appreciate the role your family now needs you to play."

* * *

The rest of their visit was taken up with discussions of how best to throw a spoke, permanently, in Moira's wheel. As Jack had hoped, the three older and eminently wise ladies took Clarice and her quest to their hearts. In controlling the ton's collective mind, they spoke as generals deploying on a battlefield. From Clarice's expression, she was enthralled; from her comments, she was learning quickly.

Despite the success of his plan to gain her the aid she needed, Jack felt a certain disquiet, a faint-yet-pervasive ruffling of his instincts, but of what they were warning him he couldn't say. At the first opportunity, he excused them on the grounds that they were due at Lambeth Palace at noon and whisked Clarice off. Once they left his aunt's house, his instincts settled.

They reached the palace to discover that despite the bishop's brother's intercession, Deacon Humphries was not available to be interviewed.

"At least, not yet," Olsen explained. "He went out this morning before the bishop could speak with him, and won't be back until late this afternoon."

Clarice grimaced. Their meeting with Jack's aunts and Lady Osbaldestone had gone so well, she'd felt buoyed and ready to take on the world, and Humphries, too. Stymied, she glanced at Jack. "Perhaps we should go over the details of the allegations with Deacon Olsen, and explain how we believe they can be disproved?"

Jack looked at Teddy, who'd joined them; she'd be safe with him and Olsen. "Why don't you explain our approach to Deacon Olsen and Teddy, too, if he has the time?"

Bright-eyed, Teddy nodded. "I'd like to hear what's going on."

"Meanwhile," Jack said, "I should check with those working on gathering our proofs. The faster we can assemble all we need, the better."

Clarice blinked, then nodded. "Very well. I take it you'll be at your club if Humphries returns earlier than expected?"

"Yes." Jack caught her eye. "But don't interview him without me."

Clarice smiled and reassured him; he listened cynically, insisted she promise, then bowed over her hand. He took his leave of the others. She watched him stride away, broad shoulders square, then allowed Deacon Olsen and Teddy to escort her to Olsen's study.

Two hours later, Jack slouched into a tavern behind Lambeth Palace. Slumping into a not overly grimy booth, then ordering a mug of porter when the barmaid sauntered up and asked his pleasure, he glanced, apparently vacantly, around, in reality taking swift stock of the other occupants.

They were as down-at-the-heels, as uncouth as he now appeared. In his rough workman's garb, cloth cap to worn boots, he doubted Clarice would recognize him, much less his aunts and Lady Osbaldestone, no matter how aware of such affairs they imagined they were.

While Deverall, Christian, and Tristan pursued witnesses for contradictory accounts of the three supposed meetings, he'd elected to pursue a set of meetings that didn't feature in the allegations yet impinged upon them most powerfully.

Humphries had to have met his ex-courier-cum-informer somewhere—somewhere other than Lambeth Palace. Teddy had learned that the porters had never admitted any visitor for Humphries but had ferried messages delivered to him courtesy of a random selection of street urchins.

Never the same urchin twice, which confirmed that the ex-courier-cum-informer was a man who knew the requisite ropes. The porters saw all urchins as interchangeable; they couldn't identify any of them. The odds of, by luck, stumbling across one of the urchins in question in a district that teemed with them were exceedingly long.

After receiving some of the messages, Humphries had left the palace, always on foot. The meeting place had most likely been near. Jack had reconnoitered, strolling up and down the thoroughfares about the palace. There were no coffeehouses or large inns in that area. Putting himself in the ex-courier's shoes, Jack made a short list of watering holes that met the obvious criteria—not too far from the palace, not busy, not successful, not the place to find rowdy crowds who might remember a clergyman and whom he met.

He'd already been to two other taverns; both had fitted his bill, but neither had held the type of person he sought. The Bishop's Mitre, in which he now sat, was tucked away down a narrow lane off Royal Street, about ten minutes' walk from the palace, most of that through the extensive grounds.

Of the three taverns he'd been in, this held the most promise. The interior was dim and shadow-filled even in early afternoon; the clientele were all but somnolent, evincing no interest in their fellow man. But there were two sets of sharp and watchful eyes—the barmaid, more wide-awake than the norm, and an old crone nursing a mug of ale in the inglenook beside the fireplace.

Both had noted him when he'd entered; the barmaid had accepted him as the workman he appeared to be, but the crone was still watching, eyes alert behind her bedraggled fringe.

Jack assumed that, as with the urchins, the ex-courier would have used different meeting places, but he only needed one clear sighting, one good description.

Rising, he picked up his glass of porter. Taking a long swallow, he walked to the small fireplace in which a fire struggled beneath a wad of peat. He took up a stance as if staring into the faltering flames; after a silent moment, he glanced swiftly at the crone on the bench tucked beside the chimney, and caught the rapid shift of her eyes as she looked away.

He looked back at the flames, took another swallow of porter, then spoke, his voice pitched low so only she could hear. "I'm looking for anyone who can tell me about a man who met and talked with a clergyman here some time in the last few months. I'm prepared to pay handsomely for anyone who can describe this man—not the clergyman but the other."

He waited patiently as a full minute ticked by, then the crone cackled softly. "How's will you know I'm describing your man? I could tell you anythin'. You'd be none the wiser, and I'd have your gold to keep me warm."

Without shifting his head, Jack looked at her, caught the bright gleam of her eyes. "If you can describe the man I want, you'll also be able to describe the clergyman."

The bright eyes widened, then the crone nodded. "A smart one, you are. If that's the way of it then, the clergyman's tall-ish, but not as tall as you. He's got precious little hair left, but what there is is plain brown and stringy. He's a fretful sort, always frowning, not a jolly soul as some of them can be. He's not fat, nor yet scrawny, and his lips pout like a woman's."

Quelling a surge of anticipatory triumph—her description of Humphries was too detailed to be false—Jack grinned encouragingly. "Right enough. Now what of the other?" If she could describe the ex-courier with the same exactitude, she'd be worth every penny he had on him.

The crone screwed up her face; she stared across the room. "Similar height, maybe a touch taller, but heavier build. Barrellike. Looked like a fighter though he was too well dressed fer that. Mind you, he weren't a gentleman, but he weren't no servant, either." She paused, then added, "Not one of those business agents, neither—not the right look fer that at all."

Jack's gut clenched; a chill whispered across his shoulders. "What of his face?"

"Pale, whiter skin than most, pasty, you might say. And round—heavy and round. Eyes round and pale, smallish, broad nose. And he spoke with an accent, not one of ours. Something foreign. I didn't hear enough to say more." The crone looked up at Jack. "That enough fer you?"

Jack nodded. He reached into his pocket, reached past the pennies and found a sovereign. He drew it out, held it out.

The crone's eyes gleamed. She took it carefully, examined it, then looked up at Jack as her hand and the coin disappeared beneath her tattered clothes. "Fer that," she said, eyes narrowing as if she was revising her view of him, "you get a warning, too."

"Warning?"

"Aye. The gent you seek, the other one. He's dangerous. They met here twice. Both times, the clergyman left first. I saw the other's face once the clergyman was out the door. He was planning something, and it weren't good. Dangerous he looked, evil, too. So if you're thinking to find him, have a care."

Jack smiled winningly. Then he doffed his cap, bowed extravagantly, and left the old crone cackling delightedly.

But when he stepped out of the tavern, his smile faded. The crone's description shared too many similarities with Clarice's description of the man who'd run Anthony off the road to doubt that it was, indeed, the same person. Which meant the crone was an excellent judge of character; that man was definitely dangerous.

Luck, he'd often noticed, visited in multiples. Heading for the club, he made for Westminister Bridge, intending to hail one of the hackneys constantly crossing back and forth. Reaching the road to the bridge, he turned and strode on, past a trio of urchins who were taking turns with a streetsweeper's broom.

Jack stopped. Turning back, he ambled up to the urchins. Fishing out three pennies, he started juggling them. When he stopped before the trio, he had their undivided attention.

He glanced at their avid expressions, worded his question carefully. "A man hired urchins to deliver messages around here. He's tallish—almost as tall as me—and he has a round, white face. And he's a foreigner." He infused the word with patent disgust and saw their lips twitch. "These pennies are for any boy who can tell me where they delivered a message from this man."

The boys exchanged glances. Jack suddenly understood. He stopped juggling for a moment, drew out another three pennies, and teamed them with the first three. He juggled again, then looked down at the faces of his audience.

They still looked unconvinced. He stopped and added another three pennies, then they smiled.

He smiled, too. Three responses. Fate was pleased with him.

"The bishop's palace, main gate," one said.

"Same fer me."

"He sent me to the porter's lodge this end, not the front."

Jack looked at all three, then tossed the three sets of three coins to them. They all snagged them out of the air, swift and sure.

"One other thing." No sense leaving any stone unturned. "Can any of you read? Do you know who the message was for?"

Again they exchanged glances. Jack sighed and fished in his pocket, careful to draw out only the pennies. He counted them. "Tuppence each extra if any of you can tell me who the message they took was addressed to."

"Some deacon." One boy tried to grab the coins, but Jack was faster; closing his fist, he raised it high.

"Aw—c'mon, mister."

Jack shook his head. "Try harder. Deacon who?"

The boy screwed up his face, frowned ferociously. His friends egged him on.

"First letter," Jack said.

The boy's eyes popped open. "An aitch—I remember that. And it was longish—an em and a pee and another aitch, a small one."

Jack smiled. "That will do. Hands out."

They promptly presented their palms and he gave each the promised tuppence more. They danced with delight; when he said good-bye and turned away, they sang back and waved him off.

Grinning, Jack reached the bridge, hailed a hackney, and rattled off back to the club.

*   *   *

"So the man who sent messages to Humphries, and the man Humphries met in a tavern more than once, was round-faced, white-skinned, tallish, heavily built, with a foreign accent?" Deverell looked at Jack.

Jack nodded. "And dresses well, but is not a gentleman. More, the same man ran Anthony, James's cousin who was driving to Avening to warn James about the allegations, off the road, and most likely would have silenced him permanently if Clarice hadn't appeared."

The thought chilled him. If the man hadn't decided that silencing Clarice as well wasn't worth the risk . . . what he then would have found on rounding the last bend on his long journey home didn't bear thinking about.

They'd all spent the day in various disguises; returning to the club, they'd used the upstairs rooms to return to their customary gentlemanly state, then gathered in the library to share what they'd thus far learned.

"My inclination," Tristan said, once they'd recounted their news, "is to concentrate on establishing that these meetings never took place. While for each instance, each tavern, we know there are those prepared to swear Altwood met this courier there, we've all also found others equally believeable prepared to take their oaths Altwood never set foot there."

Deverall nodded. "Once we have the contradictory evidence, it'll be easier to shake those who've spoken falsely. I've had a quick look at the three so-called witnesses to the meeting I'm investigating, and all are known as perennially desperate for cash."

"He'll have paid them, no doubt about that." Jack grinned, all teeth. "But where gold can buy lies, more gold can buy the truth."

"True, but I gather there's a reluctance to cross this courier. They'll do it in a flash if they think they've been found out, but having taken his coin, they need the 'excuse' to change their stories."

They grimaced; all understood the workings of the less-than-honest mind. "So," Jack said, "we'll move first to get our own, more believable witnesses."

"Indeed." Christian looked at Jack "Does James Altwood always wear the collar?"

Jack nodded. "He dresses better than your average clergyman—well-cut coats and trousers, good-quality boots—but he always wears the collar."

Deverell smiled in anticipation. "Which is to say that if he ever was in those taverns, he would have made a not-inconsiderable impression."

"And thus would have been remembered." Tristan looked at Jack. "I'd say we're well on the way to getting the evidence not just to challenge but to throw out as mistaken the three incidents central to these allegations. And with that done . . . perhaps it might be wise to explain to this Deacon Humphries on just what shaky grounds his charges now stand?"

Jack nodded. "That would seem the fastest and cleanest way to bring this charade to a quiet close. We've yet to meet Deacon Humphries, but hopefully that pleasure won't be long denied . . ." Jack looked up as Gasthorpe entered. From the uncertain expression on the majordomo's face, Jack guessed what he was about to say.

"My lord." Gasthorpe addressed Jack. "The lady who called on you here once before has returned. I've left her in the parlor."

Jack nodded and rose. "I'll go down." To the others, he said, "Lady Clarice Altwood."

All three were on their feet in a flash.

"We'll come down, too," Deverell said.

"Just to lend you countenance." A teasing glint lit Christian's eyes.

Jack humphed, but could think of no good—no valid—reason to argue. Indeed, it might be wise for Clarice and his three colleagues to meet.

However, he made sure that when he entered the parlor his

friends were at his heels, that they hadn't dropped sufficiently far back for Clarice not to immediately notice them and behave as if he and she were alone.

As it was, her dark eyes deflected instantly to his entourage. He introduced them; with her usual self-possession, she gave them her hand, acknowledged their bows, and thanked them for their assistance in exonerating James.

Then her attention reverted to him, focused on him exclusively. "I came to tell you that we won't be able to interview Humphries today." Her expression grew colder. "Apparently, he's arguing with the bishop over our involvement."

Jack raised his brows, unperturbed. "He won't get far with that."

"No, but he is delaying us. The dean said he imagines the matter will be settled in our favor by tomorrow morning. He suggested we return then."

Clarice looked at the four gentlemen arrayed before her. The room seemed much smaller with them in it. One glance had been enough to confirm that however urbane and sophisticated they might outwardly appear, underneath, they were very like Jack. She summoned her most encouragingly interested expression. "Jack mentioned you're helping to overturn the evidence of the three incidents central to the allegations. Have you learned anything?"

She'd addressed the other three; they merely smiled and looked at Jack. Suppressing a sigh at their lack of susceptibility, she did, too. With a few brief words, he outlined what they'd gleaned thus far and their current tack.

"Hmm." After a moment digesting their news, she met Jack's eyes. "Given we can achieve nothing more at the palace, I've grasped the opportunity to be seen with Sarah Haverling at an afternoon tea. Later, there's a dinner we should attend, and two balls after that." She arched a brow at him.

He held her gaze, then nodded. "I'll call for you at eight."

She inclined her head regally, then glanced at the other men, silent witnesses doing their best to appear inconsequential, or at the very least uncomprehending. The moment replayed in her mind; she wondered what they made of it, then shook aside the uncertainty that followed that thought.

Graciously, she took her leave of them; smiling, they bowed and withdrew, leaving Jack to see her to the hackney she'd left waiting.

They paused on the pavement; he raised her hand to his lips and kissed it, caught her gaze, wryly smiled. "Benedict's at eight."

With a nod, she allowed him to assist her into the carriage.

Jack closed the door and stepped back. He watched as the carriage rattled off down the street, heading back to Mayfair, taking her back to the charmed circle into which she'd been born, in which she belonged . . .

Turning, he walked back into the club and climbed the stairs to the library. He entered the room in time to hear Tristan ask Christian, "Are all marquess's daughters like that?"

Jack joined them where they stood in a circle before the fireplace.

Christian raised his brows. "My sisters do have a similar . . . aura. Not, however, to quite the same extent as Lady Clarice." Christian smiled at Jack. "I imagine turning her from her path would not be easy."

Jack humphed. "Try 'impossible'—you'll be nearer the mark."

"Never mind," Tristan said. "At least you won't have to put up with any feminine softheartedness when it comes to dealing with this villain."

Jack snorted. "More likely I'll have to keep her from visiting too final a retribution on the fellow."

"Too final?" Deverell looked surprised. "He is a traitor, after all."

Jack frowned. While they'd been chatting his brain had been turning over all they'd learned. "Actually, I don't think he is. He's not our man, Dalziel's last traitor, but only his henchman. And he's a foreigner. His loyalties lie with the other side."

Christian nodded. "A subtle but meaningful distinction."

"Catching him is one thing," Jack said. "Keeping him alive might prove useful."

Still standing, they discussed a few further speculations, then Christian and Tristan departed, at the last wishing Jack good luck in the ballrooms that evening. Chuckling, they left. Jack cast a speaking glance after them, then moved to sink into one of the deeply cushioned leather armchairs.

Deverell crossed to the tantalus and poured two glasses of brandy; returning, he handed one to Jack, then sat, facing Jack across a small table.

Deverell raised his glass to Jack, then sipped; Jack echoed the gesture.

"I'm impressed," Deverell said, a not teasing so much as appreciative light in his eyes. "I take it that's the way the wind now blows?"

Jack considered denying it, decided there was no point. "Yes, but for God's sake don't do anything to tip her the wink."

Leaning back in his chair, Deverell blinked. "Why not?"

"Because . . ." Jack let his head loll back against the leather; eyes on the ceiling, he said, "Her view of gentlemen of our class is not generally favorable. Avoid unless in possession of sound reasons to do otherwise sums it up. If you add the word 'marriage' to 'gentlemen of our class,' matters turn seriously sour."

"Ah." Deverell's tone was understanding. "Bad experiences?"

Jack nodded. After a moment, he continued, largely to himself, "I'm facing an uphill battle to convince her to change her mind."

Deverell grinned.

From the corner of his eye, Jack noticed. He frowned. "What?"

"I noticed you didn't say 'a battle to change her mind.' You're not imagining you can, not directly. Another subtle but meaningful distinction."

Jack thought, then pulled a face. "A lost cause to imagine

otherwise. With her, I can't decree. I can only make my case and pray she'll believe it, and that ultimately she'll regard my suit with favor."

Raising his glass he sipped; he caught Deverell's gaze as he lowered it. "Any sage advice would be welcome. This is not a battlefield on which I've had any experience."

Deverell grimaced. "Nor I."

Silence fell, then lengthened.

Eventually, Deverell stirred. "Surprise." He caught Jack's eyes. "Taking a tack she won't expect, or better yet would *never* expect, might help. She seems like the sort of female you need to keep off-balance if you want the upper hand. Or even a guiding hand."

Jack snorted softly. "Oh yes, that's Boadicea."

Deverell looked taken aback by the name, then realized and chuckled.

Sip by sip, Jack drained his glass.

Deverell was right. So . . . what was the last thing, the last action, the last approach that Boadicea would expect from him?

Chapter 17

❧

"Good evening, Lady Clarice." Lady Winterwhistle, seventy if she was a day, regarded Clarice through unfriendly, beady eyes. "Quite a surprise to see you again." Her ladyship glanced at Lady Davenport, whom Clarice and Jack had just left. "And in such company."

Jack's hackles had risen at the first spiteful syllable, but Clarice merely raised her brows faintly, ineffably regal, mildly returned the greeting, introduced him, then inquired as to her ladyship's daughter's health.

Lady Winterwhistle looked disgruntled, a harpy denied her prey. To Jack's surprise, her beady eyes fixed on him, then again deflected to Lady Davenport. "Ah! I *see.*"

Jack doubted it, but the expressions crossing Lady Winterwhistle's face suggested she was making a remarkable number of deductions.

Her ladyship fixed her gaze, almost gloating, on his face. "Your aunts like to think they can accomplish the impossible. Daresay Davenport dragooned you into this." Jabbing her finger at him, Lady Winterwhistle turned away, dismissively contemptuous. "More fool you."

His temper surged.

Clarice's fingers bit into his forearm. "No—don't react."

Jack looked down to see her watching him. He searched her face; she seemed curiously unaffected.

Reading the puzzlement in his eyes, she sighed and looked away. "There are many in the ton like her. After last night, word has spread, and they've had time to polish their barbs." She lifted a shoulder. "The best way to deal with them is simply to ignore them."

At her urging, they strolled on, down Lady Maxwell's crowded ballroom. Dinner at Lady Mott's had been a more select affair; while some had certainly been surprised to discover Clarice in their ranks, none had stepped back, or reacted in any adverse way. In the main, they'd been welcoming, curious yet relaxed. But he and she were now strolling through more general waters; alerted, Jack watched more closely, more carefully assessing what lay behind the nods that came their way, most studiously polite, some wary, only a few honestly friendly.

Indeed, certain ladies, all of the older generation, stiffened at the sight of Clarice. None, however, dared cut her; cutting an Altwood under the noses of half the ton would be akin to social suicide. If Clarice was present, she'd been invited by their hostess, and almost certainly at the behest of some lady of even higher rank. Yet the looks, some mean, others frankly malicious, followed them.

After a while, he murmured, "It seems very unlike you to so mildly turn the other cheek."

She glanced at him; amusement flared briefly in her eyes. "Their ability to disconcert me . . . that died a long time ago. Seven years ago, to be exact." Looking ahead, she walked on, then murmured, her voice low so only he could hear, "Even at the time, I realized that part of what drove them—those who were so ready to crucify me for refusing to marry as directed—was that I'd dared to do what they had not." Glancing up, she met his gaze. "There's always a price to be paid for demonstrating to others what they might have accomplished if they'd only been strong enough."

She looked ahead as they neared the end of the room. "My being here, once again walking among the ton, accepted into the circles into which I was born—to some that will seem like sacrilege, even now. To them, my banishment was a prescribed punishment. They couldn't have borne it if I hadn't been made to pay for my defiance."

Head tilting, she considered, then her lips curved. "But if you think my reaction uncharacteristically mild, just think of what they're feeling. The fact their censure is unable to touch me in any way, because I won't allow them any say in my life, won't recognize or acknowledge their spitefulness and so deny them all power . . . that, to them, is the ultimate rebuff."

It took a moment for him to see not just that point, but her strategy in its totality. Summoning a smile, he squeezed her fingers and met her eyes as she glanced up. "My apologies—I shouldn't have doubted you."

The look she shot him was vintage Boadicea. "In this sphere, I should think not."

They spotted Alton and Sarah and spent ten minutes in their company, then Roger fetched them to meet Alice's aunt. As Moira was not present, they grasped the opportunity to strengthen the connection.

After that, they continued strolling, stopping and chatting here and there, but only when others approached them. Most such approaches were purely curious; only a few had any deeper intent. Nevertheless, Jack detected a thread in the comments, especially those from the censorious, when, realizing Clarice was beyond the reach of their malicious disapproval, they instead suggested, in the most elliptical fashion, that the fact she was still unmarried proved that little about her had changed.

Knowing her as he did, male as he was, it took him a good fifteen minutes before the penny dropped.

They were, in his presence, accusing her of being fundamentally uninteresting to men, that males had no sincere interest in her.

He was so incensed, and not just on her part, that he'd escorted her back to the front hall, handed her into the town carriage Alton had placed at her disposal, and they were on their way to the second ball of the night before his temper subsided enough for him to think.

To plan.

By the time they were strolling down Lady Courtland's ballroom, and meeting with a similar reaction from certain members of the assembled throng, he'd decided on their response—his, and through that, hers.

One glance at her expression, at the coolly superior, faintly distant hauteur she deployed as a shield, suggested that explaining his strategy would be a waste of time; she most likely would refuse to agree to it, preferring to hold to her untouchable, dismissive stance.

Her strategy was working well against straightforward disapproval, however, he felt certain his plan would deal more effectively with that other, potentially more hurtful thread.

They hadn't bothered dancing at Lady Maxwell's; the dance floor had been crammed with eager young ladies and their partners, an uninviting crush. Now, however, the instant the strains of a waltz floated out above the milling crowd, he grasped Clarice's hand, with his usual charm excused them to the two ladies with whom they'd been chatting, and led her to the dance floor.

Clarice inwardly frowned as Jack determinedly steered her onto the floor, but, assuming him to be bored witless and perhaps wanting to stretch his legs, she made no protest. With his customary commanding confidence, he drew her into his arms; she went readily, willing enough to grasp the moment, to refresh herself, her senses, with the exhilaration of waltzing with him.

He drew her close, set them revolving, his hand heavy at her back, warming through the silk of her mint green gown. Her skirts shushed against his black trousers; her thighs briefly caressed his, slid away, returned . . .

His lips lifted lightly, then his hand tightened and he swung them into a turn. Exhilaration swelled, tightening her lungs, leaving her giddy even though, courtesy of the crowded floor, their movements were restricted, the progressive revolutions less physically charged, less powerful. Her senses still leapt, then sighed, luxuriating in the closeness, the subtle sensual empathy of the dance.

She drank it in, for those moments let all else fall away, let her eyes, her mind, focus solely on him, on them, and the attraction that pulsed between them. Warm, alive, oddly reassuring. Comforting.

He was with her, they were together, and nothing else mattered.

The music ended; she stifled a sigh as he released her, and she returned to the world. To Lady Courtland's ballroom and the inquisitive horde still waiting to interrogate her.

Her coolly collected smile in place, Jack by her side, she let them have at her. Moira was present somewhere in the crowd, which made her even more determined to carry the evening off as Lady Cowper, also present, would expect, with a high and supremely confident hand.

She was chatting to Lady Constable, the third lady to waylay her since the waltz, before she realized—realized just how revealing that waltz must have been. Lady Constable's eyes flitted back and forth from her to Jack; the particular speculation in her expression, as with the two earlier ladies, hadn't immediately registered with Clarice, but now she saw and understood.

Her practiced smile never wavered, but the instant they were free of Lady Constable, and she was strolling once more on Jack's arm, she caught his eye. "I'm not at all sure that was wise."

Any suspicion that he hadn't intended it, that he hadn't deliberately let some suggestion of the nature of their friendship show, was slain by the look in his eyes, hard and uncompromising. "Trust me." His voice was low, his diction precise. "Correcting that particular misconception was definitely necessary."

He sounded more than sure . . . indeed, she wasn't sure just what to make of his tone, but before she could question him, he added, "I can't help you with the rest, not actively, but that's one aspect I can personally address." Looking down, he met her gaze. "And I believe you'll find it won't harm your standing in the least."

She searched his eyes, that enticing medley of greens and golds, noted his satisfaction, and decided to leave well enough alone. With a light shrug, she looked ahead. "I daresay you're right."

He was. If there was one thing Jack could happily take an oath on, it was that the ton would treat her with far greater respect if they understood just how interested in her he was. How deeply she held him in thrall. A gentleman's enthrallment was a sure measure of a lady's power; his surrender would vouch for hers more convincingly than anything else.

Admitting to enthrallment. That hadn't, of course, been his intention, but he hadn't foreseen how matters would evolve. Yet if displaying his enslavement made her difficult road easier, so be it; he was, curiously, content. No matter what he wished, he couldn't slay the dragons of her past for her—as Lady Osbaldestone had so sapiently remarked, that was for her and her alone to do—but he could clear her path.

Grimly satisfied, he surveyed the outcome of their public display. A goodly number of the gossipmongers were now viewing them with eyes on stalks, understanding lighting their eyes. That Lady Clarice Altwood had made at least one notable conquest would be the latest morsel of juicy gossip passed over the ton's teacups tomorrow.

Nothing scandalous, but it would serve to slay any notion that she was doomed to die an aging spinster, that her interests, her abilities, didn't encompass snaring a husband and raising a family.

Indeed, given who she was, a dynasty.

His mind was happily exploring that notion, leaving the conversation largely to her, keeping nothing more than a watching brief on the reactions of those around, when a well-dressed gentleman pushed through the crowd to reach them, waited, openly impatient, for the lady and gentleman conversing with Clarice to move on, then stepped forward to claim her attention.

"My dear Clarice."

Clarice hesitated for a heartbeat before regally offering her hand. "Emsworth."

The chill in her tone would have alerted Jack even if he hadn't recognized the name. So this was the bounder who'd caused her so much heartache. Jack watched him straighten from his bow.

Clarice retrieved her hand, and gestured at Jack. "Allow me to present Lord Warnefleet. Viscount Emsworth, my lord."

She'd uttered the last two words in subtle but provocative fashion. Jack shook hands with Emsworth, who met his gaze with barely concealed dislike.

Something of Jack's thoughts must have shown in his eyes; Emsworth's eyes widened, and he abruptly broke the contact.

He looked at Clarice, and smiled, a stiff gesture that marked him as one who didn't smile often. "My dear Clarice, I'm delighted to see you back among the ton. If you would honor me with this dance?"

Jack inwardly swore. Emsworth had timed his approach well, but as the musical summons floated over the crowd, Jack relaxed. A cotillion. He glanced at Clarice, and sensed her inward shrug. He resigned himself to letting her dance with Emsworth.

"If you wish." Clarice gave Emsworth her hand. It was, perhaps, not a bad thing for her to be seen interacting civilly with him. He was a part of her past she'd buried long ago; she discovered she felt very little toward him, not even true anger, just a mild annoyance that he wished to take up her time.

But she would be gracious and spare him the next few minutes. That, to her mind, would lay that part of her past to permanent rest.

He led her to the dance floor, and they took up their positions in the nearest set. The music swelled, and they dipped, twirled. Throughout, Emsworth tried to catch her eye; Clarice delighted in denying him even that much notice. The figures of the complicated dance returned to her without thought. She smiled at the other dancers, perfectly content to have them see her nonchalantly dancing with Emsworth.

When the music ceased, and she rose from her final curtsy, Emsworth tightened his grip on her hand. "My dear Clarice, there's a matter I wish to discuss with you, a matter, as it were, from our shared past."

She met Emsworth's gray eyes, tried to fathom just what matter that might be.

He glanced around, over the crowd's heads. "Come out onto the terrace. We can talk there."

Without waiting for any agreement, he steered her toward the glass doors opening to a terrace that ran the length of the ballroom. Resigned, Clarice went; she'd never approved of him, of the way he treated her, but she wanted to hear what he had to say. It might give her something else she could use to spike the pistol Moira had trained on Alton and Sarah, and that definitely would be worth a few more minutes of her time.

Reaching the doors, Emsworth guided her through; just before she crossed the threshold, Clarice glanced back, and spotted Jack's burnished head moving purposefully through the crowd in their direction. The sight was reassuring; she could admit that much to herself.

Once on the terrace, Emsworth looked around, then, his fingers about her elbow, he urged her away from the knot of guests conversing just beyond the doors. They strolled to where shadows from nearby trees flickered over the flagstones, and there were no others near enough to hear.

Emsworth released her. Clasping his hands behind his

back, he took up a stance Clarice recognized as signifying he was about to make some priggish pronouncement while pretending to gaze out at the dark gardens.

She half expected him to say something disparaging about her interaction with Jack, and their unnecessarily close waltz—

"I'm really very glad to see you back in town, my dear. You've paid the price for your reckless behavior in refusing me. Clearly those hostesses who matter have deemed that incident can now be forgotten."

He'd noticed the support Jack's aunts and Lady Osbaldestone were marshaling behind her. Good—

"Of course the fact remains that you can never hope to make a suitable marriage, yet clearly you have . . . missed the pleasures of the marriage bed. I would, were it possible, renew my previous offer, however, as I am now wed"—turning, Emsworth met Clarice's stunned gaze—"I suggest that it would be best for you to become my mistress. I command a reasonable income—you would not find me ungenerous." He paused as if consulting his inner importance, then, thin nose elevating, he refocused on her. "Accepting my offer will see you safe from men such as Warnefleet and his kind."

Clarice had placed her features under the severest control the instant she'd understood his drift; now she let abject contempt flame in her eyes, let fury color her expression.

She stepped across Emsworth, backing him against the balustrade, leaving them eye to eye. "You're a nauseating specimen, Emsworth. Regardless of what pleasures I might have missed, I wouldn't agree to be your anything were you the last man on this earth."

His eyes widened as he leaned back from her wrath.

Before he could react, she brought her knee up, fast.

His eyes crossed. His lips twisted.

She stepped back, watched as he crumpled to his knees, for good measure boxed his ears as he doubled over before her, disguising the act as solicitously reaching to help him.

Sensing someone behind her, she glanced over her shoulder, and found Jack, grim-faced yet with unimpaired satisfaction watching Emsworth collapse to the flags.

"It seems Viscount Emsworth's been taken ill." She caught Jack's gaze.

He grinned fleetingly, then reached for her and shifted her to the side. "Bad health and ill luck seem to dog the viscount's family."

Jack's hands remained, reassuring on her shoulders. Between them, they largely screened the fallen Emsworth from the others on the terrace. "The viscount's first wife, for instance, pitched to her death from the top of the stairs in his house. The servants have no idea how such a thing could have happened. And his second wife is often so poorly she doesn't leave her room for days. Some unexplained illness leaves bruises all over her."

Jack leaned over Emsworth. His voice lowered and took on a hard edge. "A word of warning, Emsworth. If you don't want me and my kind to visit much-deserved retribution on you, you'd be well-advised not to show your face in London, or indeed anywhere in the ton, again."

Emsworth was quivering; his nose was running, his mouth open as he struggled to breathe. Jack met his dilated eyes. "I trust I make myself plain?"

Emsworth looked into Jack's face; what little color had remained in his drained.

Jack smiled, not amiably; straightening, he reached for Clarice's arm. "Come, we should return to the ballroom. We can send two footmen to assist the viscount to his carriage."

Clarice glanced down at Emsworth. He was all but sniveling, still unable to draw a proper breath. Entirely satisfied, she allowed Jack to turn her toward the ballroom. "I always wanted to do that, to see if it really worked."

Jack looked at her. "It works. Because you're so tall it works very well."

"Hmm."

In the matter of Emsworth's ultimate routing—being carried by two footmen around the house and deposited directly into his carriage—Clarice stood back and let Jack arrange all. His glib tale of Emsworth's being taken ill was outwardly swallowed whole, but many had witnessed Emsworth dancing with her, then leading her out onto the terrace, and her subsequent relaxed return on Lord Warnefleet's arm. Many waited for Emsworth to return to the ballroom; when he didn't, speculation ran rife.

In distracting the ton from the allegations against James, she, aided by Jack, was succeeding admirably.

They spent the next half hour circulating among the now-intrigued guests, then departed, leaving all the avid questions unanswered.

As she settled on the carriage seat, Clarice smiled into the shadows. She had never before allowed anyone to help her in dealing with a problem such as Emsworth, yet sharing such an enterprise with Jack seemed oddly right.

Something else about her that had changed.

Glancing at him, seated beside her, relaxed and confident, she wondered how he'd known about Emsworth. How he'd known to know, for he would have had to have asked; he hadn't been in London, a part of the ton, for the past thirteen years.

Looking ahead, she frowned. She was certain she hadn't mentioned Emsworth. So how . . . ?

James? She knew James's opinion of Emsworth and that episode in her life. If Jack had asked, James would have told him.

Which meant Jack had asked. And not only had he been interested enough to ask, he'd then cared enough to learn more.

Through the shadows that flickered as they drove through the streets, she studied his profile. Then she smiled, faced forward, and thought of what lay ahead. Of how they would spend the rest of the night in her suite at Benedict's.

"I'm perfectly certain my information is correct." Deacon Humphries all but glared across the narrow table at Jack.

Jack studied the good deacon. The crone's description had been accurate; his mouth was womanish, and when he pursed his lips, as he was wont to do, the effect was indeed a feminine pout.

It was noon; Humphries had resisted speaking with them as far as he'd dared, but had ultimately bowed to the bishop's decree and met Jack, Clarice, and Olsen in a small cell-like office deep in the palace.

"We understand, Deacon Humphries, that you believe your information to be the truth, but simply stating that doesn't constitute proof." From where she stood before the window, Clarice swung to confront Humphries; they'd all taken seats around the table, with her next to Jack, but then, apparently too exercised to keep still, she'd risen and started pacing.

Much to Humphries' disquiet. As he looked up at her, his priggish antipathy to being lectured by a woman shone clear in his face. "I will produce my proofs to the bishop in good time."

Before Clarice could utter the withering retort forming on her tongue, Jack cut in. "As you've heard, the bishop himself, in the interests of administering swift but sure justice, wishes you to explain to us the details of your case. Whitehall, too, wishes to know specifically what evidence you have, beyond the accounts of the witnesses you've listed, that you believe conclusively proves that James Altwood passed secrets to the enemy."

Humphries fixed his gaze on Jack's face, clearly trying to ignore Clarice. Once again Jack was grateful for her distracting, somewhat overpowering persona; it was rare that those he interviewed saw him as the softer touch. Humphries subjected him to a careful study. "I understand you're a long-time acquaintance of Reverend Altwood."

Jack inclined his head. Before he could reply to the unstated challenge, Clarice did.

"If Whitehall, knowing of Warnefleet's association with James, nevertheless deems it safe to assign the government's interests into Warnefleet's hands, then I hardly think his loyalties are open to question by anyone." Her tone declared that avenue of discussion was closed.

Humphries' lips thinned; without looking at her, he inclined his head in her direction. To Jack, he said, "The tale the witnesses tell is consistent. Taken together, they paint a convincing picture of Altwood's meetings with the courier."

Jack debated how much to reveal; in fairness to Humphries, he felt forced to say, "I've already received evidence that a number of your witnesses are unreliable. There are others, more credible, who are willing to swear James Altwood has never set foot in those taverns. Lastly, it seems likely we'll succeed in gaining unimpeachable evidence that on those dates, at the times specified, he was elsewhere."

Humphries' lip curled; his expression stated he placed no faith in such assertions.

Evenly, Jack continued, "All that aside, however, the allegations must stand not on any evidence of meetings—that at best is circumstantial—but on evidence of secrets actually being passed. My question for you, from Whitehall specifically, is: what is that evidence?" Jack glanced at the sheaf of papers Olsen had laid on the table. "To this point, you've failed to produce any details beyond asserting that such evidence exists."

Humphries did not appreciate being pressured. His narrow chin tightened; he clasped his hands, before him on the desk, more firmly. "My evidence for the actual secrets passed comes from the only *reliable* source there could be. The person Altwood handed the secrets to."

"And this person is?"

Humphries' lips set in a thin line. "I'm not prepared to divulge this person's identity prior to the hearing. However, as Whitehall is demanding, the information passed included the disposition and strengths of our forces prior to the seige of Badajoz, the same prior to the rout at Corunna, and more recently, the details of the deployment to Belgium some weeks prior to Waterloo."

Jack kept his face expressionless, briefly flicked his eyes to Clarice to warn her to keep silent. Although two of the subsequent battles had been won, the three engagements cited had each resulted in heavy losses. As a student of military matters, Humphries would know that better than most.

"The three recent meetings you've cited, what was passed at them?" They'd supposedly occurred over the early months of 1815.

Humphries hesitated, then replied, "At those meetings, Altwood passed information on, respectively, the details of the demobilization, the strengths of our troops left standing, and our ability to remobilize and the order of same. Such information would have been vital in planning Napoleon's return."

Jack inclined his head. "Have you seen any evidence yourself—lists in Altwood's hand, maps—that he passed on to this courier?"

Humphries pouted. "I haven't seen them myself, but I've been assured they exist. The courier has copies."

"Copies." Jack stilled. "Not the originals?"

"He had to hand the originals to his masters."

Clarice couldn't restrain herself. "How fortunate."

Humphries frowned but refused to meet her eye.

Jack pressed again for the courier's name, but Humphries held firm; Jack called a halt before Clarice could use her tongue to flay him. The meeting broke up; Humphries departed. After confirming to Olsen that what he'd said about contradictory evidence was true, and asking him to stress to Humphries that that was indeed the case, Jack, with Clarice beside him, walked back to the front hall and out of the palace.

As they strolled down the drive, Jack glanced back at the towering edifice. "He honestly believes he's doing the right thing, that he's been called on to carry Justice's sword."

Clarice humphed. "He needs to remember she carries scales, too, and why." After a moment, she added, "And she's a woman."

Jack smiled, but the gesture faded as he paced beside Clarice. "Whoever set this up—Dalziel's last traitor—has tied Humphries up tight. Prodded by his jealousy of James, and with what must have initially appeared perfectly plausible evidence, he's gone out on a limb. Now, even though we're demolishing that evidence, he's not going to back down, at least not before the hearing in the bishop's court."

Clarice glanced at him. "Are we going to have enough evidence gathered by then?" Olsen had told them the bishop, anxious to get the sensitive matter laid to rest with all speed, had scheduled the hearing for five days hence.

Jack grimaced. "It won't be easy, but it's possible." They reached the gate, and he halted. "Apropos of that, I must get back to the club and the others. We need to consider the order of our attack."

Clarice hid a smile at his phrasing and the distant expression in his eyes. Then he refocused on her; she felt her heart flutter, but then it settled into its normal, reliable rhythm. She grimaced lightly up at him. "I have to attend a slew of afternoon teas. Your aunts made me promise. It'll be perfectly ghastly, but"—she shrugged—"it probably is necessary. We have to make it clear I'm back, to everyone, including Moira. She's expected at two of the teas."

Jack grinned, took her hand, and raised it to his lips. Kissed. "I'd back you over Moira in any battle."

She laughed. A hackney rolled toward them; Jack hailed it, handed her up, then told the driver to return her to Benedict's. Sitting back on the cushions, Clarice watched the posts of Lambeth Bridge slide past; imagining the afternoon ahead of her, full of the social whirl, she wished instead she could remain with Jack.

She'd rather be with him than anyone else in the ton.

Over the next three days, Jack, Deverell, Christian, and Tristan worked solidly to undermine Humphries' allegations.

They first took statements, sworn in the presence of Jack and one of the others, from three witnesses from each of the three taverns named—the barman, and two regulars acknowledged as near-permanent fixtures in each case. Each swore they had never known any clergyman to set foot in their establishment; given the dates and times of the supposed meetings, they would have been present and would have seen James, if he'd been there.

That done, the four club members turned their persuasive talents on the less-reputable crew who had agreed in exchange for coins to swear that James Altwood had been present at the same three meetings. Faced with the sworn statements of the others, especially those of the barmen, and assured they would be excused from appearance before any court should they now elect to tell the truth, all recanted. And signed statements to that effect.

Jack and his three comrades were celebrating their success in the club's library when Alton arrived. Shown up by Gasthorpe, he looked around, intrigued, then reported that he and his brothers had identified at least one social event James had attended on the evening of each of the meetings, and had found ladies with diaries who could vouch that he'd been present at all three events.

"Given the times"—Alton held out his list to Jack—"it's difficult to see how James could have been dining with these people yet simultaneously in some tavern in Southwark."

Alton was invited to join the celebration.

Ten minutes later, Gasthorpe summoned Jack; a messenger from Whitehall had arrived. Jack went down, accepted the package, briefly checked the sheets of paper it contained, then, grinning, returned to the library.

Closing the door, he waved the sheets. "Not just the final nail but the hammer as well. We're ready to bury the allegations."

"What is it?" Alton asked. The others looked the same question.

Jack dropped back into his chair. "When we interviewed him, we managed to drag from Humphries the specific information the courier said James had passed at these three meetings. Much of it James would have known—troop strengths and deployments are precisely the things he researches. However, there was one piece of information I couldn't imagine James knowing—ever bothering to learn—namely the details of demobilization. As a military strategist, he's interested in battles and the preparations for those. What happens afterward holds no interest for him. Why would he have researched the specifics of demobilization?"

Christian grinned. "I take it that sheaf of papers proves he didn't?"

"Indeed." Jack smiled fondly at the papers in his hand. "I sent that friend of ours in Whitehall a list of all the military personnel James had interviewed between the fall of Toulouse and Waterloo. This is the result. Statements from all those interviewed stating that their discussions with James at no time touched on demobilization, plus statements from the staff at the War Office and Army Headquarters who managed the demobilization stating that they at no time had any contact whatever with James Altwood."

Deverell smiled and raised his glass. "When he acts, that friend of ours is nothing if not effective."

Their celebration continued for another half hour, then they all recalled it was the middle of the Season and they had social events to attend, however reluctantly. Alton left, eyes bright, saying he'd see Jack later. Closing the front door behind him, Jack grinned. Alton wasn't slow; he'd understood enough of their references to have gained a more complete and accurate view of Jack. The brotherly concern that had been directed Jack's way had largely evaporated, laid to rest. One more hurdle removed from his path.

Smiling to himself, pleased with his day and looking forward to his night, Clarice's eager questions, and her likely response to their accummulating successes, he climbed the stairs to dress for the evening.

"My dear, your return is the talk of the ton!" Old Lady Swanley beamed at Clarice. "I'm absolutely delighted that

Emily could persuade you and Lord Warnefleet to attend tonight."

Clarice smiled; confident and assured, she settled on the chaise beside Lady Swanley. A childhood friend of Clarice's mother, Lady Swanley was one who had never wished her ill; it was pleasant to be able to circulate in such company again, to relax with people she didn't need either to manage or guard against.

Gathered about her ladyship's table, they'd dined with a select group of guests, then the ladies had left the gentlemen to their port. Ranging in age from Lady Swanley's venerable years to her granddaughter's seventeen, the ladies disposed themselves on the chaises and chairs in comfortable groups and settled to their favorite occupation, discussing all they'd seen and heard that day.

Relaxed, Clarice responded easily to questions and comments about herself and her life in the country, her brothers' romances—romances the ton was only just realizing were being conducted under their collective nose—and rather more carefully to questions touching on her return to the ton and the adjustment likely to flow from that, specifically to Moira's standing.

"For there's no doubt in anyone's mind, my dear, that she'll take against your success and do her best to hobble you." Lady Swanley nodded sagely. "She was always a flighty, demanding miss. She thought marrying your father would gain her the status she wanted, and so it would have if she'd behaved appropriately."

"If she'd had any sense, you mean." Henrietta Standish snorted. She caught Clarice's eye. "Moira's idea of behaving in a manner appropriate to a marchioness is shrilly demanding all due honors." Henrietta humphed. "It's never occurred to her that respect is earned, and true status bestowed on one. Neither is given because one stamps one's foot and insists."

Every night as she moved through the ton, with Jack's aunts and Lady Osbaldestone's backing gradually, step by step, reclaiming her position, Clarice heard more of Moira's misdeeds, increasingly learned just how close to being deemed *persona non grata* her stepmother stood. There were moments she almost felt sorry, or at least concerned for Moira, but then the specter of what Moira was holding over Alton's and Sarah's heads, what she'd done to Roger and his Alice returned to her mind, and Clarice put aside such softer emotions as unjustified.

Every evening with Jack by her side she continued to juggle the balls they'd tossed spinning into the rarefied atmosphere of the ton's ballrooms and drawing rooms. Her reemergence, her reinstatement as it were, was focusing the ton's attention better than they'd hoped; most were agog to learn why she'd returned and were keeping close watch for any hint of an answer.

Her brothers' romances were of interest, too, but not, yet, as keenly watched. Few had yet realized how serious said romances were; once they did, the majority would assume that her brothers' impending nuptials were the cause of her return.

In comparison, the rumor about James, a whisper they'd succeeded in coloring as too dangerous to inflate to fully fledged gossip, had faded, almost withered away. The kernel still resided dormant in some minds, but no one felt the need to nurture it, not with so much else to talk about.

Not with the senior branch of the Altwood family so very much the cynosure of the ton's collective eye.

Later, after the gentlemen had returned to Lady Swanley's drawing room, and she and Jack had done the rounds, they left for the next event on their schedule, a ball given by one of Clarice's cousins, Helen Albemarle.

"I find it rather strange"—Clarice leaned back against the carriage's cushions—"that the family, those I've had little contact with over the years, like Helen, seem so ready to welcome me back." She glanced at the facades sliding past the window. "I hadn't thought to be so readily reembraced."

She'd been musing out aloud, something she was falling into the habit of doing when there was only Jack to hear.

Somewhat to her surprise, his hand closed more firmly about hers.

"Anthony told me that the wider family, especially the younger generation, didn't view you with the opprobrium you seemed to expect."

When she turned to stare at him, Jack smiled at her amazement. "You didn't seriously imagine I'd rattle up without knowing what we'd face?"

Put like that . . . she inclined her head, acknowledging that, knowing him as she now did, that would indeed have been a silly notion. However . . .

He'd asked, had thought to ask Anthony even before they'd set out.

He'd been thinking of her, of what she would face, if she knew anything of him, thinking of how to protect her even then.

Facing forward, she left her hand resting in his, felt the strength of his fingers surrounding her slighter bones, and felt . . . she wasn't sure what it was she felt, only that it was novel and somehow precious.

She didn't have time to dwell on it, not then. The carriage rocked to a halt before another set of front steps, at yet another fashionable address. They alighted beneath an awning and walked up the narrow red carpet laid out to welcome her cousin's guests. When they reached the ballroom, Helen came sweeping up to greet them.

"I'm so *thrilled* you could come, and that you're back with us—I mean among the ton—again." Helen beamed and embraced her, then turned to greet Jack; Clarice introduced him.

That done, Helen rattled on at high speed. She was still the talkative, well-intentioned and perennially good-natured lady Clarice remembered; it was easy to reconnect as if there were only a seven-week gap in their acquaintance, rather than seven years.

Beckoning her young daughter to attend them, Helen introduced the chit, who had just made her come-out. Clarice gave the girl her hand and a reassuring smile, and was taken aback when the girl sank into a deep, very correct curtsy. A swift glance at Helen showed her smiling with maternal pride. Clarice recovered swiftly and bestowed on the girl her most regal and formal approval, the social blessing of the family's most influential female.

That was what Helen and her daughter had hoped for; they both beamed. Parting from them, Clarice took Jack's arm, and they moved on.

Glancing at Jack, she caught the amused light in his eyes, but she doubted, male that he was, that he'd correctly interpreted that little interlude. Helen had whispered that Moira was there; Clarice only hoped Moira hadn't witnessed the moment. If she had, she'd be livid.

Clarice had accepted that to properly aid not just James but her brothers she'd have to reclaim her position in the ton. What she hadn't initially realized was that in doing so, she would forever diminish Moira's precarious and hard-fought-for standing, such as it was.

By her own actions, because of her attitude, Moira could never lay claim to the respect Clarice could, and it increasingly seemed did, command. If Helen's behavior was anything to judge by, she was all but reinstated, not just in the ton's mind but within the family, too, to the full honors by right accruing to the Marquess of Melton's daughter.

She dragged in a breath. Jack glanced at her. She met his eyes. "I hadn't thought it would be so easy. Or so swift."

He smiled; his fingers tightened briefly over hers on his sleeve, then he looked ahead, steering her through the crowd to where Lady Davenport imperiously beckoned, two older ladies beside her on a chaise.

Clarice recognized the pair; by the time she and Jack reached them, she'd metaphorically girded herself for battle, yet as, turning from greeting Lady Davenport, she curtsied before her paternal aunts, her father's sisters who had supported him throughout in his banishment of her, she let not an inkling of her feelings show.

Constance, Countess of Camleigh, looked her up and down, cold gray gaze and haughty features giving nothing away, then she raised her eyes to Clarice's. "I can't say you've grown—you always were a Long Meg—but . . ." With an effort, her ladyship held out both hands. "Welcome back, my dear."

Startled, Clarice took one crabbed hand in each of hers, and, faintly stunned, yielded to the tug and bent to touch both cheeks with her formidable, and until then she'd believed highly disapproving, aunt.

Constance knew; she humphed as Clarice straightened. "At the time, I thought Marcus was right, but later, especially after what happened to that poor soul Emsworth married, and the more we saw of Moira, well, I came to think perhaps you had, indeed, known best."

"Indeed." More fluttery than her domineering sister but just as high in the instep, Catherine, Lady Bentwood, nodded portentously. "And Emsworth's second wife is faring even worse, they say. A shocking thing it would have been had he married you."

Clarice was grateful she didn't need to reply. She and Jack remained for ten minutes; both her aunts were exceedingly interested in meeting him, and in gleaning as much as they could about James. When Jack had reached the limit of what they'd deemed fit to divulge, Clarice stepped in and excused them.

Constance sniffed but let them go.

Clarice didn't need to glance around to know that everyone in the entire ballroom now understood that she was fully repatriated to her former status.

She glanced up to see Jack battling to suppress a grin. "What?"

He met her eyes, let that grin—a dangerous one—fleetingly surface. "Why do I have the strong feeling that if Emsworth had married you, it would have been he who fell down the stairs?"

Her answering grin matched his. She looked ahead—straight into Moira's furious, flashing eyes.

Thankfully at a safe distance. Her stepmother was standing, fists clenched by her sides, almost quivering with rage, along the opposite wall. Her daughter, Mildred, stood beside her, also shooting daggers at Clarice.

Clarice met their ire, then coolly inclined her head to them. Then she looked away and let Jack sweep her into the crowd.

Chapter 18

They remained at Helen's for over an hour. Clarice glimpsed Moira a number of times, but every time she looked, her stepmother turned the other way. Inwardly shrugging, Clarice thereafter ignored her and addressed herself to refreshing her memories of the various members of her numerous and widespread family.

Time and again, she was asked for advice. Some even solicited her thoughts on the suitabililty of various matches for their daughters and sons. The irony didn't escape her, or Jack; they shared a speaking glance, but managed to keep their lips straight. Regardless, nothing could have more strongly declared that her family regarded her as their de facto matriarch, in preference to Moira.

Later, they journeyed the short distance to their last port of call for the evening, Lady Carraway's house at which her ladyship's rout was in full swing. A dashing, well-connected matron, her ladyship bade them welcome, archly commenting that Clarice would find numerous old friends among the thronging crowd.

That crowd was somewhat different to those at previous events; her ladyship's guests were primarily Jack's and Clarice's age. Consequently most of the ladies were married, and many of the gentlemen as well. Not that their marriage vows seemed to weigh heavily on most of the guests' minds, at least not in terms of momentary enjoyment.

Clarice gauged the mood in a few swift glances, a few short exchanges. There were indeed a number of guests she remembered of old, yet watching a lady who had made her come-out at the time Clarice should have flirt outrageously with some gentleman while his wife, beside him, fluttered her lashes at a gazetted rake, Clarice felt nothing beyond a vague tiredness, a wish she and Jack had simply returned to Benedict's. But Lady Osbaldestone and Lady Davenport had insisted she make her mark in even this sphere; bowing to their greater wisdom, she gripped Jack's sleeve and sallied on.

Jack guided Clarice through the crush, cloaking his reaction with his customary easygoing bonhomie. Clarice had mentioned that her mentors had strongly recommended her appearance at this event, but he suspected they hadn't made allowance for that waltz he and she had indulged in three evenings before. Since then, the attitude of certain males toward Clarice had changed. Altered. Witness Emsworth's offer.

While he seriously doubted others would make such a crass mistake—aside from all else, he'd made certain word of Emsworth's discomfiture, in all its wonderful detail, had circulated subtly through the clubs—to his mind, the male interest in Clarice had escalated to a dangerous level.

When he'd moved to throw her sensual attractiveness into the teeth of the gossipmongers, he hadn't considered that they had sons and nephews many of whom were perennially on the lookout for ladies of sensual promise.

Still, he didn't regret that waltz, not for a moment; as for the rest, he would simply ensure he remained, always, by her side.

He succeeded in that endeavor, but the night had turned sultry; the ballroom grew increasingly stuffy. Despite her upright stance beside him, he sensed Clarice was wilting; she'd been the cynosure of attention for the entire evening, and still largely was.

"There's a balcony beyond the glass doors." He turned so she could see the doors he meant. "Let's step out and get some air."

She nodded. "An excellent idea."

They moved steadily across the room. Eventually, they gained the doors. As he swung one open, Jack caught sight of a footman entering the room, balancing a tray of tall glasses. He glanced at Clarice. "Go out—I'll get us some refreshment."

She nodded and stepped through. He let the fine curtains fall over the open door, and headed for the footman.

Clarice walked out onto the balcony; the cooler night air wrapped about her and she breathed a sigh of relief. She'd been born and reared within the ton, had untold experience at events such as this, yet while she could manage such appearances easily, almost without thought, they neither fascinated nor held her attention.

There was, she knew, more to life than balls and parties.

Despite being once again received into the ton, despite having reclaimed her position in its totality, she was finding it difficult even to pretend that such things truly mattered anymore, not to her.

Gripping the balustrade, she looked out into the velvet darkness of the night, and considered what had changed. Not the ton, that was certain.

"My darling Clarice."

She blinked; it took her a moment to place the drawl. Slowly, she turned and studied the handsome man who'd slipped out of the ballroom to join her. His aristocratic features showed clear signs of dissipation, of the passage of the years.

"Good evening, Warwick." Her tone, cold and emotionless, as disinterested as she felt, pleased her. "What are you doing here?"

He held her gaze, then boldly let his lower, tracing the curves of her body, tonight displayed in magenta moiré silk. Clarice gave thanks she hadn't worn the plum silk.

"I wondered, my dear, if, having endured seven years of purgatory, you might perhaps consider the advantages of—"

He broke off at the sound of approaching footsteps. They both turned; Clarice smiled as Jack stepped through the curtains carrying two glasses of champagne. She took the glass he held out to her, with it indicated Warwick. "Lord Warnefleet, allow me to present the Honorable Jonathon Warwick."

Jack's lids flickered, yet his charming, easygoing smile remained in place. Clarice knew him well enough to distrust that smile utterly.

Warwick didn't. He smiled back, an amiable wolf expecting to negotiate a share of the prey. "Warnefleet." He held out his hand.

Jack's gaze fell to it, then he turned to Clarice. "Hold this for me, will you?"

Puzzled, she took his glass, too.

Jack turned back to Warwick—and slammed his fist into Warwick's jaw.

Clarice blinked. Warwick staggered back, then collapsed to the ground. Stunned, wits rattled, he stared up at Jack.

With a light shrug, Jack resettled his coat, straightened his sleeves, then lifted his glass from Clarice's fingers. "Thank you."

He raised the glass to Warwick. "Pleased to meet you." He sipped.

Utterly befuddled, Warwick remained sprawled on the ground. "What was that for?"

Jack smiled, this time genuinely, all teeth. "*That* was for past misdemeanors. That, and worse, is what would have happened to you last time had I been about. That, and worse, is what *will* happen to you in future, should you be so unwise as to approach Lady Clarice again, in whatever fashion." His smile grew intent. "Because I am here, now."

Taking another sip of champagne, Jack considered Warwick, then quietly asked, "Do you have that clear?"

Belligerence had bloomed in Warwick's eyes, but there

was hint enough in Jack's tone to make him look more closely. After a moment of studying Jack's eyes, Warwick paled; all aggression leached from him.

"Indeed." Lips compressing, he threw Clarice a brief glance, then awkwardly got to his feet. Straightening, he paused, as if waiting for the world to stop spinning, then he fractionally inclined his head. "If you'll excuse me?"

He started back to the door. His stride hitched as he saw the group of three ladies and two gentlemen who had followed Jack outside; from the looks on their faces they'd seen enough to keep the gossips buzzing for the rest of the week. Then Warwick continued on, passing the group without acknowledging them in any way.

Jack turned to Clarice, met her eyes, and pulled a face. "My apologies. It seemed that was overdue, and no one else seemed likely to . . ." He shrugged.

To his relief, she smiled delightedly. "Thank you." Her eyes said it even more than her words. Placing her hand on his sleeve, she turned to stand beside him, viewing the beauty of the garden at night as they sipped.

There were whispers behind them, but then the group, eager to share their news, scurried back into the ballroom.

Jack sighed. "I didn't mean to create a scandal."

Clarice chuckled. "I don't mind. Indeed, since my aim is to distract the ton from James's predicament"—she glanced up at him, lightly squeezed his arm—"I should thank you for your help."

She caught his gaze as he glanced at her. "Thank you for hitting him for me. I've always wished I could do that."

"Your way would have worked, too." Jack turned her back to the ballroom. "But you don't want to become predictable."

She was laughing, smiling, as he led her back into the ballroom, back under the glare of the ton's fervid gaze.

They didn't leave immediately, but played the game, circulated once, then departed.

Back at Benedict's, together alone in her suite, Clarice devoted herself to tendering her thanks in more tangible, much more sensual vein.

Later still, lying sated in the tangle of the bedcovers, Jack slumped beside her fast asleep, she found her mind drifting over recent events, over the changes in her life.

The unexpected shifts in her landscape, her unforeseen reactions.

That evening's incident with Warwick flared in her mind. She had no doubt whatever that he'd been about to make her an improper offer, when Jack had returned, and without even knowing of that pending insult, had dealt with Warwick as he deserved.

For her. There was no other reason that might have driven him. He'd acted not just as her defender, but as her avenger.

She'd never had anyone act for her in that sense. Not her father or her brothers. She'd never expected it of them; she wasn't even sure she'd have accepted such support from them.

Jack hadn't asked, he'd simply acted as her champion, as if he had the right.

She wasn't sure he didn't. She certainly felt no qualms, no inner difficulties over accepting help from him, over letting him stand as her defender, her champion.

The news, of course, would be all over the ton by morning, yet she couldn't summon any degree of care, of concern. She didn't care if the whole world knew that she was willing to allow him into her life. Close.

She glanced across the pillow, watched him as he slept, let her eyes trace his face, the hard planes, the definite angles. The strength inherent there, and in the heavy body half-wrapped around hers.

Her lips curved; she looked up at the ceiling, unexpectedly basking in his instinctive possessiveness.

A possessiveness that had always been there, with her, an aspect of his nature he'd never sought to hide or conceal. She'd seen it from the first, but hadn't felt threatened, still didn't. In her heart, in her bones, in her soul she knew he posed no threat to her, that he never would.

She wasn't sure why. Perhaps it was something to do with the connection that day by day, night by night, continued to grow between them. Perhaps that was why she didn't feel vulnerable, because due to that connection, he was vulnerable, too.

In the same way, to the same degree.

A mutual binding.

Reaching out, she let her fingers play in the soft ends of his hair while she considered that, and what such a binding might mean.

Her mind couldn't answer her questions. It drifted away to another change, another unforeseen reaction.

No one, herself included, could have known that, her position within the ton beyond her expectations reclaimed, she wouldn't want it anymore. That tonnish life and the constant whirl of society would no longer hold any allure for her. She'd been away long enough for the spell to fade and die; perhaps she should thank her father for that? Not for banishing her, but for forcing her to choose.

Life, as Claire had said, was a matter of making choices, then living with the results. Of choosing a road, then going forward along it, seeing where it led, enjoying the adventures along the way.

Much as she and Jack had done from the moment they'd met.

When this was ended, when they'd exonerated James, and saved her brothers and seen them each to the altar, she'd face another choice. To retreat to her previous existence, to choose society's road, or . . .

She tried to concentrate, but sleep fogged her mind and drew her down before she could decide whether she actually had another alternative, another unexpected road she could choose . . . or if she was simply dreaming.

* * *

"The bishop expects to convene his court tomorrow. I suggest we see him today." Jack looked across the table on which he'd spread their accumulated evidence and met Clarice's gaze.

It was after ten o'clock, and he'd returned from a morning conference with his colleagues at the Bastion Club to lay all they'd gathered before her.

"This"—he gestured to the documents arrayed before him—"is beyond convincing, proof positive that James never attended those three meetings, that the meetings never took place. With that established, the allegations no longer have any foundation. I discussed it with the others—we all feel that if there's a chance to avoid the matter appearing even in the bishop's court, we'd be wise to seize it."

Clarice nodded slowly, thinking it through. "That way, no formal allegations will be recorded, not anywhere."

"Precisely. So, shall we go and see the bishop?"

She met Jack's eyes, and nodded. "Let's."

Arriving at the palace, they spoke first to Dean Samuels and Deacon Olsen. The dean conveyed their message, their thoughts, directly to the bishop's ear. Ten minutes later, they were shown into a private audience.

"Well, then." The bishop looked from Jack to Clarice. "The dean tells me you have news?"

From his expression, it was plain that he was looking to them to help him avoid what for him now loomed as a political quagmire. Jack smiled. Ably assisted by Clarice, he obliged, going through each alleged meeting, citing the witnesses Deacon Humphries had named, in each case profering the signed and witnessed recanting of their stories and their tales of having been paid by the supposed courier to lie.

"The description of the man who has been meeting with Deacon Humphries, presumably giving him information, matches that of the man who paid the witnesses to swear that they'd seen James Altwood meeting with the courier in those taverns." Jack paused, then continued, "In addition, we have at least three witnesses for each tavern who will swear *no* clergyman has ever crossed their threshold, at least not in the last two years."

Looking up, he met the bishop's eyes. "Furthermore, we have confirmed information from various persons within the ton placing James at social functions on the same evenings as the alleged meetings."

Dropping the sheaf of statements onto the small table before him, Jack laid his hand on the last pile of documents. "Lastly, as to the information passed, while most of the details cited James did indeed have, and would be expected, military scholar that he is, to have, the specific information said to have been passed during one of the three recent meetings concerned details of demobilization." Jack's smile grew intent. "That, however, was information James Altwood didn't have."

Succinctly, he described the exhaustive search Dalziel had conducted. "All of which failed to find any avenue through which James Altwood accessed such information."

Clarice stepped forward. "Taken together, the evidence gathered proves conclusively that James did not attend the three meetings with any courier, indeed, was elsewhere at the time, and could not have had at least some of the information he is said to have passed to the enemy. In short, my lord, the allegations made against my relative appear entirely without foundation. More, they appear to have been constructed, either by this supposed courier or someone working through him, to ensnare the authorities, the Church included, in an unjustified trial."

The bishop blinked, but he wasn't disappointed. He nodded, his expression stern. "Indeed, Lady Clarice. Your point is well-taken." From his expression, he was clearly aware of the pitfalls involved in unjustified trials, even in his court.

He looked at Jack. "Lord Warnefleet, the Church is indebted to you, your superiors, and the others who aided you in assembling this evidence so swiftly. You have our thanks. And Lady Clarice, as well. You may convey to your family, dear lady, that there will be no further action taken in this matter." The bishop glanced at the stack of papers before Jack. "In light of all you've presented, I see no benefit in proceeding with a formal hearing. I intend to dismiss the allegations as unfounded. I will inform Whitehall of my decision."

Clarice beamed. "Thank you, my lord."

The formality preserved to that point dissolved. The dean and Deacon Olsen came forward to shake Jack's hand and exclaim over the evidence. Clarice engaged the bishop, who asked rather wistfully after her aunt Camleigh, inquiries Clarice, somewhat to her surprise, was now in a position to satisfy.

Some fifteeen minutes later, in perfect accord, they parted, Jack, Clarice, and Olsen leaving the bishop and dean to explain matters to Humphries, a solution they agreed was best all around.

Olsen left them at the head of the main stairs; delighted, he staggered off to his office, the evidence exonerating James piled in his arms.

Smiling, Jack turned to Clarice. She wound her arm in his. Side by side, they descended the stairs.

"One matter successfully dealt with." Clarice paused on the palace steps and lifted her face to the sun. "I suppose . . ." She looked at Jack. "Now we have James saved and that matter off our plate, we should concentrate on my brothers' futures." She eyed him appraisingly, assessing, subtly challenging. "Lady Hamilton is holding an *al fresco* luncheon today. Lady Cowper and Aunt Camleigh, entirely independently, mentioned it as an event I'd be well-advised not to miss."

Jack raised his brows but said nothing.

Undeterred, Clarice led him down the steps. "Of course," she confided, "they both want me there for the same reason." She caught Jack's eye. "Moira will be there, and so will the

Haverlings and the Combertvilles. After Helen's ball last night, I suspect our aunts want to ensure that Moira comprehends her revised position."

She grimaced and looked down.

Jack studied her face, what he could see of it. "It's political, isn't it? The way the ladies jostle for position and influence, band together in this faction and that?"

She glanced at him, then wrinkled her nose. "It's *like* politics, but more cutthroat. If you fail within the ton, you rarely get a second chance. Politics is more forgiving."

Jack swallowed a snort; from what he'd seen, she was right. The ornate gates at the end of the palace drive loomed before them. "Would you like me to escort you to this luncheon?"

The porter bowed and swung the gate open. Clarice stepped through, waited until Jack joined her, then smiled. "If you can spare the time. I'm really not sure what I might encounter. Having someone I trust by my side would be comforting."

Jack met her eyes, and bit back the words that he would always have time to be by her side—saw in the dark depths an awareness that mirrored his own. Boadicea wasn't in the habit of wanting the comfort of another's presence, let alone requesting it.

Lips curving, he raised her hand, kissed. "For you, I'd brave any danger, even the ladies of the ton."

She laughed and accepted his gallant offer. He hailed a hackney; they climbed aboard, and set out on their next adventure.

"Moira isn't here." Clarice met Jack's eyes, her puzzlement clear.

Scanning the gaily dressed horde thronging the riverside lawn of Hamilton House, Jack shrugged. "Perhaps she decided after last night that her presence was no longer required, that there was no longer any point. Her daughters are all married, aren't they?"

"Yes, but that won't wash. She's definitely angling to arrange a good match for Carlton. Wild horses shouldn't have been enough to keep her away from a gathering of this tone."

Clarice saw her aunt Camleigh through the crowd, caught her eye, and raised her brows pointedly. Her aunt shrugged and lifted her hands in a gesture that plainly stated she had no idea why Moira wasn't there either. Clarice grimaced and turned to view the crowd. "I suppose the truth is I just don't trust her. Know thine enemy and all that."

When Jack didn't respond, she glanced up, and saw him transfixed. Strangely wooden. She followed his gaze to a haughty matron, two young ladies in tow, sweeping toward them with the unstoppable determination of a galleon under full sail. The lady's gaze was fixed on Jack.

Sweeping to a halt before them, she smiled delightedly at Jack. "Lord Warnefleet, isn't it?"

Clarice didn't stop to think, simply acted; she stepped across Jack, forcing the lady, startled, to meet her eyes. Clarice smiled, thinly. "I don't believe we've been introduced."

The lady blinked, met Clarice's eyes, then swallowed, stepped back, and curtsied. Clarice looked at her charges; they quickly did the same.

"Lady Quintin, Lady Clarice. Lady Hamilton is my aunt."

"Ah, yes. I believe she mentioned you." Clarice looked at the young ladies. "And these are your daughters?"

Lady Quintin was clearly torn—to be first to engage the eminently eligible Lord Warnefleet on behalf of her charges, or instead gain the approbation of a lady as powerfully connected as Clarice Altwood . . . who was standing between her and her target. Her ladyship bowed to the dictates of reason, and smiled. "Indeed, my lady. Amelia and Melissa."

With a facility acquired through countless hours spent in similar pursuits, Clarice chatted with the three, then artfully dismissed them. Behind her, Jack was called on to do no more than bow. Distantly.

"Thank heavens!" He took Clarice's elbow as the three

moved away, and turned her toward the house. "Let's—" He broke off, then swore beneath his breath. "Saints preserve me—there's an army of them!"

"Saints won't do you much good, not in this arena." Smoothly, Clarice disengaged from his hold and instead wound her arm with his. Briefly, she caught his eye. "Stay close, and I promise to keep you safe."

The fraught look he cast her made her smile.

She turned that smile forward, on the mamas and their charges lying in wait. "No sense in trying to avoid this. We'll have to fight our way through."

They did, steadily moving toward the house, but each yard was gained only at the expense of an exchange with some matron and her daughter or niece, if not both. Initially Clarice wondered at Jack's reticence, at his clear wish to remain as aloof as possible rather than employ his customary effortless charm, but then she looked more definitely at him, into his eyes, and realized it was his temper he distrusted, not his glib tongue.

For some reason, the matrons pressing their charges on his notice touched some nerve . . . perhaps not surprising. They all seemed to imagine that they'd be able to manage him, to manipulate him into behaving as they wished. For a man such as he, with a background such as he, to be treated so—it was a form of contempt—had to be galling. Especially as social strictures forbade him to react as he undoubtedly wished.

People had tried to manipulate her once; at least she'd been able to say "no." For him, "no" wasn't an option; the ton didn't permit gentlemen to be so ruthless, not in public.

She, of course, could be as ruthless as she wished, but in deference to Lady Hamilton and the Altwood name, she played by the accepted rules, and repelled the predatory mamas one by one, with a smile, a swift and sure tongue, and an absolute refusal to release Jack's arm.

One couple—a veritable gorgon and her pretty but strangely nervous charge—remained in her mind. Not because of anything they said, but because of the tension that tightened Jack's muscles while they'd faced them.

It took more than half an hour to gain the terrace, then another fifteen minutes before they could fall back against the cushions in a blessedly silent hackney and heave sighs of relief.

Clarice glanced sideways at Jack, beside her. "That was ghastly. Was it like that when you were in town before?"

He let his head fall back against the squabs. "Yes. I told you I'd had enough of it, that that was one of the reasons I left."

And hadn't intended coming back. Clarice remembered. "The Cowley chit? You'd met her before."

His expression grew grimmer. "Before, she and her aunt were my absolute last straw." In a few words, he told her how they'd tried to entrap him. Even without him stating it, she could see what a near-run thing it had been.

"*Dreadful!* And then to so brazenly approach you again?" She narrowed her eyes. "I wish I'd known."

He chuckled rather tiredly. "Perhaps it's as well you didn't. The ton's focusing on you enough as it is."

After a moment, she murmured, "I'm sorry. Helping me has put you back in the matchmakers' sights."

His lips twisted; he reached for her hand and closed his about it. "No matter. You saved me. And in the main, you and the unmarried young darlings don't move in the same circles."

Clarice nodded and let the subject die, distracted by yet another revelation, with trying to make sense of yet another unforeseen reaction.

She'd been perfectly prepared to socially annihilate any lady who had attempted to pressure Jack, to force him to interact with them and their charges. It was indeed fortunate she hadn't known about the Cowleys at the time; heaven only knew what she might have done, how she would have made them pay. Faced with her determination, all the ladies had backed down, more than anything out of confusion; they were unsure what to make of her relationship with Jack. Unlike the more discerning males and the more experienced hostesses, most matrons saw her as unmarriageable, too old. So they'd bide their time and try again to engage Jack, who didn't want to be engaged.

It was her reaction to their aggression that surprised her, that left her off-balance. He—males of his class, his type—were the protective obsessives; why, then, did she suddenly feel the same?

What made the feeling even stranger was the edge of possessiveness that had crept into her thoughts, into the way she thought of him. That, too, she'd thought was an emotion peculiar to him, to males like him. But she was too attuned to her own desires, too used to acting on them not to be aware that she wanted him, wanted to secure him, hold him, keep him—possess him, too.

It was all very unsettling.

Especially when combined with the prospect of having to choose another road.

What if the road that opened at her feet didn't include Jack?

At Clarice's suggestion, they detoured via the park; from the safe confines of the hackney, they scanned the carriages lined up along the Avenue, but saw no sign of Moira.

"Something is definitely wrong." Clarice slumped back as Jack gave the order to return to Benedict's.

Her premonition seemed to be correct. The instant they swept into the foyer of the hotel, the concierge hurried forward with a note.

"My lady." The concierge bowed deeply before Clarice. "The marquess was insistent this be handed to you the instant you walked in."

Clarice took the note. "Thank you, Manning." Using the knife he offered, she broke Alton's seal, then handed back the knife, and dismissed the concierge with a nod.

Opening the note, she scanned it, then held it for Jack to read.

The note was short.

> *Dean Samuels is here at Melton House. He came look-*
> *ing for you and Warnefleet—there have been develop-*
> *ments in James's case. Come as soon as you read this.*

A.

Jack glanced at Clarice.

She was frowning. "*What* developments? The case is over, isn't it?"

"Apparently not." Taking the note, Jack folded it and handed it back to her. "We'd best go and find out."

The hackney hadn't yet left. The driver was glad to take them up again; adjured to hurry, he whipped his horses up and they swung through the streets to Melton House.

Alton and the dean were waiting in the library. Both rose as Clarice swept in. "What is it?" she demanded without preamble, waving them back to their seats.

Swinging her skirts about, she sat in the armchair opposite the dean. Jack fetched a straight-backed chair and set it beside her.

"It's nothing to do with the case against James *per se*," the dean hurried to assure them. "A mere technicality, a slight holdup, nothing more."

Clarice sat back, her dark gaze on his face. "What?"

The dean didn't look happy. "The bishop called Deacon Humphries in and explained your findings, intending, in the light of those, to ask Humphries to withdraw the charges, which would be the neatest way of dealing with the matter, you see."

Clarice nodded. "And?"

"Humphries was . . . well, *confused*. It wasn't that he questioned your findings, more that he couldn't see how they could be. He was insistent, *very* insistent that his charges were justified, that the information his informer would personally provide would prove more than convincing on its own. He'd intended to call the informer as a witness, if such confirmation was needed. He, Humphries, was still keen to present the man's evidence before the bishop. Humphries argued that without hearing that evidence, any move to let the charges fall would be premature. In short, he argued for leave to bring this man before the court."

Jack leaned forward, forearms on his knees. "We—Whitehall—would be very keen to meet this gentleman. Did Humphries tender his name?"

"No." The dean seemed increasingly agitated. "I asked, the bishop asked, but Humphries held that he'd given his word not to divulge the courier's name without his permission, because of course, as an ex-courier for the enemy, the man would be incriminating himself . . . although within the confines of an ecclessiastical court, that's not quite so clear. However." The dean drew in a deep breath. "I was called out of the room. While I was gone, Humphries pressed for, and the bishop granted him, leave to speak with the courier first, before revealing the man's name and calling him as a witness."

The dean met Jack's eyes. "Humphries has gone off to meet with the man."

Jack held the dean's gaze. "That's not at all wise."

The dean wrung his hands. "I felt so, too. I came as soon as I heard. The bishop's not pleased with Humphries, but he wants this matter settled, buried. We can all see it's a . . . well, a distraction, if not worse."

"Indeed." Clarice shifted forward; leaning across, she clasped her hands comfortingly about the dean's fretful ones. "But you've done all you can. We'll have to hope that Humphries returns soon and comes to the same conclusions as we have."

Under her dark gaze, the dean steadied. He nodded. "You're right. I'd best get back." He stood; the others followed suit. "I'll send word the instant Humphries returns."

After the dean had left the room, Clarice looked at Jack.

"Did Dalziel know we were going to speak with the bishop this morning?"

Jack nodded. "I sent word. It's possible Dalziel has someone watching Humphries. He, Dalziel, would certainly have been expecting to trace this courier via Humphries, but he might not have expected Humphries to go tearing off today." Jack moved to Alton's desk and reached for paper and pen. "I'd better alert Dalziel that Humphries has gone to meet the man."

Alton watched him scrawl a quick note and seal it, then Alton summoned a footman. Jack gave him the note and directions to Dalziel's office, buried in the depths of Whitehall.

Once the footman had gone, Alton looked at Jack. "This is truly serious, isn't it? You fear for Humphries' life."

Jack grimaced. "Whether it's reached that stage I don't know, but in this game, life and death are the usual rewards."

Clarice stirred. "Do you think Humphries knows that?"

Jack met her eyes. "No. I think he's an innocent caught unknowingly in a web spun by Dalziel's 'last traitor.'"

Clarice nodded. She saw Alton, puzzled, open his mouth to ask more questions; before he could, she asked, "What progress have you and the other two made with your proposals?"

A question certain to distract Alton. He glanced at the clock on the mantelpiece, then rose to tug the bellpull. "Let's have some tea and cakes, and the others can tell you themselves."

Edwards came in; Alton ordered tea and sent for Roger and Nigel, who wonder of wonders were both in the house. Clarice noted a certain spring in Edwards's step, detected an unusual ease in Alton, too, but she decided to let them answer the questions she'd already posed first.

Roger came striding in, and she didn't need words to know how his romance was faring; his eyes were alight, his stride carefree, his whole manner a testament to joyous expectation. He caught her hands, hauled her up, and waltzed her around the desk.

"Alice agreed. Her parents agreed. Everything is *wonderful!*" Halting once more before her chair, he planted smacking kisses on both her cheeks, then released her and heaved a contented sigh. "All is well!"

Clarice opened her eyes wide at him. "I'm delighted to hear that. However—"

"As for me—" Nigel appeared, caught her about her waist and swung her up and around, laughing when she swore and thumped his shoulder. He set her back on her feet, still grinning like a fool. "Emily thinks I'm a god. Her parents are a trifle more serious about it, but I know they think I'm remarkable, too." His eyes danced; he squeezed Clarice's hands and released her, letting her sink back into her chair. "So everything's set for the big announcement."

"Tea, my lords, my lady." Edwards, still beaming, swept in with the tea tray.

Clarice swallowed her pithy question: what about Moira? and waited while Edwards set out the teapot and cups, and a plate of cakes that her brothers and Jack fell upon like starving wolves. The instant the door closed behind Edwards she looked at Alton. "What about you and Sarah?"

Alton was struggling to keep a boyish grin from his face. "I haven't had a chance to speak with her today—she was out at some luncheon—but of course I've asked, and she's agreed. And"—he paused to draw a portentous breath—"I had an interview with Conniston at noon. He's accepted my offer—Claire had paved the way quite nicely, I must say—and so everything's now set."

He looked at Clarice; she was aware her other brothers were also looking expectantly her way. "It's really quite lucky the matter with the dean brought you here. We were wanting to ask you how soon we could hold a ball to make our formal announcements. Two days? Three? I know it'll be a rush, but we'll all help, and so will—"

"Wait!" Clarice set down her teacup, then looked at each of their faces. Not one showed any hint of a cloud on their horizon. She had to wonder . . . "What's happened to Moira?" She looked from one grinning face to the other. "Where *is* Moira?"

Alton smiled beatifically. "At the moment, she's on her way to Hamleigh House."

"*What?*" Clarice was stupefied.

A state her brothers seemed to relish. Nigel chortled. "It was really something, you know. Vesuvius erupting at the breakfast table, fireworks exploding—pity you missed it."

Roger grinned, unrepentant but understanding. "Alton's banished her."

Clarice couldn't speak. Couldn't find words, couldn't get her tongue around them. She stared at Alton. He grinned back, so transparently pleased with himself she didn't like to ask, but she had to know. "Why? And how?"

She wasn't entirely surprised when they all sobered. They exchanged glances; she held up a hand. "Just tell me. No roundaboutation, if you please."

Alton grimaced. "She waltzed into the breakfast parlor this morning in high dudgeon. She wanted—no, she *insisted*—that I banish you again."

"She screamed and moaned and gnashed her teeth," Nigel supplied.

Alton nodded. "Over the family, about how they were treating her now you were back, and so on."

"Helen's ball was the last straw, it seemed," Roger put in.

"That I can understand," Clarice returned. "But surely you didn't banish her for a little ranting."

Alton frowned. "It wasn't just a little."

"Well, you can imagine what she said about you," Nigel said.

"But anyway, that wasn't all. When I refused to banish you, she threatened us, but not just us. She threatened Sarah and the others, but Sarah most of all . . ." Alton grimaced sheepishly. "I lost my temper."

"He *roared* at her." Nigel's expression clearly stated he'd enjoyed every minute.

Clarice blinked.

"Didn't know he had it in him," Roger put in. "Not at that volume, anyway."

Alton glared at his brothers. "Regardless, it couldn't go on, her constantly threatening us, trying to manage everything to benefit her darling Carlton." His voice hardened. "She pushed me too far, and I pushed back. I told her that, given all she'd said about our three wives-to-be, she was no longer welcome at any of the family's major estates. I told her she could go to Hamleigh"—Alton glanced at Jack—"it's a small manor the family own in Lancashire—and I'd pick up the household bills and she could live off her jointure, or she could go and stay with her daughters and their husbands if she chose, but she was not to set foot in any of the family's other houses again, and not to show her face in London again, either."

Clarice couldn't believe it. "And she agreed?"

Nigel grinned even more. "That was the best part. I thought she was going to have an apoplexy right there over the breakfast table."

Alton frowned him down. "Of course she didn't agree. She ranted and raved and threatened some more, until I informed her that we understood she wanted Carlton to marry well, but that that was hardly likely to occur if we let it be known that he wasn't Papa's get."

Chapter 19

❧

Clarice knew her mouth was falling open, but she couldn't seem to stop it. She gaped at Alton, finally managed to find breath enough to say, "You *knew?*"

Alton frowned. "No. That is, I only learned of it last evening when I dropped by Gribbley and Sons to check the figures for the settlements. Old Gribbley had heard of my plans—he called me into his office to congratulate me and reminisce about how Papa would have seen the match. While doing that, he let fall Papa's views on Carlton's parentage."

"*Papa* knew?" Clarice stared even more.

"Apparently. I gathered it was more than suspicion, but according to Gribbley, with Carlton fourth in line, Papa didn't care to make a point of it—which sounds like Papa." Alton shrugged. "I daresay, if he hadn't died so suddenly, he would have mentioned it to me. As it was, I didn't know, but Gribbley thought I did."

Clarice blinked. "But Moira knew you didn't. After Papa died, she felt perfectly safe in forcing you to dance to her tune."

"Indeed."

"But *you* knew." Head tilted, Roger was studying her. "How?"

Clarice grimaced. "I was seven at the time, and Moira and

I were already at loggerheads. Meeting your lover in your own house with an antagonistic young stepdaughter about was hardly wise."

"But you never let her know you knew," Nigel said.

"No, but if she'd kept on as she was, I would have." Clarice looked at Alton. "I intended to confront her with exactly that if she didn't give way over your marriages." She smiled. "But now I don't have to, for you've taken care of it yourself."

Alton's lips twisted wryly. "Just as well I did. Conniston asked about Moira, so I told him what I'd done. Later, after he'd given his blessing, he told me he wouldn't have if Moira had still been about. He thinks she's a viper. He congratulated me for, in his words, 'coming of age.'"

Clarice studied him for a moment, then let her smile deepen. "In some ways that's true, and I have to say it's something of a relief."

All three of her brothers made rude sounds, but she merely smiled at them all.

"Now," Alton said, leaning forward, "what about our engagement ball?"

They spent the rest of the afternoon sorting out the arrangements. Jack watched Clarice rise to the occasion, even though she still seemed a trifle dazed.

James was safe, exonerated, his name unimpugned. True, Humphries had yet to withdraw the charges, but as the dean had said, that was only a minor holdup; all would soon be well.

As for Humphries, Jack entertained the gravest concerns, although he said nothing to dampen Clarice's mood. While she was rattling off instructions regarding the guest list and the invitations, the footman sent to Whitehall returned with a reply from Dalziel; Jack stepped into the front hall to read it.

Dalziel had indeed dispatched a minion to watch and follow Humphries; on reaching the palace and realizing how many exits from the grounds there were, said minion had sent for reinforcements. Unfortunately, before they could arrive and throw a proper net around the palace, Humphries left by a rear gate and disappeared.

For Humphries, the future did not bode well. Dalziel wrote that he would keep Jack informed and requested that Jack reciprocate.

Tucking the note into his pocket, Jack turned to go back into the library, only to find Alton had followed him out and was regarding him evenly.

Jack raised his brows.

Alton studied his face, then nodded toward the note. "That man in Whitehall—was he the one you worked for during the war?"

Jack hesitated; the impulse to veil his past was ingrained, still real.

Alton colored. "I—we—checked. You were a major in the Guards, but no one in your regiment remembers you at all. Yet you're hardly the forgettable type."

Jack smiled, entirely sincerely. "Actually, you'll find that I'm totally forgettable when I wish to be." He walked closer, halting before Alton so no one else could overhear. "That was my particular talent, always being able to merge in, to appear as if I belonged." He met Alton's eyes steadily. "And yes, the gentleman in Whitehall was my superior for over a decade."

Alton nodded, then smiled. "We just wanted to know."

Jack returned his smile easily. "Entirely understandable."

"Alton? Where the devil are you?"

They turned as Clarice appeared at the library door. She frowned at Alton. "Don't think to escape."

Alton looked innocent. "I was just going to send for Sarah."

Clarice nodded. "Do. And while you're at it, send for Alice and Emily, too, and Aunt Camleigh and you'd better ask Aunt Bentwood, as well. We'll need everyone to do their part if we're to arrange a major ball in five days."

"It could just be an ordinary ball," Alton said. "We wouldn't mind."

Clarice bent a look of withering scorn upon him. "Don't be an ass! You're the Marquess of Melton—your engagement ball, by definition, *cannot be* anything other than major! Now come on." She turned back into the room. "You and the others can make a start on the invitations."

Alton followed her in. Jack followed more slowly in his wake. He paused just inside the threshold and watched Clarice bustle about, setting her brothers to the task of penning invitations.

James was saved, her brothers' engagements secured and shortly to be appropriately announced to the fashionable world. All she'd come to London to do, they'd achieved. She'd decreed the ball would be held as soon as possible; he'd interpreted that as a wish to have everything done and finished with.

After that . . .

Watching her, he couldn't deny the unsettling uncertainty that had taken root in his mind. Would she return to Avening and quiet country life, or had tonnish society and her family not just reclaimed but recaptured her?

She saw him and frowned. "Come along. You aren't going to escape either."

He smiled, easily, charmingly, and ambled over to do her bidding.

They spent the next two hours immersed in engineered chaos. Only Clarice seemed to know what came next. Her sisters-in-law-to-be arrived and joined the discussions, after which Clarice sent them home armed with lists of questions for their parents. Her aunts stopped by and gave their regal blessing, promising to send a list of the more influential members of the ton to be included among the guests.

Throughout, Clarice kept him and her brothers busy inscribing invitations in their best copperplate.

Finally, she glanced at the clock, and called a halt. "We need to dress for dinner."

Alton stretched and groaned. "I'm going to collapse at my club."

Clarice narrowed her eyes at him. "No, you are not. You're going to join Sarah and squire her about." She raked her other two brothers. "And you are going to do the same with Alice and Emily. As of now, you are affianced gentlemen, and you need to act the part. If you want your engagement ball to be a success, you'll start sowing the right seeds tonight."

Nigel snorted. "Three Altwoods announce their engagements all on the same night, with their recently returned-from-banishment sister as hostess. The ball won't be a success, it'll be a riot. Everyone in London will want to attend." He caught Clarice's glare and held up his hands. "All right, all right, we'll do as you say, but there's no chance of this ball being anything other than a horrible crush."

"Actually"—Alton leaned forward and fixed his dark gaze on Clarice's face—"speaking of hostesses, you will return here now, won't you, Clary? Moira's gone, and Sarah certainly won't mind—she sees you as an older sister already. She'd welcome your help, and indeed, no one is better suited to dealing with this sort of thing." He waved at the clutter of invitations surrounding them. "There's no reason you need to return to Avening, not now. James doesn't need you, but we do. You will stay, won't you?"

Jack's heart seized.

Before Clarice could utter a word, Roger and Nigel leapt in to add their entreaties. This time, the three were more persuasive; they'd had time to plan and polish their arguments. They painted a picture of Clarice's life as it should have been, as it could now be if she wished, the life she was born to, one of privilege, wealth, and position.

Jack managed not to react, not to stiffen, not to draw anyone's attention as he sat back and listened. Calling on the skills of his past, he let himself fade into the background until the other four had forgotten he was there.

He watched Clarice. She hadn't yet suceeded in saying a word; she seemed resigned to letting her brothers put forward every last argument they could muster, pulling every string they could think of to convince her to return to the family fold.

Keeping silent and still was an effort, a battle. He felt like his heart was in his throat, but still he waited. It was her decision, and only hers.

Finally, when Nigel had at last run out of words and an expectant silence fell, Clarice smiled at them. "Thank you, but no."

Jack breathed out. He felt faintly giddy.

Clarice held up a hand to cut off her brothers' protests. "No. Don't argue. You've argued quite enough, and I must return to the hotel and get ready for the evening."

Calm and serene, she rose and turned to Jack.

Rising, too, he met her eyes, but could read nothing beyond fond exasperation with her brothers in the dark depths.

She kissed them as they farewelled her. "I'll see you all tonight."

Cloaking his feelings in his customary geniality, Jack bade the brothers good-bye, led her into the hall and out to Alton's town carriage, waiting to carry them to Benedict's. Settling onto the seat beside her, head back as the carriage lurched, then rumbled on its way, he told himself she'd said "no."

Unfortunately, it hadn't been a very convincing "no."

It hadn't convinced her brothers; he'd seen the glances they'd exchanged. It hadn't convinced him either.

Things had changed dramatically, unexpectedly. She'd been welcomed back into the ton, her stepmother had been defeated and banished, her brothers were all to marry soon. And they'd succeeded in exonerating James.

When she'd had time to consider, to think of how much had altered, would she still wish to return to Avening, a quiet country backwater, or would she choose to remain in town and live the life she always should have had?

He wasn't going to give her up. Not easily; not without a fight.

Arm braced against the mantelpiece, boot propped on the

fender, Jack stared into the fire in the sitting room of Clarice's suite. She was still dressing for the evening; he had a little time.

Her brothers' renewed push to have her rejoin the family had been an unwelcome shock. He was grimly aware of how significant a threat their suggestion posed to his vision of the future, the vision he'd been nurturing for the past weeks, that of him living quietly at Avening with Clarice by his side.

At no stage had he imagined winning her would be easy. Unlike with other females, he couldn't ride up and slay her dragons for her and claim her hand as his reward. With her, he could only clear the way, at most empower her so she could slay said dragons herself. She was that sort of woman. He could stand by her side, his hand over hers on her sword and help her, but as with vanquishing Moira, it was she who had to perform the crucial act.

Being self-determining was a part of who she was; he couldn't in any way take that from her. Not if he wanted her, and he did.

Through their time in the ton, his admiration for her had only grown. He'd seen more of her strengths, and while those dominated everyone's view of her, he'd glimpsed vulnerabilities, too. And noted them. Not to exploit, but to support, to protect.

In his heart, he was convinced she needed him every bit as much as he needed her. But how to bring that to her attention?

The only answer he'd been able to conjure was to unstintingly give her the support she needed, which wasn't always what one might suppose. She didn't need or want to be protected in the same way other women did, but assisted. Treated as an equal, not set in a gilded cage.

But he'd been doing precisely that for weeks, and while she definitely appreciated his help, he suspected she viewed it more or less as her due, which, indeed, it was. How, then, was he to shake her, to open her eyes so she saw him as him, and not just as a male who had the sense to deal with her correctly?

Deverell's advice returned to him. Surprise. He'd thought the idea worthy of consideration at the time; now, it held promise.

If he wanted to woo her, then it had to be suitably, which meant unconventionally. Others had tried conventional approaches in the past; it was no real wonder they hadn't succeeded.

Not jewels; too easy, too predictable, and she already had a horde. Something more meaningful.

"Right then."

He turned to see the object of his thoughts gliding toward him encased in a seductive confection of shimmering cerise gossamers and matching silks.

She caught his eye, and twirled. "Do you approve?"

He met her gaze, and smiled, with perfectly sincere intent. "You look . . . superb." Taking her cloak from the maid who'd followed her from the bedroom, he draped it over her shoulders. As he did, he murmured, voice low, just for her, "Quite *delectable*, in fact."

From close quarters, her eyes, a trifle wide, touched his, briefly scanned, then her lips lifted, and she looked ahead. "We'd better go."

Before he shocked the maid. He smiled, inclined his head, and followed her from the room.

Jack came down to a late breakfast at the Bastion Club, still smiling at the fond memories he now possessed of a warrior-queen writhing in naked ecstasy upon a bed of shimmering cerise silk.

The color of the silk against her skin, ruby against the ivory white, just like rose petals, had given him an idea of one gift he could give her that she wouldn't expect, but, he suspected, would appreciate.

He mentioned his requirements to Gasthorpe, who undertook to send a footman to scour the city and surrounds for what he needed.

He'd just finished a plate of ham and sausages and was savoring Gasthorpe's excellent coffee, when a sharp knock on the club's front door was followed by an inquiry in a clear voice he knew well, in a tone that brought his protective instincts surging to life. Rising, he walked out without waiting for Gasthorpe to summon him.

Clarice met his eyes, signaled toward the dean, standing beside her. "There you are. I fear we bring bad news."

Jack took one look at the dean's ashen face, and ushered them both into the parlor. "Perhaps a little brandy, Gasthorpe."

"Indeed, my lord. At once."

Jack saw the dean into one armchair. Clarice watched, then sank into the other. Although shocked, she was by no means overcome.

"What's happened?" Jack looked at the dean; the man suddenly seemed his age, much frailer than before.

"Humphries." The dean met Jack's eyes. "He hasn't returned."

Gasthorpe arrived with a tray loaded with brandy, tea and coffee. Jack gave the dean a stiff tot of brandy, then helped himself to coffee while Clarice poured herself a cup of tea.

The dean sipped, coughed, sipped again, then cleared his throat. "I wanted to send word last night, when Humphries didn't appear at dinner, but the bishop . . . I think he was hoping against hope. He's in a terrible state. We've asked all the porters, but they haven't seen Humphries since he left the palace yesterday afternoon, soon after he spoke with the bishop."

Jack glanced at Clarice, met her dark eyes. "We can hope, but I fear we should expect the worst."

He looked at the dean, who nodded, defeated. "I'll send word to my colleagues, and get a search under way." He hesitated, then asked, "Has the bishop notified Whitehall?"

The dean frowned. "I don't know . . . I don't think so."

"I'll send word there, too."

After a few minutes, when some color had returned to the dean's parchmentlike cheeks, Jack suggested he return to the palace. "Tell the bishop we'll do all we can, but if something serious has befallen Humphries, it's possible we'll never know. And if by chance Humphries does return, do let me know immediately."

"Yes, of course." The dean stood.

Clarice got to her feet. "I'll take the Dean back to the palace in my carriage." She met Jack's gaze. "I've canceled all my appointments today. I'll be spending the entire day at Melton House, organizing."

Jack nodded. "I'll send word there, and to the palace, if we have any news. That said, I'm not expecting to learn anything soon."

He saw the dean and Clarice back to Alton's town carriage, then strode swiftly back to the house.

"Gasthorpe?"

"Yes, my lord—I have the footmen waiting."

He sent word to Dalziel, Christian, and Tristan, and roused Deverell from his bed upstairs. All of them went to work, activating a network of eyes and ears, concentrating on the areas south and east of the palace, and all along the Thames, searching for any sighting of Humphries, alone or with someone else.

The Bastion Club became their base; Dalziel sent word he'd have his men report there, too.

After lunch, Jack changed into merchant garb and went down to the river. Finding a team of bargemen with no work, he sent them to search the marshes at Deptford as far east as Greenwich Reach, the traditional place for bodies put into the river close to the city to wash up. That done, he returned to the club to receive any reports and coordinate their efforts.

The day wore on, and they heard nothing. Although he hadn't expected anything else, Jack wondered if they'd ever learn what had happened to Humphries.

As the hours ticked by, he was glad Clarice was occupied, safely ensconced in the bosom of her family, surrounded by others and with too much to do to think too much about the missing deacon. To wonder if there'd been anything they could have done differently that might have deflected the sadly driven man from his determined course.

Jack knew there wasn't. That when people like Humphries were caught in a web of intrigue and treason, they were too weak to break free. In this case, the spider— the last traitor—would devour Humphries, even if, as Jack suspected, it wouldn't be he himself who did the deed.

When afternoon edged toward evening, and there was still no word, Jack left the reins in Gasthorpe's capable hands and headed for Benedict's. Finding Clarice absent, he went on to Melton House.

She was still there. He walked into the drawing room and saw her seated on a chaise surrounded by her sisters-in-law-to-be, her aunts, and a small army of female helpers. She looked like nothing so much as a general directing her troops.

Distracted, she looked up; across the room, she met his eyes. Swiftly read his expression. She didn't need to ask whether they'd heard anything.

She glanced at the clock, blinked, then turned to her helpers. "Great heavens! We've forgotten the time!"

The observation triggered a torrent of exclamations, of orders for carriages to be brought around. The female gathering broke up. Jack surmised Clarice's brothers had taken refuge in their clubs.

The departing ladies smiled shyly up at him as they trooped past him into the front hall. Clarice brought up the rear. Reaching him, she lifted a hand and lightly touched his cheek, then let her hand fall to grip his arm before moving past him.

Comforted by that fleeting touch, by the understanding and empathy it conveyed, he followed her into the hall. He nodded to her aunts as they kissed Clarice's cheek and turned to leave.

"We'll see you later," Lady Bentwood told Clarice.

Jack wanted nothing more than a peaceful evening alone with Boadicea.

When the door closed behind the last of the ladies, she walked back to him. With a sigh, she halted before him.

He looked into her dark eyes. "Do we have to go out tonight?"

She studied his eyes, then grimaced. "I'm afraid so. It's Lady Holland's *bal masque*."

Lady Holland was one of the ton's foremost hostesses.

Taking his hand, Clarice led him into the drawing room. Inside, she turned into his arms; behind him, he pushed the door closed.

"We have to go. It's an annual event, one of those must-attend events of the Season, at least among the haut ton."

He pulled a face. "And it's a masked ball?"

She leaned into him, smiled as he settled his arms about her. Raising her hands, she framed his face. "We have to go, but we don't have to stay long."

He searched her eyes. "Where am I going to get a domino?"

"I've asked Manning, the concierge, to organize one. He's terribly efficient, and for some unfathomable reason, he's decided he approves of you."

Jack humphed. "Very well. If we must, we must." That she'd spoken of "we" throughout mollifed him somewhat.

She stretched up and kissed him. Gently, lightly, a promise of things to come.

He accepted the caress, but made no move to take it further.

Ending it, she drew back, lifting one brow in patent surprise.

With his head, he indicated the door. "It has a lock, but no key."

Her expression lightened. She laughed and stepped out of his arms. "In that case, it's clearly time to leave. Let's go back to Benedict's. We can dine there."

They did, then she dressed for the evening, and they took the carriage to the Bastion Club. Jack donned his evening clothes while Gasthorpe relayed the results of the day's search, an uninspiring negative all around.

Jack grimaced and dismissed Gasthorpe with a nod. Swirling the black domino Manning had had waiting for him around his shoulders, he tied the ties across his chest, made a horrendous face in the mirror, then picked up the black mask that completed the prescribed outfit, and went down to fetch Clarice from the parlor.

During the drive to Holland House, he told her of their lack of success.

Returning the clasp of his fingers, she leaned lightly against his shoulder. "You've done all you can."

Their carriage joined the line of conveyances waiting to deposit their occupants before the arched entrance to the gardens of Holland House. Eventually, the carriage rocked to a complete halt; putting on their masks, they descended, then followed the graveled path beneath a stand of old trees to the conservatory where the Hollands stood waiting to receive their guests. Her ladyship's famed *bal masque* was always held in the gardens rather than in Holland House itself.

The terrace onto which the conservatory opened was long, and lit by numerous lamps; when, after being warmly welcomed by Lady Holland and her much quieter spouse, Jack and Clarice emerged onto its flags, the wide expanse running the length of the house was already crammed with the cream of the ton, a strange sight in their crowlike dominos, with the bright colors of gowns flashing here and there, like jewels hidden beneath, while the genuine jewels garlanding ladies' throats and winking from gentlemen's cravats glowed with liquid fire.

The impression of a gathering of fantastical birds was heightened by the masks, some with long feathers adorning their upper edges, others with jeweled or gilt nosepieces very like beaks.

At this stage of the night, masks were compulsory, as were the black dominos. In a well-lit ballroom, it would be relatively easy to penetrate such an incomplete disguise, but in the Holland House gardens, neither the flickering terrace lamps, the moon that shed a gentle radiance, nor the small lanterns scattered about the gardens cast enough illumination to do anything other than veil every figure in mystery.

As more guests arrived, those already present spilled down the terrace steps and spread out along the lower walks and lawns; like a wave, they rippled expectantly across the paved court, an improvised dance floor. Descending the steps at Clarice's side, Jack admitted, "It really is a magical sight."

Hidden in a leafy grotto, the musicians set bows to strings, and the first haunting strains of a waltz floated out above the gleaming heads. Clarice turned into his arms and he gathered her in, then set them revolving.

She smiled. "It's a magical night."

At such a ball, until the unmasking at midnight, it was possible to dance with one partner exclusively without causing a scandal; with everyone masked and cloaked, how could any of the beady eyes watching possibly be sure, sure enough to risk comment? So they waltzed, and talked quietly as they moved through the crowd. Some guests, mainly the younger crew, grasped the opportunity of anonymity to indulge in rather more risqué behavior than they would normally dare, yet the gathering was generally benign, a pleasant way to spend a spring evening.

Later, once dominos were put back and masks removed, the glitter and glamour of a ton ball would take hold, until then, a sense of subtle mystery held sway.

"That's Alton." Clarice leaned close to Jack, indicating a couple standing nearby, totally oblivious to all about them. "At least he's behaving. I haven't sighted the other two, yet."

"They're here." Jack steered her away from Alton and Sarah.

Clarice blinked up at him. "Have you seen them? How did you recognize them?"

He grinned. "They saw you. I recognized their reaction."

She studied his eyes, confirmed he wasn't joking, then humphed and looked away. Being taller than the average, she was relatively easy to recognize; spotting her through the crowd, Roger and Nigel had both headed in the opposite direction. Jack smiled, and turned her toward the dance floor; the musicians were getting ready to start playing again.

They were at the edge of the floor, waiting to step into the dance, when a younger couple, laughing, presented themselves before them.

The lady playfully wagged her finger at them. "Her ladyship says you've been dancing together far too much. You must mingle."

"Indeed." Her companion, tall and darkly handsome, grinned. "You are *commanded* to mingle." He bowed flourishingly before Clarice. "My lady?"

Clarice shot an amused glance at Jack, then gave the gentleman her hand. "If you insist, my lord."

Jack watched her step into the gentleman's arms, quelled a pang of jealousy and patently irrational concern. He looked down at the pretty blond lady, who all but bobbed before him expectantly. He smiled. "Ma'am, if you would honor me with this dance?"

She laughed, a light sound that held a measure of triumph, then gave him her hand and let him lead her to the floor.

There was nothing unusual about the encounter; the same had been happening to other couples about them for the last half hour. Nevertheless, out of habit, Jack kept a distant eye on Clarice as he whirled his partner around the floor.

Keeping track of Clarice should have been easy, yet when the dance ended and, parting from his companion, who curtsied prettily then bobbed away into the crowd, doubtless searching for her next victim, Jack focused on the lady he'd thought was Clarice, the woman turned and proved to be someone much older. A chill touched his nape. He scanned the shifting crowd, but could see no other tall and regal female.

The last he'd glimpsed of her, and been sure it was her, she and her partner had been revolving down the other side of the floor. Reminding his prickling instincts that they were in the private gardens of Holland House, enclosed within stone walls, and that the chances of anything untoward occurring were surely slight, he started quartering the crowd.

He tried not to dwell on the fact that anyone with any connection to the ton would have known that Clarice would be there tonight. Dancing with him in the poor light.

And that everyone would be masked and cloaked, indistinguishable—that no matter how he prodded his memory, he would never be able to identify either the gentleman who had whisked Clarice away or the lady who had distracted him.

When he reached the other side of the dance floor, and had still not found Clarice, he was ready to panic.

"Unhand me, you oaf!" Clarice struggled frantically, trying to break free of the rough hands that had grabbed her and hauled her back through shrubs and bushes into a dark clearing.

Her partner—the bounder!—had whirled her to an unexpected halt at the far edge of the dancing area, indeed, just a little beyond, where the paved court was bounded by thick shrubbery.

He'd released her, bowed, smiled unpleasantly, and rather ominously advised her, "Enjoy the rest of your evening, Lady Clarice."

She'd blinked, and he was gone, a swirl of black domino merging into the crowd. Frowning, she'd stepped forward to follow him, away from that distant nook where no one else stood, when two pairs of hands had reached out of the bushes at her back and grabbed her.

"Jus' be still, woman! 'Ere, Fred, where's that gag?"

Hauling in a breath, Clarice tried to wrestle free, but the man behind her, a huge brute, simply tightened his arms around her until she thought she might faint. Abruptly realizing how real was her danger, she sucked in a tight breath and opened her mouth to scream—

Her mask went flying. A huge paw slapped over her lips.

"Now, now—you don't want to do that, missy. No need to let anyone know we're 'ere."

He lifted her off her feet and started to shuffle forward, away from the noisy crowd.

Clarice closed her eyes, tried not to breathe—he reeked enough to make her feel faint just from the smell—and bit down on his palm.

Hard.

She nearly gagged, but it worked. He howled, wrenched his palm away and desperately shook his hand. She didn't wait but hauled in a breath and screamed for help.

The other man, a shadowy figure, slapped her. Almost casually, but the blow made her head sing.

"Stop that!"

The man still holding her was cursing. The other came to stand before her, piggy eyes peering into her face from beneath the brim of a dirty cap. "No point screeching, anyhows. The nobs're making such a racket no one'll hear you."

She dragged in another breath to scream again; the instant she opened her mouth, quick as a flash the second man stuffed a crumpled kerchief into it.

Clarice gagged, wheezed, and tried to spit out the material, frantically trying to clear her mouth.

Her sudden burst of struggling caused the man holding her to yelp; he grabbed her shoulder, fighting to hold her upright.

Just as Jack crashed through the wall of bushes.

Clarice redoubled her efforts. Out of the corner of her eye she saw Jack grab the second man and fell him with one blow.

Then he turned to face the man holding her, who took one look at him and instantly started to use her as a shield.

Jack went one way, the man went the other, keeping her between them. For a fraught minute, they performed an awkward dance.

The man Jack had felled groaned; he hauled himself onto his hands and knees, moaning.

"Come on, Fred! We got to get outta 'ere!"

Gathering himself, the man behind her lifted her and literally threw her at Jack.

Jack caught her, pulled her protectively to him, staggered back under her weight but steadied.

His arms wrapped protectively around her, she felt his muscles tense with the impulse to give chase as her assailants stumbled away, quickly disappearing into the blackness that was the rest of the gardens.

Unabashedly clinging to him, she knew the instant they were alone, safe; the battle-ready tension holding him faded, enough for him to move, to gently brush her cheek, cradle her face and tip it up to his.

"Are you all right?"

Not entirely sure she could trust her voice, she nodded, met his eyes, fell into them.

Watched his gaze devour her face, trace her features, saw in the moonlight the hard edges and planes of his face shift. Saw, very clearly, the Norman lord he truly was, the battle-hardened warrior stripped, for one instant, bare.

What she saw in that instant, in his face, made her heart turn over.

His eyes met hers, seemed to see into her, seemed to sense that she did indeed, could indeed see him. Then something— raw possessiveness, blatant desire—swept through his eyes. His arms tightened about her. He bent his head and kissed her.

As if he owned her. Completely. Utterly.

She was swept away on the tide; she didn't even try to fight it. Clung, instead; wrapped her arms about his neck and kissed him back with every iota of passion in her highly passionate soul.

Time stood still.

For long moments, they communed, explicit and intimate on their private plane in the dark of the night.

At last, he lifted his head, looked down into her eyes. She was plastered against him, molded to him; she saw no need to move.

Something caught his attention. He looked at her shoulder, at where her domino had been pushed aside; he frowned. "Your gown's ripped."

Freeing one hand, still holding her safe against him, he lifted the torn silk of her bodice, smoothing the fragile material up over her breast to the shoulder seam from which it had parted.

That was when they heard the first titter.

They both swung to look, Jack still holding her protectively within the circle of his arms.

A bevy of guests, old and young, stood crowded around a gap in the bushes a little farther along. Two of the males were holding lanterns aloft.

"Ah . . ." one said. "We, ah, thought we heard a scream, and . . . ah, came to look."

Unsurprisingly, that was greeted with a positive wave of titters. Some of the older guests were whispering behind their hands.

Clarice closed her eyes against the sight and stifled a groan. It wasn't hard to imagine what they thought they'd seen.

Jack looked faintly disheveled, protective and defensive. Her skirts were badly crushed, her domino all askew, her bodice torn, and she had indeed screamed. No doubt they'd arrived just in time to see that unrestrainedly passionate kiss, and now thought they understood what had happened.

Jack glanced at her; he didn't know what to say. Neither did she.

Before they could make any attempt to set the matter straight, Alton pushed through the crowd. He strode directly to them. "What the devil's going on?"

"Two men attacked Clarice," Jack said, his tone low.

"What?" Alton stared at her; to Jack's relief, he seemed to see her pallor. "My God! Are you all right?"

"Yes. Jack found me in time. But—"

"Which way did they go?" Alton raked the darkness beyond them.

Jack pointed. "But they'll be away by now. I couldn't leave Clarice to follow them."

"Of course not!"

"Alton—"

"My heavens! What is going on?" Lady Camleigh came bustling up, giving the crowd, who were starting to edge away, a severe look. She glanced at Jack and Clarice. Her eyes opened wide. "What . . . ?"

Alton explained before Jack could.

Within a minute, Lady Cowper, Lady Davenport, and ultimately Lady Holland herself had joined them, along with Roger and Nigel and their fiancées, and Sarah, too.

Jack could feel the effort it was costing Clarice, still within his arm, to remain upright, head high, her spine poker-straight. Everyone was exclaiming, asking how it had happened, whether she was all right—

"Quiet, please!" Clarice didn't shout, but her tone effectively cut through the chatter.

Everyone fell silent. Everyone looked at her.

She made no attempt to step away from Jack's side, but, clasping her hands at her waist, she lifted her chin and quietly stated, "There's something you all need to know."

Jack could feel her quivering with shock and agitation, but nothing showed in her cool demeanor or her steady gaze.

"Before you appeared, a crowd had gathered—they came, rather late, in response to my scream. But after Jack had rescued me and the men who attacked me had vanished, I kissed him, and he kissed me. Then he helped me straighten my torn gown." With one hand, she waved at her shoulder, where the bodice gaped from the seam. "That, unfortunately, is what the interested saw." She paused, and looked around the circle of their supporters. "I think you can imagine what they *think* they saw."

"Damn!" It was Nigel who uttered their thoughts aloud.

Regally, Clarice inclined her head. "Precisely. However . . . I'm afraid I really do not feel up to circulating among the guests for the next hour and more to quash the inevitable rumors."

Concern in his face, Alton stepped toward her. "You *aren't* all right."

Clarice raised a restraining hand. "I'm just feeling a trifle shaky, that's all. Jack will take me back to Benedict's. I'll be fully recovered by tomorrow. But"—she drew in a tight breath, looked around the circle once again—"I wanted you all to realize . . . what will come."

Somewhat to Jack's surprise, the ladies, both young and old, gathered closer, assuring Clarice that she could leave it to them, that they'd ensure no ill-informed nonsense was credited. Everyone accompanied them back to the house in a blatant show of solidarity.

The one who surprised Jack most was Lady Holland, their venerable hostess. She had the reputation of being an excellent friend, and a god-awful enemy; until she stood beside them while the carriage was brought around, Jack hadn't been sure which she would prove to be.

But then she patted Clarice's hand. "Don't worry, my dear. I think you underestimate your standing, and ours, too, if you think we can't scotch this, or at least nip it in the bud. It's transparent to any who've spoken with you both that the incident happened exactly as you described. In such circumstances, the rest"—with a wave Lady Holland dismissed their too-revealing embrace—"is merely to be expected."

Her ladyship turned her slightly protruberant eyes on him, and smiled. "Indeed, a gentleman such as Lord Warnefleet would have greatly disappointed us had he not reacted as he did."

Outwardly, Jack smiled; inwardly he groaned. The last thing he needed was to be cast as a romantic hero to the entire ton.

At last they were in the carriage, rolling briskly back to Benedict's. They didn't talk along the way; Clarice held his hand tightly, her head against his shoulder, and stared out into the night.

He did the same. Reliving that scene, imaging what the crowd had seen. The difficulty with Lady Holland's and the others' assurances was simple; they hadn't seen that too-revealing embrace. That kiss that had cut far too close to his bone, the inevitable reaction to a situation that had shaken him so badly his customary chameleon's mask had been nowhere in sight.

That moment, that kiss, had been far too raw, their emotions, both his and hers, far too close to the surface for any-one watching to have misunderstood.

To not have seen that they were lovers.

They might not have, as the crowd doubtless thought, made love in the gardens of Holland House, but that one fact was now unarguable.

And it was now public property.

Chapter 20

❧

*T*heir return to Benedict's was uneventful; Clarice, wrapped in her domino to hide her torn gown, passed more or less unnoticed.

Once in her suite, she shut the door, tossed her domino over a chair, then went to sit in one of the deep armchairs by the hearth. She slumped, very tired, still shaking inside. A small fire was burning; leaning forward, she held her cold hands out to the blaze. "I think Moira was behind that."

"Moira?" Jack had halted just inside the door; she could feel his gaze on her. "Not the traitor's henchman?"

"Not unless the traitor's henchman can get friends of Moira's daughters to help him." She clasped her hands and stared into the flames. "I just remembered where I'd seen that man and woman before. They were walking with Hilda and Mildred in Bond Street a few days ago."

How Moira would laugh once she realized how her vindictive scheme had played out. That Clarice had been saved from whatever horrors Moira had planned for her, but had instead been caught in an even more flagrantly scandalous situation than the one Moira had tried to create seven years ago.

Luckily, she was no longer twenty-two, and her father was dead.

A few moments later, Jack appeared beside her. "Here."

She looked up; he was holding out a glass of brandy. She took it; sitting back, she sipped. The fiery liquid slid smoothly down her throat, then spread, warming the icy pit that was her stomach.

For a moment, Jack stood, sipping and looking down at the fire. Then he shifted and sat in the other armchair. Forearms on his knees, he cradled the brandy balloon between his hands, then he lifted his head, and met her gaze. "We have to talk."

Her veins ran cold. She took another sip of the brandy. "About what?"

His gaze remained, unwavering, on her face. "About the situation that now exists."

She quelled an impulse to ask "What situation?" He wasn't going to let her avoid the subject; that much was clear in his hazel eyes. "What, precisely, do you mean?"

He hesitated; to her it was clear he was searching for words, for the best avenue to follow. "Despite the fond hopes of our supporters, regardless of what that crowd did or did not actually see, they saw enough. No amount of denial is going to erase the truth they did indeed observe."

He paused, then drew in a deep breath; she wished she could cut the discussion short, dismiss his words, simply look away, but she couldn't tear her eyes from his, from the face she now knew so well.

"There are still . . . accepted practices within the ton. We might think little of them, but they nevertheless are there. If we want to remain an accepted part of that society, the circle into which we both were born, then we have to abide by those rules, by their ways."

An even more frigid chill washed through her. She held up a hand, palm out, to stop him.

He reached out, caught that hand, held it. "No—hear me out. You've reclaimed your position within the ton. They were ready to welcome you back, to reinstate you in order to rid themselves of Moira perhaps, but time has dimmed the past, and the ton is now once more your world. With your reclaimed status, there's much you can do to further help your brothers, to establish the foundation for the next generation of your family—a laudable goal, one I understand." His voice took on a harder edge. "But to remain within the ton, you need to hold the position you've regained. You need not just to weather but quash the scandal that will inevitably flow from that moment in the garden."

He paused; she still couldn't drag her eyes from his. "I know it isn't what you want, but . . . if you wish it, you have my offer to marry you. If we agree to marry, there will be no scandal, and you'll be able to accomplish all you desire within the ton."

She wondered what he saw as he searched her eyes, then his hand tightened, gently, around hers.

"Your choice." His lips twisted, self-deprecatingly wry. "But you do have to choose. Now. Tonight."

She blinked, and struggled to pull together wits that seemed to have spun away.

I know it's not what you want.

He was wrong, so wrong. Marrying him was precisely what she wanted—if nothing else, that much was clear in her mind—but not like this. *Never* like this.

This was a nightmare come to life, not just for her, but for him, too.

"No." It was her turn to squeeze his hand. She was grateful for the contact. Looking into his eyes, she realized how close they'd grown, that it wasn't possible, with him, for her to simply decree.

It took effort to lower her shields, to look steadily into his eyes and let him see what she felt, and why. She swallowed, and found her voice. "Seven years ago, I made a stand. I refused to allow the ton to dictate my life, not when it came to marriage. That was the right decision then . . . and it's even more the right decision now. We've both been near victims of others exploiting these selfsame rules to try to control us, to marry us. You know, and I know, how we both felt, still feel about marriage in such circumstances, essentially under duress. To now bow to those same dictates, to do that to ourselves . . . no. I will not sacrifice you, or me, to their false gods, to their arrogance."

"But—"

"No—hear me out." She managed a weak smile. "I told my brothers I didn't want to return to the family fold, not in terms of tonnish life, of being the matriarch of the clan on any permanent basis." Tilting her head, she studied his face, tried to read his eyes. "I don't think they believed me, or rather they imagine they can persuade me otherwise. I'm not sure I convinced you, either."

Lips twisting wryly, she leaned back in the chair; she still held his hand. "You know I rarely change my mind, and on that subject, I never will. Once my brothers' grand engagement ball is over, I intend, most definitely, to return to the rectory at Avening. The ton won't understand, but they're not required to. It's what I want, where I want to be, and that's all that matters."

He didn't say anything for several heartbeats, then his fingers shifted over hers. "You're turning your back on what other ladies would kill to have."

"Perhaps. But unlike them, I know the true value of what I'm refusing, and what I'm embracing in its stead."

You. A different sort of life—a more fulfilling life.

"There are times when I find you very difficult to understand."

She smiled, but it was a weak effort. "Never mind." He didn't understand that she loved him with all her heart, but then she'd only just realized that herself, and she didn't know how he felt about her, either. She had no idea if anything would come of what was now between them; she could only hope. They were both complicated people with complex motives; being certain of what was driving the other would never be easy. Not unless they stated it.

And as she looked into his now-familiar hazel eyes, for once in her life, she wasn't brave enough to simply say, in so many words, what she felt.

Sometime, perhaps, but not tonight.

Tonight, the feelings were too raw, too roiling, the full realization too new.

She hadn't expected to fall so deeply in love.

Gently disengaging, he stood. Taking both empty brandy balloons, he set them on the mantelpiece, then looked down at her. Studied her eyes, her face. "If you're sure . . ."

"I am." She held out her hands. He grasped them and drew her to her feet.

For a moment, they stood face-to-face, close, then she smiled; retaining possession of one of his hands, she turned, and led him to her bed.

In the cool shadows of the night, in the soft billows of her bed, despite their ease, their familiarity, an element of something different prevailed. As if, with her refusal of his forced suit, they'd stepped beyond the bounds of regimented life and were now free, between them openly free, of all constraint.

So that he could now drive her further, harder, and she could respond, not just with passion but with an abject surrender that went deeper and meant infinitely more. As usual, they passed the reins back and forth; when it came her turn, she lavished pleasure and more, a deeper worship, an appreciation that was physical, emotional, sensual, and still something more, upon him.

The engagement started simply enough, a touch, a sigh, a kiss. But desire caught them, then spiraled until they burned, not fast and furious but strongly, steadily. Wanting more, needing more, consuming more.

Surrendering more.

Giving more.

The night shadows embraced them; in the sweet dark in his arms she finally found what she had thought she never would, the full measure of what she was truly meant to be. All she could be.

Her heart soared, and she no longer cared if it would later break. To be this way with him was reward enough.

That, and knowing that she loved him.

Jack woke in the small hours of the morning. Beyond the walls, the world was wrapped in deepest night, quiet and still; within them, peace, soft shadows and a comforting, comfortable warmth prevailed.

Beside him, Clarice lay deeply asleep, one small hand spread on his chest, the gentle rhythm of her breathing a cadence some primitive part of his mind faithfully tracked. Lying back in the cocooning softness, luxuriating in a sea of sensual well-being, he took stock.

She'd refused to marry him.

Logically, he should feel dejected, cast down. Instead, he felt as if some tricky, unexpected, unprecedented hurdle fate had conspired to throw in their path had been successfully negotiated and overcome. As if they'd somehow triumphed.

She'd refused him, but he couldn't fault her reasons. He hadn't wanted to offer for her hand like that, but had felt compelled to. Even now, in the same circumstances, he would do it again; that offer had had to be made.

And she had had to refuse it.

Somehow, that—him offering, her refusing—had freed them. Cut through the web of social dictates that had threatened to trap them. But more, the moment had lifted a weight from his heart and dispersed all lingering clouds from his mind.

The way forward was clear, and his reasons for following the road he'd selected had never been more definite.

It was time to act. To seize the moment. Every warrior instinct he possessed assured him that was so.

He glanced at Clarice, let his gaze drift over her fine features, relaxed in sleep, then carefully, without disturbing her, he eased from her side, and the bed.

Finding his trousers and shirt, he slipped into the sitting

room and closed the door. He swiftly dressed, then tugged the bellpull. When the sleepy night footman tapped on the door, he sent him to fetch the box he'd left with the concierge.

"Boadicea, Boadicea, open your eyes."

Clarice woke to the whispered words, and the sensation of fairy kisses pattering like rain on her skin. A shower of silken softness, of caresses almost intangible.

Even before she opened her eyes, she caught the scent, in a flash of evocative memory was transported back to Avening, to the folly, to the nights of passion they'd enjoyed there, free of the world, free of all care.

Opening her eyes, she saw Jack leaning over her, one hand moving above her as he rained apple blossom over her bare breasts. She turned toward him, onto her back, glanced around.

Discovered they were lying in a sea of apple blossom.

She looked up at him, caught his eyes as he shifted back, viewing her.

His lips curved. "This is how I see you—how I want to see you. My warrior-queen naked on a bed of apple blossom."

The covers were down by their feet. The pink-and-white petals were everywhere, over her, under her; they clung to her skin, but not so much to his, the light dusting of hair keeping them at bay. But as he touched her, caressed her, sculpted her flesh, and heat rose beneath her skin, the evocative scent wafted from the petals, until, closing her eyes, she could almost believe they were back at Avening.

She sighed as his hands drifted over her.

Then she opened her eyes, parted her lips—he dipped his head and kissed her. Filled her mouth with a long, sure, confident invasion. Shifted farther over her, parted her thighs, and touched her, caressed her, until she simply sighed into the kiss and let go.

Let him have his way.

Let him lift her legs and wind them about his hips, then

thrust deep into her welcoming softness. Let him fill her intimately, possess her completely.

For once, she made no move to take the reins, but let him do as he would, show her what he would. Without hesitation, she placed herself in his hands and let him take her where he wished. How he wished, as he wished.

Dawn broke, and poured its soft light down upon them.

Head back, spine bowed as he rode her, as he drove her ever higher, ever harder toward the beckoning crest of their sensual wave, she clung, sobbed, gasped through their kiss, and gave him all he wished, and took all he offered in return.

And felt, deep within, hope well and bloom, saw opening before her a landscape new and fresh, filled with possibilities, with promise.

With love.

It was a land they could have if they wished, if they would.

The wave broke; they clung as ecstasy crashed through them, caught them up, spun them into the heavens, shattered them, then re-formed them.

Welded them anew into something they hadn't been before. She didn't have words to acknowledge it, but she knew it in her heart.

Knew neither she nor he would ever be the same.

The wave of sensual joy receded, sighed away and left them, sated and boneless, wrapped in each other's arms in the tumbled jumble of her bed.

Amid the sea of apple blossom.

Cocooned in love.

She floated, but didn't truly sleep again, too delighted, too energized, too aware.

How could apple blossoms mean so much?

How could the simple act of coming together be so meaningful? So earth-shatteringly powerful?

She knew the answers. It wasn't the physical, nor the sensual, not even the emotional connections made, but what those arose from, what the item or the act represented, what it acknowledged.

Shared endeavors, shared aims, shared accomplishments, shared successes, shared joys. All those together, everything that made up shared lives.

This, she knew, was what she'd been made for, what she'd waited all the long years for.

His was the life she was on earth to share, and hers was his rightful sphere.

Lying on her back, her fingers trailing lightly through his hair as he lay slumped across her, his head pillowed on her breasts, she blinked, then squinted down at him. "What did you call me?"

He didn't open his eyes, but his lips curved against her skin. "Boadicea." After a moment, he added, "It's my nickname for you."

She stared at him, speechless, totally unsure how to respond, how she should or wanted to respond.

Apparently realizing he'd accomplished a feat few ever had, he opened his eyes and lifted his head the better to view her wordless state.

What she saw in his eyes, the soft glow that lit the gold and green, only stunned her more, left her even more bereft of words.

She knew what he was, always had known, had recognized the steel, the hardness, the shields. That he would be this vulnerable, and allow her to see it—that he would call her Boadicea, his warrior-queen—simply took her breath away.

He caught her hand, touched his lips to her fingers.

The touch anchored her, helped her feet find earth. She blinked, managed a weak frown. "Boadicea was painted blue."

Still smiling, he shook his head. "Not blue for you—pink and white. If you need anything to cover your nakedness"— he looked down and surveyed her breasts—"it can only be apple blossom."

There was a smug, supremely male expression on his face.

She couldn't help it—she laughed.

Saw answering laughter spark in his eyes, and realized that was the right response, that nothing more was needed between them.

Reaching for him, she drew his face to hers and kissed him. Then he kissed her.

Eventually, he drew away. "It's already dawn. I have to go."

She looked into his eyes, mere inches away. "Stay."

He searched her face, confirmed what she was saying, hesitated, then grimaced. "No, not yet. Not until this is over."

She sighed and let him go. His face had set; her warrior-lord was back. Her reputation was his to guard, or so he saw it.

Lying amid the apple blossoms, feeling them shift silkily against her skin, she watched him dress and knew she'd never want him to change. "I'll come to the club later in the morning. You'll be meeting with your colleagues, I expect."

He looked at her, nodded. Then he returned to the bed, kissed her witless, and slipped out of the room while her head was still spinning.

She arrived at the club at eleven o'clock and was met with grave faces all around.

"Some bargemen I'd hired found Humphries' body washed up on the morning tide." Jack glanced at Christian and Deverell, then turned back to Clarice. "We—you and I—should take the news to the bishop."

Clarice nodded.

"Meanwhile," Christian said, his tone flat and steely, "we'll check with our sources and get Tristan to do the same. Someone may have seen Humphries along the riverbanks or bridges. We might jog someone's memory now we know where to concentrate."

Solemn and serious, they parted. Jack handed Clarice into Alton's carriage, and they rattled around to Lambeth. But once admitted to the palace, they had to kick their heels for over an hour; the bishop, dean, and Deacon Olsen were all officiating in the cathedral.

Finally, the dean returned. Hearing their news, his face fell, but he quickly organized a private audience with the bishop.

His lordship was appalled. Jack realized that, however much he'd been told that Humphries had been drawn into a dangerous game, the bishop hadn't, until that moment, comprehended the life-and-death nature of that game.

"I . . . oh, my heavens!" Pasty-faced, the bishop stared at him. "How . . . ? Do you know?"

"It seems he was coshed, most likely knocked unconscious, then tossed into the water. He would have drowned quickly."

The bishop glanced at Clarice. Although pale, she was holding up better than he. The sight seemed to stiffen his spine. "Yes, well, we will, of course, do all that's necessary. If you could have the body delivered here—"

A knock fell on the door. The bishop scowled. "What is it?" His tone was querulous; he was deeply shaken.

Olsen looked in. "I apologize for interrupting, my lord, but a message has arrived for Lord Warnefleet."

Jack crossed to meet Olsen. Taking the note, he glanced at the seal, then broke it. Unfolding the note, he glanced at the bishop. "It's from Christian Allardyce—Dearne."

The bishop blinked. "He's one of you, too?"

Jack didn't answer. Scanning the note's contents, he returned to where the bishop, Clarice, and the dean waited, Olsen at his heels. "Two evenings ago, Humphries was seen walking along the river bank near Tower Bridge. He was with another man—a large man, soberly dressed, with a pale, very round face." He looked up.

Clarice met his eyes. "The same man—the courier-cum-informer we've been tripping over all along, from Avening to here."

Jack nodded.

"But . . . why kill poor Humphries?" The bishop looked bewildered.

"Presumably because Humphries knew this man too well

and could identify him." Jack sighed. "I suspect we've reached a dead end with our investigations. Unless Humphries has left any information in his room?"

He looked at Olsen and the dean; both shook their heads.

"When he didn't return," the dean said, "we searched everywhere hoping to find the name of some meeting place, some address or way of contacting this person, but there was nothing in Humphries' papers."

Jack grimaced. "Standard practice. Nothing ever to be written down."

A moment passed as they absorbed the fact that not only was Humphries dead, but that his murderer would almost certainly escape justice.

Clarice stirred. "What about the charges against James?"

The bishop blinked, refocused, then waved his hand. "Consider them erased." He met Clarice's eyes. "I'm exceedingly glad I forbade James to leave Avening. Bad enough I've lost one good man to this . . . this charade of someone's making. If I'd lost James, too, I would have been extremely unhappy. I will, of course, write to him, but I would be greatly obliged if, when you see him, you would assure him of my continued support and that we look to see him when next he ventures to the capital for his studies."

"Indeed, my lord." Clarice curtsied.

Jack bowed. "If you will excuse us, my lord, I believe I should take this information to Whitehall without delay."

Reiterating his thanks, the bishop dismissed them.

Olsen and the dean followed them out. Jack assured them Humphries' body would be delivered shortly to the palace. Teddy appeared as they crossed the front hall; he spoke briefly with Clarice, then stood on the steps with Olsen and the dean as Jack handed Clarice up into the carriage. With a salute to the three men, Jack joined her. The coachman flicked his whip and the carriage rolled smoothly down the palace drive.

Whitehall wasn't far away.

Clarice, of course, had absolutely no intention of waiting

in the carriage while Jack consulted with Dalziel. Jack was perfectly sure she wanted another look at his enigmatic superior, and he saw no reason to deny her; it might jog her memory over who Dalziel was.

He ushered her into the bowels of the building, into the anteroom that gave onto Dalziel's office. He gave his name to the unassuming clerk, to whom it meant nothing. While the clerk went to inquire his master's pleasure, Jack wondered if Dalziel constantly changed clerks; they were never the same.

The clerk returned almost immediately. "He will see you now, but the lady must remain here."

Jack knew from the way the clerk very nearly quailed that Clarice had narrowed her eyes at him. Before she could cut the poor man to ribbons, he squeezed her hand. "No point. He's a law unto himself. Wait here, I won't be long."

He left her muttering about the trumped-up behavior of scions of the nobility, of which she, of course, was one. She couldn't see his smile as he walked down the short corridor to Dalziel's room, the highly relieved clerk trotting before him. The clerk showed him in, then departed, closing the door.

Dalziel rose from behind his desk; he extended his hand and Jack shook it, a courtesy they wouldn't have exchanged before, but Jack was no longer one of Dalziel's subordinates. Now, they met more or less as equals, as gentlemen tying up the final untidy threads of a decades-long war.

Dalziel's gaze had raked his face the instant he'd walked into the room. Now, waving him to the chair before the desk, Dalziel slumped heavily back into his. "I take it you bear no good news?"

Jack grimaced. "Humphries' body washed up this morning in the Deptford marshes."

Dalziel swore, violently and colorfully. He stared up at the ceiling. "Do we know anything about the man responsible?"

Jack related what they'd learned. "So it's been the same man at every turn."

Dalziel's dark eyes met his. "No hint of anyone else?"

"Not a whisper." Jack studied Dalziel's impossible-to-read face, then baldly asked, "Have you no clue who the real traitor is?"

Dalziel held his gaze for a long moment, before replying, "Not who, but as to what . . . that's become rather clearer. This episode unfortunately won't lead us to the man—he's been too clever for that. Whoever this foreigner is, he's certainly not the mastermind behind the whole. However, the very nature of the charade has revealed that our traitor knows the ropes of government, the legal system, and society well. He made only one mistake—choosing James Altwood, who knew about you, as his target, and that was something he couldn't have known. If it hadn't been for that slip, we wouldn't have been so sure of Altwood's innocence so early in the piece, early enough to act decisively to avoid any trial."

Dalziel shuddered. "I don't want to think of what would have happened if the charges had progressed to a formal trial. The failure of the case would have been spectacular, and would have effectively ended any hope of bringing the *real* last traitor to justice. Any subsequent talk of traitors would have been completely discounted." He paused, then added, "As a way of ensuring his own safety, this charade was inspired. Whoever he is, he knew to a nicety what he was doing.

"Of course, he didn't expect to fail." Dalziel's expression subtly altered. He glanced at Jack. "For our troubles, we've learned that the last traitor is in fact real. Until now, he's been little more than a shade, a postulated being. All I had were suspicions, instincts. But now you, Dearne, Deverell, Trentham, and I all know that the last traitor exists. No shade organized all this."

Jack inclined his head. "True. So although we didn't win this skirmish, we came away with improved intelligence."

Dalziel smiled. "Aptly put." He paused, clearly reviewing. "One last thing. Did anyone get a good look at this foreigner?"

"Anthony Sissingbourne—he saw the man's face only

briefly, but at closest range. And Lady Clarice Altwood—she saw him from a greater distance, but she saw the man walk, move." Jack hesitated, then added, "Of the two, Clarice would be more likely to recognize the man than Anthony."

Dalziel nodded. "It might prove worth our time to review the foreigners known to be of similar physical description, those in the embassies, the consulates, various diplomatic posts, that sort of thing. If we turn up any likely candidates, we may need Lady Clarice."

Blank-faced, Dalziel met Jack's eyes. "If you were still under my command, I'd order you to keep her close, and guard her well." His mobile lips twitched. "However, from all I hear, you'll be doing precisely that, order or no."

His expression impassive, Jack merely inclined his head. "She says she intends returning to Gloucestershire. Regardless, I'll remain with her."

"Good." Dalziel rose.

Jack did the same. He met Dalziel's gaze, let a slight frown show. "I'd much prefer to imagine we won't meet again."

The faintest of self-deprecatory smiles curved Dalziel's lips. "Unfortunately, our instincts are independently suggesting that's unlikely to be the case." He grimaced. "Which means this is no real parting." He waved Jack to the door. "Take care of her."

"I will." Hand on the knob, Jack paused, then glanced back. "Incidentally, she hasn't recognized you yet."

Back in his chair, Dalziel met his gaze, then shrugged. "With luck, by the time she does, it won't matter anymore."

Picking up a pen, Dalziel gave his attention to a letter. Puzzled, Jack went out; closing the door, he walked back to where Clarice was waiting, pacing before the highly nervous clerk.

In the carriage, he told her all Dalziel had said; she merely humphed and frowned.

They returned to the Benedict to take stock. On the table in her sitting room, they found a note from Alton, with two tickets for that evening's Royal Gala at Vauxhall.

"I thought tickets to such events were obtainable more or less only by royal decree." Jack examined the gilt-edged vouchers.

Clarice humphed. "They are, but Alton can be as charming as some others I know when he wishes." She perused the note. "He writes that the bishop has informed him that the charges against James have been dismissed outright, and that he, Roger, and Nigel thought to use the Gala for a combined celebration of their winning free of Moira, their pending engagements, and James's exoneration, to which, of course, Alton bids us attend."

Handing the note to Jack, Clarice smiled to herself. It was patently clear her brothers thought to use the Gala—the very epitome of tonnish entertainment—to demonstrate the benefits of returning to the family fold, hoping to sway her into wanting her life of old.

They wouldn't succeed, but if she let them try their damnedest, if she attended and enjoyed, and *then* told them she was returning to Avening and her quiet country life, they would realize how futile it was to keep pressing her, that her decision was indeed final and absolute.

And Jack, too, would see and understand.

Smile deepening, she turned to him. He stood by the table, still staring at the vouchers in his hand.

"We'll have to go, of course."

Jack glanced at her, saw, very clearly, the soft light of anticipation glowing in her eyes. He inclined his head, and smiled. Charmingly.

Nine hours later, he was still smiling charmingly, but the gesture had grown thin—almost too thin to hide his feelings, the increasingly fraught urge to drop his mask entirely, seize Clarice, and whisk her away.

Away from those who wanted her to remain here, in the glittering bosom of the ton, to help them, to be a part of their family, not just the old but the newly forming, too.

It wasn't hard to see she'd be tempted.

The booth Alton had hired was in the best area, facing the rotunda with the main dance floor between. Sitting in one front corner, keeping still, being as inconspicuous as possible, Jack watched Clarice whirling through a polka in Nigel's arms.

About them, the cream of the ton circled and strolled, chatting, exclaiming, laughing. Jewels flashed; silks and satins corruscated in the light thrown by the bobbing lanterns. Perfumes and the scents of wine and fine food blended, teasing the senses; the music and chatter combined in a pervasive blanket of sound that yet managed to remain within reasonable bounds.

Everyone present was determined to enjoy themselves; their host was known as the Prince of Pleasure, and they took their cue from him. With only the highest families in the land able to obtain vouchers, the social standing of the company was assured. Consequently, the event was largely unstructured, with less rigidity, less consciousness of importance, all of which contributed to a sense of freedom, of being able metaphorically to let their hair down and simply enjoy.

Even to his prejudiced eyes, the scene was fabulous, and made even more appealing by the lighthearted atmosphere.

Alton whirled past with Sarah in his arms. Jack fought an urge to scowl. Everyone was enjoying themselves except him, and it was hard not to think that Alton was to blame. Especially as the man had pulled out all stops to convince Clarice to adopt the mantle of Altwood matriarch.

Jack had been forced to stand beside Clarice and listen to her soon-to-be sisters-in-law tell her how much they would appreciate her help in setting up their households, in establishing their own positions within the ton. He'd had to smile and nod while *grande dame* after *grande dame* made haughty overtures to Clarice, inviting her to join their circles.

Admittedly, Clarice had merely smiled and avoided giving any assurances, but she hadn't said "no."

He would have much rather she'd said "no," even though he knew such a plain and abrupt refusal wouldn't have been socially acceptable.

He wasn't feeling all that inclined to behave in socially acceptable ways.

And with every minute that passed, he only felt more driven.

More tortured.

Regardless of what she'd said, regardless of what he'd thought and hoped that morning, once she considered the evening and all it implied, plus all the arguments countless others had put to her, and most of all the persuasions of her family, would she change her mind and decide to return to this life?

It was what she'd been born and bred to.

If she did . . . it would be without him. He knew, had known for some time, that the only place he would ever call home, the only place at which he would feel at peace, was Avening. Yet . . . would he ever know real peace, real happiness, without her?

Her family wanted her; they appreciated her more with each passing day. But they didn't appreciate her, know her, as he did. They didn't fully understand Boadicea, couldn't fully engage with her, with all she was, as he did.

They didn't need or want her as much as he did.

He was watching her, as ever, when she abruptly stopped midwhirl, then stepped out of Nigel's arms. She wasn't looking at her brother, but to the side of the dancing area; Nigel appeared to be asking her what was wrong.

Jack stood. Over the heads, he watched Clarice push away from Nigel's restraining hands. Following the line of her gaze, he scanned the revelers—until he came to a man's very pale, round face.

Jack swore. He didn't wait to see more, but vaulted over the waist-high front of the booth and plunged into the crowd.

There were muted shrieks and exclamations, warnings to have a care as he shouldered through the crush. He had no concern over whose ruffle he ripped; Clarice had left Nigel and started after the man, their courier-cum-informer who had murdered Humphries.

The man saw Clarice, stared, then turned and weaved away through the crowd. With her height, Clarice could still see him; she continued to track him, her attention fixed.

Jack swore and redoubled his efforts to reach her, uncaring of what havoc he caused. But the music had ended and the dancers were streaming from the crowded floor, leaving him fighting against a human tide.

Clarice followed the man who had run Anthony off the road all those weeks before. She realized he'd glimpsed her, but by using the crowd to her advantage, she hoped he might think she'd lost him in the throng.

She wanted to see where he was going, and even more whom he was meeting. He had to be meeting someone; there was no other reason a person of his ilk would be at such a gathering.

Tacking through the crowd, she managed to keep the man in sight, gradually gaining on him. He was circling the rotunda, presumably looking for one particular booth; she was increasingly sure he thought she'd lost him.

Then he stopped. His back to the gardens, from the edge of the crowd, he looked around, as if checking one last time before he approached whomever he was there to meet.

Clarice ducked behind a group of people, thanked her stars she hadn't worn plumes in her hair as so many other ladies had. She looked down, counted to ten, then shifted to peek at the man again—just as the group before her moved on.

Leaving her staring across a bare expanse of ten yards, directly at her quarry.

His small eyes opened wide. Then with a muffled curse she heard, he whirled and plunged down the path behind him.

Clarice picked up her skirts and hurried after him.

The path was a major one, well lit by lanterns strung between the trees. There were couples and groups strolling along, enough to reassure Clarice but not enough to hide her.

Or the man. He darted along, not quite running, trying, still, not to attract too much attention, glancing behind him every now and then. The idea of screeching "Thief!" and pointing at him flared in Clarice's mind, just as he ducked down an intersecting path.

She swore, and rushed on. The distance between them had lengthened. She was almost running as she rounded the corner and started along the next path.

A minor path. An unlighted one.

Chapter 21

Clarice halted. She'd traveled less than ten yards along the path, but already she stood in dense shadow. The bustle of the crowd around the rotunda suddenly seemed far away, screened by thick bushes.

And she could no longer see her quarry.

"Damn!" She stood a moment more, debating, then did the sensible thing, turned on her heel and marched back to safety.

"Damn, damn, da—" She sucked in a breath and whirled as the man rushed toward her. He'd been hiding in the bushes a few paces farther on.

Lips pulled back in a snarl, he was on her. Before she could release the scream rising up her throat, he slapped a huge hand over her lips, trapped her against him, then started to drag her back down the path. Away from the lighted path with its occasional strollers, away from anyone who might glimpse her silvery gown.

Clarice struggled frantically. This was much worse than the previous night; this man had killed, and would cold-bloodedly kill again.

She kicked and fought, and managed to slow him, but she couldn't break free. He was not only stronger than the man last night, he was also more intent, more set on his aim, more experienced. His hand was clamped so hard over her lips, she couldn't move her jaw enough to bite.

Desperate, she used her weight, sagged in his hold, then kicked and wrestled when he swore and tried to juggle her.

She forced him to stop again, but they were too far from the other path; she wasn't making enough noise to attract anyone's attention.

The heavy arm around her middle tightened, compressing her lungs. Then the hand over her mouth shifted; he pinched her nostrils closed, simultaneously pressing hard against her mouth, sealing off all air.

Clarice stopped struggling; she went totally still. Before she could think what to do, how to pretend she'd fainted, a roaring filled her ears.

Her vision started closing in, narrowing to a central core of light . . .

Jack appeared within that halo.

She assumed she was dying, that his was the final image she would see, her biggest regret that she would take to her grave—

Her captor swore. He released her mouth, reached beneath his coat.

Clarice sucked in a huge breath. Blinking back to life, she realized Jack was truly there, rushing down the path toward them, her warrior-lord come to save her.

Simultaneously she realized her captor had drawn a wicked-looking knife from his pocket, that he was holding it down where in the deep shadows Jack wouldn't see it.

She wrenched sideways, trying to force the man to raise the knife.

The man didn't move, didn't take his eyes from Jack, closing rapidly.

Clarice remembered she could speak. "He has a knife!"

Neither Jack nor the man seemed to hear.

Desperate, she lifted her feet and flung herself to the side, trying to pull the man off-balance.

She succeeded better than she'd expected. Her flailing

foot connected with the man's knee. With a grunt, he went down, his grip on her breaking as she tumbled to the ground.

Jack grabbed her, hauled her upright, thrust her back along the path behind him. She staggered back, gulping air.

The man surged up like a spring aimed at Jack. The knife glinted evilly as he drove it toward Jack's throat.

Jack caught the man's wrist, swung so his shoulder and back were against the man's chest, holding him at bay as Jack fought to gain control of the knife or to make the man drop it.

The man drove his other fist low into Jack's side; Jack grunted, shifted, caught the man's free fist in his other hand, and held it away as he concentrated on the hand holding the knife. He put all his strength into breaking the man's grip while holding the man trapped, stretched across his shoulders.

Still giddy, Clarice watched as they wrestled. This was no clean fight; even she could see the difference. Neither was averse to using any means they could to win. They grunted, and staggered; Jack was too experienced to let the other have space enough to use his legs. Inexorably, Jack bent the man's wrist back, farther . . .

Suddenly, Jack let the man's other hand go and drove his elbow back into the man's chest. The man wheezed, and nearly collapsed on Jack.

Jack staggered. He might have been as strong, but the other man was heavier.

With a huge effort, the man wrenched himself free, flinging Jack away. He staggered, but quickly regained his balance.

They faced each other, two wrestlers looking to close, a few yards between them.

Before Jack could move in, the man abruptly fell back.

His eyes went to Clarice. He lifted his arm.

Jack couldn't reach him in time.

He flung himself at Clarice.

He caught her, let his weight carry her to the ground, didn't truly care when he felt the sharp sting of the knife, followed by blossoming pain as it lodged in the back of his shoulder.

Behind him, the man swore foully with a thick accent, European but from nowhere that bordered the sea.

Jack heard the man's footsteps as he started toward them, felt Clarice's arms wrap about him and hold him, felt her warm and safe beneath him.

Ruthlessly focusing his senses, he gathered his strength to push free at just the right moment; it would take more than a knife in the shoulder to stop him.

The man's footsteps abruptly halted. He was still too far from them for Jack to make any sensible move.

Shouts reached them, followed by footsteps rushing down from the major path.

The man swore again, more softly, then swung on his heel and fled.

Jack groaned and swore, too. "Damn it! He's getting away." He started to struggle up, but Clarice tightened her hold.

"There's a knife in your back."

He bit back his "I know"; there was a strange note, an odd quality in her voice. He reminded himself she wasn't used to fights and knives and death, but he was nowhere near dead. "It's all right. I'm not that hurt."

"But—"

He pushed back enough to sit up, disentangling from her as Nigel and Alton came pounding down the path. With his head, Jack ordered them on. "After him. I'll survive."

Clarice had already scrambled to her feet; hunkered down, her attention was fixed on him. After the briefest of glances her way, glances she didn't even register, Alton and Nigel raced on.

They were young and fast; there was a chance they might catch the villain.

Other revelers were gathering at the head of the path, but no one else had yet ventured down.

Clarice twitched the hems of her skirts from beneath Jack's legs, and scrambled around him to view the damage.

Her heart seemed to have lodged in her throat, choking her; the sight of the blood oozing from around the blade made her reel, not with faintness but with a medley of emotions so powerful she had to slam a door on them just to function. "What can I do to help?"

She laid her hand lightly on Jack's shoulder; he was obviously in pain.

He met her eyes as she peered around his shoulder. "Can you pull the knife out?"

She blinked. She was thankful the path was so shadowy; he hadn't seen the blood drain from her face.

"It hasn't touched anything serious. It's lodged in muscle, but it'll do less damage if I don't move until it's out."

She shifted back to face the knife. "How?"

"Just grab it and pull it slowly out. I'll try to relax so it comes out more easily."

She dragged in a huge breath, held it, closed her hand around the hilt, and did as he said, careful to exert only enough force to draw the knife slowly free . . . then it was out, in her hand. She blew out a breath, and slumped to sit beside Jack.

He offered her his handkerchief. "Use that to press on the wound."

She did. Just as she pressed the linen pad down hard, a shot rang out.

They both looked down the path in the direction of the sound.

Jack closed his hand around hers. "It won't be your brothers."

She looked at his grim face. "How can you be sure?"

He started to rise. She scrambled to her feet, then helped him up, keeping one hand pressed to his wound.

"Let's go and find out."

Others had now ventured down. A few gentlemen, seeing Jack's injury, offered their handkerchiefs to help staunch the blood. Clarice accepted them, adding them to the wad beneath her hand as, followed by a small procession, they headed down the path.

They traveled more than half the length of the huge gardens before they reached the scene of the shooting. It wasn't on the path, but a little way off it, in a small clearing surrounded by bushes. A shocked group of revelers, including, Clarice noted with relief, Alton and Nigel, stood staring, silent and stunned, in a wide circle around the round-faced man.

He lay on his back, arms wide, staring, sightless, up at the night sky.

A large hole in his chest bled sluggishly. On the grass beside him lay a nondescript pistol.

There was no question that he was dead.

Halting beside Alton, Jack sighed.

"I don't understand." Frowning, Alton turned to Jack. "We'd gone past on the path, then heard the shot. But who shot him?"

Jack looked down at the pale, round face. "His master—our last traitor."

Using Alton and Nigel as assistants, Jack gathered what information he could.

Nigel found a young lady who had seen a man leaving the clearing immediately after the shot had rung out; he convinced her parents that she should talk to Jack, and escorted the party to where Jack sat on a bench beside the central avenue, Clarice at his side still holding the wad of handkerchiefs tightly to his wound.

A few gentle questions confirmed that the young lady had indeed seen the murderer. Unfortunately, she was in the grip of incipient if not actual hysterics; Jack wasn't sure how to proceed.

Clarice shifted, drawing the girl's startled gaze. "Come now. This gentleman was injured trying to catch the man. You're not injured, just frightened, but you'll feel much better after you've told us all you saw. Where were you standing when it happened?"

The girl blinked, and replied, telling them she and her group were strolling the lawns just beyond the small clearing. Clarice's calm questions, asked with the transparent expectation of receiving coherent answers, steadied the girl; she responded increasingly freely. When the shot had rung out, she was the best placed of their group to see the gentleman who had walked, calmly and unhurriedly, away from the scene.

Unfortunately, beyond describing him as tall, with a well-cut evening coat and fashionably styled dark hair, she couldn't identify him. She hadn't seen his face.

"He didn't look around at all. At first, I thought he couldn't have heard the shot. Indeed, I wondered if it *was* a shot I heard, given he was so calm."

Jack summoned a smile and thanked the girl, her parents, and escort. Relieved, the parents ushered the small group away.

Alton looked down at Jack. "Should we search?"

Jack grimaced. "For what?" Slowly, assisted by Clarice, he stood. "Whoever it was is indistinguishable from the majority of male guests."

"If he's even still present," Clarice said.

Jack glanced at her. "Oh, he'll be here. Leaving, doing even that much to draw attention to himself, let alone cutting short his evening's entertainment, isn't his style. Especially now he knows that our last chance of identifying him"—he glanced back at the clearing where the garden's attendants were dealing with the dead body—"just died."

At Jack's insistence, Clarice took him back to the Bastion Club.

"Gasthorpe knows how to contact Pringle, and he knows more about stab wounds than any doctor in London."

She did as he asked and kept the emotions bubbling inside her carefully suppressed. For the moment. At least until the doctor had pronounced Jack fit enough to withstand them.

At the club, she swallowed her protests, respected their rules, and agreed to wait in the parlor.

Gasthorpe whisked Jack away; noting the majordomo's unruffled efficiency, Clarice surmised he was used to dealing with peers sporting stab wounds and the like. She humphed and paced the parlor. Dr. Pringle arrived, a sharp-featured gentleman who bowed and assured her that Jack had the constitution of an ox. He also promised to stop by on his way out and inform her of his opinion of Jack's injury.

Mollified, she sat; when a footman appeared with a tea tray, she was absurdly grateful. She sent her compliments to Gasthorpe and settled to wait.

Upstairs, Jack winced as Pringle probed the wound.

"Clean as a whistle." Pringle opened his bag and rummaged for bandages. "One benefit of dealing with professional killers."

Used to Pringle's graveyard humor, Jack merely grunted. He gripped the edge of the table against which he was leaning and kept his lips shut as Pringle rebathed the wound, smeared it with some unguent, then laid gauze across it before bandaging him up. The bandage had to wind over his shoulder and across his chest, but Pringle was experienced enough to leave him room to move reasonably freely.

Pringle was tying off the bandage when the door opened, and Dalziel walked in. Jack let his surprise show; like him, Dalziel was in evening dress.

Dalziel closed the door behind him, nodded to Pringle, then studied Jack. "There's a story flashing around the clubs of a gentleman rescuing a fair damsel in a dark walk at the Vauxhall Gala, then the villain being shot dead." Dalziel raised his brows. "I take it that was you?"

Jack grimaced. "Yes to the first, but I don't know who shot him." Concisely, he recounted the events of the last hours. "So in terms of appearance, the last traitor could be you or I. The other detail you can add to his file is that he's high enough in society to garner vouchers to a Royal Gala. The watch at the gates was strict, entry by voucher only. Our ex-courier-cum-informer couldn't have got in without one."

Dalziel nodded. "Duly noted. As to our late friend . . ." His voice hardened. "I can confirm that he was a Pole, known to have a secret loyalty to Napoleon's cause. Curtiss and the Admiralty have been watching him for years, but he's never shown any interest in military secrets, nor has he been traveling. He's been in London since '08. Unfortunately, I only learned all that this evening."

Jack blinked. "So if he had lived, you would have been speaking with him tomorrow morning."

Dalzeil nodded. "On that you could have safely staked your estate."

"So he had to die tonight."

"Indeed. That, I assume, is why he was summoned to the Gala."

"A place in which he would have imagined he was safe."

After a moment's pause, Dalziel mumured, "I fear, like many others, he underestimated his master."

There was a quality in Dalziel's voice that made Jack shiver. Even Pringle blinked.

Dalziel shifted, and the sense of menace dissolved. He looked at Jack, then smiled, and turned for the door. "If I were you, Warnefleet, I'd retire to the country forthwith. After this latest act of heroism, you're going to be at the top of the young ladies' lists." At the door, Dalziel looked back, smiled cynically, and saluted him. "And for once, their mothers will agree."

Jack blinked, stared, then closed his eyes and groaned.

Clarice had heard someone arrive, then heard him leave, but it wasn't Jack. She couldn't summon enough interest to look out.

She'd finished her cup of tea and was starting to drum her fingers on the chair arm when she heard two sets of footsteps descending the stairs. A moment later the door opened. Pringle entered, Jack followed.

She rose and offered her hand.

Pringle came forward to take it. "Just a deep cut. Nothing that won't mend soon enough, as long as he doesn't aggravate the injury."

That last was said with a quizzical look at Jack.

Who met it blankly.

She thanked the doctor. Jack shook hands with him, and Pringle left.

"Now"—Clarice hitched her evening cloak over her shoulders, and picked up her reticule—"it's time we headed back to Benedict's." So she could share her thoughts, her emotions, with him.

To her surprise, Jack frowned; he made no move toward the door. "Rather a lot of people saw us together tonight. Again. After last night, and tonight, perhaps it would be better if I remain here. I probably won't sleep all that well, and Gasthorpe's an excellent nurse."

She fixed her eyes on his, drew in a deep breath, and managed, just, to keep her temper, to keep her swelling emotions in check. "My dear Lord Warnefleet, please understand this— there is *no way on earth* I am letting you out of my sight. Not tonight, not for the foreseeable future. Furthermore"—she drew in another huge breath—"regardless of Gasthorpe's efficiency, I *defy* him to be better able to nurse you than I, and as for you suffering from any difficulty sleeping, I'm quite sure I'll be able to find *something* to distract you from the pain in your shoulder, to exhaust you enough for you to fall asleep."

Her voice had gained, not in volume but emphasis; to her horror, it threatened to quaver. She had to draw in another breath and hold it for an instant before she could ask, pointedly, "Are you ready to leave now?"

Jack blinked, studied her, and realized she was almost quivering, that a species of fine tension was thrumming through her. That she was seriously, deeply upset. "Yes. Of course. If you're sure?"

"Of course I'm sure."

She may be sure, but he wasn't, not at all sure just what she was so upset about. It could be simple reaction, even compounded reaction to the events of the last two evenings. In what he suspected was typical Clarice fashion, she might have been bottling it all up inside, trying to be her usual tower of strength for everyone else.

In the front hall, he slung his coat over his shoulders, called a farewell to Gasthorpe, then took Clarice's arm and guided her outside. In the street, he helped her into the carriage, then joined her, easing back against the squabs, aware of her watching him closely.

"It's only painful if I press on it, or lift my arm above the shoulder."

The wound truly wasn't bad, more a nuisance, and none of the rest of him was injured in any way. However, as they rattled around to Benedict's, he did wonder what the rest of the night might have in store for him.

As they turned into Piccadilly, he recalled Dalziel's visit and mentioned it; without being asked, he related all Dalziel had said.

They passed close by a street flare as the carriage turned a corner; in its glare, he saw she was frowning.

Suddenly, she looked up at him, her face clearing. "Royce."

He frowned. "Royce who?"

Her frown returned. "I don't know. I'm not sure I ever did know. But that's Dalziel's Christian name, the one he goes by—Royce."

Jack considered; after a moment, he shook his head. "Tracing one of the nobility on the basis of one Christian name is simply too hard."

But he made a mental note to tell the others. One day they'd learn the truth, the whole truth, about Dalziel. Now, however, he had another, more immediate, equally difficult member of the nobility to deal with.

By the time Clarice had succeeded in bullying him up to her sitting room—directly, with no detour via the secondary stairs—he'd decided how to deal with her.

Directly, as direct as she usually was. In the instant he'd seen their late adversary poised to hurl a knife into her heart, he'd had a revelation sharp enough to qualify as Cupid's dart.

In contrast, the impact of the knife had been rather anticlimactic.

Life was too short not to reach for love, not to seize it. If she'd changed her mind and decided to remain in London . . . she'd simply have to change it back.

In the carriage, he'd recalled her advice to Alton. People giving such advice usually spoke from their own perspectives.

So be it. He'd thought showing her how much he loved her would be enough, but . . . perhaps not. And if not, then . . . unfortunately, it was one thing to show her, another entirely to tell her. To say the words aloud. Doing so might well qualify as the hardest task he'd ever faced, but he would do it.

He had to; he had no choice.

It was that, or risk losing her, and the latter wasn't an option.

Closing the door, he walked to the fireplace while she shrugged off her cloak and set her reticule aside. In the carriage, he'd debated letting her speak first, letting her release whatever it was that was so clearly brewing inside her, but then he'd remembered how she could rant and rave; very likely she'd distract him. Best if he grasped the nettle and spoke first.

He swung to face her as she neared, and trapped her gaze with his. "Before we get distracted with anything else, there's something I want to say."

She blinked, surprised, but then he saw a certain wariness creep into her dark eyes, eyes whose expression he could now often read.

He drew breath, and spoke quickly. "The truth is . . . I love you to distraction, and will move heaven and earth, and anything between, to make you mine."

She blinked, no doubt recalling what were almost exactly her own words, but now he'd taken the plunge, he found the rest came more easily.

"I know that your family—Alton, Roger, Nigel, and all the rest—need you, that that need is real in its way, but I need you more." He held her gaze steadily, and dropped every shield he possessed, every veil he'd used through the years to hide behind, something at which he'd grown exceedingly adept. "I have a manor house that's been empty for too long, a rose garden with a bench that hasn't had a lady to sit on it, to look over the blooms and play with her children, not for decades.

"I know you care for your brothers, your wider family. I understand what they mean to you, perhaps even more because I'm an only child. Indeed, because I understand, there's nothing I want more in life than to have a family of my own, with you. A quiverful of children—little girls just like you, imperious and haughty, who'll order me around." He lifted his shoulders in a half shrug. "And a few boys, too, perhaps more like me, to keep you and the girls occupied arranging our lives."

He saw the tears slowly fill her eyes, but didn't pause, didn't dare stop to learn why she was crying.

"I suppose I should adhere to the usual prescription, but that hardly seems applicable to us." He drew breath, and hurried on, "I want you in every imaginable way, but especially as my wife. I don't want some meek and mild miss, some simpering ninny. I want *you*, just as you are, the you others don't understand and are wary of, the you I've seen so clearly over the last weeks—that's the you I appreciate and want and need.

"I want you as you are, by my side for better or for worse, in sickness and in health." He managed a small smile. "We've already encountered much of the worst of each other, and weathered it, and experienced sickness"—he gestured toward his head—"too. But more than all else, it's you I want, not some marquess's daughter, not a well-dowered bride, but just you."

Reaching out, he took her hands, shifted closer, looking down into her eyes, swimming in tears. "You know what I am. I'm not any kind of gentle man. Through the centuries, Warnefleets have always been warriors. Because of that, I don't need any gentle lady as my wife, I need you as my warrior-queen. For me, only you will do. You're the only lady I've ever even dreamed of having as my wife."

He dragged in a breath. "However, just so we're clear, although I'm wealthy and wellborn, as you are, I don't want to live a fashionable life in town. I've estates scattered the length and breadth of the country, and I enjoy running them, making them work. Taking good care of them, and the people they support. That, to me, is my rightful place. A touch medieval, perhaps, but if the cap fits . . . and in that respect, my wife needs to be an experienced lady I can rely on to sort out the roster for the church flowers, among other things."

Although her eyes had filled, they hadn't overflowed, but glowed through the tears, magical in their luminosity.

Hope welled. He essayed a small smile. "Do you think you could make do with that? With my heart, my love, and that?"

Clarice's heart felt so full she could barely speak. It wasn't his proposal that slayed her, but the manner of it, his laying of his warrior's heart at her feet.

When she swallowed, and didn't immediately answer, because she couldn't yet speak around the lump in her throat, his face hardened, just a fraction. "Will you marry me, Boadicea?"

She tried to smile through her tears, but it must have been a poor effort, because his expression changed to one of incipient panic.

"If you really wish it, I can manage the estates from town—we could live there for most of the year." He dragged in a breath. "If that's what you want, I'll do even that—anything—"

Pulling her hands from his, she waved them to cut him off. "No, no, no!" The words came out in a tear-sodden mumble.

His face fell. Then he blinked. "No to what?"

She managed to drag in a big enough breath, managed a real smile, a radiant one. "*No don't spoil it.*" She looked deep into his eyes, saw his sudden panic evaporate as he looked into hers. "That was the most perfect proposal I could ever have hoped to hear." She let all she felt show in her eyes. "I love you, you dolt. I've loved you for weeks."

He grinned, and reached for her; she let him draw her into his arms. Reaching up, she traced his cheek. "I hoped, truly hoped that you'd ask me to marry you. I've never wanted to marry anyone else, not the way I wanted to be your wife. I was going to go back to Avening with you, then do whatever it took to extract a proposal from you."

She tilted her head. "And if I failed, I was prepared to be your mistress for however long you wanted me. I'd rather be your mistress than any other man's wife."

His grin took on a distinctly male edge. He bent to kiss her; she placed a hand on his chest and pushed back.

"No—wait. Let me finish. I said I was *going to* wait and go back to Avening with you." She paused to draw in a huge breath. "But last night, and even more tonight when that man threw the knife and I thought I might die, and then you hit me, and I thought *you* might die, and then the knife struck you, and that was even *worse.*"

She searched his eyes, saw nothing but love in the gold and green. "I was going to speak to you tonight, now. I was going to tell you how much I love you, that it didn't matter if you didn't want to marry me, but I had to tell you, had to own to it"—she felt the tears come again and fill her eyes—"because life's too short to turn aside from love."

He looked at her for a moment, then bent and kissed her eyes closed, kissed away the tears that seeped beneath her lashes.

"We're not going to turn aside from love—we're going to embrace it." His words slid into her mind, into her heart as his arms slid around her and held her safe, close. Secure. "We're going to go home to Avening and fill the manor with children, and grow old watching over them and managing our estates."

Her arms stole around him and she sank against him, sniffed delicately. "What about Percy? He's sweet, but . . ."

"You'll cut him to ribbons." Jack smiled against her hair. "You can help me choose which of my other properties to make over to him. I think he'll do well, once he's trained and has something behind him."

She nodded. "Something that's his."

She drew back, and he let her. He looked down at her face, marveled at all she'd said, at all they'd shared. "You do know that I would trade everything that's mine in this life, just as long as that meant you were mine?"

Clarice reached up and framed his face, looked into his eyes. "Take me back to Avening."

He smiled, not his charming smile but the sincere expression that was so much more potent. "That will be my pleasure."

She smiled back, slowly, tauntingly. "Indeed. That, too."

Reaching up, she wound her arms about his neck, and drew his head down to hers. "But for tonight . . ."

Tonight, all that was left of it, was theirs. Theirs to share in a private celebration, and more, to go further, to take their first joyous steps into their joint future, to laugh, to play, to pleasure, to share.

In the soft shadows of her bedroom, in the warm jumble of her bed, they loved, and embraced all that flowed from that, that grew and burgeoned and welled from that. Carried in each caress, in every sighing kiss, in each moan, each surrender, the glory swelled, poured through them, filled them.

They exulted as the tapestry of pleasure and delight, of sensual glory and the overwhelming beauty of love's transcendent power spun about them, trapped them, and held them. Until, at the last, it swept them, senses shattered, from the world.

Into that place beyond reality where only true hearts and souls could go.

Into a landscape that was familiar yet subtly altered, more definite, more distinct, more sure. More emotionally certain. Together, hand in hand, they gloried in the change, welcomed it and explored; side by side, they drew their new landscape into their hearts, into their lives, and made it a part of them.

Now, forever, always theirs.

The Altwood engagement ball, held at Melton House three nights later, became the most celebrated event of the Season. Never before in the annals of the ton had four scions of a noble house announced their engagements all on one night, at one place, at one time.

The ton was beyond dazzled.

Clarice wore the plum silk gown. She wanted the ton to remember this night, her swan song, the only ball she would ever host under her ancestral roof, the ball celebrating her own engagement along with those of her three brothers.

She wanted the ton to remember her as that scandalous Lady Clarice in her daring plum silk gown.

She succeeded.

The announcements were made with all due ceremony at a dinner for sixty attended by many of the most influential in the ton, then she and her brothers and their soon-to-be spouses welcomed the army of the fashionable who had, one and all, responded to her invitation to join their celebration.

In bright satins and silks, black coats and white cravats, the crowd thronged the ballroom, flowed onto the terrace, even filled the stairs, all eager to view the most exciting moment, when the newly affianced couples took to the floor to lead the company in the first waltz.

When the musicians set bow to string and the summons rang out, the crowd quieted and held their collective breaths.

Proud and transparently happy, Alton led Sarah down the wide stairs, followed by Roger and Alice, and Nigel and Emily. Clarice and Jack brought up the rear, but when Alton reach the bottom of the sweeping staircase, he stepped to the side, and halted, Sarah on his arm. Roger followed suit, moving to the other side of the stairs with Alice, Nigel and Emily close on their heels.

Leaving Jack and Clarice center stage.

The expectation gripping the crowd abruptly cinched a notch tighter. A few gasps were heard; a ripple of whispers sped down the long room, but quickly died. All eyes remained trained on the couples at the bottom of the stairs.

On Jack's arm, Clarice stepped off the last stair. Surprised, she looked at Alton.

He smiled. "You should always have been the first. You've always given us the lead in matters such as this. Without you, God only knows if we would be here, like this, tonight." With a graceful gesture, he waved her on. "After you, sister dear."

Clarice looked into his eyes, then looked at Sarah.

Smiling mistily, Sarah nodded. "You and Jack first."

The music swelled; at Jack's touch on her bare back, Clarice inclined her head regally to her brother, then turned into Jack's arms.

She felt them close about her, looked into his gold and green eyes and saw love shining down at her. She smiled back and let him sweep her onto the floor, into their future.

The crowd let out a collective sigh.

Her brothers and their fiancées followed; the four couples alone circled the floor once. In Jack and Clarice's wake, a flurry of deliciously scandalized whispers erupted as more of the company took note of her gown, and the rest took note of what a handsome and striking couple they made.

Then others joined them; within a minute fully half the guests had taken to the floor, all eager to be a part of that very special moment.

Clarice didn't see them; she was too deeply enmeshed in the web of happiness that cocooned her and Jack. "When can we leave for Avening?"

He, too, had eyes only for her. He arched a brow. "Is tomorrow too soon?"

She smiled. "I'll order the carriage for ten. We can stop at the club on the way."

Jack grinned. "Anyone would think you didn't appreciate the ton in all its glory."

Clarice arched a brow back, haughty, a touch tart. "I appreciate it well enough, but I know what I want—Avening, your children, and you."

A wise man knew when to keep his lips shut. Jack's grin deepened into a real smile; he gathered her closer, swept her into the next turn, and started to plan how best to deliver to his warrior-queen precisely what she wanted.

They returned to Avening so James could marry them in the village church where all the Warnefleets for generations had pledged their vows; neither had considered anything else.

Mindful of Jack's injuries, not just his healing shoulder but his still-healing head, Clarice insisted they take three days to cover the distance from London, stopping for long relaxed luncheons and ending the day in the late afternoon at a comfortable inn.

They were traveling ahead of a small army. Her three brothers, their fiancées, and numerous other members of her family, as well as Jack's aunts and other family members, along with a select contingent of family friends, Lady Osbaldestone among them, were to follow in a few days.

They intended to marry as soon as may be; neither wished to waste any more of their lives. Appealed to, the bishop had been only too happy to bestow a special license and his blessing on them. The other members of the Bastion Club had been duly summoned; all would shortly arrive. Dalziel had been invited, but had, predictably, sent his regrets.

Jack suggested they ride the last stretch. Glad enough to be free of the confines of the coach, Clarice joined him in long gallops interspersed with ambling walks through countryside still sharp with the freshness of spring, down lanes wending through rolling fields, sunshine and a sense of belonging all about them.

At the last, they cantered up the Tetbury lane and reined in at the top of the rise, as Jack had only a few weeks before. With Clarice beside him, he looked down on Avening valley, on the orchards surrounding his home, at the clouds of apple blossom still clinging to the trees.

The same, and yet not. The emotion the sight and scent of apple blossom evoked in him had changed.

He glanced at Clarice, smiling lightly as she surveyed her domain.

Jack felt his heart swell. This was his real homecoming, because now, with her, his home was complete.

Reaching for her hand, he raised it to his lips, brushed a gentle kiss across her knuckles. Met her eyes and smiled when, surprised, she looked questioningly at him.

Releasing her, he waved her on. Side by side, they rode down the hill, to the village, to the manor.

Boadicea, Avening, and apple blossom.

At long last, he was home.

THE FIFTH BASTION CLUB NOVEL

*tells the story of Jocelyn Deverell, Viscount Paignton,
who, growing tired of the* ton *and his failure to find
a suitable bride, bites the bullet and asks his favorite,
eccentric spinster aunt for assistance. She knows just the right
lady to engage Deverell, one who will prove an irresistible
challenge—a young woman of strong mind, an iron will,
and a determination never to wed.*

FROM AVON BOOKS IN FALL 2006

In the Meantime . . .

STEPHANIE LAURENS's CYNSTER NOVELS

continue with

The Truth About Love

an Avon Books paperback, February 2006

Following is an excerpt from The Truth About Love,
*which tells the tale of Patience's brother,
Gerrard Debbington, and the lady
he discovers he cannot live without.*

The next Cynster Novel,

What Price Love?

Will be available in hardcover
from William Morrow, March 2006

Gerrard Debbington is faced with a stark choice—he wants to paint the renowned but highly private gardens of Lord Tregonning's estate, Hellebore Hall, in Cornwall, but to do so he must also paint a portrait of Lord Tregonning's daughter. Gerrard has no wish to paint any flighty flibbertigibbet, but with no alternative offering, and encouraged by Patience, he agrees. Jaded by tonnish society, tired of being the target of too many matchmaking mamas, Gerrard, joined by his friend the Honorable Barnaby Adair, kicks the dust of London from his elegant boot heels and journeys into Cornwall.

Gerrard tooled his curricle between a pair of worn stone gateposts bearing plaques proclaiming them the entrance to Hellebore Hall.

"It's certainly a long way from London." Relaxed on the seat beside him, Barnaby looked around, curious and mildly intrigued.

They'd set out from the capital four mornings before, and spelled Gerrard's matched grays over the distance, stopping at inns that caught their fancy each lunchtime and each evening.

The driveway, a continuation of the lane they'd taken off the road to St. Just and St. Mawes, was lined with old, large-boled, thickly canopied trees. The fields on either side were screened by dense hedgerows. A sense of being enclosed in a living corridor, a shifting collage of browns and greens, was pervasive. Between the tops of the hedges and the overhanging branches, they caught tantalizing glimpses of the sea, sparkling silver under a cerulean sky. Ahead and to the right, the strip of sea was bounded by distant headlands, a medley of olive, purple and smoky gray in the early afternoon light.

Gerrard squinted against the glare. "By my reckoning, that stretch of water must be Carrick Roads. Falmouth ought to lie directly ahead."

Barnaby looked. "It's too far to make out the town, but there are certainly plenty of sails out there."

The land dipped; the lane followed, curving slowly south and west. They lost sight of Carrick Roads as the spur leading to St. Mawes intervened on their right, then the tree sentinels that had lined the lane abruptly ended. The curricle rattled on, into the sunshine.

They both caught their breath.

Before them lay one of the irregular inlets where an ancient valley had been drowned by the sea. To their right lay the St. Mawes arm of the Roseland peninsula, solid protection from any cold north wind; to their left, the rougher heathland of the southern arm rose, cutting off any buffets from the south. The horses trotted on and the view shifted, a new vista opening as they descended yet further.

The lane led them down through sloping fields, then steeply pitched and gabled roofs appeared ahead, between them and the blue-green waters of the inlet. Swinging in a wide, descending arc, the lane went past the house that majestically rose into view, then curved back to end in a wide sweep of gravel before the front door.

Rounding the final curve, Gerrard slowed his horses; neither he nor Barnaby uttered a word as they descended the last stretch. The house was . . . eccentric, fabulous—*wonderful*.

There were turrets too numerous to count, multiple
laced with wrought iron, odd-shaped buttresses aplenty
dows of all descriptions, and segments of rooms forming
ciful angles in the gray stone walls.

"You didn't say anything about the house," Barnaby said
as the horses neared the forecourt and they were forced to
stop staring.

"I didn't *know* about the house," Gerrard replied. "I'd
only heard about the gardens."

Arms of those gardens, the famous gardens of Hellebore
Hall, reached out of the valley above which the house sat
and embraced the fantastical creation, but the major part of
the gardens lay hidden behind. Poised sentrylike at the upper
end of the valley that ran down to the inlet's rocky shore, the
house blocked all view of the valley itself and the gardens it
contained.

Gerrard let out the breath he hadn't been aware he'd been
holding. "No wonder no one ever succeeded in slipping in to
paint undetected."

Barnaby shot him an amused look, straightening as Gerrard tightened the reins, and they entered the shaded forecourt of Hellebore Hall.

Seated in the drawing room of Hellebore Hall, Jacqueline
Tregonning caught the sound she'd been waiting for—the
clop of hooves, the soft scrunch of gravel under a carriage's
wheels.

of the others scattered about the large room heard;
peculating on aspects of the nature of
rrived.

to speculate, not when she could
up her own mind.

rmchair beside the
and

ted that Mrs. Elcott's and Lady Fritham's
e capital had provided.

ogant, the pair of them, my cousin said."
ed disparagingly. "I daresay they'll think
bove us."

"I don . . . hy they should," Eleanor returned. "Lady
Humphries wrote that while both were from excellent families, very much the haut ton, they were perfectly personable
and amenable to being entertained." Eleanor appealed to her
mother. "Why would they turn their noses up at us? Aside
from all else, we're all the society there is around here—
they'll lead very quiet lives if they cut us."

"True," Lady Fritham agreed. "But if they're half as well
bred as her ladyship makes out, they won't be high in the instep. Mark my words"—Lady Fritham nodded portentously,
setting her multiple chins and the ribbons in her cap
bobbing—"the mark of a true gentleman shows in the ease
with which he comports himself in any company."

Unobtrusively slipping away, gliding silently up the long
room to the window that gave the best view of the front portico, Jacqueline cynically noted the others present; aside
from her father's sister, Millicent, who after her mother's
death had come to live with them, none had any real reason
to be there.

Not unless one deemed rampant curiosity sufficient reason.

Jordan Fritham, Eleanor's brother, stood chatting with
Mrs. Myles and her daughters, Clara and Rosa, both
unwed. Millicent stood with them, Mitch
her side. The group was engrossed
and the singular success of M
suading society's fore
Hall and favor

431
balconies
, win-
an-

There were turrets too numerous to count, multiple balconies laced with wrought iron, odd-shaped buttresses aplenty, windows of all descriptions, and segments of rooms forming fanciful angles in the gray stone walls.

"You didn't say anything about the house," Barnaby said as the horses neared the forecourt and they were forced to stop staring.

"I didn't *know* about the house," Gerrard replied. "I'd only heard about the gardens."

Arms of those gardens, the famous gardens of Hellebore Hall, reached out of the valley above which the house sat and embraced the fantastical creation, but the major part of the gardens lay hidden behind. Poised sentrylike at the upper end of the valley that ran down to the inlet's rocky shore, the house blocked all view of the valley itself and the gardens it contained.

Gerrard let out the breath he hadn't been aware he'd been holding. "No wonder no one ever succeeded in slipping in to paint undetected."

Barnaby shot him an amused look, straightening as Gerrard tightened the reins, and they entered the shaded forecourt of Hellebore Hall.

Seated in the drawing room of Hellebore Hall, Jacqueline Tregonning caught the sound she'd been waiting for—the clop of hooves, the soft scrunch of gravel under a carriage's wheels.

None of the others scattered about the large room heard; peculating on aspects of the nature of they were too busy arrived. the visitors who'd just a to speculate, not when she could Jacqueline preferred not her own mind. view with her own eyes, and make u armchair beside the

Smoothly, quietly, she rose from the a chaise on which sat her closest friend, Eleanor Fritham, and Eleanor's mother, Lady Fritham, of neighboring Tresdale Manor. Both were engaged in a spirited discussion with Mrs. Elcott, the vicar's wife, over the descriptions of the two gentlemen shortly expected that Mrs. Elcott's and Lady Fritham's correspondents in the capital had provided.

"Bound to be arrogant, the pair of them, my cousin said." Mrs. Elcott grimaced disparagingly. "I daresay they'll think themselves a cut above us."

"I don't see why they should," Eleanor returned. "Lady Humphries wrote that while both were from excellent families, very much the haut ton, they were perfectly personable and amenable to being entertained." Eleanor appealed to her mother. "Why would they turn their noses up at us? Aside from all else, we're all the society there is around here—they'll lead very quiet lives if they cut us."

"True," Lady Fritham agreed. "But if they're half as well bred as her ladyship makes out, they won't be high in the instep. Mark my words"—Lady Fritham nodded portentously, setting her multiple chins and the ribbons in her cap bobbing—"the mark of a true gentleman shows in the ease with which he comports himself in any company."

Unobtrusively slipping away, gliding silently up the long room to the window that gave the best view of the front portico, Jacqueline cynically noted the others present; aside from her father's sister, Millicent, who after her mother's death had come to live with them, none had any real reason to be there.

Not unless one deemed rampant curiosity sufficient reason.

Jordan Fritham, Eleanor's brother, stood chatting with Mrs. Myles and her daughters, Clara and Rosa, both as yet unwed. Millicent stood with them, Mitch... ...nel Cunningham by her side. The group was engrossed i... ...n discussing portraiture, and the singular success of Mi... ...itchel and her father in persuading society's fore... ...most artistic lion to grace Hellebore Hall and favor h... ...her with his talents.

Calmly, Jacqueline approached the window. Regardless of her father's, Mitchel's, or the artistic lion's belief, *she* would be the one bestowing the favor. She hadn't yet decided whether she would sit for him, and wouldn't, not until she'd evaluated the man, his talents, and, most importantly, his integrity.

She knew why her father had been so insistent this man, and only he, could paint the portrait her father required. Millicent had been nothing short of brilliant in planting the right seeds in her father's mind, and nurturing them to fruition. As the one most intimately involved on all counts, Jacqueline was aware that the man himself would be pivotal; without him, his talents, and his vaunted integrity regarding his work, their plans would come to naught.

And there was no other way to turn.

Halting two paces from the window, she looked out at the occupants of the curricle that had just rocked to a stop before the portico; in the circumstances she felt no compunction in spying on Gerrard Debbington.

First, she had to identify which of the two men he was. The one who wasn't driving? That tawny-haired gentleman stepped lithely down, then paused to throw a laughing comment to the other man, who remained on the box seat, the reins held loosely in his long-fingered hands.

The grays between the curricle's shafts were prime horseflesh, and had been well-spelled; Jacqueline registered that in the briefest of glances. The man holding the reins was dark-haired, with strong, chiseled features; the tawny-haired one was prettier, the darker the more handsome.

In the second it took her to blink, she realized how odd it was for her to notice; male beauty rarely impinged on her mind. Then she looked again at the pair in the forecourt, and inwardly admitted that their physical attributes were hard to ignore.

The man on the box seat moved: a groom appeared and he descended from the carriage, handing over the reins.

And she had her answer; *he* was the painter. He was Gerrard Debbington.

A dozen little things confirmed it, from the strength apparent in those very long fingers as he surrendered the ribbons, to the austere perfection of his clothes, and the reined intensity that hung about him, every bit as real as his fashionable coat.

That intensity came as a shock. She'd steeled herself to deal with some fashionable fribble or vain popinjay, but this man was something quite different.

She watched as he answered his friend with a quiet word; the line of his thin lips didn't so much curve as ease—the veriest hint of a smile. Controlled power, intensity harnessed, ruthless determination—those were the impressions that sprang to her mind as he turned.

And looked straight at her.

Her breath caught, suspended, but she didn't move; she was standing too far from the pane for him to see her. Then she heard skirts rustling, footsteps pattering at the far end of the room; glancing sideways, she saw Eleanor, both Myles girls, and their mothers crowding around the far window that was angled to the forecourt. Jordan peered over their heads.

Unlike her, they'd crowded close to the glass.

Looking back at Gerrard Debbington, she saw him studying them, and inwardly smiled. If he sensed someone watching him, he'd think it was them.

Gerrard regarded the cluster of faces blatantly staring from the wide windows facing the forecourt. Raising a supercilious brow, he turned away; avoiding the gaze of the single woman standing back from the window closest to the portico, he looked at Barnaby. "It seems we're expected."

Barnaby could see the goggling crowd, too, but the angle of the nearer window hid the lone woman from him. He gestured to the door. "Shall we make our entrance?"

Gerrard nodded. "Ring the bell."

Strolling to an iron handle dangling by the door, Barnaby gave it a tug.

Turning his head, Gerrard looked once more at the woman. Her stillness confirmed she thought he couldn't see her. Light spilled into the room from windows behind her, diagonally across from where she stood; courtesy of that she was, indeed, primarily a silhouette, barely illuminated. She was intelligent enough, then, to have realized that.

But she'd forgotten, or hadn't known of, the effect of painted woodwork. Gerrard would take an oath the frame surrounding the window was at least eight inches wide and painted white. It threw back enough light, diffused and soft, true, but light nevertheless, to let him see her face.

Just her face.

He'd already glimpsed three youthful female faces, every bit as uninspiring as he'd expected, in the other group. Doubtless his subject was one of them; God knew how he'd manage.

This lady, however . . . he could paint her. He knew it in an instant; just a glance, that's all it took. Even though her features weren't that clear to him, there was a quality—one of stillness, of depth, of a complexity behind the pale oval of her face—that commanded his attention.

Just like his dream of the Garden of Night, the sight of her face reached for him, touched him, called to the artist that was his soul.

The front door opened and he turned away. Outwardly set himself to the task of greeting and being greeted. Cunningham was there, doing the honors; Gerrard shook his hand, his expression mild, his mind elsewhere.

A governess, or a companion. She was in the drawing room, the doors of which he could now see, so unless she beat a very rapid retreat, he would meet her. Then he'd have to find some way of ensuring she was included along with the gardens in the other subjects he was permitted to paint.

"This is Treadle." Cunningham introduced the butler, who bowed. "And Mrs. Carpenter, our housekeeper."

A stern-faced, competent-looking woman bobbed a curtsy. "Anything you need, sirs, please ask." Mrs. Carpenter straightened. "I've not yet assigned rooms, not being sure of your requirements. Perhaps, once you've looked around and decided which rooms would best suit, you could let Treadle and me know, and we'll have everything arranged in a blink."

Gerrard smiled. "Thank you. We will." The charm behind

his smile worked its usual magic; Mrs. Carpenter's face eased, and Treadle unbent a fraction.

"This is Mr. Adair." Gerrard introduced Barnaby, who with his usual air of genial bonhomie, nodded to the two servants and Cunningham.

Gerrard looked at Cunningham.

Who seemed suddenly on edge. "Ah . . . if you'll come this way, I'll introduce you to the ladies, and inform Lord Tregonning that you're here."

Gerrard let his smile grow a fraction more intent. "Thank you."

Cunningham turned and preceded them to the double doors leading into what Gerrard had surmised must be the drawing room.

He was right. They stepped into a room long enough to boast three separate areas for comfortable conversation. At one end, no longer by the window but gathered about the chairs angled before a large fireplace, was the group of ladies and the young man who'd peered out at them, and one other, middle-aged lady he hadn't previously seen.

Directly ahead, on the chaise that faced the doors, were two matrons, one of whom was eyeing Barnaby and him with incipient disapproval.

Although he didn't glance her way, Gerrard was instantly aware of the single lady, standing alone and regarding them levelly from the other end of the room.

Suppressing his impatience, he halted beside Cunningham, who'd paused a yard over the threshold. Barnaby halted just behind his shoulder. Gerrard looked at the bevy of young misses, waiting to see which one came forward—which of the three he was going to hate to have to paint. To his surprise, they all hung back.

The middle-aged lady, a welcoming expression on her face, started toward them.

As did the lone lady on his left.

The middle-aged lady was too old; she couldn't be his subject.

The younger lady drew nearer; he could no longer resist, but looked directly at her.

And saw her, her face, for the first time in good light.

He met her eyes, and realized his error.

Not a governess. Not a companion.

The lady his fingers were already itching to paint was Lord Tregonning's daughter.

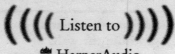

(((((Listen to)))))

📖 **HarperAudio**

STEPHANIE LAURENS

The Ideal Bride
Cassette
Performed by Clare Higgins
5 Hours/3 Cassettes
0-06-058503-X
$19.95/$29.95 Can
Coming on CD February 2006

The Perfect Lover
Cassette
Performed by Katie Carr
5 Hours/3 Cassettes
0-06-052783-8
$19.95/$29.95 Can.
Coming on CD February 2006

The Ideal Bride
Large Print
0-06-058981-7
$19.95/$29.95 Can.

The Truth About Love CD
Performed by Elizabeth Sasme
6 Hours/5 CDs
0-06-079352-X
$29.95/$42.50 Can.

www.stephanielaurens.com

📖 **HarperAudio**
An Imprint of HarperCollinsPublishers
www.harpercollins.com

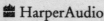

ALSO AVAILABLE
Harper
**LARGE
PRINT**
Edition

🦊 **AuthorTracker**

Don't miss the next book by your
favorite author. Sign up now for
AuthorTracker bey visiting
www.AuthorTracker.com

LAA 0905

DISCARDED

Perfume River

Perfume River

A NOVEL

ROBERT OLEN BUTLER

Atlantic Monthly Press
New York

Published simultaneously in Canada
Printed in the United States of America

FIRST EDITION

First published by Grove Atlantic, September 2016

ISBN 978-0-8021-2575-0
eISBN 978-0-8021-9010-9

Atlantic Monthly Press
an imprint of Grove Atlantic
154 West 14th Street
New York, NY 10011

Distributed by Publishers Group West

groveatlantic.com

16 17 18 19   10 9 8 7 6 5 4 3 2 1

For Kelly

Perfume River

What are Robert Quinlan and his wife feebly arguing about when the homeless man slips quietly in? Moments later Robert could hardly have said. ObamaCare or quinoa or their grand-daughter's new boyfriend. Something. He and Darla are sitting at a table in the dining area of the New Leaf Co-op. Her back is to the man. Robert is facing him. He notices him instantly, though the man is making eye contact with none of the scattered few of them, the health-conscious members of the co-op, dining by the pound from the hot buffet. It's a chilly North Florida January twilight, but he's still clearly overbundled, perhaps from the cold drilling deeper into his bones because of a life lived mostly outside. Or perhaps he simply needs to carry all his clothes around with him.

Robert takes him for a veteran.

The man's shoulder-length hair is shrapnel gray. His face is deep-creased and umbered by street life. But in spite of the immediately apparent state of his present situation, he stands straight with his shoulders squared.

He sits down at a table beside the partition doorway, which gapes into the crosswise aisle between checkout counters and front entrance. He slumps forward ever so slightly and puts both his clenched fists on the tabletop. He stares at them.

"You should've put your curry on it," Darla says to Robert.

So it's about quinoa, the argument.

1

"Instead of rice," she says.

She has continued her insistent advocacy while his attention has drifted over her shoulder to the vet.

Robert brings his eyes back to her. He tries to remember if he has already cited the recent endorsement of white rice by some health journal or other.

"All those famously healthy Japanese eat rice," he says.

She huffs.

He looks at his tofu curry on the biodegradable paper plate.

He looks back to the vet, who has opened one fist and is placing a small collection of coins on the table.

"I'm just trying to keep you healthy," Darla says.

"Which is why I am content to be here at all," Robert says, though he keeps his eyes on the vet.

The man opens the other fist and begins pushing the coins around. Sorting them. It is done in a small, quiet way. No show about it at all.

"Thanks to their fish," she says.

Robert returns to Darla.

Her eyes are the cerulean blue of a Monet sky.

"Fish?" he asks. Uncomprehendingly.

"Yes," she says. "That's the factor . . ."

He leans toward her, perhaps a bit too abruptly. She stops her explanation and her blue eyes widen a little.

"I should feed him," he says, low.

She blinks and gathers herself. "Who?"

He nods in the vet's direction.

She peeks over her shoulder.

The man is still pushing his coins gently around.

She leans toward Robert, lowering her voice. "I didn't see him."

"He just came in," Robert says.

"Feed him quinoa," Darla says. She isn't kidding.

"Please," he says, rising.

She shrugs.

This isn't a thing Robert often does. Never with money. He carries the reflex attitude, learned in childhood: You give a guy like this money and it will go for drink, which just perpetuates his problems; there are organizations he can find if he really wants to take care of himself.

Giving food is another matter, he figures, but to give food to somebody you encounter on the street, while rafting the momentum of your daily life—that's usually an awkward thing to pull off. And so, in those rare cases when it wouldn't be awkward, you can easily overlook the chance.

But here is a chance he's noticed. And there's something about this guy that continues to suggest *veteran*.

Which is to say a *Vietnam* veteran.

Something. He is of an age. Of a certain bearing. Of a field radio frequency that you are always tuned to in your head.

Robert is a veteran.

He doesn't go straight for the vet's table. He heads toward the doorway, which would bring him immediately alongside him.

He draws near. The man has finished arranging his coins but continues to ponder them. He does not look up. Then Robert is beside him, as if about to pass through the doorway.

The vet has to be aware of him now. Still he does not look. He has no game going in order to get something, this man of needs. It has truly been about sorting the coins.

He smells a little musty but not overpoweringly so. He's taking care of himself pretty well, considering. Or has done so recently, at least.

Robert stops.

The vet's hair, which was a cowl of gray from across the room, up close has a seam of coal black running from crown to collar.

Robert puts his hand on the man's shoulder. He bends near him.

The man is turning, lifting his face, and Robert says, "Would you like some food?"

Their eyes meet.

The furrows of the vet's face at brow and cheek and jaw retain much of their first impression: deeply defined, from hard times and a hard life in the body. But his eyes seem clear, and they crimp now at the outer edges. "Yes," he says. "Do you have some?"

"I can get you some," Robert says.

"That would be good," the man says. "Yes."

"What do you like? I think there was some chicken." Though he hasn't invoked the preternaturally healthful quinoa, he catches himself trying to manage this guy's nutrition, an impulse which feels uncomfortably familiar. He's trying to get him healthy.

"It needs to be soft," the man says. "I don't have very many teeth."

"Why don't you come with me," Robert says. "You can choose."

The vet is quick to his feet. "Thank you," he says. He offers a closed-mouth smile.

Standing with him now, about to walk with him, Robert recognizes something he's neglected: This act is still blatant charity, condescending in its anonymity. So he offers his hand. And though he almost always calls himself—and always thinks of himself—as *Robert*, he says, "Bob."

The vet hesitates.

The name alone seems to have thrown him. Robert clarifies. "I'm Bob."

The man takes Robert's hand and smiles again, more broadly this time, but struggling to keep his toothlessness from showing. "I'm Bob," he says. And then, hastily, as if he'd be mistaken for simply, madly, parroting the name: "*Too.*"

The handshake goes on. The vet has a firm grip. He further clarifies. "I'm *also* Bob."

"It's a good name," Robert says.

"It's okay."

"Not as common as it used to be."

Bob looks at Robert for a moment, letting the handshake slow and stop. Robert senses a shifting of the man's mind into a conversational gear that hasn't been used in a while.

"That's true," Bob says.

Robert leads him through the doorway and along the partition, past the ten-items-only register, and into the buffet area. He stops at the soup warmers on the endcap, thinking of the man's tooth problem, but Bob goes on ahead, and before Robert can make a suggestion, Bob says, "They have beans and rice. This is good."

Robert steps beside him, and together they peer through the sneeze guard at a tub of pintos and a tub of brown rice. Good mess hall food, Robert thinks, though thinking of it that way jars with a reassessment going on in a corner of his mind.

Of no relevance to this present intention, however.

Bob declines any other food, and Robert piles one of the plastic dinner plates high with beans and rice while Bob finds a drink in the cooler. Robert waits for him and takes the bottle of lightly lemoned sparkling water from his hand and says, "Why don't you go ahead and sit."

Bob nods and slips away.

Robert steps to the nearby checkout station.

A young man, with a jugular sunburst tattoo and a silver ring pierced into his lip, totals up the food, and Robert lets his reassessment register in his mind: From the clues of age in face and hair, Robert realizes Bob is no Vietnam veteran. As old as the man is—perhaps fifty or fifty-five—he is still too young to have been in Vietnam. He missed it by a decade or so.

Robert pays.

The clerk gives him a small, understanding nod.

"Do you know him?" Robert asks.

"He comes now and then," the young man says.

Beans and rice and fizzy lemon water in hand, Robert turns away.

He steps into the dining area and sets the plate and the can before Bob. The man has carefully laid out his napkin and plastic utensils and has put his coins away.

He squares around to look up at Robert.

He is not the man Robert first thought him to be.

"Thank you," Bob says.

Robert knows nothing about him.

"It's a good meal," Bob says.

"You bet," Robert says, and he moves off, thinking: *It would have made no difference. I would have done this anyway.*

He sits down before Darla.

She leans toward him and says softly, "I'm glad you did that."

To her credit, she does not ask what he's bought the man. She sits back.

Her plate, once featuring the spicy Thai quinoa salad, is empty. He looks at his remaining tofu curry. He picks up his fork and begins pushing it around.

She says something he does not quite hear.

He stops pushing.

There are other voices in the dining area. Conversations.

He thinks: *Can it have been that long ago?*

But of course it can. Even consciously thinking about it, Vietnam yields up no clear, individual memory. Images are there—faces and fields and a headquarters compound courtyard and a bar and a bed and a river—but they are like thumbnails of forgotten snaps on a cellphone screen.

"More," Darla says. As part of other things she's been saying, no doubt.

Robert looks at her.

She narrows her eyes at him.

"It's probably cold," she says, nodding at his food.

"Probably," he says.

"You can get some more," she says.

"I don't need anything," he says.

She shrugs. "Shall we go?"

"Coffee," he says. The word is a nanosecond or so ahead of the conscious thought.

She cocks her head. He went back to the stuff a few months ago after she'd wrangled a year of abstinence from him. She was reconciled to it but the one-word announcement sounds like a taunt, he realizes.

"Bob needs some coffee," he says.

"Bob?" She twists at the word in her snorty voice, assuming he's referring to his coffee-seeking self in the third person. She occasionally calls him *Bob* when she thinks he's behaving badly.

He doesn't explain. He rises. He approaches Bob. The man is hunched over his food, wolfing it in.

Robert is beside him before he looks up.

"You a coffee drinker, Bob?"

"I surely am," he says.

"How do you take it?"

"With a splash of milk."

"I'll get you some."

"I appreciate it, Bob," Bob says.

Near the buffet, Robert begins to fill a cup from a percolator urn. Framed in the center of the urn is the bag art for today's brew. An upsweep of mountains dense with tropical forest, the vista framed in coffee trees.

Somewhere along the highway to Dak To, they'd laid out the beans to dry. He is passing in a jeep, heading to an assignment that will quickly be changed, sending him upcountry. A pretty-faced girl in a conical hat, leaning on her coffee rake, lifts her face to him. And he sweeps on past.

The cup is nearly full.

He flips up the handle.

He splashes in some milk.

He returns to Bob.

The man thanks him again, briefly cupping both hands around the coffee, taking in its warmth before setting it down.

"You a Floridian, Bob?" Robert asks.

"I'm from Charleston, West Virginia," he says.

"Good thing you're not up there for the winter."

Bob nods a single, firm nod and looks away. "I have to go back," he says.

"Perhaps when things warm up."

"No choice," he says. "I've got responsibilities." His face remains averted. He isn't elaborating. His beans and rice are getting cold.

Robert still has the urge to make this encounter count for something beyond a minor act of charity. Learn a bit more about him. Offer some advice. Whatever. And this is all he can think to ask: "What sort of responsibilities, Bob?"

Robert Olen Butler

Bob doesn't look at him.

He doesn't eat.

He doesn't drink.

Robert has made the man go absolutely still. But Robert sloughs off the niggle of guilt, thinking: *He's probably been asserting these responsibilities to himself for the whole, long slide to where he is now, knowing there's nothing left where he came from, knowing he'll never go back.*

Robert puts his hand on Bob's shoulder for a moment and then moves away.

He does not sit down at their table. Darla looks up. She glances at his empty hands. "No coffee?"

He shrugs.

She nods and smiles. "Finished with dinner?"

"Yes," he says.

She gathers her things and they put on their coats. She leads the way across the floor. Darla may well glance at Bob as she passes, ready to offer him an encouraging smile. She would do that. But Bob looks up only after she's gone by.

He fixes his eyes on Robert's and upticks his chin. He says, "You know my old man, is that it?"

Robert takes the odd abruptness of the question in stride, answering a passing "No" as he follows Darla out of the dining area.

And that is that.

~

Darla and Robert are finished in town, and he drives toward home on the parkway. The two of them do not speak. This is not uncommon after dining out.

They live east and south of the Tallahassee city limits, on an acre of garden and hardwood and a dozen more of softwood, and the quickest way carries them first along a commercial scroll of strip malls and chain eateries, lube joints and furniture stores, pharmacies and gas stations. Robert finds himself acutely aware of all this. He turns south at his first opportunity, and then, shortly, he turns east again, onto Old Saint Augustine Road.

Darla humphs, though for all their years together she has alternately used this dismissive sound as a sign of approval. It is up to him to know which humph is which.

Old Saint Augustine is easy to interpret. Canopied in live oaks and hiding its residences and smattering of service commerce behind sweet gums and hickories and tulip poplars, this is a road from the state's past, a subject he occasionally teaches at the university and Darla occasionally is happy to hear him discourse upon. Though their silence persists tonight.

She switches on the university radio station.

This same ostinato of orchestral strings presses his face to a window on a TWA 707. The Rocky Mountains crawl beneath him. He is flying to Travis Air Force Base, north of San Francisco. From there he will go to war. And this music is playing in his head through a pneumatic headset. Beethoven's Seventh Symphony. The first movement has tripped and stomped and danced, making things large, as Beethoven can do, but confidently so, almost lightly so. A little bit of the summer pastoral spilling over from the Sixth Symphony. And now, in the second movement, the largeness of things is rendered into reassuring repetitions. Can Robert believe this of what lies ahead of him, this grave contentment the music would have him feel?

He is not to be a shooting soldier. He will do order-of-battle work, rather like research, rather like the things he learned to love in his recent four years at Tulane. Wherever they put him, he will be bunkered in at the core of a headquarters compound. It would take an unlikely military cataclysm—or a fluke, a twist of very bad luck, a defiance of an actuarial reality of warfare that is obscured by Cronkite's nightly report—for him to die.

He is young enough to feel confident in that reasoning.

It is September of 1967. Four months before the military cataclysm of the coming Vietnamese New Year, Tet 1968.

And if he does survive, he believes he will earn a thing he has long yearned to earn, foreshadowed only a few days ago in a bar on Magazine Street. His father shed tears over his tenth farewell Dixie, Robert's fourth. Silent tears. William Quinlan has always been a quiet drunk. A quiet man, about feelings he could not command, feelings better felt by women. Robert still thinks, as he flies away to music his father could never understand, that he knows what the tears were about.

In the car, however, this ostinato is solemn and insistent. More than solemn. It aches. He feels nothing like contentment as he races through the corridor of oaks. It is forty-seven years later.

He glances at Darla.

Her face is pressed against the window.

~

Down a pea gravel drive they emerge from a grove of pine and cedar. They stop before the house they built in 1983 from early-twentieth-century Craftsman plans, with a shed-dormered gable roof, a first floor of brick, and two upper floors of veneered stucco and half-timber. For a decade Darla's parents withheld every penny of their considerable resources from the struggling young academic couple, disapproving of the politics that brought the two of them together, and then, upon their deaths, they surprised their daughter with a will that split the parental wealth in half between her and a brother as conservative as they. She got the sprawling Queen Anne estate on Cayuga Lake and enough money to keep it up, along with the expressed hope—just short of a mandate—that their "daughter Darla and her family come home."

The parents' death itself surprised her. It was by late-night car crash on the Taconic Parkway, both of them apparently drunk. Darla immediately sold the Queen Anne and she and Robert built this new house, to their shared taste, having lately taken their places at Florida State University. At the time, their son Kevin was eleven. Their daughter Kimberly was five.

Tonight, with Robert's Clinton-era S-Class Mercedes sitting next to Darla's new Prius, they enter the house and put away their coats and go to the kitchen and putter about, she heating water for her herbal tea and he grinding his Ethiopian beans to brew his coffee, and for a long while they say nothing, not uncommon for this early-evening ritual, which occasionally feels, for both of them, comfortable.

Then, when their cups are full and they are about to go off to their separate places in the house to do some end-of-evening work, Darla touches Robert's arm, very briefly, though only as if to get his attention, and she says, "What did you two talk about?"

"Who?" he says, though he knows who she means.

"The homeless man," she says.

"The weather," he says.

She nods. "Did he say how he copes?"

"We didn't get into that."

"I hate to shrug him off," she says, though in an intonation that mutes the "hate" and stresses the "off." She therefore does not need to add "but we must."

They say no more.

They are both on sabbatical this spring, and they go to what have been their separate studies ever since the house was finished.

Robert's is on the third floor, where the Craftsman plans called for a gentleman's billiard room. His desk faces the fireplace in the north gable, with its hammered copper hood.

Dormers and window seats are to his right hand and his left. His books line the room in recessed shelves.

Early-twentieth-century American history is his specialty and he is writing a biography of a journalist, publisher, and agitator for pacifist and socialist causes, John Kenneth Turner. Tonight, he is working on a paper for a history conference. "The Prototype of the Twentieth-Century Antiwar Movement in the U.S.: John Kenneth Turner, Woodrow Wilson, and the Mexican Invasion." A mouthful of a title that he sits for a time now trying to simplify.

Darla's study is off the first-floor hallway between the living room and the dining room. Her desk looks west through the casement windows, across the veranda, and out to the massive live oak behind their house. She teaches art theory. By certain scholarly adversaries at other schools, her research is considered to be interdisciplinary to a fault. She is known for her book *Public Monuments as Found Art: A Semiotic Revisioning*. Tonight she is trying to finish the rough draft of a paper, which, indeed, she will present at a semiotics conference. "Dead Soldiers and Sexual Longing: The Subtexts and Sculptural Tropes of the Daughters of the Confederacy Monuments." The title seems just right to her.

They are focused thinkers, Robert and Darla. They would, if pressed to consider the matter, attribute some of their focus to the mutual respect they have for each other's work. They need give each other not a single thought once they are sitting in these long-familiar rooms.

But the last sip of Robert's coffee is cold. And he thinks of Bob.

He wonders what the man is doing right now. There is some shelter or other in Tallahassee, surely. Bob is there. Perhaps he is thinking, still, of Charleston, thinking of whatever it is he feels responsible for. Or perhaps Robert was right about that sudden stillness in Bob. Perhaps the man is merely hunkered down for the night in this life he's drifted to, trying to figure out how he got here.

~

After the man and his wife passed and vanished and Bob got reacquainted with the food and the coffee before him and after he ate and drank and sat for a while at the table, he has once again forgotten what he knows about what can set him to thinking, forgotten this to his severe detriment since he does not want to deal with the inside of his mind, with the thinking machine revved up, not ever, but especially not at the very same time as having to deal with finding a place to sleep, now that he's missed the deadlines for the shelters and the missions and the lighthouses and the mercy houses and the promised lands and the heavenly refuges. But tonight he has forgotten what he knows about *the situation*.

So as soon as he remembers, he stands and goes out of the New Leaf Market and it's too late, the situation is upon him:

It was light and now it's dark. It happened while he wasn't watching. It happened quick.

It launches him along Apalachee Parkway. And for a long while he just focuses on pushing his body hard to get away. Push and push. That's all there is. Too much. The ache in his legs and his back starts it all aching in his head again. He doesn't know how far he's come, how long he's been walking. A couple of miles. Maybe more. Then a landmark tells him he's making progress, even as it stirs up issues. Tillotson Funeral Home passes, its phony columns floodlit like the capitol building, its marquee making some dead body famous for being dead. Some stiff named Henry tonight. Henry something or other, the second name not even worth Bob noticing. This guy doesn't matter. Some Henry who was breathing and then he wasn't.

The dark continues to nag at Bob. Its suddenness happened early, this being the first week of January. It left a bad chill behind, which is why he's been walking east as fast as he can. In January he cannot simply vanish into the urban woodlands of Tallahassee, follow a bike trail and then veer off into the woods and find his things in a place only he knows about, through a culvert and along a drain bed and up a bank to a mark on a tree here and a mark on a tree there and a few more marks and a fallen oak and a hollow beneath, a place that was good for him all autumn long and he could go there anytime no matter how his flailing mind was trying to fuck with him, and he could get his stuff and he could find a place to sleep in the woods.

All of this is rushing in Bob again, filling his head with words, but he never thinks it's somebody else's voice.

"It's me. It's just me in here."

He says this aloud.

He's not crazy. He knows to look around right away to see if anybody heard him and nobody has. Bob's doing fine, with only cars whisking past, no people, no one to hear. He even has the presence of mind to walk against the traffic in the stretches without sidewalks. He's not crazy. He can even circle back to his previous thought, the one before the little digression that was worth mouthing.

"I could always find my way in the woods," he says. "You were okay with me there. Not that you'd let on. But you didn't fool me. I knew you were okay with me there."

This he addresses to his father. But Bob's not crazy. Bob doesn't think the old man is there with him on Apalachee Parkway to hear. The old man is just a memory to him, maybe hiding out in Charleston and yellowing from his liver or maybe spotlighted this very night in front of some funeral home, but he's nowhere nearby to hear. Nevertheless, because he's not crazy, Bob shuts his trap and does his talking in his head *where you always are, but when I'm strong—and I'm strong tonight, I know I am, in spite of the situation—I can make you behave, in my head I can take us into the woods, just you and me, and I can make it be the summer of '71, a certain day in August and I've gone and turned twelve and that was when I learned about the thing you didn't want me to know. That I was okay by you. Though it was only with the Mossberg .22 in the crook of my arm, that I was okay with the Mossberg*

18

going quick to my shoulder and I kill some animal or other that you didn't even see and it makes you drop into a shooting crouch and lay out some covering fire and then you stop and you look me wild in the eyes and inside you're going Who the fuck are you? *and then you focus and you answer your own question in your head, you don't want me to see it but I do, I listen into your head and you go,* You're Bobby, you're my son and you can shoot, by God, I been gone away a big chunk of your life to shoot in some big woods—in some fucking jungles in Vietnam—and I come back and by damn you can use a rifle just as good as any of the boys I been with *then you look where I shot and you throw a camouflage tarp over the crack that just opened and shut in your head, and you jump up, but you're not talking, not saying a word, of course not, you're not looking at me but I know what's just passed between us, no matter how you try to camouflage it, I know this thing about the two of us.*

"Goddamn you, I know it," Bob says.

I know it here in the woods even though I will doubt it when we get back home tonight, you will have your way with my head when you've got us in our single-wide and you're in your La-Z-Boy and you've got your bottle, and your silence is just your silence, and I better stay out of arm's reach while you're sitting there dealing with whatever it is you came home with a couple of years ago. Your situation.

Like Bob has a situation. Like now. Like this long, cold walk he's on tonight, trying the one thing he knows to try, concerning a place to sleep. A church building along the parkway, maybe thirty minutes by foot east of Walmart, an hour and a half from New Leaf, and longer still from the Hardluckers' center of town, and as he pushes on east, Bob can't stay in the woods in his head with his father for all that time, in fact his mind has already grabbed him up and galloped into that trailer park along the Kanawha, out past the West Virginia State campus, out where he's not okay with his father at all, and even if Bob summons up enough energy to at least drive his mind forward to when he's older, to when he's near as tall and rangy as his dad and he can easily fend off the old man when he wants to reach out and give his son a slap—it wasn't about that really, those slaps were all open-handed, always, Bob knew all along there were worse fathers by far—even when Bob skips forward, his mind only roars louder, because his real fear had to do with whatever it was inside his father that only the old man could see, the things he never talked about. Bob was afraid those things were inside himself already, no matter if his father found them in a jungle halfway around the world, because the two of them were the same, father and son, they were stretched tall in body in the same way, they had the same hands and eyes, and they were the same by that shared thing in the woods, when they were okay together. And the okayness only made everything worse because that was never spoken about either, just like the Vietnam jungle stuff. The good things between them and the bad things that could come to men like the two of them were all one in the same unspeakable place. And so Bob tries to just walk. He just strides hard and lets the pain of the pavement pound through his joints and back and temples and gums and he focuses on what's ahead.

A pastor out here at Blood of the Lamb Full Gospel leaves the outside door to the groundskeeper's storage room unlocked on cold nights. They have a food pantry, but this far out of town they do hard-luck families mostly, not the individually lost. Out here, sheltered floor space next to a John Deere is a private little bit of charity by the good pastor that often goes unused, its being attractive only to a Hardlucker without a car. Which makes it a pretty good bet to be available to anyone ready to walk six or seven miles. Especially since the space is needed most when it's the most daunting to walk, in the cold or the rain.

Two nights ago it was cold and Bob had the place to himself. It was a hard walk. Tonight it's cold again, but at the moment, with some things talked over, he feels pretty good. Pretty damn good. He's got today's newspaper folded in his pocket, a full copy abandoned on a table, waiting for him as he finished his coffee tonight. There's a light in the storage room to read by. He's not afraid to read the news. The meal and the coffee are sitting well in him, so his thoughts turn to the man who gave them to him, the man with the same name as his, the rangy older man with the John Wayne jaw: *You said it first, my name, and I thought for a second you somehow already knew I'm Bob and it turns out you're Bob, and my father is Calvin, my father isn't Bob, if you were my father I'd be Junior and I don't know what I'd think about that, I think I wouldn't like it, not at all, my father is Calvin, Cal, my mother is Marie, and what did you mean, Bob, about my having responsibilities in Charleston? Did you know me there? You another of my old man's cronies are you? What do you want me to do about it?*

"I never met you before in my life," Bob says.

He stops walking.

He's not feeling so good now.

Things are suddenly getting a little out of hand.

He realizes that.

This was a good man he met. Bob the stranger.

He needs to stop his mind.

He needs to sleep.

The church isn't much farther.

He walks on and the streetlights are gone, they've been gone for a while and the dark is even darker but Bob hasn't noticed till now. Still, it's all right, he's reconciled to the dark for this night, and up ahead now is an upspray of light as if rising from the earth, beaconing a message on another marquee, before the Blood of the Lamb Full Gospel Church: **GOD ANSWERS KNEE-MAIL**

Somehow this calms Bob for a time. Hardly from the sentiment. But he's not only not crazy, he's pretty smart. His mother was smart. Cal was too, in a shrewd sort of way. When Bob's mind is flailing with deep issues, to hear deep issues turned into banality is a kind of mental speed bump for him. He slows down.

He gives the sign the finger as he goes by, and he finds he can focus now for a time, and he keeps his eyes lowered as he passes the central spire and the fake front columns on the stuccoed facade. He keeps his face down and he moves through the side parking lot and around back and to the separate community building and around to the back of that and to the door and he's glad now it's almost over. He will sleep. He can sleep.

He is at the door and he puts his hand to the knob and he turns it and the knob yields and then the door and he steps into a darkness smelling of cedar mulch and motor oil, and he stops, and he waits a moment for his eyes to adjust and he sees a swift movement of shadow out of the corner of his eye and hears a guttural bark of a voice and he hears nothing more, not even the clang of the shovel against his forehead.

~

In bed now, Darla inserts her iPod earbuds, and she and Robert switch off their lamps. Their Kindles have their own light. The tinny spill of Bach from his wife's ears fades quickly from Robert's awareness. Soon, however, he is reading the same few sentences over and over. He turns off his book.

"Good night," she says, aware of the vanishing of his light in her periphery.

"Good night," he says, though they have long ago agreed that the formality of his reply is unnecessary, since her head, at this point, is always full of music and she cannot hear him.

Nor do they kiss.

They are so very familiar with each other. And that familiarity has become the presiding expression of their intimacy.

Robert sleeps.

And he wakes.

He has been dreaming, but he does not remember a single image of the dream.

Not that he tries.

It is enough that he is awake.

The room is dark.

He turns his face toward Darla. He can make out—more kinesthetically than visually—the topography of her. She is lying on her side, facing away.

He gently pulls back the covers, eases his way from the bed so as not to disturb her, puts on slippers and robe, and he goes out of the room and along the hallway and down the stairs. He pulls his topcoat from the vestibule closet, enters the wide dark of the living room, and passes through the French doors and onto the rear veranda.

He stands at its edge. The moonless sky is clear and the stars are bright. His bare ankles are cold but his chest is warm. He once would have snuck a smoke here. He didn't need Darla to persuade him to abandon cigarettes, even an isolated, open-air smoke or two. His father's burr-grinder cough did that.

Now he simply puffs his breath into the starlight.

His oak stands before him in vast silhouette, its lower horizontal branches thick as most trees, thick as water oaks and pin oaks. On other nights, with or without cigarettes, he felt that his scholarly discipline, his life's work, his very mind were made manifest in this tree. After all, it stood there through early-twentieth-century America, breathing oxygen into that era's air. It even likely witnessed the birth and death of the Confederacy, perhaps even Andrew Jackson's war on the Seminoles, Old Hickory's ruthlessness thwarted by the tribe's guerrilla elusiveness.

But on this night, as Robert folds his arms across his chest and squares himself to the oak, he feels the presence not of the ghosts of history but of Bob. Bob the illusory Vietnam veteran. He evoked Vietnam over Robert's quinoa at the health food store and then, being illusory in that regard, couldn't vent the war away. So it has settled back into Robert himself. For this, the veranda, facing the oak tree, is the wrong place to be tonight: a tree sits in the center of Robert's Vietnam.

He unfolds his arms, thinks to turn, to retreat to bed. But he does not move. Instead, he wakes and it's dark and a woman is beside him, naked and small, and she is waking too and the room is still heavy with the incense she has burnt for her dead. Robert has lingered with her, fallen asleep with her in a back street on the south bank of the Perfume River in the city of Hue. It is 3:40 in the morning, January 31, 1968, and they have woken to the sound of the North Vietnamese rockets and mortar rounds coming in from the mountains to the west.

Robert blinks hard against the memory.

He will not let certain things in.

He pats his pockets now, by reflex, as if he will find a cigarette, and he turns his face a little, breaking with his live oak.

But the woman lingers, still naked, in the dark of the room, lit through the window by a distant flare from across the rooftops.

And now he is throwing on his clothes. Hue was supposed to be different, traditionally spared by both sides. The targets of the North's New Year's offensive were thought surely to have been revealed in the fighting that commenced this time yesterday. Surely it was all coordinated.

He is dressed and he and the woman are standing beside the bed.

Her name is Lien. Lotus.

She hands him something heavy. Metal. He knows the thing. It is a French .32-caliber pistol that belonged to her father.

Do Robert and the woman speak?

Of course they do.

He loves her.

But he will not remember more of her now.

And he is down the back stairs into the dead-fish stench of the alley and the AK-47s are popping from across the river. The Viet Cong. Or maybe even the North Vietnamese regulars. Though his job has been to count—men, weapons, from all the field intelligence that comes in—he thinks: *We don't know jack shit about them, for all our counting.*

He goes out into the street, and far down, under the streetlamps along the river, he sees the men moving. The men he counts. He thinks: *I am a dead man.*

He turns and runs in the direction of MACV, the US compound, half a dozen blocks away. He rushes past storefronts and the passageways into rear courtyards and past the smells of mildew and dead fish and the smell of wood fires and from all directions now comes the din of weaponry, of small arms and RPDs and the whoosh and suck and blare of rockets, the sky flaring across the river, beyond the Imperial Palace walls—they are hitting Tay Loc, the city airport to the north—and now he sees men before him, as well, a squad of dark-clothed men a block up the river and gunfire is crackling everywhere and now a needle-thin compression of air zips past his head and he lunges into an alley mouth and he is running hard and figures are coming to doorways and he thinks the local communist cadres are emerging, he thinks again that he is dead, and there is only darkness around him and the alley slime underfoot and he pushes hard, and if he is to die he'd rather not see it happening, so he doesn't look right or left or feel any of the bodies coming out. He just runs and he runs and he is out of the alley and he is in a pocket park and standing before a great, dark form.

A banyan tree.

It is old and it is vast. Its aerial roots are thick as young trees and nuzzled together into their own dense forest, propping up a billowing dark sky of leaves, and there is a deep inner curve to the roots, and a turning, and in the direction of the MACV compound there is heavy small-arms fire now and he hears the AK-47s and he hears an answering M60 machine gun and the M16s and he knows what to do.

He enters the tree.

He moves into the turning and he puts his back to its roots and he sits and he draws his legs into him and he is in the dark. He can see around the out-curving columns of roots. Bodies appear, nearly as dark as the night, moving quickly past with a metallic rustle of weapons, and he pulls his head back, squeezes into himself. He closes his eyes and smells a dank wet-earth smell and something fainter beneath, an almost-sweetness, and a little sharp thing in the nose, and he thinks of the girl's incense and the dead she prays for. He knows this tree has killed another to live. These roots around him, holding him in the dark, began long ago by wrapping themselves around another tree, the strangler roots, embracing a living tree until it vanished, until it was dead inside the growing banyan. Rifles flare nearby and he presses back into the killing embrace of the banyan.

He holds the French pistol in his right hand, flat against his chest. He expects to die here.

Robert steps from his veranda.

He is panting heavily.

He has not let this happen for several years.

He moves across his lawn now, approaches his tree. He places both hands hard upon its trunk to stop their trembling.

He leans heavily there, waiting for this to pass.

But still he thinks: *I was not meant to be here. I was not meant to live this life I've led. I was meant to die long ago. Long long ago.*

~

Darla wakes, opens her eyes. Her lids are heavy, a precious, fragile state for her in the deep middle of the night. She is on her back, and above her is only indecipherable dark. She lets her eyes close. The bed has stirred and it continues to stir. Her eyes open again and their heaviness has vanished. She turns her face and watches her husband's form adjusting, arms and now legs and now arms again. She realizes he is doing this as unobtrusively as he can. He was once much worse, returning from whatever it is that he does. He is trying. She would speak, but she does not want a conversation that would wake her up once and for all. If there is something on his mind and he is choosing not to volunteer it, it can wait till morning. She turns on her side, putting her back to him.

And she sees him for the first time. It is May 8, 1970, four days after the Ohio National Guard killings at Kent State. He sits alone at a bistro table in a corner of a coffee shop in downtown Baton Rouge. She figures she has him pegged: the stretchy slacks and the button-down, short-sleeved sport shirt could simply be the sartorial momentum of the LSU student dress code, only recently rescinded, but something else about him—perhaps the longer hair on top of his head and the new growth on the sides; perhaps his quiet, two-handed focus on his coffee; perhaps just that surge of intuition about a guy your pheromones tell you you'll fall for—something—makes her figure they are PX clothes and a military whitewall haircut abandoned at last and a cup of better coffee than he's had for the past two or three years. He is an ex-soldier.

Behind her, on Fourth Street, some of the thousand people who just marched on the state capitol are drifting by, stoked and chatty with righteousness. Enough of them are also crowded into the shop to justify Darla receiving her cup of coffee and then approaching this man with green eyes and disparately dark hair and a jaw as smooth and hard as monument marble.

He looks up at her, though slowly, as she draws near, as if he were reluctant to shift his attention from the coffee.

She plays her hunch. "It looks like you've wanted that cup of Community for a long time." She learned quickly, as a New York girl first-year grad student, about the local coffee, ground and roasted on the north side of town.

"I've been away," he says.

Darla looks around the crowded room as if checking the available seating. She knows it makes no difference; she'd be doing this anyway. Still, even though she has for several years been quite comfortable with her female empowerment in this new age, she chooses to portray, with the search, a practical reason for the question she is about to ask. She nods at the empty chair across from him. "May I?" she asks.

"Of course," he says.

She puts her coffee cup on the tabletop and sits.

He stirs now in the bed next to her.

She stops this memory.

She is no longer sleepy. She needs to count bricks in an imaginary wall. She needs to take deep breaths and let them out slowly.

She thinks: *What prompted this bit of* recherche du temps perdu? *Not a small French sponge cake. Not even Community Coffee. Perhaps my Thai quinoa salad, though for its overspiciness rather than its latent nostalgia.*

She can't even muster an irony-arched half smile for herself. She would like to dismiss the past with this sort of smarty-pants joking. But that is a lifelong impulse she has lately come to see as cowardly. The fact is she clearly remembers falling in love with him. Loving him. Loving him and loving him.

And now that she is sitting before him in a Baton Rouge coffee shop with only a small tabletop of a French sidewalk café separating the two of them, and now that she is gazing directly into those eyes of his, they remind her of the emerald green of a Monet forest. She thinks to remark on this. Even in those first few moments with him. She also thinks, however, to mask her desire by immediately noting that it was the pigment that drove Monet mad. But instead, she says, "Did you march?"

He blinks those green eyes slowly, as if trying to understand.

Given her hunch about what he is or recently was, she hears herself as he might: the question could be a way of asking if he is a soldier. They are being routinely spit upon these days.

She clarifies. "To the capitol. Over the war."

"Ah," he says in a tone that suggests he was unaware of the event. "No."

"Surely you knew," she says. "We went right past that window. A thousand of us."

"I figured it was a Greek Row picnic," he says.

For a clock tick or two she believes him. The green eyes show nothing.

Then they come alive. Widen and spark, and Darla and Robert laugh together.

His eyes.

She looks toward him in the dark in the bed.

She realizes she has not been noticing those eyes for some time. She makes a note in her head to look him carefully in the eyes today.

And it occurs to her now, for the first time, after all these years: *My god. I'd actually expected an observation about the pigment of his eyes driving Monet mad to hide my desire. It would, in fact, have cried out my desire. His eyes were driving me mad.*

Did she ever go on to openly make that observation about their color?

She tries to remember.

She cannot.

She thinks not.

I never did tell him, she thinks.

And then: *Thank god. He got me into his bed quick enough as it was.*

But she did tell him. It was on their fifth wedding anniversary, spent in bed in their apartment in Baton Rouge, making love in the morning but then spending the rest of the day—wisely, necessarily, they thought—reading for their PhD oral exams. They did so, however, naked together in bed, the heat turned up high, as it was a chilly February day. In the late afternoon, as the light from the window was fading, just after Robert switched on a nightstand lamp, she told him about his eyes, thinking perhaps he and she might touch again for a time on this special day. She told him about their color. Told him that she'd planned to cut him down at once, however, with her line about Monet. Perhaps at the moment of her confession Robert's head was too full of the academic rhetoric of history. Her head was too, after all. For he simply smiled a little and offered a bland *How sweet* and he resumed his reading and she resumed her reading and they did not touch again for a few days, and when they did, the incident was forgotten.

Darla is counting bricks in an imaginary wall, pausing at each hundred to take a brisk, long breath and then letting it out as slowly as she can, trying to ignore the unconscious, restless body in bed beside her, trying simply to sleep.

Shortly after her third hundred, Robert turns heavily onto his back and sighs. Darla hesitates briefly—just long enough to realize how there is no good reason to hesitate, even briefly, to follow this impulse—and so she seeks his hand at rest between them and lays hers gently upon it. She thought he was probably asleep, and he is, but she keeps her hand on his until, just past her fourth hundred, she falls asleep.

~

When Robert wakes, there is a thin etching of gray dawn along the vertical edges of the blackout blinds. Darla's hand is long gone from his and he has missed the gesture. He is lying on his back and she is to his right, on her side, facing away. He is capable of a gesture similar to hers. He could lay a hand gently on the point of her hip now, as she sleeps, and then take it away again after a time without having to raise any issues or expectations between them. He has done so, with her sleeping, within the past week. But this morning he has woken to find Jimmy in his head and he needs to deal with that first.

Gently, very gently, so as not to wake her—for she can be a light sleeper sometimes, an aggrievedly light sleeper—he turns onto his side with his back to her.

For some years now it has taken Robert a little bit by surprise whenever he thinks of his brother. But the prompts this time are instantly clear: Robert's venture to the veranda without the purgative focus of a cigarette, particularly on a night of Beethoven's Seventh; the consequent memory of his flight from the North Vietnamese soldiers in Hue, of his refuge in the banyan tree; his taking refuge, as well, from the army, for an occasional night, in the arms of a Vietnamese woman.

Robert long ago recognized the irony of all this. In some sense he actually ran and hid before Jimmy did.

But it wasn't the same.

Even now, almost forty-seven years later, he feels compelled to repeat the litany of differences: More than a few Americans at MACV, officers and enlisted men alike, had local women to go to now and then; the communist offensive on five other provincial capitals the previous night had convinced everyone in Hue that the city's traditional exemption from serious attack, tacitly accepted by both sides, still pertained; Robert's break from the army was not even AWOL, much less desertion. And Robert had not run from the war. He did not even run from that night's battle; he sought cover and would later emerge.

He would later emerge.

And a price would be paid for not running.

Robert shuts down this line of thinking.

He does not want to emerge from the banyan. Not this morning. Not ever again. There is no need. He has long since reconciled himself to those few days in 1968.

So much time has passed. Generations. For Christ's sake, he's had his own children and grandchildren since.

And the irony about his act being akin to Jimmy's is superficial. A conceit. Jimmy did run. From the war. From far more.

Not that Robert blames Jimmy.

Not for his politics, certainly.

Not for decades.

Robert eases onto his back once again, expecting that thought to send Jimmy on his way, but instead he and Jimmy are sitting in overstuffed chairs angled toward the settee where their father is in a familiar stage of dozing off. Sitting upright, head sinking, he will soon—barely lifting his face and without opening his eyes—pivot slowly into fetal repose on the velour.

It is Labor Day, 1967. Robert is on home leave with orders to Vietnam. He graduated in June of '66 from Tulane and struggled through that summer with what to do. He went off to LSU on a graduate school deferment, but he dropped out as soon as the fall semester was finished and he enlisted.

Robert is wearing his dress greens. Glad for his father to see him in them. His father was a nineteen-year-old hard-stripe corporal in the infantry under Patton in Germany, about to become a platoon sergeant when the war ended.

But the conversation has been odd. Minimal. Tangential. Almost sullen, for his father's part. Pops is a quiet drunk. But sober, he can talk. He has the gift of gab. Even smart gab at times. He isn't well educated but he's well read. Their home has always been filled with books, and he even hounded any traces of Third Ward Yat out of his sons' speech. Still and all, Robert understands: About real feelings his father also is a quiet man. He gets drunk on his feelings and clams up.

And Robert figures there are other things going on to shut Pops down, figures the old man and Jimmy were probably fighting before Robert arrived and the fight simply has overridden everything. His little brother, fractiously self-assertive and needy as usual, has simply jumped in between him and their father.

Robert, in his bed, closes his eyes to the oak beam running above him in the ceiling as if it were about to fall and split the bed in two. He is tempted to slide forward a couple of hours, to the abrupt ending of the family's Labor Day afternoon in New Orleans.

But he does not.

He remains in the moment when he and Jimmy are themselves quiet, almost placid-seeming, with each other, as they sit watching their father fade into sleep in the front room of the family's double shotgun in the Irish Channel. When Pops bought the house—after he was promoted to stevedore foreman at the Seventh Street Wharf—he opened the common wall of the semidetached, here in the living room and in the back, at the kitchen, making a unified home of it. Robert was ten, Jimmy was eight.

As their father begins to snore, the brothers look at each other. It's been more than a year since they've been together.

Robert made his decision about the war on his own. The previous summer Jimmy was hitchhiking out west, and he spent Thanksgiving and Christmas somewhere in the Northeast with a girl he'd met on his travels.

Without a word or a nod, the brothers rise and go out the front door and down the porch steps. Clay Square lies before them, the de facto front yard playground of their shared childhood. Two years apart, they were playmates and then enemies and then friends and then largely indifferent to each other, as they sought their own independent selves, and now neither of them is sure about the other. They are ready to be what they will become on this little walk together, as Robert goes to war and Jimmy enters his senior year at Loyola after months of faux vagabondage during the Summer of Love.

They pause at the sidewalk and scan the broad, oak-edged sward of the park. The boys have too much history between them there, too much contending and screaming and too many tears and bloodied noses, long passed but with the affect still clinging to the place, and they turn south on Third Street, heading toward the river.

"So you've done this," Jimmy says.

"This?"

"The US Army in Vietnam."

Robert looks at Jimmy.

He is visibly Robert's brother, with the same jaw, their father's jaw, but Jimmy is paler in hair and skin, missing their mother's touches of darkness, which she got from her own mother, who was Italian. In spite of the confrontational quickness of his remark, Jimmy isn't looking at Robert. He's keeping his eyes ahead, down the street.

Robert says, "I did the *army*. It was up to them where they sent me."

"That's a cop-out," Jimmy says, though he still doesn't look Robert's way and his manner is matter-of-fact. "Did he put you up to it?"

Robert knows who Jimmy means. Pops. As of this Labor Day weekend in 1967, they have both always called him that. But Jimmy invokes him now as an impersonal pronoun.

"No," Robert says at once, taking the words literally to make the answer simple. No, there was no overt conversation, no request or exhortation or plea.

Jimmy says, "This isn't his war, you know. Even if he wants to make it that. Ho Chi Minh is not Adolf Hitler. Far from it."

"I told you this isn't about Pops."

"It's an evil war," Jimmy says.

Robert says, "Did your girl of the summer put you up to this?"

Jimmy stops walking abruptly.

Robert stops too, turns to him. He expects a fight now.

But even though Robert is a step in front of him, Jimmy keeps his eyes down the street.

They stand like that for a long moment.

Robert senses his brother grinding toward a choice. A fight is one option, clearly.

Now Jimmy looks him in the eyes.

From years of experience, Robert knows how to read his brother's face. It surprises him now. Nothing is there that fits the way Jimmy began this conversation. No furrow, no flare, no twitch. Nothing that fits his temper.

"My feelings are my own," Jimmy says, and his voice is actually soft. Robert cannot remember the last time he heard this tone in his brother.

"I believe you," Robert says. Though he's not sure he does. But he makes his own voice go soft as well.

"I bet he's proud of you," Jimmy says. He is still managing his tone.

"I don't hear any sarcasm in that," Robert says.

"There isn't any."

"Is she a flower child?" Robert says. "Teaching you gentleness?" He regrets it at once. No matter that he's starting to hear Jimmy's tone as an affectation, a lie. It's still a better way for them to talk, surely.

Jimmy doesn't answer. His cheeks twitch slightly and release, twitch and release. He's grinding his teeth.

If a woman is indeed gentling his brother down, the attitude deserves nurturing. So he makes himself a little vulnerable to his brother, offers an admission. "He isn't showing it."

Jimmy stops working his jaw. "I don't follow," he says.

"Pops," Robert says. "His approval. He was never going to actually show it. We both know that."

Jimmy furrows again, briefly, and grunts a nod of sympathetic recognition.

"My decision was my own," Robert says.

Jimmy nods again, in assent, looks away, beyond Robert to the square. They are silent for a few moments. Then Jimmy says, still looking into the distance, "She's bringing it out in me."

Now Robert doesn't follow.

Jimmy turns his face to him, sees his puzzlement.

"Gentleness," Jimmy says. "She's only bringing something out in me that's already there." He pauses, then adds, "And she's not a flower child." This last, however, comes out devoid of gentleness. Not quite angry, but sharply firm. Still, in an earlier time, Jimmy would be in full-flighted umbrage now.

Robert says, "I didn't mean to insult her."

"It wouldn't be an insult anyway, if she were," Jimmy says.

Robert thinks: *If you didn't take it as an insult, you wouldn't have hardened up in the denial.* But he doesn't let it out quite that way. He says, "I was just asking. Trying to assess what degree of criminal you both think I am by putting on this uniform."

"I thought you were asking to source my gentleness."

"Those two things often go together these days. The gentleness and the judgment."

"We're judging a government."

"By embracing another," Robert says. "North Vietnam's oppressions are even institutionalized. Read a little history. No government, no country in this world has spotless hands."

A quick clench comes to Jimmy's face, furrowing his brow and tightening the margins of his eyes. But he unloosens at once. His forehead stretches tight in willed calm.

Robert finds this oddly touching. His brother is still working hard to please his girlfriend.

"I won't argue Vietnam with you," Jimmy says. "Personally, I can't stand the politspeak and jargon and sloganeering. I can't stand the drug-addled vapidness either. But I'm sorry for the war coming to our family like this. I am."

"It will come to you, as well." Robert says this softly, not as a willed effect but from an ache that he is surprised to feel this keenly. He has even brushed aside his brother's implicit rebuke. Talk was starting that graduate school deferments were about to vanish. The war could come quite personally to his brother next May.

Jimmy does not answer. But he does not look away. He and Robert hold their gaze for a long moment. Then, as if they'd spoken of it and agreed, the two of them turn and continue south on Third Street.

They will not speak again about the war. Not on this day. Not, as it turns out, ever again.

In his mind now, in his bed, Robert has had enough.

The room is cold.

He wants his first cup of coffee.

He draws back the covers.

He sits, puts his feet on the floor.

But he has come this far on Labor Day, 1967, and the rest of it must play through him so he can drink his coffee with the past relegated once more to the past.

Much of that final scene is a blur. It wasn't about him, after all. He was simply a witness, standing apart. He's not even sure where they all are in the house. He can see only Jimmy and Pops. They're shouting at each other. Likely they're in the kitchen, because Mom walks out, brushing past Robert. He should follow her. But he doesn't.

He stays, though for a long while only in body. He tunes out the words, as Jimmy is drawn by his father into the polit-speak he said he despises. High-decibel politspeak that goes on and on.

Until abruptly the voices cease.

For a moment the room rings with silence.

Robert takes notice.

Jimmy and Pops are standing close, facing each other.

And then Jimmy begins to speak, but softly.

Robert listens. He misses some of the words, but he gets the gist. It's about a murderous war. It's about those who defy their country. Then Jimmy's voice rises and Robert hears clearly: "Those are the real heroes."

And William raises his right hand and slaps his son across the face. Jimmy's face jerks away from Robert's view.

The gesture has been flash-powder fast and William's hand has vanished. Robert's mind is lagging way behind. He saw what happened, recognized it. But Jimmy has quickly brought his face back to his father's, and for a moment Robert doubts his senses, wonders if he saw correctly. For all his bluster and working-class manliness, Pops has almost never used his hands on his sons.

And it happens again. Robert sees a movement at William's left shoulder and hears a sharp sound and Jimmy's face jerks this way, showing itself to Robert. Pops has struck him with his other hand, and he barks a single word: "Cowards."

Robert's body is startled into immobility while his mind revs up to understand. And it comes to him: It's General George Patton, Pops's beloved high commander. It's Patton's infamous gesture in a field hospital in Sicily in 1943, slapping a shell-shocked soldier across the face as a cowardly malingerer. The press got hold of it and Eisenhower stepped in, reprimanded Patton, took him out of combat command for a crucial year. Pops has spoken more than once about the bum deal this war hero got for a righteous act. Pops absorbed this gesture over the years. His muscles memorized it. And finally what seemed a familiar circumstance reflexed it.

All this tumbles through Robert's head as more words are spoken from across the room, as Jimmy then moves away, as he passes Robert, whose body is still inert. Nothing in Robert's thoughtful understanding of the situation suggests what action his body might take.

Jimmy is gone from the room. He will continue out of the house. He will not return.

It's all over. The end.

But for Robert in his father's kitchen, and for Robert in his own bedroom, what ended was simply that Labor Day in 1967. Jimmy would go on to his senior year at Loyola. It would be ten months before he'd go to Canada.

What Robert does not see at the time and what he does not see now is Jimmy's face after the second slap. The blow brought Jimmy's eyes to Robert's. But at that moment Robert was seeing only what was in his own head: an imagined image of Patton slapping a mind-blasted soldier in a hospital ward; Pops sitting somewhere with a beer, bemoaning Patton's unfair fall from grace.

Robert missed Jimmy's eyes fixed on him, missed what they asked.

And so he puts the incident away, as he always has: Everything happened very quickly; there was nothing to be done; it was all about these other two men anyway.

Robert rises from the bed.

Soon, in the kitchen, ready for the morning in khakis and cardigan, Robert burr-grinds his coffee beans, trying to return fully to this house, to the winter morning, to a day of work ahead in an America of a century ago. To do so he considers this Ethiopian he is grinding as if he were a Starbucks Foundation Endowed Professor of Coffee writing a monograph on these complex beans, washed and sun-dried in a cooperative in the village of Biloya, grown in deep shade more than a mile high in the surrounding mountains by a thousand farmers on less than two acres each, a coffee comprised of a dozen heirloom varieties, Kurume and Wolisho and Dega and more. Roasted last week in Durham, North Carolina, just a little past medium, the beans just beginning to turn dark.

As he waits for the water to pass through the filter of his Technivorm Moccamaster at exactly two hundred degrees, however, he marvels: *All this stuff in my head is prompted by that man in New Leaf. Not even him. My first mistaken impression of him. He has nothing to do with Vietnam.*

"You were restless last night," Darla says.

He turns to her.

She stands in the doorway in black running tights—she still has fine legs, this Dr. Darla Quinlan—and red fleece jacket. She holds her watch cap, her hair pulled back and bunned up, the pull of her hair smoothing the wrinkles in her face enough for them to nearly vanish at this distance. If he were nearer, he would touch the bottom of her chin with his fingertip, lift her face just a little, and even her incipient jowls would vanish.

"No more than usual, I think," he says.

"Perhaps not," she says.

"Sorry I disturbed you."

"It's not about me. I wondered if you were all right."

"I am."

They look at each other in silence, each feeling the wish to have more to say but unable, for the moment, to think what.

"Tea first?" Robert finally asks.

"I like to run first," she says. But she does so without a trace of a dumb-shit-you-should-know-that-after-all-these-years tone. Robert wonders if that means she's considering putting the running preference aside.

"Just this morning," Robert says. "It's cold out."

She hesitates, but says, "That makes it better to take the tea when I return."

They fall silent a moment.

"You'll be working by then?" she asks.

"How long will you be?"

"I don't know," she says. "I didn't sleep well."

"Sorry," Robert says.

"It wasn't you. I knew you were restless because I was already awake."

"Does it make you run longer or shorter, not sleeping well?"

"Longer, usually."

"Tough girl," he says.

"Tough girl," she says.

"We'll see," he says.

She angles her head to indicate she doesn't quite understand.

"Whether I'm working when you get back," he says.

They are silent again, but not moving.

"I can stay," she says.

"You should run," he says.

"All right."

She puts her cap on. She turns. She turns back. "You could have a second cup. You love the new beans."

"The second cup goes to my desk," he says, though without a trace of a tone—or even a trace of a feeling—that she should know that after all these years.

Darla goes.

How is the silence of this kitchen consequently different because she is out running somewhere on the dirt and macadam remnants of a WPA road instead of still sleeping upstairs? Somehow different. Felt several times lately by Robert, like a newly, faintly arthritic knuckle. He cannot say why.

He takes up the coffeepot, and now, in order to work, he has to try to put Darla out of his mind along with Bob and

Jimmy and Lien and Dad and the others who hover around them.

Perhaps because his work often leads him to consider the smallest semantic details, he hears the shift in his mind from his earlier memory to this present moment: Pops stopped being Pops somewhere along the way. He is Dad now. And to his face, there was rarely an occasion to address him with a name at all. *Dad* to his mother, when they spoke of the man.

But this is exactly the hovering of others he needs to resist. Semantics—his *mind*—snagged him on his father just now, so he thinks it will be a simple matter of the will to return to this kitchen and his coffee and the scholarly day to come. But a woman slips into him. To his surprise, it is not Darla.

Lien. She came to him last night beneath the oak tree, across all these years, and he left her last night just as he left her when the Tet siege began. Now, she comes to him as she always did, silently, gently. Borne not on a thought but a river.

The sunlight flares from the water and he turns his face to her, pressed chastely against him in the narrow bow of her uncle's sampan, the man out of their sight line behind them, beyond the bamboo thatch shelter in the middle of the three-plank boat. He is their chaperone, working the long sculling oar, bearing them on the river past the Citadel, past the coconut palms and the frangipani, toward Ngu Binh Mountain. Robert and Lien met only a few weeks ago in her cousin's tailor shop, where she works. He came again and again as if to consider a tailor-made suit until finally she said, *I am happy Robert never choose,* and she invited him to float with her upon her river in this season that gives it its name. And indeed the water all around them fills him with a ravishing sweetness possible only on the cusp of rottenness. The blossoms of fruit orchards upriver—litchi and guava, breadfruit and pomegranate—have fallen into the water and decayed in their passage to the South China Sea. The sunlight flares from the water and he turns his face to her and she turns her face to his and they hold each other in this gaze, before they have ever kissed, ever embraced, weeks before they will make love, and the perfume of this river fills them both, and she says to him, *Mr. Robert, your eyes are the color of water drop on lotus leaf,* and he says, *Miss Lien, your name means "lotus," yes?* and she turns away from him, glances over her shoulder toward her uncle, to make sure he cannot see. Then she looks at Robert again with her eyes the color of a black cat turned auburn in sunlight, and she leans to him, and they kiss.

He has not had this memory—has feared and resisted this memory—for years. He knows how to let go of it. He reinhabits this: Lien offers him the French .32-caliber pistol that belonged to her father, and he takes it and he turns and he heads out her door and down the stairs and into the war. This is a memory he can put aside without needing his willpower.

He closes his eyes.

He smells the coffee he has brewed.

He opens his eyes.

Once again he takes up the carafe. He pours his Ethiopian in small circles, listening intently to the purl of it, leaning in, flaring his nose to its smell, isolating the notes of peach and blueberry and cocoa. He thinks, reflexively, to carry the cup to the living room, as he often does, to sit in the reading chair that faces the French doors to the veranda. But the oak tree is framed in those doors.

He sits instead on a counter chair at the kitchen island. He puts his back to the casement window looking out to the veranda. This will be only about the coffee. He puts his hand to the mug handle.

The telephone rings.

He straightens sharply, inclined not to answer, short of its being Darla on her cellphone, in distress out in the woods. The answering machine is within earshot, in the hallway between kitchen and living room. At the second ring the machine's synthesized woman's voice says, "Peggy Quinlan."

His mother, on her cellphone.

Robert looks at the clock over the kitchen sink.

Barely past seven.

She has insomnia. She has unreasonable worries about Dad. She has reasonable irritations with him. She gets lonely, even with him always around. She never thinks what time it is.

Another ring and the answering machine announces her name again.

The coffee is hot.

Robert will let the machine answer. He can call her in a quarter of an hour.

He puts both hands around the mug, warms them there. He will take his first sip when things are quiet again.

Shortly the machine answers and his mother's voice, strained and short of breath, says from the hallway, "Robert, pick up if you're there. Your father has fallen. We're at the hospital. He's broken his hip."

Robert releases his cup of coffee, rises.

He crosses the kitchen, feeling he's moving too slowly. He's adjusting to this thing. His father turned eighty-nine in November. He's had trouble with his heart. A broken hip is bad.

His mother has gone silent.

He reaches the kitchen door, and just before the machine cuts her off, his mother says, "Okay. Call me as soon as you get this. I need you, Robert."

His parents are less than an hour away, forty miles north, in assisted living in Thomasville, Georgia.

He enters the hallway, passing Darla's study, glancing through the open door to the empty desk across the room, the oak tree beyond, and he stops at the telephone table opposite the vestibule.

He picks up the phone and dials his mother's cell.

"Thank God," she says. "Where were you?"

"How is he?"

"Not good, honey. Not good. The doctor is very concerned."

"We'll talk when I get there," Robert says. "You're at Archbold?"

His mother does not reply. Then her beat of silence turns into a choked-back "Yes" and she begins to cry.

"It's all right, Mom. He's a tough guy. I'll be there."

"Hurry," she says.

And Robert does. He pours his coffee into a thermos and dresses and writes a note to Darla. He tapes it to the front door: *My father has broken his hip. I'm in Thomasville. Don't worry. Work well.*

He turns onto Apalachee Parkway.

His mind roils with anticipated scenes at the hospital and he cuts each one off, tries to think of things he can manage. Like whether and how to make the connection, in his paper, between John Kenneth Turner's partisanship in the Mexican civil war and factions of the Vietnam antiwar movement siding with the North and lionizing Ho Chi Minh. Easy things like that. Things not having to do with family.

In this struggle of mind, Robert seeks distraction, so he turns his eyes to the Blood of the Lamb Full Gospel Church, which he is approaching. Here he routinely finds ironic amusement on a marquee that presumably intends to persuade the fallen to enter therein and learn the absolute truths of the universe, but doing so with messages that veer in tone between fortune cookies and one-liners from a born-again Milton Berle. But this morning his eyes slide past the new message to a Leon County EMS ambulance parked in front of the church, and then to a pair of white-coated men lifting a dark-clothed blur of a third man from a wheelchair into the back of the vehicle, and then past them to a fourth man, tall and nattily topcoated and standing stiffly upright, watching nearby and seeming, given the context, to be the pastor himself, the benighted editor in chief of that marquee.

51

And the church has passed and Robert thinks of his father, how he would share his son's amused disdain for the man in the topcoat, how his disdain, unamused, extended as well to Mama's priests. Robert wondered if that would be so even now, as his father finds himself on the cusp of some absolute truth of the universe, a truth you could learn for certain only by dying.

~

In a room over a clothing and leather goods shop on Baldwin Street in Toronto, Canada, Robert's brother Jimmy is waking. He lies on his side, at the edge of his bed. The panes of the window before him are groved in fern frost. He owns the building, has owned it for thirty years. The shop is his. These winters are his, finally, more or less. The room is cold but he's been sleeping with the covers sloughed down to his chest.

He pulls them up now to cover his arms, his mind filling: windowpanes overgrown with ice; an upstairs room in a two-story brick row house; he and Linda clinging close in a sleeping bag on a futon, the ice lit by the streetlight on McCaul. This was their first winter in Canada, spent only a few blocks from where he now lies thinking. The house was rented by an earlier wave of American resisters and deserters and the women who fled with them. They'd turned it into a commune and a crash pad for other exiles newly arrived. He and Linda had crashed there the previous summer but were permanent by that winter night, the night they celebrated the occasion of their meeting, eighteen months earlier. They had done so with a sweet lovemaking—slow and quiet, as there were two other couples asleep in this room—and with a trembling from the cold that never quite stopped, even after they'd spent themselves and lay clinging.

Jimmy blinks at the daylight brightness of this ice before him now.

He closes his eyes.

He thinks: *That was the closest we have ever been. In that moment.*

This is perhaps true.

His mind declines to fill with details of subsequent events, from only a few weeks later: Linda's hand on the commune founder's arm, sounds behind a closed door, the smell of him on her skin. Nor with the subsequent principled conversation he and Linda calmly had, after a few hours of shouting, about the liberated soul, male and female, alike and equal, about a new age and a new culture and the freedom of love. Which was like their principled conversation in San Francisco during the Summer of Love, about war. And like their principled decision, as his student deferment expired the following spring, for them to begin anew together in this place. This cold place.

All of that so long ago.

They've stuck to their principles.

He is weary now. In the legs, in the hips, in the groin, in the chest. In the eyes.

He opens his eyes once more to the ice on the window.

And he sees only the floaters. The lifelong accumulation of all the little crap between him and the world. Sometimes he can see through them as if they aren't there. Sometimes they are all he can see.

He is glad he will be with Linda tomorrow in their home on Twelve Mile Bay. Next month they will have been married twenty-four years, at last for more than the number of years they were together unwed.

He hunches his shoulders and draws the covers closer.

He owns the building but the room is cold.

He'll have Heather call someone to look at the furnace. And he sees her now, sees not floaters, not ice, not the scenes of principled compromise between him and his wife, but sees Heather sitting before the iMac in the back room downstairs, just yesterday morning. He stepped into the doorway from the front of the shop and she realized he was there and he could see a little smile come to her face. A smile because he was there, because it was him. And she did not care if he could see. She smiled to her own purpose, her own intentions, her own unvoiced willingness, before she let him know she knew he was there.

Then she touched command-S and swiveled in her chair, and her skin was as white as a new snowdrift, though the smile she gave him directly was meltingly warm, and her usually heavy-lidded dark eyes widened with the smile. She was somewhere in her thirties, a single mother of an early-teenage girl, but his head filled with the talk of Heather Blake: how she thought it was very cool, very very cool he'd been a hippie;

how her benighted parents had despised the hippies but she longed for that life, because as free as things seemed to be in her generation—and God help us how free it was for teenagers today—it was free only in blow jobs and loose talk; how the spirit wasn't free, how it took an old spirit to be free, a mature spirit, like his. All of which talk had accreted over the couple of months she'd worked for him. Never a pointed discussion. But bit by bit. Yesterday morning, confronting Heather's smile and the history of this talk, he sagged heavily against the doorjamb. But he simply asked, *How's the website going?* She laughed. As if she read his mind. As if she were saying, How silly you are. But she said, *It'll be back up within the hour.*

Jimmy is still lying on his side, facing the window.

The principles they spoke of, he and Linda, their freedom to love, those were never undone. Not even on their wedding day. Not overtly.

And the marriage has lasted. Canada has lasted.

He is keenly aware of two things now. The stalks and leaflets of the fern blades on the window seem hoary but alive, even though they are an illusion, merely a cold replica of a living thing. And the bed. He is aware of the bed.

He eases from his side onto his back.

He turns his head.

The bed is empty.

Not that she is gone, Heather Blake. She has never been here.

He lifted himself from the doorjamb yesterday morning and stood straight and thanked her for her Internet expertise, and he turned away from that little cocking of the head she gave, as if she'd expected him to say something else. Lately she always seemed to be waiting for him to say something else. But he turned and went about his business.

Through the years he has acted three times on the principle of personal freedom that he and Linda agreed upon. Briefly acted. The incidents were discreet but never intentionally hidden; they simply were never spoken of. That deceptionless silence also was decided between them. There'd been no need to say anything; their daily lives, each with several separate friendships and separate responsibilities in their business, especially during the two decades on Twelve Mile, made that easy. The commune founder seemed to have been a brief thing for her. Jimmy is not sure if or how often she has exercised her privilege, since.

But why exactly is his own bed empty now?

He does not quite regret it. If he has regrets, he could still act. But he does briefly wonder why.

The answer, he senses, lies in the image of the fern frost lingering deep in his chest like a nascent cough. Long ago he and Linda left their parents' religion—left all religion—behind. But for the past few years there have been things Jimmy's been trying to work out in some other way. Most recently he has been telling this to himself, which, indeed, he does again now: *It is only science of the past hundred and fifty years that has shaken our belief in our consciousness surviving death. But elemental science gives us examples that confirm the ancient and abiding paradigm. The caterpillar, for instance, does not even have the sensory mechanism to perceive the butterfly it will become; but it will be transformed nevertheless.*

He is sixty-eight.

He coughs, drily, from the chill he carries inside him.

Surely the pale nakedness of Heather Blake would be a more certain hedge against death.

And yet it isn't, somehow. The young feel they are immortal. *Must* they, to care so much about fucking?

He is to have lunch with his leather tanner today. But Jimmy wants simply to drive the three hours home. The lunch is mostly a social meeting. Maybe he can pull the meeting forward to a morning coffee.

And he does.

So shortly after one o'clock he turns off the Trans-Canada Highway onto Twelve Mile Bay Road. For nearly a week there has been no snow and the road is clear, the drifts and plow-spew mounded up on both sides of the narrow pavement, tunneling him home. After seven miles he takes the fork onto Harrison Trail along the north side of the bay, and six miles farther he turns off Harrison toward the water and into his ten acres, thick with snow-swathed white pines.

He emerges from the tree line, and off to the right is the south-facing, two-story, board-and-batten, Italianate house he and Linda restored from a century's worth of battering by Lake Huron winters. The place is a homely architectural idea, especially in its simplified farm version, a box with a low-pitched hip roof and a runt of a front porch. A Birkenstock of a house. But perhaps even because of that, it has always felt right to them, and they've made it their own.

He took their Volvo to Toronto and he parks in their adjacent garage. Linda's Forester is gone. He hoped to catch her at the house before going out to the barn. He didn't even have a thought of what they might do. Just sit together for a while. Talk about small things.

He walks the hundred yards west along their asphalt connecting drive to the leatherworks, their converted and expanded three-bay English barn where they still make their own high-end handbags and purses, satchels and briefcases, portfolios and backpacks, sketchbooks and journals and Apple appurtenances. The car, the two SUVs, and the pickup of the four women who work for him are aligned before the barn. There are no marked spaces on the asphalt skirt but most days the order of the vehicles is the same, the spacing even. His Gang of Four is meticulous in everything.

As he approaches, the low roiling of his mind subsides. There should be laptop satchels and messenger bags ready for edge finishing. When the pieces are intended for shelf stock it's understood Jimmy will always do the finishing himself. As he's become successful and volume has increased, he's let all the other work go to his gang. But this near-last thing, this labor-intensive thing, subtle to the eye but a hallmark of a quality bag, this he has kept for himself on as many of the bags as possible: the application of his special formula of beeswax and paraffin wax and edge paint layered and heated and sanded half a dozen times and sometimes more, sealing the leather tight from rain and snow and the moisture-laden air itself. He has occasionally wondered, but never tried to calculate, the number of hours of his life that he's been sealed inside the doing of this thing. Jimmy's Zen, the women of the leatherworks call it.

He steps through the middle bay door.

As soon as it's shut behind him, before he deals with people, he pauses and takes in the smell of the new leather, thick in the air from a recent shipment of top-grain sides. The leather that he buys, from the man he saw this morning, is special: trench-cured, packed tight in rock salt and buried in the earth for three months; and bark-tanned, bathed with oak and hemlock. Gamey still, this smell, fatty, faintly briny, but with an undercurrent of a smell like hazelnut. He closes his eyes to concentrate on that deep-current scent, a promise of the settled, sweet-fumy leather smell to come, something his customers will want to put their faces against, to breathe in.

He opens his eyes.

In this central barn space, the women, knowing his ritual, are looking up from their stations, waiting for him. Two of them have been cutting pattern pieces, skiving edges—the skiving the only thing done by machine on the best of their bags—and the always laser-focused Mackenzie twins have been hand-stitching.

"Good afternoon, Gang of Four," he says.

"Good afternoon, Jimmy," they say in unison.

All but Mavis immediately return to work.

She leaves her patterns, steps around the table, and approaches him.

She has worked for him for a dozen years, living alone for ten of them, during which decade she was a divorcée from a man and lean of build, but two years ago she married a woman and she filled out with happy fat, which she has since been pleased to keep. In those ten previous years she would not have been the one to rise to greet him, but she is the one before him now and smiling.

"How are you, Mavis?" Jimmy says.

"Fine," she says.

"Have you seen Linda this morning?"

There is a brief stopping in her. This registers on Jimmy, barely, but he assumes—though the assumption is as slight a thing as the stopping itself—that Mavis is simply trying, given the intense focus of her work of a few moments ago, to distinguish this morning from yesterday morning.

"No," she says.

A beat of silence passes between them.

For his part, this silence is not in expectation of more from Mavis but in idle curiosity over where Linda might be.

Mavis, for her part, is moved to elaborate. "I didn't expect her and didn't think to look for her."

"Ah," says Jimmy.

Another beat of silence and she says, "We've got some bags for you."

Jimmy thinks to call Linda on her cell. Or to go into the house and see if she left a note. But instead he says, "Good," and he moves off to the far end of the central bay to his worktable and his pots of wax and paint, his trimming tools and heating wand, his sander and his various favorite buffers—the tine of a deer antler; pieces of sheep wool and blue denim and brain-tanned camel hide.

He works a while, and in his concentration he does not even register the buzz of the intercom and the murmur of Mavis's voice, and then she is standing before him. This he is aware of, and he lifts his face.

"Linda is home," she says.

He's a little slow to react and Mavis is very quick in turning away, so his acknowledgment is nodded to her retreating back.

But he goes out at once.

As Jimmy nears the end of the connecting drive, he sees Linda emerge from the front door and come down the few steps of the porch, her focus on him. He approaches.

It was not so long ago that he began to think she was starting to seem her age. Not that he could quite say why. She is still white-oak-hard and sturdy and upright, a thing she was when he first met her on a beach in Alameda with flowers in her hair and flowers painted beneath her eyes and with her breasts bare in solidarity with some other young women on the shore. He would soon feel the toned hardness in her body when they were in each other's arms, hard enough that he was surprised at how gentle she was with her hands and in her voice and with her mouth. And in her eyes. They were as dark and fetching as a seal pup's, but her brows were thick and severe in their arch. In heart and mind, as well as body and face, she was so very much a child of that era. An era of militant gentleness, judgmental tolerance. Over the

years, paradox continued to shine through her, and it masked
the inevitable weathering and wrinkling and sagging of her
body. Masked them utterly. She still seemed to him young.
She remained interesting. And so the source of this recent
sense of her aging was surprising and hard to identify, and
it came clear to him now only in its abrupt absence: She is
striding to him and there is a thing about her that those of
the Summer of Love would have called an aura. An aura. Yes.
He is, in this moment, acutely aware of an aura about her, of
energy, of something like youth, and he realizes that for the
past weeks, months even, it was something else.

And as she draws near, she says, sharply, "How do you
think your mother got our home number?"

"Did she?" he says, thinking: *So that's the transformed aura.
Anger.* Thinking too that the discovered phone number might
be a simple thing, an oversight on his part committed sometime
along the way; perhaps it did not occur to him to register the
number as unlisted when they moved up here to Twelve Mile.

She sets her arms akimbo. "She left a message on the
machine."

"What did she say?"

"You need to hear for yourself."

They head off toward the house, side by side.

"You're home early," she says. "Did Guy cancel?"

"No. We had coffee instead."

"I was at Becca's. She's not good. She and Paul may be
through."

Her anger at his mother seems to have dissipated quickly. She's put the whole thing off on him now, and he's okay with that. He says, "Is somebody dead?"

"Dead?" She looks at him.

He realizes she's still thinking about their friends. He's asking, of course, about his mother's message.

They go up the porch steps.

He concedes to her agenda. "This is nothing new, is it?" he says.

They've reached the door, and they pause. She gives him another look. He's confused her again.

He clarifies: "Becca and Paul."

She shrugs. "Not yet," she says.

Now it's he who's lost the thread.

She reads it in his face. "Dead?" she says. "No one's dead yet."

He leads her inside and into the front parlor, which they've filled with Mennonite furniture. He approaches the sideboard.

He stands hesitating over the answering machine.

He could simply erase the message. Right now. Erase it and change the number. His mother knows his wishes in this matter. It has always been best for all of them.

But he touches the play button.

Her voice wheedles into the room. *Darling Jimmy. It's your mother. I'm sorry. I can't tell you how much I regret how things went between us. Between your father and you. I've always loved you, my son. He has too. That's important to say. He has too. I don't mean to push my way now into your life when I know you're trying so hard . . . Not trying. Succeeding, I'm sure, in your new homeland. I don't mean to . . . I'm sorry. But your father is in a bad way, physically. The doctor is very very concerned about him. He may not live long. Whatever that might mean to you. At least just for you to know.*

This all came out in a blathering rush, and then she fell silent, though she did not hang up. Perhaps she heard herself. Perhaps she knew that all she could do next was ask directly for something he'd long ago made clear he had no intention of giving. Not that his father wished to hear from him, even if he was dying. His mother was no doubt doing this on her own. He could hear her breathing heavily. *The machine will cut her off soon*, he thinks. He waits.

But before this can happen, she says, *Your brother loves you too. We all do.*

She pauses again. Then: *Does your phone give you my number? Maybe not.*

And she speaks her phone number into the message. Jimmy has no intention of remembering it.

In case you want it, she says.

And the answering machine clicks into silence.

He hesitates.

Humming in him is an apparatus of thought he assembled years ago. For him at least, blood ties are overrated. It's only people who have a deeply intractable sense of their own identity—an identity that has been created through parents or siblings or grandparents, through those of their own blood—it's only people like that who can't imagine an actual, irrevocable break from family. But you drift apart from acquaintances. You even drift apart from previously close friends. Why? Because your interests and tastes, ideas and values, personalities and character—the things that *truly* make up who you are—shift and change and disconnect. Indeed, it's harder for friends to part: you came together at all only because those things were once compatible. With your kin, that compatibility may never even have existed. The same is true of a country. You didn't choose your parents. You didn't choose your land of birth. If you and they have nothing in common, if they have nothing to do with who you are now, if you are always, irrevocably at odds with each other, is it betrayal simply to leave family and country behind?

No.

Fuck no.

Jimmy extends his finger, touches the erase button. With only a quick sniff of hesitation, he pushes it.

~

Bob is on his back. And he starts to slide, feeling the movement first in the front of his head and then running down his body like nausea. He opens his eyes. He was upright a moment ago. Under a sky. After a talk with Pastor Somebody. After a sleep. But a cold sleep. Very cold. He's been outside somewhere. Now, though, there's a low, dark ceiling above. It's not just him moving. Everything is moving. A face looms suddenly over him.

A jowly, red-cheeked face, a bulbous nose. They are moving together, Bob and this man. From the front of Bob's head: a knot of pain pressing there, pressing outward.

He tries to lift himself up at the chest.

"Hold on, sport," the face says.

Bob lets go. Falls back. He begins to spin slowly. He closes his eyes against this.

That nose and those cheeks. A rummy. *This is the guy who did it*, Bob says in his head. *The son of a bitch who brained me.* He tries to rise up again, and even though he knows he's not prepared, he thinks, slowly, carefully, meaning each word: *I will kill you.*

A pressure on the center of his chest. He falls back.

"Hold on," the voice says. "I'm here to help you."

Help?

"You're on the way to the hospital."

The pressing in his forehead. He's stretched tight there. Thoughts congregating, trying to break through skull bone, trying to leap forth.

Bob opens his eyes, thinking he might catch sight of them.

That's crazy, he realizes.

His mind is clear now. He believes the face.

Okay. Okay okay okay. You're not the guy.

For a moment Bob loses track of exactly what man he is trying to find or why he should care so hotly.

"Can you hear me?" the face asks.

"Why shouldn't I?" Bob says.

"Good." The face narrows its already narrow eyes. "I need to ask you some questions. You understand?"

"What's to understand?" Bob says. The man is an idiot.

"We have to see if your head's okay."

"My head."

Bob thinks he has filled those two words with sarcasm.

To the emergency tech he sounds dazed. "What's your name?" the EMT asks.

Bob's first response is to himself: *My name. All of this about my name suddenly. Not just with this rummy. Too much about my name.* He's not sure how he got that impression. So the first thing he says aloud is, "Why is it too much?"

The face cocks sideways.

Bob is simply trying to figure this out. Not that he expects the face to have an answer to the question.

And then Bob remembers. The other Bob.

"Do you understand what I'm asking?" the face says.

"What are you asking?"

"What's your name?"

"Hello, I'm Bob," Bob says. "Bob isn't so popular anymore."

"Bob," the face says.

"Bob," Bob says.

"Bob what?" the face says.

"Bob what," Bob says. "Bob fucking what." A sharp thwack of pain in his head. Not in the forehead. At the back of his head. From his father's hand. *Tell the man your name,* his father says. *If you're going to sneak around in the night, little motherfucker, you're going to get captured and then it's name, rank, and serial number.* Bob has followed Calvin from their single-wide. It's the middle of the night, but in a fourteen-by-sixty every sound kicks around in your head even if your bedroom is on the opposite end from theirs. All the words, jumbled and blurred but clear enough tonight about his mother's fear of his father meeting up with somebody, a buddy, somebody up to no good. Now Bob's standing in front of a man with a hippie-wild beard, an army field jacket dappled in piss-colored street-light, a First Cav patch—horse's head and diagonal slash—at the shoulder. *Name.* And another slap at the base of his skull. *Bob,* Bob says. One more slap from his father: *Do it right.* Bob says, *Robert Calvin Weber.* A beat of silence and his father barks, *Rank.* Bob looks at him. *Damn straight,* his father says. *You don't have one. Lower than a buck private.* And then his father does a thing that he sometimes can do. He abruptly puts his arm around Bob, crushes him close. And he says to the man in the field jacket, *But he's a crack shot, this one. He's a goddamn killer in the making, my boy.*

"Do you remember your last name?"

The face.

"Weber," Bob says.

"All right, Bob Weber. Where are you?"

The fuck. "Hell," Bob says.

And the man gives Bob *that look.* Every man jack of the Hardluckers knows that look. The look when the upstanding asshole—the Upstander—in front of you can't find or never had or gives up on or runs out of patience for a guy who looks and smells and just plain exists like you. He gives you that tightening and tiny lifting of the upper lip under just one faintly flaring nostril, that back crawl of a gaze, that little lift of the chin, all of this so slight you could easily feel it wasn't him at all, it was you, it was you shrinking, a shrinking that's been going on in smooth, small increments for a long while and you only just now can see it, like staring so hard at a clock's minute hand that eventually you can watch it move. *That look* says what you're in fact witnessing is *you* growing *smaller*, and this son of a bitch giving it to you has seen it all along.

Bob wishes he had the will to lift a hand and make a fist and punch this face. Not the will. He probably has that. The strength.

The look vanishes now. This man and Bob both know it was there and will always be lurking, but it vanishes, so the two of them can go on.

The face says, "If you're messing with me, I need you to stop so we can know how to help you. Tell me where you are."

Bob is weary. His head hurts. "Seems like an ambulance," he says.

"Okay. Where did we find you?"

Where.

The pastor crouched before him, a dense mane of shovel-blade gray hair crowning his head. Bob was sitting upright, probably this man's doing. He was beneath a tree. The church community building squatted across the yard. *I'm Pastor Dwayne Kilmer,* the man said, putting a blanket around Bob's shoulders. *Call me Pastor Dwayne.* Bob's ears rang loudly and a small angry animal was trying to claw its way out of his forehead, but things were coming back to him already. *Who did this?* Bob said, raising his hand to his head. *I don't know,* Pastor Dwayne said and started to add, *In the . . .* But Bob interrupted, waving his hand: I was in *there.* He could not remember the name for it, though the door was in plain sight. *It was empty,* Pastor Dwayne said without even turning to look in the direction of Bob's gesture. He knew more than he was saying. *It's a sin to lie,* Bob said. Pastor Dwayne rocked backward in his crouch. *Now Brother Bob,* he began. *Do you know me?* Bob said, sharply. *How do you know my name?* Pastor Dwayne said, *You told me a few moments ago.* This stopped Bob. He couldn't remember. Then he thought of a question he needed to ask. *Who did this to me?* The pastor patted him on the shoulder. *I don't know who did it, Brother Bob. That's the truth.*

"Can you say where it was that we picked you up?"

Bob blinks hard at this question. For a moment he hears it coming from Pastor Dwayne. But it's the face.

The face is waiting.

Bob figures the face probably has some power over him for now. For ill or for good. Bob's hungry. His bones ache from the chill. He probably needs this guy to help. Bob should answer.

"Bloodied by the Lamb Hospital," he says.

Instantly he knows he somehow bungled it. Wrong sort of place. "Gospital," he says.

Not right. "*Gospel,*" Bob says. "The Bloody Lamb Full of Gospel."

Clarity. Clarity.

The face has *that look* again.

"That's close enough, isn't it?" Bob says. "I'm not crazy and I'm not stupid."

The face fixes itself and says, "Okay. Just rest." It drifts away from Bob's view.

Bob closes his eyes. He feels the motion all around him. He is being carried along fast now. No bumps. A straight line to somewhere. And he feels his father's arm go around his shoulders, like it can sometimes do. As always, that gesture only makes Bob ache. Ache and ache. And he thinks of standing in the night in front of their single-wide, lit by street-light, standing side by side with his father, the man's arm around him, and there's a tree growing nearby, a jungle tree that sprung up there in the trailer park and nobody gets wise to it till it's too late, and in that tree is a Viet Cong, a sniper, a helluva shot of a sniper, and the VC squeezes his trigger and sends out a single round that crashes into one side of Bob's head and out the other and then into his father's head, and he and his old man die together, right there and then, standing there just like that next to each other.

~

And as that phantom sniper's bullet spins through Bob's brain, Robert passes the concertina fence at the federal prison on Capital Circle, half a mile north of the parkway, the fence a thing his mind has always known to ignore, in its evocation of a military perimeter. But it's not ignorable with the issues of

71

this past night and this morning. His eyes know to hold on the road ahead, know to prevent even a glance to the side, but the periphery is always there for the seeing, and he is quite aware now of the four rows of razor wire spiraling along beside him, and with them Vietnam spins near, and a deep-driven voice inside Robert whispers: *You are a killer.*

He does not acknowledge it. Does not let this event play itself over, as it has done a thousand times in these five decades, in dreams, in near-sleep, in full waking obsession. It is this he fights off as he drives to his hospitalized father: Robert is huddled in the deep dark of the banyan tree. Outside are the sounds of pitched battles, none of them immediately nearby, the heaviest across the river. He wraps his left arm around his drawn-up legs, hugs them closer, and they press the pistol in his right hand more tightly against him, the fit of the weapon in his palm and the weight of it upon his chest making him feel oddly calm. Though his mind knows how foolish this is. The enemy is rushing through the city, filling it as if the Perfume River has risen and breached its banks. The tree and the pistol will soon fail him. If he is to live, he needs to think this out. Surely the North's night offensive is focused on the key military positions in the city: the airport; the South's division headquarters in the old Citadel across the river; and the place where Robert belongs, the MACV compound. If those places fall, particularly MACV, Robert is dead anyway. If they survive the night, Robert is dead if he cannot make his way back. Finding his way back will be vastly more difficult in daylight. He cannot stay where he is.

He must use the cover of night to at least find another hiding place, nearer MACV.

All of this is preamble. Usually when the event coils through Robert's head like concertina razor wire, the decision to emerge has already been made. The next few essential moments travel on their own. He closes his eyes. He turns his head, cocks it, trying to focus his hearing in the direction of MACV: AK-47s, M16s, grenades launched and exploding. Robert pushes those sounds away into the background. He listens nearby. Nothing. The rush of dark-clad bodies just beyond the tree seems to have ended. He takes a deep breath. He lets go of his legs, stretches them out, takes another breath. He rises. He clicks the pistol's safety lever forward. He holds the weapon before him, ready to fire. He steps from the tree. Though his eyes are dilated to the dark, nothing is clear on this overcast night, not pocket-park sward or trees or alleyway beyond or huddled city shapes all around, everything is smeared together in the tarry night. He must find his way through. He pauses. And from somewhere behind him and to his right a white flare rises, rushing to its apogee, far enough away that its light simply dapples through the trees and so Robert can see but he cannot see, and there is movement to his left and he looks and a shape is there, half a dozen paces away and it is a man clad in shadow and instantly Robert's hand is moving and he is squeezing at the trigger and the pistol pops and jumps a little in his hand and it levels and pops again and again and the shape flies back into the dark and Robert hears the shape—the man—hears the man thump onto the ground, and Robert turns and runs.

And why should this man whose face he never saw, who surely was a Viet Cong, who surely, moments later, would have done the same to him if Robert had not shot first, why should this man thrash still inside Robert? *You are a killer*, Robert whispers again to himself from somewhere deep in the dark, somewhere invisible in the trees. But so many men have had to reconcile so much more, so many killings, so much blood that they have spilled in some far place where there was no alternative except to let their own blood be spilled, brought into this situation by their country, in the name of and for the protection of all that they and their families, now and for generations before, have held dear. And later on this day in Hue and on the next day and on the next, first in the streets and then safe among his own in the MACV compound, Robert will shoot and shoot and it is not entirely clear if he has killed again but he probably has. But this one, this one dark figure will not simply die, will not allow himself to be buried in the psyche the way most of all the millions who have died in wars have been buried inside most of all the millions of their killers. Why? Because Robert did not go to Vietnam to do this. Because he had a graduate school deferment and he let it go and so the army gave him a choice: to enter into officers' training and risk a combat assignment or enter as an enlisted man and select his own army occupation. So he chose not to kill. He went to Vietnam to slide away to the side, to land and work and fly home as one of the eight out of ten who goes to war and never kills, who never experiences any actual battle, who never fires a weapon. Who goes to war to cook or repair or fuel or type or drive or warehouse or launder or telegraph; or goes to study and analyze, like doing the research he loves; who goes to war and sleeps and eats and drinks and writes letters and listens to music and falls safely in love in another country with an exotic girl and writes a resume and plans a future life and goes home; who goes to war to please your dad, to receive your dad's approval, to make your dad proud, to win your dad's love.

You didn't have to kill to do that.

Robert has never told his father about the banyan tree. About the man he shot in the dark.

You are a killer.

Still. Still. So many men had it figured out that way, thinking they would be one of the eight in ten who never engaged in actual combat, but ended up having the fight come to them, having an army—not just men, not just a solitary man but an army—having an enemy army come at them and their pals, and then everyone did this thing together, so many men ended up killing, ended up killing other men, ended up turning into killers, many times over. But somehow so many of those men—surely so many; just look at all the veterans who apparently are leading routine lives, more or less happy lives, lives full of all those values we putatively fought for—so many were able to figure out how their killings were outliers, were acts apart from who they really are, so many somehow figured out how to live the rest of their lives as men who are not, in fact, killers, are anything but killers.

But when Robert emerged from his tree, this was not an enemy army before him. This was one man. A solitary man. A few paces away in the dark. A man who simply was there.

A man who simply moved. A man who could have been any-one. Maybe a frightened boy. The Viet Cong recruited boys. Maybe he was solitary because he was running away, ready in that moment to make some sort of separate peace, one man to another. Worse: maybe not a Viet Cong at all. Maybe no enemy at all. Maybe a man who minutes ago had been hiding in his home in the alleyway. Or hiding in another tree.

Robert had not seen a weapon.

Though that proved nothing. It was too dark. And the North's soldiers who had only recently passed through would certainly have killed Robert. What the hell was that man doing there? The great likelihood was that he was a soldier like all the rest, and for Robert to have hesitated would have been for Robert to die. Nearly a decade ago, Robert's own Florida passed the first stand-your-ground law: If you find yourself in a situation where you reasonably fear that someone is about to kill you or seriously injure you—no matter where you are—you have no obligation to retreat. You can kill. You can kill and you are innocent. You are innocent.

Robert and Darla have spoken several times about how they despise this law.

Robert has not spoken with Darla about how he has qui-etly invoked this law over and over to try to make that voice inside him fall silent.

He has never told Darla about the killing.

Five miles of urban-sprawl businesses have passed like white noise and now Robert crosses over the interstate. The faint quaver of the overpass, the rush of traffic beneath him, snap him back to the car, to his hands white-knuckled on the steering wheel.

"It was a fucking war," he says aloud. And to himself: *What's wrong with you? What kind of man are you? It was the Tet Offensive. I killed a Viet Cong who would have killed me.*

He loosens his grip.

He takes a deep breath.

He considers the gravity of his father's situation. Eighty-nine years old. A broken hip. A bad heart. A smoker's lungs. And this thought surges in Robert: *At least I didn't let him down. I went. Especially with Jimmy doing what he did. If Dad dies now, at least there is that.*

Robert doesn't quite go so far as to say to himself, *He was proud of me.* Though he lets himself assume it. William Quinlan never went so far as to say that. Not in those words. But the things he might have said, the things Robert wanted him to say, by the very nature of those things—intense, tender, vulnerable feelings unbecoming to a man of the era and of the sort that his father was—those very things kept him quiet.

And as the incident in the dark in Hue recedes in Robert, he notes that neither has his father ever spoken of the killing he himself did. He did kill. Unquestionably so. He was an infantryman. Indeed, William has rarely spoken of the war at all to his family, other than to say he was there, other than to speak generally of its grandness and its righteousness.

Robert stops at a red light.

Rarely to his family. But not never. His father puts an arm around him. And an arm around Jimmy. Robert is nine years old, his brother seven. Pops is sitting in a chair on the porch of the house on Clay Square and the two brothers are standing. He pulls them to him, then lets them go, but it is clear they are to stay where he's put them, at whisper distance. He says to them, low, *Boys, it's time.* He smells of bourbon. It's late on a spring afternoon. The shadow of their house has crossed the street and entered the park. *You know I was in the war. You should know what I went through for you. Can you imagine how scary it was? I want you to think of this, boys. I was with the Third Army under a great American general named Patton, and we were sweeping toward Berlin. We were in the outskirts of a city called Bingen. The Nazi troops were falling back. The enemy, you understand. So there was a house we thought they'd been using as a headquarters. A small house but with an upper floor. I went up. No one was there. Nothing of interest, and so I was ready to come back down the stairs.*

Their father stops now. Takes a deep breath. Puts his arms around them again, draws them closer, and he says, *Now pay careful attention.*

He lets them go, but delicately, so that they remain even nearer to him.

So I am still in the upper room and I head for the stairway and I start down. Not particularly hurrying. Down a few steps, a few steps more. Then I'm on the bottom floor. And I've been thinking maybe I should look around down here as well. But I don't. For some reason I think to hell with it and I go to the front door and I step out.

He stops one more time and says, *Now, boys, I want you to start counting seconds. You know: One Mississippi. Two Mississippi. Like that. You know?*

They nod.

And while you count I want you to imagine me moving across a little porch of this house and down into the yard and then taking a few more steps. But not many, not big. I'm going slow, 'cause everything was okay inside. Are you ready?

They are.

And they begin to count.

After *Three Mississippi* he says, *I'm stepping off the porch.*

Four Mississippi.

I'm barely in the yard, he says.

Five Mississippi.

I took a step.

Six Mississippi. Seven Mississippi.

Two more steps.

Eight Mississippi. Nine Mississippi.

BOOM! Pops barks the word and claps his hands together and the two brothers jump and cry out.

Pops waits a moment. Lets them calm down. Then he says, *An artillery round hit the house and the whole place and everything in it was blown to smithereens. I was that close to being dead.*

He pauses so he's sure they get it. They get it. They're still quaking.

As it was, the blast threw me about twenty feet and I ended up bruised and scuffed and my head was spinning for an hour. I was alive. Barely. It was that close, boys. You know what else that means. You two were that close to never being born. Never even existing. Think of that.

Jimmy is weeping. Robert is still shaky in the legs but he's making sure he stands up straight before his father. Jimmy

begins to tremble and the weeping turns to sobs. Pops is looking off down the street, toward the river. Robert puts his arm
around his brother.

A horn honks.

And again.

On Thomasville Road, north of I-10, at the traffic signal
before Walmart, the light has turned green.

Robert shakes off the past.

He thinks: *All of that is done with. He will die now.*

~

On the cusp between the tumbledown houses of Thomasville's
poor and the bespoke dwellings of Thomasville's moneyed,
along an avenue of attendant health care enterprises—for pain,
for feet, for teeth and hearts and vascular systems, for flu shots
and for lab work—Archbold looms large in a six-storied complex of cream stucco walls and red-tiled roofs. Robert parks
in the landscaped lot before the hospital's main entrance. As
he steps from the car, his cellphone rings. He reads the screen.
Home. Darla is back from running. He closes the car door, leans
against it, and answers.

"You got my note," he says.

"I'm so sorry," Darla says. "How is he?"

"I just arrived. I'm still in the parking lot."

Darla is standing, sweating, in the foyer, just returned. It
occurred to her to shower first. But she carries a memory, not

so much in her mind as in her body. She stood in the doorway of the bedroom in their first house in Tallahassee, a rental near Lake Ella, and there was only darkness before her. She'd just spoken to her brother Frank on the phone downstairs. *Dead.* His voice. *Both of them.* And she'd said *Oh.* She stood in the doorway and she realized that this single word might not have been the right one. Perhaps she'd said more. But she could not remember any further words with her brother, nor any details of her passage from the phone downstairs to this doorway. She thought: *We need an extension up here.* She stood there waiting for something, but she could not imagine what. And then he emerged from the darkness. Robert. She blinked hard at him. She thought: *I haven't been seeing him very clearly lately.* And Robert knew to say nothing, he knew instead to step very close. He smelled of Ivory soap and flannel and coffee on his breath. *He should brush better.* And his arms came around her, one at her waist, his hand coming to rest in the small of her back; the other under her arm and angling across her shoulder blades, that hand landing on her shoulder, cupping her there, and his hand on her back rose and moved farther around her and he drew her against him, and as soon as he did, she could remember what had happened, and she fell into him, fell a long way into him. Their first death. The first close death that comes to a man and a woman who are sharing a life. The first death brings all the future deaths with it. Brings all the deaths in all the world. And he held her close.

She does not remember this consciously now, as an event. Her body remembers, in the muscles, on the skin, simply as something it owes. Darla knows what the broken hip in Thomasville likely will mean for Robert, who has gone deep into his life without a close death of his own, and so she has not showered before making this call. She says, "Shall I come?"

"Thank you," he says. "But no. Not yet. He's probably . . . I don't know. It's going to be all about Mom. It'll be about her. You don't need to come. Please just do what you need to do today."

She says, "Perhaps I need to be *there*. Not for her. For you."

"Weren't you doing something? A field trip?"

"Did I say?"

"Last week. Something."

She thinks. Then, "Ah. Monticello."

"You want to meditate there, yes?"

"Yes."

"Go. Be a Southern belle."

"Not quite."

"Whatever you need."

She doesn't answer for a moment. From the prompting of her body, she tries to think if she should ignore what he's saying. If she should go to him anyway. But her body also feels a sharp-scrabbling chill. He keeps the thermostat too low overnight. Always. She should turn it up before she runs, but she never seems to remember. She doesn't want to go to Thomasville. "All right," she says.

"I'll see you later," he says.

"Are you sure about this?"

"I'm sure."

They fall silent. But they do not immediately hang up. They aren't good at ending phone calls. They both hate phones, in fact. They can't read each other's body or face, which is crucial to them, to inflect their silences.

"Really?" she says.

Just enough silence has ticked by between them that it takes a moment for Robert to place the *really* into its proper context.

While he tries to, she interprets the few beats of his silence to mean he's not really sure.

"I'll come," she says.

"No," he says, figuring it out. "I'm really sure. Thank you."

And he hangs up.

I do that too, she says to herself about the abruptness of his ringing off. She won't worry anymore about him for now.

She touches the off button on the phone and places it in its cradle.

~

Robert finds his mother sitting on an upholstered couch beneath the skylight halfway down the entrance corridor. Peggy Quinlan rises at his approach and comes to him and they hug in the way they've hugged for decades, leaning to each other at the waist, cheek to cheek, patting each other behind the shoulders, as if always consoling each other. The patting is firmer this morning.

"Thank goodness you're here," she says. "They're preparing him for surgery. The doctor is coming down to talk to us."

They let go of each other. She takes his hand and leads him to the couch. "I need to sit," she says.

They do.

Robert turns mostly sideways to face her.

"Are you okay?" Robert says.

"A little shaky. I didn't eat."

"Ma," he says. "You have to eat."

"After the doctor."

"How's Pops doing?"

She smiles faintly at Robert.

He sees it. "What?"

"'Pops,'" she says. "It's just good to hear you call him that again."

He was unaware. He's not sure it's good. "How's he doing?"

"He's pissed," she says. Then she quickly adds, "I put it that way because it's how he says it."

Robert wags his head at her. "You can say 'pissed' for yourself." And he regrets niggling. Why make a point of this now? But he knows the answer. The artifice of her. This is not the time for her to be working on her image.

As she often does, Peggy quickly co-opts Robert's irritation with her by claiming it for her own, criticizing herself. "Of course," she says. "What a silly time to hear the whisper of the priest. Piss piss piss. There. I'm pissed too."

Though part of him recognizes her self-deprecation, antically adorned, as just another strategy of image-making, Robert gives her credit for it. "Good girl," he says.

"But he's more than pissed," she says. "He's scared, darling."

"He's a tough guy."

"You don't see him like I do. He's not so tough."

This is hardly the first time she's claimed this. Robert has always doubted that it's so. He has understood her assertions about the inner life of William Quinlan simply as her taking the opportunity to project *herself* onto the blank screen of her husband.

"He's faced death before," Robert says.

"It's not about the dying," she says. "It's about leaving other things unresolved."

"Jimmy."

"That," she says. "And more."

Robert nods at this. But he does not even try to think what those other things would be. They could be legion.

Peggy waits.

Robert stays silent.

She says, "I called Jimmy."

"What?"

"I called him."

"How?"

"Your grandson."

She waits again, and Robert can only do likewise in response. He refuses to drag the story out of her. She is prone to this sort of drama.

She says, "I asked Jake if there was a website. He found one. It's like the white pages for Canada."

"Didn't you already try to find his phone number?"

"Years ago. But this time, there he was. Not in Toronto anymore. A town called MacTier. It was his voice. I recognized his voice on the answering machine."

"So you didn't talk to him directly?"

"No."

"When did you call him?"

"This morning, though I've had the number for a little while. I knew how losing Jimmy continued to hurt your father. Even if he wasn't talking about it."

"I'm not so sure."

"I don't expect him to call me back. At the end I was too much on your father's side. How could I not be? But it wasn't so bad between the two of you, was it?"

"Bad enough."

"Still." Peggy picks up her purse from beside her and opens it and draws out an index card. She offers it to Robert.

He lets it hang there between them.

"Please," she says. "His number. He may listen to you."

"I'm not sure it's a good thing, even if Dad wants it."

"For me then." The throb in her voice sounds genuine. Still Robert doesn't take the card.

A figure appears in Robert's periphery.

"Mrs. Quinlan." A baritone, but not as warm as you'd expect from the pitch. A scalpel-edged voice. Robert turns to it. A man in blue scrubs, young-seeming somehow but with his managed scruff turning gray and with wrinkling at brow and eyes.

Robert and Peggy rise.

She uses the moment to thrust the index card into Robert's hand.

He pockets it.

"Dr. Tyler," Peggy says, "this is my son, Robert."

He shakes the man's hand. It feels faintly oily.

"Please sit," the doctor says.

They do, and Tyler perches on the front edge of a chair set at a right angle to Peggy's end of the couch.

Robert sees now that Tyler holds a plastic ziplock bag of almonds in the palm of his left hand. The man dips in and takes a few and chews them as he speaks. He lifts the bag a little, to draw attention to it. "Forgive me," he says. "These are part of my prep. Good protein and good magnesium. To be at my best for Mr. Quinlan."

Peggy gives him a nod of permission, not that he was asking. "Go right ahead."

"I have to tell you honestly," he says, drawing the sentence out slightly so he can look both Robert and his mother in the eyes as he speaks it. He pauses briefly, chewing his almonds, swallowing his almonds, though presumably the intent of the pause is to let these two family members have a moment to prepare themselves for the implied bad news.

It has another effect on Robert, a little to his surprise: He wants to slap the almonds from the man's hand—*eat them in the goddamn elevator on your way to the operating room if you must*—and to grab him by the front of his scrubs and shout, *Out with it.*

Tyler says, "The statistics are not good. Of those who break a hip after the age of eighty, one in two will not live more than six months. And Mr. Quinlan has two complicating factors beyond the hip. His heart issues, of course. And unfortunately, the fall has broken his right wrist. This will make rehab very difficult. We can put the bones back together. But having a man his age on his back for an extended time can lead to fluid buildup, which can lead to complications, most commonly pneumonia or congestive heart failure. We will be vigilant. But you need to know the special risks."

He is done. He takes more almonds. Robert and Peggy understand that he's waiting for questions. Does he want them to ask the obvious one? *So will he die now?*

The doctor will evade.

But he has just said it.

Even Peggy knows this. Her question is simply, "When will we be able to see him?"

"It depends on how things progress this morning," he says. "But understand he'll be on morphine at least through tonight. He won't be fully aware. You can go home and rest. Call us mid-afternoon."

As if simultaneously hearing the same cue, they all rise.

They shake hands, and Doctor Tyler is gone.

Robert and Peggy do not move, do not speak. They struggle to absorb the official version of a prognosis they both already knew well enough, from common knowledge. Now it's personal, however.

Finally Peggy says, "I came in a cab. Can you take me home?"

"Of course."

Her eyes are full of tears and she steps to Robert and now the two of them hug with no bend at the waist, with quiet hands upon each other's back, with no artifice or mulled memories or sense of family failures. They hold each other quietly, mother and son, and though Robert is a man capable of them, he finds he has no tears to shed.

~

At their kitchen table, Jimmy sits facing the window, the afternoon shadows bluing the snow. Behind him Linda is making chamomile tea. He stares at the darkening bluff of white pine. He's also standing in the center of his parents' kitchen in New Orleans. Robert is nearby, in his uniform, ready to go fight in an unholy war to please the man Jimmy's been furiously arguing with about the issues of the United States' bloody interference in Vietnam. An argument that has kept Robert in the room, their mother having fled, after taking care to turn off all the pots on the stove. Robert did not flee but he hasn't said a word. He's just standing there. If he's ready to go kill for their father's disastrously distorted patriotism, he should at least be ready to argue the justifications. He may have found some semblance of physical courage to decide to go—likely to vanish when the reality of the carnage is upon him—but he is an intellectual coward.

But no. That's present-day thinking. At the time, Jimmy has some crazy little hope. He and his brother talked about these very issues a couple of hours ago. Just the two of them. In the midst now of the old man's fury, Jimmy has a fragmentary hope about Robert's silence, that their own discussion—civilized compared with this present one—had opened his brother's mind.

Jimmy is weary from the fight. He is all shouted out. His father seems weary too. They have both suddenly fallen silent, standing nose to nose, breath to breath, but Jimmy finds one more point to make. Voice pitched low, the sudden quiet after all the noise making it seem even more emphatic, he says: "The real heroes in all this are the men and women who've said *No* to their country. Instead of becoming part of an illegal and murderous war, they've gone to jail or gone into exile. Those are the real heroes."

The blow comes quick. Jimmy doesn't even feel it the first time, not the slap itself, only a force, a pressure flipping his head to the side.

Though he knows what's happened.

He brings his face back just as quick.

The eyes before him, his father's eyes, are seething.

The next blow he feels, a flare of pain shooting up through his temples and down to the roots of his teeth, and his face turns and his brother appears and his brother's eyes are upon him and upon this pain and upon their father and Jimmy's eyes lock on Robert's, and there is only quiet around them and there is only this moment of their eyes, holding, and Jimmy realizes that in spite of the clash of their philosophies and their politics, in spite of a childhood strewn with older-brother petty cruelties—he was himself guilty, after all, of younger-brother cruelty—in spite of one of them being not just the older but the favored son and one of them being the lesser son, the redundant son, in spite of all that, Jimmy finds he now expects something of his brother, expects the bond of shared blood and shared tribulation of family and zeitgeist to pull taut and to hold.

But these eyes. His brother's eyes witnessing this defining moment with their shared father. These eyes are empty. They are dead. Behind them is nothing.

The clink now of cup and saucer before Jimmy. The smell of herb and steam and Linda. He is happy for the interruption. But he stares at the cup, decorated with roses, and he has let go of his brother's eyes and he is facing his father once more and feeling empty himself now, wondering if there will be another blow from this man, but wondering this from a great distance, and his father's mouth is moving, shaping words Jimmy does not hear.

Except for the final few: *Then you are no son of mine.*

Clarity.

The end.

"You okay?" Linda's voice.

"I'm okay," Jimmy says to Linda.

She sits at the table with her own cup of tea. Usually she sits opposite him. They have always looked unflinchingly into each other's eyes to speak of important things. Now she sits to his right. *Nearer to me*, Jimmy thinks.

He appreciates this. He puts his hand on hers. She puts her free hand on top of his. But only for the briefest of moments. She rushes the gesture. She pats him there and takes both hands away, arranges her cup of tea into some imperceptibly precise position before her. She lifts the cup and sips.

Jimmy does not notice any of that. He's standing at a pay phone outside a diner on Elmwood Avenue in Buffalo, New York. He and Linda have been handed off by the New Orleans Draft Resisters to the Buffalo Resistance and they are about to enter Canada forever. It is July of 1968. Jimmy graduated from Loyola in June. It has been five months since the North's Tet Offensive showed Walter Cronkite and therefore American television and therefore, at last, any right-thinking Americans what was really happening in Vietnam. Jimmy's student deferment is no longer renewable. His induction is imminent. He and Linda are ready to leave. They will go into Canada as visitors and stay as landed immigrants and eventually become Canadians and this is their last hour in the United States.

His parents will find out eventually, he supposes. He doesn't give a damn how his father hears. But he gives a partial damn about his mother, enabler of William Quinlan though she be.

So Jimmy is dropping quarters into a phone and calling the house on Third Street.

His mother answers. He says what he must, and things clearly are hurtling toward a final good-bye. Before he realizes his mother has fallen silent not from lovingly conflicted emotion but for this other purpose, she has put his father on the phone and the man says, "Your mother is crying."

"I'm sorry for that," Jimmy says.

"What the hell are you doing?" his father says.

Jimmy finds that the prospect of even speaking the words to this man makes his mouth clench. That he and his father have not spoken of Vietnam since Labor Day—have hardly spoken at all—makes him confident this is true: "You know what I'm doing."

That William Quinlan is making no reply confirms it.

The silence ticks on, filled with long-distance static and now a distant car horn and now Linda's hand falling upon Jimmy's shoulder, squeezing gently there, and remaining, remaining as he waits for a last few words that surely will come.

And then they do, though more simply than Jimmy expected, and therefore more final.

His father says, "Good-bye then."

And through the thousand miles of telephone wires comes the click that was the last sound from his father through the forty-six years since.

Jimmy sees the pines, as if he has just opened his eyes from sleep.

He looks at Linda.

She is staring into her cup of tea.

Jimmy looks at his own cup.

So.

He picks up the cup. Sips.

Puts the cup down. The faint tap and scrape of china upon china.

"I wish I could help you," Linda says.

He looks at her.

Her eyes hold on him now.

"Why do you think you need to help me?" he says.

Something seems to release in her. A tension he did not notice. She nods.

"Why do you think you can't?" he says.

She sniffs. Looks at her teacup. Drinks from it.

"You and your father," she says without looking at him. She says no more. That is answer enough for both questions.

He studies the tree line.

He senses how comfortable he and Linda are together. At last. For how many years of their marriage would this event have prompted a spirited conversation, a recitation of shared beliefs, a problem-solving debate about families and politics and ethics. A loving, respectful debate, but a debate.

Now they are quiet.

From that sense of comfort he feels he needs to reassure her. "I'm fine," he says.

"Truly?"

"Truly."

"Of course," she says, as if reassuring herself this could be true. "After all this time."

"Yes," he says.

"Good," she says.

And they are quiet for a few moments more.

Then Linda says, "Then can I ask a favor?"

They are looking at each other again.

"Of course," Jimmy says.

"Don't let your father's situation get you started," she says.

One debate topic has not dissipated with their long-accumulated closeness, one that began only a couple of years ago. He has already ceased to speak of the subject. He's told her he has. She doesn't need to lean on it at this moment.

Thinking these things, he remains silent for a few beats.

She clarifies, unnecessarily. "Your recent interest in a supposed afterlife."

Jimmy thinks: *Ah, my darling, you are still young, as you have once again begun to seem. You still have faith in nothingness.* And he hears himself beginning to debate her in his mind, where he concedes: *I envy you your faith. It is worse to wonder.*

Linda says, "I'm sorry. That sounded harsh. Particularly under the circumstances."

"No," he says. "It's all right."

She nods. And she seems to be waiting. For what? He's absolved her for harshness. He has already pledged to keep his thoughts on this subject to himself. He says no more.

She says no more.

They drink their tea and then, side by side, carry their cups and saucers to the sink.

~

Darla parks in front of the nineteenth-century brick opera house just off Monticello's traffic circle. In the center sits the Jefferson County Courthouse, in the Classic Revival style of the town's namesake. She crosses the street and turns to her left to circle the building, her eyes on the monument for the Confederate dead at the north side. From this approach, only its eight-foot base is visible beyond the waxy, evergreen crown of a century-old magnolia.

She has come here to fight against her mind. The semiotician part—studying signs, the signifiers and the signified—is prone to jargon-driven incomprehensibility; the art scholar part—studying created objects—can easily be stricken aesthetically blind. Both parts constantly threaten to cut her off from fundamental human life as it is lived, first and foremost: in the moment, through the senses. Not that she doesn't love her mind. It is always quick, for instance, to see a good irony, such as this very distrust of her mind having itself begun as an *idea*. And it was her analytical self that challenged her to look more deeply at these monuments, issuing the challenge in this very town after she and Robert came here with friends for roadhouse food and antiques and found this relic of Old South, lost-cause passion and laughed at its excesses and, yes, at its unintended semiotics.

To give voice to this monument's signified meaning, both in its own era—the last years of the nineteenth century—and in this era, she needs time to stand and meditate on the thing. She is convinced that at the deepest level its meaning is essentially a meaning of the body. Of the bodies of this monument's creators. The bodies of the women of the Ladies' Memorial Association of Jefferson County, Florida, and of the United Daughters of the Confederacy.

As Darla approaches she is surprised to find her own body trilling a little at the longings signified in the part of the sculpture hidden behind the crown of the magnolia. But even with her empathy already engaged, in the next few moments, as the centerpiece of the memorial becomes visible, it is difficult for her to see the thing in terms other than those that make for easy, companionable, derisive twenty-first-century laughter: a monumental shaft rises long and straight there, condomed in a Confederate battle flag, showing itself to her suddenly from behind the tree like a Johnny Reb dropping his pants, his man-part ready for action, its condition even captioned in marble at the base: ERECTED 1899. Erected still, a hundred and fifteen years later, in perpetual frustration.

She draws near the monument.

She grows still inside.

This is not just about facile Freudianism.

The frustration commemorated here is real and deep and human. It is not simply the outcome of a failed political cause but of failed human connection. These were women trapped in a male-driven time and culture that both inflamed and suppressed their passions, intellectual and physical. Inflamed and suppressed and thus redirected and inflated them.

And these were women whose men were savaged and broken and traumatized and distorted and reinvented by war. It is not lost on Darla, as she stands before the western face of the monument, that she is herself part of just such a generation of women.

And without votes, without clear forms of influence, but in bodies and minds roiling with nascent independent identities and with passions that cried out for self-driven expression, these nineteenth-century Southern women created clubs. Became clubwomen. To think and feel and organize together. History clubs and travel clubs and library clubs. Improvement clubs and betterment clubs and advancement clubs. A Ladies' Memorial Association. The Daughters of the Confederacy. And in this town, as in almost every other town, a literary club. Darla could see the women of the Jefferson Country Literary Club convening in the parlor of one of their Carpenter Classic homes on a weekday afternoon, just the women, in shirtwaists and Newport knots, sitting together, dreaming together, creating words together, writing them down, these purplish, engorged, sublimating words before which she now stood.

Let this testimonial of woman's deathless fidelity to man's imperishable valor speak to the sons and daughters of this Southland for all time to come.

Darla stops reading.

She sits up and it is very dark. She and Robert have been living together for less than a week. He is beside her in the bed. She struggles to disentangle her mind from a trivial dream and to animate her sleep-heavy limbs, but her hearing is fully awake and she recognizes a snubbing of sobs in him and then a strangled gasping and then a wrenching in the dark and his body moving. The sounds that woke her dissipate, and only a heavy, trembling breathing remains. She can make out Robert's body, sitting now, turned with his back to her.

She lifts her hand, hesitates, moves it to him, touches his shoulder.

He starts.

"Sorry," she whispers.

He stands abruptly.

But he does not move off.

He breathes heavily, and then not at all, and then a little less heavily, making an effort to control himself.

He lies back down.

He does not explain, not even to say he's had a bad dream.

Not on this night, not ever in the decades to come, does he speak of the nightmares of their first couple of years together.

She's not supposed to be party to them. But surely she knows them well enough. They are of Vietnam. They are of what he has seen, what he has done.

This first time, he's been out of the army for barely four months. Is she moved on that night to think of his *imperishable valor*? No. Right and wrong are clear to her at age twenty-three: Perhaps he stood against the horrors he faced in Vietnam; perhaps he did not run. But for this to be achieved in service to a cause not only lost but utterly wrong, the act would be stripped of anything she'd call courage. His true valor could be found in his having marched with her against their own government. But in her growing fidelity to Robert Quinlan, when he dreams and awakens to his guilt, to his shame, how is she to help him? He has already done whatever it is he has done. She wrestles with all this and then with a rush she has an answer: His valor, expressed by protesting in the streets of Baton Rouge, is even greater for its first having been challenged and wrecked in this unholy war. The longhairs who duck all that and hide and then prance their own righteousness are not half so brave as he.

Darla blinks her way back to Monticello.

The longhairs. Her father's phrase.

She does not want to consider her father.

She concentrates on the text of the monument.

Let this mute but eloquent marble testify to the enduring hardness of that living human wall of Florida soldiery that stood during four long years of pitiless war — a barrier between our homes and an invading foe.

She is making a familiar argument to her father. "You talk like Ho Chi Minh is threatening to invade Ithaca and march up our shore and into our parlor," she says. The two of them are sitting on wicker chairs on their front veranda overlooking Cayuga Lake.

Resisting still, Darla turns from the Confederate monument and walks a few yards away, stops beneath a cabbage palm, its lower fronds burnt brown by last week's freeze.

Her father is here too.

He's blathering about the domino theory.

Why does she even bother arguing?

As he goes on, she continues for now to accede to the family tradition for discussions: You at least pretend to look at each other. But she can't believe he's insulting her intelligence by spouting this nonsense. Demanding she believe that when Vietnam turns communist it will immediately topple to Chinese control and then Cambodia will fall and then Laos and on and on.

She's heard enough. She says, "Our country is totally ignorant about who it's dealing with." This much she says to his face. She is ready to make the case. But the face is so familiar. Once, she voraciously studied every twitch and glint and moue of it for approval. But now Darla's First Law of Parental Physics has prevailed: Every obsessive daughterly action to find her identity through her father will eventually result in an equal and opposite reaction. The idea of speaking to this face repulses her. And his eyes make it worse. They are the blue of a clear sky starting to go dim on a late-autumn afternoon. They are *her* eyes.

So on this day, sitting on the veranda of their upstate Queen Anne with a man who is used to being the patriarchal boss, who won't listen to reason, who spews the domino theory to justify a country gone mad, she breaks with the family tradition.

She lowers her face a bit without taking her eyes off his, just to signal that what she is about to do is conscious and meaningful, and then she turns her head away. She even shifts her shoulder a little in the same direction, to make both points: She is enlightening him and she is turning her back on him. And then, as if to the forest of hemlock and sugar maple that surrounds their house, she says, "Virtually every city and town in Vietnam has a statue of a hero. They all have one thing in common. They honor Vietnamese heroes who threw the invading Chinese out of their country. It's preposterous to argue that a unified Vietnam will turn into a puppet state for the Chinese. They have two thousand years of invasion and resistance between them."

Markus Kallas, Darla's father, grew up in Hell's Kitchen. As a teenager he helped his storefront-butcher father create and market a sideline of Estonian blood sausage. As a twenty-three-year-old, with his father's death, he took over the business. As a thirty-year-old he began making his fortune by canning meat and finding a better way to keep it moist through the heat processing. He is old-country, old-school, and self-made. However, with Darla's words, Markus Kallas—who finds the showing of strong feelings to be unseemly in such a man as he— even Markus Kallas cannot hide an involuntary softening and beaming in his face. In spite of his daughter's odd and insulting gesture of talking as if to the trees. She's not like all the rest of that hippie crowd. She has done her homework. She even has the right kind of backbone, stiffened by study and thought. She is old-school. His political opinion does not change because of her reasoning, for he did not reason himself into the opinion, but his feeling for his daughter, in some fundamental way, does. Moments later he layers over his newly altered feeling with the seemly reserve he is devoted to, though the feeling itself will abide till his death on the Taconic Parkway.

What will abide in Darla, however, is an unaltered feeling about him, for in those few moments she was looking into the trees and she did not see what was briefly evident in his face.

So she returns to the shadow of a cabbage palm four decades later with this thought, directed specifically to her father: *After Vietnam was unified it took only three years to prove me right. The first war they fought was in Cambodia, where they kicked out a genocidal communist regime supported by the Chinese. The second war they fought was on their own northern border with the Chinese themselves. You never understood a thing.*

The veranda and the house on Cayuga Lake linger in Darla's head even as she reflexively pulls back from a road tractor wheezing its way past in the traffic circle, its semitrailer stacked with pine tree trunks. She cannot imagine her father's leaving her the Queen Anne in his will as anything but a ploy. As an effort, even from beyond the grave, to bend her to his will, his way of life, his way of thinking.

The semi is gone. The smell of pine lingers. She rouses herself. She moves back to the Confederate monument. *Focus*, she thinks. Focus.

Let the young Southron, as he gazes upon this shaft, remember how gloriously Florida's sons illustrated their sunny land on the red fields of carnage, and how woman—fair and faithful—freshens the glory of their fame.

Ah, Freud. The young men gazing upon the monumental shaft of their fathers. Encouraged to do so by their mothers and their grandmothers. The ladies of the club. Darla will certainly elicit laughs at the Semiotic Society of America annual meeting. What will the laughter of those mostly male semioticians signify? The following year she might do a paper on *that*. But her very purpose, in the paper and on this day, is to find and speak the significance of this monument that brooks no laughter.

Darla closes her eyes and listens. Listens to the overwrought voice of these women, their prose bepurpled with passion for their men. In the parlor that Darla imagines, where the Literary Club of Monticello crafts this prose, most of the women are Darla's age. Their men are dead. Their husbands. Dead from the war. But dead even if they survived. Even if they still sleep beside these women each night, three decades later. For the men have grown small. The cause in them has been lost to self-pity and pettiness, to meanness and an oppression of their women. Or even simply lost to a quotidian life after the war was over, a life of bricklayer or cabinetmaker, mule driver or lumberjack, haberdasher or druggist or barber. Or teacher.

And Darla asks: *How did these women, fair and faithful, preserve their passion?*

Not just preserve. Amplify.

And she knows. Their passion was for the dead. And being dead, those men could never disappoint.

~

On this night, at his insistence, Robert and Darla go to their studies and work, he being all right, his father being eighty-nine after all, his mother bearing up just fine. Darla appreciates the chance to massage her notes from the day. They act as if this were any other evening. But when they finally enter their bed, neither of them picks up a Kindle from a nightstand, and she forgoes her iPod as well. And as soon as they are arranged in their places—side by side with a forearm-length space between them in the king bed—as if on cue, they both stretch up and turn off their lamps and lie back.

The room is still but for a faint buzz from an LED electric clock, a relic of their first year in this house, preserved by Darla on her side of the bed.

After a time, he says, "The children."

"I called them," she says.

"You did?"

"I did."

"Good," he says. "It only just occurred to me."

"I called them," she says.

"When?"

"This morning. While you were at the hospital."

A beat of silence.

She asks, "Are you sure you're okay?"

"I'm okay," he says.

"If you're not, I hope you'd say so."

"I would."

A few beats more.

Then Robert asks, "How did things go in Monticello?"

"Fine."

"Did you think like them?"

"The ladies?"

"Yes," he says. "The Daughters."

"The daughters?"

"Of the Confederacy. Did you get inside their heads? Like you wanted?"

"Yes," she says.

"What was it like?"

One more beat.

"Passionate," she says.

And now their last waking silence of the day begins.

Darla does not linger with the Confederate women. Her fading consciousness somehow veers to her grandson, Jacob, who answered the phone this morning when she sought Kevin, mistakenly dialing her son's home number rather than work.

She recognizes the boy's voice, though it sounds different to her. It's been nearly a year since she spoke with him. He was skiing somewhere at Christmas. He's twenty. Not a boy. His voice surely hasn't changed from nineteen. But there's something in him that's new. Maturity maybe.

"Is that you, Jake?" she says.

"Grandma?"

"Yes."

"How are you? I've been meaning to call Granddad." She hears him pause a beat, catching himself. "Call you both." She smiles. Jake's a good young man, not wanting to hurt her feelings.

"I wish I could put him on the phone," she says. "But he's at the hospital up in Thomasville. It's Grandpa Bill. He's fallen and broken a hip."

"Oh fuck." Jake catches himself in the curse but, in doing so, utters an almost inaudible *Oh shit*. Almost.

Darla smiles. He's still a boy.

"Sorry, Grandma," he says.

"It's okay."

"I'm just shocked, you know?" he says. "Jeez. I've been wanting to talk with him too."

"Honey, you'll have a chance. I'm sure he'll be all right."

"Both of them," Jake says. "You know?"

For a moment she doesn't know. Then: Bill and Robert both. Jake's been thinking of them, wanting to talk with them. While there's time.

"They're both fine," she says.

Fine. One has a broken hip at nearly ninety. The other has turned seventy. But fine. They're fine. Her mind is slowing now. *Lugubrious*, she'd say about her mind. The word *lugubrious* presents itself to her as a little surprise from someone. She thinks: *I'm falling asleep.*

She turns onto her side, and the movement stirs one last moment of clarity in her. The conversation with Jake was not a veer from Monticello. Robert's mortality is a matter of someone's active concern. Robert could vanish in a moment, this man who she met, who became a part of her life, only because he went to war. She is sitting at a desk, rather like her desk downstairs, but it sits in the middle of a parlor in Monticello, with her ladies of the Literary Club gathered around. She holds a quill pen over a blank sheet of paper. Motionless. She can think of no words to write, though she clearly understands she must compose a tribute to her dead husband, the Southron Robert Quinlan, veteran of a lost war, who is dead.

For Robert, as well, this silence is a waking silence. The past courses through him as spontaneously as if it were the dream imagery of incipient sleep.

Lien stands in a bower of blooming flame trees on the bank of the Perfume River, waiting for him. It's June, a rare cloudless day, fiercely hot. On Le Loi Street along the river, Operation Recovery has expunged the rubble of razed buildings and the bodies of the dead. The trees are splashed with flowers the color of arterial blood.

She vanished with the Tet Offensive. Word of mass graves of civilians was spreading through the city and it was understood what sort of people were slaughtered by the North in Hue: government officials, freethinking university teachers and students, those who could identify the embedded Viet Cong, those who had worked with and those who had lain with the enemy Americans. Bargirls. Girlfriends. Robert feared Lien was dead.

When restrictions eased and he could leave the MACV compound, he went at once to the site of the tailor shop. The building survived but the shop was closed and boarded up. When the sampan community near the central market reassembled, he walked its banks over and over, searching for Lien's uncle, trying to remember the man's face, hoping he would himself be recognized by the man.

And then, one afternoon, an old woman stopped him outside the MACV compound and said Lien's name to him and told him a day and a time and this place, and he approaches her now.

She wears a white *ao dai*, the tight-bodied Vietnamese silk dress with its skirt split up the sides from feet to waist, revealing black pantaloons beneath, a dress she has, on special nights, worn privately for him without the pantaloons, naked beneath it from waist to feet.

He holds a brown paper parcel tied in hemp cord.

She turns her face at the sound of his approach, comes forward. She makes no move to touch him but explains this with her first words. "I do not touch you like I wish from people that see us."

"I understand," he says.

Her dark eyes focus on his, but dartingly: his right, his left, back and forth, as if she does not believe the one and seeks something in the other, then seeks it in the first again, hoping what she saw a moment ago has changed. Or has not changed. *Her* eyes seem anxious. Only that. Their lids are rounded some by French blood. He longs to ask her to close her eyes for him to kiss her there. Surely she can read in him the feelings that produce this longing. But he senses already he will never kiss her again.

"I was afraid they killed you," he says.

"I hide," she says. "I have one place to hide and then I run away."

"When did you return?"

"Few days before now," she says. She seems to begin to say more—a taking of a breath, a lift of her chest—but she lets it go, does not speak.

He does not dare to ask the questions flaring in his head. Will she stay? Can they be together? Instead he feels the weight in his hand.

"I brought your father's pistol," he says.

She takes the parcel from him, saying, "I was afraid also they killed Robert."

She looks again into his eyes. She studies him closely but with her own eyes steady now.

In the center of his chest he trembles. Standing before her gaze, given that he feared for months that she was dead, he is slow to fully understand the trembling. He takes it simply for passion.

"He did help you?" she asks.

Robert does not understand.

She sees this.

"My father," she says, lifting the parcel a little.

"He saved my life," Robert says, wishing he could believe it was as simple as that.

She nods. Her eyes are growing bright from nascent tears.

He aches to lift a hand. To touch her face. But he knows what's next. It was always to come to this. Surely it was. But they've lost so many nights already. And those nights still before him in this country—eighty-seven more, the count on the calendar on the wall beside his bed—now that she is safe, now that she is here, at least some of those nights could be made to feel as if he were never going to leave her. As if she could somehow go with him.

But he already understands there will be no more nights.

"I am glad," she says. "My father can like you."

"Could have liked," he says. The man is dead. The correction is a wistful reflex. She has always asked that he correct her English. She has always wanted to be perfect in her English for him.

"My father could have liked you," she says.

They wait.

He feels something shift in her.

"You understand," she says. You must. You should. You will. You can't.

"That you must go?" he says.

She smiles. She has heard herself leap in her words in a way that he should not have been able to follow. But he has. They have always understood each other. And so her smile quickly fades. And the tears begin to fall.

She does not wipe them away. She does not avert her gaze.

"I understand," he says. And he feels his own eyes growing warm.

"I cannot see this," she says. Very gently. He knows she means his tears.

He looks away to the river to hide them. The seemingly incessant clouds of Hue keep the water the color of cheap jade. Today, beneath an empty sky, the Perfume River flows blue.

He says, "You'll leave Hue?"

"Yes," she says.

He thinks he is in control of himself now. He looks back to her.

"I love you beaucoup much forever," she says.

Before they can laugh at her irony—she has used the catchphrase of the bargirls—she touches his hand, a fleeting wisp of a touch, and she turns and walks quickly away.

Watching her go, he understands his earlier trembling. It was not entirely passion. The trembling would also have had him speak to Lien about the man he killed. She was the one person who might have been able to absolve him.

But it's too late. And as he watches the white flutter of her *ao dai,* the long drape of her black hair as she leaves him, his trembling returns. Now, though, it is indeed passion. The last feeling he will ever have while his eyes are actually upon her is this ache to take her in his arms and hold her as close as he can.

In the following months, his active passion for Lien slowly faded. She was gone forever, irretrievable, this woman he'd loved. Whatever was uniquely left of her within him, he could not, would not consider. Dared not.

That was in another country. A country at war. He worked hard to see Lien as a *Vietnamese* woman. He focused on the *otherness* of Vietnamese women, on the seemingly universal kinesthetics of them—the feeling in his chest and arms and loins for their smallness, for their softness of parts and hardness of will, for the glide of them. And so all of those qualities faded from him once he returned to the States and to the women who had shaped his desire from boyhood. These Americans were the women—in their diversity, in the scale of them—who were imprinted on him. Then, in a coffee shop in Baton Rouge, Louisiana, he felt his physical desire embed itself in a long-shared culture, in a shared cast of mind, in another woman's uniqueness, an American woman. He was ready for Darla.

And now, in this dark room, on the night his father fell and began to hasten toward death, his remembrance of lost passion flows on in him like a river of cerulean blue and enters the sea: Darla, earlier this evening, as she emerges from her study. He stands at her door, as is their way. Whoever of them first notices that it has passed a certain hour will go to the other and wait at the door. And she emerges as she always does, with a faintly startled look as she returns to him from the realm of her mind, and she gives him a soft sigh, as if yes, the workday is through and there you are and I am glad. And he feels, as he sometimes does at this, a swell of tenderness. He felt it when he stood in her office door this evening and he feels it again now, in this moment, in this bed, and Robert wishes to take Darla into his arms and hold her as close as he can.

He turns onto his side.

She is lying with her back to him.

He pauses.

Between Robert and Darla, when did sleep begin to trump desire? It has. And thoroughly enough that even as he desires her now, this is not a question he asks himself. He simply pauses from the fact of it. Perhaps it began after a certain number of years together, after they had come to a certain bone-deep familiarity; perhaps there was a crucial time or two when he turned to her and she was sleeping and, in waking to his touch, she simply patted the beseeching hand and coiled back into unconsciousness. Or perhaps it was she who first touched him in this way. For neither of them was it understood as a general policy. But something soon shifted. Being of a certain age, perhaps they indeed preferred their sleep and respected this preference in each other. And telling themselves it was only about this or that particular night, they did not realize what else might come of it.

~

Bob knows where he is. He is inside his head and his head is a deer tick swollen fat and he dare not move or a gnarled and hairy hand—it's the hand of God, if you want to face facts, and Bob is ready to face facts—the hand of God will reach down and take his head between thumb and forefinger and He will squeeze and Bob's head will explode with blood. All Bob can think to do is put his own hands on his head and try to hold it together. He draws his arms out from beneath the sheets, and he knows where he is. A thing he must learn over and over today, it seems. He's in the eight-bed observation unit off the emergency room. He's been here before for something or other. The place smells of his mother. Her Clorox. Her sponging it on kitchen cabinets, on counters, on the sink in their single-wide. Her hands smelled like this place. Always. Softly, she would grunt and growl and wheeze at the sponging, she would weep at the sponging. He puts his hands on his head, a palm over each ear, his fingers reaching up, pressing hard until the bed can take him and he sleeps.

Then he wakes, and nearby a voice says, "Brother Bob."

Bob begins to turn his head in that direction and the pain rushes like a breaker of blood into his right eye, crashing and foaming there.

A hand is upon his head.

This will be it. Finally. The big squeeze.

But the hand simply rests on him, and Bob focuses his eyes to see Pastor Dwayne, who is in the midst of a prayer, the details of which elude Bob. But presumably they are to fix all this.

"In the name of Jesus," Pastor Dwayne concludes, and he draws his hand away. He smiles.

Bob's head still hurts.

Pastor Dwayne says, "How are you doing, Brother Bob?"

"Brother Bob's head hurts like a sonofabitch," Bob says.

Pastor Dwayne maintains his smile. Even warms it a little. "The Lord spared you from serious harm."

Bob says, "Have you found out who it was the Lord spared me from?"

"I'm afraid there's no way to determine that. The man was long gone when we found you. As you well know, we freely offer that space to anyone in need."

Bob's body wants him to sit up in umbrage, but the pain in his head checks that impulse instantly.

"Be still now," the pastor says. "I'm here to help you. The hospital will keep you for only twenty-three hours. That time is almost up. But I've spoken with the social worker. They'd normally find you a halfway house for a few days. I've asked if I might take you in at the church, and they've agreed, if that's all right with you."

Bob pops a little breath in halfhearted assent. You always take the handout in front of you.

"After your head feels better, perhaps we can find you some work," Pastor Dwayne says. "Our Heavenly Father brought you to us for a purpose."

Bob would dispute this now if another sea wave of pain weren't rolling through his head. *Heavenly or not, a father just wants to fuck with you.* Bob knows the pain has helped him out. Don't push back at the old man if there's anything more to be had from him.

And so by mid-morning Bob has an inflatable futon and a reading lamp and a New International Holy Bible in a conference room off the church office, converted to a temporary living accommodation so readily that he knows other Hardluckers have preceded him in this place. Bob is wearing flannel and denim, new to him, with the smell of cheap dry cleaning layered over intractable Goodwill funk. He has showered. He used the talcum powder set out for him. He has new underwear. He knows he better not stay.

Pastor Dwayne has blessed him and encouraged him to rest and to read today and to take his pain medicine, and he has promised a nice chat later this afternoon, when he has finished his day's errands. In the meantime, Sister Loretta, the church secretary in the next room, will help him in any way he needs.

Sister Loretta, buxom and no doubt well talcumed, was standing in the conference room doorway beaming and nodding at him in assent through all of this encouragement, though now that Pastor Dwayne has gone on his way, she has returned to her desk and is presently on the phone talking to a friend. Her voice pitches suddenly lower, though Bob, bending near to the frosted glass panels edging the door, can still hear her speaking kindly of the poor unfortunate in the conference room who the pastor feels responsible for, but it's okay, the friend should come pick Loretta up at noon, as the poor man is fast asleep. She can take an hour away. Pastor Dwayne won't mind.

Shortly after noon Loretta is gone and Bob steps from the conference room. A distant corridor rings with hammering. A man in coveralls carrying a ladder passes by on the gravel beyond the office windows and Bob steps back to put the conference door between him and any possible glance.

The footsteps on gravel recede and all is quiet. Even the hammering stops for a few moments, and Bob stays where he is till it resumes.

He crosses the room, passes Loretta's desk, and he opens the door into the pastor's office.

Bob is not a thief.

He has not been a thief for decades, and even then it was for only a few years in his late teens. He never used a gun. Never a gun. He was quiet. He was an amateur. He stopped after a couple of whiffs of jail but before he had a permanent record.

He does not enter Pastor Dwayne's office with the intent to steal anything. He does not have even a flicker of a thought to do so.

Now that he's standing in the room, the door closed behind him, the bright chill silence of the January morning pressing against the windows, Pastor Dwayne's massive mahogany desk crouching before him, Bob could not say why he's come in here. Better simply to put on the sweater and overcoat and watch cap and gloves they'd gathered for him from some donation bin and to walk away right now, while no one is looking.

But this man Dwayne has found an empty La-Z-Boy in Bob's head and has taken a seat and put his feet up. Though he's playing it smarmy for the moment. When he stood before the fresh-scrubbed and newly clothed Bob, he explained about his errands and what he expected of Bob for the day's activities, and then he stopped talking and he took a moment to look at Bob, up and down, and he said, "I see something in you."

Maybe that's why Bob is standing in the man's office now. *Do you know me? Who the hell are you that you know me?* Bob will turn the tables on him. Figure *him* out. *I bet I know you.*

The wall beyond the desk, between two windows looking into a tree line, holds a bronze cross up near the ceiling, and beneath are frames and frames.

Bob circles the desk and approaches.

A cluster of color photos. Dwayne and wife. Bob does not look at her face. Dwayne and his sons: young Dwayne and child boys; older Dwayne and teenagers; old Dwayne now and men. Arms around one another's shoulders.

Bob moves his eyes sharply away from the family photos, all featuring that Jesus-aping loving father, Pastor Dwayne Kilmer. Bob's gaze lands on another arrangement.

A diploma for a Master of Arts in Theological Studies from Bob Jones University.

A photo of Pastor Dwayne shaking hands with the governor of Florida, the two men grasping hands but looking at the camera, the governor a bald man with a lunging, sappy smile like the smiles of the Hardluckers you need to watch out for in the shelters at night.

A typed letter, framed in gold plate. At the top is an eagle sitting on crossed rifles, the NRA logo. *Dear Pastor Kilmer. I am grateful to you for your support in our efforts to protect our Second Amendment rights. What our opponents do not understand is that we have a First Amendment only because we have a Second. Men of God such as yourself . . .*

Bob skips to the signature. He cannot read it. The first name appears to begin with a great, curvy *P* and the rest is a tight march of undifferentiated letters that could be all *u*'s or *m*'s or *n*'s or *l*'s. Then Bob's eyes slide to the right, to what he realizes is a companion frame, and he thinks he recognizes the square-jawed man speaking behind a lectern. Back to the letter. The logo. And yes. The man's name is printed in small type beneath it. Not a *P*, in the signature. A fancy *C*. Charlton Heston. Bob's old man loved this guy. Moses the gunslinger.

Bob looks abruptly away from this wall, turns around.

He starts, as if someone has snuck in behind him.

But it's the high back of Dwayne's desk chair.

Bob circles it.

Sits in it.

He puts his arms along the arms of the chair.

He settles himself. As best he can, for his head is quick-thumping in pain.

There's nothing to do for that. Just push through it.

He begins to open drawers.

Center drawer. Ballpoint pens. Paper clips. Cluttery little crap.

He's having trouble concentrating, trouble seeing things clearly. But the thumping slows a bit. Bob knows it's his heart beating in his head. It's his heart driving the pain.

He opens the top drawer in the desk's right-hand pedestal. More clutter. Brochures for the church, a bottle of aspirin, a granola bar, a phone-charging cord. In the second drawer are pristine envelopes, stamps, a stapler.

Bob hates this guy. As if he were lying to Bob's face. This bland daily shit. It's all lies.

He slams the second drawer and pulls at the bottom one. It won't yield.

Bob pushes back in his chair and looks at the drawer. It's the deepest one. Files probably. *Who gives a damn?*

But Bob doesn't like Dwayne keeping his secrets. The drawer has a simple pin tumbler lock. And Bob still has a small skill from his teenage thieving days.

He opens the central drawer and removes two paper clips. He bends one to work as a torque wrench, the other as a rake.

He has to leave the chair. His head and his knees begin to scream at him in pain but he makes himself crouch down. He is determined now.

He draws near to the lock. He inserts the first paper clip, turns it, holds the tension, inserts the second, and he begins to rake the pins inside the lock. His fingers fumble a bit for a moment, but long ago he had a good feel for this, and his muscles quickly remember and he rakes again and once again and the last pin slips into place and the lock yields.

He opens the drawer.

Vertical files, but they're pushed to the back. Forward, lying at the bottom of the drawer, is a Glock 21 pistol, and a box of .45 auto cartridges.

And Bob thinks: *Dwayne, Dwayne, Dwayne. Pastor Dwayne. Dreaming of ISIS sending a few boys over here to Tallahassee to bust in and rape Loretta and grab you and cut off your head, but you're ready to defend your First Amendment church with your Second Amendment Glock, you're ready to protect your flock like a good father should, like a good shepherd, like a Heavenly Father.*

Heavenly Father my ass.

Bob's own voice in his own private head has clambered heavenward to the oldest old man of them all.

Sneering all the way, of course.

And another sea surge of pain swells in him and crashes behind his eyes and tumbles down his face and into his throat and into his chest.

Punishment for the sneer, no doubt.

And he hears a voice.

Not his own.

A loud voice.

A big fucking loud voice.

I'VE BROUGHT YOU HERE FOR A PURPOSE.

Bob's not crazy. Bob knows he's hearing this voice in his head. But just because it's inside his own private head doesn't mean it's not a voice. A real voice. Talking to him. Every voice you ever hear when you're right there in the room with it still has to pass through your head. Even if you close your eyes and make the face and the mouth saying the words vanish, the voice remains, talking away. So where is it *then*? In your head. Your own private head. Just because it's in your head doesn't mean it isn't real.

I BROUGHT YOU HERE.

The voice pauses.

A beating pulse of pain in Bob's head.

An invitation to litany.

I BROUGHT YOU HERE.

And Bob responds: *To make me okay.*

YOU HAVE A PURPOSE.

To be okay.

I BROUGHT YOU HERE.

To you. To you.

YOU HAVE A PURPOSE.

To arm myself.

And Bob takes up the Glock 21 and its box of cartridges. He closes the drawer, and he uses his boyhood skill to reengage the lock. And he thinks: *Dwayne'll never know. He won't even miss his weapon till the Viet Cong bust in and then he'll know and he'll go* Oh shit *and they'll cut off his head.*

~

Earlier this morning, as Pastor Dwayne negotiates Bob's release into his care, Robert reassures Darla that she needn't go to the hospital today—his father would surely be embarrassed to be seen in an invalided state—and she goes off on her run. Robert is drinking his coffee at the kitchen island, aware still of the spot on his cheek where Darla kissed him good-bye. A utilitarian kiss, surely, conveying gratitude for a courtesy rendered, but it landed wetly there, as if her lips were parted. Perhaps not so surprising; she is, after all, *ardently* grateful. He can well understand her gratitude. He doesn't want to go either, for a low-grade dread won't stop niggling at him over this visit.

He takes the last sip of his coffee and carries his cup to the sink. The dread is not just about his father, but about his mother as well. And thinking of her, he thinks of the index card.

He turns from the sink and realizes where the card is. He puts his hand in his pocket and draws it out. She has written *James.* What was in her head? Is her use of his never-used formal name a rebuke of her other son? An attempt to distance herself, shield herself? But the card was intended for Robert's eyes. It's just another dramatic pose. Beneath is a phone number with a 705 area code.

This will be a day rife with choices between one unpleasant option and another. The present decision: call his brother after all these years and risk actually having to deal with him, or incur further implorings from his mother to help reconcile the family. The latter will be tedious in a familiar way. The former is disturbing in being so unfamiliar. But the prospect of a call to Jimmy at least stirs Robert's morbid curiosity. If the conversation goes badly, so be it. Robert will simply hang up the phone and that will be that till they're all four of them dead.

Robert takes the phone from its cradle near the foyer and carries it to the living room. He sits in the recessed window seat at the opposite end from the French doors to the veranda.

He dials.

Jimmy grasps the phone at the first ring.

He is sitting at his kitchen table, facing the forest. The phone was already beside him. Linda rose early and was gone when he came downstairs. Her note said that Becca was having a meltdown. Jimmy has been expecting Linda to call and check in, as the two of them were intending first thing this morning to discuss a long-overdue switch from DSL to UPS Canada. The expectation of her call was strong enough that he has not looked at caller ID.

With a voice thick with spousal familiarity he says, "Yes?"

The resultant beat of silence straightens him up in his chair. Somehow he knows it's Florida again.

Robert was expecting—was hoping—to leave a bare-bones message on an answering machine and put the burden of all this onto his brother. But the sudden, surprisingly familiar, surprisingly warm voice ratchets instantly into their shared past. Robert knows the warmth isn't for him. Not that this disappoints him. His brother was simply expecting someone else. For a moment Robert thinks to hang up.

But instead he says, "Jimmy?"

Jimmy doesn't recognize his brother's voice immediately.

Robert understands the next few moments of silence as *It's you, is it? What the hell are you doing, calling me?* Robert almost hangs up.

But the voice registers now on Jimmy. "Robert?"

"Yes."

They both fall silent.

The same impulse stirs in Jimmy that prompted him to simply erase yesterday's message. Touch the button. Keep the dead in their graves. He does not consciously consider this, but the years have worked away some of the softer rock of his brother's estrangement. It's still bouldered up in his head. But not like his mother's. So he says, "Mom put you up to this."

"Of course." As soon as he says it, Robert hears the easily inferred subtext: *I would not be speaking to you otherwise.* He did not intend it.

But Jimmy does make the inference. "You did your duty," he says.

In the thumping finality of Jimmy's tone, Robert hears his brother's subtext—*So now that you've done it, hang up*—and Robert regrets his part in turning the call so quickly into this. They're on the phone together after forty-something years. No matter how it came to pass, why not say a few things?

Robert does not hate his brother. He is not angry with his brother. Or even disappointed in him. Over the years Robert has come simply to feel nothing. As if his brother died. Died pretty young—right after college—before the two of them had a chance to mature comfortably into an adult, brotherly friendship. He's dead, and whatever grieving that entailed is long over with. No one even visits the grave anymore.

But his brother is alive at the other end of the line. So Robert says, "This isn't about her." He pauses, not quite knowing how to further soften things.

Jimmy says, "Is he dead, then?"

"No."

"Is it all overblown?"

"No. Just not dead *yet*."

"I have no interest in seeing him. Dead or alive."

"I suspect he feels the same way." This didn't come out the way Robert wanted.

Jimmy does not reply. He thinks: *At least he's saying it straight.*

But Robert tries to fix it: "Not that it means a damn thing to anyone, what he feels." And he thinks: *That sounds sarcastic. Critical.*

And Jimmy thinks: *So much for straight.*

Robert says, "I admire that in you, not giving that particular damn."

"What?" Jimmy draws the word out to clearly mean *Bullshit.*

Robert considers bailing now.

But he doubles down. "I admire it and I share it."

"When did that happen?"

"We're neither of us twenty-two anymore."

"You figure you actually grew out of trying to please him?"

"The price was too high," Robert says. He has not put it this way to himself. The banyan and the man in the dark have been too close to him lately. They were big-ticket items on the bill he paid.

The words surprise Jimmy too. This is an admission he could not have expected.

The consequent silence between the brothers persists long enough that Robert finally says, "Are you there?"

"I am," Jimmy says.

Robert realizes he is standing at the veranda doors. He does not remember rising and crossing the room. He is looking at his live oak but has not seen it till this moment.

Jimmy is standing at the kitchen window. A hundred yards off, the white pines are jammed close, side by side, like a cordoned crowd before a burning building. For many years he understood his brother's defining act that Labor Day afternoon as a betrayal. He thinks: *Not from his point of view. It was an act of loyalty. Behind his eyes, he was being William Quinlan's loyal son. His only son. Of course the price was too high.*

"I won't come," Jimmy says.

"I understand," Robert says.

"You know it was different for me with him."

"I know."

"It was different for me because of how it was for you."

Robert might have expected this from Jimmy but not so simply or directly. Where they both now are, in mind and heart, is the result of way too much life lived incommunicado. Robert realizes they're teetering on the brink of forty-six years' worth of unexpressed blame and justification, anger and regret, jealousy and insecurity.

Jimmy has come to much the same realization.

Neither wants to tumble into all that.

Both, though, in spite of the telephonic silence swelling in their heads, are reluctant simply to hang up.

This time it's Jimmy who says, "You there?"

"I'm here," Robert says.

They know a little something about each other, the knowledge having been arrived at in the same way. At some point in the last few years, at some moment late at night, pajamaed and weak-willed, caught up in the technogeist and visited by a soap-operatic curiosity about the past, each began to Google names. For Robert: the lenient commanding officer at MACV in Hue, who had his own girlfriend in a back alley room and who was glad just to get Robert back alive at Tet, and who died in 1998 after two decades as an insurance executive in Omaha; Lien, who was untraceable; a sloe-eyed girl from high school; and Jimmy. For Jimmy: Mark Satin, the director of the Toronto Anti-Draft Programme; the first woman Jimmy slept with after he and Linda sensibly established how freely free love would remain in their lives; Heather, whose Facebook picture album was full of pub parties and her child; and Robert.

Jimmy says, "I understand you teach."

Only for a moment does it surprise Robert that Jimmy knows something about his present life. He realizes, from his own knowledge of Jimmy, that there need be nothing sentimental about this, much less affectionate.

"Yes," Robert says. "At Florida State University. History."

"Sounds like where you'd go from Tulane."

Robert hears, as well: *Not to Vietnam.*

Though Jimmy did not intend this.

Robert says, "American history. Usually Southern. Early-twentieth-century particularly."

"I saw your bio at the school site."

"And you make leather goods," Robert says.

"I do."

"Bags."

"And other things. But bags are our specialty."

If Robert knows about this, so does their mother, and Jimmy almost adds: *So does she own one?* But there is no way to ask that and make it simultaneously clear that he doesn't give a damn.

Robert almost says something about the glowing reviews and press coverage at Jimmy's website, about the special things Jimmy does to the leather, but Robert can't immediately shape those words concisely or clearly and maintain the appropriate tone of benignly tepid small talk.

And so they fall silent one last time.

Both men turn from the windows they are facing.

Then Jimmy says, "You understand?"

"That you won't come to see him."

"Yes."

"Of course."

"Tell her to let go of this."

"I'll try."

Both houses tick with morning silence. The brothers feel the vague impulse to say a little something more before they end the conversation, but neither can possibly imagine what it might be.

"Good-bye then," Jimmy says.

"Good-bye," Robert says.

They disconnect.

Each takes the cordless phone away from his ear and looks at it for a moment as if it were a faded Polaroid found in a shoe box.

~

Jimmy's four women workers have gone off together for their monthly lunch at Mavis's house and he is glad now to be able to sit at his worktable and have the barn to himself. Linda has not yet checked in with him. It must be going badly at their friends' house.

He has taken up his deer tine and his softest square of camel hide and has hunched into the furious burnishing of the edges of half a dozen messenger bags, filling himself with the smell of warming beeswax and edge paint, emptying himself of Robert's voice and the family he has left behind.

But shortly he hears the middle bay door creak open and closed. He looks across the floor.

It's Linda, and he thinks: *Good. The antidote.* Whatever of Robert and Peggy and William he has not been able to burnish away will vanish in five minutes with Linda.

She is flushed from the sun and the cold and sheds her quilted coat as she approaches. Beneath, she is turtlenecked to her chin and is long-legged and slim-hipped in black dress–up jeans.

She stops before him.

She strips off her knit hat and shakes her hair down. "Your women are gone," she says.

"This is their day for Mavis's wife to make them venison stew."

She obviously hasn't noticed the phenomenon.

"A start–ups tradition," he says.

"Ah," she says.

She grows still, her coat over her arm, her hat in her hand. She is staring at him but he has no sense that she's seeing him. She's considering something, he senses.

Becca no doubt has confided in her. Linda wants to speak of it but has probably made a vow not to. Linda takes that sort of pact seriously.

"You've got a tale to tell," he says.

She makes a small sound, deep in her throat. Not quite a sound of assent. More meditative.

Jimmy waits for Linda to figure out what she's free to reveal.

Then she says, "When will they be back?"

He's thinking of their friends splitting up and hears this wrong. His puzzlement must be showing. Linda clarifies. "Your women."

"My women . . ." he says, drawing out the phrase to add an unspoken *as you oddly insist on calling them*, ". . . usually take an hour and a half or a little longer on stew day. They make it up at the end of the afternoon."

"And they left recently?"

"Twenty minutes perhaps."

Linda nods and lays her coat and hat on the near edge of Jimmy's worktable, and she says, "Then let's go sit on the couch together for a few minutes."

"All right," Jimmy says.

He follows her to the south end of the barn and into the break room next to their office.

"The coffee's fresh," he says.

"I'm good," she says, and she heads for the flannel chesterfield. He follows her.

She arranges herself sideways at one end, her legs drawn up beneath her. A long story to come.

Jimmy sits in the middle of the couch, within reaching distance, holding distance if need be. He turns toward her and waits.

She is still working something out in her mind. Then she says, "They're finished, Becca and Paul. Forever and for the best."

"I'm sorry," Jimmy says.

"No," Linda says. "It *is* for the best. For everyone concerned."

A recent image of the couple flickers into Jimmy's head: a restaurant in Toronto, the two of them side by side on the bench seats, Paul's pugilist jaw and horn-rimmed reader's eyes, Becca's ballerina bun and Bardot pout. They are nearly two decades younger than Jimmy and Linda but the four of them are joined together by New Democratic Party politics, halibut fishing on Hudson Bay, and a couples' chemistry that synthesizes compassion and snark.

Before Jimmy can consider this image, it flickers out again with Linda reaching into his lap and lifting his hand toward her. She leans to it and kisses him on the very spot where a wedding ring would be if they were to wear them.

"My darling," she says as she replaces the hand in his lap.

But he instantly senses what is happening.

"I need to go away for a week or two," she says.

If he objectively considers this, there is the possibility that she will, as Becca's best friend, simply stay with her or go away with her to help her through the first wave of trauma over the dissolution of her marriage. Paul is once divorced; Becca has never been.

But Jimmy understands. Linda is invoking the agreement that allowed the two of them to officially wed. A quarter of a century ago it was what they both wanted, equally, philosophically. It was how they'd sorted out the world together—before marriage and after—with regard to equality and rights and interpersonal power and the nature of love. All these things freely given and received and shared.

Jimmy has always been content with this.

He has wanted it.

But now in the center of his head he feels a hot dilation, like the frame of a Saturday movie serial sticking in the projector and its image splitting and searing and burning through.

"I'll be back soon, my sweet Jimmy," she says.

He does not say anything.

This declaration is clearer than is their custom.

She keeps her eyes on his. Nothing intense in her gaze. This is how it has always been for them. They have always treated each other's lacunae with loving tact. It is what they want.

The conversation is meant to stop here.

They will hold hands. They might kiss. They might even make love now, here on the chesterfield, to assert their abiding connection.

But the burning is done in Jimmy's head and there is only a blank screen. A tabula rasa. And from it he asks, "Were you the reason for the breakup?"

Minutely—but minutely is significant for Linda, Jimmy knows—minutely she flinches. Then she composes herself once more.

She takes his hand again. "They've never meant as much to you as to me," she says. "You're not worried about the breakup."

She's right about that. Nor is it the issue. But he does not say so.

"Nothing has changed between you and me," she says, squeezing his hand gently.

Then he hears himself ask another question. "Which of them is it?" He realizes only in the asking that he does not know, could not guess.

She lets go of his hand, but her voice remains gentle: "I think the way we've always handled these things is best, don't you?"

Now he asks, "Does the other one know?" But obviously not. Otherwise none of this would now be a surprise to him. He would surely have heard from the excluded one.

Linda straightens before him, taking a deep breath. Her eyes do not narrow or harden or flare, as they can do when he and she argue. If anything, they soften for him. He feels a twist of admiration over this. Then a tighter twist, of tenderness. And then a sudden chest-clamping regret.

She says, "Are we wrong, my darling? Surely not. We have always been so smart about this. Love on this earth is not a singularity. It is a profusion. As simple as a kind word at a checkout counter. As complex as you and I. But love always has boundaries. By the parts of us—mind, body, heart—that are involved, or not involved. And to what degree. And for how long. I feel certain this is a partial thing now before me and a brief thing. Our love for each other—yours and mine—is the bedrock for any other experience in this fleeting gift of my life. It's the same for you, isn't it? We've said so to each other. Often. Aren't we grateful for that?"

And at this she lifts her hand and touches his cheek and says, "Whichever of us dies first, I want our lips to touch in that moment."

She pauses, and she says, "I love you, Jimmy."

She waits, her fingertips lingering on him.

He can think of nothing to say.

He is not moving.

He can't imagine what's showing on his face.

She withdraws her hand.

She shifts her legs, squares her shoulders to him a bit more.

She says, "Why don't you spend a couple of weeks with that girl Heather. She would like nothing better, I'm sure."

He still can find no words.

She says, "Maybe she'll help you stop worrying about what's next."

~

Just before noon Robert answers the foyer phone. As he expects, it's his mother. "Darling, he's off the morphine drip and starting to wake up."

"I'll be there within the hour."

Peggy rightly takes these as his last words and jumps in. "Before you hang up. I'm out in the hallway. I need to ask. Did you try?"

"Jimmy?"

"Of course Jimmy."

"Yes."

"And?"

"He's not coming."

Robert hopes that will be it.

He waits for her.

She waits for him.

Not for long. "Why are you doing this to me?" she says. "What did he say?"

"Do you really want details?"

"Yes."

"There aren't many. We didn't instantly turn into chums." Robert hesitates only very slightly before the lie: "I don't recall the exact words." He recalls them quite clearly. "But it amounts to this: Nothing has changed. We all need to let him go."

Robert waits for a dramatic sound on the other end of the phone. A stricken word. A sob even. But there's only silence.

This troubles Robert more than her usual emoting. Better for her to be angry. She needs to be fighting. He says, "We're still toxic to him."

"Did he say that?" This comes out sharply. Her dukes are up. Good.

"No," Robert says. "Not those words."

"What words?"

"I'm not going to be his proxy in an argument with you, Mom. I'll see you in an hour."

"Toxic," she says.

"Listen. The only way this thing could have been made right was for Pops to reach out. Not Jimmy. Years ago. At the latest when Carter gave the amnesty. Pops should have told Jimmy to come home. Told him—God forbid—that he understood, that he didn't condemn him."

Robert has said all he intended to, and Peggy delays only long enough to draw a breath. She says, "I am so sick and tired of the men in this family."

Robert lets her have her big curtain line unchallenged.

But she stays on the phone.

So does he, though she's no longer on his mind. He wonders at Jimmy, at how firmly he grasped his own life and held it close all these years.

"Are you still there?" Peggy finally asks.

"Yes."

"Why? Come up here to me."

And a short time later he is passing the Blood of the Lamb Full Gospel Church. He turns his face to it, puzzles over what that was all about yesterday morning. A man in coveralls is carrying a ladder along the side of the church building.

And then the church vanishes with a run of pine along Apalachee Parkway.

Peggy is waiting for Robert in the hallway outside his father's room. She steps toward him.

"Have you been waiting out here all this time?" he says.

"No," Peggy says, keeping her voice hushed and flapping her hand at him to do the same. "It's been an hour. You've always been punctual."

"Is he still awake?" Robert accepts her tone, has kept his own voice low. A private conversation in the hall would cause an argument for her and Pops.

"*Fully* awake," she says.

They've already been arguing.

Robert says, "So what do you need to say on the sly?"

Peggy's head snaps ever so slightly. It always comes as a surprise, that he sees through her.

"Yes, well," she says, "I just wanted to remind you he's in a delicate state."

"Of course."

"Not just in his body. His mind. He's lost his mind."

"The drugs," Robert says.

"He's lucid," Peggy says. "Just mad."

"Let me guess. He doesn't want a priest to come visit."

"I won't even tell you how he put it," she says.

"It's his choice," Robert says.

"So please don't let him get worked up about anything."

"I'll do what I can."

Peggy clutches Robert's hand. Somehow it feels real, this gesture. "I know you will."

He takes both her hands in his.

She says, "I'm just so afraid I'm going to lose him now."

"He's a tough guy. He can beat the odds."

"God knows I'll miss him," she says. "Even at his worst."

Especially at his worst, Robert thinks. *His worst has kept you happily energized.* But he gently compresses her hands and says, "The best thing is for you to go on downstairs and get some coffee and a Danish. Linger over them. I can handle Pops better if it's just the two of us."

Peggy searches her son's face, seems to reassure herself about something, and then nods.

They let go of each other, and without another word Peggy is gone.

Robert approaches his father's hospital door.

He steps in.

At first the only sound he recognizes in the room is his father's heart, digitized into a soft monitor beep. And now the faint hiss of the air flowing from the wall into his father's lungs. Pops lies in his bed, his torso angled upward, his arms laid out on top of the blanket, the left one wrapped thickly from hand to elbow. He is watching out the window: the bright afternoon sky and the distant tops of longleaf pines.

Robert hesitates. His father keeps his watch. Always clean-shaven, as if he were standing for inspection by Patton himself, his cheeks and chin are covered now in dark scruff.

Robert says, "Pops."

William turns his face abruptly to his son. "Sorry," he says. "I thought you were Mother."

Robert approaches the bed, wondering briefly if his father's mind has indeed gone wrong, if he was expecting his own mother, the long-dead Grandma Quinlan. But of course he meant Peggy.

"I sent her away for coffee and pastry," Robert says.

"Good," William says. And then his eyes wander off, as if the exchange has set him thinking.

Why does Robert have the immediate impression he knows what's on Pops's mind? Perhaps it's the recent, vivid reminder of the daily struggle between his father and mother. That and the coffee and pastry. These stir the past in him, not as recollections, but enough to give him his impression as he arrives at his father's bedside.

What has worked covertly in Robert are two events. In one of them, a decade ago, on an otherwise routine phone call from New Orleans, his mother suddenly sounded real, sounded vulnerable in a way unalloyed with dramatic artifice. Robert had just casually mentioned that Darla was at school for the afternoon.

"She has a class?" Peggy asked.

"No."

"For what then?"

"Whatever."

"She's often away."

"Away?"

"At school."

"Of course."

And Peggy's voice shifted now to that authentic-seeming place, though he didn't pick up on it yet. "Does it bother you sometimes, this regular separation, when you're so close to someone? When you don't really know what's going on in their life? What they're doing?"

"Oh, I can easily guess," he said. The tangle of students and colleagues and papers and bureaucracy.

"Your father goes off every afternoon like that," Peggy said. Her tone pitched downward, inward. "He's done it every day for years. Ever since he retired. No one's around to notice but me."

She paused.

Robert was clearly aware now of the authenticity of this riff.

She went on, trying to figure it out as she'd apparently been doing for some time. "He loves to drive his car, it's true. He's always loved to drive his cars. He's driven since he was eleven, after all. There were no licenses back then. This love grew with his bones. I understand. But it's more than that. He's going for a little drive, he says. He's going for coffee, he says. Every day. He goes away for hours. I understand I can be a burden. Just to be around me. He wants to escape. But I wonder how much coffee you can drink. I wonder if he's alone."

Now a long silence. In moments like this, Robert usually knew when she was waiting for him to give her something back. But this silence felt different.

Then she said, very softly, "I sometimes wonder if he has a woman."

Another silence.

To his surprise, the notion of Pops carrying on a flirtatious friendship at his age did not strike Robert as ridiculous. So although a laugh would have sufficed, he felt the need to deny this. He began to shape a reply.

But she said, "You wouldn't know."

"I'm sure he doesn't," Robert said.

"No one would know."

Robert tried to find more words.

But she intervened, her tone breaching into avid reassurance, "Not that I'm suggesting anything about Darla."

"I didn't think . . ."

"You've got a peach there, Bobby boy. You better take good care of her or you'll have to answer to me." And Peggy laughed a loud, sharp laugh.

And then, a few years ago, Robert and Darla drove the six hours together to New Orleans for a semiotics conference. While Darla did her panels, Robert went off to see his parents. This was a last-minute decision. William and Peggy had visited Florida the previous month. There would be no sustainable small talk left between them for a while. But Robert felt guilty to be this close and not spend a few hours. He would surprise them. If they were out, at least he'd tried.

It was a quarter to two on a Friday afternoon when he turned onto Third Street from Magazine and crossed Annunciation into his parents' block. Up ahead he saw Dad's Impala pulling away from the curb. The afternoon vanishing act. Robert could simply take his father's place at the curb and visit his mother. Or he could follow his father.

At the foot of Third, William turned uptown. Robert stayed close, not taking any chances of losing him. Over the intervening years Robert had given very little thought to his conversation with his mother about all this, other than to conclude she'd never have said those things to him in person. The disembodiment of the phone had put her into a deep-seated Catholic frame of mind, as if she were in a confessional booth, speaking to an invisible priest.

This was probably quite simple. It was about coffee and a chance to escape the bickering. But if Dad was having an octogenarian tryst, Robert wanted to get a glimpse of the woman in the affair. Mom would never need to know.

William stayed on Tchoupitoulas for as long as he could, for the whole length of the river docks, till the street ended at the zoo. This he skirted, and then he followed the levee into Carrollton, turning onto the area's eponymous main drag. He drove only a short distance farther and turned into a strip-mall parking lot.

Robert pulled into a spot down the row and watched his father get out of his car. If Dad had bothered to look around he would have seen Robert's head and shoulders among the car tops down the way, but he did not look, was not the least bit furtive. He did not move to the sidewalk along Carrollton Avenue, but struck out along the parking lot lane toward the side street.

Robert followed his father.

He was impressed by the man's vigorous stride. Perhaps the stride of a man meeting a woman. Certainly the stride of a father who, from this distance, seemed not to be aging. Who might live forever.

He crossed the side street and turned away from Carrollton. A couple of doors up was a coffee shop. Chicory Dickory, Coffee and Beignets. At least the coffee part of Dad's story was true: he went in.

Robert neared the shop, slowed drastically, approached carefully, and paused in the doorway. His father's back was to him. He was standing before a table with three other men who were standing as well, their chairs pushed away as if they'd just risen. They were all of them old. Their right arms and hands were frozen in a sharp military salute, and they were swiveling slightly at the hips so that each could direct his gesture to each of the others.

They sat.

The clock on the wall said precisely two o'clock.

Immediately a waitress arrived with a tray of beignets and coffee for four. She lowered the tray and they all served themselves from it, making small talk with her, calling her by name. These guys were regulars.

Robert pulls a chair to his father's hospital bedside. He's aware now of how he knows what his father was thinking. Coffee and pastry and the irony of Peggy getting away from him for that. Coffee and pastry and the company of men, and how those things are likely gone forever. Till yesterday his father was still driving. He'd surely found a coffee shop in Thomasville. Did he find a new band of veterans as well? Robert hopes so. He kept his father's actual secret through the years. Peggy would have nagged a stop to those afternoons as surely as if they'd been filled with a mistress.

Seated now, he leans toward his father. The initial covert working of the past in him—the phone conversation with Peggy and his shadowing of his father—is done. But the memory of the New Orleans coffee shop emanates on. As Robert stood in the doorway, he thought to turn and vanish. Simply, quietly.

But instead he stepped in and sat down at a table near the four men, with his father's back still to him. Robert ordered a coffee with chicory and sipped at it, hearing fragments of their talk. They spoke of the weather and the Saints and their aching joints and Obama and al-Qaeda and eventually they arrived at Patton and Eisenhower and at how they lost the peace by letting the Russians into Berlin. And then Robert's coffee was gone and he'd pushed his luck already, not really wanting his father to catch him here, and not really wanting an answer to the question that had lately gnawed its way into the center of his brain. Which was: Would his father get around to the story of a small, doomed house in Bingen? Robert's thoughts were getting ragged enough for him even to wonder if Dad would have his Good War cronies start counting, *One Mississippi, Two Mississippi.*

Robert left money on the table and went out into the street, thinking: *No. That's the stuff he and his pals take for granted. Bingen was a story made for fucking with the minds of a couple of little boys.*

You share a war in one way. You pass it on in another.

All this swifts through Robert, though in his father's room at Archbold Memorial Hospital he is washed by its wake.

But small talk prevails for the moment. He says, "How do you feel?"

William snorts. "Better a few hours ago." He groans and gingerly shifts his shattered arm, which lies between them. "For the first time in my life I'm beginning to understand drug addicts."

"Impossible," Robert says, and he hears a taint of anger in this. He softens his voice. "How'd that come about?"

"Twenty-four hours on morphine and four hours off it," his father says.

Robert has had, for some years, two modes of conversation with his father. Most of the time he listens, unchallenging, serious of manner, letting his father set the conversational agenda and its tone. Or, occasionally, when he reaches his limit of tolerance for the man's hypertraditional thinking and right-veering politics and blue-collar attitudinizing, Robert becomes ironic, contrapuntal, engaging with his father but in a manner that tugs at the man's points as if he could be pulled to the left.

Robert knows he should let this conversation roll out in the most comfortable way for a very old man in a hospital bed with a broken hip and a shattered arm. But he does not. He says, "A little morphine in all the air. It would be wonderfully refreshing for everyone."

"Are you quoting or just selfishly getting sassy with a badly injured old man?"

"D. H. Lawrence."

"Was he an addict?"

"I don't think so."

"I was always an addict," his father says. "For the caffeine and the sugar."

Robert is a little surprised to hear this admission in those terms, even if his father is in a mood to sling the irony back at him. "That's a serious confession."

William snorts at this. "Don't be flip about that. Your mother wanted to get a goddamn priest in here."

"I take it you said no." Robert tries to twinkle this. Not very successfully.

William looks at him as if he's being goaded. Which is closer to the truth. "I told her if she let one in, I'd beat him to death with my cast."

At this he tries to gesture with his broken arm and barks in pain and then coughs deeply and grindingly, which clenches his body, which further agitates his arm and now even his hip.

Robert puts his hand on his father's shoulder. "Easy," he says. The gesture is futile and the coughing and clenching go on, though Robert keeps his hand where it is. "It'll pass," he says. "You're a tough guy," he says. And finally, "Should I get the nurse?"

William manages a sharp shake of the head. *No.*

Finally the coughing stops. His body calms. Tears are streaming down William's face.

He seems unaware of them.

"Fuck," he says.

Robert finds his hand still on his father's shoulder. He gives him a gentle squeeze there and withdraws.

"I wouldn't even be able do it," his father says. "Goddamn cast isn't hard enough."

Things shift in Robert. But to a complicated place. Not to banter. Not to an encouragement to rest. Not to soothing palaver. His father is indeed a tough guy. That Robert believes. But his father may soon be dead.

Robert sits back in his chair.

William is quiet now. He blinks his eyes. His good hand comes up quickly to his face and wipes at the tears. He sees Robert noticing. "From the pain," he says.

"You shouldn't let yourself get worked up over her."

"That's our life."

"She's probably going to try again to get the priest in here."

"She thinks I'm going to die," William says, but almost gently. "She says she won't know who she is without me."

"Are you beginning to understand her?"

"Drug addicts are easier." William turns his face away, toward the window.

Then he turns back.

He holds his gaze steadily on Robert. His eyes seem heavy-lidded, as if he's struggling to keep them open. But the impression is not weariness. These strike Robert as the heavy eyes of sadness. And he feels himself to be the object of the look.

Robert does not ask what's behind this. Instead, he says, "Were you still a Catholic in Germany?"

William snorts softly. His eyes relax. "You mean, 'There are no atheists in foxholes'?"

"Something like that."

"Whoever thought that up was full of shit. Either they were never in a war or were in the priest's pocket to start with." William begins carefully to rearrange himself at the shoulders. "Not that I'm an atheist. That's just another religion."

He stops arranging. He sucks up the pain.

"Should I get a nurse?" Robert says.

William shakes his head sharply *No*. He takes a deep breath, and pulling from the shoulder he adjusts his broken arm just a little. He closes his eyes to the pain.

Robert stifles his hands, his voice. He will offer no help. Pops has to be Pops.

When the pain has passed, his father says, "What was it for, my Good War? And what was our national humiliation for?"

He means, by the latter, Robert's Bad War.

William says, "It only brought us to this fucking world."

Robert says, softly, "There it is." The phrase catches him by surprise. He hasn't used it in decades. It was a meme among the enlisted men in Vietnam. Its meaning slid upon a long continuum from *I am content* to *We're all fucked*. In this case: *You said it, brother*.

William begins to cough again.

But he stops it. With a sharp intake of breath and a brief flinch of his body and a sneer. A sneer at the cough and at the pain. He takes a moment to let out the breath, fight off a little after-tremor of hacking, and he says, "Who wouldn't be happy to die tonight? Give me the political wars of the twentieth century any old day. At least your communist or your fascist gave a shit about this present life. The religious wars are going to take us all down. Behead the other guys and blow yourselves up. Sure. If you really read the holy book they believe in—that we *all* supposedly believe in; the first part of it for all of us is the *same book*—then what they're doing makes perfect sense. That book's full of genocide, on direct order from the

Commander in Chief in the Sky. With Moses himself leading the dirty work. Every holy battle gets around to it. Not just by the punks in the ski masks. Even the New Testament believers get around to it. The Catholics and the Pilgrims both had the stake and the torch."

William falls silent.

Robert has never heard any of this from his father. Was it new? Did it take the breaking of his body for him to come to this? Or did his little band of brothers look up over their coffee and beignets one afternoon and know?

Robert has to work hard now not to put his hand on his father's hand. The man wouldn't recognize the gesture, so he dare not. But Pops's words have fallen upon Robert like a shared thing. Like an understanding between them. Even like a backdoor expression of fatherly pride. Pops went to war. Robert went to war. Both of them came to this.

Robert embraces this understanding. And with it returns the moment at a corner table in the bar on Magazine Street when it was late enough and they both were lubricated enough and the lights in the place were localized enough and dim enough that he and his father seemed all alone in a dark recess, but there was still enough light from somewhere that when his father turned his face slightly, Robert saw the man's eyes beginning to fill and he thought to reassure him, even though Pops surely understood already, from his own war and from what Robert had just said about his job and duties in Vietnam, but Robert was moved by his father's worry, and he added, "It's all right. I've got a job inside the wire. I'll be safe in Vietnam.

It'll be like research. I'll get home safe." His father did not speak, did not turn back to him, and the tears that had come to his eyes began to fall. Robert had never seen his father weep. Robert could easily have wept then as well, but he was keenly aware that the pride and appreciation in his father's tears would be diminished by tears of his own. Robert needed to maintain the composure of a soldier. And he did. He cut the tears off, and he waited for his father to be himself again. Which, slowly, silently, the man became, and they drank some more and then some more, and they did not speak to each other again of war. Not on that evening. Not ever. Not about their personal experience of it.

But now.

As a seventy-year-old Robert finds himself as needy and eager to please this man as an adolescent. So he edges his chair as close to the bed as he can. He leans toward his father. He says, "Whether it's over politics or over religion, it all comes down to whatever nasty gene humans carry that makes us go to war. But once a war's on, it takes warfare to stop it. From a distance both sides on a battlefield look alike. That doesn't mean one of them isn't justified in being there."

Though animated by his teenage self, Robert has spoken in the voice of the man he is. And he has heard himself. He thinks: *I don't believe half of that. Not in the way it came out.* And his fuller belief hurtles through him, that the very waging of a righteous war, even the very winning of that war, can trigger the dark gene. So the winners go on to fight unrighteous wars.

And maybe that's the real gene that causes all the trouble. The one encoded for righteousness. Politics and religion and just the pure waging and winning of wars all share that.

But it makes no difference. The Robert who edged his chair toward his father didn't want to make a nuanced point. His intention was deeper and simpler. Two men. Sharing what they did, what they are. *That* Robert finds his voice now: "Pops, it's okay. For us both. We had to go to war. You and I did what we could."

And this turns Pops's face back to him.

They look at each other.

Robert waits.

William struggles with something. Then he says, "I've held this inside for a long time."

He pauses.

Robert quickens.

And William says, "I lost one son utterly."

Jimmy.

Robert regrets that it has to be in contrast to his brother, but he longs for what's next so much that he puts this regret aside. He even draws a good breath now at how Jimmy has made him even more important to his father.

And William says, "So I've held my tongue. But the truth is you didn't go to war. You went through the motions. But you turned it into graduate school. You contrived a comfortable place on the edge of the action to go study. You didn't even let the army decide your fate. You wangled your safe little job with a pre-enlistment deal and avoided the real thing. You told all the others who manned up, 'Better you do the dirty work, not me. Better your blood than mine.'"

Robert falls back in his chair in enervated stillness. He would rise, he would go, but he remains.

His father says, "And look where you put me. What could I have said to you? How could I argue for my son to risk death? How could I do that to your mother? And what would it say about you, that I should have to talk you into it? You already chose."

William stops talking.

He keeps his eyes on Robert.

Robert is looking at the distant tops of the pines.

"I probably should have taken this to my grave," William says.

Robert does not reply. He thinks he sees the trees quaking. Even from this distance. The wind must be strong today.

"It's all over anyway," William says.

Robert turns to his father. "I'm sorry I disappointed you."

He regrets saying this. He should argue the point. Or he should rise and go without speaking. He should not give a damn what his father thinks. They are both old men. But he has said it. And now, though he regrets this even more, he waits for his father to dispute him: *No, Robert. No not at all. I'm not disappointed. I've come to be glad. Glad you're alive. Your brother's act is my only shame. You did go to Vietnam, after all. I'm proud of you.*

But his father says nothing of the sort. He has already made himself clear.

Tet comes to mind.

But Robert has never said a word about what haunts him. His father would only be critical of that. Of course the scholar, having tried to create his comfortable little place, would be haunted by an act that any real soldier, any real man, would have understood as necessary, inevitable, righteous. Would have done proudly.

When Hue was secure and the men queued through one long night for a phone call home, Robert told his parents only that he was okay. MACV was not overrun. He was safe.

And later, when the family was safely reunited in America, there were no Vietnam war stories. None offered. None sought. As it had been, mostly, for his father and his war. Robert convinced himself that his own silence was another thing that bound him to his father, that made the man proud.

And now Robert's words hang in the air between them. Robert looks away from this man. Back to the trees, the sky.

William isn't speaking.

Robert finally looks at him.

His father's eyes are squeezed shut. He is writhing minutely in physical pain. Silently.

"I'll get the nurse," Robert says.

He rises. He walks out of the room. He stops at the nurses' station and tells the first nurse who looks at him that William Quinlan is hurting.

Then he goes down in the elevator and crosses the lobby and pushes through the door and finds his car and gets in.

He sits for a moment quaking like the tops of the pines all around him.

And he drives away.

~

Darla sits at her desk, fingers poising over her keyboard and then falling away, again and again, trying to signify with her words what it was that she felt before the Confederate monument yesterday, what it was that she understood; but trying first to distinguish her understanding from her feeling; and as she fails at that, trying to decide whether trying to distinguish understanding from feeling isn't, in fact, a fallacy, whether the very act of intellectualizing what was signified by the monument doesn't, in fact, miss the whole point. Which brings her to the kiss. The kiss she gave her husband this morning.

She parted her lips to him. But she placed the kiss on his cheek. Would she have preferred his lips? Yes. Is that preference associated with her fingertips poised but inoperative once again over the keyboard? Perhaps. Yes. After her communion yesterday with the fair and faithful ladies of nineteenth-century Florida, the ardor of her lips longed this morning for Robert's mouth. But she understood him: With his father on his mind, it was hardly the right moment. Her thought trumped her feeling.

Her hands fall.

Still, if she'd kissed him on the lips would she have the right words now for this thing her ladies built?

She lifts her hands once more, curls her fingers over the keys.

The front door latch clacks. He's home.

She has left her office door open for this. An invitation to him.

The rustle of him now in the foyer.

She puts her hands on the desktop.

She waits.

She hears nothing.

She turns in her chair.

He has not silently appeared. Perhaps he assumed the open door of her office meant that she was elsewhere.

Or perhaps he needs to be alone. This is an interpretation she expects to wish to be true. She shouldn't want to hear about his hospitalized father, a man she has always found insufferable. But, in fact, she wishes Robert had understood the open door and rushed to it.

He has done no such thing.

And her mind, following along in its own path, yields this: *William Quinlan is the product of a* victorious *army, its monuments boilerplated with conventional self-congratulation.*

She turns back to her computer. But she looks beyond its monitor, through the window, out to the live oak. This tree was already massive when her ladies were composing their words. She invites them. She arranges them beneath her oak, their skirts spread out around them, basket lunches at hand.

Unexpectedly, they turn their faces to her.

And she rises to look for her husband. She steps from her office. She moves along the hallway, past the foyer, and she stops at the bottom of the staircase. She listens upward.

But the sound that catches her attention is the ricochet chirp of a cardinal. Distant, but not a sound to be heard from where she is standing.

She steps into the living room.

At the far end a French door is open. Robert is framed there, his back to her. He stands very still, looking out to the oak.

She remains still as well. She watches him for what feels like a long time.

Then his head dips abruptly down. Something has finished in him. He turns and starts at her presence.

"Sorry," she says, moving toward him.

He steps in. "I didn't know where you were," he says.

They approach each other but stop short, not touching for a moment as she tries to read him and he tries to collect himself. She looks him carefully in the eyes, his green eyes, which she resolved to do night before last in the bed, in the dark, drawn into a long-set-aside memory. How deep their color seemed to her when they first met, but they are paler to her now, green but not Monet green at all. Were they ever? Have they diminished over the years, gradually, she simply never noticing? Were they never what she thought? Or is this grief she sees in them?

She steps into her husband, putting her arms around him, turning her face and laying her head against his shoulder, telling the ladies beneath the oak to hush.

He pulls her gently close.

The two of them say nothing till they pull apart just as gently.

She looks again into his eyes. They are saturated but unblinking, refusing to express a tear.

"What's happened?" she asks, instead of asking more directly, *Has he died?*

Robert's eyes stay fixed on hers but his head twitches ever so slightly to the right. She takes this as: *Happened? He broke his hip is what happened.* What he's really thought does not, of course, occur to Darla: *Happened? How do you know? Has he said these things about me to you?*

She tries to clarify. "I thought perhaps he took a turn for the worse."

"He's bad enough."

"I understand," she says, feeling clumsy, caught in the implication that Robert's sadness could be caused only by his father having died. She assumed that mere suffering would simply bring out the abrasive worst in William Quinlan, a worst that would primarily irritate Robert. "He must be in a lot of pain," she says.

Robert simply shrugs.

Something has *happened*, she decides. *Just not death.* Now she assumes it's something William has said. But other than expressions of quotidian grumpiness or reflex jingoism—none of which, surely, would affect Robert like this—she cannot imagine what.

Robert turns away, wishing to sit down. Only once, many years ago, did he voice his delusion to Darla. He submitted to

159

her his father's pride in his Vietnam service to help explain how he ended up a soldier in the war that this beautiful and righteously impassioned woman despised. And he submitted it along with a manifestly mature clearheadedness about his need for his father's approval, which allowed the delusion to be unquestioningly shared by them both.

His first impulse is to sit in his reading chair. It's angled away from everything in the room except the French doors. It faces the oak, which is on his mind. He has never said a word to Darla about killing the man in the dark. He has never said a word to anyone. He is weary and he wants his chair for the privacy of his present thoughts. But he does not want to snub his wife. So he moves to the sofa, which also faces the veranda, and he sits there at one end.

Darla has watched him make this choice. She senses he's made it to acknowledge her presence. But he does so without looking her way, without saying a word, and he has placed his back to her. So she circles the sofa but stops at the far end. "Would you prefer some privacy?" she asks.

He looks at her. "No," he says. "Sorry. I just needed to rest."

She sits too. Not next to him but not quite apart.

They say nothing.

Darla will not press him for words.

Robert's mind is full of them: *It would be better if I'd fully earned his scorn in the way he pictured me. If I'd stayed behind the walls of MACV that night and never killed. Or simply killed from there in an indeterminate way, as I may have done sometime during the next few days, spraying rifle fire with others into trees and building facades and down the street, aiming at muzzle flash. It would even be better if I'd not gotten lucky that first night: not found my way to the gates of MACV; not arrived in the middle of a battle lull with the right cries and somebody to hear them so I could make a dash to the gate; not dodged, at the last moments, some surprised enemy fire. Better if I'd simply died that first night trying to get back. Would my father, to his surprise, have perceived some sort of courage in a dead body in the street with a pistol in its hand? Would he? Of course he wouldn't. Of course not. He would have known my actions for what they were: headlong flight into cover, more proof of my instinctive cowardice. But at least I never would have heard about it. Fuck you, Pops. Fuck you.*

And in the lull from a heartfelt fuck-you, Robert becomes aware of his wife next to him. He turns his face to her.

Gazing beyond the veranda as a pair of mated cardinals spanks across the yard, Darla senses Robert at once and looks at him.

And the lull in him ceases. He looks away from her, but she has replaced his father in his head. *It wasn't until we'd had sex, until we were quiet at last and slick with sweat, that I explained my work in Vietnam, my work so like research, my work so unlike that of a man who was ready to kill for his country. But when she'd finally asked how it was for me there, my carefully arranged job was all I spoke of. All she wished to know. She was relieved. I was no killer but I was no coward. I was perfect for her. She was glad I was alive. What would she have thought if I'd gone on to tell her about my man in the dark? If I'd told her how I killed a man when he might have been anyone? How he frightened me, so I shot the man down.*

Decades later she would bitterly criticize two high-profile Florida cases of men acquitted of murder for standing their ground. Back then, at the beginning for us, in her antiwar passion, would she have gotten up at once and gone to the bathroom and closed the door and washed me off her body forever? Or because she was already falling in love with me would she have been glad I hadn't taken the risk?

Something in Robert fillips a perverse little impulse into his mind: *Tell her. Tell her now. Tell her you killed this man. But tell her as if this were your old man sitting here next to you. Give it to her with the spin he might actually respect, a spin I fervently wish were true: I was alone on what constituted a battlefield in Vietnam. So I did what men do on a battlefield. I may have gone to Vietnam to minimize my risks, but when the real war came to me, I stood in the dark alone and raised a steady hand and I killed and I'm content with that.*

The impulse lingers in Robert for a few beats. If in response she flares at him, if she throws aside her supportive concern for him, even as his father is dying, and vociferates the politics of pragmatic pacifism, if she declares her deep disappointment in him and vanishes into her office for the night, then Robert would know: By the same tale his father might soften; his father might approve; his father might reconsider.

And all of this suddenly sounds crazy to him. Crazy that he still gives a goddamn about his father's regard. Crazy that he'd even fantasize about saying something that risks his wife's love. Crazy that his obsession over the first man he killed—with such mitigating circumstances—should have renewed itself all these decades later. Crazy to think that the twenty-three-year-old

in 1968 has anything whatsoever to do with the man he is in
2015. And this last thought instantly seems crazy to him the
other way round as well, that the twenty-three-year-old should
have anything but a deep connection to the seventy-year-old.
He is a historian, after all.

This facile chaos of thoughts beclouds a simpler truth he
has ignored for decades: He could never have won the respect—
never have won the love—of both his wife and his father. He
always had to choose.

He lifts his arm, presses his wrist hard against his forehead.

Darla watches. She edges closer to Robert and arrives at
the wrong conclusion about the gesture: He is moved by his
father's suffering.

Robert is wrong about her, as well. If he were to say what
he thought to say a few moments ago, even spun for his father's
approval, he would not have risked her love. Would not even
have done so in 1968. She did not ask for the details of his
military service—though she knew she must eventually—until
she could sleep with him at least once.

She wanted him strong-handed and even rough and she
wanted to feel in the midst of it that this man might have been
a killer. Wanted him that way but it was okay because it was
by her desire, by her initiation, by her permission that he was
fucking her. She was in control of the pounding of him inside
her. It was she clutching him tight and it was she crying out for
more and for harder and so it was okay, she was the boss. And
she could assume he'd been a killer, but that was in another
country, and here and now, in this bed in America, she had

the power to reform him. She had the power to forgive him, a man who killed and maybe killed some more and killed and killed. Dangerous as he was, he needed her. He needed her to bring him back even from that.

Not that all this was conscious in her. It resided in her breathlessness, it was in her hands that took his and closed the bedroom door and drew him to the bed and stripped his clothes from him and allowed him to strip the clothes from her, and it was in her hands that ran over the stubble of his whitewalled hair, that grabbed him down there, grabbed the part of him that may even have known Vietnamese women like this, that hurt these women and left them, women she could forgive him for, women she could forgive.

None of this was in her conscious mind. Not then, not since. But the first time they made love it was certainly present in her hands and her breath and in the tremors of her and the grinding in her and in the rushing and release in her and in her sweat afterward and in the lull.

On that night, after she and Robert had sex, when she was led to ask him what he'd actually done in Vietnam, when she heard how his job had been like research, how he was in a safe place counting and assessing men and weapons, how it was so very unlike combat, after she heard these things and then showered and dressed and came back to him and sat beside him on the bed and hooked her arm in his, after all that, she lied to him. And to herself. She said, "I'm so glad."

Not entirely a lie. Her rational mind was glad. If she was to be with this man forever, as she already felt she might, and if she believed in the righteous cause of her generation, it was better that he had not taken part in the fundamental act that makes war evil. Her mind was content with that. Even grateful.

But she had expected the answer to be different. In her body, something was let down, something had lessened. Her body feared—her body knew—that even though her love for him would grow, having sex with this man would never again be as good.

His wrist falls from his forehead.

He looks away, out through the French doors.

Darla says, "Is he giving up?"

"I don't think so." Robert turns to her.

"How's your mother?"

"Wallowing in it."

Darla holds her tongue. About both of Robert's parents.

"I spoke with Jimmy," he says.

Darla gapes. "What?"

"My mother found his number."

"You actually talked with him?"

"I did."

"Wow."

"She loves her melodrama."

"But you called him."

"I did."

"For her?"

"*He* made the break permanent. Not me."

She grunts softly in assent. "And he actually talked with you?"

"Talked. Some. It ended as you might expect."

"He has his father in him. I can't see him ever forgiving."

Robert snags on this, though not about Jimmy. He masks it from Darla by turning his face away toward the veranda. He stays silent.

"You don't think so?" she says.

He still doesn't speak.

"I know it's ironic," she says.

"But true," he says. "He'll never forgive me for going to Vietnam."

"And your father will always love you for it," Darla says, overexplaining the irony to reassure him.

Robert rises abruptly, crosses to the French doors.

"You don't need Jimmy's forgiveness," Darla says, thinking she's read his gesture.

Robert turns back to her.

She cannot see his face with the afternoon sun in the trees behind him.

He braces himself to let go of his father. It's easier to start with his brother, so he answers her, "I know that. I don't even miss him, is the truth of it," thinking, *Nor will I miss Pops.* Pops: The word belies his assertion. *I won't,* he insists. But the man won't let him go. Maybe when he's dead. Surely when he's dead it'll all be over.

And Robert has another impulse. No. Not an impulse. More considered than that. When his father is dead, what is unfinished will not die with him, it will simply stay unfinished. Robert thinks: *Tell him. Whatever the outcome. Go to him.*

Tomorrow. Tell him about the man in the dark. And tell him the truth. Tell him you can't get over it.

~

Jimmy despises napping in the daytime. It is, for him, a lying down to a small death. But after Linda has made her announcement and made her suggestion and they have fallen silent, and after she has risen and bent to him and tried to kiss him lightly on lips that he will not lift to her, and after she has, instead, pecked him on the forehead and gone out of the break room and stopped at Jimmy's worktable and put on her quilted coat and knit cap, and after she has closed the barn door behind her and, no doubt, gotten into her car and driven away to either Paul or Becca, Jimmy finds his eyes bloated with the wish to close. He lifts his feet and turns and stretches out on the sofa. Expecting sleep, he sees before him a vast expanse of meadowed snow, the tree line etched thinly at the far horizon, the sun low behind it, setting there he realizes, and he turns and turns and it is the same in all directions: He is alone; he is utterly alone. So he turns and turns and when he is once again facing the setting sun he can see something, far off, tiny still but recognizable as three figures against the snow. At first he is lifted by the sight of them, but then he knows who they are and he cannot imagine how they have come to be here, in this landscape of snow, in his Canada, but here they are, his mother and his father and his brother, and they're coming this way. He thrashes. He sits up.

Mavis's face is before him, her brow furrowed, her gray gaze gone sad.

She waits in silence as he squeezes his eyes shut briefly, clamps his two temples between thumb and fingers, waits for the wooziness of daytime sleep to fade. Finally he lifts his face again, looks at her.

"Are you okay?" she asks.

"Just the effects of the nap."

"I mean otherwise," she says.

Her manner with him over the past weeks, particularly when Linda was the seemingly routine subject between them, finally clarifies itself. "You knew," he says.

She looks at him for a few beats, filling in the unspoken words between them. "Only guessed," she says.

"This won't affect any of you," he says.

"I'm not worried about that."

"I'm all right," he says.

She nods, minutely, as if she's doubtful.

"It's an understanding," he says.

"I don't mean to intrude," she says.

"Thanks."

They stare quietly at each other for a moment.

Then he asks, "How was the stew?"

She flickers a smile. "I brought you some."

"Good," he says. "I'll have enough for two nights."

She puts her hand on his shoulder, squeezes it gently, and she goes.

He rises.

He crosses to the coffeepot, pours a cup, drinks. It's no longer fresh. At the pay phone in Buffalo in July of 1968, after the click of disconnection from his father, Jimmy hung up the receiver, turned his back on the phone, and he looked at his watch. He didn't need to know the time to know it was time to go. In the break room Jimmy does not consciously remember that gesture, but it and the reflex that animated it, that propelled him to the life he's lived all the years since, is the same now: He looks at his watch. It is five minutes to one. He can be on Baldwin Street in three hours. Before the shop closes and Heather goes home. It is time to go.

Less than three hours later, Jimmy steps into his shop, the entry door's retro brass bells jangling above him, the smell of mellowed-down leather filling him, two things that always give him a surge of pleasure, this space he has created, these things he has made. And the long drive has done him good. He quickly ceased thinking about Linda and instead revisited all of Heather's knowing looks and admiring words, compressing them into an underlying narrative that reassures him he's not about to make a fool of himself.

The shop is empty, including the checkout counter. He moves along the center aisle with a sudden and acute sense of Heather: In a place empty where he expected her to be, he misses her.

Then she appears in the doorway to the back room.

She's wearing her sales-floor outfit, a jacket off the rack—today a lambskin bomber—over a black crewneck T-shirt. Black on black makes her dark eyes even darker, her skin even whiter. She brightens. His narrative falls apart. He will make a fool of himself.

She comes to him.

She stops just beyond reach. A bad sign.

"I didn't expect you," she says.

All he has is small talk. "Things seem slow, eh?" he says.

"Winter Wednesdays. I let Greta go home. She's working up a cold."

"Good," he says. He hears the ambiguity. He quickly adds, "That you let her go."

She smiles at the correction. Then she softens the smile at the edges and lifts her chin. An inquiry. A prompt.

Such things were part of the Highway 400 narrative.

She is saying but she is not saying.

An insistent part of him wants simply to thank her vaguely and claim that he only dropped in to see how things are and he's meeting somebody down the street and has to leave.

So he tries to drag himself in the other direction by the improbable strategy of nodding at her chest. He means to indicate the bomber jacket. He says, "You're modeling today."

"I sold its mate this morning. The lady took one look and said, 'I want what you're wearing.'"

"On a Winter Wednesday to boot." He knows he sounds lame.

But, generously, she laughs.

Overloaded with prompts, Jimmy is mystified why this should be so difficult for him. He's never been awkward approaching a woman. And he offers himself an explanation: *It's too important, is why. This is different.*

"You look beautiful," he says.

Heather soughs, as if she's been holding her breath. She gathers herself and says softly, "Thank you."

And he finds himself needing to explain. To her. To himself. "You've admired how my spirit seems free," he says.

He has more words but the effort of just these makes him pause.

She fills the pause, again softly: "Yes."

"Free by ideology," he says. "Free by protocol. Free by . . ." He searches for a word now. ". . . devaluing it," he says. "*Thus.* Thus it's devalued, the freedom."

He stops. Tries to clear his head.

"I'm having trouble," he says. "Putting it into words."

"Do you have to?" she says.

Another invitation. He won't ignore it, but he trusts it will stay valid for a few more moments. "I have to," he says. "I think I understand. I was free because what my wife and I decided we were free to have wasn't worth all that much."

He finds that Heather has moved closer to him.

They are in each other's arms.

And in the room above his shop Jimmy lies on his side, the fern frost on the window jaundiced by street-light, Heather spooned into him, her arm draped around his chest. He closes his eyes, discerns the soft touch of her nipples just beneath his shoulder blades.

He and Heather are quilted over, the room still cold. He'll have her call someone to look at the furnace.

It seems to have been such a long long while since he had that thought yesterday. The flex of time.

And he thinks of dark matter, dark energy. How astrophysicists now understand that all visible matter—from the galaxies to our bodies to the strands of our DNA—makes up only a tiny percentage of the mass of the universe. How all of the rest of the matter and energy—unobservable, unrecordable, the dark 95 percent—somehow resides in the spaces formerly thought to be empty. How quantum physicists are beginning to theorize the existence of parallel worlds to explain the bizarre mechanics of matter in its smallest particles. How, as well, it's known that our bodies are made up of atoms, electrons orbiting nuclei, with empty space in between, that our bodies themselves are mostly empty space. And so if dark matter and dark energy exist in the empty space between the stars, why should they not exist inside our very bodies? Are we not ourselves mostly dark matter and dark energy? And what if that's where those parallel worlds reside?

Linda was wrong. Being with Heather won't stop me thinking about what's next. Linda was stupidly wrong: It's not worry. For millennia we've all been thinking there's a place for us other than the one we're in, this savage place where we fight each other, consume each other. This place we must escape. From the sun to the moon to the earth, from Heather's nipples to my shoulder blades, from her atoms to mine. In all the empty space within and between, there is consciousness, there is existence. Impervious to war and betrayal and hardness of heart. It's the place we all will run to.

"Are you awake?" Heather whispers.

"I am," Jimmy says.

"What are you thinking?"

Only in his wish to answer her does he realize: "How it was I came to Canada."

Heather tightens her arm around his chest. "I can't hold you close enough," she says.

~

The next morning Heather and Jimmy rise late, her daughter having spent the night with the grandmother, who is accustomed to sending the girl off to school. They have to rush to get ready to open the shop on time, tussling for first use of the bathroom basin, pausing to laugh at feeling like a couple already. Robert and Darla rise in their usual manner, having gone to sleep in their usual manner, Robert distracted, this time by his intention to speak to his father, and Darla sublimating with Bach. She is to go for her run and drive to the hospital on her own in the late morning. Robert will head up earlier, though after Darla has left the house he lingers for another bean-grinding and brewing and a second slow sipping of Ethiopian coffee, in his reading chair facing his oak. Peggy sleeps late in her one-bedroom assisted-living apartment at Longleaf Village, exhausted by her husband's pain, sorry the twin bed next to her is empty, dreading when it will not be. Bob is up early from his bunk bed at the Mercy Mild Shelter. He's happy that North Florida is behaving in the way it often suddenly can, throwing off the cold, warming the morning. He makes his way to the woods near Munson Slough, where he will spend a couple of hours dry-firing his Glock, getting back his trigger control.

And a physical therapist at Archbold Memorial named Tammy, a former softball star at the University of Georgia, uncovers William with encouraging chatter about how tough he looks and how he's going to muscle through this little episode. She unwraps his compression leggings and she straps a thick cloth belt around him, and she starts to get him up, get him vertical, get him on his feet with her help, just for a little bit, to prime his body to heal, to engage him in staying alive, to get him used to the cost. This is her specialty. She is a champ at this.

William is grumpy but compliant. He might think this is a good time in history to die, given what the world has come to, but he's too pissed about it to succumb. So he is vertical now. And he feels something begin in the middle of the calf of his right leg. A pulling loose. Like an adhesive bandage that's been on for too long being stripped off, beginning there in his calf and running now upward, behind his knee, and then curving to the inside of his thigh. It's a good feeling. A letting go. But the rushing changes, as if the bandage finishes breaking away and something emerges from beneath it, a goddamn night crawler burrowing its way past his broken hip and up his spine, and William thinks, *What the hell is that doing inside me?* but it moves too fast for a worm way too fast and the blood clot hits his heart and the engine seizes *in Papa's Ford Runabout pickup, which is as old as me, and maybe this is when it finally dies, on this dirt road along Bayou Bernard and Papa has stripped off his shirt and has the hood up and he's cussing like Mama won't stand for, and now we're sitting beside the bayou letting the Ford cool off and Papa cool off, and I'm a little behind him and sneaking peeks as usual at the slash of a scar below his left shoulder blade, and I been warned by Mama since I was toddling not to ask him, since the scar was from the Big War and full of bad memories, but today I do ask and he turns on me and his hands come up but he doesn't hit me, he just gets quiet and he gets sad and he takes me by the shirt and pushes me over backward, but not hard not to hurt me just to tell me to shut up, and he's weeping like a baby with me at the train station and I'm in my uniform and there's another Big War, and as I put my duffel over my shoulder it hits me like a rifle shot in the brain what it is that he's been carrying around all this time, the fact that his battle scar is in his back, it's in his goddamn back, he turned his back, and so I turn my back on him, I turn my own goddamn back and I run away from this man and I'm going up the stairs in a house in Mainz, and it's just mop-up, we haven't yet found a living soul on this whole block, it's only us Patton boys tidying up with the Third Army that's about to cross the Rhine, and I'm checking the second floor, just for procedure's sake, and I'm at the top of the stairs and there's a doorway to my left and I step into it and across the room the window is bright behind him and he's sitting tall there and I can't see his face, I can't read his face for the shadow but his Schmeisser is crosswise in his lap and his hands are down but I don't check where they are I just know they're down but I don't check if his shooting hand is near the grip and it's all fast and my M1 is up and I'm squeezing and squeezing and the Kraut's chest blows open and he flies back and he's dead, and then I notice some little thing, no I don't, not then, I just see it but I don't really notice it, not then while I'm rushing inside over killing the enemy, rushing sweetly at that moment, sweetly like happens in a war, and it's only years later, when my sons are about ten, about the age I was myself in the dying Ford, and it's hot summer in the Ninth Ward and the afternoon thunderstorm has just passed and my boys take off their shoes to run barefoot in the wet grass, it's then that I really notice the German soldier's boots, which are sitting there beside him, the two boots straightened up side by side and his socks draped over them, his feet hurt, this guy, his feet hurt and he took off his shoes and socks so whatever is going to happen to him on this day at least his feet won't hurt him so bad, and I turn away from my sons so there's no chance they'll glance back at me and see my eyes filling with tears, and not a week goes by for the rest of my years that I don't think about that man and I squeeze the trigger and I squeeze and there is no rushing in me, no fucking sweet thing, my own chest cracks open and my heart seizes, and I come up the stairs and I step into the doorway and I see him sitting there and I notice his boots, and I take my hand off the trigger, I don't squeeze the trigger, and the light behind him gets brighter but the shadow on his face fades away, and we look each other in the eyes, and it's just two fellas in a sunny room*

And William Quinlan is dead.

~

When the phone rings in the foyer, Robert is still sitting in his reading chair, his coffee mug empty for a while now. He's not actively dreading his father. He's not wavering in his intention to tell him. He's just inert. Intending to overcome that. The dread driven deep. The wavering converted to dozy distraction: wondering if this lot of coffee beans is depleted yet at the roaster; watching the flash of cardinals beyond the veranda; thinking the room too warm and suspecting the weather has changed overnight. It takes a second ring of the phone to make him rise, and still there is no urgency in him, no sense of dread. Just the phone ringing.

Doctor Tyler himself. Very sorry. A saddle embolism is not uncommon in spite of doing everything possible. Death certificate signed. In the hospital mortuary awaiting instructions. Have you done this before? Do you have a funeral home?

"No," Robert is finally saying, "I'll have to see about one."

"Not a problem. Call here and tell us when you decide. The home will take care of everything from this point on."

"All right," Robert says.

"I'm very sorry," Doctor Tyler says.

"Yes," Robert says. "Thank you."

"He didn't suffer."

"That's good."

And the conversation is over.

Robert puts the phone down.

He finds himself inert again.

He does not miss his father.

But something got misplaced.

177

He looks around him. "Darla?" he calls.

No answer. Again, louder: "Darla?"

Nothing. She's not back. She sometimes gets inspired and runs a long time. He understands that. She has to go up to the hospital afterward and she wants to run thoroughly first.

No.

She won't have to go to the hospital.

There's a beeping. Distant. But nearby.

He looks. It's the cordless phone. He's forgotten to push the off button. He picks up the phone. He pushes the button. He puts it down.

He drifts back into the living room, looks at the French doors, moves to them, opens them, steps into a morning that feels almost warm.

He looks to the live oak standing massively before and above him. He walks to it, turns his back to it, and sits heavily down in the crotch of two roots. He presses against his tree even as his limbs feel their tone fading. They waver, and he wills his legs to stretch flat and he lets his arms fall to his sides.

The oak's trunk is rough, touching him hard in the back in long, uprunning ridges. He is glad for its hardness against him and he is glad to smell the sudden Florida warmth in the air. He is glad he is in his own country now and did not die. But he aches. He aches for the dead. For one man he did not know at all. For one man he knows too well.

He sits like this until he hears Darla calling for him from inside the house.

"Out here." He does not move.

She appears in the open French door, sweating in her running clothes, a towel around her neck. "What is it?" she says.

"He's dead," Robert says.

She steps to the edge of the veranda, but pauses.

She doesn't want to force him to stand by coming too near the tree. He seems propped there as if after a beating in a ring. "Are you okay?"

He rouses himself, flails a little with his arms, drags at his legs.

She presents a palm. "You don't have to . . ."

"I'm fine," he says, making it to his feet.

She steps closer, ready to hold him but not initiating it, regretting her sweat.

He's not ready for the ritual of this. He holds still, looks down to the space between them.

The phone rings, a small sound from the foyer but it lifts Robert's eyes to hers.

He knows who it is, and from his look, she knows.

Darla says, "Would you like me to talk with her?"

He considers this.

The phone rings again.

"Thanks," he says. "But I better."

He moves past her.

She remains.

Not just in the small of her back, the touch of his hand; not just in her chest, the press of his; but in her conscious memory now, his arms come around her in the darkness of their bedroom with both her parents laid out in a hospital morgue a thousand miles away, and he pulls her close. She should have done that for him just now, instantly, as he did it for her, not pausing in the doorway or on the veranda. But he surprised her, the tableau of him and the tree. She did not expect him to be stricken by the death of such a difficult man, a man who would no longer be able to disappoint him. She'd needed a few moments to get over her surprise. Then the phone intervened.

Darla needs to be close to him now.

She turns, steps through the French doors, crosses the living room toward his voice in the foyer: "Of course, Mom . . . Of course . . . Try to be calm till I'm with you . . . Say a prayer. Say a rosary."

Darla hears these last few words trying to stick in his throat. She stops before she becomes visible in the living room doorway.

"Soon," he says. "Yes."

He listens. He says, "Of course. Very safe."

Moments after this she hears the phone clack into its cradle. She steps into the foyer and he turns to her. She comes to him and puts her arms around him.

He draws her close, but only briefly, and he gently pulls away. "I have to go up there now."

"I'll follow as soon as I can," she says.

An hour later Robert is sitting on his mother's sofa, his arm around her, her head on his shoulder as she weeps. Across the room the leg rest of his father's overstuffed brown velvet recliner remains raised from the last time he sat there, barely more than forty-eight hours ago. Whenever Peggy's tears swell into sobs, Robert murmurs *I know, I know* until they ebb. She has not reminisced or eulogized or criticized but has simply wept, which makes her grief seem to him unadulterated and keeps his arm around her, gentles his grip on her shoulder, makes him long for his mother to show this part of her more often. He wonders if Darla's arrival, the expansion of the audience, will put her back onstage.

He tightens his hold on her as if to prevent that.

As he does, Robert grows conscious again of the leg rest on the recliner. Whenever the old man figured he was returning soon, he kept it raised and worked his way out of the chair at an angle. He'd hobble then. He never spoke of them, but surely those knees hurt him. Most likely arthritis. They hurt him to push against the leg rest to lower it, though they probably hurt him as much climbing from the chair so awkwardly. But he'd gotten it into his head that this was the best way to do it, so by damn he'd do it this way forever. The last time he sat here he struggled to extend one leg off the chair and to drag his butt on the cushion till he could get the other leg over and then to drag some more to put both his feet flat on the floor and then he braced himself and he rose. He'd done this thousands of times and he thought he'd be right back. He was wrong. He'd be dead before he could do it again.

Robert finds his eyes filling with tears.

He does not feel as if they're for the man himself exactly. Maybe some. Maybe for the father Robert wished he'd been. But these tears seem mostly about knowing this small, commonplace thing. How his father got out of a chair. True to his character. Stubbornly. Hurting himself trying not to hurt himself. Someone Robert comprehends in this small but telling way has vanished from the world: That's what these incipient tears are about. And he raises his free arm, drags his wrist across his eyes, refuses to shed them.

He feels his mother's face turn upward toward his.

She will get this all wrong.

That pisses him off.

He abruptly drops his arm. He does not look at her. He says nothing.

He feels her face turn downward again.

Good.

Peggy Quinlan gently disengages her son's arm from around her, raises the handkerchief she's been fisting, and dabs at her eyes, wipes her nose.

She tucks the handkerchief into a pocket of her sweater.

Robert is still not looking at her. Not looking at the chair either. His eyes have drifted to a Currier and Ives print of a sleigh in the foreground of a snowy countryside, its pair of horses in a synchronized trot, the sleigh holding a mother and father and two children. This print has hung on his parents' living room walls through his whole lifetime. Robert long ago stopped even seeing it. He sees it now. And he remembers that as a child he took the two children, bundled similarly, to be brothers. They are not. One is a girl.

"He loved you," she says.

Damn.

Robert regards her. He wishes he could offer the reflex reassurance that has been so easy for the past half hour. Just one *I know* and she might refrain from making the case for William's love. In the absence of any overt avowals from the man, Robert made his own faulty case for that over the years. Those tears in the bar, for instance. And none of it carries weight anymore. Not after yesterday. He tells himself: *After yesterday I can't lie about this even to say those two words.*

But he considers the alternative.

She is brimming with bullshit reassurances.

"I know," he says.

And he thinks: *Fuck me. I'm your son. So there's the lie we can agree to between us, so we can just go on.*

She lays her head on his shoulder again.

She does not resume crying. Robert feels her working up to more words, though this intervening silence makes him hopeful they won't be intended proofs of his father's love for him.

But before she speaks there's a knock at the door.

She rises and moves off.

Robert flexes the ache out of his mother-hugging arm, rolls the kink out of his shoulder. As his mother and his wife linger just inside the door to embrace and murmur, Robert rises from the sofa and steps to his father's recliner. He looks for a moment at the man's indent in the backrest and seat cushion. Then he lifts his foot and pushes the leg rest down till it snaps into place.

He cannot imagine how they will all get through the next several hours. But Darla squeezes Robert at the elbow and sits with Peggy on the sofa for a time, and soon enough things grow as much practical as mournful, seeing as William waits in the basement of Archbold. He needs a funeral home to carry him away and this leads to Peggy's entreaty that they bury him in Tallahassee so that when she joins him they will both be nearer to Robert and Darla. This leads them to a choice of a funeral home and a cemetery and then to details of a wake and a service and then to a locating of Peggy's desk copy of the will and of papers for insurance and Social Security and, in the process, the finding of a box of family photographs and the consequent reminiscences and criticisms cast as endearments and Peggy weeps some more and grows weary from weeping. Darla tucks her in for a late-afternoon nap while Robert wanders into the living room, weary himself. He stares at his father's recliner and sees no reason why he shouldn't sit there and put his feet up, but he finds no capacity to do so. And then Darla is beside him.

"Why don't you go on home," she says softly.

She puts her head against his shoulder. The same spot that has been occupied for a long while already on this day.

She says, "I suspect this is harder on you than you realize."

He puts his arm around her, squeezes her gently, and lets go.

"I'll work on her papers," she says.

"Thanks," he says.

"We need to make some calls."

"Yes."

"Shall I do them?"

"No. I'm fine."

"Let's divide up the close ones," she says.

Robert nods.

Darla suggests she call their daughter and Robert their son.

He speaks what suddenly strikes him: "We're getting to this late."

"We needed some arrangements first so they could make plans." Again she speaks softly.

She's being patient with him.

Robert takes Darla in his arms, kisses her on the top of the head.

She turns her head, lays it on his chest, and exhales deeply.

She says, "In his own way, I'm sure he loved you."

He makes himself wait for a few moments before ending the embrace so she won't suspect anything is suddenly amiss. He thinks of something to say: "I really appreciate what you're doing here." And he goes out of the apartment and fumbles with the key in the door lock of his Mercedes.

On the Florida-Georgia Parkway he places a call to his son in Atlanta. Kevin's voice sounds cheery on the answering machine. Robert simply asks him to call back. He hangs up. He turns his headlights on in the thickening twilight. He decides to stop at the New Leaf Co-op for a quick dinner.

~

Bob sits at an outside table in front of the New Leaf, watching the sky darken. He won't let it sneak up on him this time, the dark. If it wants to come he will wait for it and he will own it. He is strong enough. Till a woman's voice. Rushing by Bob, a woman talking rapidly on a cellphone, a fluttering jabber beating outward like something you're planning to shoot, flushed from a plum thicket. Then she stops at the curb, invisible to him behind a support column on the arcade over the front of the co-op. She talks, she laughs, unseen. Laughs. Sapping him. Through a thin wall a woman's talk, a woman's laughter. Bob is fifteen. He is naked. Against this sound, from the past and from the present, he crosses his two arms before him at the wrists, pounds his chest once and again, hard, but the woman yammers on into her cellphone and Bob knows he can't just get up and step out beside her on the curb to deal with her, he has to let her be and take care of it in his own head, and so he sings, he grabs a few words from the first song that comes to him and he sings them over and over—*There's something happening here*—at first only inside his head but then they find their way into his mouth and into the chill of the dark, looping over and over *There's something happening here* and the voice of the woman at the curb before the New Leaf abruptly moves off and fades away. The words slide back into Bob's head. He listens outward while they play, and he realizes they can stop and he stops them.

All around, the darkness has taken over but he didn't let it catch him off guard. He should go inside now. He has some coins. But he finds he cannot move. Somebody has turned the flame up inside the knot on his forehead. The pain has his full conscious attention, but inside him, coming upon him while he's distracted, like the night overtaking the day, he is still fifteen but he's not yet naked, it's earlier in the evening and he's staring at the flicker of the TV screen in the living room, and beyond the kitchen, at the far end of the single-wide, from behind the closed door of his parents' bedroom, their two voices are grappling fiercely and then they stop and all that's left is his mother weeping and now his father emerges and slams the door and Bob steels himself, waits for it all to turn against him. But his father stops in the kitchen, and beyond the thin wall his mother weeps on and Bob wants to go to her and try to help her stop, but his father is between him and the bedroom and so he stays where he is, keeping his eyes on the TV screen, seeing nothing. The refrigerator door opens and closes. A bottle cap hisses off and falls. And another.

And now Calvin looms over Bob. Bob keeps his eyes where they are. He braces himself. But the man simply stands there. Waiting. Bob looks up. *Here*, his father says. He's holding two Blue Labels and he extends one of them to him. His father's in that middle ground he sometimes can get into when he's buzzing with beer and not hard stuff. His mother's weeping has faded. Bob takes the beer, and as quick as that, he knows *this* is what he wants. His father sitting down in his chair nearby and the two of them drinking a beer together. It's happened a couple of times before, and this is what Bob wants.

And when their beers are done, his father rises and says, *It's time for you, boy.* Bob does not ask what that means. They go out of their trailer and the night has come on. It's July, a few days after the Fourth, which Calvin celebrated in places unknown. Then they're in his pickup running south on 119, and after a long while he actually talks. *It's still Independence Day for you, boy. You're with me and I can draw the day on out. Fourth of July is my Christmas and Thanksgiving and fucking Arbor Day all in one, 'cause of what I went through for this country. We still got some fireworks to shoot off, you and me. I went through shit for this country and you know what it was all for? Five days. Five fucking days by the seaside. The US Army can blow your mind. They put you in a jungle to kill and be killed and then by God they pluck you right out of there for five days and nights and they put you in a pretty little city right there in-country, right on the South China Sea, and it's like Jesus himself went down into Hell with His winnowing fork and nicked you out of there and put you in Heaven where you belong and you're walking down a street and it's not paved with gold, it's better than that, it's paved with pussy, in bars and in massage parlors, and this pussy isn't mama-san pussy, it's the real pretty ones, even though the day before, if you see girls like this in a village you're clearing, you can't trust to turn your back on them much less drop your pants. The day before, you might have to blow their pretty asses away. But now you go right on in for a massage and more, and you just fuck your brains out, you fuck your fears out, you fuck your goddamn blood-and-gore memories out, and you're doing it with the enemy—that's the thing—you're doing it with the prettiest little Co Cong in the whole shithole country.*

And Calvin Weber stops talking. He just drives. And what he does not say to his son, though it is the feeling he has just come to, unexpectedly, what he could not even shape into words in his own head is this: It has never been the same since. Not sex. Not intimacy of any kind. With a woman. With a buddy later, the two of you drinking and trying to laugh off the experience, trying to crude it down but failing and falling silent and sitting in that silence in a bar in Vung Tau, Vietnam, knowing the same thing, that being with a woman, being with a buddy, being with anyone, will never be as good as that again. And the price isn't worth it. Not for what you have to go through. Not for what you're left with.

But for Bob the next thing is his father whooping softly and pulling off the highway toward a crimson neon sign through the trees: **MASSAGE**. Calvin says, *See what we got now, right here in West Virginia? You'll finally be a man tonight, Private Weber.* Then Bob is with a woman and he's naked. And his father is in the next room. Even as Bob finds himself naked with a naked woman and finds himself ready for her, he can hear his father's voice through the thin wall. He can hear his father talking big and laughing big and he can hear the woman in there laughing with him. And Bob knows what's about to happen to himself will not be good. Knows nothing will ever be good.

And a figure is emerging from the dark in front of the New Leaf a tall and rangy figure and it's almost upon him and Bob knows all too well who it is and he might as well get this over with and his hand starts to move, though his reflexes aren't so quick anymore, his hand is moving toward the right-side pocket of his overcoat, moving too slow but moving for goddamn sure and he knows once it's there at least he's got his trigger control back, he can end this thing between him and the old man once and for all, but a voice comes from the figure *Hello Bob* and Bob knows the voice and he can make out the figure now and he recognizes this man and Bob's hand wants to keep on going anyway, wants to pay somebody back for something, but it comes to him that this isn't the right place or the right time or the right man, and he stops his hand, and it's the other Bob standing over him now, and Bob answers him: "Hello, Bob."

~

As Robert approaches the New Leaf in the early dark he does not immediately recognize the shapeless hulk sitting at a table near the door. Robert's old man is too much with him, though his overt thoughts have taken refuge in the trivial: how chilled he feels though the air is mild; how fragile his eyes have been this past year or so, with the lights inside the co-op seeming far brighter than they likely are. But as the hulk becomes a man and clarifies its face, Robert's recognition of him instantly evokes a recollection of Bob's parting question three days ago: *You know my old man?*

Perhaps this should make Robert keep on walking. Perhaps he should avoid Bob this time. But only his mind engages this option. His body veers at once toward the man of hard times, the man a decade too young for Vietnam, the man of responsibilities in Charleston, the man whose father can come sharply and unbidden to his mind. Robert stops before him and says, "Hello, Bob."

"Hello, Bob," the man says.

Bob's bandaged forehead fully registers now on Robert. "Are you all right?" he asks.

Bob pulls back tight at the chest, as if the question is out of line.

"Your head," Robert says.

Bob loosens, humphs. "My head. My head got assaulted by a mystery man with a shovel."

"Damn. How'd it happen?"

"Not worth saying."

"You got help?"

"With my head. Not with the son of a bitch."

"You need anything for it?" Robert figures to buy him something for the pain.

"Revenge would be good," Bob says.

He sounds serious. Robert hesitates, recognizing the need for caution in replying to this, though nothing comes to mind. He's saved by his cellphone ringing.

"Sorry," he says to Bob, pulling the phone from his pocket and lofting it in explanation of his apology. He turns, paces a few feet away in the direction of the parking lot.

The cellphone screen says: Kevin Quinlan.

As often happens with grandfathers, William was warmer with his grandson than he'd ever been with his sons. As Robert is well aware. Kevin and the old man were close. Robert should have planned this out. How to say it.

The phone rings again. He answers. "Kevin?"

"Dad. What's the news?"

How even to begin? Here at the end of this difficult day, it eludes Robert for a moment that Darla already talked to the kids, right after the accident. "Your grandfather fell," he says.

"Mom said. We've been Googling broken hips."

It's going on three weeks since Kevin last spoke with Robert, normally a weekly Sunday tradition. His son has been busy with work, no doubt. Which is very good. As a boy more a Lego kid than a book kid, as a man Kevin saved his small architectural firm in the recession by guiding it into associated general contracting. Robert longs simply to ask him about that, about how his work is going, about how busy he must be. Robert knows he can't. And for what he *must* say, he's far from having *any* words, much less the right ones.

"Looks serious," Kevin says.

"Yes."

"Did the surgery go okay?"

"The surgery itself went fine." Robert hesitates.

"Itself?"

Restless with his clumsiness, Robert rolls his shoulders, turns around. "He's dead."

Robert is now facing Bob but is unaware of him. Bob is quite aware of Robert. This abrupt announcement has rung clearly in the dark. Someone is dead.

Kevin is silent for a moment. And a moment more.

Robert turns around again, faces the parking lot. "I'm sorry. Sorry for your loss. Sorry for just blurting it."

"No," Kevin says. "It's okay. I know this must be hitting you hard. Harder than me. Your Pops."

Now Robert goes silent.

"What happened?" Kevin asks.

"A blood clot, as I understand it. First time they stood him up, it went straight from his leg to his heart."

"Jesus."

More silence. Robert grows restless again, paces the edge of the sidewalk in front of the New Leaf.

Kevin says, "How's Grandma?"

"Being Grandma."

"Holding up then."

"Holding up."

Robert hears sounds on Kevin's end of the phone: a door slam; sharp voices, recognizably his grandson and daughter-in-law.

"Excuse me," Kevin says to Robert, and then, muffled, "Jake. I'm talking. It's important."

Jacob lately turned twenty. And yes, as grandfathers can be, Robert is unreservedly warm with him, though in this case he has nothing to make up for, as he has always been warm with his son as well. For most of Jake's life, however, the warmth has flowed mostly from a distance. For those years, Kevin and his family have lived a long day's drive away, which in practical terms has meant Sunday phone calls and four visits a year, diminishing in the past decade to two.

Kevin returns to Robert. "Sorry," he says.

"Jake is home?" After two years at a community college, he's been away on a construction job.

"Temporarily," Kevin says in a voice fraught with something it isn't ready to get into.

In the following beat of silence Robert stops pacing.

He prefers to talk now about his grandson.

But Kevin says, "When's the visitation?"

Robert's restlessness returns, propels him in the direction of Bob. "Monday evening. The funeral's Tuesday."

"Where?"

"Tallahassee."

"I've got a crucial meeting Monday morning. We may have to come straight to see him."

"Tillotson Funeral Home on Apalachee," Robert says.

Bob hears this too.

Robert becomes vaguely aware he's within earshot. He stops, turns away again as he adds, "Anytime after six. There'll be food. Your grandmother wants it to feel like a real wake."

"Granddad won't like that," Kevin says, though Robert hears no irony in his voice, only sadness.

"No he won't."

"I won't be telling funny anecdotes about him," Kevin says.

"He'll appreciate that." Robert hears his son puff at this, no doubt ready to weep. He thinks Kevin will want to do that privately; he'll want to keep the tears from his voice. So

Robert says, "Sorry to be abrupt but I have to go now. I love you. See you Monday." And he ends the call.

Robert puffs too.

He stares sightlessly into the parking lot for a few moments, puts the phone in his pocket, remembers Bob, and turns back toward the man, half expecting him to be gone.

But Bob is there.

Robert approaches again, stops before him.

Bob raises his face. "Someone's dead?" he says.

"My father," Robert says.

Bob feels a rising in his brain like the first rise of gorge, a dizzying bloat, but he forces it down. Far down, without even identifying it.

"Have you eaten?" Robert asks.

"Not for a while. Not tonight."

"I haven't either. Shall we?"

Sometimes when Bob's next meal is certain; sometimes when an Upstander acts natural around him, like this one is acting, with nothing even vaguely resembling *that look* going on in his face; sometimes when Bob has just struggled for a while with the way his life has gone and the poison that recently wanted to rise has been pushed back down; sometimes when any of these things happen but especially when they all happen at more or less the same time, Bob can find himself suddenly thinking straight like he used to and having acceptable words to speak and making a pretty good impression on somebody. This is one of those times.

Bob says, "It's my turn to pick up the tab. But I'm afraid that'll make for slim pickings tonight."

Robert is surprised at Bob's banter, but Robert's consequent smile contains no incredulity, no irony, no patronage. For Bob, his banter has carried a risk: Making an unexpected good impression on an Upstander can also provoke a version of *that look*. But the other Bob shows no trace of it, only a smile like he'd give anybody, and Bob is grateful for that.

"I've got it covered," Robert says.

As Bob rises from his chair, something occurs to Robert. When the man is standing, Robert extends his hand. "We never got past 'Bob.' I'm Bob Quinlan."

"I'm Bob Weber."

They shake on this.

So the two Bobs find their way to a corner table inside the New Leaf, well away from the handful of other diners, and they sit with beans and rice before both of them.

"I'm glad you made me think of this," Robert says, nodding at his plate, though he chose it out of sympathetic deference to Bob's teeth. "I used to love beans and rice."

Bob has never loved it. "When was that?" he asks.

"You'd think it'd be growing up in New Orleans. But my mother was more potatoes than beans. It was in the army. Basic training."

He's army. Bob's straight thinking suffers a little blip. This man before him has already blurred, now and then, into Calvin.

Robert says, "Of course in basic, you can fall in love with a tepid shower and dry socks and sharing a cigarette, though you don't even like to smoke."

Bob is working hard now to keep straight. He's got a little litany for this from some counselor or other. *This is this; this isn't that. This is now; this isn't then. It seems the same but it's different.* Okay.

He thinks he has a grasp on things and he can move on. But he hears himself lingering. "So you were in the army?"

Robert nods. "Fort Polk, Louisiana."

Bob looks hard into Robert's face. This is not his old man. This is another guy. He's not even an Upstander but an actual stand-up guy. They're eating food together. They're talking straight. Bob can ask this thing. "Did you go to war?"

Robert falters, briefly, but long enough for his voice to thicken and sadden and soften from the past twenty-four hours. "I went to Vietnam," Robert says.

And Bob, who still fears dark hints about unspeakable secrets, instead has just heard a tone in this voice he never expected, hears this other Bob clearly going: *Let's not make a big thing of it.* And going: *There may be guys who get fierce over this but it sure ain't me.* And going: *I'm just fucking sad about the whole fucking thing.*

Bob is fucking sad too. And Bob feels his mind straighten. He says, "Your father died?"

The man hesitates again. Bob clutches up. Maybe he shouldn't have asked. And though he expected his own father

197

to show up a few moments ago over Vietnam, it's now that Calvin steps into the room and strides this way. He stops just behind Bob's shoulder, and Bob is afraid this sad man before him will suddenly see Calvin and he'll go holy shit and he'll bolt. But instead the man says, "He died this morning."

Now it's Bob who goes holy shit. He thinks: *So what are you doing having beans and rice tonight with the likes of me?* But he asks, "How?"

"A blood clot to the heart. He was in the hospital."

Calvin vanishes. *Fucking poof.* "I don't trust hospitals," Bob says.

"That's probably smart."

For a time now, they eat their food in silence. Robert feels odd. Finally he has spoken of his service today, though spoken to a stranger, to a man of hard times, to a man who could not have known Vietnam directly. Though Robert has spoken of small things. But small things bind men at war as well, bind them just as certainly as they are bound by spilled blood. The man he has spoken to: Did he serve in another war perhaps? Unlikely. By the look of him, he was of the wrong generation for Afghanistan or for either Iraq, unless he was a lifer. Robert almost asks, but he doesn't.

The two men go on eating. And Robert goes on wondering about Bob. The way Bob's father came upon him a few days ago, Robert figures his neglected responsibilities in Charleston might have to do with his old man.

Robert works at his basic-training food for a few bites, trying to put all this aside. But he knows Bob is a man of suffering, of wrong choices, of lost chances. Also a man with limited options. Robert is keenly aware that no one's options to redeem a lost chance are more limited than his own. He does not quite think of it this way, he simply follows the impulse, but the effect is the same: To deal with your own problem, meddle with somebody else's.

Sensing, however, that the meddling needs tact, Robert begins, "So you're from Charleston?"

"Yes."

"Been gone a long time?"

"Years."

"Any folks back there?"

That is a sore point for Bob right now. A sore point anytime. He shrugs.

"Your father still alive?" Robert asks.

Okay. Okay. This other Bob's own father died just this morning. Bob is still thinking straight enough to see that. But he wants to stay straight and the question is starting to drag him aside. He realizes time is passing. He realizes he's not saying anything. He touches his forehead, where the sizzle has resumed.

Robert finds himself ready to buy Bob a bus ticket. Send him back to Charleston to find his father. Advise him to use the bus trip to figure out everything he's got to say to the old man before it's too late. Even if it's *Fuck you*.

But Bob's still not talking. He's flailing in his head for things to think about other than what the other Bob and his dead father would have him think, and the oil drum fire in his forehead gives him something: Maybe on the next cold night he'll take a little walk to check out the groundskeeper's storage room at the Blood of the Lamb Full Gospel Church. Check to see who might have returned to the scene of the crime.

Robert senses the shift in Bob. He senses his mistake. Pressing about a father is wrong. The bus ticket is wrong. But the impulse to fund Bob suggests another plan. A way to actually help. "Have you got a place to sleep tonight, Bob?" he asks.

Bob's reflexes on matters of food and shelter are strong. This question, in that tone of voice, from a stand-up guy, casts off, for the moment, both Calvin and revenge. "No I don't, Bob," he says.

"Can you make good use of a week in a motel?"

The answer to that, for Bob, can be a little complicated. But on balance, yes. "Yes," he says.

Instantly a practical problem presents itself to Robert. He hesitates, recognizes a likely expert sitting before him, but doesn't know how to ask. "Do you have a place in mind . . ." He gets this far and realizes he could have just made that the question. Unfortunately his tone kept the thing open-ended.

Bob understands. He finishes, declaratively: ". . . that will take a guy like me." Before the other Bob can feel awkward for asking, Bob goes on, "Sure. You know the Prince Murat Motel?"

Through this day, from his awakening to the revelation of his father's death to the hours with his mother to this unexpected dinner, Robert, unawares, has been winding tight inside. Now it all seems to snap loose and he nearly gasps with relief as his safely scholarly mind seizes on something familiar. "I do," he says, leaning toward Bob. "It's my favorite business establishment in Tallahassee. Prince Achille Murat was a nephew of Napoleon Bonaparte and the son of the King of Naples. He was exiled with his family to Vienna after Napoleon's final defeat, and then he emigrated to Florida. By the age of twenty-four he was the mayor of Tallahassee. He was a Jacksonian Democrat, though he never really made much of a political career outside the area. He became a bosom pal of the young Ralph Waldo Emerson, who called Tallahassee in 1826 a 'grotesque place,' by the way. But Murat eventually was known mostly for his eccentricities."

The first of these that comes to Robert's mind is Murat's reputation for washing his feet only after he wore out his shoes. Robert leaves this unspoken. He's beginning to hear himself.

Bob has no idea what Robert is talking about. Bob has even begun to wonder if Robert has troubles like his own.

After a moment of silence between them, Robert says, as if to explain his little lecture, "I do know the Murat."

Still silence.

"I teach history."

"They'll let me in there," Bob says.

"Then it's the Murat," Robert says, and he says no more. What seemed to loosen in him is again wrung taut.

~

After Robert leaves his wife and mother on the day his father died, as the January late afternoon wanes into darkness and Darla works in the next room sorting through papers and arranging the wake, Peggy finds herself unable to sleep. She turns her face to the ribbon of parking lot light edging her window blind. She closes her eyes. And she is standing very still, trying not to sweat, not to swoon from all the cheap perfume—like hers—on all the bodies of all the girls as they wait—like her—along the platform of the inbound track, wait for the troop train, wait for the long wait to be over. Their men will return to them on this day. Bill will return. The rest of Peggy's life will begin. She is wearing her daisy-print sundress. Her arms are bare, and her hair falls to her shoulders in long curls and mounts high above her forehead in a pompadour. Little Bobby is elsewhere. He is up and running already, at thirteen months, always running, and talking as well, babbling an hour at a time to a framed photo of his father, he and the image sitting together in the center of the living room floor, the glass perpetually smudged with Bobby's fingerprints. He was conceived on Peggy and Bill's wedding night, which was also their last night together. Bill has never seen his son. But he won't see him on this night either. The boy is at Mama's and Papa's, where the four of them have lived these two years. And Uncle Joe is happy to go on a bender for a few days with his buddies at the Industrial Canal so Peggy and Bill can have some time alone in Joe's shotgun on Constance Street. So they can make love for the second time.

Peggy opens her eyes. She has turned and is facing her husband's empty bed, barely visible in the dim room, as if this is the memory and the train platform is her life in the moment.

She closes her eyes again. Briefly she watches the splash of phosphenes there, the color of street-light. Then there is only bright New Orleans sunlight beyond the shade of the railroad shed. And now cries at the far end of the platform. Someone sees the train. The bodies around her begin to move, to surge. She holds still. He will find her. She has always known he will return and he will find her.

And she says to her nineteen-year-old self: *Oh, baby, don't get your hopes up. He's been off fighting a holy war against the legions of evil, an evil so pitiless that it would have one day crossed the ocean and come to our own front porch. He has seen things and done things that required a bravery beyond your imagining. You have been faithful to him. You have trusted in the noble cause he fought for and you must make him feel how proud you are. You must try to hold him close. But don't be surprised at the things you both have sacrificed. This night will be one of them. And the next. And the next. Try not to be disappointed in him.*

~

Later this same evening, Jimmy turns off Harrison Trail and into his Twelve Mile Bay property. He has returned to pack his bags. He will stay in Toronto till the future is arranged with

Linda. Heather is beside him. She becomes abruptly quiet as they enter the half-mile approach to the house. In the city, when he told her he needed to come up here for his things and it was best to do it right away, she did not speak of the reason but she insisted on coming along. She stirs now, leans toward the lights they push before them.

"She won't be here," Jimmy says, offering a hand.

He has read her correctly. She grasps his, holds on tight.

They emerge from the pines. The house is lit by the moon. There are no lights within. No car in the driveway. Heather lets go of his hand.

Barely through the front door, she brings the two of them to a stop.

"Sorry," she says.

"Why?"

"Cold feet."

"No need . . ."

"I know the place is yours too," she says. "But it feels like *her*."

"Then you should wait. I have to go upstairs."

She looks at him.

Outside it's January in Canada.

Jimmy nods to the nearby door. "The parlor. You won't find much of her there."

Heather steps before him, squares him at the shoulders, pulls him to her. They kiss.

"Soon," he says.

And soon he descends the stairs with two large leather Pullmans. By the time he reaches the bottom, Heather appears in the parlor doorway. She has not turned on the light.

She steps from the room as Jimmy approaches. He puts the suitcases on the floor.

"What?" she says.

"I just want to kiss you once more. The last thing I do in this house tonight."

Before they can move, the phone rings.

They both look toward the parlor door, then back to each other.

"Do you think it's her?" Heather says.

"No."

"I want that kiss," she says.

The phone rings again.

Jimmy starts to explain that it has an answering machine. That to do the kiss they will have to listen to whoever it is. But he does not have time even to shape the words. Apparently there is another message already on the machine because it kicks in now, after the second ring.

And a woman's voice begins to speak in the parlor. "Hello, darling."

Even before Heather can flinch, the voice says. "It's your mother."

Peggy pauses.

"Come on," Jimmy says.

And Peggy says, "Your father died this morning."

She pauses again.

Jimmy picks up his suitcases.

Heather touches him on the arm. "Wait, baby." He explained his family to Heather last night, in the long rush of shared backstories between them.

Peggy says, "I know your feelings about him."

She hesitates once more.

"At least listen," Heather says.

"I don't blame you," Peggy says. "I'm free to say that now. I don't blame you at all. For anything. You had to deal with his feelings about you."

Jimmy sets the bags down.

"They weren't *my* feelings. You have always been my son, who I love. You always will be. But I was married to your father, who I loved. I was his wife."

Peggy begins to weep.

Her tears are for the man she loved, for his vanishing from this earth and from her life, for that loss. They are also in release—they are even in relief—at his vanishing from her life, for that loss. They are in guilt for that relief. The tears are also for the love of him, for the thrill that faded but never vanished at his unexpected smile and at the trailing of his fingertips along her neck whenever he passed unexpectedly behind her, though she always feigned a leap of ticklish discomfort, knowing that was necessary to induce him to continue the gesture through the years. The tears are for that necessity too. And the tears are from the belief that there is a next life as the Holy Catholic Church describes it and that he won't do so well in that regard.

They are also for herself, for having to lie and manipulate to maintain the coherence and happiness of the family; for having to do these venial sins on so many occasions that she has consequently neglected to sufficiently acknowledge them, much less reconcile them, in the sacrament of confession; that she will not do so well herself, therefore, in the next life. The tears are for the possibility that in the place where those sins must be dealt with, she will find herself once again wed to William Quinlan, and the struggle will resume in much the same way. And the tears are for Jimmy as well. So he can understand that things have changed. That he can come home. That he has always been her son, whom she loves. Because she does truly love him. Which is to say, in part, that her happiness is not fully possible without his being happy, though she cannot rest assured he is happy unless it is in a way she herself can recognize. And manage. So as she weeps, she does not hang up. She does not take the phone away from her mouth. And she takes care to weep loudly enough that the phone message will not cut off.

Heather is moved by her tears. "Can't you speak to her?" she says.

"No," Jimmy says. Though he recognizes how drastically things have changed in the past thirty-six hours. How in this chosen country of his, a vast and leveling snow has fallen over his convictions about family, about connectedness. He awoke to that yesterday. He dreamt of it and he woke to it. Convictions constructed and refined again over five decades have been overwhelmed as if overnight. And a new conviction, seemingly as strong, has bloomed over the same night: his love for this woman before him who was not even born when he exiled himself from the United States. He has either been something of a self-delusional fool through most of his life or he has suddenly become a fool of an old man; or both; or neither.

Heather says, "So many of her generation were loyal wives before everything else."

Jimmy thinks: *So many of mine accept instant love. With no exclusions, age included.*

He wants to hold Heather close.

Peggy's tears are snubbing to a stop.

Jimmy opens his arms and Heather falls into them.

Peggy says, "I'm sorry. I'm so sorry. This is a difficult time. But if some good can come of this. If I could see you. Wouldn't it be a closure for you as well? For us all."

She pauses.

"Whatever you decide, my darling," Heather says.

Jimmy does not move.

"Just in case," Peggy says. "Tillotson's Funeral Home in Tallahassee. The wake begins at six Monday evening. The funeral's at ten on Tuesday morning. Please think about it."

She pauses one last time.

Jimmy waits for more drama from his mother. More tears. Effusive avowals of love, in spite of her sticking by the man who rejected Jimmy to his dying day. But instead she says, "Let's put him in the ground, my son. Together. We both need that."

And she hangs up.

~

Peggy has made her phone call to Jimmy from the kitchen, with Darla sitting at the dining table beneath the pass-through. She'd emerged from the bedroom a few minutes before, after sleeping for several hours.

"I'm glad you could rest," Darla said.

"I feel clearer about things," Peggy said.

"I ordered Chinese while you were sleeping. Plenty of it. Can I warm some for you?"

"No, honey. I'm fine."

"Tea?"

"I have a call to make before anything," Peggy said. The second phone was in the bedroom from which she'd just emerged, but she moved past Darla and into the kitchen.

Darla handled the papers in front of her but did not see a thing. Naturally she listened. Till Peggy suggested to her long-lost son that they put William in the ground together and hung up.

Darla sets the papers down. No faking. She waits.

A cabinet door opens. Pots clatter. The door closes. Water runs. A pot lands on a metal stove burner. "I've changed my mind about tea," Peggy says. "You want some?"

"Thanks," Darla says. "Yes."

A few minutes later Peggy emerges with a tea service on a tray and she leads Darla to the couch, putting the tray before them on the coffee table.

In this quotidian matter they are equally imprinted by the old school of female propriety, so they hold both saucer and cup to eliminate the unseemly stretch to the coffee table. They sip and sip again in silence.

Darla has never felt particularly close to Peggy. She has witnessed the woman's poses and dramas—experienced them, indeed, as lies and manipulations—for as long as they've known each other. But Peggy's words to Jimmy and her clear intention for Darla to overhear them and now simply her silence over tea somehow don't feel like manipulations. This feels like a different Peggy.

So Darla puts her cup and saucer on the coffee table, and she says, "Why did you let me hear that conversation?"

As the woman's face turns to her, Darla still expects the old Peggy. A look of faux surprise perhaps. *Did I? I'm so stricken I wasn't even thinking.*

Instead, Peggy offers Darla a quick but restrained smile. "I wanted to share my clarity with you," she says.

Darla's surprise is genuine. She masks it, and says nothing.

Peggy stretches to the coffee table, puts down her own cup and saucer, and sits back. She lays her hands side by side on her lap, as if this revelation was expected and what follows has been thought out.

She says, "I hope I didn't sound harsh. I loved Bill. I'm going to cry over him again and again in the coming weeks. Please don't doubt the sincerity of those tears. But Jimmy needed to hear this other part of it."

"I understand," Darla says.

"Men have their ways," Peggy says. "How they communicate with each other. How they bond. My husband and yours, for instance. Their father-and-son bond was so strong. But after all, they both went to war. Is this why men make wars, do you suppose? To share something like that? Is it the only way they can truly feel close to each other?"

Peggy pauses, as if she wants Darla's opinion on this. Darla sees her Confederate men sitting around the barbershop through a long, hot summer afternoon, getting drunk on Old Forester and war stories, as their women sit in a parlor, sipping blueberry shrub and writing their impassioned prose.

But before Darla can say *Yes, you may be right*, Peggy says, "Jimmy never had that. As a man, he had to know instinctively what he was giving up when he went to Canada. That may have been the hardest thing about what he did. I feel free now to fully respect him. For his courage to walk away from what sons usually want."

This all strikes Darla as sincere. She covers one of Peggy's hands with her own.

Peggy looks Darla in the eyes, holds the gaze quietly. Then she says, "I feel like I've always been held back from you as well. You're my daughter. Truly you are."

Even as the woman invokes a newly liberated self, a frank and direct self, Darla hears this as the old Peggy, hears a lie crafted to serve a false image of the family. A newly revised, freshly reconstructed image, sans patriarch. But then she thinks *No*. Peggy's eyes do not waver in the following silence. The woman may well feel this way about her. But to Darla, Peggy has never felt like a mother. Not even close. And now Peggy's unwavering eyes themselves—the very sincerity of them, if sincere they be—seem like a mode of manipulation. These eyes expect Darla to proclaim a corresponding daughterly feeling about her. Even if it's a lie.

Darla does find this to say about her daughterhood: "I intend to be a good one." Not that this isn't also more or less a lie, knowing, as she does, Peggy's standards for a good daughter.

Peggy turns her hand to Darla's, palm to palm, meshes their fingers. She chuckles. A willed chuckle, brittle with rue. And she says, "Why did God choose to surround me with men all my life? Gracious me. I would have been such a good mother to a daughter." She lets that sit between them for a moment. Then she gently squeezes their entwined hands and says, "I feel ever so close to you, my dear."

Darla has exerted her own will to keep from imagining a lifetime as Peggy's actual daughter. And she doesn't believe this climactic declaration for a moment. But she accepts it with her own little squeeze.

Peggy doesn't need belief, doesn't even try to assess that. Acceptance of her assertion is all she seeks. But she does hear the plunk of one more venial sin dropping into her bucket. *Ah well*, she thinks. *It can't be helped.*

~

When Darla finds Robert, he is sitting in his office, in his desk chair, before his computer showing an Apple icon doing an endless Pong bounce. After calling for him from the foyer and hearing his answer from up here, she has approached quietly. His door was open. Before he knows she's there, she stands for a long moment, feeling tender about the back of his head, his overcast-gray hair going shaggy at the collar.

Finally, she says, "Hey."

He looks over his shoulder, turns a little in his swivel chair. "Hey. How is she?"

Darla crosses to him.

He stays seated.

"She's doing remarkably well," she says.

"Good."

She nods at the screen saver. "You've been like this for a while."

He turns back to the bounce of the bitten apple, as if to confirm what she's said. "It's been a long day."

He stares for a few more moments.

"I'm so sorry," she says.

She lays her hand on his shoulder.

"Thanks," he says.

He doesn't move.

"Better to sleep in bed," she says. "With your eyes closed."

He rises.

They say little else until they are beside each other beneath the covers.

No Kindle.

No iPod.

Darla's lingering tenderness for Robert stops the grating in her, leads her quickly to the cusp of sleep. As her longing drifts into vagueness on its way to unconsciousness, it offers a final, spoken "If there's anything I can do" even as she sees her own dead father's face pause over his lifted soup spoon, his vast and shaggy brows rising, and he says, *You will grow old simply canvassing for Democrats and bloviating at dinner parties, doing far less for the world than the manufacture of a fine sausage,* and she remains mute before him, mute but eloquent on the red fields of sausage, a woman fair and faithful, and Robert, his head shaved into whitewalls, takes her in his arms for the first time and there are so many things she does not know about him, so many things she need not know in order to love him.

"You've already done it," Robert says, in answer to her sleepy-voiced offer. "Thank you." And he turns onto his side, away from his wife, falling toward sleep himself, and the homeless man sits across the table and he asks, *Did you go to war,* and Robert answers, *I went to Vietnam,* and the man says, *Show me your scars,* and Robert raises his hand to his forehead and he finds a bandage there and he works his fingertips under its edge and he rips it away.

~

The handouts bite Bob on the ass. That and the Murat being closed for refurbishing into a Budgetel. The other Vietnam vet had to put him in The Sojourner, near the bus station, a sizable step down from the Murat, it being the only other place that would take him. Which might've been okay, for the sake of warmth and a sure bed, except for the handouts. Only yesterday Bob acquired new blood-of-the-lamb clothes from skin outward and a full-gospel shower and even a coating of goddamn talcum powder, so after he walks into this room and hangs up his Goodwill coat and sweater on the clothes rack and places his Glock on the nightstand and stacks the pillows for his head and takes off his shoes and lies down beside the pistol and looks up at the ceiling, Bob discovers that the shower and the clothes and the talcum have separated him from his own stink sufficiently so he can smell the stink of the motel—the musty smell of roaches and air conditioner mold in the air, and a couple decades of cigarette smoke and spilled food and spilled spunk and women smells in the carpet and drapes and bedspreads—and all this puts him in another motel room and he's sixteen years old and he's traveling with his father because his mother has had enough, which she's had a couple of times already, and she's gone off to Wheeling to see her sister for an indefinite period and Calvin has decided he and Private Weber need to get out of town, need to go hunting up in the mountains, and on the way they find this cheap motel room, but it's got one beat-up luxury, a television, and Calvin makes the mistake of turning it on. A big mistake, because it's April 30, 1975. The picture flickers and flips into focus just in time for Harry Reasoner to say, *The Viet Cong flag is flying over the Presidential Palace in Saigon today just a few hours after the South Vietnamese government announced its unconditional surrender.* And Calvin jumps up from where he's sitting on the foot of the bed and he says, just once, real low: *Motherfuck.* After that he's just pacing and glancing at the screen and not making a sound, which backs Bob up against the headboard and tucks him tight and scares the shit out of him more than if his old man was raging full-voiced, because once more it's all about the things he's not saying, the things he knows that men have to face down, and Bob understands that it's got to do with killing and being killed and your buddies being killed, of course, but it's not that simple and maybe what makes it complicated *can't* be said, *has* to stay a secret, so it's forever a black hole you carry in the center of you, swallowing everything, not just the killing and the being killed but the living on, swallowing your whole fucking life as well, it's about voices and laughter through a wall when you damn well know there's nothing to laugh about and there are no words to say, and so the old man is pacing back and forth saying nothing while on the TV Americans in civvies and Vietnamese with their women and children are crowding into buses and then running to helicopters and then a door gunner on a chopper is looking down on the roofs of Saigon and then it's roofs along a beach and then it's the sea and a voice on the TV is saying, *The helicopter passed over small fleets of boats leaving the coastal city of Vung Tau* and Calvin stops pacing abruptly at this and whirls to the screen and then he backs away from it and now he's across the room and he's got his Winchester 70 and he squares around to the TV and it's nighttime on the screen and a tall man in a suit and sunglasses with his hair flying shakes hands with admirals in ball caps and the voice is saying it's Ambassador Graham Martin stepping from a Marine helicopter onto the deck of the command ship *Blue Ridge* and he's closing the final chapter on America in Vietnam and Calvin works the bolt on his Winchester, chambering a round, and the voice from the TV says, *When this correspondent asked what his feelings were, Martin would only say that he was hungry,* and Calvin whips the rifle up on his shoulder and Bob turns his face away and the room explodes. And how long does he go on after that, the old man? A little over two years. Quieter than ever, even when drunk. So quiet that Bob's mother, who's come back, seems almost happy. So quiet that Bob feels it's okay to slip out one night and hit the road and end up in Texas for day labor and landscaping and restaurant work, okay to be a West Virginia wetback. And one night the old man himself slips out. He heads into the pines behind the trailer park and chambers a round in his Winchester and sticks the muzzle in his mouth and blows off the back of his head and all his secrets with it.

~

Framed tastefully in brick and Portland pilasters, Tillotson Funeral Home's floodlit marquee beacons into the evening dark:

William Quinlan
Husband, Father, Veteran
Visitation 6 to 9 PM

Two hundred feet away, up the landscaped parking lot, Tillotson's wide, double-winged, hip-roofed Georgian house is similarly lit. In the front foyer a grandfather clock begins to strike six.

As it does: In the visitation extension behind the main house, Peggy is alone at last. She stands before the buffet table, the caterers for casseroles and cold cuts just departed through the rear porte cochere, and her church-lady friends busy cleaning up out of sight in the Tillotson kitchen. They have chatteringly helped her with the Irish stew and the Irish potato soup, which steam now in their own special row of food warmers. Peggy thanks Mary the Holy Mother of God for this moment of quiet. Robert and Darla turn in at the marquee. Darla thinks of those very women—Peggy and her friends from church—and that very row of food warmers, with Peggy putting on her *birth-name-is-Pegeen* persona to make Irish food; and she thinks how much Peggy wanted her to be part of that project, the two of them bonding in the Quinlan family's reconfiguration, with the church ladies as witness; and Darla thinks how she should probably feel guilty at having declined Peggy's invitation but how, in fact, she does not. Not in the least. Robert focuses his thoughts on the Georgian house itself, built in 1922 by Horace Naylor in the Great Florida Land Boom, lost by Horace Naylor in 1926 in the Great Florida Land Bust, restored for the benefit of the dead and their kin by Howard Tillotson in 1934, and repeatedly expanded and modernized by two generations of Tillotsons to follow. Robert is, of course, a historian. And he happens to live in the middle of a city that sits in the middle of many of his interests. But even as he sees the personal excesses of the house's speculator builder in the half dozen two-story Corinthian front columns, Robert recognizes that his mind is simply trying to avoid his father's face as it waits for him in an open casket inside. A mile away, heading east on Apalachee Parkway, Jimmy is driving a rented Impala to the funeral home from a room in the downtown DoubleTree. Heather is beside him. Just before stepping out of their hotel room, Jimmy stopped Heather and suggested they simply close the door, have an ironic night of sex and HBO, and then go back to Canada; and Heather reminded Jimmy of the conclusion they'd struggled to together in Toronto, that he's seeking closure not renewal and if things go badly they can escape at any time. Jimmy knows that conclusion was grossly oversimplified, but he can't begin to say what the full truth is, except that even though it brought him here, it is now urging him to turn around and go home. They have been silent in the car. Heather lays her hand on Jimmy's thigh. He puts his hand on top of hers. And they pass Bob, a dark and bundled figure striding along the sidewalk, also heading east, silhouetted against the neon of a liquor store. Sometime in the deep predawn dark of this morning Tallahassee turned cold, and it's been cold all day long, and it is cold tonight, and Bob has a score to settle. So he pushes his aching knees and he accepts the radiating pain from knee to back to mouth, his remaining teeth throbbing with each step. He accepts this pain on the way to the Blood of the Lamb Full Gospel Church, accepts it because he wants to be waiting in the groundskeeper's storage room when the nameless faceless coward returns. Bob has something more effective than a garden tool for him. Bob touches just below and to the side of his heart, touches his coat where, inside, his Glock waits.

Robert and Darla step between the center columns, past Cracker Barrel rockers deployed along the portico right and left, through the front doors, and into the hushed, condoling greeting of two black-suited Tillotsons tanned like winter corpses. One of them breaks off and leads Robert and Darla across the welcome foyer, past a spiral staircase, through a doorway, and into the visitation room foyer. Here they cross a dense Oriental rug toward an open double-wide doorway as **William Quinlan** floats brightly, unsettlingly out of the dark at Jimmy, who averts his eyes. He steadies himself in the empty lane ahead of him and then glances up the long, dim expanse of parking lot to the funeral home. There seem to be very few cars. He does not pull in but accelerates past.

"We're too early," he says. "I don't want to be the center of attention."

"That'll be hard to avoid," Heather says.

"Not in a crowd."

"So we'll take a little drive," she says.

They rush on along the parkway as the accompanying Tillotson discreetly falls away and Robert and Darla step through the doors of the visitation room. They stop. Robert scans the place. It's large and could be made larger. To the right, an accordion wall creates a doorway into a somewhat smaller, separated space, where trays of cold cuts and sides wait on a table whose other end, out of sight from Robert's angle of vision, holds the Irish food before the tranquil-at-last gaze of Pegeen Quinlan. Informal settings of chairs and divans are arrayed all about, most of them facing to the left, where Robert has so far declined to look, though Darla's head is already turned that way. The chairs and divans are empty but for two elderly women in hats on a chesterfield in the center of the floor. But it's barely six o'clock. Kevin and his family are still on the way from the airport. Robert's daughter Kimberly is arguing a case before the Connecticut supreme court in the morning. Peggy is nowhere visible, probably overseeing the food. That's it for the immediate family, who are the only ones, by the protocol, you'd really expect to be here at the opening bell.

Robert needs to get this out of the way before all the others begin to arrive. He turns toward the left-hand wall, where Corinthian half columns flank the casket and ceiling spotlights shine softly down on its contents in what the Tillotsons no doubt have in mind as the gaze from Heaven. The contents at six o'clock, however, are presently blocked from view by the backs of two old men in dark suits. Not Quinlans. Not likely to be Tillotsons. Still. So be it. Get it over with.

Robert touches Darla on the arm. "Give me a minute," he says.

"Of course," she says.

He moves off in the direction of the casket, and as he approaches, the two men begin to turn. He realizes who they must be. These veteran faces are different in detail from the beignet boys, but they are the same in wizened ethos. These are Bill's coffee buddies from the Thomasville chapter of the Greatest Generation.

"You must be his son," one of them says.

Robert takes the man's offered hand and says, "Yes, Robert," thinking, *He didn't say "One of his sons." Of course not. Jimmy never existed.*

But it surprises him that his father acknowledged *his* existence to these men, given the recent revelation.

He has missed hearing the name of the first veteran and finds himself shaking the hand of the second as the man finishes the last couple of syllables of his. ". . . field."

The first vet says, "Harley and me served on the Western Front the same time your dad did."

"We all had coffee and Dunkin' Donuts pretty near every week," Harley says.

"In Thomasville?"

"Yep. He loved his Glazed and his Original Joe."

"He was very proud of you," the first man says.

This flips Robert's face sharply back to him.

Confident he understands the look in Robert's eyes, the man says: "Not that he said much about your experience. He respected your silence."

And the second vet says, "But the little he did say . . . Well, we all understand the tough job and the short life span of infantry lieutenants in Vietnam." He gives Robert a knowing nod and offers his hand for another shake. "Thank you for your service."

Robert does not take the hand. If the refusal hurts the man's feelings, it's his donut buddy's lying fucking fault. *That wasn't the service I rendered. I was a cowardly specialist fourth class hiding in a bunker counting beans.*

But the man thinks he understands Robert's hesitation. He straightens up, withdraws the offered shake, and turns it into a salute, holding a strack pose. "Sergeant Harlan Summerfield offers his gratitude, sir."

Shit. Shit. Robert can't keep up the rebuff. It's not this man's fault. But neither can he explain. So Robert returns the goddamn salute, forced to buy into the lie of his humiliated father, whose body Robert is suddenly, acutely aware of. It's presently reduced to a chest-to-crotch view by the frame of intervening vets, laid out in his one wearable but outdated suit, a dark gray pinstripe with padded shoulders and wide lapels, his hands crossed over his bowels.

The two men pick up on the shift of Robert's attention.

"We'll leave you with him now," the first one says.

"Just wanted to pay our respects," the second one says.

Robert is clenching in the chest as if he were about to step out of a banyan tree in the dark.

"Good to meet you," one or the other of them says.

And the two men step aside and vanish.

Robert moves forward into an aura of dry cleaner perc and mortuary pancake, and he stands alone now in front of his dead father.

Beneath the veneer of a Tillotson tan, William Quinlan's dumb Sunday-doze face is fixed for eternity, the face that always seemed to Robert, in its own parsimonious way, to allow that nothing was terribly wrong between the two of them. The face that said, without actually saying it: *Even though I don't offer any details, you're sufficiently okay by me that I can simply sleep in your presence in this apparently unperturbed way.*

The old man sleeps that way now. Couched in that lie. But even if he were suddenly to wake, brought back for just a few climactic moments, and if he were to look Robert in the eyes and say to him, *I know what you really want to do, so okay, go ahead, punch me in the face if you got the balls, take your best shot,* Robert would not be able to lift an arm or make a fist, would not even be able to lift a lip into a sneer. All he has is a handful of words: *Go back to sleep, Pops.* Robert feels weary. Deeply weary. Simply weary. He feels seventy fucking years old. *Go back to sleep.*

A hand on his shoulder and he starts.

He's done with the casket anyway.

He turns.

It's his mother.

She opens her arms.

He is as little inclined to accept this gesture as he was Sergeant Summerfield's salute. But he is even less capable of brushing it aside. He puts his arms around her, telling himself, *This embrace isn't about my feelings for him. It's about her. It's just for her. That's her dead husband in the casket and she loved him, in her own way. In her own way she loved him very much, so I can hold her and kiss her now on the cheek.* Which he does, and he says, "I'm so sorry, Mom."

"I know," she says.

She kisses his cheek in return. Then she brings her mouth very near his ear and whispers, "Who are those people?"

Robert whispers in return, "A couple of his World War Two buddies."

"Really," she says, with a thump of a tone, meaning *How come he never mentioned them to me?*

She lets Robert gently disengage the embrace.

"They're casual coffee buddies," he says.

Darla has drawn near.

Robert sees her over Peggy's shoulder, turns his face to her.

Darla, however, is focused on her mother-in-law. The back of Peggy's head; her ashen hair rolled plain and tight; her arms falling from the embrace of her son into a slump of her narrow shoulders; her usual wiry vigorousness transformed abruptly into a bony dwindling, like a twentysomething cat. And she thinks of all the recent mother-daughter words. All the grief words. And the riddance words. And the Irish food prep. These things suddenly signify for Darla. Signify in a way that can, in a century-old monument, elicit her compassion for women long dead. So why not here, for this flesh-and-blood woman?

"Peggy," she says, the consideration of using *Mom* having flashed into her and out again in a nanosecond. *Maybe another time.*

Peggy turns to her, brightens, throws open her arms, embraces her, pats her.

"I'm so glad you're with me tonight," Peggy says.

"I am too," Darla says.

"Can you help me greet people now and then? Not to monopolize you. Robert needs you too."

"Of course," Darla says.

Peggy lets go of Darla, pulls back a bit, looks her in the eyes. "Thank you," she says. She lets that register, and then she says, "Would you like a few moments with Bill now?"

Peggy Peggy Peggy. How do I say No *to that? You have a talent.* Darla says, "Of course."

Peggy nods, steps away, revealing Robert still stuck standing where he was, looking at his wife with one side of his mouth and the corresponding curve of his cheek clenched in irony. "I'll give you a few moments," he says, and he too moves away.

Darla wants to rap him in the arm with a knuckle as he passes. She wants simply to follow him.

But she steps forward.

Her father-in-law's face is a crude likeness, molded in hand-puppet rubber. But it's him. No doubt. The distortion is simply death. It's the stuff he's pumped full of instead of blood. It's all the makeup. And yet: *I envy Robert.* This thought surprises her. She does envy him. Her own father went face forward through his windshield and into an overpass pier. Darla and her brother, far away from the bodies, made the decision by telephone. It was logical. *Don't wait for us. Close the caskets. Seal them up. We don't need to see our parents in that state. I don't need to see the wrecked face of my wrecked father.* But she did. And she didn't know it until now, as she looks at the face of this boring, emotionally obtuse, river-dock-macho, son-bullying, simplistically jingoistic man lying here dead. As altered as the man's face is, this moment with William Quinlan still feels like a kind of existential intimacy, and much to her surprise and a little to her horror, she ardently wishes she'd had a chance for these concluding moments of closeness with her own father. As bullying and politically knuckleheaded as he could be. As passionate over sausages and conservatism but reticent over her. So why does she long for that lost opportunity, to see his final mask of reticence? Her mind replies: *Perhaps because it would say to you: This is the ultimate him and so it was always him. A him apart from you. A him he would have arrived at whether he felt tenderly about you or not. Whether you ever existed or not. You did not create the chill in him. You did not earn it. If he could give no more in life, it was only because he was destined to die. That dark wind was already upon his face. If you'd had these final moments with him, perhaps you could have understood all that for yourself. More than understood. You could have actually felt it.*

But as she stands before this other father, these are only thoughts.

And so she aches.

Her eyes fill with tears.

She rues them. Rues they'll be construed as mourning William Quinlan. Rues they could not fall upon her own father's face.

She waits for them to subside.

She glances over her shoulder.

Robert is disappearing through the door into the visitation room foyer. Peggy is approaching two elderly couples Darla does not recognize.

And Peggy reaches these strangers now, the two old men and, apparently, their two wives. The women are rising from the chesterfield.

"Hello," she says.

The two men turn.

"Thank you for coming." She speaks with the exaggerated brightness of decorous disdain: These men are the first outsiders to mourn her husband, and she has never heard a word about them.

"I'm Peggy Quinlan," she says.

At least they seem to recognize who she is. As soon as they all finish fluttering their names and their condolences at her, Peggy ignores the wives and looks from one veteran to the other as she says, "Remind me where Bill first met you."

"Over at the American Legion hall."

Neither has Bill ever mentioned the American Legion, much less its hall.

Peggy certainly has no intention of revealing her ignorance of all this. Fortunately, her three friends from church have finished in the kitchen and are now entering the room through its double door from the back hallway.

Peggy nods in the direction of their arrival. "You'll excuse me."

The strangers clamor their understanding.

She takes each of their offered hands and says, "Please step into the next room and have some food. There's Irish stew. It was Bill's favorite. Perhaps you knew?" She does not pause to have that confirmed or denied. Either way it would piss her off. "Or there are plenty of other things. Please."

The veterans and their wives all agree to eat.

Peggy moves off toward her friends from St. Mary's Catholic Church. They've taken a turn toward the casket, but the steps of her pursuit slow as she finds her mind accelerating to a thing she thought she left behind in New Orleans, a thing surely already dead, dead on its own, a thing that certainly has no business in her life now, not with the man himself dead, but it does have a life. It very much does. Because if he moved to Georgia and found these two men for friends and she never heard a word about them, then it proves he was capable of a private life full of people he kept from her. Worse. It proves everything she feared in New Orleans, feared for decades: His going off most every afternoon wasn't simply for a drive and some coffee. It was for a woman. A woman he loved. Loved instead of her.

She has slowed now to a stop.

Ahead of her, the three friends are lined up before Bill.

She turns her back on them.

The strangers are heading for the food. Robert has vanished. Darla is in the process of vanishing as well, out the entrance door of the visitation room.

And Jimmy once again nears the Tillotson Funeral Home, featuring William Quinlan like the star of his latest movie—*Husband, Father, Veteran*. Jimmy and Heather have been chased back by the Impala's open fresh air vent. A few miles down Apalachee Parkway it sucked in the nighttime stink of the tree-shrouded Leon County dump, a clear sign to both of them that they should give up the drive.

He pulls into the first empty space, far from the few other cars and the floodlit house.

He turns off the engine but does not move.

Heather says, "Cold feet?"

"The back of the crowd at the cemetery is one thing. But doing this . . . I don't know."

"Baby," she says. "You want to put *him* in the ground, not just a casket. You need to see him in it, don't you think?"

Jimmy shrugs in a slow-motion, exaggerated, high-shouldered way.

Heather smiles. She's known him long enough to understand the gesture as pouty assent. She finds it endearing, which makes her suspect she's falling in love.

He says, "We're still too early."

"So let's sit here and make out for a while," she says.

Jimmy barks a laugh at this.

But he turns a little in her direction and regrets the ubiquity of center consoles in modern cars. "We'd have to climb into the backseat to do it right," he says.

"So?"

"On the way out," he says. "After getting him into the casket."

Heather laughs and leans across the console to him. She initiates a kiss, which they draw out for a time and end with as much of an embrace—of shoulders and chests—as they can manage. Jimmy's attention drifts up to the funeral home. But it's far enough away that he does not even register the figure silhouetted in the open front doorway.

Robert has only moments ago slipped his cellphone into his pocket, having absentmindedly carried it in his hand from the visitation room to this place in the doorway. The text message that brought him here was sent by his grandson. *Almost there.* The message pleased Robert, and surprised him a little. If they're almost here, there's no reason for Jake to text, except that he's eager to see his granddad.

Far down at the parkway, lights have just turned into the parking lot, but they immediately pull into a spot and go dark. Clearly not Kevin. Nor is it Kevin at the opening and shutting of doors much closer. Figures from school are emerging there.

"Are you okay?" This is Darla's voice from just over his shoulder.

He glances at her. "Yes. Thanks. I got a text from Jake. They're almost here."

Darla steps up beside him.

Four FSU colleagues, three of Robert's, one of Darla's, are heading this way.

She feels Robert fidget a little. "I'll handle them, if you like," she says.

"Thanks. Yes."

And after the commiserations, she does, taking them away to the food and alcohol that make this a wake and not a funeral.

More lights turn in now from the parkway and keep approaching until they angle into the nearest parking spot. Robert goes out into the chill and down the front steps to meet Kevin, who is striding forward, looking young in the dim light, not forty-two, looking like a college boy. He embraces Robert. Grace follows and puts her arms around both of them. A tender woman. Good for Kevin. Robert withdraws one arm from his son to include his daughter-in-law in his embrace.

The death of his father is grieved more simply by these two, who did not know the man, who knew an alternate man. Robert looks beyond this wordless huddle. Molly is on her cellphone; she's eighteen, after all. Jake is standing nearby watching Robert closely. Their eyes meet and the boy nods to his grandfather.

How has this boy gotten so big? This man. Twenty now. He's taller than Robert. Maybe not when Robert was twenty, not before his septuagenarian shrinkage. But tall. A man. And Robert wonders how this is now a surprise. As the hug goes wordlessly on, Robert tries to think of the last time he saw his grandson. A year. Maybe two. Jake's been elsewhere during the family's last couple of visits. Growth spurts have their limits. The last time, Jake surely was some significant fraction of this man who stands before Robert. But it was long enough ago that the near-man has been composted into this present surprise.

Grace begins the exchange of condolences. "I'm so sorry, Dad," she says.

The three end the embrace and exchange ardent words as they all gather and turn and move off toward the front door.

Bob cannot distinguish the words but this faint flurry of sound floats down the parking lot to him. He has just stopped abruptly at the foot of the Tillotson driveway. The lights of the marquee have drawn his eyes up from their focus on the sidewalk and have stopped him, and now these distant voices come at him like a past incident that troubles you in the middle of the night but you can't quite remember what it was. And the lights. This sign. **William Quinlan**. Quinlan. Bob thrashes in his head to understand. Just recently a Quinlan. A handshake. I'm Quinlan. The Vietnam vet. *Vietnam. America's last chapter. Bang. Done.*

Bob's head snaps back at the sign.

Quinlan's dead. *He only just shook my hand. That was quick. Done. Bang. It doesn't make sense.* So Bob tries to do in his head what he can do with his eyes. He squeezes at these thoughts like they're the blur of words in a newspaper. He squeezes till they clarify, just a little, just enough to make them out. The Quinlan who shook his hand was Bob. Not William. He's Bob. A Vietnam vet. In that, too much like the old man. *But this one is Bob like me.*

And now Bob remembers the rest. The father of the other Bob has died. A blood clot in a hospital. Tillotson Funeral Home. Bob looks again at the sign. Tillotson. And this Quinlan: *Husband. Father. Veteran.* Another veteran. This makes Bob stir a little. Too many veterans. But the other Bob is okay. They ate together at New Leaf, the two of them. *But he put me in a hotel with my father. Did the old man arrange it? Did he get his Vietnam buddy to put me in a room with him?*

No.

This is Bob the son of William, who is dead.

Bob looks toward the distant house. Shining.

Dead in this place shining in the dark.

Respects.

Bob can't just walk up to the front door.

He understands that.

Nearby. Twenty yards away. The woods. Bob knows his way through woods. These run up toward the shining house and then past and around back, surrounding the place. Bob heads off. Laurel oak and water oak and sweet gum, dark and dense, and Bob enters them, moving swiftly, silently.

Hushed, Robert and his son's family enter the visitation room. Robert is before them. Kevin steps up now beside him, scans the room, sees the casket at the far wall, keeps on looking around. Robert figures he knows why. When Kevin's gaze arrives at the buffet room, Robert says, "I suspect they're in there," meaning Peggy and Darla. When Kevin looks at him, Robert nods back to the partition doorway. "Serving your grandmother's food."

Kevin turns to his family and says, softly, "This is a good time to pay our respects."

Grace steps beside him, takes his arm. Molly has put her cellphone away and takes her mother's arm. Jake is standing a little apart, and when the others move off toward the casket, he stays put.

"Granddad," he says in a near-whisper, "can we have a little talk? I need some advice."

"Of course," Robert says, reciprocating the whisper. He nods toward his grandson's retreating family. "Perhaps a little later."

Jake understands. "Thanks." He follows the others.

Robert moves off toward the buffet room thinking how Jake has gotten to age twenty without the two of them ever really sitting down to talk about life in the way a grandfather and grandson often can do. Will this be a night full of ironies? Full of people assuming Robert's unadulterated sorrow, for instance; full of the tender, approving warmth—as one might receive from a loving father—that those assumptions will earn him. And likely this irony as well: The old man has reminded Jacob that families can dissolve, so if you ever want a heart-to-heart connection with your grandfather, you better get it while you can. Not that any of this was William Quinlan's benign intention. He just happened to die.

Robert steps into the partitioned room with his mother's food unfurled on platters and in pots and stainless warmers and with herself stationed behind the row of tables ladling Irish stew and brightly complaining that Tallahassee is muttonless.

"But the lamb is good," she says, tapping the serving spoon in the air over the filled plate of Darla's colleague. Peggy turns her face at Robert's arrival.

"Kevin and Grace and the kids are here," he says.

And Bob pushes on through the trees. Why does he feel a rushing in him, why is he beating up his legs and lungs and elbows and shoulders trying to get through a thicket of oak in this big fucking rush? As if something is pursuing him here in the woods. No. He's doing the pursuing. That shifting of the dark up ahead, shaping and shifting and vanishing and shaping again *You can shoot, by God Bobby, you can shoot* and Bob pulls the Glock from inside his coat, snug in palm and crotch of thumb and forefinger, his fingertip lying easy on the trigger, perfectly fitting its curve, perfectly placed for Bobby to be okay by God, a hell of a shot. The old man was worthless in the woods. He was worthless. Maybe he was worthless in the jungles of Vietnam as well, maybe that's what pissed him off so bad at Bob, Bob being okay when the old man wasn't. Maybe Calvin Henry Weber, sergeant—or whatever his rank really was—serial number whatever-the-fuck, was scared of his okay boy Bob. When Bob has a Mossberg or when Bob has a Glock, Calvin Henry Weber is scared. And Bob moves on, dodging the trees, aware, though, that he's not just chasing, aware that he has a destination, aware of a building being sliced into fragments by the trunks of the oaks, a building passing by and passing by and finally vanishing, replaced by the stretch of a sodium-vapor-lit drive, covered along the back edge of the building by a hanging porch. And Bob changes his bearing, which has been north. He now turns east, and the building is passing again through the trees to his right. He has circled behind it and now there is a wide doorway in its rear facade, bright lights inside.

Bob stops.

Things clarify for him.

He has come to pay his respects to a dead man. A father of a Bob. The other Bob. Bob the Vietnam buddy of the father he's been following through the woods.

Keep it straight.

Bob tucks his Glock back inside his inner coat pocket.

But the door is opening.

And while Bob has been making his way through the woods to this place behind a particularly large-trunked laurel oak: Peggy and Robert emerge from the buffet and cross the room to wait for Kevin and his wife and his son and his daughter to finish their shoulder-to-shoulder encounter with the corpse of William Quinlan, which they soon do. Kevin and Grace draw their children closer in an embrace and they turn to find Peggy and Robert. They all huddle in condolence. Beyond them the visitation room is beginning to gather visitors, arriving from a flow of cars into the parking lot, including, mostly recently, a minivan from Longleaf Village. The minivan prompts Jimmy and Heather to look at each other and nod and emerge from their car, though unhurriedly, as they want all these recent arrivals to have a chance to populate the room. Jimmy flexes at his qualms as if they were morning-stiff muscles.

Inside, Peggy abruptly declares to Kevin and his family, "You're straight from the airport. You must be famished. I've got just the thing." She steps between Kevin and Grace and arranges herself shoulder to shoulder with them, hooking their arms and conveying them toward the buffet room.

"Come on, kids," she says over her shoulder.

Molly says, "I'm famished," and follows.

Jake glances to Robert, who nods at his grandson and waits for the diners to make some progress toward the partition door. Then Robert says, "Let's go." He leads Jake across the visitation room, looking first toward the exit into the foyer. But people are coming in, some of whom he knows, and he looks away to the back wall and the doors there. No one has gathered near them. "This way," he says.

Jake follows.

They say nothing to each other as they cross the room and enter the back hallway. It's lit brightly with torchiere floor lamps. Double doors directly before them lead outside.

"Inside or out?" Robert says.

"Out," Jake says.

"Good man," Robert says.

Bob has already stopped in the trees across from the back doors of the funeral home. Things have already become clear to him. He has already tucked his Glock away inside his coat.

The door is opening, and he hangs back, fades into the darkness like the ghost of his father that he's been chasing through these woods. No doubt also like his father's ghost, he keeps a careful watch.

Robert and Jake step into the chill air, stop beneath the porte cochere roof, turn to each other, and Jake says at once, "I've been intending for a while to do this the next time I saw you." He extends his hand.

Robert accepts Jake's hand and they shake. His grandson's grasp is firm, ardently so but not strained.

Jake says, "Thank you for your service."

The puzzlement that Robert felt but did not show when Jake offered his hand must be flickering now in his face because Jake quickly adds, "For our country. In Vietnam."

Their hands are still clasped and Jake renews the shake with this.

Robert nods, trying to block out the voice of the corpse just inside the doors, trying to quash the same impulse he'd felt with the old man's donut buddies. He manages: "That's good of you to say."

The handshake ends.

Jake says, "We've never talked about any of that."

"I tend not to."

"I respect that," Jake says. "But if it's not an absolute thing. 'Tend,' right? I mean, I've never asked. But I'd like to. I'm older now. I'd like to sit down and talk about war with you. I mean, you're my grandfather and you've been through that and it's crazy I shouldn't find out what you know."

His grandson's intention, especially now, should rattle Robert. But upon this rush of words, Jake the boy frisks into him, Jake from the few years he lived close by, the three-year-old out with his granddad for a walk but the boy never walking anywhere, always taking off and running ahead.

Not that Robert ever wants to discuss Vietnam, but for now he says, "Maybe not tonight."

"No no," Jake says. "I understand. We'll make another time."

"Of course."

"Soon."

"Sure."

The two of them are standing here growing a little chilly now up the sleeves and down the collar and beneath the tie because of Jake and his interest in their talking together. So when his grandson pauses, Robert simply waits, glad he's put off Vietnam. For some years the two households have had ongoing good intentions to get together more often and soon, but it never seems to happen. Robert regrets that but hopes the phenomenon will at least save him from ever having this particular grandfather-and-grandson conversation.

Robert assumes that asking for this was the purpose of tonight's private talk. He expects Jake to take them back inside.

But he doesn't. Jake is working up to something else. He looks away, toward the trees, where Bob is watching closely.

He's spotted me. But Bob doesn't react abruptly, as much as his hand wants to duck inside his coat. Just in case it's okay. Just in case the darkness that Bob is standing in is sufficient, he simply moves backward, deeper into the shadows, but without seeming to move, in minute measures, steadily, his hand ready to leap if necessary. The boy's head turns back to Cal's buddy.

Jake says to Robert, "There's one other thing. Maybe we can talk now just a bit? They're okay inside without us for a couple more minutes, aren't they?"

Robert hears a different sort of rush in Jake's voice, an urgency, a pressing private need. "Whatever you need, Jake."

"I just need to say it. I'm joining the Marines."

Robert steels himself instantly to show no reaction. Though he's staggered.

Jake rolls on. "Dad is freaked. But I've made up my mind. He sees me as a child. Always will, probably. At least till I'm forty or something. I'm smart, Granddad. I've been thinking about this for a long time, you know? The war you fought—we can talk about all that another time—but that one was fucked up. Sorry for the language. That's a thing too with Pop. But Jesus. It's just a fucking word. In the Vietnam War we got mixed up with another country that was trying to decide for itself who they were, and they had no intention to make anybody else think the same way. Much less kill you if you disagreed. You know? They weren't about to send the Viet Cong over here to hijack an American Airlines jet and fly it into a New York skyscraper. Hell, how did the dreaded communist Vietnam end up? They're filling clothes racks at Walmart and Target. But this war now is different. The jihadists of the world are cutting off the heads of anyone who disagrees with them. Not just Christians. Even other Muslims. Over what?

Over a fourteen-century-old beef about who should carry on Muhammad's work, a cousin or a caliph. And they're coming for us. They say so. They mean it. If they had the technology and a modern country and the governing chops of Adolf Hitler, they'd out-Hitler Hitler. This is a real cause to fight for. If we don't become the new Greatest Generation, then the jihadists will turn us into the Beheaded Generation."

Bob has stopped retreating into the dark. The boy's voice has risen and it's angry and though it takes too much from Bob to make out the words at this distance, too much squeezing in his head, he knows the boy is telling off his father, standing up to him, and Bob is breathing hard, his right hand is itchy but he keeps it at his side for the moment. Still he owes it to the boy, so he strains to hear, and there's *Viet Cong* and there's *jihad* and there's *Hitler* and there's *beheaded* and Bob can't draw his next breath because there's just too much in his chest to get past.

Jake has stopped talking. He's panting a little.

Robert wants badly to have words now. His life, his work, is about words. None come to mind. Jake *is* smart. Robert has listened to him carefully. He's heard him. He understands how Jake can see the world in this way, how he can see this cause as just. But how to reason a young man out of going to war? As reasonable as Jake's words sound, his decision itself isn't about reason. But now that the babble in Robert's head has quieted, the only words he commands can't begin to address Jake's rush, his passion.

It may be too late anyway.

Robert says, " Have you already joined?"

"I've taken the aptitude test. And I've passed the medical. I make it official next week."

"What do you need from me?"

"If you can talk to Dad, help him through this. He's really upset. He won't get off it."

Kevin is smart too. He's surely said it all. Robert despairs of finding a way to dissuade Jake.

"Your dad isn't making any sense to you?"

Jake shrugs. "It's not really about sense. He loves me."

"I love you too, Jake."

"But you made the same choice when you were my age. For a worse cause."

Another irony for this night. That was also about a father's love. A worse cause indeed. And Robert suddenly has relevant words: "Are you sure you're not doing this because he *does* love you? Because you need to be your own man, separate from him?"

Jake turns his face away to the trees. To think this over.

Bob straightens sharply. Something's happened across the way. Since he resumed his breathing, Bob has held himself very still, in body and mind, trying to understand what was before him and what he should do about it. But either the words faded or his mind has. And now the boy has looked away again. As if he's been slapped across the face. Things can change quickly. Bob puts his hand inside his coat. Holds the Glock but keeps it inside there for the moment.

Jake turns his face back to Robert. He says, "I'm sure. Living with what I believe, how I feel, I couldn't bear to watch the future unfold if I don't do what I can."

Robert does love this boy. Loves this smart, tough, quick Jake, who has not gotten enough of his grandfather in his life. Robert lifts his hands to grasp Jake at the shoulders.

Oh no you don't. Bob slips his Glock from his pocket, takes a breath. *Breath control. Trigger control.*

Robert cups Jake's shoulders and he begins to pull him toward him.

Bob's right hand comes up strong, steady, brings the Glock to bear, tracking the side of Robert's head.

Jake could take one breath more, could have one more flicker of a thought, he could hesitate for the briefest moment to accept from his grandfather what he has resisted over and over in the past few weeks from his father, but Granddad can do this because he was a soldier, because he went to war, Granddad knows what it means because he's been there, and so Jake rushes now, he opens his arms to Robert and they hug.

And one flicker, one breath, one moment away from squeezing the trigger, Bob's right forefinger freezes, and a deep recoil of air rushes into Bob, drops his right arm, pushes him back as if a Viet Cong sniper has been following him through these woods and has squeezed off his own round and shot Bob through the center of his chest. Because this father and this son have embraced.

Bob leans against a tree. Closes his eyes.

Robert and Jake say nothing but hold the embrace for a few more moments. Then they let each other go and they turn and head back through doors, into the hallway.

They pause before entering the visitation room.

"Thanks, Granddad," Jake says.

Robert reaches out, cuffs his grandson on the shoulder. He fills with a thing too complicated to call *regret*, though his insistently abstracting mind would be content with that. "What are you going to do for them?" he asks.

"The Marines?"

"Yes."

"That's what the test was about. Whatever they want. But you know the first thing they teach in the Corps. Every Marine is a rifleman."

Robert manages a nod.

Jake says, "Well, time to deploy." He opens the visitation room door, holds it for his grandfather.

Robert finds himself immovable with the thought that Jake would have made his Grandpa Bill proud.

He flicks his chin to Jake to send him on in. Jake winks and says, "Cover me." And he disappears.

The door swings closed.

Robert reboots.

He goes in.

Near the door Peggy is quickly closing in on Jake. She reaches him, hugs him, releases him while giving Robert a tilt-headed frown, and she propels her grandson toward the buffet room.

She does not follow but comes to Robert. "Where were you two?"

"Jake wanted to talk."

"Is he okay?"

"He's okay."

"I'm sure it's hard for him," Peggy says. "Losing his Grandpa Bill. He's not experienced death before. That's a blessing, of course. But now he's got to face it."

"He's fine, Mom."

"Your father loved that boy."

"I'm sure he did."

"He was so *full* of love."

Robert doesn't have any words for that.

Peggy's eyes are filling with tears. But not about Jake. Or the old man. She's fixed on Robert now. She lifts a hand and touches his cheek.

He accepts it. Waits.

She withdraws the hand, looks over her shoulder.

Several dozen visitors are arranged now in small, softly murmuring groups about the room.

Peggy turns back to her son. "I'm weary of them, Bobby. Can we talk a little?"

"Of course," he says, hoping she won't speak to him as *Bobby*. "There's a place through here."

He leads her into the back hallway. For a moment they pause between the two sets of doors. "This is nice," she says.

Beyond the porte cochere doors, beyond the back driveway, in the darkness of the trees, Bob has settled to the ground at the foot of an oak, his back against the trunk. The Glock is still in his hand, though he is presently unaware of it. His head is full of a high metallic whine. It's often there. Words can cover it over. Or other sounds. But he has no words to speak, for the moment, and the woods around him are silent. So he listens to the whine. Idly. An oscillating whine. Though its highs and its lows are very near each other, he can distinguish them. He's smart that way. He begins to count in his head. At each peak. One. Two.

Robert and Peggy step away, toward the end of the hall opposite the kitchen. They stop in the amber bloom of light of a torchiere. They face each other. Peggy initiates a hug, which Robert returns. They hold this for a long moment and then Peggy pulls away, but barely a half step, maintaining the connection of their eyes.

She says, "I keep thinking of when he came home. You and I were living with Mama and Papa, you know. In that creole cottage in the Irish Channel. You were two years old and he was thunderstruck at the sight of you. He picked you up and put you on his shoulders and that's pretty much where you stayed for a couple of weeks. He'd carry you everywhere from up there. 'Let him see far,' is what Bill would say. 'Let my boy see far.'"

Robert has heard this story often enough that any capacity it once had to move him is long gone. Besides, the old man as a young man was already the man he was and forever would be. A toddler son was easy to sling around. Easy to give a damn about when you could overpower him absolutely.

Peggy says, "He wanted to name you William Junior, you know."

This is not the first time he's heard this either.

"He loved you that much," she says.

What Robert wants is to avoid arguing with his mother on this night. However, he says, "What he wanted was his firstborn son to be just like him."

She brightens. "You see?"

He has said this to her as if to disprove his father's love. But he realizes she hears it as a demonstration of that love.

Her bright smile of QED beams on. And the smile suddenly strikes Robert as one of her lies.

Does she know about his father's deep disappointment in him? The man kept it from his son. Did he keep it from his wife?

Robert and his mother look at each other for a long moment in silence. Her brightness fades a little. He struggles, wanting to let this pass but wanting to know if she knows, wanting to ask but wanting to keep the truth strictly between him and the dead man if she doesn't.

So he says, "But I wasn't just like him."

He expects a spin now, or an evasion or a lie.

She even hesitates.

Then she surprises him. "It was me who talked him out of naming you William," she says.

The family explanation—Robert can't remember the exact moment it was offered him but he's sure it came from her— was that his father realized that his son, to be kept distinct in conversation, would become "Billy" or even "Junior," and he thought both sounded sissified.

Robert narrows his eyes at her. "You said he talked himself out of it."

"Did I tell you that?"

"You did."

"For his sake. He didn't like admitting my influence."

"You didn't like biting your tongue."

"I bit it as an act of love." She squares up before him and doesn't flinch: "It was me. I told him, 'This boy needs to be his own man.'"

"Did he understand that?"

"Well, who knows. He was a father, after all, with strong ideas. He gave you a love for books. This soldier and dock-worker gave his son that."

Robert does not really expect to learn if the old man revealed his fatherly disgust over Vietnam. He probably didn't. But she did witness his disappointment in Robert. Listen to her: Your father may not have loved you for what you became but he made you read. That was the substitute from childhood onward. Isn't that an outcome worthy of actual love? Aren't you grateful?

He says, "He gave me the love of books expecting me to come to the same conclusions from them that he did."

Her face puckers in puzzlement. "You seemed to."

She's right.

"I often bit my tongue," Robert says.

She smiles at him, half smiles. "An act of love."

Well, the act never won his. He catches himself before this comes out of his mouth. She's tried the same tactic all her life long.

Her eyes are fixed on Robert's but restlessly so.

"He loved all of us," she says.

And he understands. If she can convince Robert of William's love for him, then she might believe that the man loved her as well.

Because she doesn't believe it.

Of course she doesn't.

And it abruptly occurs to him: He hasn't told her what he knows about the old man's secret trysts.

Her priests would nail me for a sin of omission. A big one. Sure it was for his privacy. It was his place to tell her. It was between them. It had been going on for years when I found out. She would have stopped him. She would have nagged him back home if she knew it was something that didn't threaten her so profoundly she preferred the lie. But still. He wasn't worth keeping it from her. He was never worth it. Mea culpa.

"Mom," he says. "I'm so sorry. I should have told you sooner. But it wasn't so long ago I found out. All those afternoons, for all those years, that he drove off on his own in New Orleans: It wasn't a woman. It was guys like those you met tonight. It was Dad and his army buddies doing beignets and chicory coffee."

Peggy's face goes blank. Then she blinks, and for a few moments more she shows nothing. And a few more.

Robert doesn't understand.

So he says, "He loved you."

She blinks again. Then she begins to cry.

Oh shit: Robert should have told her long ago. Or he should have figured out a better way to tell her now.

He lifts his hand to touch her shoulder, perhaps pull her to him.

She catches his hand in hers, lifts it, and squeezes it.

"Are you sure?" she says.

"I'm sure."

"It's time for me to cry a while," she says. "Thanks for this."

"I'm really sorry," he says. "I should have told you at once."

Peggy struggles to manage her voice, hold off the tears. "You were caught between us. I totally understand, sweetheart. You loved your father too."

She looks around, lets go of Robert's hand, sits down on an overstuffed chair beneath the torchiere. "I'll be in soon," she says.

Robert stands over her for a moment more, but she has lowered her face to weep.

He turns and moves along the hallway.

He pauses between the two sets of doors.

He thinks to head outside, to get away from all of this.

He faces the porte cochere exit. His hands go to the push bar.

Beneath the tree Bob's eyes are open again. The whining has been fading. It's almost gone. The numbers are gone. He's done these countings before. He wishes he could decide when they happen, could make them happen. The whine, the numbers are better than the voice and the words. *Hello, Private Weber. Let's talk.*

Robert's hand is on the push bar.

But he knows this is futile. There will be no escape tonight.

He looks back down the hallway to his mother, her torso, in profile, bent forward, her head bowed, her hands clasped, resting on her knees.

He turns around, crosses to the doors into the visitation room, pushes through.

Darla appears before him.

"Hey," she says. She must have been standing nearby, expecting him.

"Hey."

Darla glances over his shoulder, sees that Peggy isn't appearing. "Is she okay?"

"She's crying alone for a while," Robert says.

"That's good."

"I hope."

"I saw you two go out."

"There isn't much privacy at a thing like this."

"It's what a wake's for. So you're not alone."

"What have you been doing?"

"Serving food."

"Is it going over?"

"The Irish stew is a big hit."

"That'll please her."

"So it will."

Robert looks away, into the room, whose numbers seem to have increased since he stepped out. Not that he sees anyone in particular. They are all blurring together now.

Darla says, "Can I make a suggestion?"

"Sure."

"I never saw my own dad after he died. Did I ever tell you that?"

He looks at her. "No."

"Well. I didn't. It was a closed casket. I needed to look at him. It's a good way to get things straight in your head so he won't hang around in there."

Robert tries to take this in. He's not sure. He stalls by quibbling.

"Still waiting for the suggestion," he says.

"You weren't with him at the casket for very long," she says. "Just make sure you did enough tonight."

Robert looks off in the direction of the far wall. In the middle of the room, a clump of assisted living visitors with plates of Irish stew blocks his view of the casket beyond. But he's thinking Darla may be right.

She says, "It's not about good guys. I had as much trouble with my dad as you did with yours. More."

"Okay," he says. "You're right."

Robert and Darla would both agree: This is one of the paradigms of the two of them at their intellectual best with each other. A difference. A discussion. Patience over a semantic quibble. One sees the other's point. And concurs. Sealed with a moment of contented silence.

That moment ends, but before they part she says, "Does she need me, do you think?"

"Mom?"

"Yes."

"Not right now. I think she needs to be alone."

"I'll go dip some stew."

"I think you're starting to like it."

"Please," she says.

She begins to turn away.

Robert puts his hand on her arm. "Hey."

She looks back at him.

"Thanks," he says.

She nods.

He heads off toward the wall with the casket.

She moves in the other direction, toward the buffet room. But she puts only a few steps of separation between her and the back door of the visitation room before her department chair intercepts her and hugs her as if the dead father were Darla's own. Darla figures the warmth is mostly about department politics, which means a conversation is imminent. She gives up the hope of hiding immediately behind the stew.

Robert veers wide around the group of old women in hats and old men in wide ties from Longleaf Village. He keeps his face averted; he's met a couple of them and this is not a time to chat.

He's past them now and he looks toward the casket.

A man is standing there, his back to Robert.

Robert does not recognize him.

Just a man. A lanky man wearing a leather jacket, his hands clasped behind him, his pewter-gray hair thick-curled and shaggy at the collar.

Robert stops. He'll wait till the man moves off.

Robert looks about to see if anyone else is waiting to view the body.

A few steps off to the left is a pretty, pale-skinned woman, her dark hair spilling from beneath a knit cap. He takes her for an art theory student of Darla's. Perhaps she has a concealed sketchbook, waiting to capture a dead man.

Robert thinks to walk away now.

But he returns his gaze to the man.

He has not moved.

Well, yes. His hands, in their clasp, have begun to twist, have grown fretful.

And now Robert has a thought. This man is not from FSU. Not from assisted living. Not one of Bill's generation. Wearing leather at a funeral home visitation, he's not from Peggy's church. Robert looks at the woman again. Her gaze is fixed on the man. They are here together. And she's older than he thought at first glance. Robert looks closely at her jaw, looking for his father's, his own, his brother's. Looks at her eyes. He's not recognizing a Quinlan, but he's never met Linda. This woman's features could be from Linda's genes. He follows her eyes back to the casket. The man's hands cling to each other to quell their restlessness. Robert suspects his own hands were just as restless when he stood there. *It's him.*

Jimmy has not been here for long. He is still breathless, standing in the presence of death. Not realizing, not quite yet, that its immanence in this casket is a major reason why he's here. All he presently understands is that the face of his dead father is largely an unrecognizable face. Not a man at all. Not even a good caricature. All the features are bloated and blurred and slathered over. Features he last saw forty-six years ago. Features that would have been nearly as unrecognizable last week, when Bill was still walking around, unawares, in death's anteroom. Jimmy once more asks himself the basic question: *What the hell am I doing here?* And since the dead body is not providing an answer at the moment, Jimmy works his way along. *Closure. Sure. But I'm here because Linda left me. I'm here because I found Heather. Here because I found her only very recently and she's not yet enough. Blood ties are overrated. But that's about the inefficacy of blood, not about the need for ties to something. The something was once Linda and Canada. I still have Canada. Oh Canada. Unarmed, universally doctored, killingly polite Canada; grumbling-not-hating Canada; minding-its-own-fucking-business-in-the-community-of-nations Canada. Tolerant, come-find-a-refuge-and-your-own-identity-here Canada. Not enough. I know that. Canada and Heather may eventually be enough. But for some reason I had to come stand here before this man. Only blood connected us. Not part of the real equation. I did dream of him. And my mother. And my brother. But you can dream about an old girlfriend or a high school teacher or a crooked auto mechanic and it doesn't mean you need to seek them out before they go into the ground. Still I came to this man, his corpse waiting to rot. Because he's dead; he's dead so he knows something important, something no one alive knows. Right now. What is it? Is he wedged into the dark matter, pressing his face against mine? Has he run off to be someone else, somewhere else? Or maybe he's nothing at all. Or just made new. Maybe death is like when they knock you out for a colonoscopy. You're counting backwards one second and awake the next*

*and they tell you it's all done and you don't remember a thing. Maybe
you die and you wake and this life you lived is utterly forgotten like that
lost hour. Life in the USA and life in Canada. Life on planet Earth.
Life is just the camera up your ass that you won't even remember. So
what actually happens after death is fucking academic. If there's nothing
afterward or if it's something that you'll totally forget, then it's all the
same. Okay. What the hell am I doing here? I'm here to look at the bag
of bones my father has become so maybe I can stop thinking about this
thing I can't stop thinking about. I came to face death.*

Another thought, flowing from these, begins to shape
itself. About his brother.

And someone is standing next to him.

"Hello, Jimmy."

Jimmy turns to his brother. Jimmy's impulsive few nights
of Googling—yielding images of Dr. Robert Quinlan at academic conferences, on a book dust jacket, from the university
website—have prepared him only a little for the changes of
nearly five decades. The abrupt, palpable presence of Robert's
graying and slackening and weathering, his leap from twenty-
three years old to seventy: These twist the knife of mortality in
Jimmy's brain. His own face in the mirror each day is much the
same as this one. But even as he's struggled with the thoughts
of death, he could look in the mirror and convince himself,
I'm pretty good for my age. I can put off dying. But he got to that
understanding of his own face gently, gradually. Jimmy regards
this man before him, this man of Jimmy's blood, this man in
the same pretty good shape as he, and sees him as mortally old.

"Hello, Robert," he says.

"I didn't expect you."

"It was last-minute."

They need a little break from each other already.

They have a corpse for that.

They both look in its direction.

All the possible small talk coming to Robert's head sounds potentially touchy or argumentative: *So what changed your mind? Mom will be very pleased. Is Linda with you? Who's the woman? Well, there he is. Was it worth the trip?*

He resists all of these.

And perhaps for that very reason, perhaps because he refuses to choose one of these superficial, calculated things, what he does say is from quite a different part of him. "If you want to slap him across the face, feel free."

They turn and goggle at each other.

Neither can think of a thing to say.

They look back to William.

Robert reboots. "Well, there he is."

"There he is."

"Was it worth the trip?"

"Not yet."

"Is there anything I can do?" Robert asks this with a little surge of animation, a vague impulse, which he stifles to offer forward his hands. He even finds himself about to say, *I'm glad you came,* but he doesn't want to stir up Jimmy's scorn. He's lived with a bellyful of scorn these past few days and he wants to keep things calm with his brother.

Jimmy says, "Answer a question if you can, without looking around."

"All right."

"Where's our mother?"

"She's taking a few minutes alone. I can get her. She'd be only too glad . . ."

"No." Jimmy says it sharply. He softens his tone but with it justifies his sharpness: "That's why I didn't want you to look around."

"So *there's* something I can do," Robert says. "Help you slip out unnoticed."

The words could be construed as sarcastic. Would have been in the life they lived together before each went away. But Robert has also softened his tone.

"I haven't decided yet," Jimmy says. "I may."

Still another matter of tone. This fastidious one in Jimmy makes a warmth rise in Robert, from his cheeks and into his temples, replacing sympathy with pissoffedness.

"Look, Jimmy," he says, but quietly, calmly. "Why don't *I* just slip away and let you do what you need to do. If Mom appears I'll run interference for you. Distract her so you can get the hell away."

Jimmy sucks a breath, pulls back ever so slightly.

Robert thinks: *It was the 'get the hell away.' All right. All right. I'm not in the mood. Let's get it on, brother.*

But Jimmy says, "I'm sorry. I sounded arrogant. I'm here because I want to be here. But it's complicated."

Robert feels animated again. He may need to slip away for his own sake, just to stop the mood swings. He says, "I get it. Not a problem. It's always been complicated."

He looks at William. It wasn't such a crazy thing to say. About the slap. It was Jimmy's fretfully clasped hands. He says, "Not long before you appeared, I stood here and I thought about him waking up and daring me to punch him in the face."

"Did you do it?"

"No."

"Not even in your head?"

A beat of silence between them now. And another.

"No," Robert says. "Wish I could've. But it's just a corpse."

Another silence.

But brief. For Jimmy, this too is spoken from an impulse. "We should make a pact," he says. "We'll fight no fights from the past. If we get angry at each other it needs to be about something right in front of us."

"Man, I agree with that," Robert says. "But the past is all you and I have. If we're going to speak at all, things may come up. But not to argue them."

"Fair enough," Jimmy says. "And this can't be a sentimental agreement. It's not mindless make-nice. You know what I mean?"

"I do." Robert offers his hand.

Jimmy takes the hand.

They shake.

The thought of adding their other hands to the ones shaking occurs to both men but only in the abstract, only to be recognized as sentimental and set aside.

When they let go of their hands, Jimmy says, "I'm going to test our pact right away. I came here because of a dead father. But it's not just about him. Maybe not about him very much at all anymore."

Jimmy hesitates. He hasn't planned this. Never imagined relating it to his brother. But he's glad for the chance. He says, "You were precocious when we were kids. And I think you had something dark in you. Can I ask? Did you go off to Vietnam to face death? Did you have to get into the very presence of death to figure it out? Is that what I didn't recognize about what you did?"

This is not the question Robert expected. He wants the answer to be *Yes*. To square himself with Jimmy. To put his motives beyond the criticism of his father, who would never understand such a thing. But the answer isn't yes. Isn't even partially yes. He says, "Since we've agreed not to argue the past, is it possible for us also to be entirely honest?"

Jimmy waggles his head a little at this sudden complexity. "Good question. At least we need to try. Otherwise you might as well just go ahead and help me get the hell out of here. But perhaps we can have it both ways, eh?"

"Perhaps," Robert says. "So then. No. I didn't go off to face death. Not at all."

And he thinks: *Simply that much honesty may not result in an argument, but it will preserve, everlastingly, the estrangement between us.* And he knows: *I can say the thing that the man lying next to us nearly took to his grave.* A thing Robert would just as soon take to his. *Do I want a brother?* If Robert says no more, he will lose Jimmy forever. If he speaks fully, Jimmy might have a way to understand him, even in light of his own drastic deed of the sixties. *Do I want this man for my brother?*

Perhaps.

Robert says, "You were right long ago. It was all about Pops. About winning his love. You were smart to give up trying. I can see that now. I didn't go to Vietnam to confront death. I did everything I could to avoid it. Not to see it. Certainly not to inflict it. I voluntarily enlisted so I could choose an army job. A deep-in-a-hole faux research job. And in doing that, I destroyed the thing I wanted most from Pops. I got its opposite. He'd expected me to go off eagerly to the killing, as he had. So he despised me for the rest of his life. Silently. I never knew. Not till he told me himself the afternoon before he died."

Robert finds himself relieved not to take that to his own grave. Even if Jimmy doesn't get it.

Robert turns his face away, in the only direction possible. To his father. To the death mask of his father. Concerning his brother, Robert thinks, *I don't trust him. But he's the only person alive who can possibly understand. The only other son of my only father.*

"Bobby."

Robert looks back to his brother. Jimmy stopped calling him that before they were teenagers.

For Jimmy, though what seems to be happening here is new to him, though the army part mitigates his worst assumptions about Robert, his mind could easily swirl on now in its accustomed way. With no mitigations possible once you become part of the war machine. With the established legacy of his father's blows and Robert's silence. But the other part of all this surges in him: their shared father, who betrayed them both. And Jimmy thinks: *Do I want a brother?*

And he says, "I didn't know any of that. Never imagined."

Then a pause between them.

Long enough for Robert to turn a corner in his head and find another abyss to leap across. *But I did confront death: I inflicted it.*

This he cannot tell his brother.

Jimmy says, "If I were you—if I were the big brother—I probably would've courted the old man the same way. At least you kept the blood off your hands. I hope I would've been smart enough to do it the way you did."

Robert struggles now with one more irony: As fine as his brother's reaction is, Robert's remaining secret about Vietnam would've had a better chance for absolution from Pops. If Jimmy were to know, Robert would lose him again.

"Thanks," Robert says.

But that is the only show of sentimentality between the two brothers, who both turn now to look at their father's dead body.

Together they eye him silently for a few moments.

"Crappy suit," Robert says.

"He needs leather for the grave," Jimmy says.

And Bob is standing at the edge of the woods. Calvin is in him. Saying things he hasn't said before. *So Private Weber, you're in the woods tonight and you see the enemy and you're quick like you've always been, quick to lock and load and aim, 'cause you're my boy and you're good at what I'm good at. Yeah, I said good like me. Good like I used to be. I know all you ever saw was how wrecked I was. They fucking beat us down. Not the enemy. The brass. The government. They did it to all of us. They humped our asses through the jungles of Hell, blew us apart, body and mind, and then they just up and quit. Turned the last page. Gave the whole thing away and turned us into chumps. Dead chumps. Maimed chumps. Batshit-crazy chumps. Sure you saw me already broken like that, even with a rifle in my hand, which is a fucking shame. That wasn't me. Not like I was in the heat of it, not while I was waging war. You need to believe that of your old man. You're like the me in Vietnam. But tonight you were quick and ready and then you backed off. Why? A fucking hug. You had your target in your sights and you let him get away because you turned it into this bullshit jungle village scene. A father giving his boy a hug. There's a lot you don't know about life. I can't even begin to tell you. But you walk into the prettiest little village with bananas in the trees and clucking fucking hens in the doorways and you can get your ass blown apart there just like anywhere else. These are tough lessons to learn, boy, things you have to learn for yourself. I can't say I'm sorry I learned them, even as fucked up as it was. That's better than being a chump who stays stupid all his life, thinking things are gonna turn out fine. Go on through those doors over there. You'll see. I'll come with you. We'll see together. I can't give you a hug. Grow up. I seen too much in this world to do a thing like that. But I can slide on inside your head and your heart and your itchy good right hand and ain't that even better?*

And Bob is crossing the driveway.

He feels his Glock lying heavily against his heart.

And he's through the porte cochere doors and it's not what he was ready for. A long room. No, a corridor. Piss-colored light and easy chairs. Just an old woman down the way. Just one old woman. Looking up now. Looking at him. *What's to see here?*

She's looking Bob over. With *that look.*

She rises.

Bob waits for his father to tell him what to do.

She's heading this way.

And Bob hears Calvin again: *I can slide inside your head and your heart.*

He takes a deep breath.

He fills himself up.

Like breathing in a ghost.

The old man.

Bob feels light as air.

And she's before him. Cocking her head. Pursing her lips into a tight line.

But an odd thing. Her eyes are red. From crying. Her cheeks glisten. *Hold your horses, boy. I've seen this in my wife. I didn't mean to hurt her but I have. Hanging with people she doesn't understand. Drinking too much. Getting a little rough. She's not the enemy.*

So Bob is calm.

"Yes?" the old woman says.

"Yes," Bob says.

"Can I help you?"

"I don't know."

"This is a funeral home."

But see how dense she can be sometimes? What the fuck am I supposed to do about that?

"I know that," Bob says.

She looks at him closely. She uncocks her head. She unpurses her lips, which she has repursed after stating the dumbshit obvious.

"Do you know someone here?" she asks.

Even with Calvin inside his brain, he is still Bob. That's good. So he remembers. "Bob Quinlan," he says.

This makes the woman smile. "Bob?"

"Yes."

"I see. Where do you know him?"

"From Vietnam," he says.

And something enters her. That look vanishes. Her eyes soften. "You're a veteran," she says, lifting up the word as if she should have known all along.

"Yes," Bob says.

"Please wait," she says.

She moves past him. He turns and watches her step to the inner doors.

She pauses before going in. "I'll find him for you," she says. "What's your name?"

"Bob."

And she changes again. Her face crimps up like that's impossible, the name's already taken. "Bob," she says.

"Bob," he says.

"Why don't you wait here, Bob," she says. "I'll get Robert."

She pushes through one of the doors and it swings shut.

He's clearly not wanted in there. *Too fucking bad.*

Peggy pauses. Takes in the room. She was afraid of a visitation space this big. Afraid Bill would look unloved. But there are people. Dozens. He looks loved. If he's nearby, hovering around before finally departing, he'll see.

She has let the man in the hallway slide to the side of her mind. He's probably homeless. He has the clothes, the whiff. But he's a veteran. Of her son's war. She looks to the doorway to her food. She should make the man a plate of food. From this angle she sees the beginning of her special row of warmers, a glimpse of Darla moving, out of sight now, serving Peggy's dishes to Bill's mourners. This is good.

She should find Robert for the veteran. Is Robert helping this man? She scans the crowd, ending at the far wall, the casket. She sees Robert there, talking to a couple. She moves off toward him, thinking, *Bob. You've never been Bob.*

And Bob steps through the doors into the visitation room. The woman has just passed by, not noticing him. Just as well. She's moving briskly. She would have him stand around waiting on her like a bum at the back door.

He turns.

He follows her.

But more slowly. Taking in all the people as he goes. *Look at them. Hats and ties and rouged cheeks and jowls and stubble and crimson lips and scarfs and sweaters and throats and hands, it's that simple, boy, like feathers and fur and claws and hooves, like jungle jackets and rucksacks and pith helmets and VC pajamas, like white faces and black faces and yellow faces, this is what you learned there, all these are the same, people and their bodies and their uniforms and their skin, all of them are a zip of lead or a burst of flame or a tumble of shrapnel away from dead. Or a round of .45 Auto from the Glock in your pocket. You are a walking, talking, swinging dick of a reminder that it's all just a wisp of smoke that the least little puff of air will blow away, and all the politics and all the ideas and all the scheming and raping and robbing and conquering, all the grunting and raving and wailing and weeping by every last one of these creatures is for nothing, because just that simple thing in your pocket there, boy, if you hold it steady and you aim it true, can turn any one of these poor motherfuckers into maggots and bones.*

"Oh my God," Peggy says, close enough now to recognize the other man, who is turning to her voice. "Jimmy," she says. "Oh Jimmy."

She rushes and she throws open her arms and Jimmy expected this moment if he came, if he stayed, and he decides to set aside all the years of his mother's loyal-wife silence so that he can go through these motions. He opens his arms too and he takes her up and she embraces him. He looks at Heather, who is smiling the same smile he's seen in quiet moments over coffee in their three breakfasts as a couple—even as Peggy looks at Heather thinking, *I have another granddaughter and I didn't even know she exists*—and Jimmy looks at Robert, expecting from his brother a mutual lift of the eyebrows over this other difficult, shared parent. But Robert is beginning to turn his face away, to look into the room.

And as he draws near, Bob understands. *You see what we've learned? What I gave my life to learn? At every moment, no matter who we are, we are all of us on the brink of being fucked. Nothing to save you from that. Nothing you can do. There it is. I am hugging you close now, my son.*

And Robert sees Bob. Half a dozen strides away.

Their eyes lock.

Bob stops.

They look at each other.

Bob lifts his right hand, moves it up to his chest, and then reaches inside his coat. He pauses. For a moment Robert thinks Bob is feeling his heart. Is he in pain? But Bob's hand is moving again, emerging.

A pistol, in profile against his chest, moving now, turning, the barrel coming round, and Robert is moving too, pushing forward in chest and shoulders sensing in them the placement of mother and brother and brother's lover and of Bob and the vector between and Robert steps and the muzzle appears now and Robert steps again veering right, lunging between Bob and the others, the muzzle stopping, steadying, and Robert stops and squares and centers his chest on the killing black hole at the tip of the pistol.

"Bob," he says.

They wait for a single breath.

And Bob understands.

He lifts the pistol and puts the barrel in his mouth and he holds his father close and he pulls the trigger.

~

Robert slips into the bed and pulls the covers to his chest. Only his table lamp is lit. Darla is in the bathroom. The door is closed and a thin fluorescent line shows at its base. The water is running. And then it stops. Not a sound from where he knows his wife to be. Not in this moment, not in the next. His limbs quicken. They would have him jump from the bed, rush to her. But now he hears some small sound. Unidentifiable. Perhaps a bottle-click on porcelain. Something. It is enough. The electric clock whines softly from her nightstand. He did not lose her. He did not lose any of them. Except for Bob.

It's been a week.

Bob has appeared each night but one in a dream. His eyes are oddly warm and wide upon Robert even as the back of his head explodes. And each night Robert has awakened in a thrash of regret: *I stopped to take a bullet when I should have lunged onward to take your gun.* Last night, for the first time, Bob did not come to him.

Robert has not dreamt at all of his father. Or he has utterly forgotten him before waking. After all, he and his brother, side by side, watched the box that held the old man vanish into the earth.

But he is keenly aware: *One dead man still lives.*

In the bathroom Darla has cleaned her face and she stares at its nakedness and thinks, *I am old.* She closes her eyes. She saw nothing of the event itself, arriving in the doorway after the gunshot, Robert rushing to her while all around him the crowd surged backward, breaking apart, wailing. Robert took her in his arms, spun her into the buffet room, shielded her from the sight, as witnesses said he shielded his brother and his mother from the gun.

She can still feel his arms upon her.

She will ask Robert to turn out his light before she enters the bedroom. They have held each other every night since, but silently and inertly and only for a few minutes. She opens her eyes. She cannot bear to see herself. She looks away. Her lipstick sits on the cosmetics shelf beside the sink. She reaches out, puts her hand on it, hesitates, picks it up.

After she is ready; after she is all right again in the mirror, looking pretty good for sixty-seven; after she feels his arms around her, turning her away from harm, lifting her with the sound of a gunshot ringing in her head; after she feels his mind working beyond this door, his fine mind that she sometimes senses in his study when she is in hers; after she can picture him sitting alone at the bistro table in the corner of the coffee shop in Baton Rouge; after she is ready, she turns to the door and puts her hand on the knob and she pauses. She has felt this present desire for him often in these past few years, when her hand wished to rise to him, when her body wished to press against him; but then she has paused to consider the moment and her body and his body, to consider the day just passed and the day to come and the lateness of the hour, to consider the words that may have lately been spoken between them over some trivial thing. And she has not acted.

But in this pause now, she thinks of something to do. She grasps her nightgown at the shoulders and lifts it from her body and over her head and she tosses it to the floor.

She opens the door only wide enough for her voice and says to her husband, "Turn out the light."

He does.

She does the same with the bathroom light and steps into the darkness.

And she crosses the room feeling like a fool, her body naked but her face made up. But no. It's not foolish. She wants her face as beautiful as possible for him in this present moment even if he can't see it, and she wants him to remember her body from the past, when he first loved her. This present nakedness is for herself: She can't reason herself out of it. She must stay in her body. She must act.

Darla slips into the bed.

She keeps a small separation between their bodies, letting the dark continue to mask her intention. This is sweet to her, to let that be for a few moments. This imminence.

As for Robert, he is lifting his face from his coffee while protesters are streaming by in the street outside, but one of them, this woman with blue eyes, is standing over him, bantering at him from the start, and he hears himself speak the first words he ever said to her: *I've been away.* And he thinks now of her, of them: *I've always been away.* He turns his face, seeing only a vague shaping of the dark beside him, and he says, "If I tell you something I did in Vietnam, a thing I deeply regret, will you stop loving me?"

She answers by rising up and moving over him and descending into an embrace.

And as they make love, Darla is very glad to be connected to her husband. She is comfortable, though the parts of her that ache each day are aching now and the parts that once were vivace are now andante. But she is old. She knows him so well. And she senses her Confederate women nearby, perhaps sitting out in the yard, in the dark, perhaps under the live oak tree near the veranda, waiting for her, understanding.

Robert, too, is glad for this connection, glad to be inside his wife once again. And when they are finished making love, he will tell her his secret from Vietnam, about the man he killed in the night, and he knows, from this answer of her nakedness, that she will continue to love him. The only secret he will keep from her forever is what fills him now, unexpectedly, as he moves within her: his first days in the city of Hue, in the autumn, in the midst of a war, the air full of the perfume of fruit blossoms floating downriver, heading for the South China Sea, and the woman he met and loved and lost, and the fear he has carried ever since that the smell of the air and the love of a woman would never again be as good.

Acknowledgments

It took me sixteen years to sufficiently compost Tallahassee and Florida State University and Jefferson County into my imagination to remake them into this novel. It took me seventy years for all the rest. I offer my abiding gratitude and affection to my friends and warm acquaintances, to my colleagues and students here in Northern Florida. You have all nurtured me. And this book, as with several of my recent books, owes a serious debt of thanks to my friend and physician, Wesley Scoles, for his medical expertise as my characters dealt with life in their bodies.